BUTTERFLY
CHANGES

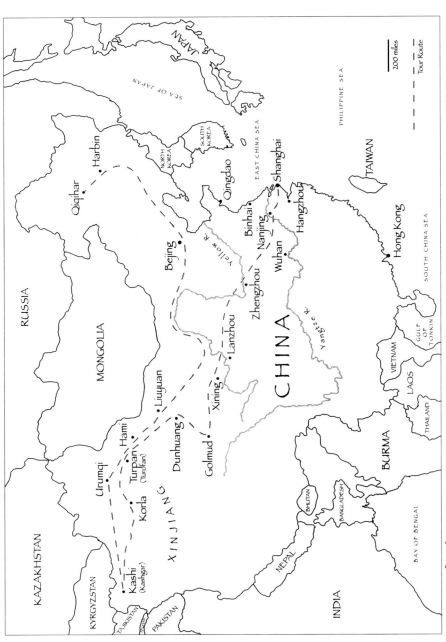

200 miles

Tour Route

RUSSIA

KAZAKHSTAN

KYRGYZSTAN

TAJIKISTAN

PAKISTAN

MONGOLIA

Qiqihar

Harbin

SEA OF JAPAN

JAPAN

NORTH KOREA

SOUTH KOREA

Beijing

Yellow R.

Qingdao

EAST CHINA SEA

Shanghai

Binhai

Nanjing

Hangzhou

TAIWAN

PHILIPPINE SEA

Urumqi

Hami

Liuyuan

Turpan
(Turfan)

Korla

Dunhuang

Xining

Lanzhou

Zhengzhou

Wuhan

Yangtze R.

CHINA

Hong Kong

SOUTH CHINA SEA

Kashi
(Kashgar)

XINJIANG

Golmud

NEPAL

BHUTAN

BANGLADESH

INDIA

BURMA

LAOS

THAILAND

VIETNAM

GULF
OF
TONKIN

BAY OF BENGAL

Tour of China 1987

BUTTERFLY CHANGES

A Novel by R. Vision

Ackowledgements

Thanks to Haizhen, who inspired everything; Lindi, who patted me for encouragement; Bonnie Evans, who edited "Butterflies;" Joanne Torvaldson, Michael Hudson and Mary Reed, who read it; and Lynn Yost, who read it and decided to produce it.

Credits

Cha Cha and Fred Hampton, Chicago 1969 © R. Vision
Chinese Cultural Revolution, courtesy *www.etext.org*
Lake Louise, Canada, ca. 2004, courtesy Dr. Alexander Gottesman
The White Snake, illustration ca. 1935
Shanghai map, ca. 1939
North American Man and Chinese Woman, photo used with permission
Covers, book design, butterfly art & map © 2006 L. Yost
Typsetting/Adobe® InDesign®: Papayrus (heads) TT;
11/13.2 Goudy Old Style (text) OTTT; Kai (Chinese characters in text) TT

Published by Valley Vista Press
1225 Ghaner Road
Port Matilda PA 16870 USA
info@valleyvistapress.com

First published in the United States of America by
Valley Vista Press, 2006

Despite extensive use of fact and characterizations of persons both living and dead, this book is a novel, a work of fiction.

To order additional copies, please contact us.
BookSurge, LLC
1-866-308-6235
orders@booksurge.com

Dedication

To Haizhen, for Haizhen, always Haizhen

献给海珍，为了海珍，永远海珍.

TABLE OF CONTENTS

Sit by my side,
Come as close as the air,
Share in a memory of grace,
And wander in my world,
Dream about the pictures that I play of changes....

The world's spinning madly,
It drifts in the dark,
Swings through a hollow of hate,
A race around the stars,
A journey through the universe ablaze with changes....

Phil Ochs (1960s)

* * *

Dong (East) Pass

Peaks as if massed,
Waves that look angry,
Along the mountains and the river lies the road to Dong Pass.
I look to the West Capital
My thoughts unsettled.
Here, where the Qin and Han armies passed, I lament
The ten thousand palaces, all turned to dust.
Kingdoms rise,
The people suffer;
Kingdoms fall,
The people suffer.

Zhang Yang Hao (Yuan Dynasty, 14th century)

BUTTERFLIES

by Jack Freidman

Call me Zhuangzi, the ancient Chinese butterfly who woke one morning from a vivid dream and never after knew whether he was a butterfly dreaming he was a man or a man who had dreamed he was a butterfly. I love a modern Chinese butterfly, Hai Bao, who has fluttered across the Pacific Ocean and lives in a dreamworld of mountains and snow, always wondering which is real, the Canada outside her window or the China inside her mind. For the two have little connection – except me sitting here writing of her. So she must test me, see if I am man or butterfly, solid or flighty. Except she knows from reading Zhuangzi that she'll never figure that one out. Why put ourselves through such changes? Because change is the lot of us poor butterflies.

Chapter One

Damned if I know how a side street in Chicago can intersect with an alley in Shanghai. But you can bet your long underwear in the middle of a Canadian winter I'm going to find out. I can figure out anything if I write enough. That's the way I've always done it. I write until I understand what I'm saying. I like to think I can figure out how to build a bridge across the Pacific Ocean if I have to. Maybe I'll discover I've already built it because in my mind crooked, stunted Bissel Street runs straight into winding, narrow Pushan Lu.

I grew up on the west side of Chicago, far from Bissel Street — forget about Pushan Lu. I was raised in an apartment box in a building of apartment boxes in a block of apartment buildings separated from similar blocks by straight, elm lined streets. The buildings were big and brick and I was young and unhip, so I didn't see them for what they were. Somewhere along the way to Bissel Street I heard the song and recognized them right off: "little boxes made of ticky tacky." But as a kid I only knew I felt out of place, Jack in the wrong box. I went to school and to summer camp and then to the university. In fact I went to six universities before I copped out just before I climbed into the Ph. D. box, but all I'd learned to do was teach in another one. That's what I was doing when I drove a colleague to his apartment. He lived on Bissel Street. Man, what a revelation. If my overly literal mind would let me, I'd rename Bissel Street Revelation Road. Then I'd rename Pushan Lu Ge Ming Lu. So my intersection would be the meeting of Revelation and Revolution. Sounds neat, eh? That's why I'm a bad novelist: too many facts, too little imagination.

You don't get imagination in a box. I had never imagined Chicago could look like Bissell Street. My box trained eyes made like Popeye the Sailorman, and thirty years later the shock of that first impression still vibrates in my mind like a speed freak in an opium den: cockeyed Victorian buildings shoved slapdash together in pairs, one long wood porch pasted to each pair, everything compressed so tight together that gables bulged out all over and crazy corners and cornices stuck out in crazy places, seemingly the product of air pressure, not carpentry. But the main impression was color. Who the hell painted brick buildings? On Bissel Street, apparently, anyone who could get hold of enough paint, brushes and ladders. The whole mass was painted in clashing colors and crammed with people in clashing colors and sizes from clashing cultures and lifestyles, blacks, browns, whites, reds, African Americans, Latin Americans, Italian Americans, Slavic Americans, hillbilly Americans, native Americans and at least one WASP college professor. So many folks, so different, in such close quarters, yet they seemed to be thriving on their contact. Adults jammed the porches boozing, gambling, singing, dancing, arguing, loving, yelling advice and admonitions to the children who jammed the sidewalks eating, playing, crying, rolling, quarrelling, flirting, yelling back at the adults yelling at them.

Although my middle class eyes and ears caught little that was familiar, I caught on. This was what I was searching for. This was life. The conviction flashed surefire through my mind. In years filled with doubts and changes I have never doubted it, it has never changed. Even after the people had been driven off Bissel Street, leaving the buildings like Victorian haunted houses. Even after the porches had been ripped away, the gaudy paint stripped away, the exteriors sandblasted to reveal the still more ghastly fact that despite the eccentric seeming architecture with its bizarre angles and bulges, the buildings were all exactly the same. The tacky paint and tacked on wood had been masking a Vickytickytorian assembly line subdivision.

Bissel Street made my vague dreams concrete. (Okay, only asphalt, which turns soft under heat. I thought they were hardrock American too. I only hit on how mushy and unamerican most of them really were after the heat hit in Lincoln Park.) So what if it deadended at the high wrought iron fence around the lush lawns and marble halls of McCormick Seminary and turned crooked in the slums south of Willow? At the time I would have pledged allegiance to the inclusiveness of its short run, branded its very crookedness a peculiarly American straight and narrow. Who'd have thought runty little Bissel Street would wind through the mountains of British Columbia and wind up in Shanghai?

In 1965, soon after my first sight of Bissel Street, I moved into its neighborhood. Lincoln Park. I couldn't find a flat on Bissel so I settled for Dayton, two streets over. By 1968, after a brief interlude teaching in North Carolina, I had made it to the next street, Fremont. That's when I met Cha Cha Jimenez, a Puerto Rican teenager, exgangleader, exjunkie, exjailbird, future revolutionary leader, future junkie, future jailbird. He lived on Bissel Street. Where else? the kid was another revelation. I thought I was teaching him, but he taught me – and drew me into the world I had glimpsed three years earlier. In order to try to save first Bissel Street, then Lincoln Park, then the world I got into politics. I was carried along Bissel Street into a sea of protests, demonstrations, tear gas, jails, bullets, funerals of friends murdered by the cops. It's a long story.

I told it once in a novel in which the main character is modeled on Cha Cha.

I was also carried across the sea into the land of Chairman Mao, whose writings we young revolutionaries read, whose thoughts and actions we dug. That's another long story. Eighteen years it took me from the time I got on the road on Bissel Street to the time it led me to China, and in that time I had changed and China had changed. I did fall in love with China but not for any reasons I would have dared to struggle for during the heyday of Chicago's *wenhua da geming*.

It was my second year living and teaching in Shanghai. The city was bursting with life and crowds which made Chicago seem pastoral yet somehow calmed my nerves. As I write my way out of Chicago now, I can feel that calm returning, my prose style relaxing into its natural contortions like an old man released from the tension of having to dance like a young one but needing to pirouette a bit to prove to himself he is not dead. Back then although I wandered and ran and rode my bicycle through Shanghai's life and crowds, I was not part of them. I was walled out as well as boxed in. I lived on the wrong side of the high walls of the luxurious Jin Jiang Hotel, protected from the life I wanted by guards I did not want, served by servants I did not believe in, locked inside the prison of my ignorance of the language. Yet despite all the walls I had made some friends, learned a little of the language and culture, desired more.

Then Zhang Hai Bao laughed at my Chinese, a most unchinese thing to do. My spoken Chinese was – still is – laughable, but no other Chinese listener had ever laughed. Chinese courtesy demands flattery, not honesty. "Oh, how wonderful; you can speak Chinese," people would gush after I grunted *ni hao* (hello). Four young Chinese and I were shoehorned into an art teacher's tiny campus studio cluttered with big Western abstract paintings, but when I looked at the woman laughing her unchinese laughter, she was leaning toward me and I knew I was looking over all the walls that all of Chinese history had built to keep foreigners like me from seeing into the heart of China.

I slept little that night and at first light I started running. I did not know where the writer I had met lived, but I knew it was within walking distance of the school at which we met. I liked to explore Shanghai and that was a neighborhood I did not know. It was a long run: half an hour there, half an hour back, two hours or more in the neighborhood; from the Jin Jiang Hotel, whose night sounds always put me back in the Chicago of my childhood, up Shimen Er Lu, whose long, arching bridge was the only place in flat Shanghai where I could have the illusion of running in the mountains of British Columbia, down into reality, the tenements and factories of the Zha Bei district. From atop the bridge the east glowed red as ever Mao said while to the north gray Zha Bei steamed pink beneath a sky dyed pink and orange: air pollution begets spectacular sunrises. It was June, the season when stationary objects molder and moving people sweat. I don't think I have ever sweated so much, and I am sure I have never loved sweating so much. It made me feel one with the working masses and with Hai Bao. I ran down many streets, alleys and lanes, but I kept coming back to one, Pushan Lu. I was running, running, looking, looking, loving what I was seeing even if I was not finding what I came looking for. Pushan Lu looked nothing like Bissel Street. Its buildings were low, rectangular, unpainted. These really were little boxes. Insubstantial. But not a smidgen of ticky tacky. They and their street were swarming with the same sort of activity and life as Bissel Street. I caught on again: ticky tacky is in the mind, in the mental taffy of mediocre, middle class ambitions. People make buildings; buildings need not, must not be allowed to, box in people. That's why I fight my birthright: to break out of all boxes. Revolution flashed as revelationary as revelation had been revolutionary. I felt the same emotions I had felt on the Chicago street twenty one years earlier. And I knew Hai Bao lived there. She belonged on Pushan Lu as surely as Cha Cha had belonged on Bissel Street.

Life does not hesitate to return to Pushan Lu after a rain. One might expect some caution after the summer downpour which flooded the street in five minutes, but before the foreigner figures out it is safe to shut his umbrella, a heavy set youth clad only in blue shorts plops into a wooden tub whose rainswollen six inches of water overflow into the tributary of the Yangtze flowing down the gutter, a willowy young woman sprinkles newfangled detergent powder into a similar wooden tub which holds a wooden scrub board and dirty clothes, and several brittle old women commence rubbing away in their own tubs with more traditional bars of brown soap. Tipped off, the foreigner sets down his suitcase and struggles to lower and fold his umbrella. It is not easy to hold up an umbrella in a hand also bearing two loaded baskets. He automatically notices the various styles of washing as well as the various stages of food preparation and the other action happening all over the sidewalks and street. Some folks are carrying chopping boards and cleaver like knives while those more advanced in the dinner process are hauling pots and charcoal grills shaped like short sections of stove pipe out of places of shelter. Across the road a huddle of men tinker with the rear of a pick up truck body perched on four wooden pedestals which straddle the rushing gutter from sidewalk to street. Two women march down the street in stiff step, connected by a long bamboo ladder they are carrying, and call out to the men. The huddle breaks. The men scatter. The coach must have called in a new play: dinnertime. The foreigner hesitates a moment, salivates, cogitates. Then he takes the baskets and umbrella into the hand which had been carrying the suitcase and squats gingerly to pick up the suitcase with the freed hand. Shanghai summer rains bring little cooling and only add humidity to the close quarters people are crammed into. All the relief, all the life, is on the streets. And even on Shanghai's teeming streets Pushan Lu's fertility of life is extraordinary.

But today the foreigner is too exhausted to appreciate the life. He notices and plods on. Even the realization that the men were actually constructing the truck body, that he has passed them before without realizing this, that he has just gleaned another grain of Pushan Lu's life, cannot lighten his steps. He had rested as he waited out the worst of the storm under shelter, but he bears a big Western pack on his back, a heavy Chinese cloth suitcase in one hand, two bamboo baskets and the umbrella in the other hand, a peasant fisherman's cone rainhat on his head. He is wet from both rain and sweat, tired, hungry, bedraggled. He stops to switch the loads in his hands at shorter and shorter intervals. Exhaustion is threatening to lead to anger, for although everyone stares and a few people can't help laughing, no one offers to help. On one of the tourist streets of Shanghai someone would surely relieve him of the suitcase in return for an opportunity to practice speaking English. But Pushan Lu is far from the tourist districts. The English experts here know "hello" and "bye bye." The most proficient perhaps have added "thank you" and "velly goode" to their vocabulary. Since none of these words fit this situation, the people are too shy to offer to help while he is too angry and proud to ask, for he knows they will laugh even more at his screwed up pronunciation and confusion of tones.

Suddenly a Chinese woman rushes up and takes the suitcase. The suppressed laughter turns to suppressed gasps. Not that the two embrace or show their emotion in any obvious way: this is China, not the West. Yet every gawker can feel the emotion. The tired foreigner is instantly happy, at peace with the world. He no longer minds the stares, for now he can admit how funny and out of place he must look. The laughter was the honest laughter which originally drew him to Pushan Lu, and how can he blame the curiosity? He himself cannot keep from wondering what a nice Jewish boy from the west side of Chicago is doing walking down Pushan Lu side by side with a Chinese wife, coming home.

Once we got home Hai Bao allowed me to drink, eat and rest a few minutes before ordering me to bathe in a wooden tub like the ones I had observed up and down Pushan Lu. She assured me (more gently than she has many times since) that no Chinese could sweat and stink like a Westerner.

Chapter Two

Damn.... There I go again. I wanted to start my novel with a bang, but I never intended to start every chapter with the same bang. Then last night the lake of blood surged over me again. Damn, damn, damn. Even my mother, who had a cliche for every occasion, might be tempted to swear. My worst nightmare. I saw the lake after Manuel Ramos's murder, but it didn't begin haunting me until after Fred Hampton's murder. Then it kept me awake every night for months. Until I ran from the Lincoln Park I loved. That let me sleep a little, but for years the nightmare still haunted that little. Then I discovered my mountains and left the blood behind. Or so I thought. The mountains are still there, right outside my window, but last night the lake of blood was there too. Damn. The irony is about as subtle as the comic books I read as a kid.

Mom didn't approve of most of the comic books, only the *Classics Illustrated* ones she bought me. But her saccharine optimism was but a different dose of the sugary American ethic the comic books dished out. The superheros, constantly thwarted, always prevailed in the end. "If at first you don't succeed, try, try again," mom would advise me now. "He who hesitates is lost," she would add when she saw how doubtful I feel. But if I do try again and fail, her only solace would be, "That's life." Damn. If that's life, mom, life's a cheat. I'm supposed to dream of butterflies, not get stung by life when I'm not looking.... "Flit like a butterfly, sting like a bee," (or something like that) said Muhammed Ali. I'm better at flitting than stinging. The one place I wanted to sting in, Lincoln Park, stung me. When all my dreams turned to nightmares, I flitted to the mountains of British Columbia and wrote everything down, wrote all the nightmares out of me. At least that's what I thought until last night, when I dreamed of the lake of blood again, the blood of Manuel Ramos.

Ok, mom, I'll go for it. But allow me one last "damn." For what if writing, once the solution, is now the problem? Maybe writing, which I once used to untie the knots in my mind, has become one of those strings you were always

telling me to tie around my finger so I wouldn't forget. Maybe when I write
I remember and when I remember I dream. Once I dreamed a street could
become a world, but the street led into a lake of blood. When I dream a butterfly
can be immortal, will it metamorphose into a worm? Why can't I write of what
I love without remembering what once I wrote to forget? Why, when a dream
dies, can't I let it lie? Why pursue it to the ends of the earth? And why does the
dead dream keep pursuing me when, at an end of the earth, by some miracle, I
find life? Real life, mom, not a cliche.

It seems I cannot write without remembering. It seems that writing isn't
magic and memory doesn't vanish simply because writing has tricked the mind
into forgetting. To write again, even to write of Hai Bao, is to remember again,
and the gates of memory, once unbolted, swing wide however rusty the hinges.
No fierce Chinese door gods guard my gates, no spirit wall protects me from
myself. So be it. Fling the gates open wide. I'll risk everything for Hai Bao.
Wring out the bloody rag and run up the red flag. Chinese stories need symbols.
Moral lessons too, so here's one on me, one Chairman Mao himself couldn't
dig: Bissel Street's life was fed by death, its beauty by blood. The Chairman
said, "Politics is war without bloodshed." He never played politics in Chicago. If
Bissel Street led me first to Mao, then to China, then to Hai Bao, it was because
I flitted against the flow, for in Chicago all roads led to the lake of blood which
inundated my dreams. Not that China has much to brag about: the last time a
lake of blood flooded my mind was after the Tienanmen Massacre of 1989. At
that time I had been dreaming of writing a novel about Second Sister, but both
that dream novel and the nightmare one which the massacre prompted washed
out: I had not been in either place. To write it seems I have to be, to live, not just
flit and dream. I have been and lived on Pushan Lu, but to write of it, it seems, I
must deal with Bissel Street. They intersect in more ways than I would like.

So welcome to Chicago in my novel about China, bloody Chicago where
life is as lurid as any comic book, where words and bosses are crude. I was
crude too. I am a Chicagoan too even if during my youth I knew nothing about
life, nothing about power, nothing about all the things that are supposed to be
second nature to every Chicagoan, all the things my mother neglected to teach
me. I saw little of mom during my days of socialist protest politics in Lincoln
Park, but whenever I saw her or talked to her on the phone, she invariably asked
me when I was going to grow up. Growing up, to mom, meant much the same it
means in China: getting married and raising a family. I did grow up in Lincoln
Park but not in any way that either mom or I wanted. Some changes come too
abruptly for even the most revolutionary advocate of change. All my youthful
dreams and images, youth itself, ended one early morning in May, 1969. Must I
remember all that? *Do you have eyes but no eyeballs? Hai Bao would ask.* Must I lump
myself with Daley? *The wise man looks like a fool.* Shit.

Bosses are as traditional in Chicago as emperors in China, and Bissel Street was too much for Chicago's bosses, too much life, too much variety. Tough to line up votes, tough to control and unprofitable to boot. So they gave it the boot. A peacefully integrated low rent area like the Lincoln Park I loved undermined the real estate interests which run the bosses who run Chicago. The land was too central, too valuable to be wasted on poor people. The neighborhood became a moving target, the weapon to riddle it urban renewal and the real estate speculation urban renewal triggers. Real guns were used too. The life I loved on Bissel Street has long been dead, murdered like Manuel Ramos.

I didn't know Manuel. Or Pancho, who got his head bashed in by a gang of Anglo kids with baseball bats. Or Juan, who got bumped off by a cop in a dispute over priority on a shitter in a public john. They were just kids in purple Young Lords berets I had seen hanging out with Cha Cha, first around Halsted and Dickens, then around People's Church. Hell, I didn't really know Cha Cha though I wanted to believe I was the Great Liberator who was fostering his revolutionary growth. I lent him books and "rapped" to him. Maybe that's why none of us knew each other. Words got in the way. We were too busy rapping to talk, too busy spouting propaganda to notice we were getting slugged in the mouth. That happened to me soon after I moved to Lincoln Park. It may have been my introduction to the Young Lords. I tried to act as peacemaker in a fight outside George's hot dog stand at the corner of Halsted and Dickens, and one of the kids decked me. It might have been Cha Cha. He and his gang hung out on that corner. Someone drier behind the ears than I might have worked out from the blood in his mouth and the tooth dangling from a shred of flesh that those kids and their lives were dangerous. Not me. Not the Great Liberator. Even after five years of watching kid after kid killed or maimed I was still planning to save them and the world. Even into the Seventies, when Juan got his and yet another cop got away with murder, I didn't get it. Only long years later, after I flitted out of Chicago and wrote everything up so I could forget it, did I begin to catch on.

One of the first effects of urban renewal is to dry up available housing. In Lincoln Park people who couldn't pay big bucks were forced out. Young adults who wanted to start new households couldn't make it in the neighborhood they grew up in. Some young Latins found places in Bridgeport, a working class Irish neighborhood, Boss Daley's neighborhood, where rents stayed cheap. They didn't want to live there. They wanted to live in Lincoln Park, but the mayor's plan to lure back wealthy whites who had fled to the suburbs meant turning communities like Lincoln Park into upper middle class suburbs within the city. It served him right that his plan drew the very people he wanted to get rid of into his own neighborhood. It served the people wrong.

Orlando was one of the leaders of Cha Cha's old street gang, the Young Lords. He was one of my favorite rap victims because he usually took everything

I spat at him without batting an eye. The one time he talked back, I was too busy rapping to listen and the Latin lilt in his voice seemed to belie his words. He told me how fucked over he felt when he moved out of his parents' place and couldn't find anywhere to live in Lincoln Park. He found an apartment in a Bridgeport basement along with a job pumping gas at a local filling station. "Right on," I cheered, but I wasn't really listening. As far as I was concerned a job meant money for the revolution. Few of these kids had jobs, and the revolution needed money. Minor matters like rent, food and transportation didn't concern me. But Orlando interrupted again. He bitched about his exile and the hatred he could feel in his Bridgeport neighbors and on the street as he walked home after work. I remember now what I couldn't acknowledge then, the lilt quavering, the voice hesitating, the bravado we all used dropping away, fear. Then he recovered and vowed to tough it out. For the apartment was cheap and he made enough money to buy an old junk of a car. Wheels confer freedom: he could drive back to Lincoln Park after work.

On his twenty first birthday in May, 1969 Orlando didn't drive to Lincoln Park. He threw a party at his Bridgeport apartment. Cha Cha and I left early because Cha Cha had business at the Black Panther office. He didn't drive and I was his number one chauffeur. I had intended to drive back to the party, but work before pleasure, my mother always told me. After dropping off Cha Cha, Priscilla, the woman I lived with, and I headed home to hit the hay so I could try, try again, work, work harder the next day. And once I hit the hay, once I thought it in those words and closed my eyes, I was back in the comic book world I grew up in. Comic book dreams of comic book patriotism, comic book stereotypes. So it shouldn't have come as the shock it did when at about three a.m. the hay and my dreams got jabbed with a pitchfork. Yikes, groan, grunt, oof, shazam. Just the way it always happened. My boyhood comic book world was full of formulae and sureties. One of them was that if someone, even the Great Liberator, attempted to hide or sleep in a haystack, in the next cartoon box a cartoon farmer would appear with his pitchfork. That was about to change. In the nightmare world into which I was about to wake nothing would ever be certain again.

Came a banging on my door, a pounding which still pulses through my nightmares. I tried to ignore it, but it grew louder. Finally, after the requisite comic book moans, the Great Liberator dragged out of bed to open the door and face his fate. I figured it was cops coming to bust me, who knew what for? I gave Priscilla the phone number of our lawyer before I staggered to the door. But it wasn't the cops. It was Angel Sanchez, the Young Lord with winged feet who always managed to escape arrest. He had a hell of a story to tell me. He always had a story to tell. But this was one he couldn't tell to Manuel Ramos' wife.

The Bridgeport coming of age bash for the Lincoln Park street kid had been drunken and loud. Normal for Lincoln Park, but this wasn't Lincoln Park. Unfortunately for the merrymakers half the cops in Chicago lived in Bridgeport and half those who didn't had an aged parent who did. Across the street from the party an off duty cop was painting his mother's apartment. He decided to turn off the noise disturbing his art. The partyers crammed into the tiny vestibule of Orlando's apartment to taunt the dude in the paintstained teeshirt who was claiming to be a police officer – "pig," they would have called him. His epithets for them would have been even less kosher. As kids will do, they overplayed their hand. Inevitably someone in the crowd packed a Saturday night special, and the piece got passed around to piss off and scare off the partypooper. The gun had reached Manuel when the cop decided to prove to the spic punks what and where he was. In the well trained manner of Chicago's professional police force he stepped back, whipped out his forty five, dropped to one knee and commenced firing into the jammed vestibule. The first shot blew away Manuel Ramos' brains. The second shot ripped through Raphael Ortez's neck, barely missing the windpipe. The third shot went wildly into the ceiling because Sal Santos, an ex Young Lord just back from a tour in Nam, leaped from the crowd, grabbed the cop's arm and wrestled the piece out of his hand. What has always amazed me is that none of the gang kids, six of whom were later charged with assaulting an officer of the law, picked up either of the two available weapons and gunned down the bastard who had tried to blow them all away.

Back in Lincoln Park Angel elected me to break the news to Baeta, Manuel's wife. She had not gone to the party because she had to care for two babies, one only a few months old. I suggested Angel and I go together to tell her, but he pointed out that phone calls would come to me: he didn't exactly think of me as the Great Liberator, but I was middle class and white, which fitted me for raising bail money and getting people out of jail. Besides, Manuel and Baeta didn't have a phone. So Angel, squirming out of yet another tight spot, went to roust the mother from bed and remained at her place to mind the babes. He dispatched her to my place. In nightmares Baeta seems a child herself, her eyes huge. I had to look into those astonished eyes and tell the fragile looking girl behind them her boy husband was dead. At first I couldn't do it. I couldn't even be sure Manuel was dead. Then the phone rang. It was John Jonas, a teacher at Waller High School and a friend. He had been at the party and was middle class enough not to be busted when every cop in Bridgeport turned out and turned up. He was calling from Mercy Hospital. Manuel was stone dead.

I thought Baeta knew. How could she fail to figure it out from the furor which had yanked her out of bed in the middle of the night and thrust her into the house of a stranger, from Angel's evasiveness and my embarrassment, from my words over the telephone, from my face? I thought Baeta knew. Not that I would ever admit tragedy without being forced to. Not that I would admit to myself that my Lincoln Park days were a tragedy, not the long march of history I hailed them as at the time, before writing forced me to think clearly, not in cliches. I thought Baeta knew. She was standing, black eyes pleading into mine.

She spoke to me only with her eyes. Those eyes. Those wide, open eyes. Had I ever looked into a baby's eyes, I might have known that she didn't know. I might have seen what I was seeing. Probably Baeta's eyes were just out of kilter from fright and from being waked and sent blindly from light to night and back into light again, but I wanted to believe they looked knowing, not innocent, eyes which had been there and back, which had already seen what I could not tell her. So I told her. Words came too easy in those days. In my waking life propaganda raps had replaced comic books and scholarship. Too often I used words to deceive, myself more than others. *"How come a man with such big eyes can't see?" Hai Bao often accuses. "How can a man who can't see what's in front of his face call himself a writer?"* "He's dead," I blurted out. Then I did see. In the instant my words took shape in Baeta's eyes. Which contracted in shock, then bulged with horror before glazing over. Priscilla – not me: I was too surprised to move at the discovery Baeta had not known – caught her before she hit the floor and got her into a chair. I guess I've always needed a woman to catch for me.

Or to catch me. A few hours later I was elected again, this time to go to the Bridgeport apartment with our lawyer and a female law student. My function was to be a witness. I witnessed enough to supply my nightmares for a lifetime. The vestibule was a three foot square sunk six or eight inches below three doorways: to the outside, to Orlando's apartment and to an upstairs apartment. The night's blood was all there, covered with a thin sheen of Chicago dust. The quantity amazed me: a little silvery lake. But under the silver surface the lake was thick and putrid red. I stared into its depths. I had never seen anyone faint before Baeta did it, but the technique need not be studied. The law student snatched a chair, caught me and pushed me into it as my knees buckled.

I recovered and witnessed the legal profession at work. Lawyer and student dug the flattened shell of the third bullet from the ceiling and took measurements and photographs. Finally we examined the back porch. Here we were accosted by a neighbor who screamed at us, "You dirty spics. Didn't you learn your lesson last night? Get the hell out of here. I'm calling the police." We spics, two Jews and a WASP, got the hell out of there. We got the hell back to Lincoln Park, where we thought we were safe. I didn't know it heading back to Lincoln Park because it took more blood to get my nightmares surging, but I was beginning to run or flit or whatever the hell I did to get out of Lincoln Park.

Chapter Three

Speaking of hell, how the hell did Bissel Street lead me to Xinjiang? Surely Shanghai was far enough. Shanghai was heaven, or at least under heaven. Xinjiang was only under the sun. A primitive desert of the heart. Why the hell hit that deadend now?

Perhaps because, like so many of my deadends, like Bissel Street itself, it was a beginning, a setting out towards a new intersection, towards Second Sister, in whom Shanghai and Xinjiang intersect in the Subei, in whose blood 1949 and 1989 China intersect in me in 1969 Chicago. Although I don't remember ever having a nightmare about Xinjiang, as soon as I wrote "hell," I saw it, the desert in the west of China, the desert in which my love dried then flowered anew, watered in the blood of Second Sister. Blood you don't have to look at can be romantic. It is literary blood, not literally blood; it has even enabled me to write the mandatory prologue about Hai Bao's antecedents which must begin a Chinese story. Yet how can a Western narrator give a damn about ghosts or ancestors or even parents when he falls in love with a beautiful woman? I'll have to slip on the inscrutable oriental mask I found in China's too scrutable occidental desert and preach a history lesson.

Zhang Hai Bao was born in the year of the *su fan* movement. Politics, not numbers, is the measure of time in China and anything significant is named. Numbers, when used at all, are subsidiary. Scenic views an emperor paused to admire, the knoll on which a communist leader rested, the rocks which threatened a general's boat and a vast assortment of ghosts all carry specific names to commemorate their fame, and years have names based on events, usually political, which occurred (or which the emperor wanted to occur) during imperial reigns. This, like most things in this ancient land, has been true since ancient times. If our Western penchant for numbers forced us to assign to China a year zero, a beginning of the modern era, it would come two hundred twenty one years before Christians begin their numbers game and would mark not the birth of a god and religious leader but the success of a political movement, the year Qin Shi Huang irretrievably changed history by bringing the Chinese Empire under unified rule – his own. He became a god and political leader. His movement featured mass deportations and executions, vast armies of workers engaged in enormous public projects such as building The Great Wall, the burning of all books, especially histories, which did not support his rule. It was much bigger than the *su fan* movement, a minor rectification campaign. It was the *wenhua da geming*, the Great Proletarian Cultural Revolution.

In order to conquer and rule the vast land Qin Shi Huang had to annihilate the old order, the old aristocracy, the old power. To do so he opened a bottle that loosed violent winds of change. Once he consolidated his power, he needed to recap the bottle to prevent further change. He proclaimed himself "First Emperor," proclaimed that his dynasty would last ten thousand years. Historians claim he miscalculated by nine thousand nine hundred eighty five. We all make mistakes. Even the Communist Party of China admits to a few although, like Qin Shi Huang, it does not permit histories of its rule. But don't worry about trifles; the new age has dawned red. Mistakes can be rectified and rectification campaigns are a specialty of the Communist Party of China. The future is bright even if there is no present. The past has been rectified; Qin Shi Huang lives! Historians who mocked him are hereby convicted of following the wrong line and sentenced to rehabilitation through labor. He succeeded in bottling up the winds of change. After he was dead and his son and dynasty overthrown, when the leaders of that overthrow attempted to restore the old system which Qin Shi Huang had destroyed, they could not (if they really tried: as the Communist Party would discover, attaining absolute power alters the perspective on change). It no longer worked: Nothing but Qin Shi Huang's stoppered bottle worked for two thousand years. Or, at least, when it cracked it could be repaired by replacing its owners just as Qin Shi Huang's son and legalist advisors had been replaced. Dynasty succeeded dynasty with little basic change except the names. Until even changing dynasties no longer worked. Stagnation set in, but still no one dared reopen Qin Shi Huang's bottle. Finally Mao Ze Dong dared, and he had to go it alone, for every time he turned his back his coleaders tried to cap the bottle. "Change," cried Mao. "Stability," echoed his party of the altered perspective. Quietly. Mao grew old pulling corks out of bottles; his government grew up pushing them back in. Eventually Mao died and could be bottled himself, worshipped under glass in Tiananmen Square without being heeded. He joined his illustrious ancestor Qin Shi Huang in – let me calculate – in the year of their lord 2197. Seven thousand eight hundred three to go. Fortunately patience is a traditional Chinese virtue.

All powerful is the grip of traditional culture in this land where that grip has held on for millennia. Chairman Mao felt the grasp of Chinese culture and set out to break it. As had Emperor Qin. Indeed, Mao followed the method laid down by Qin, politics. And like the First Emperor, Mao achieved spectacular

initial successes. He united the country and built a Great Wall of morality and
ideology to protect China. This not only walled out and eliminated imported
vices such as opium addiction and prostitution but actually seemed to loosen
the vise of Chinese tradition. And out popped Zhang Hai Bao, a true child of
the communist revolution. Westerners call it *Anno Domini* 1955, but it was the
year of their lord Qin Shi Huang 2176, the year of the rule of our Party 6, the
year of the *su fan* movement

Hai Bao's parents could not even have met in traditional Chinese society.
Her father was too poor to marry but strong enough to push a wheelbarrow
loaded with produce across the Subei, from Binhai to Xuzhou, six hundred
li (three hundred kilometers) to the west, to help feed the communist armies
during the decisive battle of Huai Hai, the battle which sealed Chiang Kai Shek's
fate. A million soldiers fought for sixty five days, but the battle was won not by
strength of arms but by strength of legs and wheelbarrows. The communists
were able to cut the nationalist supply lines while keeping their own troops
fed. Hai Bao's mother didn't do much walking. She was from a small country
landlord's family who bound her feet when she was a child. The bands mangled
her feet and hobbled her walking but made her a valuable ornament, and when
she was eighteen her parents arranged her marriage to a merchant's son from
town. His family doubtless paid a good bride price. The coming together of
the strong legged but poor bachelor peasant and the prosperous merchant's
boundfooted wife is the story of new China's coming together which is rightly
called liberation, for no failure after power was won can obscure the grandeur
of its winning, of the most massive mass movement known to history. Qin Shi
Huang may have established a scenario when he conquered the land, constructed
the Great Wall, reconstructed Chinese society and consigned history to the fire,
but the twentieth century populated the drama on a whole new scale.

Everything about the Chinese Revolution staggers the imagination: its
scale, its scope, its complexities, its contradictions. Mao revelled in contradictions
and wrote much about them; the Western mind wishes he had written and
spoken more specifically about the contradictions within his own movement.
Yet because Mao's movement was modern as well as massive, we can still dig
into it and find real people, not terracotta statues. Real people like Hai Bao's
mother. Her merchant husband had taken a concubine and moved with her to
the Sunan, six hundred *li* to the south. He left Hai Bao's mother raising
two children in a house in his family compound. She saw him only a
few times a year when he visited on business and attempted to assert his
rights. The rest of the year one of his brothers attempted to assert his
rights. Hai Bao's mother became a tough, angry woman, but that made
her life even worse, for Chinese women of her class were expected to
be soft, compliant. And their feet were bound to discourage them from
running away. Then liberation blew into the Subei.

The winds of change had been too long pent up. When Mao pulled the cork they broke loose in a raging cyclone. The earth was disturbed, the red dust of China blowing in the wind. Chiang Kai Shek and his corrupt government were blown away. As liberation swept south and the dust began to settle, a new marriage law swirled in. The very idea of law in a land so long ruled by custom was new, and this law was laid down by raw, untraditional leaders who sprang up everywhere as if from under the ravaged ground. Mainly they were young peasants who had originally been recruited as Communist Party guerillas to fight the Japanese. Liberation lifted layers which had pressed them down for longer than history could remember, and they burst from underground full of joy and enthusiasm for change, their eyes directed toward the red sun in the new sky above, not the earth which had held them prisoner. When word of this unheard of thing, a marriage law, came down from above, they passed it on enthusiastically, for many of them would have been too poor to marry in the old society and others could have expected only marriage to a woman they had not chosen and never seen. To fighters for change few things in Chinese culture seemed more in need of change than marriage traditions; now old, oppressive customs were to be blown out by the same wind which had blown them, the old fighters, the new leaders, in. No longer was marriage to be a financial matter arranged by families, the addition of a family servant and a childbearer to carry on the family name more than the taking of a wife, let alone a lover. Individuals were to become free to marry whom they chose, and those who had married without love were free to seek divorce. That was the law. What a wonderful thing was this new thing, the law. The new leaders were making the same discovery Qin Shi Huang had made almost twenty two hundred years earlier, when legalist philosophers advised him that law could be used to change culture and tradition.

The Western imagination strives to picture the Chinese breaking the chains which have bound them for millennia, to see in the grand drama of the Chinese Revolution the triumph of good over evil, of the people over their oppressors, of the new over the old. Why else did I fall in love first with the Chinese Revolution, then with New China, then with Zhang Hai Bao? But the Western mind, especially that of a historyless North American, often fails to grasp the Chinese reality, the force, still very much alive, of its long dead history.

No culture has a longer unbroken history than China, and no people have a greater knowledge of and respect for their history than the Chinese. Yet few histories are murkier than China's, and the more recent the history the murkier it becomes. The reason, as usual, is politics. History is what the emperor declares it to be. One asks no questions of the son of heaven, and one writes no histories of his times before his coffin is closed or while those loyal to him retain power. So the greatest of Chinese historians, Sima Qian, more than two thousand years ago wrote his history from stories and legends handed down to him, wrote, so far as has come down to us, nothing of the fascinating times in which he lived. The Western mind insists he must have wanted passionately to write about his own times, to revenge himself on his emperor, who ordered him castrated. But the servant serves the master: he did not write a critical history of his emperor's reign, and after his castration he went on serving, went on writing only safe, ancient history. Just as Communist Party members did not resign after the Beijing massacre of 1989. Just as the history of China after 1949 is not taught in China. Not that the history of Chicago in 1969 is taught in Chicago.

Hai Bao's mother came from spunky stock, but the brutal power of the ancient Chinese culture can be seen in the story of one of her sisters. At least some of the story of Hai Bao's second aunt survives. We should be grateful for that. Hai Bao's father's family, after all, has no history. He is descended from nameless peasants who for countless generations worked land seldom their own until they were laid under the land which had pressed them down in life. Because Hai Bao's mother came from a landlord family, however small the landlord, some names and an outline of the family history have come down to us despite, in this case, efforts to muddy it beyond the common muck and murk.

Hai Bao's aunt's name has not come down to us for the simple reason that she did not have a name. Unlike knolls, rocks and ghosts women in old China were rarely important enough to be named. They were subsidiary, numbers who didn't count: 1,2,3 within the family or first sister, second sister, third sister in polite conversation. Hai Bao's mother was fourth sister. Second sister died before Hai Bao was born, but I was with Hai Bao when coincidence and a sharp ear for language first piqued her to unearth her aunt's history.

It was the summer of 1987 and she and I were occupied with the traveler in China's most common occupation, waiting in line for train tickets. The place was Urumqi, the capitol of remote, desolate Xinjiang, three thousand kilometers west of Hai Bao's ancestral home. I was sick, and we were near the end of a tiring journey through a desert which had destroyed ancient cities and civilizations yet preserved their shapes for a thousand years, literally an outline of history. The ticket line, as usual, moved little faster than life in those long dead cities, and we practiced the Chinese art of sleeping on our feet, faces cast down at the dirty concrete floor of the dreary concrete station which, like everyone in it, seemed weary of its role in Han China's effort to cast its concrete block civilization upon the foreign cultures of an alien desert which only the map and the government could call China. Suddenly Hai Bao's nose lifted. She had detected familiar accents. She sidled over to a woman several places ahead of us in line and soon led her back, declaring her not only to be from Binhai but a distant relative. We got our tickets a little sooner, since the woman bought ours with her own, and received a relaxing meal at the kinswoman-stranger's home. (What made the meal relaxing was that Hai Bao felt no need to supervise food preparation as the Han worship of cleanliness demanded she do in every Xinjiang restaurant in which we ate.)

The woman we met at the station was from the family of second sister's first husband. The older members of this family and of Hai Bao's mother's family had been feuding for the forty years since second sister's death, but Hai Bao and her in-law had both been born after the event and were little involved. The woman informed us that the Communist Party had recently declared that second sister's husband had been a secret member of the Party, an allegation, like many others in this case, which Hai Bao has never been able to confirm. Previously the man had been known only as a bandit who was shot dead attempting to rob a rich man's house. Confusion between bandits and communists is traditional, more shifting sand on which to build history. The history of what occurred after the bandit or communist's death is like the outline of those dead cities in the desert, fascinating but full of holes. The accepted facts are that second sister remarried, but shortly thereafter her son suddenly sickened and died; the first husband's family accused her of murdering the boy, got her daughter, then twelve, to testify against her mother and the local government of the day to side with it; as a result the authorities turned second sister over to her first husband's family, who executed her.

After being piqued in Xinjiang Hai Bao made a trip to the Subei to try to fill in the story. It was her first visit to her hometown and she learned much about her own roots. But little about her aunt's execution. She could find no records or reports of the event, and her own aunts and uncles would tell her nothing. An old woman, a stranger on the street who must have heard she had been inquiring about second sister, fed her rumors that she could not swallow. But under my mask I am from Chicago: slurp. The old woman whispered that second sister was executed in the public marketplace by hacking off one limb at a time and finally carving her heart from her breast. Eventually the pieces of body were given up for burial, but the killers kept the heart. That part sounds apocryphal, even to me, even after research revealed that one Chinese tradition claims eating a human heart confers courage. Then I remember Chicago. Maybe if the heart was not eaten immediately and not eaten during the three terrible years or confiscated as a feudal tail during the Cultural Revolution, some old codger in Binhai still cherishes it as a memento of the days when men were men. Or maybe the bugger fled the Subei during land reform, took the heart with him, moved to Chicago and joined the police. The few facts Hai Bao learned came from second sister's daughter, but Hai Bao dared not press her cousin about the matter. The woman's apartment is kept so spotless that even where cleanliness is worshipped few are brave enough to enter a shrine in which the wrath of Buddha is incurred for allowing in a speck of dust. Hai Bao entered and helped sweep the floor, but she dared not dig beneath the cleanliness.

Everyone agrees second sister was a beauty. I wonder if I can imagine her as she actually was?... roundish – almost, perhaps, fat: folks in countries where starvation remains a living memory do not admire skinny women, and plumpness has been a mark of Chinese beauty since at least the Tang Dynasty. Yang Gui Fei, the most famous beauty in Chinese history and literataure, beloved of an emperor, tragic heroine of countless dramas, operas and poems, even Yang Gui Fei is always described and painted as plump. Hai Bao's mother, second sister's daughter and most of the women in the family are stout. Even a Westerner brought up on very different standards can imagine second sister's type of beauty: a full moon face peeping over a full earth body mounted on mincing half feet; ample flesh for heavy labor, labor decreed mainly horizontal by the mutilated feet. She was created to be a mass of contradictions, contradictions designed to the specifications of a leisure class's conspicuous consumption. She belonged in an emperor's harem but was born as the emperor was being evicted from the palace. Emperor or no emperor, she was given as girls of her class had always been given, to a rich family to be a rich boy's bride. Who knows why the boy turned bandit? The age piled contradiction on contradiction until no one's role was clear. Only the traditional rules of conduct remained clear; because the place was the same as in the days of Qin Shi Huang, no one dared notice how utterly out of time the rules had become.

All we know is that Second Sister's husband led his little family and his little bandit band until he met his fate and left his wife to hers. Hers was the traditional Chinese widow's trap. Her husband was dead, what was she supposed to do? She had lived with him, loved him, depended on him. Perhaps she would have been willing to die for him or die with him, but he had died without her. What was she supposed to do?

Whoops. My mask slipped off. It takes a Westerner to ask such a question. Every Chinese knows what she was supposed to do. She was supposed to live on serving her husband's family. Since time immemorial China has been cluttered with memorials to virtuous widows who did so. Indeed, First Sister, the oldest daughter in the family, was widowed at the age of twenty eight and now, sixty years later, remains an honored member of her husband's family. Seeing her older sister's life must have had a bearing on second sister's resolution to remarry. But she had been chosen and purchased not by a man but by his family. She belonged to it first, him second, herself never. Her duty was what it had been for at least three thousand years, to work for the family, to raise her son to carry on the family name, to raise her daughter to fetch the family a good bride price.

So her real crime was insubordination: after burying her husband she refused to bury herself in her husband's family. Such unfilial insubordination is called immorality in traditional Chinese culture, and it was of immorality she was actually convicted, of immorality even her daughter knew she was guilty. The daughter, raised in the bosom of her father's family, had been made to feel so much shame for so long over her mother's immorality that she could be persuaded to testify against her mother. How could a child know that once her father's family and her community had achieved their revenge, she would be left for the rest of her life to wrestle alone with what she had done – with a ghost she knows well although this Chinese ghost has no name.

The death of the boy provided a godsent pretext: for the husband's family members to indulge their blood lust, for the girlchild to expiate her shame, for the community to redeem its morality. No one except second sister's birth family and her new husband sympathized with or attempted to defend her. To this day Hai Bao's father, a kind hearted man who sympathizes with anyone in trouble, has no sympathy for his wife's sister although he does not believe she murdered her son. She had no motive for killing her son. The husband's family would have claimed the deed was done from spite, that she murdered her son for the same reason she remarried, to cheat the family of its due; the boy bore its family name, not hers. The only evidence offered of poisoning was the ancient superstitious test of quicksilver: the dead body rose or sank or discolored or something when placed in mercury or some other substance. No one really believed this proved the use of poison. But the family had only to pretend it was proving murder. The woman was obviously guilty of immorality, and immorality has always been punishable by death in China. The local government gave the woman to her first husband's family to be punished because she belonged to it, had sinned against it, not her son. The government could make such a decision because the community believed her a whore even if not a murderer.

A bit gruesome to a Westerner, even one wearing a Chinese mask. We would prefer to deny the strength, unanimity and consequences of belief in China, the bloody grip of traditional Chinese morality. Still, a febrile Western brain might be forced to accept it, might even be able to revel in the blood so long as it can be seen as the blood of old China, not new. What no Western mind – certainly not mine – can grasp is the continuing power of Chinese tradition. We believe in laws and government, believe that a change in government can transform society. On what evidence? In China there have been many complete changes in government. Each has led to a new dynasty, a complete change in name usually accompanied by a temporary change in bureaucratic efficiency, little else. Nothing has really changed since the days of Qin Shi Huang: the local authorities who presented second sister to her first husband's family did not serve an imperial government or a warlord government or a puppet government set up by the Japanese or a landlord or *Guomindang* (Nationalist) government inspired by Confucianism, but one of the transient liberated area governments set up by the communists and full of the ideals of new China. Like many other places in the north of China Binhai was captured first by one side, then the other during the civil war. Its government changed frequently and the Western mind wants to agree with the communist interpretation of the changes as vast and momentous. The *Gongchangdang* (Communist) and *Guomindang* governments are imagined to be opposites, the former supporting the lower classes, the poor, the helpless; the latter supporting the upper classes, the rich, the traditionally powerful. Isn't that what a revolution is? So the mind balks, but the fact remains: a communist inspired government handed over the helpless widow to the wealthy family to carve her heart from her breast.

What an alluring country, what a seductive culture! But body armor might be in order while making love.... The problem is, how's a foreign barbarian supposed to know this before he has been disarmed and disarmored? The mask China wears is not like mine, new found. China wears the mask of four thousand years of civilization, of beauty, of control, of morality. How can any hairy foreign devil, even a Jew from Chicago, learn before he has been shorn like Samson what every Chinese knows: the mask is intended to disguise, never to hide, savagery as primitive as Qin Shi Huang's or Genghis Khan's? Shortly before the Tiananmen (Gate of Heavenly Peace!) Massacre Deng Xiao Ping quoted the old Chinese proverb, "Kill one, frighten a hundred." A few years after second sister was made an example, the new local communist government, the direct descendant of the one which connived in her butchering, probably led by most of the same men, declared that women were free to seek divorce and to remarry.

There was not an instant deluge of divorce applications, but, scandalously, in Binhai one woman did apply. Second sister's little sister, Hai Bao's mother, applied to become an example of a different kind. Binhai is not an ancient town, but since its founding in the Song Dynasty no woman had ever sought such a thing as divorce. The very word had an alien ring. Confucian ethics proclaim men the unquestionable leaders of families, so a man (and only a man) could send his wife packing and do so without consulting her or any court. After the newfangled divorce was granted – the woman receiving custody of her daughter while the son was sent to the father – life became harder, not happier for Hai Bao's mother. Old friends shunned her, and while the divorce settlement had awarded her the house she lived in, that house was surrounded by the houses of her exhusband's family and that family hated her with the special hatred reserved for a pariah, the hatred which had killed her sister. She survived amidst that hatred for two years before she followed the wind south to Shanghai, which was in the flux and flush of its postliberation boom. In a city where exprostitutes were being given new jobs and new lives no one was likely to harass a divorcee.

Hai Bao's father had also made it to Shanghai. Impressed by his dedication – after delivering the food he stayed on at the battle of Huai Hai as a stretcher bearer – the communists sent him to a cadre school. Had he stayed on there he would no doubt have become a full party member and, in due course, a high ranking cadre. The Communist Party operates on the seniority system, and those who joined up before 1949 have long been at the top of the seniority list. But, typically says his daughter, he got sick and went home for a rest. When he returned the cadre school was gone. During a time of civil war such secret institutions moved frequently and did not leave forwarding addresses. So a promising official career was lost and a wife was gained: if he had gone with the Party, he would not have come to Shanghai.

Shanghai, the city which had always dealt from both sides of the deck, where Western money and dissipation had traditionally mated with Chinese poverty and desperation to spawn mansions and slums, factories and brothels, luxury hotels and opium dens, gambling palaces with the longest, busiest bars in the world and streets shuffled with beggars, pickpockets, pimps, card games and the fastest moving morgue going. Shanghai, void of hearts and long in everything black, suddenly trying to lay its cards on the table and become a red city, liberated from its old traditions in 1949 and attempting to build new traditions, to reform the prostitutes, gamblers, pimps and junkies, – and eliminate any who proved unreformable – to build on its base of Yangtze mud and foreign filth, of feudal oppression and capitalist sin, new China's model socialist industrial capitol. Chinese had been flocking into Shanghai from the countryside ever since the Opium Wars established it as China's capitol of capitalism, but the winds of liberation frightened the flocks into a stampede. Two very different bunches were blown loose from their tethers to the land and raced for the salvation which popular rumor ascribed to Shanghai: jobs, food, money, anonymity. First came the poorest of the poor, many of them near starving. Second came what in China had passed for rich, the landlords, though not the richest of the rich, for they fled farther, to Taiwan and beyond. The same storm stampeded poor and rich toward Shanghai: land reform. For the landlords land reform meant loss of the land which had been their living, perhaps loss of life itself, for the poor on whose backs they had built their lives had suddenly stood up and so thrown them down. If they failed to get up and run, they might be beaten to death, and even if they survived they could continue to live only by cutting their long fingernails and bending their straight backs like peasants. Better far the anonymous risk of the great city. Yet however sudden was the disaster for the landlords, it was not sudden enough for the starving. They could receive land, but how could they survive on it long enough to reap their first harvest now that they could no longer hire themselves out to a landlord for immediate food? The food grew faster in Shanghai than it did on the land.

So the winds of change blew poor and rich together into the same pile called Shanghai. In Shanghai's cultural chaos, the crazy cradle of confusion city dwellers accused of being the birthplace of the future, country folk found security in the only way they knew: home. In Shanghai the poor bachelor peasant who had been a communist in training could marry the divorced daughter of a landlord because they hailed from the same place. They could not even have met in the Subei, yet that place where they could not meet drew them into marriage. Locality is crucial to identity. In a big, new city like Shanghai there are little hometown organizations of people from every county in China significantly represented in the city population. Even after a family has inhabited the metropolis for generations, its official hometown remains the birthplace of its ancestors and is so recorded on all legal documents. Urbanites who have never seen their "hometowns" proudly call themselves Shaoxing *ren* (persons) or Wuchang *ren*. Or Binhai *ren*. In Shanghai Binhai too had its local organization. Of course it had: don't the two place names mean approximately the same thing, by the sea? And of course when the hometown folks discovered two unmarried Binhai *ren* of a similar age and opposite sexes, the Chinese penchant for matchmaking asserted itself. It was not a fablebook romance. The two were already in their forties, lonely country folks in a huge city, grateful to find a companion with the dialect and memories of home. Nevertheless, the two did get to know each other before they committed themselves. Maybe China had indeed changed. Hai Bao's mother first saw her first husband on her wedding day.

In Shanghai during the early Fifties nothing looked as it had a few years earlier. Everywhere new housing was going up. Some of it was decent housing, but much of it was labeled "temporary." Northwest of the main train station, North Station, an area of fields was converted to temporary housing. The most elementary of concrete rowhouses were thrown up. People were told that in five years these would be torn down and better, permanent housing would be constructed for everyone living there. It sounded plausible given the pace of change. Meanwhile, two hundred *yuan* could purchase two matchbook sized rooms in a row of two storey boxes. The newlyweds from Binhai had been renting a half matchbook sized room. They did not have two hundred *yuan*, but Hai Bao's mother told her new husband to get their names on the list. Then she took off for the Subei. There she sold her old house – or at least the materials from which her old house was built. Wood is valuable in China, for the forests were cleared centuries ago. Perhaps she could have sold the house back to the merchant's family for more money than she received for the materials, but she did not speak to them. They were furious to see the house go down, an ugly hole gape up in the middle of their compound, but they were powerless to stop it. The money from that house plus some her husband had saved purchased the little rowhouse in *Pushan Lu Yi Cun*, Pushan Road Number One Village. The name sounded like the countryside from which most of the inhabitants were newly arrived. The flat was a bit damp and dingy, as concrete always is, and it flooded every year during typhoon season, but the government had promised to rectify temporary inconveniences, to build something better in a few years. The happy couple whitewashed the walls and had a home. The next year, during the *su fan* movement, Hai Bao was born. Until she married in 1986 at the age of thirty one, Hai Bao knew many other political movements but no other home.

Chapter Four

I was sixteen when Hai Bao was born. My middle class family expected me to become a surgeon, but I was already figuring out that real blood was a lot scarier and less romantic than the red stuff splashed around my comic books. I craved romance, poetry, not Shelley yet, but the image of a beautiful but ineffectual butterfly beating its wings against a luminous void would have turned me on even if the idea of becoming one turned me off. So I announced a change of vocation. I wrote a poem, very bad, very long, long lost, thank god. It featured two Asian peasants and was inspired by (more likely borrowed from) Markham's "The Man with the Hoe." One of my peasants was Chinese, one Indian. Each country was newly recreated in "the whirlwind of rebellion." I pictured the fate of the human race along with the hoes in the peasants' browned hands. Whichever peasant best succeeded in throwing off "the burden of the world," "the silence of the centuries," would "judge the world," determine its future.

It was 1955 and my poem was a typically simpleminded Fifties cliche. I might as well have written it up as a race: India ran for the first world, China for the second. The winner would pass the baton (not the hoe) to the rest of the third world. In keeping with my origins I rooted for the Indian peasant, not the Chinese one, because I admired Gandhi more than Mao. No ineffectual angel Gandhi: his dreams were as real and political as Mao's yet moral as well. Middle class ambition I might forsake, but not middle class morality – *go ahead and laugh, Hai Bao, but my conduct with you proves it's true* – and Gandhi was selfless in a way even Mao must have admired. Gandhi declined political office and died tough and skinny while Mao was already growing flabby with power. In addition, India possessed depths of mysticism which proffered relief from the shallowness of the Fifties, exotic depths of mysticism into which a bored teenager could dream of sinking.

Holy cow....

I try to look back tolerantly on a world weary sixteen year old's lick and a promise fling at mysticism, the vegetarianism and recitations from the Bhagavad

Gita that drove my mother wild. "You get what you pay for," mom always told me. I got more than I asked or paid for, especially since books were cheap and talk cheaper in those days and years later I used what I got from the books to talk my way out of the Viet Nam draft, the mystic as conscientious finagler. But the real reason I was writing poems in 1955 was that I was planning to be an articulate mystic, to record for posterity unprecedented and beautiful revelations of the unfathomable and beautiful godhead deep within me. The real dream of that period was to be a writer, and although I later neglected that dream for others, it was forever calling "wait up" like the boy inside me, and I always intended to come back to it.

But even if I'd been a wildly imaginative novelist instead of a poet back then, I couldn't have foreseen that thirty years later I would marry the Chinese peasant's daughter and become the ancestor of his grandchild. How could I have imagined that? How can I comprehend it even now, now that it's real, not imagined, now that I know she is not only the peasant's daughter but the martyr's niece? Maybe I shouldn't try. For once I don't have to write. When I started writing this book, I had no awful memories or nightmares to purge from my psyche, no new compulsion to justify myself to myself. I thought I could finally write as I wanted to when I was young, as a writer should, to exalt life and love. Then I started dreaming of blood instead of butterflies. Apparently writing is neither the simple literary exercise I imagined I imagined as a teenager nor the complicated psychological trick desperation turned it into as an adult. For me writing is a gamble, a risking of what I have to get more. I thought I gave up gambling long before I learned to write my fears out of me. So why risk writing my love out of me now? Why risk discovering that my present life totters on a fiction, on the bridge across the Pacific Ocean? that I am but attempting to buttress one fiction with another?

Yet write I must. *She knew that from the start. Writing could bring us together when culture or morality drove us apart, drove her to tears of anger and despair: "I'm sorry I loved other women. It was long ago and I was young. I couldn't have become a writer if I hadn't. Because I'm no good at making things up, I had to write novels based on my own life. I needed love stories. But I only told them after they were over, after the love had ended. They were all flashback novels." "I don't care.... What means flashback?" "I don't know the Chinese word. 'Flash' is a sudden light, hen kuai, hen ming de guang. You know 'back.' 'Flashback' means the writer jumps back to an earlier time, remembers what happened in the past." "You can't write me flashback. Our love story not allowed to end. Must write flashfront." "No, no. The opposite of 'back' isn't 'front' here. Back in time. Duimian de 'back' shi 'forward.' Dong bu dong?" "Understand. You must write us flashforward."* I can no more throw poor words away and be content to live with Hai Bao than I could have become a silent mystic. I must write to understand myself, my dreams. Not her: I married for love, not scrutability, and loved China without understanding it before it turned into her. But she flitted into my dreams, became my dream. She and her world transformed my world. To fathom that I must recreate her and her world in a way I can at least pretend to imagine I understand, become a part of even if I remain myself. Her life, my novel: a marriage of cultures.

Yet I was not there. The Shanghai which grabbed me in 1983, the China I struggled to see before she opened my eyes, were not the ones she grew up in. And I still can't catch the nuances of a language which thousands of years of history have built into a many levelled pagoda. Think of the sticky mess a sucker for words like me can make of a language like Chinese: when I try to buy salt, shopkeepers offer cigarettes; once I noticed a strange look when I was talking to a neighbor on Pushan Lu, and Hai Bao later informed me that I had called her mother a horse. Schlemiels like me have been executed for pronouncing or interpreting Chinese words as I do. Fortunately Hai Bao is a princess, not an emperor. Not only does she spare my life but she tells her stories in my words, my language, deadly as that is to her nuances. Those flat English words for her intricately tiered Chinese stories are all I have. Somehow I must turn my words into hers, her stories into mine. Were I blessed with imagination, perhaps I could create a complete world, a perfect past, a Shanghai and a China worthy of her and her stories, terraced with colors, odors, sounds, meanings, presence. But I was not present and lack the facility to create existence from air. There are not even photos of her or her family before her teenage years. Sometimes the events or environment which reminded her of a story can help me feel it; sometimes I can theorize about what she does not know or cannot remember. But usually, I expect, I'll end up doing what I usually end up doing in life, playing it by my tin ear, saying what seems best under circumstances which are seldom what they seem to me to be. Being married to someone from so different a world has not been easy, but neither has it been dull. And the main difficulty is not lack of mutual understanding. We did great during those wondrous early days when we muddled along for hours, she with a Chinese-English dictionary in her lap, I with an English-Chinese dictionary in mine. We often understand each other less now that we understand each other's words more. Still, I am again what I was when I was sixteen, a writer, so I must use words to shape the facts of her life into a fiction I can pretend makes sense. And on this fiction – on this pretense of sense which I know is nonsense, a bridge of words over the Pacific, words, words, words, raising me up when I seek the ocean's depth, casting me down when I reach for the sky, failing to convey or connect feelings because feelings are real – build a mansion for our life together, my translations of her English stories back into the Chinese they live in then forward into my English, words and stories, languages and literature, past and present, cultures and characters coupling, arching, merging, building somehow – mystically? – into an architecture of feeling, binding us somehow – securely.

But how secure can I be? What if one day she writes of me?

Chapter Five

She was born the last day of July. Thus, she was swaddled all through sweltering August, for Chinese tradition even today demands that babies be swaddled for the first month of life. Immobilization has always been a technique to teach lessons. In ancient China adults learned lessons in pillories. The more extreme contraptions led to cruel public deaths which taught the result of nonconformity and immorality. Lesser ones, like that favorite of the opera stage, the cangue, (a hinged board locked around the neck, wide enough to prevent the hands from getting food or drink to the mouth, long enough to prevent the mouth from getting to food or drink) allowed their prisoners to walk into exile, preaching a silent but unmistakable sermon all along their sad, slow way. Little Hai Bao learned early and thoroughly two basic lessons of existence: the constant necessity to bemoan one's fate and the eternal futility of bemoaning one's fate.

Despite her plight and the noise she made about it she was loved. Her parents were over forty and had not dared hope for such a blessing. Even when her mother became pregnant, both parents announced loudly that a baby conceived so late in life was bound to be ugly and stupid. Of course, such proclamations were part of a pageant orchestrated to lull the jealous gods into ignoring the baby. Nevertheless, they sprang from real fears, fears which grew through nine months of reiteration. When the baby was born bright, lovely and normal, the elated parents named her Hai Bao, sea treasure. The character *hai* (sea) was part of both their hometown and their adopted city, but the name referred mainly to Shanghai. The infant was their Shanghai treasure, their proletarian princess, and all the humidity of their dank concrete bunker of a home, all the sweating discomfort of the mother, doomed by tradition to languish in bed next to the child for that first month, not permitted even to brush her teeth or comb her hair, all the exasperation of an evacuation of the ground floor when the annual typhoon flooded it and forced people and furniture into the airless, sloping dormer above could not stifle or even diminish the joy and love the parents felt for their new and most wonderful of treasures. The father cut a hole in the roof and installed a trap window which let a little air and light into the attic and kept a little of the rain out of it, and they were happy although mother and child continued to bemoan their fates and the futility of their complaints. Despite discomfort the parents were happy because of the baby but also because the future was bright. The revolution to improve the lot of workers like them had triumphed; the new government was young, honest and respected by all; if it made an occasional mistake, the *su fan* movement showed it had methods to change and purge itself. What if their new home was too hot and let in water from both top and bottom? It was a considerable improvement over what they had before, and in four or five years the government would build new sewers and dwellings in which they and their neighbors could live happily ever after. What could be finer than to have a baby born at the most auspicious hour of recent Chinese history? a new life to grow up with new China?

Bounce, bounce, bounce; jounce, jounce, jounce. In, out, up, down. Bounce, bounce, bounce; jounce, jounce, jounce. The cockeyed rhythm must have been her first memory. Indeed, she didn't know the memory was inside her until thirty years later, when making love in a sitting position bumped it out. She remembered it as a single adventure although it must have happened more than once. I tried to get her to remember more, but she had only been three years old and memory can no more be forced than love. I must have jammed my body into that sitting position half a dozen times trying to force her to remember more. It was a godawful position, gave me a charley horse in the back of my calf every time. Every time except that lovely first time, the time she remembered. We got into it that time because Hai Bao was always curious to try new positions. When she initiated the lovemaking it was natural, so naturally the rhythm, however unnatural, was right. I must have got the rhythm wrong the other times, jounced when I should have bounced. It was the rhythm, not the adventure, which jogged the memory, so the rhythm must have been jogging in place in her memory all those years and the adventure darted out because it was part of the rhythm, not vice versa.

Naturally rhythm would be her earliest memory and an unnatural rhythm would stand out ready to spring out when jolted. The little girl was accustomed to others' rhythms: her mother's swift shuffle or constant repositioning of her as she slid from task to task in her housework, her father's longer, more purposeful flow, her sister's jerking grab and panting dashes to seek out friends, the big Shandongese neighbor woman's effortless rush. These motions were a part of her, more natural than independent movement. Chinese children are held and carried constantly during their first year's waking hours and almost constantly long after they can walk. This is a sign of love but is also motivated by necessity and the availability of unpaid porters. Babies never crawl because they never have the opportunity to crawl. The very idea of setting an infant on the floor (which is usually tamped earth in the country or concrete in the city) would dismay any Chinese parent or grandparent. Conveniences such as playpens and infant seats were still unheard of in the early Nineties, when Hai Bao and I brought our baby to China, and when we told Chinese about such contraptions they were aghast. "Put a baby in a cage? Tie her up? Terrible. And how can you train the child if you aren't holding her?" Chinese babies are toilet trained by the time they can walk. They seem less energetic and independent – calmer and less selfish, a Chinese would say – than Western babies. Carrying becomes a habit around the house and remains a necessity on crowded city (or village) streets, for sidewalks are nonexistent or narrow and commonly piled with building materials, furniture being aired or repaired, cottage industry workshops and stuff in general where they are not wholly taken up by people hanging their wash across them, preparing dinner or cooking it on charcoal stoves, playing cards or practicing *tai ji*. People going places compete for the streets with busses, cars, trucks, tractors, bicycles, an assortment of three wheeled pedalled conveyors of freight and each other. The crush in the neighborhoods, while not the breathtaking immobility of the local market or the great shopping streets like Nanjing Lu in Shanghai, is dangerous for small children. The duty of Chinese adults is to protect children from danger until the children marry and so become adults themselves. Therefore, little Hai Bao, like other Chinese children, was accustomed to being carried, lived in harmony with the rhythms of others.

But now she was in her safest, most familiar refuge, her mother's arms, yet the rhythm was new. Never before had her mother attempted to run, and running on her mother's tiny, crippled feet created the strange, jarring rhythm. She wasn't certain whether it was the uneven running or her own efforts to see what was going on which kept moving her away from her mother's body. She only knew that every few jumps her mother would gather her back in so that the rhythm alternated between jolting jounces when her mother's arms alone supported her and cushioned bounces when she was nestled into her mother's soft body. Her mother had more bosom than most Chinese, so Hai Bao felt comfortable and secure when pressed to that body, but she wasn't a baby anymore and she wanted to know what was happening around her.

Her mother was racing, along with many others, from one communal dining hall to another. Each hall was empty of food but filled with rumors of its presence at another hall. So off the crowd rushed from one to another, and thirty years later the babe in arms remembered the movement and the excitement: high adventure, new rhythms and dissonances, great waves on a sea hitherto calm, the treasure previously protected suddenly battered by storm. Without the customary lectures Hai Bao was learning another lesson that duty compels Chinese parents to teach their children: adventure is not something to be sought. At each port in the storm the story was so similar that in memory all drift into one. And when Hai Bao remembered she suddenly understood the vague disgust she'd always felt when she entered a restaurant or other closed in place where the odor of refried oil saturated the air.

Ma, I'm hungry."

"Aiya, no food here. I'll find you some. Come." She bent down to pick the little girl up.

"Ma, I can smell food."

"That's from before."

"I smell it, I smell it."

The smell clung to the pillars of the cavernous dining hall, hung from the rafters and high ceilings, flung its tantalizing invitation at the little girl from every vast corner until it wrung from her tears of want, tears of hunger, tears of futility, tears which seemed to come from her nose, not her eyes. Until all the tears and all the odors condensed into petulant, footstamping temper: "I smell it; I want it; right now. Right now." And her mother pulled her back to the breast, again braved the storm, and the bouncing and jouncing of adventure, of the Great Leap into a hazardous sea resumed, repeated itself, doused the anger as it drenched the memory of the child. (Who when she grew up was courted by the son of one of the neighborhood leaders – no bosses in China but lots of leaders – a woman who had held authority in the local dining hall. The woman liked to laugh as she reminisced about the good old days, for they had been good for her family: no adventure for her kids, only food. When the dining halls opened and there was no shortage of food, the family members of the leaders and workers perhaps received slightly larger portions, little else. But when food became scarce, much of what little there was found its way into the mouths of leaders' and favored workers' families.)

Even if Hai Bao's family could have bought food – which it couldn't because stores no longer sold food, all of which went to the communal dining halls – they could not have cooked it. Their pots, cooking utensils and small charcoal stove had gone into the neighborhood backyard blast furnace to be converted into "steel." Every urban neighborhood and every rural commune had such blast furnaces. "The spirit of the people" was harnessed to increase China's steel output tenfold during the Great Leap Forward of 1958. The furnace in Hai Bao's neighborhood was conveniently located next to the local school so school kids could participate in the process by bringing their families' metal goods to be smelted. Hai Bao's father had proudly helped Jie (older sister) deliver the goods, virtually everything made of metal in the house. By the time Hai Bao started school in 1961 the furnace was gone, but a miniature mountain of its twisted product remained in the playground for many years. Unfortunately the children were not permitted to climb or play on it. It was too valuable. Also too dusty. The children would have liked to play on it, might even have claimed they had a right to, for a large chunk of the mountain was made from their playground equipment, which had been among the first items smelted.

The Great Leap was leapt without looking. That was its downfall – and its soaring glory. Think of it as an existential leap of faith by over half a billion people, sponsored by a government which considered the very word "existentialism" a synonym for corruption and decadence (*when the word was allowed at all: in 1983 I was told not even to use it in class*) and banned all discussion of the idea. Yet the people of the world's most populous nation stood together, linked hands, shut eyes and leaped into the unknown. Picture them arm in arm, row upon row atop the entire length of the Great Wall with Mao incanting "*Yi, bei,...Chu,*" ready, set,... go. Everyone leaps. No one drops hands at the last second and breaks the chain. No one in what is probably the most cautious country in the world plays it safe. (Of course "playing it safe" would have been dangerous, as everyone knew. The previous year, during the Hundred Flowers Movement, the government had begged for criticism. To play safe, to stay on the right side of power, many intellectuals did offer criticisms. Then the government recalled its altered perspective and launched the Anti-Rightist Movement, which condemned many of those who offered criticisms to prison camps.) Even today the memory of the Great Leap's boldness, avidity, adventure and innocence inspires many Chinese of my generation, Chinese who have returned to traditional caution because they know too well the calamities caused by the Leap's blindness and stupidity. The Party would force them to take many another leap, but only the original one was voluntary and enthusiastic.

The Great Leap was mainly a rural movement, the movement which accomplished in a few months the collectivization of the peasantry. Talk about quick change artists. Has history ever seen a greater one than Mao? Imagine changing half a billion peasants who had hardly changed in two thousand years into communalists in a matter of months. Everywhere peasants merged or were merged into communes comprising thousands of families, communes which took over many functions of the traditional family. For the Great Leap was a leap toward communism. Although it was leapt without looking, was a leap into the unknown, Mao had popped another cork and the "communist wind" was blowing again, blowing the leapers in the left direction.

Although the Great Leap was mainly rural, communal dining halls landed in the cities too. Talk of urban communes was in the air, and communal dining halls were first steps toward them. No doubt the speed of such steps would have increased to a run and climaxed in a second leap had not the first one stumbled badly and so signalled a false start in this race to replace traditional Chinese values with communism. There would be many another try. As Hai Bao put it on our first date alone, "The Party wants to be feudal father to the nation." *She said it first in Chinese, then translated it into perfect English. I now realize she must have consulted Mei and got it down in advance. That did not occur to me at the time. I was too impressed by the vivid image and the, to me, original idea, pleasures in themselves since most of my Chinese friends and students seemed to vie to see who could cram the most cliches ("idioms," they called them) into their English speech. Although I had thought I approved of Mao's ideas, I did not consider arguing. I was far too taken by her and, now, by her expression of a new idea. Besides, we both had a long way to go in our language development before we could engage in philosophical debate. I was forced to think out and rethink my own ideas. She still has that effect on me.* The goal was to contract traditional extended family functions to enable the Party to replace the patriarch as provider and controller. The cohesion of the traditional family had held Chinese society together for millennia, but the power of the oldest generation had also exerted a conservative influence which had helped prevent significant change since the revolution of Qin Shi Huang. Now Mao wanted change. Making food and its preparation the responsibility of the Party, not the family, and sending everyone out of the home for meals would weaken the influence of the family. It would also free women from kitchen chores and enable them to work outside the home, to "hold up half the sky" as Mao put it (and Western feminists still proclaim on buttons). Many women would work in the dining halls, but many more – Hai Bao's mother for one – could work in industry. So the communal dining halls were planned to change the role of the family, change the role of women and ensure equality in eating.

I still rather like the theory – or would if the communal meals were voluntary and tasted more like the ones Hai Bao's mother served me and less like the ones dished out in my school cafeteria. The problem lay in the practice, in rigidity and in the quickness of the change. Virtually no preparation or education. A little propaganda and a lot of sleight of foot. The Great Leap attempted to vault over intermediate educational and economic stages, from feudalism to communism in a single bound. Education was to be gained by doing, and the doing was to advance the economy so it could supply all the people's needs. Enthusiasm was expected to overcome lack of structure and planning. "The spirit of the people is greater than the man's technology," we used to chant, quoting Mao, in the Sixties. Mao was more a romantic poet than the Marxist theoretician he fancied himself. The Great Leap was poetry in action and is still remembered by the leapers for the beauty of its daring. But since poetry is not edible, the Great Leap is better remembered for mass starvation during the three terrible years which followed it. The economy broke down, there was not enough food to go around and what there was was ransacked by family selfishness in the very halls intended to abolish family selfishness. The city dining halls had to be closed within a year of opening. They have not been mourned. They did not leave behind even a hope that someday the experiment might be repeated at the right time and with proper preparation. They left nothing but memories: memories of innocence, memories of beauty, memories of adventure, memories of failure.

Ah, to have shared the adventure. Even had I known then what I do today, I know I would have eagerly exchanged my dull teenage existence for a share in the Chinese adventure.

"Aiya, when is the last time you were hungry to starving?" inquires Hai Bao, who did share in it.

"As a matter of fact, during the Great Leap I spent a summer in Greenwich Village, my first extended time on my own, and when I ran out of money I subsisted for weeks on a ten cent knish every second or third day." Unfortunately she has heard this story before.

"Yes, and you had relatives you could go to for a big meal when you got hungry enough and a return bus ticket to Chicago when you overgluttoned and got sick."

It's true. I may have been young and adventurous, but I was older and wiser than the Chinese government. I craved adventure and, later, revolution but took no existential leaps. Changes yes, burning my bridges behind me, no. During the Cultural Revolution Cha Cha got a three week tour of China on the basis of his revolutionary credentials. When I was invited to China in the early Eighties, it was for a year, and it was on the basis of my academic credentials.

So why did a popular government, one doing well rebuilding a devastated economy, leap into an adventure which risked all its accomplishments, risked the entire country and population? Adventure is not to be sought. Except by romantic poets. Mao had resources far greater than brush and inkstone. Did he set out to see his ideological and romantic ideals realized in his own lifetime even at the risk of destroying them? Or did he simply fall prey to absolute power? What does popularity mean to a man with absolute power? to a country without democratic traditions? And why did Mao remain popular after his adventure led to mass starvation?

Chapter Six

As Jack awoke one morning from uneasy dreams he found himself transformed in his bed into a gigantic insect. After earning undergraduate academic credentials in literature I had dropped out of school to write the Great American Novel. A dispiriting year later I enrolled in graduate school, changed back into a student having learned I had nothing to write about, no life experience and no imagination to compensate for the lack. It felt like becoming a cockroach. Listen to the culmination of this metamorphosis:

"What is the key word in the penultimate chapter of Sir Thomas Browne's *Hydriotaphia or Urn-Burial?*"

I had been slinging around my own sesquipedalian words, orally exhibiting the spacious sweep of my erudition, my profound, perspicacious penetration and esoteric insight into the capacious speciousness demanded to qualify for the Ph. D., when Morton Dauwen Zabel put that question to me. I couldn't answer it. I couldn't answer any question the three wise men examining me asked thereafter. If they had asked "What is your name?" I would have flunked that one too. They assisted me out of the room and sat me on a bench so they could assess my performance. Fortunately a fellow student happened along and helped me stand up so I could reenter the room and face the music.

When I was informed I had passed the exam, the requiem I had been hearing on the bench did not turn to triumphant jazz. Somehow its strains grew louder. I staggered to the nearest bar and, for one of the few times in my life, got drunk. *Oh shit, now I'm going to have to explain this to Hai Bao. She's never seen me drunk – or stoned or tripping or paranoid. She doesn't even like it when I say "shit." I remember her puzzlement the first time she saw one of our Canadian friends drunk. "Why is he acting that way?" she kept whispering to me. Although all kinds of booze, most of it very potent, are available in China, public drunkenness is taboo. Looking foolish, even admitting to past foolishness or errors, simply isn't done. I almost ended the romance before Hai Bao and I were married by trying to tell her about my previous romances. I wanted to be honest and she hadn't blinked when I told her I had been in jail. What I didn't understand was that in China everyone knew of good people who had been in jail for political reasons. Political persecution was respectable; immorality was not.*

The more I drank the madder I got: "*Dies Irae,* day of dread. Bastards. Empty encyclopedists. No, encyclopidiots. Encyclopidiotic bastards. You were toying with my mind. You wanted to see how far into your arid realm you could lure me. My mind didn't fail me. It quit working because it refused to follow you. *Lacrymosa,* mournful me. I've spent my life studying words and the sum of my knowledge is that I now know that 'diurnal' is the key word in the penultimate chapter of Sir Thomas Browne's *Hydriotaphia. Tuba mirum,* the trumpet will sound. My mind, my knowledge, mine. No dried up mental dinosaur is going to drag my mind into its oblivion. No damn, dusty pedant is going to play with my life because he never lived his own. *Confutatis maledictis,* confound the wicked. To hell with you. To hell with my dissertation. *Libera me,* deliver me. I'm young, I'm alive, I'm American." With the alcohol swilling and the music swelling within me, it didn't occur to me that I was selling out mysticism: my thesis topic was "Heterodox Mysticism in the Works of D.H. Lawrence and Aldous Huxley." I had bought into the American dream: independence, freedom, give me liberty or give me death.

As I added scotch and beer to my declaration of independence, Clark Kent entered the phone booth. I had learned I had little skill with words. A good writer requires either mastery of words or imagination. She does not require both – we can't all be Shakespeare – because mastering words enables him to make subtle points which appear to imply imagination while possessing imagination renders the most obvious words dynamic. In the bar I forsook all such literary cerebrations. The phone booth opened. Shazam! The great mystic had become the great liberator. Down with words and imagination. Up with life. Life is short. Time present and time past are both present in time future. Seize the day. Quit studying and live. The world is not enough with us. Change the world in which the few boss the minds and bodies of the many. Toss the bosses out on their asses. This is the way their world ends. With a bang, not a whimper. That's the spirit. Hail to thee, blithe new spirit.

Yes, uncreative me resolved to recreate the world. Only after the world was changed utterly would I have leisure to write, and then I wouldn't have to create. I would simply write about how I had done it. Well, maybe I wouldn't be able to do it alone, but the Fifties had become the Sixties and for the first time I had the sense there were others out there who might help. The hunter had not yet turned into a butterfly, but at least I no longer felt like a cockroach. As a confirmation of my new dreams and excellent intentions I sprang to my feet and stretched my young body. Then I staggered down to Forty Seventh Street and listened to Trane.

After I sobered up it occurred to me that I didn't know what to change the world to. Nevertheless, I did not return to the University of Chicago. *Shit again:* *I quit a few months after Hai Bao began her school career. Writing this is supposed to make us one, her oriental portrait in my occidental frame. I wish it didn't keep dividing us. In this case it's more than age: I was twenty three when I wrapped up my school career, younger than she was when she finally earned her high school certificate. She didn't start university until she was twenty eight and received her M.A. when she was forty, almost double the age at which I received mine. I've worked most of my life not to be a scholar; she's worked most of hers to be one.* Yet although I had lost the illusion I was a creative genius with a novel inside me, I knew no more of life than I did when I was failing to dig out that elusive novel. I didn't know what I wanted beyond independence. As a result the American dream led me nowhere. In leaping a tall building in a single bound, I stumbled. I simply began playing with my mind in new ways. I played cards, mainly bridge, became one of the better bridge players in the United States. Nights I did not play cards I went to the race track. I was a good gambler, won more than I lost, but I knew I was wasting mind. Then I discovered Bissel Street.

Chapter Seven

Only Mao, the romantic, failed to learn the quintessential Chinese lesson that adventure is not to be sought. Hai Bao learned it well. Her adventure in the dining halls was a prelude to years of adventures in not eating: days of scouring fields near her house for edible weeds; meals of soup which consisted of water thickened with a little flour or doufu wastes formerly reserved for the pigs; old, moldy rice which Ma said should have been tossed to the pigs; rumblings and protests by her stomach.

Her sister learned the lesson better. Jie was thirteen years older than Hai Bao. In 1960 Jie set off on a great adventure. She went to Anhui Province to study medicine. That an eighteen year old girl from a poor family could do this was a measure of how much China had changed. There was no tuition and the government paid living expenses. Jie and her generation were the first literate females in her family, and Jie was the first member of her family to graduate from high school. Now she was going to become a doctor. But what she saw becoming one was a measure of how little China had changed.

Jie was the brightest, most beautiful girl in all of *Pushan Lu Yi Cun*. Yet although she was a member of the one generation in Chinese history in which young people, at least in the big cities, actually could select their own mates, Jie had no Shanghai beaus. Of course she was still young when she left and there has never been a tradition of casual dating in China, but even had she been older the local boys would not have dared approach her. She was too bright, too beautiful, too proud, one to be worshipped but only from afar. A glance was enough to tell a boy this was a girl who would choose for herself, not one who could be chosen. And in her mind Jie had already chosen. She had the traditional Chinese reverence for scholarship plus the modern admiration of science. Hefei, where she would be studying, was the site of New China's premier scientific university. Jie planned to choose a brilliant young scientist for her husband, and Jie was not one who failed to accomplish what she planned. She had a bit of Mao's perseverance.

When Jie returned home for the holidays six months after she left, Ma took one look at her and cried. Although food had been in short supply in Shanghai, Jie had left stout, a quality Ma, like most Chinese, admired. Now you could see her bones and in her hand she carried a black bun, a solid block of sorghum, powdered yam and husks. Ma had not seen its like since the days of the Japanese occupation. Rumors of starvation in the provinces had been swirling around Shanghai, but Ma was not one to pay much attention to that sort of talk. The coarse black thing in her daughter's hand was another matter. In Shanghai flour, what little was available, was white and fine textured. "Pig fodder," Ma wailed before she even said hello to Jie.

"The pigs have all been eaten," Jie muttered in reply.

Shanghai's fine textured cloth interested Jie more than its food. Her body's new shape, whatever her mother might say, was perfect for a *qipao*, the traditional slit dress which did not tolerate bulges. Even before the Cultural Revolution decreed blue Zhongshan suits (*in the West we called them Mao suits*) for the entire population, the Party frowned on pretty clothes. No one except Jie wore *qipao*. Dress was encouraged to be simple and utilitarian. "What could be more simple than a *qipao*?" Jie asked Ba ingenuously. "I can make one in an evening." Jie had quick fingers on the sewing machine and light feet on the treadle. Ma took Jie's side and Ba felt too embarrassed to mention how a *qipao* exposed the girl's legs. Jie stocked up on cloth in Shanghai, and the *qipao* she made were most utilitarian: they attracted every eligible bachelor in Hefei. After the Cultural Revolution Hai Bao inherited many of those *qipao*; Jie had regained her stoutness.

The Sunday after Jie returned to Shanghai guests began to arrive, two of Ba's coworkers and a husband and wife from several rows over. The visitors were all from Anhui. Everyone had heard the rumors and all the rumors ranked Anhui as one of the worst hit provinces. Formalities were quickly concluded: courtesy forbade the guests to accept the offer of tea and snacks which courtesy compelled the hosts to make. Things were not so bad in Shanghai that the offer could not be made or that it could be accepted, but they were bad enough that neither side insisted. A famine is not a tea party.

Ba walked over to Jie, who was not wearing or doing anything likely to attract attention. She wore several layers of clothes covered by khaki pants and a plain white sweater and sat hunched unobtrusively in a corner reading to Hai Bao. Jie pretended not to notice Ba. "Our friends are waiting," he whispered when she failed to look up.

"The monkey king plucked out a handful of hairs, bit them into small pieces and then spat them into the air, crying 'bian' (change)," Jie read to Hai Bao. "*Bian,*" Hai Bao repeated.

"Sorry to interrupt, but you must come," Ba said.

"Oh," said Hai Bao, who was waiting to see what the change would be. Jie pointed plaintively to the book. She was in the middle of a chapter, in the middle of a battle. "Part of growing up is learning to do your duty even when you don't want to," insisted ba.

Jie rose reluctantly. She looked down regretfully at Hai Bao, as if she wished she could perform one of the monkey king's seventy two transformations. Then she shuffled behind ba to the adults, sat down warily, a lamb in the wolf den, and studied the concrete floor.

The others seemed unaware of her trepidation. The older worker turned to her: "Tell us about conditions in Anhui." It was an uncharacteristically direct beginning, an indication of the gravity felt by the guests and even then possible only because Jie was still considered a child. Marriage, not years, conferred grownup status.

Not surprisingly Jie squirmed. Chinese youngsters were not accustomed to being consulted, even indirectly, by their elders. "Please. I do not want to talk," she mumbled. The others acted as if they had not heard, waited. Jie knew something of Chinese patience. She knew how long these people were likely to wait. "It's not too bad where I am, in Hefei," she finally brought out meekly.

"And in the countryside?" The people gathered were all from the countryside and had families there.

Jie squirmed some more. Her voice was almost inaudible. "I stay in Hefei, don't often go to the countryside. Only when I'm sent out to improve my practice." School, for communists, was a formal combination of theory and practice.

"Tell us what you saw there, and even if you didn't see much, tell us what you have heard. You must have heard things."

"Too terrible," Jie whispered and stopped.

"Too terrible what's happening or you feel too terrible to tell?... Tell us," the man demanded when Jie did not answer.

Jie looked imploringly at Ba. "We're all friends," he placated. "Truth always comes out. No one can be blamed for speaking the truth. You're the only one who has been there."

Jie still attempted to hold back: "In Hefei no one is starving."

The implication behind her words so changed, so charged the frigid air that even the five year old child in the corner looked up from her play and tried to comprehend what was being said. Could the electric atmosphere mean a transformation was imminent? No one spoke; the visitors stared at Jie, their eyes full of awe. Jie shrank down in her hard seat as if to escape those awful eyes, but she also raised her own slightly as if to check out the change. Had she suddenly been granted power over her tormentors? Jie was born just a little ahead of her time. Had she been born six years later she would have been among the first to grasp the new dynamics of power and become a Red Guard organizer. Now and here her overwrought auditors must have begun to sense a conflict in her – or perhaps they became more fearful of hearing what she had to say now that it appeared she would say what they most feared – for they became more reticent, more polite, Jie's suitors rather than her interrogators.

Jie tested the air: "But I really don't know anything. Why do you think the rumors I've heard are any more true than the ones you've heard?"

"Comrade, please tell us. Please."

And Jie responded to the supplication despite the fact that her training cried out that for an adult to entreat a child was improper, indecent, shameful. For the first time she looked at her interlocutor. "Really, I don't know much."

"But you have heard things."

"We hear too much, know too little." Jie almost smiled, as if aware she had said something clever.

"Please tell us, comrade. We know much less than you."

"You musn't blame me. Probably most of what I've heard isn't true. You know what rumors are. Mistakes pass from mouth to mouth." She sat straight up in her chair, crossed her legs and.... And *bian,* the transformation was accomplished. It was all the little girl could do to keep from shouting *"hao"* as she saw her sister transformed from child to woman, from beggar to empress. Jie ruled the room now and the others kowtowed to her. If they did not actually throw themselves on the ground and kiss her feet, that was only because the game they were playing had different rules from the ones Hai Bao knew. Her majesty graciously vouchsafed her subjects a smile. "We feed on rumors because we can't get facts."

Not one guest looked anywhere but directly at her, feeding on her words. The spokesman became obsequious: "Please comrade. How could we blame you? We'll be grateful for whatever you tell us, no matter how terrible."

Jie nodded, accepting his tribute. "The newspapers say mistakes have been made, that too many people were making steel or working on irrigation projects when they should have been harvesting grain, that there are shortages, that the communes can provide only bare subsistence."

"Comrade, we can read the newspapers ourselves."

Jie was silent a moment, weighing the sufficiency of his petition. When she spoke her voice was firm. "The talk is that the peasants have no rice."

"What are they eating, comrade?"

"Not much. Ground husks mainly. A bit of cabbage though most of that's rotten. Grass and weeds when they can find them. Rats when they can catch them. I've heard that some people eat tree bark, sawdust, even dirt. Maybe it's not true, but that's what I heard."

"Are they dying? The old people?" The pain in his voice suggested he was thinking of his own parents.

That same pain suggested something else to Jie: "The little babies too. I've heard...." She stopped abruptly. *Aiya,* something is wrong, thought Hai Bao.

"What?... Please."

"I really don't believe it. It can't be true. It's only a story. People like to exaggerate and spread false stories."

"What stories? Please."

"Stories about people eating...." She stopped again. No one prodded now. No one moved. "Babies." She blurted out the word and with it her moment of sophistication and control. "They say the babies would die anyhow because mothers have no milk. They say there are too many children, so families sell their children. They say some people exchange babies so they don't have to eat their own." She uncrossed her legs and stamped her foot on the floor, a child again and petulant. Good, thought Hai Bao. Now she can play with me. "They shouldn't eat babies."

"How can it happen?" someone lamented.

He wasn't addressing Jie or anyone in the room. It was a question for the gods, but it would have taken the gods to halt Jie now. "I'll tell you how it happened. The communes didn't harvest enough food. They haven't for years. But the commune leaders are scared to tell anyone. They're scared they'll be criticized or punished. They're scared of losing face. So they lie. They compete with each other to tell the biggest lie. They brag to the government that they've had a record crop and the government collects all they have because the officials think there's plenty more. So the people starve and Chairman Mao doesn't even know about it. Chairman Mao said every child is precious. The leaders haven't lost face, but the precious children are losing their lives."

Ba was trying to stop her and suddenly Jie's body seemed to be swept up in the flood of her words. She ran over to Hai Bao's corner, snatched the child up and rushed out the door with her. She carried her little sister to a friend's home. Then the friend and her little brother and Jie and Hai Bao raced to the fields and chased each other around until they collapsed in laughter. When Jie and Hai Bao returned home, the guests were gone. Jie did not work on making *qipao* that evening and neither shopped nor sewed the next day. Then it was Spring Festival.

How can it happen? Did it happen? I don't know. Hai Bao was only five. When she told me the story, she could remember the occasion but few of the actual words. Now she seems to have forgotten even those few and charges me with typical foreign exaggeration at the expense of her people's reputation. It's wonderful: I'm being accused of possessing too much imagination. "No Chinese would ever write this," she cries, throwing the pages at me. I'm sure that is true. But many Chinese would say it. Several have said it to me – in private. And every Chinese has heard stories of starvation and at least rumors of cannibalism. Most of the stories and rumors I have heard are centered in Anhui, China's traditional center of famine. I've never attempted to ask Jie what she saw and knows because I doubt she would tell me. She too may have forgotten: the Chinese memory is a fabulous beast capable of performing feats of forgetting every bit as prestidigitatious as the everyday magic of remembering required by the Chinese language. Being accused of excessive imagination is bad enough. I would hate to be the cause of sorcery.

No one starved in Shanghai, and probably Hai Bao fared better than most because both her parents skimped on their own meager rations to add bits to hers. Nevertheless, the three terrible years were anything but majestic for the little girl who was accustomed to being treated as a pampered princess.

The dining halls had closed and Hai Bao had turned five. That meant graduation from *tou er sou* to *you er yuan*, from nursery to kindergarten. Although she wanted to learn to read and was probably ready for more than the few characters she would learn in kindergarten, regulations decreed that she would not begin first grade for two more years. Attending kindergarten meant leaving the friendly confines of *Pushan Lu Yi Cun*, and this meant problems.

The main problem turned out to be a quilt. At the kindergarten all children were required to provide their own quilts for the daily nap – the midday *xuixi* is conventional even for adults in China: Shanghai almost closed down in the noonday sun, for there were no dogs and few Englishmen. All the children had a quilt except Hai Bao. Hai Bao had her father's old padded greatcoat, salvaged at the battle of Huai Hai. It was more than big enough and more than warm enough to cover her. Both her parents worked and there were no grandparents or other relatives in Shanghai to make a quilt. Probably her mother could have sewn one, but her mother worked six days a week and didn't need unnecessary additional work; certainly the family could have hired an older neighbor to make one, but the coat was there and served the purpose perfectly. Her mother was not one to be bound by conformity instead of logic. The coat would serve and the coat it would be however many hints about its inappropriateness the kindergarten teachers might drop.

Little Hai Bao had not mastered the Chinese knack of sleeping anywhere. *Big Hai Bao still isn't much good at it.* Usually she couldn't sleep at nap time, and sometimes she would overhear the teachers making fun of her greatcoat and her family. For only peasants – and even a foreigner can feel the contempt for peasants and the dirt they wallow in when Shanghai *ren* pronounce the word – would use an old coat for a quilt. But that was not the worst of her inability to sleep. One teacher seemed to take a special dislike to her. When this teacher patrolled the sleeping children, stick in hand, Hai Bao always lay as still as she could and kept her eyes tight shut, but the teacher invariably spotted her eyelids fluttering. "Go to sleep," the woman would command, and enforce her order with the stick. It was not a method calculated to enable her to sleep an untroubled sleep, and the child lived in dread of naptime.

Hai Bao does not remember whether she told her mother what was happening in the kindergarten, whether her mother guessed something from the way she acted or whether her mother argued with the teacher over another matter. She only remembers that there was an argument — her mother was not one to reply politely to anything perceived as a slight — and she was removed from the kindergarten.

It was a welcome change. Hai Bao got to swarm all day with the other children in the concrete passageways between the rowhouses of *Pushan Lu Yi Cun*. It wasn't a bad place to play in or grow up in, *Pushan Lu Yi Cun*, this concrete square nestled in a concrete block of low houses jammed together as if all had set within the same forms. It was, perhaps, four *mu* in area (one hectare equals fifteen *mu*, one acre six *mu*), ten rows of ten concrete boxes per row, two rows sharing a single rear wall, four paved five meter wide passageways between the rows. When Hai Bao was young the concrete gave way to fields to the north and a park to the west, but before she turned ten the fields surrendered to more housing and the park, fittingly alas, to a cement factory. It had been a lovely park with tall trees and a gurgling stream whose water was drinkable — after boiling of course. All drinking water in China must be boiled. Hai Bao heard many a cautionary tale about the effect of drinking cold (i.e., unboiled) water: death, usually of children or maidens. Children were not permitted to go to the park alone: too dangerous, and not only because of the water. The most unimaginative Chinese parent could imagine all kinds of disasters which might befall an unattended child on crowded streets or in crowded parks which seem to a Westerner safer (and less boring) than a church. Hai Bao had been instructed from an early age to scream loudly and unremittingly if a stranger ever attempted to grab her. That this had never been necessary was, no doubt, only because she was never allowed out of the sight of some adult protector. Her visits to the park usually occurred when she accompanied her mother or the big Shandong woman next door to fetch water. The women used carrying poles, an almost full bucket hung from each end of a skinny stick slung across the shoulders. The verb for this, *tiao*, is similar (only to a foreigner, Hai Bao would insist: the tones are different) to that for dance, *tiaowu*, and it required a graceful balancing act to stand up and move off plus a gentle bouncing gait to keep the water from spilling. It looked easy and natural; only when Hai Bao attempted to use a carrying pole as a teenager did she learn to appreciate her boundfooted mother's ballet.

Still later in life she learned to appreciate the sensual music which was *Pushan Lu Yi Cun*. The mountains of western Canada, she discovered, sated the eyes - "too much," *I remember her crying and covering her eyes: where I beheld grandeur, the sun reflecting brilliantly off new snow, she saw potential avalanches* - but starved the nose and ears. "*Too much snow, too much mountains, too much trees, too much pretty.*" Nature should be artistic; it should inspire but not the wild romance I carried on with the mountains of British Columbia. *We could laugh back then - at her English and my wild romance. She was in my land only to visit, to see my past. Our future was in China. Six months later Deng Xiao Ping would have the last laugh, but we didn't know that then. Still, I felt joyful when she stood before the big*

*window which looked out over the white valley and the whiter mountains which defined
the valley and the world I loved. I thought my world was winning her over. Until the
time I crept up to her at the window. She was transfixed, but not by my world: her eyes
were closed, the lashes moist; her nose was twitching, her fingers picking invisible strings.
I remembered a photo of her – a dreamy young woman sitting on the grass of Hongkou
Park, willow trees and a stone bridge over small waters in the background, strumming a
pippa as tall as a harp – and slunk away as stealthily as I had come. I thought she had
not noticed my presence, but hours later, as she was cooking dinner, she called out over
the sizzle and clang of stir frying, "I was remembering Pushan Lu Yi Cun. I learn from
here how good there was." "For a child," she added, sensing my disappointment. "Lots
of children, not trees. I could smell the food cooking; I could hear the children singing. It
makes a music inside my heart."*

Chinese memories must be like Chinese music: at first both ring false to
the foreign ear. When I remember *Pushan Lu Yi Chen*, the first sound I hear is
anything but musical, is the hawking which precedes spitting, a noise as loud
and startling as thunder and, in China, as natural, as much taken for granted in
a culture which believes it essential for health to get phlegm out of the body as
the roar of automobiles (a sound even today screened out by *Pushan Lu Yi Chen's*
insular construction) in my culture. Yet even assuming this thunder failed to
clap in Hai Bao's brain, her childhood was no idyll and its smells and sounds no
symphony. Mornings were a stinking cacophony, the gongs and cymbal clashes
of Beijing opera, meant to rouse, to activate the drama of the new day: shouts of
reveille to lazy men and children upstairs punctuated by the percussion of pots,
chamber as well as cooking. While grandmothers prepared breakfast, mothers
slopped the night's catch into the vault which preserved the precious elixir with
floating islands to invigorate peasants' fields, then squatted on tiny stools in the
passageway, banging, scraping, jabbering as they scrubbed enamelled receptacles
with stiff bamboo strip brushes. The noise startled Hai Bao awake and the odor
made sure she stayed that way. Day dawned yawning before the sun. It peaked
as the sun prepared to set. The hammering of heavy knives on chopping boards
was a drum roll proclaiming the end of the workday. Enter the *zheng*, plucked
across its wide range of simultaneous sounds and emotions: scratchy squeals of
children welcoming returning parents; strained, varied chants of pedlars (almost
continuous in her earliest memories, declining in number and tunefulness as
the Cultural Revolution advanced); arpeggios of anticipation of the evening
meal, a family feast even when the fare was scant. Harmonic and discordant
twangs mingled with succulent aromas of charcoal smoke and frying food from
a dozen portable stoves lining the passageway. Waking and dining, the daily
concert's fortissimo movements, were unmistakeable, unforgettable. But arriving
in Canada in the dead of winter, when even the fragrant forests lie frozen and
still, vibrated forgotten strings in Hai Bao's memory, for between the crescendos
of morning and evening the aromatic melodies of Pushan Lu muted but never

ceased. Day performed a rapid but delicate *pippa* scherzo of fast floating, quick changing scents blowing in the wind or exuding from articles hung out to air or spiralling from roasting snacks or frying lunches. The pippaist picked against the reedy whoops of children and a full bowed *erhu* continuo drone of insects. Dinner may have marked the dramatic climax of the music, but for Hai Bao culmination came with night, an adagio of faint smells rising from leftovers cooling in nearby windows and faroff odors drifting in on the breeze, played on a bamboo flute. Not the *dizi*, famous for its high pitched birdcalls, but its lesser known, lower pitched elder brother, the *xiao*, able to murmur and coo like the pigeons in the coop on the roof across from her bed, to pipe soft lullabies to put babies to sleep, to whisper like the adults attempting to keep them asleep. Then sudden cymbal crashes when the babies awoke. Always somewhere a baby was awaking, making its dissonant desires known to everyone in the flimsily constructed village within the great city, then subsiding as suddenly as it began. If the baby was quite close Hai Bao could sometimes catch the first greedy slurps as mouth closed on teat. And when all these sounds faded away, the flick of a foot or the unsyncopated wheezes of her parents or sheer anticipation woke her again and she lay waiting for the creak of wheels which announced the grand finale of pungency when the night soil collectors emptied the contents of the vault into their carts and rumbled off into the coming of the new day.

Six days a week Hai Bao played in the passageway as grandparents watched over the children. Most of the time she was with the Shandong family next door. She was a great favorite there because the family was blessed with seven sons and no daughters. But occasionally — and these rare times were the ones which stuck out in her memory — all the neighbor families would take their children elsewhere. Then Hai Bao was left alone, sitting behind her locked door trying to teach herself to read. Always the door had to be kept locked. No one had ever stolen anything from any of the houses, but the people who lived in them were sure this was only because they always locked their doors. Consequently Hai Bao sometimes experienced a feeling almost unknown among Chinese children, loneliness. *When I taught in Heilongjiang the subject came up and I was amazed to discover my students knew nothing of it. I did a quick survey of the class of twenty year olds, and not one of them had truly experienced loneliness. Toward the end of my survey a few of the students must have taken my astonishment for unhappiness and began coming up with incidents of loneliness, like coming home from school and having to wait a minute outside the door because a grandparent had fallen asleep and did not respond to the first knock.*

The Chinese view history as cyclic, but within each cycle are the peaks and valleys familiar to us Westerners, who view history as a line on a graph. The three terrible years marked the peak of absurdity of the Great Leap Forward. No one laughed at this absurdity, and only one man in the Communist Party leadership was brave enough to try to tell a little of the truth to the emperor. That man, Peng De Huai, was kicked out of the leadership, ostracized and eventually beaten to death during the Cultural Revolution. The Cultural Revolution would mark unimaginable peaks in the mountain of absurdity piled up to justify the unjustifiable, an emperor. Mao's words would be used to excuse actions so ridiculous and bewildering that the clear sighted could not see where they were going and what they were doing and the clear thinking stopped thinking. Expressing only the emperor's opinions leads first to lack of candor and honesty, ultimately to lack of opinions. While governments may think it is good to have citizens without thoughts and opinions of their own, the Cultural Revolution proves it is a disaster.

But before the Cultural Revolution there was a lull, a pleasant valley between the mountains of absurdity. Mao's Great Leap from peak to peak had crashed, and he had tumbled into the valley, where he lay recuperating and preparing a greater leap. Meanwhile, the communist wind abated and the communes began growing food instead of statistics. After the three terrible years came four nervous but relatively good ones.

Hai Bao's primary school years were happy, occasionally glorious although the glory was not occasioned by school. At least once a week Ma took her to an opera: Subei Opera, Beijing Opera, Shanghai Opera, Shaoxing Opera, in a theater, on the streets, amateur, professional, whatever was on wherever it was on within walking distance. Pushan Lu, like every other neighborhood in Shanghai, sang and danced and somersaulted with opera, and mother and daughter took it all in, even when this meant staying up long past the child's bedtime. They were fans, not connoisseurs, and if they missed some of the subtleties they missed none of the spectacle. They trembled when Cao Cao guffawed and shouted "hao" (good, well done, bravo) when Zhuge Liang outwitted him, laughed with Sun Wu Kong, cried for the white snake and sympathized with all xiaojie (maidens). They loved the magnificent costumes, the hideously beautiful face paint, the pageantry, the movement, the dance, the mime, the acting, the acrobatics. They liked the music and story too, of course; yet although traditionally drama was opera and opera drama and the writers of opera were China's greatest dramatists and some of her greatest poets, Chinese opera is much more than music and drama. It must be the most all embracing art form in the world. Its actors train from childhood, practicing every art, learning to traipse through and vault over many levels of meaning and emotion. It is both high art and mass entertainment. Its excitement buoyed Ma above her humdrum routine and sent Hai Bao soaring into spaces she little understood but greatly loved.

Ba marched to a more down to earth beat. His legs were as strong as ever and took him to and from work and on long walks all over the city but never to an opera — or a movie, concert, art show, sporting event or any other kind of entertainment. He didn't play cards or chess or games. Besides walking his most exciting activity was discussing world politics with his cronies. Long ago he had accepted the communist ideal of plain living and hard struggle, and if Shanghai and marriage and fatherhood had muffled the bugle that called him to hard struggle at the battle of Huai Hai, every pulse of his blood resonated to plain living. Boring living the opera fans considered it. He didn't even come out in 1963 when a first rate modern opera company, which combined politics with entertainment, set up its tent almost outside his door. Actually it wasn't a tent, only canvas walls to keep out those who didn't pay one *jiao* (ten cents) for admission, but the walls were erected just inside the little park outside *Pushan Lu Yi Chen*. The lucky people whose houses bordered the park clambered onto their roofs and looked down on the opera, which was about the underground struggle of the Communist Party against the Nationalists. But not even this revolutionary subject matter and the offer of a free rooftop seat by one of his pals could tempt Ba. Ma and Hai Bao paid for tickets, but Ma was rather disappointed by the paucity of costume and pageantry and Hai Bao was too young to appreciate the banter with its burden of political innuendo. Mainly she liked the novelty: the soft but impenetrable walls, the jammed rooftops, the air of anticipation and the drums and gongs as the company paraded through the streets, pied percussionists leading the masses toward the performance and the Cultural Revolution.

At school Hai Bao was a success. She was bright, pretty, popular and, most important, from a good class background. Having no ancestors who were not poor peasants or proletarians was the first key to success in Mao's China. So Hai Bao was a favorite with the teachers, always near the top of her class, always a class monitor, which allowed her to wear an authoritative looking red and white armpatch to match her handsome red pioneer's neckerchief, always chosen for school performances. Because there were so many pupils (fifty four per class, six classes in Hai Bao's grade with another school only three minutes walk away), universal participation in concerts and delegations was impossible, and the same students were selected (mainly on the basis of looks and family background) year after year. She was also the rich kid of her class. China had evolved an egalitarian society in which everyone from a good class background — and around Pushan Lu this meant almost everyone — was assigned a secure job. Workers earned more or less the same salary, which increased gradually with years on the job while prices remained the same. The difference between Hai Bao and her classmates lay in family size. With Jie away and supported by the government Hai Bao was an only child. Virtually all her classmates had sisters and brothers, usually many. *I recall a conversation with a man a few years younger than Hai Bao who was the ninth child in his family. "I am literally one of Chairman Mao's little children," he said. "If Mao hadn't been encouraging people to have more and more babies, I wouldn't have been born." As he spoke Hai Bao gave me a wink which I knew referred to feudal fatherhood.*

Because of her small family Hai Bao was comparatively wealthy. She wore new, pretty clothes because her parents could afford them and had no source of hand-me-downs. Almost every day her mother gave her a *fen* (penny) or two. This added to her popularity: a *fen* would buy a bag of goodies (generally fruits marinated with licorice and salt, then dried; almost never candy, which the girls of Pushan Lu considered much inferior to the sour fruits); or it would enable her to rent a miniature comic book from a sidewalk library, then squat, flanked by two or even four friends, on a miniature stool and read, point, giggle, read, point, sigh, read, read, read. How different were those comic books from mine, from anything I read as a boy. She did not leap tall buildings in a single bound, brave typhoons in far off seas, witness human civilization extinguish races of noble Martians, fall in love with ancient white goddesses in darkest Neverneverland. What need had she for far flung adventures when she could squat amid stacked scatterings of her culture's classics, columns of her history's solidity, cross sections of her present's heroism constructing her future's inevitable grandeur? In the spirit of that rich wreckage and epic socialist construction she shared generously with impecunious friends every pennyworth of knowledge.

She learned generosity by studying Lei Feng. Not that she read about Lei Feng on her stool. She didn't have to. He was her school's, her society's major course of study. Everyone studied Lei Feng, China's model Young Pioneer, a soldier who spent every spare minute performing good deeds, helping others, praising and supporting Chairman Mao. Study meant emulation. Hai Bao would go with a group organized by the school to a local bridge, the only hill in the area, to help push heavy hand carts and bicycle carts up the slope, or she would plunge into the rain with an umbrella to find and protect unfortunates without umbrellas. She often sought out a neighboring family which had many small children and held the baby or helped with the housework. As everywhere in China the tapping of a cane was a signal for children to compete in helping the old or blind person across the street.

The fact that children were encouraged to compete in the emulation of Lei Feng, the Chinese symbol of the new, kind, noncompetitive socialist society, bothered no one. What bothered people was the old society and its unchinese forms of individualism, exploitation and greed. School brought with it a parade of old folks "speaking bitterness," telling tales of their horrible lives under the old capitalist regime. The tales came to sound so similar that the children soon knew what was coming and hardly had to listen. But once an old woman speaking of the terrible *fupi mianbao* (bran bread, black bread) she was forced to eat described it in more detail than was customary: black, coarse, solid, hard to chew. Hai Bao saw a sudden vision of the bun Jie had brought from Anhui. She had an urge to say, "But it tastes good." Of course she didn't. Children learned early not to say such things, indeed, not to speak in class unless invited to and even then to be careful. Making fun of the bitterness speakers was just the sort of thing which might lead to problems. It was both an insult to the aged and a challenge to the new social order and so a political crime. Although a child was unlikely to be punished severely for such an offense, it might cause her family to be investigated. If anyone in the family had a bad class background, the whole family would be in trouble.

Chapter Eight

The revelation of Bissel Street led me away from Lincoln Park as surely as it led me to it. All my life I had dreamed of breaking out of the boxes I had been born into. Once I saw a way, I broke loose every which way. I was the American dreamer dreaming the American dream, no butterflies yet but lovely dreams in which I became people other than myself in worlds other than my own, people better than myself in worlds better than my own. I would have followed my dreams wherever they led me, although I never dreamed they might lead to China. I think I had discovered Mao by this time, but because I discovered him on the back of a Phil Ochs record album, he was a poet, not a politician. Gandhi was still my political ideal although I knew Lenin too, knew that the state was an organ for the oppression of one class by another. It never occurred to me that none of these guys were American because I was all American in how I used my knowledge: as words to show off with, not reality to act on. At parties I alternated between the Great Liberator quoting Marx and Lenin and the Great Lover quoting Omar Khayyam and Marvel. Like most American males I was a games player and fan: a bridge expert, a gambler on cards, horses and sports, a spectator of any kind of competition. I couldn't walk by a playground in which kids were playing baseball or basketball or hopscotch and not stop to watch. Then I stopped to watch the state of North Carolina send in armored personnel carriers to defeat half a dozen black kids throwing bottles.

Even dreamers need cash. Nothing is more American than money, yet the need turned me unamerican. Not that there's anything new about American dreams turning unamerican: America was founded in revolution, but that founding dream began to turn unamerican after the French Revolution added *egalite* and *fraternite* to good old American liberty. To me, who always wants more – more ideas, more cultures, more people, more worlds, better worlds – this seems a natural addition: equality is necessary if liberty is to be universal; fraternity is necessary if it is to be joyous. But Patrick Henry cried, "Give me **liberty**," not "Give **me** liberty." Today me first libertarians scorn us bleeding hearts who dream of liberty for all, not just ourselves. "Quit dreaming. Get a job," they solemnly advise. My mother gave me the same advice. Her American dreams were of money. Is abandoning other dreams to make money American or unamerican? Has it become unamerican to dream of anything but making money? Mom may have thought so, but I was too naive even to ask the questions. I got a job.

I didn't abandon my dreams and I didn't abandon Bissel St, only flitted away temporarily, migrated like monarch butterflies. They flit thousands of miles every year. I didn't make it as far south as the butterflies do, to Mexico, but I got to Greensboro, North Carolina, birthplace of the civil rights sit-in movement. I got a job teaching at North Carolina Agricultural and Technical State University, a black school. On this winter range I could test my dreams of equality and fraternity. Not long after landing I invited a black woman to take a walk with me in the country. Those eastern mountains, west of Greensboro, are mere bumps, but I didn't know these British Columbia mountains then, and those were magnificent in autumn colors. "Are you nuts?" the woman replied. "They'll murder us." Only years later, after I had migrated back to Chicago, did I learn how right she was: a bunch of nigger lovers like me was murdered in Greensboro.

As I taught others how to use words, Shaw's, "Those who can, do; those who can't, teach," often jangled in my mind. I didn't love teaching, but I loved my students. They were oppressed, poor, poorly educated, but eager to learn. They knew few of the things I knew about words, but they knew how to use words to fight for their rights in ways I knew nothing about. Rapping they called it. Unlike anything I had heard. Unlike anything I would do when I began rapping myself.

The day after Martin Luther King's assassination I was driving home up Market Street. Market Street is the main east-west drag in downtown Greensboro, then cuts by the A and T campus on its way to the black ghetto, where I lived – lived joyously, one northern honky among thousands of southern blacks, amidst equality and fraternity. As I approached the campus several students were trying to wave motorists to the side of the road. Being the token honky I was, I stopped. The students told me it wasn't safe to drive by the campus, so I parked my Volkswagen and walked ahead to see what was happening. *When I told her this story, Hai Bao asked why I – and everybody else – didn't just turn around and drive home by a roundabout but safe way. How wonderfully Chinese. Americans, especially Americans behind the wheels of cars, are not so easily intimidated. Some black drivers did stop and talk to the waving students. White drivers disdained even to notice the waves.*

At the school hundreds of students were milling about on the campus side, flinging around words, debating and orating with the passion of the young and beautiful and black, rapping. They were mad and wanted to be bad, so they were also laughing at the action triggered by a small pack of younger boys on the noncampus side of the road. These neighborhood kids were hurling bottles and an occasional brick at passing cars. The students didn't throw anything, but they cheered whenever a car was hit. Only cars driven by whites, the fancier the better, were targeted. Since bricks were not plentiful, they were reserved for Cadillacs and Lincoln Continentals.

I must have stood an hour with the students, who were angry but aimless. Eventually traffic on Market Street ceased. I reckoned the police had blocked off the street and wondered why they had taken so long. Action eased for five or ten minutes. Speechifying softened. Students started to drift off. Then a sight I had never dreamed of in my short, 'til then sheltered, life: an enormous machine, then another loomed out of the twilight. Tanks I called them. Armored personnel carriers I was corrected by brothers who knew more of modern warfare. Unreal! Hollywood, not Greensboro! Mechanical monsters the size of a house cumbering up a city street, telephone pole sized guns pointed at my heart! Instinct yelled, "Run." I assume that is what the authorities expected the students to do. They didn't. *"Why not?"* interrupted Hai Bao. *"Because they're Americans,"* I retorted instantly. *"Aren't Americans human beings?"* she inquired. *That question gave me more pause.* The students ducked behind the nearest class building and waited.

It was April, 1968. I had already been to my first demonstration at the Pentagon. I was on the road even if I did not yet know where I was going. "America, love it or leave it," proclaimed some bumper stickers while others trumpeted pot, acid or political change as the means of national salvation. My car did not sport a bumper sticker. No advertising for the pure of heart. My life would be my bumper sticker. Life: Bissel Street. I was a young dreamer in a young land. I did not yet know how cheap life was along Bissel Street. I had not yet met Manuel Ramos, Bruce Johnson, Fred Hampton, three friends, Latin, White, Black, who would be murdered in 1969. (I cannot call Bruce's wife Eugenia my friend. I knew her no better than I knew Baeta before I looked into her eyes after telling her her husband was dead. But Eugenia was murdered too, as if the America love it or leave it crowd wanted to advertise its lack of sexism along with its lack of racism.)

It was the time of the Vietnam War so Americans had a name for what happened next in Greensboro. Escalation, LBJ had called it. Hundreds of toy soldiers trooped out of their mechanical toy chests and stood, shouldering their toy guns, in the shadows of the monsters. Now the students had something to aim at. As I watched, a spectator as usual, a fan rooting for the home team, first a few, then more and more stole from behind the building to behind a hedge, pitched whatever objects they could lay hands on, then raced for home and safety behind the building. The soldiers remained in lines in the open, standing ducks. Soon some students quit the front lines to search out more and heavier missiles. Earlier only a handful had played at stoning cars. Now everyone joined the team, the less daring or less athletic passing missiles to the pitchers. The crowd grew as the word spread. In the South almost every family owns a gun or two: for shooting squirrels – or toy soldiers. Before long young black sportsmen with twenty twos began showing up and taking pot shots from cover. It took a while for the puppeteers to figure out their toys were being popped at, but soon their bigger guns began to boom. I was surprised to discover you really could hear bullets whizzing, but whiz they did. And ricocheted off walls. Although they were outgunned, the blacks had plenty of cover and none of them were hit. It dawned on me that spectators were as much targets as players, but it was also clear that the home team would win unless the visitors mounted their iron steeds and charged onto the campus. (They didn't and the final score was three to zip: three national guardsmen wounded, none seriously. But in the rematch a year later the guardsmen did charge the campus in tanks and a student was killed and several wounded.)

I watched the game until the late innings, then trudged into the night. Above me the sky was alight with stars and behind me it was striped with gun flashes. It must have been beautiful – oh, say can you see? – but I didn't pay much attention. I walked around not knowing where to go, for the troops were between me and my car and home. I ended up at the house of a young white woman who also taught English at A and T. We had been flirting with one another, but that night I forgot to flirt. I narrated what I had seen, she poured a beer down me and tucked me into a couch on her porch. I fell asleep instantly. Far out: I had just waked up.

Chapter Nine

Wenhua da geming. *"Da"* means big or great and is never omitted when Chinese speak of the Cultural Revolution: the Great Cultural Revolution. The name encompasses greatness of extent, greatness of scale, greatness of repercussions, greatness of disaster. It can still evoke the same kinds of emotions in China that "holocaust" evokes in Jews, but while many did suffer and die, neither the overall depth of suffering nor the number of deaths can be compared to the holocaust. This, of course, is an outsider's view, and an outsider Jew's view at that. An outsider Jew who, at the time, supported the goals of the insiders. Indeed, we Westerners tried to make the Cultural Revolution even more magnificent: The Great Proletarian Cultural Revolution we called it. Not that I or my fellow American Maoists had any way of knowing what was really going on in China. We only knew that our own native liberty was being slaughtered, so we hoped that a better way to *liberte* was through the *egalite* and *fraternite* we thought we saw in China. It seemed reasonable that the liberty which came first in our wide open spaces (and which had not led to equality and sisterandbrotherhood) would come last in crowded China. No doubt Chinese who experienced the death or serious injury of a family member or close friend take the Cultural Revolution much more seriously than I, the outsider who finds it easier to love China than understand it. To me children who torture remain childish even when their tortures are anything but. And childish actions, accusations and invective cannot be taken fully seriously even when they are committed by adults, cause great pain and have long lasting consequences. Part of my difficulty probably has to do with losing face. Public humiliation, which many people suffered during the Cultural Revolution, is awful to Chinese in a way a Westerner cannot fully comprehend and may make events which simply seem childish to me deathly to Chinese. The loss of face is greater just because the perpetrator was a child or a fool.

At the time of the Cultural Revolution we in the West heard little except rumors and propaganda. Now we have been barraged by stories: true stories, short stories, novels, movies, virtually all from victims who were silent or silenced from 1966 to 1976. The Chinese have given a new name to all this new material. They call it *shang hen*, "scar literature," but it is nothing new. The authors learned the theory in school listening to old folks "speaking bitterness," but they had to wait to practice their lessons. It is traditional after the old emperor dies or is overthrown and his old cronies are dispossessed of power to flood the land with accounts of how bad they were, how good the new regime is. Sima Qian, the Han Dynasty historian castrated by his emperor, might have written scar literature instead of ancient history had his emperor lost power. One of my students, a former Red Guard, told me a story of hundreds of thousands of volunteers digging a river with shovels and passing the muck up from the river bed via hundreds of half kilometre long bucket brigades. The new river opened the huge steel mill at Baoshan to ocean going ships. No scars in my student's story, just mass heroism. Had Mao's faction maintained power after his death, we would be hearing stories like that, not the ones we hear now. But the scarless river diggers were neither powerful nor articulate while many of the scarred were both, for the Cultural Revolution's attacks were mainly directed at people with wealth and power and at intellectuals. Deng Xiao Ping, the new emperor, used their scars to consolidate his power.

For Hai Bao, as for all Chinese, the effects of the Cultural Revolution were many. Yet the main effect was simply postponement. She had to abandon hopes and ambitions she grew up with, but because no new hopes were substituted, as soon as the Cultural Revolution ended she went back to the old ones. She ended up doing most of the things she wanted to do, but she did them about ten years later than she should have. She wasted ten years. To my surprise – for by 1983, when I got to China, I knew more than I had known during the Sixties – most Chinese I have talked to about the Cultural Revolution, when we get past the famous horror stories and the cliches, speak of it less as a terrible time than as a waste of time. A great waste of time. However, it was a waste of time during which a lot happened.

Ma and Ba's arguments were part of the everyday cacophony in which Hai Bao grew up. They did not argue about the efficacy of the Great Leap Forward, the dismissal of Peng De Huai or the split between Mao and Liu Shao Qi. We radicals debated such subjects in the West, but in China they were not controversial. Ba and Ma did not even have the class conscious arguments I wanted to assign them as a matter of dramatic correctness, – surely both politics and art cry out for one over second sister – arguments which would have provoked Ba to accuse Ma of bourgeois values and Ma to insult Ba's peasant ancestors, but Hai Bao denies that they ever fought about anything profound or historical. Ma and Ba argued exclusively about mundane matters, food for example. Ba's stomach had become delicate during the three terrible years and did not take well to oily foods, but

Ma liked to use as much oil as could be obtained on their ration tickets. "Cook your own food," Ma would tell him whenever he complained.

Sometimes Ba would do so. Then he would proudly offer it to the rest of the famly. "*Aiya*," Ma would exclaim, "*Xiao Mao* (little cat: Hai Bao's nickname) and I aren't going to eat that poison." Ba's food wasn't oily, but it never looked very appetizing. "If I want to kill myself, I'll use the knife."

"I'll get it for you," Ba volunteered. And the fight was on. It seldom ended until Ma declared that she had divorced one man and wasn't afraid to do it again, Ba offered to go with her immediately to the divorce office and Ma assured him she'd take him up on this as soon as Hai Bao was old enough.

Another favorite argument concerned reading. As a child Ma had attended school for six months, learned a few Chinese characters and always wanted to learn more, to learn to read. She was constantly nagging Ba to teach her. Periodically Ba would make the attempt, but Ma was not quick to learn and Ba, who was praised in the neighborhood for his patience, was anything but patient with Ma.

"No, no, no. This character is '*hong*' (red). It only is '*gong*' (work) when it doesn't have a radical in front of it."

"*Ai*, I got confused again. They look almost the same."

"They don't look anything like each other. One has a radical, the other doesn't. It's hopeless. You can't teach a turtle's egg to be a frog."

"Well, you're proof that you don't need four legs to be a turtle."

Soon they were shouting at one another, and later Ma threatened divorce, Ba accepted and Ma postponed the event until Hai Bao was old enough.

During the Cultural Revolution, from all accounts, fear was in the air and a single misstep could mean disaster. People trod warily. Not Hai Bao's mother. Her hobble almost became a skip. She loved the Cultural Revolution. Not that she knew or cared much about the socialist road and the capitalist road, but the Cultural Revolution brought political education to Pushan Road, and this compensated even for the loss of traditional opera. After all, she had been able to see an opera only once or twice a week while political education sessions happened daily. Since the Great Leap Ma had been employed with many of her woman friends and neighbors at a small local factory which made cardboard boxes. *I may never have conceived that I'd marry a Chinese peasant's daughter, but I had always believed that if I married I'd be getting myself into the product of a boxmaker.* She liked working and earning money, but putting boxes together was not exciting. The political education classes not only broke the boredom but also were a boon to Ma's chances to learn to read. The classes consisted of readings, mainly from Mao's *Red Book* or *People's Daily*. At every session Ma planted herself at the reader's side and peered intently at the page trying to make out the characters. After a while she got pretty good at recognizing some.

One day a new reader was reading. In the middle of a sentence the reader suddenly leaped to her feet, pointed an accusing finger at Ma and announced, "She can read. She's saying the characters before I do. She must be from a landlord family." Ma had been found out: the only country women of her generation who had learned to read were from rich families.

Ma was quick to realize her predicament. Although she hadn't really learned to read as a child, she was from a landlord family and that was a serious crime. She protested her innocence, her ignorance: "I can't read. I always follow the reader's finger, so I've learned some characters. The same characters get repeated in every lesson." Ma thought of the political education sessions as reading lessons.

The other women never paid attention to the readings. They sat quietly knitting or dozing. It took a while for them to figure out what was happening, but when they did Mrs. Wang declared, "I always knew she was a class enemy." Mrs. Wang and Ma had been feuding for ten years.

No one else believed the accusation. "Old women like us don't have ink in our chests; it's hard enough keeping the blood there," one stated. "She can read? I can fly," offered another.

Nothing would have come of it had not the reader been a young and zealous partisan of the latest leading political faction. She knew a class enemy when she heard one. She had caught out a traitor and was not about to let her get away. Ferreting out spies was the duty of every citizen. She accosted the factory leaders: "You comrades have let down your guard. Why have you allowed an enemy agent to infiltrate the ranks of the proletariat?"

The factory leaders, duly horrified, contacted the neighborhood leaders. That evening all the leaders and more followers, curious to see what was going on, came in a body to the house. "*Lao* (Old) Zhang, what's this about your wife being from a landlord family? *Xiao* (Little: everyone in China is either "little" or "old") Hong claims she can read."

Ma hadn't told Ba about the incident at the factory. They had argued the night before and weren't speaking to each other, but instead of seizing an opportunity for revenge Ba was outraged at the accusation. "Her read?" he spouted. "It's about as likely as finding a fish in a tree. I've wasted years trying to teach her. It's hopeless." He was so offended at the very suggestion that all attention was focused on Ma's reading ability and no one thought to question him directly about Ma's class background. Ba was respected for his honesty and the leaders did not really believe the accusations.

Nevertheless, the charge was a serious one and they knew they had to conduct a full investigation. They turned to eleven year old Hai Bao. Chinese schoolchildren were raised on tales of perspicacious "little friends" who had detected their parents spying and promptly squealed on them, but visions of glory and of medals for saving the country did not dance through

Hai Bao's head. The child of new China chose filial piety over patriotism, automatically saved her mother, not her motherland. Softly and shyly she followed her father's lead and said her mother was always trying to learn to read but only knew a few characters.

The struggle continued for weeks but never reached the stage of a struggle session in which Ma was formally accused. After all, this was Pushan Lu, not Hengshan Lu, not a place one unearthed the accouterments of bourgeois life and the cow spirits and snake demons who lived it. Even when an escaped landlord was unearthed, he was invariably old, feeble looking and without material possessions which could also be unearthed. The young reader, *Xiao Hong*, kept calling for a struggle session, and at her insistence factory and neighborhood leaders alternately threatened and wheedled Ma attempting to pry out a confession, but the more they tried the more stubborn Ma grew. Even Ba, who wrote letters to relatives and friends in the Subei requesting documentation (slightly doctored if necessary) and testimonials which could help Ma and supported and rehearsed her every day, learned to respect the stubbornness he had previously hated. "Leniency to those who confess; severity to those who refuse," the leaders intoned. "I come from a poor peasant family. I know a few characters because I always sit next to the reader and follow her finger. Should I be punished because I'm the only one who listens intently and tries to learn from the Great Cultural Revolution?" Ma responded. She spoke this piece so many times that the leaders tired of hearing it and the accusations gradually faded away – except from Mrs. Wang, who was still at it when I began coming around to court Hai Bao. Mrs. Wang triumphantly pointed to me as evidence that Ma was indeed a spy.

The only lasting change from the incident was Hai Bao's position in bed. Crowded countries create crowded beds. Hai Bao had slept with her parents from birth. The Chinese custom is for unmarried people to sleep head to foot. This position works – so long as tall people don't stretch out full length – because the Chinese do not use sheets, only quilts with changeable covers. For years Hai Bao had been sleeping in the middle, her head between and above her parents' feet. Ma said being in the middle would keep her warmer. After the struggle was over ma declared that Hai Bao was old enough – old enough so she didn't need extra protection and could sleep next to the wall. During the next few years the frequency and intensity of Ma and Ba's arguments decreased. Their Cultural Revolution years may not have been great, but they were relatively happy and secure.

Of course children experienced the Cultural Revolution quite differently from their parents. How they experienced it depended on their age. Had Hai Bao been born a few years earlier she would have been a full participant in China's greatest adventure. She would have been a real red guard instead of a "junior red guard" and done all the famous things red guards did, rode the rails for free, attended mass rallies in front of Mao, gone on raids to wipe out the four olds, done battle in factional strife. She would have written the big character posters that denounced landlords who had fled the countryside and come to Shanghai (most of these, in her neighborhood, from the Subei, where land reform had begun in 1946-7, not 1950 as it had in most of the country) instead of merely reading them, amazed to discover bad elements among her classmates' parents. She could have drained the cup of the Cultural Revolution instead of being left with the dregs. On the other hand the dregs contained a bit of the flavor and little of the danger: adventure is not something to be sought, even when the emperor endorses it. Her post as a young student leader, a prospective hero of a second generation of red guards, involved little more work than monitoring classmates to make sure each was wearing a proper Mao badge and gave her occasional insights into the adventures she had missed.

Once she was taken to a struggle session with a young man who had refused to "go down." He was only three or four years older than Hai Bao. The year was 1969, three years after the Cultural Revolution began and its most famous adventures took place. Disruptions created by the red guards had gone too far and what was left of the government decided to get the young zealots off the streets and into the fields. *If one forgot who popped the cork that released the kids from the traditional discipline which had kept them bottled up, it would be hard not to sympathize with the government. I remember a broad hillside littered with stones above Kunming being pointed out to Hai Bao and me. The stones marked the tombs of hundreds of people killed in a battle between opposing factions in the Cultural Revolution. Interestingly, Shanghai, the most "revolutionary" city of the day and home of the Gang of Four, was spared this sort of large scale violence, which was common in many other cities.* Youths were being sent to the countryside "to learn from the peasants" and stay out of trouble. The exception was that one child in each family was allowed to stay home and help mom and dad. This exception kept Hai Bao in Shanghai except for short excursions with her class.

Shanghai *ren* are city dwellers to the core. They loathe the countryside and look down on the peasantry. It is hard for me, a city boy who voluntarily and happily went up into the mountains, to imagine the depths of antipathy aroused in Shanghai *ren* by the notion of "going down" — being sent down, they invariably called it, although technically they volunteered — to the countryside. Even Chairman Mao, who still inspired the enthusiasm of the young, could not make them enthusiastic about leaving the city, perhaps permanently. Nevertheless, they went. There was no law forcing them to leave, but China has never functioned on the basis of law. Public pressure is the real force.

Children are part of the public and thirteen year old Hai Bao, although too young to realize it at the time, was part of the pressure applied to a neighborhood teenager who neglected to volunteer. At the invitation of her teacher she went to the boy's apartment after school. A large group of teachers, school and neighborhood leaders, Party functionaries, classmates of the boy and younger students all crowded into the boy's living room. Like most Shanghai rooms it was small and overcrowded with furniture before they arrived, so the crush of people exerted a pressure of its own. The boy did not look up when the crowd filed in. He had been through this before. Hai Bao wondered where his parents were.

The boy was squeezed into a defensive position between a table and a tall wardrobe, his back to the wall. The school principal stepped out of the crowd and the ritual attack began: "Yu, have you reflected upon what we told you?"

Yu nodded.

"Have you decided to do your duty?"

Yu shook his head.

The principal stepped back. The Party secretary of the school stepped into his place and delivered a long, perfunctory speech about Chairman Mao. Every other sentence was a quotation and every sentence which was not a quotation contained phrases which were. Hai Bao had heard the speech's equivalent dozens of times. It was not particularly tailored to the specific situation, and had the secretary been looking at the boy he was speaking to, he would have quit after the first sentence. Yu never looked up, never changed expression or indicated he had heard. Hai Bao noticed her teacher watching her. The speech was actually directed at her and the other students in the room. One reason they were there was to make sure they volunteered for everything when their turns came.

The end of the secretary's speech acted as a signal for students to take over. The session became less orderly as their accusations sprang from every corner.

"Yu, you're ruining the reputation of the whole school."

"Yu, you're letting down Chairman Mao."

"Yu, you're betraying your motherland."

"Yu, you're opposing the working class."

Yu never replied, never looked at the speakers, never looked up.

A woman stepped forward waving an unsealed letter. "Yu, I've got a letter from your parents. They ask you to do your duty." Yu looked up for the first time, accepted the letter and began reading slowly and expressionlessly. It was not the first such letter he had received. The noisy room gradually quieted as he read. "Listen to your parents," the woman, an aunt someone whispered, exhorted when he finished. "You can't help them this way. You can't do anything here."

"I can study. I want to study." The words, the first Yu had spoken, were almost inaudible. He looked at his aunt but must not have liked what he saw, for he looked down again immediately.

"Study the *Red Book*." "Study Chairman Mao." Everyone including Hai Bao was shouting at the boy. The noise went on for several minutes. Classmates were waving *Red Books* in his face.

Then one of the teachers, a history teacher, was standing in front of the boy. Hai Bao could not hear him at first. The room was noisy and he was speaking quietly, hesitatingly. "... History is also now.... And history is Chairman Mao, Chairman Mao..., the greatest figure in all history. His revolution is the most important one since Qin Shi Huang.... More important than Qin Shi Huang, of course. Qin Shi Huang benefitted only one small class while Chairman Mao's revolution benefits the great mass of workers, peasants and soldiers.... History...."

"Down with history," a student called out. Others snickered.

"Yes, down with history," mumbled the teacher worriedly. Then, louder, he said, "Let's stay with the present. Where would you be now, Yu, if it were not for Chairman Mao? I'll tell you. You would have no chance to study. Probably you wouldn't even know how to read. You would be working fourteen hours a day in a factory. Perhaps you would already be dead from overwork and undereating or from an accident in one of those unsafe factories.... Now you can benefit your mind while you work for your country. In the countryside you can also study."

"Down with studying," called out another student, and several more took up the cry. "Teachers should be sent down too," one ventured.

"Certainly," the teacher agreed when the noise died down. Something seemed to have snapped into place in him. He stood taller and his voice grew louder, deeper, oratorical. "We all know that theoretical study without practical work is useless, worse than useless, harmful. Chairman Mao says theory must be based on practice and in turn serves practice. Gorky went to school for only two years, yet he became a great writer. Chairman Mao tells us we should not read too many books. Reading too many books leads to becoming bookworms, dogmatists or revisionists. We comprehend only when we are engaged in practical revolutionary work. A revolution is not a dinner party or writing an essay or painting a picture or doing embroidery; it cannot be so refined, so leisurely and gentle, so temperate, kind, courteous, restrained and magnanimous. A revolution is an insurrection, an act of violence by which one class overthrows another."

"Maybe Yu is a class enemy," ventured a voice, but no one else took up the cry. The teacher was using Mao's words now. Inside every Chinese lies a mnemonic snare. Anchored by the weight of thousands of years of remembered history, baited by the need to memorize thousands of characters to read the alphabetless language, set by a system of education and government which relies on repetition, not reason, it is sprung by what it hears and reads frequently, for this is automatically learned by heart. Every Western advertiser knows the formula: a catchy jingle plus repetition, repetition, repetition equals the mind set to buy. Chinese does not even require the jingle. Its tones supply the melody, insure that phrases, sentences, paragraphs jangle in the mind the same way every time. *When Hai Bao told me Yu's story, her concern was with what came after the meeting. She didn't attempt to repeat the teacher's speech, which would have bored her now. But she didn't have to. I knew it well. I only wonder if its effect would have been different if I had heard it in Chinese, not English.* Every person in the room had been hearing, reading and reciting Mao's words every day for years. Few could have manipulated them as the teacher was beginning to, but all had to respond to them. Even an opponent of Mao could not resist their hypnotic effect. Most of the people in the room were already caught, so the schoolboy interrupter, who must have been listening to his own desire for action, was met with silence and so silenced into listening only to the words, which meant being gripped by the spell which was gripping the room. The teacher was not interrupted again.

"Remember," he resumed, "the only way to settle questions of an ideological nature is by the democratic method, the method of discussion, of criticism, of persuasion and education, and not by the method of coercion and repression. We must win over the backward elements. We must serve the Chinese people heart and soul. However active the leading group may be, its activity will amount to fruitless effort by a handful of people unless combined with the activity of the masses."

Suddenly Yu looked up searchingly at his teacher, who immediately looked down and began to stumble over his words. The boy lowered his eyes again, as if out of sympathy, and the older man grew even more passionate. "Now...now.... Now, Yu, you say you want to study, but you know that Chairman Mao tells us we must learn not only from books but mainly through class struggle, through practical work and close contact with the masses of workers and peasants. Learn from the people. Serve the people. Integrate yourself with the broad masses of workers and peasants and do it in your practice. Intellectuals tend to be subjective and individualistic, impractical in their thinking and irresolute in action until they have thrown themselves heart and soul into mass revolutionary struggles or made up their minds to serve the interests of the masses and become one with them. Don't drop out of the revolutionary ranks at a critical moment and become passive. You can overcome your shortcomings only in mass struggles over a long period. Be resolute, fear no sacrifice and surmount every difficulty to win victory. Successors to the revolutionary cause of the proletariat come forward in mass struggles and are tempered in the great storms of revolution. Take my hand, Yu. We can assuredly build a socialist state with modern industry, modern agriculture and modern science and culture. Play your part. Take my hand and with me follow Chairman Mao into a future of incomparable brightness and splendor."

He held out his hand and Yu instinctively stepped forward and began to raise his own hand. Hai Bao felt tears in her eyes; indeed, there was not a dry eye in the room. Except for teacher and student. "Dare to struggle, dare to win," barked the teacher. Yu's hand dropped and he jumped back to the wall. A collective groan filled the room, which had been silent except for the spellbinding voice of the teacher. Now the spell was broken. People began surging toward Yu, but the teacher was still in command. "Wait," he cried. "Chairman Mao says no violence." When they halted he turned back to the boy. "What do you want to do, Yu?"

"I want to study," muttered Yu, eyes cast down.

The session should have ended there, but it dragged on another hour. Neither kindness nor shouts, exhortations nor threats could break the boy's weak seeming resolution. He never argued back, never defended himself, never looked up, spoke no words except "I want to study" and "no."

On the street on the way home Hai Bao's teacher consoled her: "I'm sorry you didn't get to see a more successful outcome, but don't worry, we'll persuade him. Chairman Mao tells us never to give up and we won't. Every person is precious."

Hai Bao has a talent for forgetting things. She forgets something almost every time she goes out. The talent was obviously developed early in life. After she arrived home from the struggle session she realized she had left her book bag at the boy's apartment. What should she do? She didn't want to go there and have to talk to the boy. The next day was Sunday. Maybe she could get her father to go.

The problem solved itself. Before she got out of bed the next morning, the boy brought round the bag, which contained her name and address, and gave it to her mother. When Hai Bao opened the bag she discovered a letter:

Xiaojie: (This means "miss" and was a strange, old fashioned form of address. In those days everyone was called tongzhi, comrade.)

Please pardon me for writing to you, but I have not talked to anyone for three days and I am afraid to write in my diary. It seemed like fate left me your book bag. Please forgive me, xiaojie. Tear up my letter if you want to, but I need to talk to someone. I hope you won't show this to anyone, but maybe you will think you have to. It doesn't matter. It is my fate to suffer. Maybe they will kill me, maybe they will make me kill myself. If something happens to me, you must not blame yourself. I am not a class enemy. My parents are both Party members and I was one of the first red guards in our school. I went to Beijing and I saw Chairman Mao. I saw Chairman Mao, xiaojie. I will always love Chairman Mao, but how can I love the lies being told in his name? Chairman Mao is a poet. How could he want us to destroy beauty? When I returned from traveling, I participated in raids to smash the four olds. On one of those raids I had an experience which changed my life. I want to tell you about that, xiaojie. I uncovered an old Ming Dynasty vase under some garbage. I was about to smash it when I looked at it more closely. I liked its shape. It was fat and graceful, strong yet delicate. It was blue and white and pictured a sparkling river and a path leading up into tall mountains. In the background mists you could just make out a city. The vase was inscribed with a poem by Chang Yang Hao of the Yuan Dynasty. Maybe you know it:

Dong Pass

Peaks as if massed,
Waves that look angry,
Along the mountains and the river lies the road to Dong Pass.
I look to the West Capitol
My thoughts unsettled.
Here where the Qin and Han armies passed I lament
The ten thousand palaces, all turned to dust.
Kingdoms rise,
The people suffer;
Kingdoms fall,
The people suffer.

I could not smash the vase and I would not steal it. Although I have done many bad things, I am not a thief, *xiaojie*. I put the vase back in its hiding place and left, but I kept it in my heart. After that I did not go on any more raids. I began to study on my own. I studied ancient history and poetry. We are only taught about the evil. We never learn about the good and beautiful things in China's past. I want to know everything. My brother and sisters were marched off to the countryside, but I was allowed to stay here to help my mother and father. My parents were being struggled against. Finally they were sent to a May Seventh Camp and I was told to prepare to go to the countryside. I know how terrible the countryside is and I know there are no books. I will not be bullied. In the past I bullied too many people myself. I will not go. They are doing everything they can to make me. If I refuse, maybe they will break me like I was supposed to break that vase. It is not because I am needed in the countryside. It is because they cannot bear for anyone not to follow their orders. They have to break everyone who thinks for himself. They make my parents write letters telling me to go. It is the only thing they are allowed to write to me. You heard Teacher Wu, *xiaojie*. He made the speech they wanted to hear. He did not believe a word of it. They were already starting to criticize him because he is my teacher and they said it was his duty to make me go. If he did not do that, they would have struggled against him. There was not a word of his own in that speech. I was stupid, I almost believed he meant it. (The next two lines are blacked out and can't be read. Hai Bao thinks they said something that might have got Teacher Wu in trouble if she showed the letter.) Maybe I will be forced to end my life, but I will not waste my life. Thank you for listening to me. I think you are a kind girl, *xiaojie*. I hope so. I will conclude by quoting another poem. It is by Han Shan:

I make my way up the Cold Mountain path;
The way up seems never to end.
The valley so long and the ground so stony;
The stream so broad and the brush so tangled and thick.
The moss is slippery, rain or no rain;
The pine trees sing even when no wind blows.
Who can bring himself to transcend the bounds of the world
And sit with me among the white clouds?

Hai Bao was already a beautiful girl. I think this poem was intended as an invitation to her, but Hai Bao doesn't think so even today. She gets angry if I suggest this. Nevertheless, she did not show the letter to anyone and she has kept it to this day. She saw Yu on the street a few times but never spoke to him. Apparently he avoided the countryside. The ardor of the masses to struggle tended to cool when it did not meet quick success. There were too many easy ways to win revolutionary victories.

Before she turned thirteen Hai Bao's skinny body had ceased to be a child's. Her puberty rite consisted of a tight band her mother made to encircle her chest and conceal her budding breasts. Hai Bao felt ashamed every morning when she put it on, but she would have felt more ashamed without it. She was relieved when winter came and the bulk of several layers of clothing made the band unnecessary, but when spring came she was appalled at how much her breasts had grown and feared the band would no longer conceal them. No one told her what was happening to her body and she asked no questions. Such things were not discussed. When she began to menstruate her mother gave her soft paper to absorb the blood. Nothing more.

Was it this lack of education which turned her into the woman-child I married? formed the mind within the perfect yet childlike body, the mind so refreshingly innocent of the world worldly me knew? Except I, not she, was the innocent one on that wonderfilled night, the night we had both been waiting for, forever it seemed although we had known each other less than two months, our wedding night. Watching her remove her clothes, piece by piece, slowly, shyly was the most powerful, the most private experience of my life. Too private to write about, too powerful not to. For too long I had been holding myself back, holding my instincts in, forcing myself to comply with what my lack of imagination imagined to be Chinese custom, Chinese morality. There was nothing Chinese about it: I was acting out the Victorian heritage and Fifties upbringing I had spent my adult life rejecting. The little red folder with Mao's image on the cover, the marriage certificate we posed holding so proudly in the wedding photo I snapped with tripod and self timer, means nothing. What seals a Chinese marriage is the banquet. Of this I had no inkling until a year later, when I heard the full story of her friend Qiu and my friend Mei, our matchmakers. Before he met Mei, Qiu had gone through the legal marriage rigmarole with a previous girlfriend in order to get placed higher on the waiting list for an apartment. He was able to marry Mei because there had not been a wedding banquet. He encountered no problem with Chinese law, only with his danwei (work unit), which awarded him an apartment based on the first marriage certificate, then attempted to repossess because he was living with a woman other than the one on that certificate. Custom, not law or even sex, binds a Chinese marriage. My excruciating efforts to preserve the bonds of the Victorian morality I imagined to be Chinese had kept me too busy to notice I was breaking the real bonds, and Hai Bao, who spent much of our early life together showing me the ropes, said nothing. So I knew nothing of her sacrifice, thought nothing of it when she dropped plans for a traditional wedding banquet as soon as I expressed my desire for speed and her. I reviled her friends and relatives urging caution, urging compliance with the tradition I was violating as I agonized imagining I was obeying it. I was as proud of my forbearance as I was ignorant of hers as I waited for the clothes to drop, thinking only the most literary of lustful thoughts. For weeks I had been stroking her body, feeling the exotic, self forbidden fruits wrapped in the extravagant silk of her skin. Oh, that skin! After I was finally allowed to touch her – we had brushed accidentally as we sat down on a bus going home after our second meeting; she jumped back as from a bee sting and barely spoke to me the rest of the trip – I could not keep from running my hands over it. Western women occasionally have a patch of it on the back of the thigh, but all of Hai Bao's skin was like that, perfectly smooth, irresistible. I asked no questions, never considered why, only knew I had never known reality could be as tactile as those legs, that body, couldn't stop touching, stroking. Yet somehow I had restrained my appetite, refused to taste until after the unceremonious civil ceremony. I'm sure she offered. She was as impatient as I for sexual fulfilment (as my sophisticated Western concupiscence labelled her too long innocent curiosity). Yet when the moment came – after the bureaucratic procedure and after the bike ride back to the Jin Jiang and after the photographs and after the tea – she had wanted to talk. So we had lain in bed, embracing but fully clothed, and talked, memories of childhood mainly. Fascinating stuff. The stories were beginning in earnest, for it was the first time she tried to tell them without the aid of a Chinese-English dictionary. And the only time I was less than fascinated. If chapter five or seven lacks detail, blame it on my inattention on our wedding night. She must have noticed my inattention, for after a while she stopped talking. At last, I gloated to myself. Then, to my vast surprise, I started talking, telling her about my childhood. It's only fair, I thought at the time. I owe her that much, I told myself. The fact is, I must have been as scared as she was. I had no more experience with a woman like her than she had of a man. I might have talked longer than she did. And she might have been less attentive than I was. Eventually she announced she was going to take a shower. At last, I once more gloated to myself, shed my clothes and lay in bed, my mind abuzz with carpe diem poetry, eager to gather rosebuds while I may. After an age at least she emerged from the bathroom – still fully clothed. Almost the first thing I had been told about her was that she was chaste, but this was going too far. This smacked of childishness, not chasteness. "Had we but world enough and time," I began reciting to myself. She glanced at me, looked down modestly, and commenced removing her clothes, as self conscious as a child in her first gym class. Slowly the body began to appear and.... And bian, the transformation was accomplished. This was no child. My hands had already told me her body was beautiful, but seeing it was something else: O, my China, my new found old land. I wanted to worship, to kowtow, to kiss the slender feet. Then she was standing bashfully in panties only and all the literature dissolved, all the sophistication derived from all the women I had ever known vanished, and I was a teenager again, staring raptly at my first copy of Playboy. Wow! I had married the centerfold. Was I really going to be allowed to take this celestial body into my dirty arms? Get ready, I panted to myself. Then the panties dropped and.... And another transformation was accomplished. The goddess was a child after all: delicate, hairless. I was stunned. Her skin was smooth for the same reason a baby's was. How dared I touch this girlchild I lusted after? How dared I dream of kissing those baby feet and working my way up the silky, sensual legs? I couldn't move. So she came to me.

In her ignorance of everything to do with sex Hai Bao was like other Chinese adolescents. But she was worse off in one way. How she wished she had a sister she could talk to. Because she didn't, she spent a lot of time at friends' homes. She was still friendly with the Shandong family of boys next door, and most of her friends had older brothers, some of whom Hai Bao grew accustomed to talking to. Conversation between boys and girls was considered immoral, but it was hard to avoid when families lived so close together. At school was another matter and Hai Bao was more careful there, but even there she occasionally violated the taboo. You could talk about different things and in different ways with boys. She didn't do it often, but to do it at all could lead to trouble.

It was safer to walk alone at night, and she liked to steal out when she had no friends to play with. She avoided walking during the day. Adolescent boys, with little schoolwork and without adults in their home to discipline them, had taken to clumping together on streetcorners and calling out to passing girls. Hai Bao tried to cross the street, to ignore them, to not hear their lewd words, but the mere knowledge that they were calling at her made blood rush to her face. At night the boys were gone, the streets peaceful. She always headed toward town, away from the blank, black fields. There were just enough streetlights so the city felt neither too dark nor too light, just enough people so she felt comfortable, among others without being pressed by them. When she returned home she fell asleep easily, a rare pleasure.

Jie got married just before the Cultural Revolution began. On her last trip home she and Ma had held many discussions. Hai Bao listened sometimes, but she was only ten, too young to be very interested. Many men wanted to marry Jie, but Jie had narrowed her choices to two. With Ma's approval she chose a brilliant young geologist four years older than herself.

If only she had waited. When the Cultural Revolution got rolling, it was revealed that her husband had been sent down as a rightist in 1957, and although he had been rehabilitated subsequently, the Cultural Revolution reopened all such cases. It appeared there were landlords in his family background as well. This was all a terrific shock and setback for Jie (both of whose parents had been landlords). The man had revealed none of this before he married her. After a long ordeal in Hefei her husband was sent off to the Northeast for reform through labor. Jie wanted a divorce, but her husband would not agree, and there the matter rested for several years. The two saw each other for only three weeks a year, when he received his holiday.

China has never been a mobile society and the only times Hai Bao had been outside Shanghai were on school field trips, i.e., class trips into the fields around the city to help with the harvest. So when she was fifteen and Jie invited her to come to Hefei for Spring Festival, it was a progress of a thousand *li* in a day. She would travel on her own and in Hefei have only Jie, whom she had not seen in years but remembered as a pal, not an authority figure, to supervise her. Being allowed to go proved she was no longer considered a little child, and she looked forward to great fun. Her suitcase was loaded with cloth to make new clothes. She had shared Jie's passion for fashion since the days she had watched her sister making new clothes, helped her in small ways and been asked for her opinions. Now, unfortunately, she would not often be able to wear the clothes in public, but surely that would change someday, and during Spring Festival in a distant place perhaps no one would object. What fun it would be to strut the streets of Hefei and let the locals wonder who she was. If only it weren't winter, when cold would restrict what she could wear even inside. In Shanghai Hai Bao and her girlfriends liked to dress up in their own homes, and sometimes they would sneak over to have photos taken at a local studio where someone's older brother or cousin or neighbor worked. The photographers laughed at the outlandish costumes which had once been fashionable and the girls giggled. It was a delicate feeling, a dance of daring and desire on a wire sagging between morality and maturity. She knew she couldn't reach either side because Chinese tradition and the Cultural Revolution, not her own actions, determined destiny, but she didn't care so long as she didn't fall in front of her friends. Knowing how easily the wind could change directions and blow her over made the feeling all the more irresistible. And with every twenty six *fen* photo Hai Bao received a bonus. From Ma she had inherited a most unchinese characteristic, hair which curled. How her friends envied her for it. Other girls foolishly used heat to induce curls and for their troubles got severely criticized and forced to make public apologies for their bourgeois individualism, but Hai Bao couldn't be blamed. She always let a friend pick up the photos, and the friend always reported that Hai Bao's photo could not be released until the photographer examined her hair. So everyone was reminded of her curl and the photographer certified that it was natural and gave her the snapshot. She was as proud of her ethereal curls as she was ashamed of her earthly breasts.

Once there had been many little photos, but only one survives. It displays a thin girl in a long cloth dress which makes her look tall and hints at womanhood by concealing it. And there, beneath the beautiful, beckoning face, at the tip of the shoulder length hair, winks the famous curl. Being accustomed to Western hair, I had never noticed it until Hai Bao told me the story which focused my attention on it.

Jie had undergone a new transformation. Her blue Zhongshan suit was trim and well fitted, but it emphasized the fact that she was a married woman of twenty eight, not a girl. She was less excited than Hai Bao had hoped when the cloth was produced. "We can make you some clothes," Jie explained, "but you can't wear them out. I'm trying to get a divorce and that's just the sort of thing which can spoil my chances. You've got to act very proper." When she saw her little sister's disappointment she laughed and said, "Don't worry, I'll help you make them. You can admire yourself in front of my mirror as much as you want." She pulled Hai Bao to a rosewood framed full length mirror. "Why do you think I bought this in Shanghai and shipped it up here? I must have known the Cultural Revolution was coming. These days my high life of red lights and green wine goes on exclusively in front of this mirror, and you'll have to do your showing off here too. You can start now; take off your jacket. You've really grown up, haven't you?"

Jie's best friend lived next door. The woman's father had died a few months earlier and her mother was visiting from Beijing with her youngest son, who was a year and a half older than Hai Bao. When the two older sisters visited, Hai Bao and Andi, the boy, were thrown together, but they found little to say. It was much easier, Hai Bao discovered, to talk to boys she had grown up with than strangers. That was too bad because Andi was good looking and you could see he was from the city. Most of the people in Hefei looked like peasants to Hai Bao.

Two days after her arrival Jiefu, Hai Bao's brother-in-law, walked in. Jie had been talking about him and her problems with him, but Hai Bao had never given him a thought. He never gave her a thought either, never seemed to notice her presence. Not that he was rude: he was a courteous man whose body had grown strong but whom no amount of physical labor could make anything but a scholar. He was preoccupied. During his long isolation in Jilin Province, during long hours of work which exhausted his body but made no demands on his mind, he had thought about little except how to get back to his young wife and how to win her back once he did. He had a plan; indeed he had many plans. None of them took into account his wife's young sister. Which was what Jie had been counting on.

There was only one bed in Jie's apartment, a big one. The three of them would share it. People in overcrowded, underhoused countries are used to such arrangements. In fact Hai Bao had never known any other style of sleeping. Jie would sleep in the middle with Hai Bao's head by her feet. She had instructed her little sister carefully: "If I kick you, you cry." Hai Bao did not understand. "You're not supposed to understand, you're too young. Just remember, when I kick, you cry."

Hai Bao went to bed first. Traveling in China is slow and wearing, and Jiefu's entrance had prevented her midday nap. She was very tired. Jie and Jiefu stayed up late talking and arguing. Hai Bao could just make out the rise and fall of their voices as she fell into sleep, deep sleep. The next thing she felt was a sharp pain in her shoulder. Instinctively she squnched down in bed, under the quilt. This succeeded only in causing Jie's next kick to strike her in the mouth. She cried out and bit Jie's big toe. Jie also cried out. "What's going on?" boomed a man's voice. Hai Bao screamed. The room was completely dark, darker than it ever got in Shanghai. Hai Bao was afraid of the dark and more afraid of the strange man with her in the dark. She jumped up and her shoulder hit the framed portrait of Chairman Mao above the bed. The picture clattered down, the Chairman adding his reprimand to those of her sister and brother-in-law. She had no need to remember her sister's instructions to cry: she was more scared that she had ever been in her life.

By the time Jie got her back into bed, she was not sure whether she would die of cold or fright and didn't much care. Jie had to switch positions, to lie with her and comfort her, which was just fine with Jie. If her husband wanted to fondle her, he would have to settle for her feet, and if necessary she could kick him. *I'm beginning to get the message, Hai Bao — ten years late. Chinese stories always have a moral, and you told this one after we had kissed and made up after one of our first quarrels. Needless to say, I didn't catch on then, so after our next quarrel, when I awoke in the middle of the night desiring to kiss and make up again, desiring you, I was granted the wish I had failed to seize on our wedding night: I groped for your lips and kissed your feet instead.*

Hai Bao lay in the bed, unmoving and miserable, until it was light enough to get up. When she crept out of the room, Jie followed her. Once they had escaped the bedroom Jie looked at Hai Bao and began laughing. She tried to control herself, but the harder she tried the harder she laughed. Hai Bao grabbed a long coat and shoes and dashed from the house.

Outside stood Andi as if he were waiting for her. "Good morning," he called, and she practically ran to him. She didn't know what she talked about, for it wasn't until the next day that she asked all the normal questions one asks a Beijing *ren*: do you really have to wear surgical masks to keep the dust and sand out of your lungs? how cold does it get in winter? have you ever seen Chairman Mao or Premier Zhou? do you really eat noodles instead of rice? But talk she did. They walked and talked for hours.

From the next night on she did better. When Jie's first kick came, she dutifully cried and Jie dutifully switched positions in bed to comfort her. In the morning she went out, met Andi, who was always waiting for her, and they walked and talked. Afternoons she slept in preparation for the long night. The routine of it, although it lasted only a few days, made the torture bearable. Dinnertime was the worst time. Jiefu noticed her presence now and scowled as if he wanted to eat her, not his rice. Her fear of him made her crying at night easier and more real.

On the eve of Spring Festival Jie and Jiefu stayed up late, long past the barrage of firecrackers which greeted the new year. That night Jie did not kick Hai Bao, and Hai Bao slept right through the barrage of firecrackers which greeted the new day. She woke up late, crept out of bed alone, put on her nicest new clothes and went out. Her heart sank; Andi was not waiting. He must have been watching for her out the window though, for he soon hurried out in his new clothes, a shiny grey Zhongshan suit. "Happy New Year," he said, and she impulsively grabbed his hand and shook it the way she had seen foreigners do in the movies. They strolled longer than ever through streets carpeted in the thick paper plush of spent firecrackers. A few days later, when Hai Bao was about to leave for the train station to return to Shanghai, Andi shook her hand. It was the second and last time they touched.

The new year was to be a good one for Jie. She gave up her divorce plans, got permission to move to Changchun, near Jiefu, and in the autumn gave birth to a son.

The year was not to be a good one for Hai Bao.

She was ambitious. The drive ran in her family, at least on her mother's side. It had driven her mother to get a divorce and leave her home village, decisions which were previously about as possible for a woman as fishing the moon out of the water. It had driven her sister to college, a medical career and a scholar husband. Scholarship, not commerce, was the traditional Chinese high road to success, the one her sister drove down without looking left or right. For Jie there had been roadblocks and detours, but she got where she was going. (Her husband is now not only a prominent scholar but a leader of his university and a member of the Chinese equivalent of a provincial legislature.) For Hai Bao that road was closed. During the Cultural Revolution intellectuals were scorned; "stinking nines" (their number in a list of undesirable categories), they were called. When Hai Bao was caught reading *Hong Lou Meng* (*A Dream of Red Mansions*), China's most famous classical novel and a favorite of Mao, she was roundly criticized by her teachers. Her mother got into trouble for knowing a few Chinese characters. The universities shut down. (Most would reopen, on a very limited basis, two years later, in 1973.) At this time finishing middle school – not really graduating for the final two years had been lopped off – usually meant being sent to the countryside to learn from the peasants or assigned to a factory to learn from the workers. Hai Bao would finish in 1972 and the factory would likely be her fate since her family situation would keep her in Shanghai. However, there was an additional element in the three in one alliance, workers, peasants and soldiers, which controlled the country. Joining the army seemed the most promising path. This was the conclusion she and Andi had agreed upon. It had been a main topic of discussion during their long walks. It was the sort of thing it was easier to talk about with a boy. Andi was clear about it and Andi knew, for he lived in Beijing, the seat of government and the heart of political knowledge. The army's prestige had always been high and had now reached its peak. It was the army which had won the revolution and, more significant now, won the Cultural Revolution or at least ended its chaotic period. Army men held many of the highest positions in government and the leader of the army, Lin Biao, was Chairman Mao's closest comrade-in-arms and designated successor. Although this would change later in the year with Lin's death and disgrace, even after much of the military leadership was displaced or demoted, the prestige of the army itself remained high. (As it had to with real threats of war with both the Soviet Union and the United States, which was now bombing all over Indochina.)

After middle school the best students, the ones their teachers recommended for their high scholastic and moral standards, could join the army. That was Hai Bao's plan, and there was no reason to think it would not succeed. She was at the top of her class and a favorite with the teachers, a monitor with authority to send home any student in the school not wearing a Mao badge, a member of the only two extracurricular teams allowed during the Cultural Revolution, the ping pong team and the swimming team. (The swimming team was there because Mao was a swimmer. Its main activity was to leap into the *Changjiang* [the long river or Yangtze] and emulate Mao's famous swims, not across the river as Mao swam – the river was over fifty kilometers wide near Shanghai – but as far as he swam.) She sang whenever the school presented songs from the eight approved operas and was always selected to help welcome visiting dignitaries such as Prince Sihanouk and Zhou En Lai when they came to Shanghai. (The Zhou En Lai visit had been the high point of her young life. He was her hero as he was for most Chinese. The pictures on her and everyone's walls were of Mao and she always wore the requisite Mao badges, but Mao was a god and unapproachable. Zhou was human and handsome and kind and good, a man to be looked up to like a father, a father not of a child but a newborn nation and all it stood for. Although Hai Bao never got within twenty meters of Zhou, just being that near made her unable to stand still, and the adult overseers repeatedly had to order her – and many others – to calm down. For weeks afterwards she dreamed of Zhou En Lai every night. And woke up just as he was about to touch her.)

That summer Hai Bao's class went on its annual field trip to learn from the peasants and help them with the harvest. Unfortunately the peasants did not much appreciate the help of a bunch of city kids who didn't know how to do the work, couldn't have cared less about it and felt no need of further edification. They gave their young helpers little work yet objected when the kids tried to be kids, to play games and have fun. It was a boring, unpleasant time. Even walking was dangerous. One afternoon Hai Bao and a girlfriend took off for a walk, holding hands as young people always did. They were escaping a political lecture, but night stole up and fell suddenly upon them like a reactionary spy. Soon the world was black as the heart of an imperialist. There was no moon and when Hai Bao sought it the sky was spattered with specks of light which shed less light than a revisionist polemic. Suddenly one star streaked across the sky toward her. She squeezed her friend's hand, shut her eyes tight, froze. The star never hit and she never dared look up again. The girls trudged on in silence, two timid shadows surrounded by black, spooky fields. Being alone terrified them, but far more they feared being saved, discovered by some wild peasant hero. They got back safely, but the fright kept Hai Bao awake all night. From then on she stayed with the group.

The days seemed like years and one way she filled them was by writing letters. Among others she wrote one to Andi and one to a neighbor boy. They were simple letters with no hint of impropriety , but they were letters to boys. Her teacher must have gone through the mail bag before the letters were sent out and seeing letters from a female to males opened and read them. In them Hai Bao had talked about how poorly organized the trip was and made fun of the teacher.

Traditionally teachers in China had enormous power over their students. The Cultural Revolution initially took away their power, reduced them to objects of ridicule, handed the power to students whose prior tradition had been passivity. But by 1971 teachers had regained their power even if they had not regained respect from their students. In fact they had more power than ever over the now restless students, for they were required to control student activity they remembered and feared even more than did the government which had restored their power. Questioning authority was out and so were Hai Bao's plans. Her last year of school was calamitous. Her class ranking plummeted although she studied harder than ever. Teachers who had previously favored her treated her with contempt. She was grilled about her relations with males and pointed to as an example of immorality. She did attempt to apply for the army, but a month before work assignments were handed down a classmate who was in her main teacher's good graces informed her she would not be recommended and therefore had no chance. The student told her the teacher had said he would certainly have recommended her before the letter incident. Hai Bao knew he had told the student knowing word would get back to her. It was an extracurricular lesson, one of many she received that year.

At least Hai Bao did not lose any sleep or weight over her job assignment.

Almost all her classmates did. For weeks they looked tense and terrible in anticipation of the day of judgment, when they would each receive an envelope in the mail, an envelope containing their future. Would they be sent down, sentenced, perhaps for life, to the primitive countryside? Would they be raised up, rewarded with a cushy job in one of the massive and modern federally controlled factories? The pressure was that of the old imperial examination system but with no second chances. In the ancient tradition of those exams the decision which determined a person's fate would be made by faceless judges who did not know whom they were judging. At the highest level the assignments were rigidly fair. The imperial impartiality of the bureaucrats who made the decisions could be influenced only by Party policy and teachers' reports. Hai Bao knew enough about both to know within narrow boundaries where she would wind up.

If she did not want to cry, she might have laughed at the reverse which had occurred. Like all Chinese children she had been taught to fear but expect reverses. Except the reverse which had happened was not the one she had expected. She had always feared that Party policy might change, as it often did, and cause her to be exiled, ostracized or demoted in some unforeseeable way despite her outstanding scholastic record. Now it was Party policy which was protecting her. She was not going to the army or even a good factory: her teachers' reports would see to that. However, Party policy would prevent her from being sent down (since she was the only child who could care for her parents) or forced to do one of the awful jobs reserved for class enemies, jobs like emptying toilets or cleaning streets. *Street cleaning – "clean road," I believe, were the words she used. They sparked what I think was our first big argument. It was a few months after our marriage and Hai Bao was telling this story, laboring in my twisted foreign tongue. I laughed and she bristled. Naturally she assumed I was laughing at her English. I assured her I was not, that her words had suddenly solved a little mystery for me. I had understood something I had witnessed when I first came to Shanghai in 1983. I had seen a class enemy. There were still class enemies seven years after the Great Cultural Revolution ended. I used to run in the early morning and once, far from the city center, I encountered what appeared to be an apparition: a young woman in skin tight Levis, spike heels, plunging V neck blouse, large jewelled earrings, bracelets and rings. She was strutting and sweeping the streets with a big straw broom. I had to run by two mornings in a row to believe what I had seen. The second morning I passed close enough to confirm the Levi tag, the jewels and the fact she was Chinese. (Westerners might possess such an outfit, but they seldom swept the streets of Shanghai.) I passed close enough to be spotted and smiled at, but I managed to keep running and refrain from returning a third morning although I never stopped wondering about what I had seen. At this point of my explanation Hai Bao's jealousy kicked in: "Why not stop? why not go back next day?" "Because I was waiting for you." It was intended as a joke, but for all I knew it was true. I'm still not sure why I didn't stop or go back. In those days I – or my bushy beard – drew plenty of smiles but never a smile like that. And from a beautiful woman. I like to believe I*

kept going because one of the reasons I went back the second day was that I couldn't believe she was Chinese: had she been wearing a silk qipao I would have stopped. "This three years before you meet me. You not know Qiu even. Qiu not even meet wife. Bu keneng, bu keneng." *Impossible, impossible, she was shouting at me, in Chinese now, for she was too angry to twist her tongue any more. At the time I figured it was the insult to her speaking ability and jealousy which set her off. Jealousy – or was it morality? – had nearly ended our courtship when I insisted on telling her I had had sex with women other than my first wife. I squirmed out back then by switching the subject. She was more tolerant in those days, and I could sometimes transform her mood simply by throwing in a new word. She was very serious about learning English. When I stayed serious I might get by, but my jokes in serious situations constituted yet another kind of insult. Nevertheless, as I write now I know it was pride, pride in herself, her people, her civilization, her history, which I would not, would never understand. And shame, loss of face: somewhere among the thirteen million inhabitants of Shanghai was one – the worst kind of one, not so much a class enemy as a traitor to her culture – who knew what Hai Bao had stooped to, for she knew I had smiled back. Aiya. Maybe I should quit trying to understand. What has love to do with understanding? Call it all inscrutability and get back to my writing, her real words.*
Hai Bao was trapped in a new kind of middle realm, unable to follow her ambition up but also safe from being cast too far down. So when the envelope arrived, the only unknown it contained was the specific name of her fate. She was assigned to a municipally run middle level furniture factory, one neither too large nor too small, too modern nor too old, too good nor too bad, mediocre in every way. *Ma ma hu hu* (an untranslatable idiom, literally horse, horse, tiger, tiger; "mediocre in every way" renders the sense, not the essence, the verve). *Suanle* (forget it).

Chapter Ten

My first novel is a shroud of words wound around three 1969 funerals. Three times the shroud wraps the body politic as my own body grips, then slackens its hold on politics. At the first funeral, Manuel Ramos', we raised tight fists toward the sky in defiance. At the second, Bruce and Eugenia Johnson's, we clapped our hands and pretended to celebrate our friends' lives. At the third, Fred Hampton's, our hands hung limp at our sides, and had we been flung into his grave, we could not have lifted them to save our lives. We were in over our symbols.

I had flitted back to Lincoln Park from North Carolina in time for the Democratic Convention of 1968. We were chanting, "Two, three, many Vietnams; bring the war home." The Chicago police took our words seriously: Lincoln Park became a war zone. The beatings I witnessed, the tear gas which blanketed our neighborhood as well as our park, the guns in my gut forced me, and many others like me, to understand the words the cops made us eat. The end of innocence was accepting the burden of our own words. It was not the end of naivete. Pinned beneath our metaphors, we did not holler uncle; we hollered Fred Hampton's battle cry: "I am a revolutionary." Then Chicago's Cultural Revolution really got rolling. When the blood got flowing, I got lucky: it's hard to kill a butterfly with a gun and Chicago cops don't consider flyswatters manly. Some of my heavier friends were not so lucky.

The Democratic Convention also helped convert a young Methodist minister named Bruce Johnson. Late one night he peered through clouds of teargas around his church and spotted me and two female friends surrounded by cops who were entertaining themselves tickling our ribs with M16s. We were not laughing. Bruce loped from the church in full ministerial garb and asked what was happening. He didn't say much – maybe a preacher who seldom preached was doomed amid the shouting and slogans of Chicago in the late Sixties – but the cops soon hopped back into their squad cars and faded into the pungent fog. It was the beginning of a short friendship. Bruce offered the basement of his church as headquarters for the newly formed Young Lords' Organization. His church became known as People's Church, but his Christian charity split the people of his congregation and made him one of the most controversial figures in Lincoln Park. I often met him at the Eighth District lockup when Cha Cha or other Young Lords had to be bailed out. Once, when he was sitting on the bare wooden bench in his collar with an unlit pipe stuck in his mouth upside down, I couldn't resist commenting that he looked out of place. He smiled and mumbled something about a jailhouse being the proper place for a man of God in our American society. He should have stayed there. A few months after Manuel Ramos's murder someone carved him and his wife up with a knife, killing them in their own home in front of their own small children.

Bruce and Eugenia's murderer is unknown. Fred Hampton's assassins are well known: FBI agents and Chicago cops. In emulation of Mao, Fred's title was Chairman of the Chicago Chapter of the Black Panther Party. He was a poet like Mao but less literary, more spontaneous, more contemporaneous, more outrageous, more combustaneous. He was the molotov cocktail who ignited our movement in Chicago. His raps roused our ires and stoked our fires. He was inspirational, the king of rappers. He inspired because he was inspired, because he loved life and words, because he talked and laughed and stalked truth in meter and rhyme. He was irrepressible. In the heat of summer he ripped off ice cream vendors and passed out the spoils to cashless kids in the park. He was indefatigable. Dead tired in the dead of winter he rapped on to heat the cockles of a gaggle of white radicals. He was not invulnerable. I was one of the gaggle the night of December 3, 1969. We had gone to the Black Panther office to ask Fred how we could help to ease the persecution and stop the raids on the Panthers. We listened, discussed and left determined to help. In Chicago? As we left Fred confessed, "I am one tired revolutionary." Rest in peace, Fred. A few hours later he was machine gunned as he lay drugged, unable to get out of his bed despite a police raid.

And then there was Cha Cha, Cha Cha Jimenez, a blond haired, blue eyed, baby faced Puerto Rican gangbopper who was released from his annual stint in jail just in time to check out the action in our park during the Democratic Convention. Watching white kids defy the cops and be beaten changed his view of the world, he told a dozen local radicals and Puerto Rican streetkids sitting on the sidewalk around the kids' hangout, the corner of Halsted and Dickens, shortly after the convention. He said he now wanted to work with white and black radicals – "dudes" he called us – to liberate Puerto Rico and empower – my word: his was "help" – his Puerto Rican community in Lincoln Park. So shy was his manner, so round his eyes, so homespun his words, that I, a decade his elder, could not believe he was for real. Even now, thirty years later, I find it necessary to put my words into his mouth. Yet back then a gang of gangkids would have followed him to the death, and after a month or two of loaning him books, then learning what they were really about as I chauffeured him around the city, I understood why, even believed I would die for him too. This plain speaking grade school dropout could penetrate swiftly to the heart of any idea, understand its implications and put it to use in his life. And he didn't hesitate to risk his life, for strangers as well as friends, anyone who caught his eminently catchable sympathies. A year after I met him Cha Cha's Young Lords' Organization was the most powerful force for Puerto Rican independence in the United States and an ally of the Black Panther Party. This soft spoken boy the police did not murder. They supplied an agent with junk and sent him to hang around the Young Lords and wait for the right moment – it came after the murder of Fred Hampton – to put the monkey back on Cha Cha's back and drag him down and out of the struggle. The dude inside the boy, the dude I would have died for, lived for less than a year and a half.

In my novel I tried to give my Cha Cha character the humanity politics kept me from reaching out for in the real Cha Cha. I failed. That's when I found out I didn't really know him. The Cha Cha I admired in life because he was unlike me, was the man of action I couldn't be, in my novel became me, a man of words, because words were still failing me as I wrote. Not only did we radicals too often fail to bear the burden of our words, but we used words to escape the burden of our humanity and to hide the deeper realities of our world from ourselves. Our words added to the surface noise of an already too noisy world. As my words are doing now. The Cha Cha I loved so briefly had no time to play with words. He was working with people, helping them fight eviction, helping them kick junk, risking jail himself to keep others out of jail. Had The Great Liberator I fancied myself heeded Cha Cha's simplicity as attentively as Fred's poetry, I might have learned to do more with words than rap. That would have come in handy when I tried to write. I might have been able to realize the life I felt in Cha Cha, the life I had discovered without words when he might have been one of the children rolling on the sparse grass bordering Bissel Street.

And I wasn't the worst of us radical rappers. Some of us never considered shouldering the burden of our words. One guy, a kid from a wealthy Chicago suburb, a university dropout who spoke with a thick hillbilly accent and always wore a *Little Red Book* sticking out of a shirt pocket, took a paternal interest in my revolutionary growth. He had me pegged for an intellectual, so any time he caught me reading he felt duty bound to lay one of his half dozen predigested raps on me: "Hey, man, ya know what Chairman Mao tells us about books, don'tcha?" Into the fashionably frayed pocket went the fashionably dirty hand and out came the shiny red bible. There was no way short of violence he could be stopped. "We must learn not only from books but mainly through class struggle, through practical work and close contact with the masses." He always read the first sentence, to show these were truly the Chairman's words, I suppose, but once underway he had it all down by heart. "Theoretical study without practical work is useless, worse than useless, harmful. Chairman Mao says theory must be based on practice and in turn serves practice. Learn from the people. Serve the people. Integrate yourself with the broad masses of workers and peasants and do it in your practice. Gorky went to school for only two years, yet he became a great writer. Chairman Mao tells us we should not read too many books. Reading too many books leads to becoming bookworms, dogmatists or revisionists. We comprehend only when we are engaged in practical revolutionary work. Ya dig, man?"

"In sailing the seas we must depend on the helmsman," I would reply. I would have been ashamed to admit that the words he quoted were not words I treasured, that his Helmsman was more imperial than mine, that mine dreamed of liberty, equality, fraternity, pre Marxist poetry to my overworked ears, not rhetoric. I didn't dare let such guys suspect I was a dreamer, that my Mao was not the god/emperor on their polished red and gold Mao buttons but the poet I had discovered on the back of that Phil Ochs record jacket (which translated a group of Mao's poems, not the dogmas of the *Little Red Book*, then asked rhetorically, "Is this the enemy?"), now animated with Chairman Fred's outrageous spirit. The Great Liberator used to hold sycophantastic dialogues with that bard about revolution, joy, empire, and victory as I walked to and from work in those sanguine days when life seemed larger than life and Mao sang Chinese folksongs to me in English.

That all changed when a taxi driver friend called me in alarm at 5:00 a.m. on December 4 to say he had heard on the radio that Fred Hampton may have been killed. I told him that was impossible because I had just seen Fred. I went back to bed and dreamed of Mao.

We were swimming together, breaststroking against the current. Up ahead Fred was hollering for help. I tried to get to him, but the water turned thick, red, turned into a lake of congealed blood. Not only could I not reach Fred but I could not swim myself. "Red is beautiful," sang Mao, and corpuscles changed into ruddy mermaids, weighing me down, sucking me into welcoming folds of dark, pulsing blood. Blood beat like Mao's words in my ears; I screamed in my sleep, seemed to wake, somehow failed to escape the dream, for the beat drummed on. Now I was standing on the shore, trying to wipe the blood off me with a rag, and the sound was the surf breaking, breaking, throbbing through my head. The noise muffled Fred's weakening cries. Searching for him, I saw the lake was littered with human flotsam. Although the bodies were floating face down, I recognized Manuel, Bruce, Eugenia, others. Finally I thought I spotted Fred, but then I saw that the carcass wore my clothes.

The pounding in my ears changed again, quickened. It was not the surf sounding but Mao waving my bloody rag and orating. Fred was dead and Mao was quacking like a Peking duck. I could no longer make out words. Maybe it was my idea of how Chinese sounded. And maybe the Peking duck turned into a Mongolian tiger, for Mao's voice grew into a roar which kept growing, louder and more shattering until it really woke me. (I had finally made it to Bissel Street. Its greatest advantage turned out to be that its back was to the el tracks: long, loud trains rushed by in the early morning and sometimes shook me out of my nightmares.) Waking was as bad as sleeping, for waking I knew what the Great Helmsman had been hammering at me, and it clanged in my head all day: "A revolution is not a dinner party or writing an essay or painting a picture or doing embroidery; it cannot be so refined, so leisurely, so gentle, so temperate, kind, courteous, restrained and magnanimous. A revolution is an insurrection, an act of violence by which one class overthrows another. Intellectuals tend to be subjective and individualistic, impractical in their thinking and irresolute in action until they have thrown themselves heart and soul into mass revolutionary struggles or made up their minds to serve the interest of the masses and become one with them. Don't drop out of the revolutionary ranks at a critical moment and become passive. You can overcome your shortcomings only in mass struggles over a long period. Be resolute, fear no sacrifice and surmount every difficulty to win victory. Successors to the revolutionary cause of the proletariat come forward in mass struggles and are tempered in the great storms of revolution."

Mao had ceased singing to the Great Liberator and begun rapping at what was left of me. No more metaphors, only messages raining down like hammer blows. The replacement of Mao the poet by Mao the dogmatist marked the end of joy – no, hope: joy ended at the "Celebration of the Life of Bruce and Eugenia Johnson," which is what their funeral was called – in my political life. I lost heart. With Fred's poetry dead the revolution became a bloody duty. I trudged on, attempting to walk upright, attempting to do the things I had done before, but my spirit was stooped. I could no longer bear the burden of the words I believed in.

No doubt I had not been sufficiently tempered. Had I been, I would have stood my ground when, a few days after Fred's murder, a cop I had never seen before greeted me by name, patted his gun and smirked. I turned tail and fled.

The cops put me through changes, they did, but it was the change in Mao, my master of changes, the alter ego who reflected my own changes, that freaked me out. Literally: I joined the "freaks," grew a beard out of sympathy for their gentler, more personal approach to change. But few of them had much political perspective. I wanted everything: the political and the personal, the romantic and the rational, the poet and the emperor, the American dream and the communist dream. What I got was a dream tableau in which I was forever wiping away the blood and Mao was forever prating and waving the red rag. "Two, three, many Chicagos!" Did the Weathermen really chant that slogan or did it come from my bloody nightmares?

Fred Hampton might have chanted that slogan, but he would have grinned his big, lovable grin doing it. He was one rapper who could laugh at his own words. Fred was the molotov cocktail who ignited our movement in Chicago, and without him the movement and the Sixties sputtered and fizzled out. Like the molotov cocktail I threw into Cha Cha's old house the night before I left Lincoln Park. I had carefully studied a pamphlet on homemade weaponry to construct my farewell present. The Bissel Street I loved had long been silent, the tenants evicted, the buildings sandblasted to expose their tawdry nature, then boarded up and remodelled inside. Soon they would be ready to let as townhouses at many times the rent the victims evicted had paid. The night was dark. I crept into the alley behind Bissel Street. Not a ghost in sight. I lit my gas soaked rag, hurled the bottle into the building and ran like hell.

I guess that's when I began running. I knew I was running from everything I loved. And, shame, I had to run down the alley, not Bissel Street itself. What I didn't know but had learned by the time I collapsed exhausted on my floor was that I wasn't ready to run. My body had gone to pot. Or maybe the burden of my raps was dragging me down. Despite exhaustion I stayed awake all night, listening for sirens which should have come but never did, afraid to sleep, to dream, to see my words take shape.

"Do you really need all this stuff about Chairman Mao?" Hai Bao asks when she reads the manuscript. "It's boring."

Chapter Eleven

She hadn't expected the dirt. She had expected the factory to be dreary and unpleasant, but the dirt surprised her. She and everyone she knew, everyone around Pushan Lu, dwelt in small, dark quarters, but the homes were always clean. You may not have been able to turn around without brushing the walls or furniture, but when you did you didn't come away with a smudge on your skin or clothes. The factory, while not one of the big ones, had plenty of room to move around. It should have felt luxurious, or at least comfortable, after a lifetime in cramped spaces, but it only felt grey, dull, dusty. Shanghai *ren* hated dirt and dust. Why wasn't a place in which they spent almost a third of their lives kept clean? There were slogans on the wall extolling diligence and frugality and condemning waste and extravagance but none extolling cleanliness or condemning dirt. The slogans themselves, newly painted on red paper for the arrival of the new workers, quickly gathered dirt. The paint on the older slogans, painted directly onto the walls, was peeling. Even the paint on Chairman Mao's name was peeling. People moved slowly. Did the dust weigh down their diligence? By watching others Hai Bao developed the habit of bringing a clean cloth from home. She used it to wipe the places she sat or touched. She never wiped any place else.

The foreigner in China does not lack for tours of factories. I remember being guided around one in Qiqihar. It was an enormous, echoing concrete cathedral of the proletariat designed by the Russians to make people feel insignificant before the forces of production, the wave of the future. I shuffled along sluggishly, felt weighed down by the place. But Hai Bao was at home. She traipsed over to a huge contraption – the sort with massive gears rotating, heavy rods spearing sliding plates of armor, mechanical guillotines slicing loaves of steel like salami, clanks and roars resounding – and engaged its tenders in technical banter. She had operated the same kind of machine, a smaller model, to be sure, but otherwise alike in almost every detail. She explained how the machine worked, pointed out the dangerous part of its operation, the place a whip of metal flicked out and split open the face of an inexperienced worker, a beautiful young girl, scarring her for life. Our

guides in Qiqihar ceased talking down to us and I felt proud. I had joined the proletariat
at last, a member by marriage.

Hai Bao appreciated great machines. Operating the one whose big brother
we saw in Qiqihar was the cushiest factory job she attained. All it required was
pushing the occasional button and keeping well away from the moving parts.
During most of its long cycle she could sit and read or knit. But it took eight
years for her to work up to that monster, to that luxury.

She started with lower, less luxurious tasks. She entered the factory, a
danwei (work unit), the urban counterpart of rural communes, as one of seventy
new workers, all fresh out of school on their first job and assigned by a process
which combined mass bureaucracy with individual whimsy. A central agency
kept files on everyone who had completed middle school according to the
level of workplace for which each was eligible. Leaders from factories delegated
someone to pore through the files and select the allotted number of workers.
I was hired to teach in China in much the same way. I applied to the Chinese
Embassy in Ottawa, which forwarded my application to the Foreign Experts'
Bureau in Beijing. My school in Shanghai dispatched someone to Beijing to
consult the files and choose an applicant. If I had declined the job offer, the
school would have sent someone else to Beijing to seek another candidate. It is
an efficient method for assuring paid vacations in Beijing. The side benefits of
Hai Bao's hiring were less obvious since her bureau was in Shanghai and those
chosen could not refuse the job, but the factory leaders appointed a selector
whose lecherousness could be depended upon. As a result fifty of the seventy
new workers were girls and pretty ones at that. The files were quite complete and
included photos.

However she had got there, she was there. However dirty it was, it was where
she was. It wasn't what she wanted to do – "I want to study": she remembered
those words, that goal – but it was better than the countryside and it was the
only thing she could do for now. At least she had escaped the petty prying of
her teachers, had ceased to be a student who neither studied nor contributed to
production. She had become a member of the proletariat, and she had grown up
hearing too much glorification of the role not to feel some pride. But although
she had heard this glorification all her life and both her parents were factory
workers, she knew little about factory work or how factories worked. It was not
the sort of thing about which adults went into detail to children. If she could
have asked me, the outsider reading about the Cultural Revolution in Chicago,
I would have graciously filled her in. I would have explained why she and the
other new workers were ushered around the factory for the first several weeks,
spending a few hours at this machine, a few days in that department. This was
in accordance with the Maoist ideal that all workers should be familiar with all
jobs in a workplace and able to do as many as possible. She knew nothing about
this ideal. No one mentioned it, and no one did much about it after those initial

weeks. Hai Bao only knew she liked the drawn out tour because it was easy. She tried to act bright and interested and pretended not to hear the older workers' innuendos and dirty jokes, most of which she didn't understand anyhow. There were new and old areas in the factory, and all the incoming workers hoped to be assigned to one of the newer, shinier sections and machines. When she was assigned to an ancient, dingy section which required shiftwork, she cried. She couldn't comprehend why she had been slighted. The reason was simple: assignments were based not on brightness and interest nor on Maoist theory but on the files. Her teachers' reports during her last year of school continued to control her life. But wait, the great authority in Chicago would have protested: this is the dictatorship of the proletariat; the hold of the scholars has been broken; the proletariat judges with the heart as well as the mind. Indeed, her tears elicited sympathy and she was reassigned to a smaller section. It too was dirty, but it did not require shiftwork. She was grateful. Six months later she was transferred to the section to which she had originally been assigned. She had proved herself ready for it, she was congratulated. The Chinese do not make the distinction between heart and mind Westerners do: *xin* can mean either or both. Her heartfelt tears had persuaded her mindful leaders that she needed additional training. She received it. Then for the next eight years she worked shifts amid shabbiness, one week mornings, one week afternoons, one week nights.

Actually it was not so bad. The spiffy modern machines demanded constant measuring and care. The slightest mistake ruined an entire piece and earned the worker a reprimand. Where she worked standards were less exacting, and there were few leaders about when she was not on morning shift. In her first assignment she had been trained as a solderer, a skilled worker. She received no more pay than the unskilled workers, but the work was easier. Also her calligraphy skills had been recognized, and whenever a new slogan was required she was given time off to paint it. Still, she never did get used to sleeping at odd and constantly changing hours and in the daytime din of Pushan Lu.

She was lucky she did not get what she wished for. The two girls she envied most were the ones assigned to work in the clinic. The clinic was the cleanest place in the factory and the work was light. The doctor was about twenty years older than the new workers and, because he was from what had been an upper class family in the old society, the most cultured man in the factory. He could discourse about literature and art and opera and history as well as science. How Hai Bao would have liked to work in the clinic. Until the first time she felt sick. When the doctor examined her, he put the hand holding the stethoscope under her brassiere. She was too surprised and shy to say or do anything and later too embarrassed to tell anyone. None of the young girls said anything, but soon they stopped going to the doctor when they felt ill. Eventually Hai Bao learned a satisfactory method by watching *Xiao* Wang, one of the cleverest of the new workers.

When being examined by the doctor, *Xiao* Wang stood in front of a large window which overlooked the main courtyard. There were always scores of people there, so anything the doctor did would be very visible.

One of the girls assigned to the clinic was beautiful, innocent and stupid. Soon she was also very happy. Everyone could see it: she was in love. The doctor may have been much older than she, but age is an attribute in China and the doctor was handsome, witty, cultivated, respected. A flower blossomed in the girl's heart for more than a year before it began to fade as she began to suspect the doctor's attentions were not leading toward marriage. When she finally figured out that she was being used, she lapsed into a state of depression that lasted for years. She was well over thirty before she married, the last of the group of fifty girls to do so. Hai Bao kept track because she was the next to last.

The doctor did not marry until the year before Hai Bao, when he was around fifty. He married a woman professor in her early forties. A few months after the marriage they were divorced. The Chinese *danwei* is one tentacle of the Communist Party's all embracing paternalism. It controls one part of every worker's life and participates in the rest. Hai Bao had to get her *danwei's* permission to marry me, and the factory leaders tried hard to talk her out of it before signing the necessary documents. The doctor also required *danwei* participation in his divorce. One of the leaders attended the hearing, then rushed back to the factory to report that the doctor's wife was divorcing him because he was impotent. The *danwei* acted as over the wall gossip as well as feudal father.

There was much to gossip about, and gossip took up much of many workers' time. Morals were not up to the exalted standards Hai Bao had been lectured about at home and school, the standards preached in the frequent political education sessions and over the ubiquitous loudspeakers. Many of the older workers were peasants, men who had been delegated by their families to make money by joining one of the mass migrations to Shanghai of the early Fifties, when such mobility was still allowed. They lived in the *danwei* dormitory and usually saw their country wives but once a year, during Spring Festival. For the rest of the year they chased female coworkers, married or unmarried. Many of the women, especially those with unskilled, laborious jobs, appreciated their attentions. The women could enjoy a bit of levity and get someone else to do most of their heavy work. It was common to see a woman lounging on the side while a man labored for her. "*Ai laodong*," the man would laugh when questioned. *Ai laodong* (love labor) was one of the most prominent of the slogans posted on the walls. The peasants were strong and experienced. They were quite willing to do two jobs in return for favors from females. Many of the leaders used their positions for similar purposes. They had power to assign favored women easy jobs or take them along to banquets and conferences, which tended to be scheduled in famous scenic and resort areas.

So dissipation flourished amidst the dust. Some of the younger workers, encouraged by traditional Chinese morality to be busybodies or encouraged by the new morality of the Cultural Revolution to be busybodies or to get away from a boring job and have a good time and a good laugh, delighted in gossiping about the goings on and catching couples at it. One married man, caught in the act with a young girl in a storeroom, got six months in jail for adultery. The girl got an abortion. The leaders were not so easily caught. They had keys to lock doors. However, sometimes a group would assemble outside a door and shame those inside until they came out, redfaced and considerably less authoritative than usual. After one such incident someone scrawled *"ai guniang"* (love girls) under an *"ai laodong"* sign near the leader's office. For once the wall was quickly cleaned.

Hai Bao avoided such antics, but she was not above benefiting from the immorality. Young workers were considered apprentices for many years and always had an older worker assigned as their mentor. This was an influence of traditional Chinese didacticism and modern Chinese paternalism – or was it traditional Chinese paternalism and modern Chinese didacticism? Whatever it was, Hai Bao's mentor, a married woman, developed a relationship with one of the factory leaders and was able to obtain favors for Hai Bao as well as herself. It was through this woman that Hai Bao finally got off shiftwork and onto the great machine. Later her mentor opened a back door which led her into the factory school as an instructor.

All that was still far off. In the beginning it took Hai Bao a year or two to understand what was going on around her. The disparity between her working class upbringing and the working class future she had been brought up for was too great to be overcome quickly. It is a disadvantage of overprotecting children and educating them on pious platitudes and slogans. At home the princess was still treated as a child. When she began work her parents decided it was time her father moved out of the bed. He now slept on a cot downstairs. That was their only acknowledgement she was growing up. At first Hai Bao simply went to and from work – soon she had saved enough money to do it in style, on a bicycle – and made a few friends among the girls of her group at the factory. There was *Xiao* Wang, the wisest of the bunch yet quite uninterested in books or further education; *Xiao* Xiang, impulsive and outspoken, forever butting into trouble, then talking her way out of it; and *Xiao* Yang, thoughtful and impractical enough to have been an intellectual in other times. The four had different temperaments, but they shared a liveliness, intelligence and interest in events outside their circumscribed world. As they grew up, this interest grew with them and set them apart from most of the other workers. Although they avoided the factional politics swirling around them, by the middle Seventies they were known as the little gang of four, a little joke, about as far as most people dared go openly at this time. The big Gang of Four consisted of Jiang

Qing, Mao's wife, and three Shanghai followers. They led the dominant faction in the Chinese government of Mao's last years.

The Cultural Revolution was about politics, not culture. It concluded that the cultural is the political. *The difference between "cultural" and "personal" is why East is East and West is West. Culture is societal, as opposed to individual.* In many ways there was a dearth – death, it is often claimed – of culture. For most of the eleven years from 1966 to 1976 only eight modern works (five operas, two ballets and a choral symphony) could be performed on the professional stage. Almost all the professional drama and dance companies were disbanded. But culture did not really die or even go underground. It went amateur. Workers, peasants and soldiers were officially encouraged (which amounted to an order) to form performing arts groups. Folk arts were particularly promoted. Every factory had its own song and dance team, and in Shanghai there were higher level teams which combined groups of factories. For Hai Bao this meant a low level factory team, a middle level team for all municipal furniture factories and the highest level team representing the Bureau of Light Industry. All the teams benefited from the dissolution of the professional companies. Dancers and singers had to join the proletariat, and they were spread around to serve as coaches of the various teams. Hai Bao was quickly selected for her factory team, and then the coach, a former Suzhou Opera star, recommended her for the Light Industry troupe, bypassing the middle level. If nothing else this assured her of less factory work, for her *danwei* was required to grant her time off for all rehearsals and performances. At least three times a year (May 1, International Labor Day; October 1, National Day; and Spring Festival, the Lunar New Year) elaborate concerts were scheduled for which Hai Bao would get two weeks to a month off work. She came to enjoy the grudging way the leaders gave her leave when confronted by the official notice and liked to mimic their bumpkin merchant faces to her friends.

She enjoyed the leave even more. It gave her the greatest measure of freedom she had known since her parents had left her alone in lieu of kindergarten. How grand to pedal her bike downtown instead of away from town. Whenever she had inclination and time she could park her bike and dive into the tide of shoppers flooding Nanjing Lu. Once she made a special trip on a Sunday and let herself be carried along in the current of the crowd, awash in a welter of bodies and faces crushed together, blurred together, smelted together into a molten mass, the masses become a mass and she an element of it, flowing with it almost without needing to use her own muscles. That plunge she took only once. Those Sunday shoals, she knew, were not, for the most part, Shanghai *ren*. People flocked from all over China mindless of the crush, even enjoying it, for nowhere else in China could such a quality and quantity of goods be found. It made her proud of her city, proud to be part of the place setting the pace for the nation. But she wanted to be able to move freely, to set her own pace, to outpace others when so moved. So usually she stopped on her way home from rehearsals and walked Nanjing Lu during the week, when it was more Shanghai, less China. She liked to outstride the flow, slithering and sliding between the masses, one of them yet not quite among them. Shanghai *ren* dressed well, looked sleek, almost shiny, on Nanjing Lu. She loved looking at them as she sped past, their faces animated, their bodies taut with purpose. Here people did not drag and droop as they did in the factory or saunter aimlessly and leisurely as they did in the neighborhood. No, these people knew what they were doing, what they were seeking, where they were going. And so did she. Always she ended up at the great silk store, looking, touching, asking to be shown this roll or that, admiring the designs, mentally feeling the silkiness stroke her entire body, even its innards, the stomach muscles which had been tense in the street now lithe. She seldom bought, but always her mind made lists: this one and that for quilt covers, this one for a skirt, this one a full length dress, that one a blouse. She was planning a trousseau, though not consciously for she would have laughed even at a dream embodying such premature desire. Neither she nor the times were ready for that.

Such sensations were for the future. The present was for dancing: to move fully, as her body was meant to move; to join her rhythm to the rhythm of others and of the folk; to dress in light, bright, lovely costumes instead of heavy work clothes; to whirl, to glide, to soar across the stage instead of lumbering around the factory. It was glorious. She loved every dance, every song, every area of China which contributed its art to hers. Even at home she found herself doing dancesteps and singing aloud, softly but constantly, as she moved about, a habit she maintains to this day. She loved Chairman Mao and his Cultural Revolution for giving her this joy, for lifting her to this higher, moving life.

The Chinese love to do things on a vast scale. Think of the Great Wall. Or Qin Shi Huang's tomb, now being excavated near Xian. The tomb is an underground world defended by huge armies of terracotta soldiers, the dead emperor served by great teams of terracotta concubines, officials and servants devised to keep him comfortable for all the ten thousand years of his descendants' reign. Not to be outdone by the ancients, the modern Chinese have constructed an artificial heaven to roof that underground world, an immense edifice to allow excavation in comfort and safety. Think of the Cultural Revolution as a similar edifice, a monstrous single roomed structure into which the entire population of China was jammed, perhaps Kubla Khan's stately dome infinitely enlarged. Along the rigid walls of the dome were niches into which a few people could fit in relative comfort. Hai Bao and her folk song and dance team had squeezed into one such niche, but most Chinese were doomed to try to survive in the middle of the great dome, constantly colliding with others. Under the vast, vaulted roof privacy was impossible, comfort rare and, at best, transitory. If one slipped one might easily be trampled beneath the mass of milling feet.

Mrs. Ling held her scream until she was certain the police were out of earshot. As a result the noise which finally exploded from her mouth resembled a thunderclap more than a cry. And like a thunderclap it was heard only after the lightning had already done the damage. It announced the end, not the beginning, of tragedy, and the wails which followed were like emergency sirens after the catastrophe. Hai Bao, tossing in bed attempting to sleep, knew at once that something terrible had happened and there was nothing she or anyone else could do to help. Of course she still tried to help. She had learned the importance of the gesture studying opera and dance. The gesture, be it ever so futile, is as basic to Chinese life as it is to Chinese opera. Hai Bao had learned that bemoaning her fate in swaddling bands.

By the time she had thrown on clothes and rushed downstairs, the ground floor room of the big Shandong woman next door was crowded with the daytime inhabitants of *Pushan Lu Yi Chen*, old people and small children. They were all staring open mouthed at Mrs. Ling, who stood straight and stiff, wailing now at less regular intervals. "*Xiao Tuzi* (Little Rabbit) has been arrested," old Mrs. Zhou, the busiest busybody in their row, announced to the latecomer. Mrs. Zhou had obviously been listening at the window when the police were there. "*Ling Da Ma*" (Mama Ling), Hai Bao called, and the big woman barged through the crowd and flung herself on Hai Bao. The weight nearly knocked the girl over. Mrs. Ling cried in Hai Bao's arms but would say nothing. Hai Bao knew she had to get the others out to get Mrs. Ling to talk. She signed with her hand, then called for people to leave, then pushed at those standing near her, but no one budged. Finally she eased Mrs. Ling into a chair and began leading the children out. Once outside the children recommenced running and shouting, and their yells soon summoned out their grandparents. Only Mrs. Zhou and Mrs. Li were left. Hai Bao shoved them out as gently as she could. After she shut the door, they remained standing at the window, peering in and listening. Mrs. Ling rose from her chair like a wraith, but her weight was all too real when she again threw herself on Hai Bao, who helped her onto a cot in the corner farthest from the window and sat down beside her.

At first all Mrs. Ling could say was , "My Little Rabbit, My Little Rabbit." It sounded silly in the atmosphere of tragedy, but all the children were known exclusively by nicknames, usually those of animals. *Xiao Tuzi* was the last and best loved of Mrs. Ling's many sons. Although – no, because – he was more than two years younger than Hai Bao, he was her best friend among the boys of Pushan Lu. They were confidants. He called her big sister and she called him little brother. It was he to whom she had written one of the letters that got her into trouble with her teacher. He was a slim, handsome boy, rather like his nickname, very quiet and very smart, quick in his movements, quicker in his thoughts. When his mind took off on one of its flights, his eyes turned impish. Only Hai Bao could follow his flights, for he would reveal his fantasies only to her. He craved adventure, wanted to travel, to be a sailor, an explorer, to go to places no one else wanted to go. Chinese are generally not people who enjoy travel. Traditional life has always revolved around the home, tending to one's family affairs and ancestors' tombs. Hai Bao knew no one else like Xiao Tuzi, and she liked him for that. And he liked her and would talk only to her because he was sensitive and she never made fun of his ideas despite the fact that she was older and better read. His latest goal was Xinjiang, another place no one else wanted to go. During the Socialist Education Movement, before the Cultural Revolution, thousands of Shanghai youths had been induced to volunteer to settle in Xinjiang, to build another new China in the underpopulated west. Now they were forbidden to return and wrote pathetic letters back to their families. *They are still there, still desolate as the desert around them. On our bus trip across Xinjiang in 1987 Hai Bao found them at every oasis. She would descend from the bus, listen a moment, lift her nose and head straight to the local group. Oh, the joy with which she was greeted and pumped for news by the scraggly pioneers, briefly happy to hear of home in the dialect of home, their faces and Hai Bao's reflecting for the first time in my memory a radiance brighter than the desert sun, one I would come to recognize and love after she came to Canada, the chance to speak* Sanghayeehwu (Shanghaihua *in putunghua* [common dialect, Mandarin], Shanghai dialect in English) *in a foreign land. Oh, the pathos she drew from those ex "educated youth" who had volunteered to go west to build the new China, the tales of woe, the scorn for their adopted land and the government of the putative fatherland which had abandoned them to it, the schemes to get back, or get their children back, to Shanghai, the heaven where they could speak and live as nature had intended and fate had denied them.* Shanghai ren shuddered at the thought of Xinjiang, but, typically, *Xiao Tuzi* desired to go, to explore the ancient desert. He didn't plan to volunteer, just zip out and check it over. When Hai Bao gently pointed out that it was four thousand kilometers, that the train didn't run all the way, that train tickets were expensive and you couldn't buy one or stay in a hotel without the red seal of official permission from your *danwei*, he simply smiled the impish smile which meant he was working with the wind and lightning to deal with such minor problems.

Now he had major problems. He hadn't returned from work last night, and his mother had been too worried to go to her job. The police had arrived and searched the house. They had taken the clock he had recently given her and several small items of his. They informed her he had been caught stealing materials from his factory and had already confessed. They knew exactly what things he had obtained from the proceeds of crime.

What he had done was a common enough practice: workers would pilfer raw materials from their factories and sell or barter them. It was not what Lei Feng would have done, but because most materials were rationed, there was always a blackmarket for them, and since salaries and prices were both low, a little extra cash went a long way. The goods confiscated from *Xiao Tuzi* were worth perhaps ten yuan (less than seven dollars), not much, but the monthly salary for a starting worker was seventeen yuan. Hai Bao knew the boy well enough to know he didn't care about the stuff he bought. Stealing would have been an adventure, the sort of thing he would do as a lark. Or perhaps he was trying to get money for his trip to Xinjiang. But he was inexperienced; he had got caught.

There was nothing anyone could do. Arrest was tantamount to conviction. *Xiao Tuzi* was sentenced to twelve years in jail. He was sixteen years old.

Several months later, right before Spring Festival, *Xiao Lu* (Little Deer), *Xiao Tuzi's* older brother and Hai Bao's former classmate, crept into the house and whispered to Hai Bao, "*Xiao Tuzi* has returned." She hurried next door, and there in the shadows, more a shadow himself than the playful young animal she had known, crouched *Xiao Tuzi*. The rest of the family moved away deferentially and wordlessly and Hai Bao sat next to her friend on the cot where she had sat next to his mother. She was bursting with questions, but the atmosphere was too hushed for them to be asked. She waited.

"*Xiao Mao*," he said at last. His voice was full of tears, but his eyes were dry. She did not have to see them to know they had lost their impish gleam.

"*Xiao Mao*," he repeated. And stopped again. "I wanted to see you again."

"Of course you can see me," she replied, trying to fill the silences. "I'll always be your friend." Now she wanted to cry. But she didn't either.

There was another long pause, as if he had to remember how to speak again. Then he did. "I had to run away. I.... Soon there won't be anything left of me."

"No," she tried to protest.

"When they catch me, maybe they'll kill me, but that's better than dying from the inside. I'd rather really die than what they're doing to me. One of the older convicts told me that if you escape right before Spring Festival, maybe they won't come after you until after the holiday."

"What do they do to you? Do they beat you?"

"They beat me. It's their favorite pastime. But the beatings aren't the worst. I could take them." He hesitated and searched for words. "It's.... It's being alone.... It's not being able to...."

"What?" she urged very quietly.

"To.... Everything.... Nothing.... To talk."

"But you never talk much."

"But I could. If I wanted to. I used to talk to you."

"I liked to talk to you."

"Now I'm afraid to say anything. They hear everything."

"How?"

"Oh, they don't listen. They don't have to. Everyone's a spy. It's what you do in there. You can't trust anyone. Everyone believes spying's the only way out, but no one gets out. And you can't be sure of anything. You do something every day and no one says anything. Then one day they beat you for doing it. You can't even think. If you look thoughtful, they beat you and tell you to get to work. You can't dream. That's it, that's the worst. I don't even know why. I can't dream anymore, at night or in the day. I used to dream all the time and now I can't. I don't know how they stop me from dreaming, but I can't. Maybe it's because I know I'll never get out alive."

"But you're out now. Why don't you run far away? Run to Xinjiang."

He didn't answer immediately. Then he said, "I like to talk to you, *Xiao Mao*. You're the one I really like to talk to. But I can't explain because you've never been there. It's not the same world. You can't know how it is. Right now they know where I am and they know they can come and get me in a few days. But if I'm not here…. You can't imagine what they'll do to me if they don't find me here when they come. I can't imagine. I know them. I don't know myself, but I know them. They'd do something I couldn't stand. They'd…." He tried to say more, but he had no more words.

Hai Bao was glad she could hardly see his face. She wished she could comfort him like a child. Then she had an inspiration. "Can you come out? In two nights my song and dance team will perform at the municipal concert. I can try to get you a ticket."

"I can't," he began and halted. She waited. "I want to come. Maybe you can get me a very bad seat, off to the side where no one will notice."

"Good. I'll try. I hope you'll like it."

He actually laughed, a sort of humorless snort. "After reform through labor there's nothing I wouldn't like."

She had to be at the hall early, and naturally he didn't want to arrive until the last minute, but she knew where his seat was and positioned herself backstage where she could occasionally peek out at him. He seemed to be watching eagerly although he sometimes looked around nervously. Her group was the second to perform, and she was aware of dancing for him rather than for the troupe and for herself as she usually did. She felt she was dancing better than usual and was happy. She wondered if he would leave after her performance, but he stayed to the end and looked eager to the end.

She hurried to meet him outside after the concert and they biked home together. "Good or bad?" she had asked him when she saw him. "I liked it" was all he replied, but they were in a crowd and he was nervous. She expected him to say more as they rode, but he said nothing. Yet he seemed happy and sometimes she thought he was just being his old bashful self, but then he would forget to pedal until his bike wobbled. Once when this happened she suggested they walk for a while. They stepped slowly and silently along the dark street, she with her bike on her left, he with his on his right. Their elbows touched.

"Excuse me," he apologized quickly.

"It doesn't matter," she said and deliberately bumped his elbow again.

"I want you to be the last person to touch me before they take me away."

"Maybe they won't come."

"No, they'll came. I just don't know when. I hope not for a few more days."

"Don't talk about it."

"I don't want to."

She felt sad. As they walked on, she wanted to touch him again. She felt he wanted it too, but when she reached out and patted his shoulder, he jumped.

He started to apologize. Then he started to thank her. Then he cried. They stopped walking. If only she could hold him, comfort him like a child, but she just waited with him. It was late, but because it was Spring Festival there were quite a few bicycles on the street. She felt they looked terribly conspicuous standing still holding their bicycles. She feared someone might ask if they needed help. "Tomorrow night we'll walk together, OK?" she asked. "I have another performance, but I'll come home right after our number."

It was what he needed. "Good," he said, and they remounted their bikes and rode home.

Xiao Tuzi seemed almost normal the next night. Although the impishness was gone for good, and its passing made him seem grown up. As they walked along, instinctively choosing back lanes and alleys and sprinting across streets, they remembered how this block had been a field and how that building had been constructed. The neighborhood had altered greatly in the time it took for them to grow up. They recalled the lovely little park near their house and how it had been uprooted to build a cement factory, the big trees carefully dug out with their roots and replanted in other places. Hai Bao recollected the modern opera she had viewed there and a time she had accompanied her mother and him and his mother to fetch water from the clear stream which had bubbled through the park and the rising red sun set the city aflame as they watched from the woods. *Xiao Tuzi* was too young to remember those times, and this reminded Hai Bao that she was older. She had almost forgotten. *Xiao Tuzi* had always been a child, a very intelligent child, to her. Now jail had made him a man. For the first time in her life Hai Bao was walking with a man. Yet if he was a man, why did she want to hug him as if he were a child?

"You looked nice in that minority costume." It was the first time he had brought up the performance.

"I felt cold," she replied. "We all had to dance very energetically to keep warm."

"I liked it.... No, more than that. It made me alive again. To see so many people move freely. I.... I can't explain how wonderful it was."

"Moving freely. That's right. That's just what I love." She felt he had understood her. How wonderful, indeed: to feel understood about something she had never mentioned to anyone.

But his thoughts were of himself, not her. As they should be, she reprimanded herself. "I dreamed about it last night. It's the first time I've dreamed since I started sitting in jail. If I hadn't dreamed last night I wouldn't feel this way. It proved I was still alive inside. I dreamed I was in the desert. You were there too wearing that little minority costume." He hesitated, then said softly, "It's the first time I felt that way."

She wasn't sure exactly what he meant. What she was sure was that she wanted to hold and protect him. Again. Like a child although he was no longer a child. They had come to a street and he was carefully peering up and down at bicycles a long way off. "Come," she called, grabbing his hand and pulling him rapidly across. On the other side she did not let go of his hand.

They strolled to a small square. Here they dared not hold hands for fear of being taken for lovers and followed or questioned although this was unlikely during Spring Festival. Most people were too busy with their own families to worry about other people's morality. Still they were automatically cautious – and being cautious together brought them closer together, made them feel conspiratorial, as if they really were lovers. Soon after they entered the square they glanced at each other and broke into laughter, hushed laughter, about this. Without a word they both knew what they were laughing at. Hai Bao's face felt hot; she was blushing.

They did not speak about what they were thinking. Hai Bao was trying to persuade *Xiao Tuzi* to escape, to run off to Xinjiang. It was what he was always wanting to do before he was arrested. Then she had tried to discourage him. Now their roles were reversed. At first she made little progress: he was scared. But feeling so close to him, she seemed to sense what arguments to use. "If you escape you'll be able to keep dreaming. You'll dream new dreams. It will be odd because your dreams will be the opposite of what they were. You'll keep dreaming about coming back to Shanghai. And maybe if you stay away long enough your dreams will come true. After a few years they'll forget about you and stop searching for you."

Her argument was silly, but she could tell she had said the right thing. For the first time he was considering the idea seriously. "To dream," he murmured. "I need to dream." He was talking to himself, not her. After a silence he addressed her sadly: "Maybe one of the reasons I can't dream is because I can't escape. They say Xinjiang is almost as bad as Qinghai. There are prison camps and you can't run away because the desert is all around. They just have to watch a few bus and train stations and sooner or later they're bound to catch you. I can't get away from the prison camps. All China is my prison camp now."

"But they don't look for people going to Xinjiang, just ones trying to get away. Remember our dance? It's from the north of Xinjiang, from the Tianshan

(Mountains of Heaven), not the desert, up by the Soviet border where it rains in summer and snows in winter. I hear that in the mountains the brush is very thick and the moss is slippery even when it doesn't rain. They'd never think to look for you there and they'd never find you if they did. Once you're up there you're beyond the bounds of the world, free as a cloud."

He thought about that. "No, not free," he finally mourned. "I'd never be able to come back to the world. The neighborhood leaders will never forget me and never stop searching for me. The police will tell them to look out for me, and they'll look forever."

"When you come back you would have to stay with one of your brothers who doesn't live in the neighborhood."

"Would you come to see me?"

"Of course."

"No, I mean in the mountains. Would you come to see me there?"

Although the question was difficult, the answer was easy. "Of course I'll come. After you're settled and sure it's safe, write me at my *danwei*. Use a false name. Let's see. You can call yourself *Han Leng Shan* (Cold Mountain Han)." She felt a tug of conflict within herself. Even feeling as close to him as she did now, she didn't believe she would really come. But even more she doubted he would really go. That was why she had to agree.

She thought he would see through her lie, but he was already dreaming. She let him. When he finally looked shyly at her, the desire to hug him became overwhelming. She even glanced around slyly to make certain no one was watching, but when she looked back she looked into his eyes and saw with certainty that their gleam was no longer impish and innocent. He held her with his eyes. And she him. In the chill air her face was burning. They stood staring into each other's eyes, not moving but meeting somewhere up the Cold Mountain path. For years she would continue to meet him there in dreams.

She had no idea how long they stood that way before they heard voices. People were coming. They looked down and resumed walking. There was much to discuss. He was confident he could sneak onto a train during the post Spring Festival crush, but for now trains were empty and he would stick out like a fish on land. He would have to wait at least two more days. Would they come for him before then? There was no telling. Should he hide at his oldest brother's house? If he was seen that might arouse suspicion, and it was far from the train station. They discussed such problems as they walked home. They decided he had better stay put and hope for the best. Things had gone well so far and he wanted to be near her. He felt hopeful and happy.

The police came the following evening. Hai Bao was thankful she was not there to see it. When she returned home after her performance, the neighbors were still gathered in the passageway gossiping about it and her mother was with Mrs. Ling. The officers had twisted his arms behind him and handcuffed him, all the while beating him with their fists. He did not resist. When he fell they kicked him and dragged him along the cement. As they hauled him away, one of the policemen lectured his family and the crowd about the just punishment of enemies of the Great Cultural Revolution.

She did not see him for eight years although *Xiao Lu* occasionally gave her news about him. Once he escaped again, then was recaptured. When he did come home he was being carried in a chair by two of his brothers. He could not walk. He had been released from jail because of illness, because he was useless for labor. His brothers carted him to the hospital every afternoon, and after a few months he began to hobble on his own. His legs gradually improved, but his back was permanently twisted, and his face wore a twisted, vacant look. He never talked to Hai Bao, never looked at her when she tried to talk to him. He never talked to anyone outside his family, and, his mother told her, he said little to them and little of that made sense. He was paranoid, and when, after a year at home, a group of neighborhood leaders came to speak to him about working in the neighborhood, he bolted like the scared rabbit he was. He was never seen or heard from again.

1976, the year of the dragon. The Chinese dragon is not the fierce monster of Western lore, but in 1976 the dragon was angry and breathing change more violent than fire. In January, even before its ascendancy at Spring Festival, the dragon breathed out and Zhou En Lai was sent to meet Marx. The dragon breathed in and the country reeled in the vacuum at the top. The dragon breathed out and Zhu De joined Zhou at Marx's side. The dragon stamped its foot, the ground shook and three quarters of a million people perished in the Tangshan earthquake. When the dragon breathed out again and blew Mao away, the country was in shock. But there was still the power vacuum created by the inbreath to fill. The upheavals in the power structure were so momentous that the upheaval in public opinion was little noticed. Probably a transformation in the public mood had started earlier, but it became a silent mutiny after the death of Zhou En Lai.

At Hai Bao's factory everyone was in tears. I have never met a Chinese who could speak of Zhou En Lai without volunteering the information that she or he cried when Zhou died. Mao was a god, so discovering he was mortal provoked shock, not tears, but Zhou was all too human. Although he had been a revolutionary, he was admired for traditional Chinese virtues, mainly intelligence and fidelity. He was the only one of the top leaders who lived all his life with the same wife, and the fact that he was considered handsome while she was considered ugly and produced no heirs made him all the more admirable for doing it. Jiang Qing and her Shanghai followers (the Gang of Four) made their most serious error by criticizing Zhou as he lay dying and after his death. It revealed their vindictiveness. For too long they had watched

Mao command public opinion. They forgot that people could think and that public opinion could be something other than what they ordered it to be. An outpouring of mourning for Zhou became a method of expressing revulsion against the Shanghai faction. The Qingming demonstration, when thousands of people lay wreaths and posted poems in Tiananmen Square to memorialize Zhou, is famous, but the revulsion was countrywide and unorganized, and when soldiers were ordered through the Gate of Heavenly Peace and blood flowed in the square as it has so often, the revulsion rapidly grew into hostility to anything or anyone from Shanghai.

It was against this backdrop that *Xiao* Wang, *Xiao* Xiang, *Xiao* Yang and *Xiao* Zhang, the little gang of four, set off on a trip to Hangzhou for their Mayday holiday. They went only a few weeks after the Beijing outrage. As soon as they left Shanghai they found people glaring and scowling at them. Attractive young women are unaccustomed to being scowled at, but when they heard people muttering under their breath about stinking Shanghai *ren*, they figured out the reason. For the rest of the trip they spoke *putunghua* instead of *Shanghaihua*, not something Shanghai *ren* do willingly. I once travelled across Xinjiang with Hai Bao and two Shanghai friends and spent an entire month asking, cajoling, pleading, begging, ranting in an unsuccessful effort to get them to speak *putunghua*.

Hai Bao thought she gave up her music in order to go to Hangzhou. For the Mayday concerts the song and dance team decided to spotlight new, younger members. Although Hai Bao had been on the team almost three years, she was not yet twenty one and did not like to think she was over the hill. What she could not know was that her team was. The Mayday, 1976 concerts would be the team's last. Before the October concerts Mao died and the nation went into mourning. In October the big Gang of Four, featuring Madam Mao, Jiang Qing, was arrested. The amateur cultural policies were closely connected to Jiang Qing. Her arrest marked their demise. Soon the professional companies were regrouped, the model revolutionary dramas were banned and traditional opera flourished once more. *Briefly. When I reached Shanghai in 1983 different operas could be seen almost every night. By 1990 you were fortunate to be able to find one new one a month.*

Not performing with her team enabled Hai Bao to go to Hangzhou with her friends. It was the most scenic city in China, and once the four had mastered the trick of not speaking *Shanghaihua* in public, they were having a pleasant vacation. They were all of an age between girlhood and womanhood. In the countryside they would have been preparing for marriage, but in Shanghai no one married before the age of twenty five. Of course even Shanghai girls thought about it earlier, but modesty kept most from acting upon such thoughts. Modesty, however, was not prominent in Xiao Xiang's make up. As the friends approached Lingyin Si, Hangzhou's most famous temple, she fell in with a bunch of boys from Shanghai.

The other three at first accepted this as natural. Then *Xiao* Wang hurried over and pulled her back. "*Xiao* Xiang, how many times do we have to remind you not to speak *Shanghaihua*?"

"Don't get upset. Those guys were all Shanghai *ren*."

"And being guys too stupid to speak *putunghua*." *Xiao* Yang was definitely not yet one who thought well of young males.

In this case she was right. The gatekeeper had heard them. As the boys drew near, the big gate closed. "Lunch time. Everyone rests," the gatekeeper announced. The boys wandered away, but *Xiao* Xiang was not so easily intimidated and minced up to the gatekeeper to work her charms on the man, who was about fifty.

"Hopeless," declared *Xiao* Wang. "She can't even speak *putunghua* without a Shanghai accent. The only way she'll get him to open that gate is to take off her clothes."

"Don't put it past her," laughed *Xiao* Yang.

"He's too old. She's given up. We'll have to take Tiger Mountain by strategy," *Xiao* Wang said.

This was the title of one of the revolutionary operas. It is set in the frigid Northeast of China. *Xiao* Yang, who was on the factory song and dance team, launched into the aria which gives the opera its name.

Poor Hai Bao wound up in Canada, but she always hated cold and snow. "Forget those northern songs. We're in the land of fish and rice." She sang her favorite aria, one of Sister Ah Qing's from *Shajiapang*, another revolutionary opera but this one about the land just north of Hangzhou. She sang out loudly, performing now, singing in *putunghua*, hoping the words might influence the gatekeeper:

My stove is built for business,
My kettle doesn't ask where the water comes from,
My tables are used by travellers from everywhere;
Whoever comes here is a customer
And I have to be pleasant to him....

To her surprise the song had its intended effect. The gatekeeper ambled down to them to listen. Hai Bao sang her best, emphasizing the irony of the words in the present situation. When she finished the gatekeeper bowed and declared, "The temple is open." The girls looked at each other in astonishment but did not neglect to follow him and enter quickly.

"The world is changing too fast for me," muttered *Xiao* Xiang after they were inside. "A pretty voice has become more important than a pretty leg."

Twenty minutes later, as they stood contemplating the famous statue of the Buddha surrounded by a montage of a hundred and fifty faces, each different, each striking, many startling, the gatekeeper reappeared leading a woman somewhat older than they.

He let them look awhile, then gave them a modern history lesson: "This place should have a plaque commemorating Premier Zhou. The Red Guards were determined to smash the whole temple, but Premier Zhou ordered it saved. Without his intervention you wouldn't be able to see this." It was a political speech, the girls knew, an attack on the Gang of Four, perhaps, they feared, a prelude to an attack on them as Shanghai *ren*. But the man had done his duty by making the speech. He now introduced the woman, his daughter.

After the requisite pleasantries the woman got to what she had come for. She looked directly at Hai Bao and sang:

> I've just heard about you from the commander,
> Sister Ah Qing you are out of the common run.
> I admire your coolness, cleverness and courage....

When the aria ended Hai Bao sang the reply:

> Please don't praise me so, chief of staff....
> I keep a teahouse and hope for good business,
> So I must observe the code of brotherhood....

The woman applauded. "Good, good. My stove is built for business too, and my kettle also does not ask where the water comes from. I have a problem. I'm one of the comrades responsible for a production of *Shajiapang*. We put it on every year for International Labor Day. This year we want to dedicate our performance to the memory of Premier Zhou, but several of our singers have bad colds and won't be able to sing. We need replacements. If you agree to sing with us, we'll telegraph your unit and get you all permission to stay longer in Hangzhou. We'll also provide guides who can take you around and make sure you see all the sights of our municipality."

Hai Bao did not get to sing Sister Ah Qing, the leading role and her favorite character in all the new operas. She had to settle for *Xiao* Ling, a minor role. Nevertheless, she enjoyed it immensely. She was treated like a visiting celebrity. Perhaps she would have received even higher honors had anyone known she was making her farewell appearance. She was also a hero among her friends although *Xiao* Xiang claimed credit for setting the stage with her Shanghai accent. They got three extra days in Hangzhou, some fine meals and tours of so many beautiful places they could hardly take everything in. Also many more elegies to Zhou En Lai.

One thing the little gang of four stayed out of was politics, but leaving Shanghai at this time had thrown them in whether they liked it or not. Politics was in the air as it hadn't been since the early years of the Cultural Revolution, but what a difference between then and now. Then the politics had been enthusiastic and people competed to show theirs off. Now the politics were below the surface, sullen, and people were fearful.

The holiday was over; the crowds had diminished. It was the gang's last day in Hangzhou and they were strolling the Su Causeway over West Lake one last time, alone and happy and therefore speaking *Shanghaihua* again, albeit quietly amid the hushed politics beneath the beauty around them. *Xiao* Yang feared for Hai Bao, for there had been a passionate dedication before the drama: "Can *Xiao* Zhang get in trouble for acting in an opera dedicated to Premier Zhou?"

"Impossible. Everyone loves Premier Zhou," *Xiao* Xiang insisted.

"Not everyone. You know what happened in Beijing," *Xiao* Wang reminded them. The grapevine within a country without an open press is an awesome plant. Although nothing had been reported in the media, everyone knew everything about the Qingming Festival demonstration and its bloody suppression. People spoke of it softly and only among friends, but their knowledge and their admiration for Zhou En Lai coupled with the official silence created the sullen atmosphere.

Hai Bao remembered the time she had been near Premier Zhou. In her memory she was closer than she had been in life. "Why can't they leave him alone? He's dead."

"Don't be naive, *Xiao* Zhang," *Xiao* Wang instructed her. "It's because he's dead they're attacking him. When he was alive he was too smart for them."

"But what is there to gain now that he's dead?" asked *Xiao* Xiang.

"He's got lots of followers. They don't want one of them to gain power," answered *Xiao* Yang.

"Right, they're worried about Deng Xiao Ping." *Xiao* Wang paused to reflect, then continued, "But they've made a mistake. It's not Deng they have to worry about. It's Zhou's ghost. His ghost is everywhere. At least it's everywhere we've been since we left Shanghai. And the main reason Zhou's ghost is here is because they roused it. If they had let him lie and be mourned they would have had a chance. If they had joined the mourning they would have had a better chance. They made a big mistake and now their only chance is for Mao to save them. But I've heard two things about that, one that he's too sick to save them, two that he doesn't want to save them. If either of those is true, they're through."

It was the shrewdest summation of the situation Hai Bao heard, even after the events had played themselves out. (Even much later events, for when Deng Xiao Ping massacred his own reputation on June 4, 1989, this did nothing to rehabilitate the reputation of his enemies, Jiang Qing and her Gang of Four.) It made Hai Bao realize she had indeed been naive, unseeing, but she would be no longer. *Well, that's what she told me she thought at the time. Then we looked at each other and laughed simultaneously. We both know she'll no more lose her naivete than I'll lose mine. It's a trait we share, the trait which more than any other brought us together. We were each surprised the other wanted to live in China. We were each naive enough to think we could pull it off together. Deng Xiao Ping massacred our plans as surely as his people and his reputation. Yet we continue to plan a life together separate from the place and culture which brought and holds us together. The two rules of naivete are that one never understands what is happening until it happens, but then one is convinced the naivete will never happen again.* Hai Bao felt the trip had opened her eyes. And by opening her mouth to sing out in praise of her hero, she had become a part of the ghost her friend had named. Most of the people of China had become a part of it.

Chapter Twelve

"The unexamined life is not worth living." In my youth I vowed to live according to that Socratic tenet, and now, having tried to examine my life in Lincoln Park, perhaps I am try, trying again? I quit even pretending to try when I lived in Marquette Park because I didn't dare examine Lincoln Park. Is the unexamined life worth writing? Once I wrote to avoid examining, to forget. That got me through Lincoln Park. But first Ruby had to get me through Marquette Park. If not for her, writing might not have got me through an open door. This time around I am writing to examine and remember, and that too seems to have got me through Lincoln Park. Maybe writing really is magic. Or maybe I am just farther away: "Time heals all wounds." Another of my mother's gems. Writing is certainly making me remember all sorts of things. Some of them not worth remembering. Maybe some of them not worth examining either. For the more I examine the more I conclude that love, not examination, is what I live for. An unlovely conclusion, Hollywood, not Socrates. Not Jack either, I would like to protest. But I, Jack, would not be writing if I did not love Hai Bao. And god knows where – or whether – I would be living if I did not love Ruby.

One needn't love a person. I loved a place and a purpose, but I lost both when I lost Lincoln Park. I hardly remember what came next. I hardly remember Marquette Park. Yet try I must. Memory is the string that binds a life together, and writing can tie and untie the strings of memory. My mother once actually tied a string around my finger to remind me to remember something or another. What I remembered was to untie the string as soon as I got out of her sight. Memory is not so simple: Lincoln Park is knotted around my brain, but Marquette Park never got tied at all. Even with two thousand pages of field notes to work from, my Marquette Park novel is less than half the length of my other two. And I wouldn't have been able to write a short story without the field notes. Even while I was living in Marquette Park I couldn't remember it. Those field notes were originally spoken into my tape recorder as soon as I left the field. I found that if I waited until the next morning to record them, my mind was blank. One night dreaming of Lincoln Park - and I dreamed of Lincoln Park every night - wiped Marquette Park clean out of mind.

I had always chased my dreams; suddenly they were chasing me, and I was running scared. My mother always told me, "It's better to be lucky than smart," and I got lucky. As I was about to collapse from exhaustion and fear, another woman caught me, and with Peg's help I managed to flit out of Lincoln Park. I was too weak to flit far, only to the southwest side of Chicago, to Marquette Park, a neighborhood of faded brick bungalows and faded block people. That such solidity looked flimsy says more about my state of mind than those middle class homes and middle European people, I suspect. But I can't remember. Them or my state of mind. The dream world I was living in was sharp to the point of wounding, perhaps killing, me; but the world outside my dream was a dull haze, and I was too occupied by the dream and too tired from dreaming it to attempt to penetrate the haze. It was pure luck that I found a job researching youth in Marquette Park, a job which allowed me to make money doing exactly what Peg and I wanted to do, organize kids for the revolution. The tidal wave which had swept over my life had done nothing but show me that the Lincoln Park I had loved was a tiny island surrounded by a vast sea. So there we were, Peg and I, attempting to reshape the ocean instead of swimming to safety. We needed all the luck we could get.

I was about to continue writing about Marquette Park by ridiculing one of my mother's favorite songs. The lyrics claimed, "It's easy to remember but so hard to forget." Ruby may be what I remember of Marquette Park, but what keeps coming out of my pen is mom, who died just before we moved to Marquette Park, who never saw our house there. I didn't notice through the haze because Marquette Park didn't look like the neighborhood I grew up in, but its little bungalow boxes were made of ticky tacky. The neighborhood threatened me then and still does now because it represented my mother's values, all the things I spent my youth reacting against and trying to escape. No wonder I wanted to forget Marquette Park. No wonder I still want to forget it. No wonder I fell in love with Lincoln Park, British Columbia, China, places which seemed nothing like the place I grew up in, places which seemed to take me farther and farther from my family. Marquette Park was a step out of my getaway, a step back into security I wanted to get away from.

I needed to rest, so, typically, I ran. I learned how to run in Marquette Park, taught by a guy I initially judged the same way I judged his neighborhood, a guy whose name I forgot daily although we ran together frequently, forget now. I was jogging around the park when a runner who looked like a redneck powered up alongside. I tensed for an insult or attack, but he simply asked why I was pumping my knees so high and gave me a few tips on running with less effort. He made me realize that I didn't want running to be easy, that I had been running to punish myself for running from Lincoln Park, for running from my dreams. I ran from Lincoln Park to save myself, and once away I had to keep running hard enough to leave myself tired enough to sleep a precious few hours before I began to dream. Dreaming meant the lake of blood. Being lucky meant waking up at the first dip.

My second novel bore the snappy title "The Nuclear Family in Marquette Park." I did not write it there; in Chicago between nightmares I could write nothing but propaganda and field notes. I wrote it in British Columbia, and, like my first novel, I wrote it to forget. Sifting through field notes to write about Marquette Park let me forget that the worst thing that happened to me there was dreaming of Lincoln Park, let me pretend that I had really lived there in the Seventies when in fact my mind had remained in Lincoln Park and the Sixties. As my beard and long hair loudly (and the pot and acid I did only slightly more quietly) proclaimed. Not that I had looked like that or done much dope when my body inhabited Lincoln Park, but I was down and could find no better way to pull myself up than by my own beard hairs. (On her deathbed my mother had asked me to shave and I had claimed I needed my beard to do my new job well. My paying job: fortunately money could mollify her, for I certainly couldn't say that since I was no longer living in Lincoln Park I needed my beard to continue escaping her. As if there were any way short of the one she was using to escape me.) Even now, when writing has made me remember both mom and nightmares, I can remember little of the dull days and lively teenagers who helped me get through the nightmares, can remember little of Marquette Park, my hidden valley between the mental mountains and abysses of Lincoln Park and the tangible mountains of British Columbia.

The "nuclear family" part of my title came from the Marquette Park community, which was famous for what are today labelled "family values." But my teenaged informants (whom I remember only because I still have my field notes) related stories about their solid, middle class families that told me their families' values were about as sound as my memory. I sided with the kids, not their parents, although I was no longer dreamer enough to doubt that most of them would grow to be tyrants like their parents. Indeed, that is why I was on their side. I despised what their families were doing to them, despised the family as an institution – *I confess it, Hai Bao: I lack filial piety and feeling for my own family* – because it was a fortress against change in children and society. *Witness China.* It was lucky for us but not chance that Peg and I were starting a family as we moved to Marquette Park. The Sixties were over. Most of our revolutionary friends were also becoming parents. The political had become the personal. *It happened in China too. Patterns of consciousness seem to spread across the world like flu. Not that the personal in China resembled American style apolitical individualism. Not that Mao's government switched from propaganda to field notes. No, politics remained in command; the people simply ceased to listen. Most Chinese say they just got tired of political movements: there had been too many for too long. Like the natives I grew* progressively less interested in Chinese politics as the Seventies regressed, and as I reach this stage in Hai Bao's history, I find myself going through similar changes, becoming more and more interested in her, less and less in the politics around her. She is growing older, growing into the woman I love. As her personality develops, her stories become more personal, her memories more detailed. Flighty creatures like butterflies, especially butterflies masquerading as political heavies, don't mate for life, and our dislike for the nuclear family had made Peg and me resolve never to marry. We did not marry, at least not until Canadian immigration authorities forced us to get a marriage certificate to avoid deportation, but we lived together for twelve years and raised a daughter.

If Peg and I shared houses more than a passion, we also shared tastes and ideas to a remarkable degree. Our nonmarriage was the opposite of Hai Bao's and my marriage, in which mutual passion often got in the way of getting to know each other. Peg and I had our fights, sometimes fierce ones, but we fought over how to achieve what we both wanted so the fights didn't last long, which gave us time to agree on ideas and plans since we seldom ended up in each other's arms when we weren't tripping. Indeed, one reason we tripped so often was that we wanted a child. And once our daughter, Ruby, was conceived, we began planning a nonacidic trip. China. If Grace Slick, one of our heroes, hadn't beat us to it, we might have named our daughter China. To tell her she deserved a better world than Marquette Park. Mao, the ogre of my nightmares, remained the symbol of equality and sorority in Peg's and my waking goals. We had no idea how to reach those goals, but maybe by the time Ruby was eleven or twelve she would be old enough to appreciate China and China would be more appreciative of visitors. Meanwhile, we would organize in Marquette Park. For Peg and I shared political as well as personal reasons for wanting a family. Our family was to be as untraditional as our neighborhood was traditional. It was our way of trying to change both.

By the time Ruby – Ruby the Red, we called her – was old enough to sit up she was developing a head of blond ringlets, and I was developing a monotonous relationship with our community. Every morning I strapped Ruby into a seat behind my bike and rode her to the park, which was famous to the rest of Chicago for its neo-Nazi activities but was famous to Ruby for its slides. Every morning my next door neighbor, who was always on his porch, called out, "There go Beauty and the beast." Every morning I called back, "Don't call my daughter a beast." I can remember this because we must have spoken these words a hundred times or more. They were the only words we ever exchanged, and they never varied a syllable. The bushy black beard and hair hanging halfway down my back, which made me in the eyes of teenagers, made me the neighborhood nigger to adults in a neighborhood where blacks who wandered in after dark were arrested, where a black changing a tire on his car was beat to death. I could be The Great Liberator to my teenaged buddies by being the Enemy of the People to their elders, and I reveled in the second role as much as the first....

"Revel" may not be the right word for my halfhearted tragicomedy. No number of bad memories and worse nightmares could make my mind quit Lincoln Park and the Sixties. So I did not mind that hatred bore into me from the eyes of strangers, eyes which turned away when I stared back. When I bothered to recall that I was on stage being stared at, I was proud of being a stranger, a freak, proud of the gulf between me and my audience. When I stared back over the gulf, I was seeing them no more than they were seeing me. Daily I learned, then forgot, the lesson of my little melodrama: prejudice is not quite blind; both our eyes glared and saw something but never the one at whom they stared. Total blindness would have been kinder.

The unloving life is not worth living. Ruby kept me going when hope was being murdered nightly inside me. Only when I strapped her to my back or bike did I cease to be a stranger, an outcaste to be shunned. I could go anywhere and talk to all the people who turned from me when I was without my little beauty. With her on my back I could walk the picket line in front of Gage Park High, the public school which was being boycotted by whites for admitting blacks, and paranoid parents who refused to utter a peep to a respectable journalist lined up to proclaim racist justifications and obscenities into my tape recorder. With her on my back I could stroll the halls of Maria High School, probably the most conservative Catholic girls school in the city, chat with the nuns and whisper abortion information to frightened students in the cafeteria. With her, now off my back and being passed around and fondled, I could shoot the breeze or engage in philosophical discussion with any group of teenagers in the community. How could I not love her? She accompanied me to meetings of the publicly funded organization I worked for because she accompanied me in the gathering of many of the research notes which my bosses held up as examples to my fellow ethnographers (and which I eventually used in my novel). And when the Red called me "mama" at one of the meetings and my main boss freaked out, I could lecture this learned anthropologist about the nuclear family, explaining that a single word used directly and decisively said more than a scholarly treatise, that even a one year old being raised in an untraditional unfamily could gloss the family roles in our society and thus when she wanted something use the term "mama" generically to mean servant, disregarding such irrelevant factors as sex and kinship. How could a butterfly masquerading as a heavy not love her?

As is usual for me, I had no foreknowledge of what it meant to take on the family by having one, had not even known I liked babies until I watched Ruby drawn from her mother's womb. She entered the world to cheers from the spectators gathered around our kitchen table, but she came out blue and limp, and the noise quickly died while the doctor dangled her upside down and snapped snapped snapped, snapped futilely at her livid, lifeless soles. Then, as if she realized her undignified position, she let loose a howl and her body convulsed into angry pink life. In that instant transformation from blue to pink, from death to birth, I too was born. Anew, alove. In Lincoln Park I had been laid low and left dangling by the murder of friends and the place I loved. Ruby slapped me to my feet and let me resume life. But it was probably lucky I didn't live long in Marquette Park.

Good god, after writing that last sentence I did some arithmetic: I lived longer in Marquette Park than I did in Lincoln Park.

Chapter Thirteen

Change in modern China looks dramatic, for it swings from pole to pole. Yet it can feel painfully slow. The poles are far apart and the social structure so ossified that change cannot effect change until that structure cracks, and even when it falls away it may be that a nearly identical structure lies beneath it so that what looks like change changes little. The dragon of '76 decreed change; Chairgod Mao died, the Gang of Four was arrested, and the Cultural Revolution ended. What greater changes could have occurred? The Cultural Revolution had ended, but what had begun? No one knew and life went on. China waited. The traditional power struggle after the death of an emperor needed to be resolved.

Hai Bao waited as well. The child of new China waited in a new Chinese interregnum while the government and the nation waited in the old one. The new had been created by Mao's policies as surely as the old had been created by his death. A Western youth has an alternative to living with parents or marrying. Individual independence is possible, is often encouraged, may even last the rest of a lifetime. Until Mao exalted the role of youth, independence in China had been a function of age, reserved for patriarchs and matriarchs. For a female the traditional interval between being a girl in her father's family and a woman in her husband's lasted the length of a sedan chair ride between the two. But Mao, for all his personal romanticism and individual power, for all his desire to weaken the traditional family and strengthen the position of women and young people, never intended to empower the individual. He levered young people free from their families – to settle underpopulated areas, to become Red Guards, to learn from the peasants – then squeezed them into groups. His policies were designed to create a new collectivity. They might have succeeded had they evolved naturally from a combination of education and youthful idealism, ardor and curiosity, but as orders from the emperor they failed. For Hai Bao they simply created inconvenience and a longer wait for the sedan chair. *Words, words, words. I'm cooked in my own thickening stew of languages and cultures. Now my words force*

me to imagine a red palanquin emblazoned with Chinese double happiness characters
halting in front of me: the bearers set down their burden; the curtains part. But before
my bride can step out, I jump in.... I'd probably find it crowded but cozy, but I wouldn't
have to live in it.

There was literally no room for individual independence in China. The
population increase had so strained housing that individual living quarters
were out of the question. There were dormitories in work units and schools,
but these were usually more cramped, less comfortable and less private than the
family matchbox. In Shanghai there were long waiting lists for apartments. The
first question a woman asked about a potential husband concerned his housing
situation. Some young couples procured marriage licenses knowing they could not
live together, for the earlier they got the license the higher their place would be on
some waiting list. Others remained unmarried so long that their love evaporated
before their apartment materialized. Late marriage was often forced and by the
late Seventies was being encouraged as a method of population control in cities
bulging with young people returning from the countryside. Chinese tradition
favored early marriage, even child marriage when the husband's family wanted
an unpaid servant. But as marriages ceased being arranged, the age of the couple
rose: it took more time to meet and decide upon a mate. By now an older age had
been all but institutionalized in the cities; in Shanghai one married between the
ages of twenty five and thirty. The years preceding the coming of age at twenty
five were spent seeking and waiting, pretending to be a child at home, repressing
messages to the contrary from body and mind, pretending to be an adult when
one could, repressing frustration at lack of training and guidelines. They might
have been restful years, but how many twenty two year olds want to rest?

Hai Bao loved to move, but a visit from Andi, her old friend from Hefei,
showed her how limited movement was in her land of movements. And how
hard finding a boyfriend could be in her land of bureaucracy. Andi arrived
shortly before the Cultural Revolution ended. He accompanied his mother, who
was considering marrying a Shanghai widower. For three days Hai Bao and Andi
took long walks reminiscent of and reminiscing about Hefei. On numerous
occasions he assured her he liked Shanghai, Shanghai girls and eating rice. Their
other topic of conversation was the recent Tangshan earthquake, which had
brought terror to Beijing residents like Andi and tragedy to Hai Bao's family.
When the earthquake struck Jie had been away on her annual stint of doctoring
in the rural areas. Jiefu, like every other geologist in China, was ordered to
Tangshan. Ba was hastily summoned to care for their six year old son, but Ba
was too old to keep up with the wild independence typical of children of the
Cultural Revolution, too mild to have much sway over the boy. While romping
with friends the boy fell into an unfenced, unprotected campus swimming pool
and drowned. He was neither the first nor the last child to drown in it. Hai Bao's
family grieved deeply; not only was the boy lovely as well as lively, but he was

the only member of the new generation. Their grief was not assuaged when the authorities conducted the customary investigation and reached the customary verdict: the family was to blame for failing to give proper supervision to an infant. Andi expressed indignation and the same sympathy he had shown Hai Bao at the time of the child's conception.

The two of them rapidly recaptured the feelings of the earlier period, and Andi's protestations about his love of rice grew vehement. Then Andi's mother's wedding negotiations broke down and Andi had to return to Beijing. The government strictly controlled movement into the major cities. Andi might have been able to move to Shanghai because his mother's suitor had a back door. Andi didn't know but suspected one reason the marriage plans foundered was that the man was not willing to accept Andi, and his inevitable wife and family, into the household. Given the regulations, Hai Bao had little chance of ever moving to Beijing. Andi moved out of her life.

Hai Bao grew up in an era in which the Communist Party urged abandonment of many age old marriage practices, yet her one offer which resembled a traditional marriage arrangement came from a Communist Party official. The traditional method of arranging marriages was to send go betweens between the families. But Han *Tongzhi* (Comrade Han) was a revolutionary. No feudal go betweens for him. He proposed the match with his son directly to Hai Bao's father.

Hai Bao had never had much to do with the Han family. She was not revolutionary enough. Han *Tongzhi* was a leader of his *danwei* and his wife was a neighborhood leader. She had been in charge of the neighborhood communal dining hall during the Great Leap, had recruited volunteers to settle in Xinjiang during the Socialist Education Movement and had organized the placement of big character posters during the Cultural Revolution.

Although the Cultural Revolution had ended, the movement that would replace it had not yet begun, so the members of the Han family and most people in China still wore the approved blue Zhongshan suits in extra baggy sizes. Hai Bao wore slimmer Lenin style jackets and army pants that fit and so were too narrow, too tight, too stylish. This marked her as a right winger in the left looking eyes of comrades like Han *Tongzhi*.

So Hai Bao was surprised when one of his many daughters turned up at her door and invited her to their home. From then on she was a frequent visitor. She liked it there because there were so many sisters, some older than her, some younger, one her own age. And one brother. He was five years older than she, just back from the countryside, intelligent if vain, pleasant to talk to when he did not talk too much, subtle enough so she did not realize that he had orchestrated his sisters' interest in her. Then his mother began offering her longans and other delicacies and bragging about her family's open door (no back doors for them) to such goodies. Hai Bao would have liked the goodies but not their price. She became cooler and more careful about talking to the boy.

Too cool and careful for Han *Tongzhi*. He was used to getting what he wanted and getting it quickly. Probably he was not enthusiastic about his son's choice for a wife, but if it was what his son wanted, it was what his son should have. He went to Hai Bao's father: "Zhang *Tongzhi*, I have good news for you. My son is willing to marry your daughter. No hurry, of course, but you and I should begin making the arrangements. Your daughter's ideology needs reformation, but the influence of spending more time in our home should raise it to a high level in short order. No sugar coated bullets from us! There's no teacher like the communist spirit!"

Ba was nonplussed, but he was not one to argue with or insult a neighbor. So he stammered out something about Hai Bao deciding for herself.

Han *Tongzhi* controlled his laughter. "Her? What does she know? She's very young, needs guidance. You'd better take her in hand. Make it clear to her what a golden opportunity this is. During the Great Cultural Revolution I would have consulted the Party, and it sets extremely high standards for the wives of future leaders. But now, frankly, times are changing. There are even rumors that comrades may be permitted to start private businesses. A pretty face like hers might be an asset in a restaurant or something."

Ba was appalled. No one had been more vocal in opposition to any kind of private enterprise than Han *Tongzhi*. "You're not serious! A restaurant!"

"Probably it won't happen. Socialist roaders like me and you find the idea shocking, but Chairman Mao is dead now and change is in the wind. The vast ocean may dry into farm land. We have to be prepared for anything. Whatever happens this is a golden opportunity for your daughter. Talk to her."

Ba was not as persuasive as Han *Tongzhi* expected. After he talked to Hai Bao, the two of them had to restrain Ma, who was all for going straight over to Han *Tongzhi's* and turning the turtle out of his shell. Fortunately the boy was more sensitive than his father and abandoned his campaign after Hai Bao refused all invitations from his sisters. He always smiled wistfully when he passed Hai Bao in the passageway. Hai Bao kept her distance though sometimes she couldn't help smiling herself. Her smile was not wistful. It was because after she stopped visiting his house she noticed that he had a long face, rather like a horse. Maybe she wouldn't have noticed this if it had not been for his sisters. Whenever they passed her they turned their faces away and their noses up. Once one of them passed when *Xiao* Wang was with her. "Who's that crane among the chickens?" giggled *Xiao* Wang.

Although Hai Bao still respected the boy, she fell in with *Xiao* Wang's mood and giggled back, "A crane with a horse brother and a tiger father."

"Their house must be a zoo," remarked *Xiao* Wang, and from that day Hai Bao laughed whenever she thought of the family. And when they opened their restaurant she mentally named it the *dong fang hong dong wu yuan* (The East Is Red Zoo).

Hai Bao was following in her sister's footsteps. Like Jie she was extremely popular on Pushan Lu, and like Jie she knew she wanted another, a better *lu*. But unlike her sister she was unsure what she wanted, where her road lay. The times were too uncertain for certainty like Jie's. Had Hai Bao been born a few years earlier she might have sought to marry a Party official, a few years later a businessman. However repellent such prospects seem to her now or seemed then, people are shaped by the pressures of their times, and in a packed country like China the pressures have always been tremendous, resistance usually futile. And leaders like Mao and Deng increase those pressures for their own ends, to alter society's traditions. Perhaps our child of new China would have felt otherwise had she been born five years earlier or later, had to seek under either Mao or Deng. Different roads lead to the same destination. Perhaps her only firm requirement would have been that her husband be an intelligent official or businessman. But being born when she was and coming of age when she did, in the interregnum between Mao and Deng, she hesitated to seek and tended to wait, to see who sought her, to choose wisely. Uncertainty was the certainty decreed by her times. The voices around her, the propaganda she had been raised on, still extolled the glories of the working class. But she was a worker in a family and factory of workers and saw only grime, not glory, on the hands of her fellow workers. After work she never failed to avail herself of the factory showers to wash the day's dust from her body. The voices inside her, the voices of her culture, directed her toward Jie's road, the traditional Chinese way, the way of scholarship. In times when the future is uncertain the past attracts. In her dreams the only stains on the alabaster hands and arms which held her were inkstains.

The universities were reopening to the public and young people with ambition were cramming for the newly reinstated entrance exams, the first in eleven years. In the confusion of the times mature men and women who had been sent down as youths were coming back to Shanghai without permission to study for the exams, and those who couldn't get back were writing their families to mail books and studying avidly where they were. Getting into a university was the sure way of getting out of the countryside. Those who came back and couldn't get into a university could not get jobs. Hai Bao lacked the motivation of those who had been exiled; besides, she and her peers first had to pass exams for the last two years of middle school, which the Cultural Revolution had lopped off the curriculum. So everyone seemed to be studying for one exam or another. Studying? Reading? Hai Bao had almost forgotten what these were. The whole country had almost forgotten. Yet now she started as automatically as she had stopped after completing school. Directed study rapidly led to less purposeful reading – poetry, fiction, philosophy, history, whatever struck her fancy – and this seemed as natural as brushing her teeth in the morning to spit out the musty taste of night. So why had she stopped? On the street she was beginning to encounter old friends and classmates just back from the countryside. One well groomed and scrubbed young woman had said to her, "I feel clean for the first time in years. Out there you even stop washing and brushing your teeth." Like this girl Hai Bao had unthinkingly done what everyone around her was doing. Few books which were not political propaganda had been available, and only fools (those who hoped for advancement into or within the Party and those who eschewed all hope of advancement) read. Now everyone was reading again and so was she. But now, at least, she was thinking about why. And thinking led to writing. In this too she was not alone. China was suddenly flooded with stories which relieved the long cultural drought by depicting its victims. Hai Bao was not sure she had much to say, but writing was something to do while she was waiting and looking, something which might help prepare her for what she seemed to be looking for, a man who had passed the university exams.

Usually the men spotted her, but one she spotted was a philosophy student, a distant relative of *Xiao* Yang, who showed her his photo and told her about him. Every Chinese has scores of distant relatives plus a mental catalogue of what each is likely to be useful for. This one sounded too good to be true: twenty nine, brilliant, handsome and the sole son in a family with a relatively spacious apartment, but such men were now floating free after having been caught in the currents of the Cultural Revolution. He was too good not to be incredibly popular, but he obviously approved of her photo and what *Xiao* Yang told him about her. *Xiao* Yang met them in front of Hongkou Park, introduced them and vanished. Although Hai Bao had decked herself out in her only silk skirt and blouse, she had expected to be disappointed. But he turned out to be as intelligent and charming as her friend had said. And tall and handsome, even better looking than his photo. For over two hours they walked about and chatted like old, fond friends. Then he inquired about her family. When he heard it was from the Subei the light in his eyes blinked out. The conversation suddenly flagged and soon he led her to the park exit and said goodbye. She never again wore fancy clothes on a first date. *Not even to meet a foreigner. I remember well the simple cotton dungarees and blouse she wore to our first meeting. Although they were clean and pressed, they were obviously the clothes of an ordinary worker. She couldn't have chosen better to impress me.*

If what happened hadn't been so unusual, she might have taken it as a warning, as evidence that prejudices were changing, reverting, with the changing times. But he was the only man who failed to ask her for a second date. Usually she had to make excuses. So the experience simply confirmed her passivity. She would let the men court her and select the one she wanted.

That one was Bianji. Perhaps he was not as brilliant and certainly he was not as handsome as *Xiao* Yang's relative. He was rather short, not much taller than Hai Bao, who had always preferred tall men. But he was sensitive, artistic, honest and rich. His family had been capitalists. They had suffered in various campaigns but had survived, and when Deng Xiao Ping ordered wealth previously confiscated from capitalists returned, they had suddenly become rich again. Hai Bao liked Bianji immediately, so she made a point of quickly informing him about her family background. He laughed and told her frankly that his parents might object but he did not and that he made his own decisions and did not intend to let his parents run his life. She liked him all the more for his answer. She knew he liked her when, on their second date, he chuckled and told her he had already argued with his father over her. His father had asked where he was going and when he told him asked where the girl was from. This had led to a disagreement, and he had defied his father by coming to meet her.

They tried to avoid talking about their families. They had too much in common themselves to worry much about others. Their main topic was the arts. Hai Bao had always enjoyed that topic, but they talked of it in new ways, exciting ways, elevating ways. Art became the stilt which supported life, raised it to prominence, lifted the petty struggles of petty beings above the muck from which they sprang. For too many years China had wallowed in the muck. Suddenly art had the potential to shape it, to make life beautiful. Suddenly art was themselves. Bianji had been in the countryside for eight years. There was nothing uncommon about this; most of the men she met were newly returned from the countryside. What was uncommon was that he had some good things to say about his stay there. Hai Bao had never before heard anyone say anything positive about time in the countryside. Bianji actually appreciated the boredom. It had given him time to think, something he had rarely done in Shanghai, and it had given him time and inclination to observe. He had observed city youths reacting to the alien and confining environment, to their peasant keepers and to their peers pacing alongside them. He had observed the daily life of the peasants, its many limits, the masked reactions to interlopers from the city who seemed so free and acted so caged. Now he was writing his observations into short stories, stories which struck her as original and new because they were not black and white. After a virtual ban on literature during the Cultural Revolution, stories and novels were pouring from Chinese pens, but mainly they were "scar literature" which displayed physical and mental scars inflicted by the Cultural Revolution. His stories were gentle. They presented vignettes of people and relationships and quietly raised questions instead of loudly proclaiming judgments. Bianji considered them mere snippets from the canvas of his observations and said regretfully that they were all he could write for now, that he was learning, that he wanted to write in new ways and in old ways which had been neglected. Most of his stories were piquant rather than poignant and could be funny, especially when he wrote of himself. There was, for example, a hilarious account of his first use of a carrying pole. On the other hand he was not awed by the tragic. There was a portrait of a girl who committed suicide; it explored her dilemma and mind and judged neither her nor the society. It astonished Hai Bao because it led her to accept the girl's decision. That made her realize how much talent Bianji had, but he was dissatisfied with the story and vowed not to write on such subjects again until he had gained confidence and craft.

"What's wrong with it?" Hai Bao protested. "It's.... I almost said it's beautiful. Death is ugly, but your portrait is anything but ugly. It's absorbing. It almost becomes comic when she weighs the advantages and disadvantages of the various ways to kill herself. I can't believe anyone would really do that, but you slip into her mind so naturally that you make me believe it. And you use the comedy to intensify the tragedy. It's a simple idea, but I would have never thought of it. Did she tell you she was doing that? You must have known her well."

"I hardly knew her at all. That's why I had to write it that way, to get to know her. But getting to know her seemed to mean ignoring the serious issues her death raised. I kept trying to do both, but it kept coming out sentimental. So I had to oversimplify. I always end up oversimplifying."

"I think I see what you mean. Maybe it's because for so long in our country we've oversimplified everything, then pretended we had done or said something profound. At least you don't pretend. Slicing to the bone with a sharp knife is actually more simple than pounding with a bludgeon. True simplicity isn't oversimplifying, and by not pretending to raise serious issues you may imply them."

He started to reply. Then he stopped and stared at her. "Where did you learn to think like that?"

"Think like what? I never learned to think. I was educated during the Cultural Revolution. Remember? No one ever expected me to think. If I'm thinking now, it's only because you force me to. I never wanted to think about things like death before. And now...." She laughed. "Why now I even know the proper way to plan suicide. Before I could only dance."

"Ahh. You underestimate yourself. Dance expresses everything, including thought. It's much more expressive than writing." And they were laughing together and talking about dancing, about her. He had a way of turning a conversation back to her. She realized that after all his years in the countryside she was an exotic creature to him, yet he was interested in her as a human being, not just a woman. Realizing this told her that no one she had met previously had been genuinely interested in her. He could speak at great length, yet he preferred to listen to her.

They grew close in only a few dates. He took her to restaurants and to operas. It was a wonderful time for opera, a special time. After a decade of compression and suppression culture exploded, and opera provided the gunpowder. Everywhere traditional opera cartwheeled and banged, tittered and twanged, pantomimed and clanged, undulated and sang. Every style flourished, including older, less popular styles like Kun opera. Hai Bao and Bianji couldn't keep up with them all, but they had fun trying. He claimed he learned a lot about opera from her, but she suspected she learned more from him. The things she knew about opera were based on Cultural Revolution oversimplifications. She could catch the gestures, but he could dig out deeper meanings. The highlight of their opera going was scenes from *Mudan Ting (Peony Pavilion)*, the greatest of Kun operas. *Shortly before I met Hai Bao I too saw a performance of excerpts from* Mudan Ting. *Probably I saw the same scenes Hai Bao saw seven years earlier since it was the same company, the Shanghai Kun Opera Troupe, performing. I hope Hai Bao saw the same actress singing Du Li Niang. The one I saw was magnificent. I fell in love with her and Kun opera. I had seen and enjoyed a small town opera during my winter vacation, and when I puzzled over enjoying its strange sounds in one of my classes, a student whose husband was an opera expert took on the task of educating me. They shepherded me to a series of operas.* Mudan Ting *was the one that won me over. I cannot remember the name of the woman who acted and sang and danced Du Li Niang, but I remember every graceful movement of her ever graceful body, every wonderful expression of her wonderfully expressive face, a face that could leap from tragedy to comedy in the blink of an eye. Indeed, I think I stopped blinking lest I miss anything. We had excellent seats, but everyone in that small theatre could see the actors' faces. How different, I later reflected, from my experience of Western opera. In my youth I loved Renata Tebaldi and never missed one of her operas at Lyric Opera of Chicago. But I sat in the top balcony, where I couldn't see her face. Many people up there brought opera glasses, and I was occasionally offered a peek through one. I always refused. In fact, I usually closed my eyes during Tebaldi's best arias. She had the voice of an angel, but it was easier to picture her as the delicate heroines she sang if one did not look at her. Chinese opera is what Western opera claims to be but never quite is, a grand melding of the arts, drama and dance the equal of music (with lesser arts from face painting to mime to acrobatics to add to the effect). Singers don't try to shatter glass or project to a gallery half a kilometer away. The music serves the drama, not vice versa as in Western opera. And* Mudan Ting *is the greatest opera of China's greatest classical dramatist, Tang Xianzu. It tells of Du Li Niang, a sheltered maiden who dreams of an unknown young scholar handsome as a willow in spring, then sickens and dies of longing for this phantom; so great is her passion that her ghost cannot rest until it finds the actual man, makes him desire her as she does him and teaches him how to bring her body back to life and love.* Hai Bao and Bianji spoke not a word during the performance, hushed by its constant, gentle, flowing movement; its subtle music and rhythms; its ancient, unworldly beauty; the seamless stitching of realism and dream, tragedy and comedy, history and superstition in its story. Even outside after the performance they walked in silence until they had left the theater crowd behind. Then Hai Bao sighed at the beauty and the way love conquers all. But Bianji laughed at the comedy and pointed out the passion in the love which lifted it far above the average Chinese opera.

"Isn't love passion? Is there a difference between them?" Hai Bao asked.

"There is a difference. I can still love, but I don't think I have any passion left in me," Bianji lamented. "Du Li Niang was never allowed to express passion and had so much left in her it could even overcome death. I used mine up slinking at the tail of the Red Guards trying to prove I was as revolutionary as they, spouting slogans, bombarding the headquarters, repudiating the bourgeois reactionary line, storming the capitalist roaders' Workers' Red Militia Detachment, supporting the peasants and adoring the red sun in my heart and the great helmsman of my spirit, Chairman Mao. The terrible thing about the Cultural Revolution was that it squandered our strongest emotions on idiocies; it took advantage of our youth and wasted our enthusiasm. Now there's nothing of that left. That's why I can only write miniature sketches, nothing deep or long. I'm trying to get it back. You're helping a lot."

"Me? What can I do?"

"Just be you. You're like Du Li Niang. You've still got all your passion inside you. You're lucky to have been born later. Just being with you I can feel the spirit I once had, the passion the Cultural Revolution robbed me of. When I'm with you I almost feel it can pass from you to me." They were walking down a dark street. He took her in his arms and kissed her quickly but solidly.

Magic is eternally brief. There were too few of those magical first encounters when, under the cloak of discussing art and everything under heaven, they transmuted it all into their own feelings. By discussing them Hai Bao uncovered a new world in Bianji's feelings, another in her own. He opened her up, made her aware of much hidden inside her. She knew much no one had taught her, much teachers and parents had attempted to prevent her from learning. She related how she was caught reading Hong Lou Meng (A Dream of Red Mansions) at the age of fifteen, how the teacher confiscated the volume and informed her parents, how ma and ba lectured her not to waste time on trash but to concentrate on schoolwork. She had never really understood the fault in reading China's greatest novel, Mao's favorite. Telling Bianji she suddenly did: it was all about feelings and roused her own.

"Passion," Bianji responded immediately. "All that passion Tang Xianzu and Cao Xueqin understood too well. Passion from time immemorial knows no end, and from time immemorial it has caused artists no end of trouble. It's still getting us in trouble with the scholars."

"Not only scholars," Hai Bao rejoined, inspired as usual by his understanding and carrying it farther than she knew she knew. "My teacher was no real scholar. What was the Cultural Revolution about? Lots of propaganda and posturing, no genuine passion."

"It's what all Chinese history is about," Bianji agreed. "The scholars and the politicians and the moralists, all the authorities who have always run our land and lives: they have always been afraid of passion, afraid to accumulate debts of breeze and moonlight."

And Hai Bao found herself dreaming of Du Li Niang at night and wanting to study during the day, to understand Chinese history and literature. She told Bianji about Yu, the beleaguered ex Red Guard who so deeply desired to study, and how the teachers and leaders had hectored him. What passion must have lurked beneath his silence. Yet she did not tell him about Yu's letter, and that told her more about her own feelings. There were some things she would share only after marriage. She instinctively held them back even as so much inside her was being released. "The Communist Party hates Confucius because it wants to be the new Confucius. It's not freeing us from feudalism. It's trying to become a new feudal philosopher and moral authority, a new feudal father." Where did such ideas come from? How could they be so clear in her mind without her knowing they were there? It was Bianji, she knew. He brought out what was in her, conjured open a window which let fresh air into her mind and circulated ideas out.

If only she knew the trick to keep the window open. Didn't he want it to remain open long enough to let the passion behind the ideas follow them out? If only he could have waited to tell her of his feudal father. Did he have to hurry so? Did he kiss her before he told her to tease the passion? to imply that love would indeed conquer all? to say goodbye? It was his third kiss. (The second had added to the romance by satirizing romance. He had described Hemingway's description of a french kiss and attempted to insert his tongue into her mouth. She had pulled away in distaste and they had both laughed.) Before this kiss he looked around and after it he looked away, as if to see if anyone had seen. Then he said, "My father has forbidden me to see you and I've moved out. I'm staying with a friend in a dormitory. It's very temporary. There's not much room, but I hope it will show my father I'm serious."

"Please don't fight with your parents over me."

"Please don't be polite. It's the wrong time for it. I have to fight for us. And I have to fight for me. I can't let him run my life. He'd like to. He'd like to run everyone's life."

She wanted to ask how they could live in his family's home if he couldn't live there alone, but she didn't know if a kiss entitled her to such a question. "What are you planning to do?" was all she asked.

"I'll stay away a few days, then go back. I don't know what will happen, but I promise I won't hide anything from you. I'll fight for us. I'm not afraid of him."

The next time they met they went to People's Park. They had tickets for a Beijing opera but he wanted to talk. She could see something was preying on his mind, so she said little and waited. He sighed and began a story without a preface: "My little sister will get married soon."

She knew he had a younger sister and two younger brothers although they had never spoken of them. "Why does that make you sad?"

"She's in England and there's a boy here she loved and who loves her very much. He saved her and my whole family during the Cultural Revolution. He's a Party member from her *danwei*. He kept her from being sent down and kept my parents from being sent to a labor camp. She was just a girl when he befriended her, and he stuck with her all through the Cultural Revolution, when he must have been under tremendous pressure to wash his hands of the capitalist class. He's gentle and good and loves her very much, and, as I said, my parents owe him a lot, possibly even their lives. Compared to their capitalist friends they had an easy time and didn't lose much during the Cultural Revolution, so they couldn't refuse her permission to marry him. What they did was arrange a trip for her. My father has an older brother who escaped to England in 1949. My sister didn't even want to go, but her boyfriend insisted she might never get another chance and persuaded her. His trust was touching. My father and his brother had it all planned out. His brother is rich. I suppose the luxury overwhelmed my sister, and when she was introduced to a rich overseas Chinese and given the chance to live the rest of her life in it she couldn't resist. She must have tried to resist a little because my parents had to phone her several times to pressure her to do it. They've been celebrating since she gave in. Heaven knows what the poor boyfriend is doing. I doubt she even had the courage to write him. I wrote him and apologized, for all the good that will do. He came to the house and talked to my parents, who put on a big sympathy act for him. It made me sick to my stomach."

"Do you think your sister is happy?"

"May happiness found as easily as turning a hand rot in the hand that found it. The stuff communists say about capitalists isn't just propaganda; it's all true. I'm ashamed."

"Why? You certainly didn't do anything wrong."

"I'm ashamed to be walking with you, with a girl who's pure and clean like my sister's boyfriend. My hands are dirty, but what's worse is that they're tied. I can't do a thing."

Hai Bao saw he was not talking only about his sister. He was talking about them. "It doesn't matter. I don't expect you to do more. It's disgusting, but it has nothing to do with us."

"But it does. Don't you see? You would have to live in that family"

"I would live with you. It doesn't matter about your family."

"When you say things like that it reveals your innocence. It proves to me that I'm right. I can't bring you into a family like mine."

Hai Bao looked into his eyes. Even now she seldom did this; it was not considered proper. "Now I know how you wrote the story of the girl who committed suicide. You can talk yourself into anything."

He was taken aback, whether by the look or the words she did not know.

"What do you mean? What have I talked myself into? Do you want me to be proud of a family like that?"

"I want you to let me decide for me. I've heard what you said about your family. Obviously it's not something to be proud of, but you're you, not your father. And not me. I'm glad you told me. It gives me a higher opinion of you, not a lower one. Don't turn it into something it isn't. It isn't something between you and me."

Now he looked at her. Then he quickly glanced right and left and she almost laughed because she knew what it meant. He kissed her. She decided for herself: she liked kissing. She wanted to kiss him back, but he looked so forlorn she laughed instead. "You had decided to use this to split us up, right?" He nodded sheepishly. "On our first date you told me you think for yourself and you didn't intend to let your father run your life. Remember your own words. Decide for yourself. And let me decide for myself."

He glanced around again.

She thought they had settled family problems for a while and could get back to writing and opera. She liked him very much, but marriage, if it was to happen, was several years away. There was time to worry about peripheral details. They had watched a Shaoxing opera. It was Hai Bao's idea although she was not a fan of Shaoxing opera. She hoped something light and romantic would set the mood she wanted. So when, after the opera, he began to speak of his father, her disappointment was so tangible it stopped him. "What's the matter?" he asked.

"Excuse me," she replied. "I was hoping we wouldn't talk about our families tonight. Didn't we exhaust the topic last time?"

He smiled. "This is Shanghai, not Shaoxing. Shanghai ren like to settle the details before they get down to romance."

"And Subei ren," she groaned, "work too hard ever to get down to romance."

He was light hearted the rest of the evening, recited poetry, made jokes. It was a side of him she had seldom seen and one she quite liked. But she knew he was acting, that something was weighing on his mind, so when, on their next date, he requested permission to speak of his family she agreed.

For all his claims to be a typical Shanghai ren he didn't speak like one. He was far too blunt: "My father swears that if I marry you he'll disown me. No house, no money, nothing."

"After what you told me about him, I can't be surprised. Is there anything we can do? Maybe if I could meet him...?"

"He told me if I brought you to the house he would disown me immediately."

"Would he really do it?"

"He would."

"What will you do?"

"I don't know. I need more time to think. What's your opinion?"

"My opinion is what I told you before. You have to decide for yourself. I just didn't think you would have to do it so soon."

"Maybe it's better sooner than later. I was content in the countryside when he had no power over me, but I'm older now. I'm not sure I want to live that way permanently. I have to consider the rest of my life. And whatever you say I have to consider you. I always thought I'd be overjoyed to escape my family, but not this way, not with nothing. I want to write, but writing is no way to earn a living and support a family. Should I ask my wife and children to drink the northwest wind? How am I going to write when I have to watch them suffer from poverty and cold and hunger?"

She didn't think she needed to remind him she had a job. Besides, housing would be a worse problem than money. Put as he had just put it, it sounded hopeless. They walked on in silence. Then he felt her despair and took her hand. "I.... I respect you. I respect you too much to lead you on. Give me time to think. When I've thought it out clearly and come to a decision, I'll let you hear right away. I can't see you until I'm clear. I'm too much of a Shanghai *ren*."

Like a good Chinese she told herself there was no hope, and like any person anywhere she secretly hoped. The waiting was awful: she didn't hear from him for more than two weeks. She kept telling herself she had to learn patience, but she had never been patient. Then a note asking her to meet him at Hongkou Park. Impatient as ever she arrived early. She wanted to see him before he saw her. That look confirmed her fears. "It's hopeless," she told herself, and those were his first words.

"I tried to talk to him, I tried to talk to ma, I tried to talk to myself. No one was listening. I'm sorry, Bao. I'd love to live with you, but I couldn't live the way we'd have to live. I wish I had been born poor, I wish we had lost all our money. But I can't give it up voluntarily. Life is too hard in China. I can't give up having an easy life. I can't give up being able to write without having to worry about money. Because I can't I don't deserve you."

She must have prepared herself well. She didn't cry and she didn't curse, even to herself. He had been too honest for her to hate him or be surprised. She had had her day. They had had several days, good days. Good days were over for now.

He couldn't even give her a farewell present. He said he had wanted to give her a copy of *Mudan Ting*. He said he wanted to inscribe it In Memory of Passion. He told her this because he could not have written it anyhow. He wanted her to know, not others to see. She would have to settle for his good intentions. His family's copy of the book had disappeared and he could not find another anywhere. The Cultural Revolution spared few such relics.

"But passion does not die so easily," I want to shout. "That is what *Mudan Ting* is all about, passion overcoming even death."

"And marriage can overcome even life," someone shouts back. It is the matchmaker. You might think that allowing people to choose their own marriage partners and marry for love would render matchmakers unnecessary. No. Marriage is more important than people. Allowing people to choose enabled anyone to be a matchmaker, and once bitten by the bug, never shy. The woman who had introduced Hai Bao and Bianji now wanted Hai Bao to meet Bianji's sister's jilted lover. "It's fate," she insisted. Hai Bao and the man both resisted, but both were too weak to resist long. After months of pestering the two rejected suitors agreed to meet. The matchmaker met them in front of Hongkou Park, introduced them and vanished. They walked for ten minutes, each wanting to repeat the proverb that what has a beginning has an end, neither willing to speak out loud.

Hai Bao never saw Bianji again nor did she ever see a story he wrote in print although she read all the literary magazines which might have printed one. But years later she met the Party official who had been rejected by Bianji's sister. He had become a businessman.

Chapter Fourteen

Two places I have loved since I lost Lincoln Park. And the butterfly dream connects them. The first place I loved because it was so unlike Chicago, the second place because it was so like. Yet the butterfly dream connects them.

Color drew me to the mountains as powerfully as it had drawn me to Bissell Street's rainbow buildings and people. But what the colors drew from me was not at all the same. "Escape," the mountains cried out to me when they were but hazy purple swellings beneath clear white clouds in a pure blue sky. I had lived for years without comprehending the dread I had come to feel in and of Chicago's flathued flatlands. Escape. The jagged border between mountain and sky was snow, not cloud, but after years of fear and days of driving through 105 degree prairie drought I was not about to believe in snow until my mind could no longer deny what was captivating my eyes. In Lincoln Park cops who had murdered my friends swore they would get me. In Marquette Park neighbors called the cops every time a black friend – once, even, a curly headed Italian – visited. Escape. One look at the many blued glacial waters and ices of Glacier Park in Montana held me there for three days. I refused to continue on towards Peg's ancestral Canadian home although she kept telling me the Canadian Rockies were even more beautiful. The mountains shouted that freedom was too tightly swaddled in the land of the free, that it was time to unwind from the tension of life there, to admit that I was not brave enough to continue making it my home. Escape. High above the surreal depths of color and unreal grandeur of Moraine Lake in Canada's Banff Park we discovered a little hollow where the earth exhaled in tiny bubbling springs which fed the slightest, softest, brightest tinted, realest mosses anyone ever stripped and rolled in.

That was my first view of the mountains, my first inkling of my need to escape. From then on we drove to them every summer. Once, driving from the prison of Chicago, we stayed a night with a friend who lived in rural Minnesota and passed Sandstone Federal Penitentiary, where another friend was incarcerated. I stopped the car, wrote a description of the dreadful walls and vowed, "The revolution will smash all such stone walls back into sand." Then I drove full speed away from where my revolution was happening, toward the freedom of the mountains.

Every summer it became harder to drive back to Chicago. In Marquette Park I dreamed of those white mountains and blue lakes – only to have them dissolve into blood: two, three, many Chicagos. Finally Peg found a job, and she, Ruby and I shovelled and sang our way through a Dakota blizzard to arrive in the Kootenays in March of 1975. And the mountains were indeed white, the lakes blue, not blood.

I had escaped. My finest flit. Relief overwhelmed me, colored my sight as completely as the new colors around me colored my imagination and cleared my mind. It was as if the tear gas in which I had lived in 1968 had remained a permanent part of the atmosphere of Chicago, a part of me as long as I stayed. In the mountains words gushed out of me, many about glaciers or rivers and falls of ice which, I discovered the following winter, froze only in my mind. But the ink they inspired to flow from my pen washed the smog of Chicago from my head.

Although my subject was Chicago, Cha Cha, Lincoln Park, my novel was filled with descriptions of mountains. It had to be, for I could never have written about Chicago in Chicago. The mountains gave me sanctuary, vision and freedom to write, so my words gave them thanks:

> I cannot understand how both my recent lives can be real. Surely, I keep thinking, if all I lived through in Lincoln Park was real, then this world of thick spring snows in the night, of hail blasting down from a bright sky which was sunny a moment ago and will be sunny again in ten minutes, of mountains which ascend into the sun and descend into clouds over the river, this magnificent last of winter world I walk and run in night and day trying to prove it is really there, cannot be real.

> Snow is falling, big wet flakes dropping slowly, straight down. The first snow of fall down here in the valley though it has been snowing up in the mountains and working its way down for a month. Not much is accumulating here since the temperature is right at freezing but enough to cover the ground lightly and tip the trees. It's a lovely scene yet strangely two dimensional because over the river a fog of falling flakes hides the mountains, becomes an oriental screen on which snow and trees are painted. The big ponderosa pine towers above the bare birches and aspens, above the almost bare tamaracks, above the cedars springing up in its shade, above the smaller firs, pines and spruces, all green and white, as if the artist had only those two colors on the palette: green and white

painted on a screen of grey, illuminated faintly from behind the screen. How beautiful it is. How much I feel both outside it, a spectator gazing at a painting in a museum, and part of it, the solitary figure often found in such paintings.

I wrote that description nineteen years ago, and as I write today I am looking out the same window at much the same scene, an early snow, perhaps the earliest snowstorm since that one. I am back here in the Kootenays, the mountains still my inspiration. How much they gave me. The day I first arrived I started writing and stopped dreaming entirely, or stopped remembering my dreams, which amounts to the same thing since I slept well for the first time in years. After a little more than a year I finished the Lincoln Park portions of my novel and began dreaming again – of mountains, not lakes of blood.

Escaping to these Canadian mountains gave me back my dreams and enabled me to live both the American dream – I live independently on the land, growing much of my own food, heating with wood that needs to be cut on my own land – and the unamerican dream, as testified to by six years in China. As well as the one I forgot when I was originally dreaming the other two. I had failed as a doer, but that failure had finally given me life experience about which to write. I had more material than I wanted for a tragedy, yet I couldn't end the Lincoln Park novel because my life in Lincoln Park had never ended properly. Not being able to roll with the punches, I had simply rolled out of that life and into another and then another. The climax toward which my life in Lincoln Park and the plot of my novel about it built was death, for part of me had surely died. But if I killed off the main character and narrator of my novel, how could he write all my loving descriptions of the mountains? I learned to hate plots, to refuse to build my novels around them.

But it wasn't easy, and it took a long time. I had failed as a doer, both outside the system in Lincoln Park and inside it in Marquette Park; nevertheless, at first I felt compelled to justify sitting with a pen in my hand, to persuade myself that writing, not fighting, was a better way to change the world. But as the peace of my raging mountains settled over me, words came to be their own justification and I was writing for myself. Then, slowly, just being, being among my mountains, seemed to be enough. Maybe I had the makings of a silent mystic after all. Every morning my mountains changed their cloud clothes: sometimes they wore elegant toques, sometimes fleecy shawls, but usually the clouds blanketed their toes. My legs became more powerful than my pen. I could run up into mists which formed above the Slocan River, up through the fog into the sunlight, down again into the ocean of cloud which engulfed my valley. If legs could carry me from worlds of mist to worlds of light, why write? If dreams could transport me to worlds I wanted, why keep searching, why keep scratching? It took seven years to complete a first draft of that endless first novel I started so feverishly, and it probably wouldn't have been completed at all had not the mantle protecting me amid my mountains unraveled, had not the family I didn't believe in fallen apart and so revealed – although it took writing two more novels and hearing Hai Bao's laughter to figure it out – that I was not the solitary figure I liked to imagine myself, that I needed a family.

Strange to say, the mountains which calmed insanity in me gave Peg scope to explore long repressed insanity in her. Late one night she awoke me and announced, "I've decided to go crazy." The atmosphere in our house was already so mad that it didn't occur to me to question her decision. My catcher needed me to catch her. I tried. For a year I stopped dreaming and tried. And wrote furiously when Peg's insanity took her beyond my depth. I completed the Lincoln Park novel and wrote the Marquette Park novel. What I wrote stunk. But it kept me sane. No, there was nothing sane about that period, even my writing, for I ended the Lincoln Park novel with the narrator, me, returning to Chicago. But writing gave me just enough sanity to see the insanity in me, around me. Around Ruby. We had to get away. We had to escape our escape. Peg couldn't do much worse on her own.

So one night I became a butterfly. Not Zhaungzi. Not yet. I had the dream before I read the book. That I know. On the other hand I did do a course in oriental philosophy as an undergraduate. At that time my interest was only in Indian philosophy and mysticism, but we read Chinese philosphy as well and Zhaungzi's dream is famous. So perhaps I read it then and it fell into some forgotten crevice of my mind and, with typical Chinese patience, bided there for twenty five years. "The mind is it's own place and in itself can make a heaven of hell, a hell of heaven." Milton said that, and "Its Own Place" is the title of my third novel. The second draft. The first draft was called "Insanity for Beginners." But I'm getting ahead of myself. As usual. And speculating too much. Yet I don't consider it speculation to say I know what kind of butterfly Zhaungzi would have been if he lived in the Kootenays. Canadian butterflies are usually solitary, but one day, hiking near Little Slocan Lake, I happened upon a congregation of hundreds of big, beautiful swallowtails who clouded all the crowded air yellow and black.

That night I became a butterfly. When I awoke I felt so light, so fine, so natural that I wondered whether I had always been a butterfly and had dreamed all the bloody nightmare of Lincoln Park. That momentary doubt upon awakening, that silly doubt, set me free. I didn't have to return. I didn't have to save the world. I didn't even have to escape my escape. But maybe I could. "We are such stuff as dreams are made on," I battlecried, leaped out of bed, threw on some shorts and ran ten miles or more, through my dreamlike mountains and their mists, down my dreamroad, away from the insanity gripping my life, toward Bissel Street as I first saw it, will always see it, with all its crazy confusion of colors and turrets and people. And back in bed at night I found I also could flutter toward a mysterious land behind the mists, a land I loved without knowing, inspired by Bissel Street's crowds but crowded with sounds and sights I had never heard or seen, fascinating dreamscapes, mountains calmer than my mountains, streets wilder than the street which led me to them. Another night, the night after a friend showed me an ad in a teachers' magazine seeking English teachers in China, Mao reappeared in a particularly crowded butterfly dream and I knew where my mysterious land was. I also knew I was all right, for Mao was reciting poetry. *In those days he recited in unaccented English. He rarely appears now, but when he does, I am proud to say, he speaks* putunghua – *without the heavy Hunan accent he had in life.* Soon Ruby and I were flitting across the Pacific Ocean.

A year teaching in Shanghai taught me I had new things to write out of me, so I returned to my mountains. I had the technique down by now, and I wanted to hurry back to China. I wrote more than six hundred pages in less than a year. Twice: two very different drafts. I had brought back many books to learn more about China. In one of them I discovered Zhuangzi. What a wonderful surprise to discover that the butterfly dreams which led me to China were really Chinese. As well as really me. Zhaungzi, a Daoist before Daoism became a religion, loved nature. He would have loved the Kootenays. And laughed to see that my congregation of swallowtails was worshipping over a patty of moose turd.

I was dreaming of China, I was dreaming of butterflies, I was dreaming of women. But I never dreamed of Hai Bao.

"Why are the mountains so close?" asked Hai Bao, the rock on which a rolling stone had founded his new family, the first time she saw the Kootenays. My father had asked the same question the first time he visited. Flatlanders! They can appreciate mountains only as part of a distant vista. And I? I suppose one reason I love the mountains' nearness is because it means Chicago is a distant vista of my past.

But Hai Bao does not want Shanghai to become a distant vista. Even now, as Pushan Lu and the Shanghai we both love are being urban renewed more utterly than Bissel Street ever was.

Chapter Fifteen

Handpainted on my most silken memory is the first time Hai Bao kissed me. I had been wanting to kiss her but holding back for several dates — it seemed forever — afraid of frightening the modest creature who had won my love with her immodest laughter. Since the language barrier prevented delicate discussion of delicate feelings, I hoped to convey mine by the lightest, gentlest, most delicate of kisses. I expected at least a modest blush in return. I prayed she would not flee. What she actually did was kiss me back. Not passionately but certainly more firmly than I had kissed her. I guess I didn't blush either. The naturalness of her behavior throughout our courtship made it the most beautiful time of my life. Having experienced many Western women, I could not believe that love could be so simple, so genuine. Nothing was false; there was neither coquettishness nor simulated passion and protestations of love. Under unnatural circumstances she did only what came naturally and I will always remember and love her for having done it.

Where did she learn to act that way or, more correctly, where did she learn not to act? Was it cultural? In a culture which praises euphemism, lying, flattery and falsity to avoid losing face and wears a mask of prudery to cover its face? which traditionally forbade meetings between young, unmarried women and men and generally portrayed such meetings on the stage in falsettos and the most artificial of gestures? in which mates for life met on their wedding day, followed immediately by their wedding night? Did it run in the family? Consider the examples of love, murder, marriage, divorce and attempted divorce in that family. Was it learned from personal experience? Consider Hai Bao's big romance. It began in 1980, was a true romance of the Eighties, the decade of Deng. I don't claim to understand this true romance I have to report. I don't even claim I tried hard. Although I do not hesitate to work at understanding Mao Ze Dong, I am not willing to work at understanding Huang even though he is essential to my novel, involved with its single character, and Mao is not. Maybe I'm just prejudiced against Ningbonese. I don't try to understand Chiang Kai Shek either. As for Hai Bao's romance, I can see why it would leave her willing to marry me, but hell if I can see how it led to the kind of love she gave me.

If a country has no minorities does it have to invent one? China does have minorities, over fifty of them, but they are almost entirely located on the peripheries of the country. Most of the heartland lacks a minority population sufficient to support racism. This creates a problem for the majorities. Majorities? Well, if there is no minority, the solution is to divide up the majority.

Huang was Ningbonese, Hai Bao Subeinese. Such regional identity is maintained in official records generation after generation in spite of place of birth and upbringing. Regional identity is even more important unofficially. In modern Shanghai there is less physical segregation than in South Africa or Chicago (or old Shanghai, which was divided into "concessions" ruled by various nations, zones in which Western "democracies" often enforced segregation with armed guards and barbed wire), but regionalities identify with each other as closely as nationalities in Chicago or races in South Africa. Each has its own stereotype and its own place in the local pecking order. Ningbo *ren* were among the first immigrants to Shanghai after the Opium War treaty forced it open to foreign trade and foreigners. Ningbo was near Shanghai, a mercantile city, an open treaty port itself although it had no foreign settlement. Many of these early immigrants made their fortune in trade and established themselves near the top of the local pecking order. Subei *ren* were latecomers. Their area was farther from Shanghai, isolated and backward in the ways of international commerce. Even today there is no railroad in the eastern Subei (from which Hai Bao's parents hailed) and no boat link with Shanghai although both "Binhai" and "Shanghai" mean and are "by the sea." The Subeinese immigrants came as factory and menial workers at the bottom of the pecking order. They became the niggers of Shanghai.

Hai Bao grew up knowing this. Schools in post liberation China fed children "eating bitterness" lessons about how bad life was before 1949; Subei children in Shanghai received dessert at home and on the streets: lessons about prejudice against them in the city of their birth. But until she approached marriageable age all these lessons remained just that, history lessons to be stored in the memory because, hypothetically at least, Chinese know that history is never wasted, is constantly recycled, and didn't the imperial examinations seem to be coming round again? Bianji made the lessons real, moved them from the back of her head to the center of her stomach, yet as time diminished the pain of Bianji's loss, so did it dull the sharpness of the lesson. Bianji's case, she could not help thinking for she often thought of Bianji, was extraordinary because his class was. His family was a relic of a dead age. She was brimming with life, the child of new China. She considered herself and all her friends Shanghai *ren*, and she thought the old pecking order was just that: old, outmoded. The Communist Party had been top cock all her life and treated all the hens the same, was feudal father to the nation. But times were truly changing and the new recycling of history was never quite the expected one. Mao had popped his last cork and Zhou En Lai, the greatest Subei *ren* of them all, was long gone too. This was the era of Deng Xiao Ping's reforms, and egalitarianism was becoming less fashionable. While the Party was out building new skyscrapers, over at the chicken house all the old prejudices were coming home to roost.

We foreign teachers in Shanghai developed our own theories to account for the ways the Chinese behaved as a mass. One of my pet theories held that on their twenty fifth birthday all Shanghainese were administered an inscrutable oriental love potion the effects of which lasted exactly five years. How else to account for the fact that none of them were married before twenty five and all of them were married by the time they turned thirty? The official explanation (offered up in more than one of the innumerable "brief introductions" to various aspects of Chinese life to which foreigners are subjected) of the phenomenon was that late marriages were encouraged as a means of population control. End of explanation. At this point we foreigners invariably had to point out that the explanation accounted for only half of the phenomenon and invariably were stared at with incredulity, as if the idea of delaying past thirty were inconceivable. Anyone who reached thirty unmarried or without an imminent marriage scheduled was obviously reprobate, a confirmed bachelor or old maid.

The love potion worked for Hai Bao. She met the man of her dreams late in 1980, after her twenty fifth birthday. Of course by Chinese standards she was already twenty six: even the numbers game is loaded in favor of age in China. And Chinese dreams are loaded in favor of attainability. So Huang was the man of her daytime dreams; nighttime dreams, even when shiftwork produced them by day, too often cried *bian*, change: presto, Bianji magically appeared

Huang was three years older than she. They met in the usual way. A mutual friend brought some of his photos to her and some of hers to him. He was a hydraulic engineer about to enter his last year at Tongji University, Shanghai's best scientific school. He was a member of the first post Cultural Revolution class, the first class after the universities were fully reopened. This was a high recommendation in itself. Since college entrance exams had been forbidden for ten years, there were ten times as many applicants as usual and only the brilliant passed. Huang's parents did not have too big an apartment, and apartment size was always a key consideration for a woman considering marriage: she would have to live with his family, and in one of Shanghai's matchbox apartments this could get mighty uncomfortable. However, the matchmaker pointed out the favorable circumstance that Huang was the only boy in his family – he had three sisters, all married – and that even with five people living in it – the single child was the new fashion – the apartment would contain .4 square meters per person more than Hai Bao's present living quarters. Not only that but the apartment was located in the downtown area, crowded but very convenient for shopping and much higher class than Pushan Lu.

The matchmaker met the two in Hai Bao's usual spot, outside Hongkou Park, the big park nearest her house, introduced them and disappeared. They walked in the park and talked. Hai Bao did most of the talking. Huang was obviously a quiet man, but he spoke enough to show his intelligence and that he was listening closely to everything she said. He was also looking at her closely – out of the corner of his eye. She noticed because she was looking at him out of the corner of her eye. They had mutual interests. Hai Bao told him about the song and dance team. This was a test. In public she dared not speak of the team since praise of it might be construed as praise of Jiang Qing and her policies. Even now she was careful to add how happy she was that the old Beijing operas could be seen again and to mention her final performance in honor of Zhou En Lai. Huang passed the test. He did not react to her approval of the team. He said that because he had been in the countryside for seven years and then had to study hard to get into university, he had not had time for music and culture, but he hoped to change that. He particularly wanted to learn about Beijing opera since the only style he was presently acquainted with was Zhejiang opera. When she spoke of her factory, he asked if she was satisfied with her work and seemed satisfied himself when she admitted she was not, that she had much preferred the song and dance troupe. He even asked if she would like to go to college, a secret ambition which no other man had ever inquired about. Perhaps because Hai Bao was directing the conversation, they avoided the usual business matters: family, family income, family prospects for advancement and the like. Of late these had come to be major topics of first dates. Both Hai Bao's parents were now retired, and while their pensions were adequate they were not wealthy nor had they any prospects of becoming so. When Hai Bao asked Huang about his studies, he said little and spoke modestly. She liked that. All in all she was well satisfied with this first meeting and sure Huang was too.

Yet he did not ask for a second date and did not contact the matchmaker. She did. More than once. It was courteous and polite to let the matchmaker know one's feelings, even if those feelings were negative. It seemed he considered himself above such old fashioned conventions. Well, Hai Bao was not used to such treatment and was not beneath saying so. She wrote him a short note criticizing his behavior. He phoned her at work, said he had been very busy and had been intending to call her but had lost her number. How convenient you found it now, she thought, but did not say. He seemed genuinely apologetic and suggested they go to an opera of her choice.

They went to a program of Beijing opera excerpts. She would have preferred a complete opera, but this was better as an introduction for him.

She provided a running commentary for his edification and, she had to admit, enjoyed the authoritative position this gave her. She felt she was the leader in their relationship, for even after the opera he deferred to her, let her control what conversation there was. And because he gave her this control she deferred back to him and said less. They walked together quietly along quiet streets.

From then on they dated occasionally but regularly, once or twice a month. His studies did not allow more, but Hai Bao was satisfied. In summer he would have more free time and she knew they would see more of each other, but he would not chase her as other men did. She knew this and was glad of it, glad to know it was her hand that would take charge of things. For now they went mainly to movies and lectures at his school. She did not try to hurry matters. His calmness and control of his feelings settled her own. He was nothing like Bianji, and to her surprise she discovered she had learned patience, that Bianji had somehow bequeathed her the patience she needed to deal with Huang.

In summer, as she had known, they saw more of each other, meeting once and often twice a week. Toward the end of his summer vacation she asked him to pick her up at her house. Hai Bao did not go to the factory and spent the day fixing up the place, but there was not much to be done with an ancient concrete floor, cracked walls in need of a new coat of whitewash, rickety old furniture and steps little better than a ladder leading into a hole in the upper floor. She cleaned house thoroughly, put up new pictures clipped from magazines to replace the maps they had used to cover the bare places where Mao's portraits had once reigned, borrowed some solid chairs from a neighbor, dressed her parents in their best clothes and made *hun dun (won tun)*. But she could not clean up Pushan Lu and the depot which sorted junk for recycling outside the entrance to *Pushan Lu Yi Chen*, and she could not teach her parents not to speak Subei dialect. As soon as Huang arrived he wanted to leave. He didn't sit in the chairs. He didn't even taste the *hun dun*, which she had made without garlic, the way Ningbonese liked it. He gave his paltry gifts – *I knew nothing, brought nothing, years after we were married Hai Bao informed me that she bought presents for her parents and told them the presents were from me, for an old Chinese saying says a marriage offer will be granted if it comes with handsome gifts* – and uttered the minimum of words to her parents to satisfy the demands of courtesy, then led Hai Bao out the door. Characteristically he made no complaints. Indeed, that evening he was even more taciturn than usual. From then on they went back to meeting on the street near where they were going. Hai Bao had hoped that inviting him to her home would lead him to reciprocate, but he never spoke about his family and home, and after the fiasco at her home she could not ask.

When school restarted they were seeing each other every Saturday evening. They didn't do much, a movie, a lecture, a stroll in Hongkou or Heping Park or just around the Tongji campus, which was like a park. They didn't say much either, mainly made small talk. They felt comfortable that way, doing and saying little, and there was no reason to break the pattern. Indeed, Hai Bao was discovering that controlling the relationship, as she still felt she did, had a disadvantage. It meant she was responsible for them, that if she tried something new she might interrupt their slow progress, cause some sudden lurch which might throw the relationship off the tracks. Better not rock the rails on which they were gliding smoothly. Control of the relationship instinctively extended to control of herself. Even her nightdreams ceased – or at least she stopped remembering them, which, she told herself, amounted to the same thing. This seemed to make daydreaming more intense. Since direct questions were forbidden, she got to know about Huang, his strengths and weaknesses, his likes and dislikes, mainly through daydreams, got to know all about him without knowing him. She knew he knew much about every branch of science but little about art and literature, knew he was proud to consider himself an intellectual but uninterested in politics or philosophy, knew he loved *hun dun* but despised garlic or any spicy food, knew without his saying so that he preferred her in skirts and dresses rather than pants, in soft colors rather than loud. She even knew about the family of which he had never spoken a word. His parents would be careful, conventional Ningbonese whose house was unblemished by a spec of dust, who liked money but were not ostentatious enough to get into trouble during the Cultural Revolution, who were not interested in literature or politics but read the newspapers daily to know the direction the Party was taking then followed it without belief merely to avoid problems, whose major concern at present would be finding a back door to buy a television set but waiting until enough neighbors owned one so they would not stand out. They would dislike Subei *ren* but dislike trouble even more and dote on their only son and so, Hai Bao hoped, not oppose him if he took a strong stand. But she did not know this. She did not even know Huang well enough to be sure he was capable of standing up to his parents. Nevertheless, if they had strong objections Huang would have told her by now. She thought. But she could not even be certain he had told them about her. She wished she could see a family photo, at least, but even asking for this seemed too daring. When alone she derided herself for timidity, but with Huang she felt comfortable in it, felt it would be foolish to disturb their contentment. They slid contentedly through the mild autumn into winter.

Huang's graduation drew near. In the rush to get universities into full operation the first post Cultural Revolution class had begun at mid year, so he would graduate in January, 1982. Hai Bao assumed she would be invited to the ceremony, but Huang said nothing. Finally she asked him. He stammered a reply about it being a small hall with only family invited. Hai Bao checked this out and was informed the hall was not particularly small and that no limits on attendance had been set. It was the first time Huang had not been truthful. The little gang of four sat close and talked freely about the matter over lunch. *Xiao* Xiang was already married with a child, *Xiao* Yang was married and *Xiao* Wang would soon be married, so the gang seldom saw each other outside the factory,

but they regrouped to deal with what all agreed was a serious problem. Since
Huang continued to see Hai Bao, the problem must be with his family. Hai Bao
must have been deluding herself about his parents. Huang's silence about them had
been too total and had lasted too long. *Xiao* Xiang was for immediate confrontation,
but the others advised caution. They would make inquiries. Shanghai was the world's
smallest large city. There were no secrets from the nosy.

The results of the inquiry were as expected: Huang's mother objected to
Hai Bao. What to do? *Xiao* Xiang offered to accompany Hai Bao to Huang's
house to confront his mother. *Xiao* Yang suggested they all go to the graduation.
But Hai Bao preferred *Xiao* Wang's idea: *Xiao* Wang would invite Hai Bao
and Huang plus her own boyfriend for dinner at her house. Her family was
Ningbonese like Huang's. Ningbonese were reputed to be wise in the ways of
subtlety and indirection. If anyone could bring the matter out tactfully it was
Xiao Wang.

By the time of the dinner *Xiao* Wang knew all there was to be known
about Huang's family and quickly had him chatting about mutual acquaintances
and friends of friends of his family. Her father, and her mother when she was
not in the kitchen, joined in. Of course they too knew all these people. Wine
flowed freely. Hai Bao learned more about Huang's family each minute they
talked than she had in a year of dating.

After dinner *Xiao* Wang suggested the four young people go for a walk.
Outside she breathed a deep "Ah!" and changed from *Ningbohua* (Ningbo
dialect), which they had been using with her parents, to *Shanghaihua*. She said
that she wanted to get away from her parents because it was difficult to speak
candidly in front of them. They were so old fashioned. She cited details. Huang
did not immediately take the bait: family wash should not be aired in public, he
philosophized.

"You must have a lot of moldy clothes around your house then," *Xiao*
Wang rejoined quickly, and everyone laughed. In Shanghai people hung clothes
wherever there was room; there were no private places.

"Let it all hang out," laughed Huang in English. He was the only one
who spoke the foreign language, and the wine seemed to incline him to show
off. Even speaking *putunghua* when only Shanghai *ren* were present was acting,
a formal performance reserved for the movies, the radio or the classroom. Hai
Bao was tempted to respond to his English by singing archaic Kun Opera.

Xiao Wang was up to a contemporary performance: "Did you say *hán* or
hǎn?" The former meant to keep something in one's mouth, the latter to call it
out loudly.

"*Hán hu chi ci,*" laughed Huang switching to *putonghua.* "Be vague."

"*Bu. Hǎn yuan jiao qu,*" shot back *Xiao* Wang. "No. Shout out your
grievances."

Xiao Wang had won the little contest. Huang gave in and began to air grievances. Soon it came out that his mother refused to let him marry a Subeinese and a poor one at that. In addition, his mother considered the family immoral because Hai Bao's mother had divorced and remarried.

"Just bring Hai Bao home. She'll win your mother over. I'll coach her."

"I know. I've been trying to persuade ma to meet *Xiao* Zhang, but she refuses. She said she wouldn't even come to my graduation if *Xiao* Zhang comes. What am I supposed to do?"

Xiao Wang was feeling confident. "Let's go over to your place right now," she suggested.

Huang was tempted but in the end wouldn't agree: "It's my problem. If I tricked ma like that, she would never accept *Xiao* Zhang. I have to convince her myself. I'll try harder."

Try he did. Now that the problem was in the open, Huang seemed to delight in describing every detail of his attempts. They saw each other more frequently, and on every date he had a new story, a new way in which he had asked, cajoled, kidded, prodded, pleaded, assured, reassured, argued, shamed his mother. At first he joked about it, for he felt certain of eventual success. How could his mother refuse even to meet the woman he wanted to marry? How could she judge someone she had never met? Twice he sent Hai Bao letters — telephones were rarely found and less rarely used in Shanghai, but letters mailed in the morning were delivered the same day — proclaiming that his mother had agreed, then met Hai Bao and sheepishly told her Ma had changed her mind or become ill. Finally he fell to his knees and begged his mother. She requested time to think. He couldn't refuse that, could he? he asked Hai Bao. So they waited. It wouldn't be long, he assured her.

This occurred right before his graduation and meant Hai Bao could not attend the ceremony, but it also meant they were openly discussing their relationship. Around the same time Huang was assigned to teach at Nanjing University. This was a blow. He had been hoping to teach in Shanghai, but such assignments were few and coveted by everyone. Huang now rued aloud, even to his mother he asserted, that he had not married Hai Bao. Had they married several months before he graduated, he would have been assigned to work in Shanghai as a matter of course. The regulations decreed that if they married now, she would have to go to Nanjing and they would not be able to live in Shanghai. His only hope was to be admitted to graduate school at Tongji. Then they could marry and live in Shanghai. He would have to teach in Nanjing at least one and a half years before he could even take the exam, but he began studying for it immediately.

The primary benefit Hai Bao received from his study was a series of letters — in English. English would constitute an important part of the exam and was his weakest area. Of course Hai Bao's knowledge of English was limited to phrases like "Chairman Mao is the red sun in our sky" and "a long, long life to Chairman Mao." That was the sum of what she had learned in her middle school study of the language. He never used any of her outdated phrases and she never attempted to read his English letters. Years later I got to read them. They rated a C– for grammar and mechanics but were failures in content. Then again I may be the wrong judge. He did have an academic calling: he could say nothing in more words than some full professors of social science.

He also wrote letters in Chinese. These were briefer, simply saying he was studying and could not meet her. During the early part of his campaign to sway his mother Huang had been more talkative, animated and ardent than ever before. They met two and three times a week, even when he was studying for final exams. On several occasions when they walked in the park he kissed her. This made her happy although kissing no longer was an act of courage. On park benches lovers entwined, necking even in midwinter. Huang found this disgusting. They did not neck on park benches, but those who did made it easy for them to kiss. Without the bench lovers Huang sneered at he would never have dared to kiss her openly, so when he criticized once too often she defended them. It was almost Spring Festival. If his mother was going to relent, the holiday would have been the time to invite her. She understood what his silence on the topic meant, and when she defended the bench people as lovers who could not marry because they had no home, no place to express their love, he understood her meaning. He did not reply, but his first Chinese letter arrived the following day, cancelling their next date.

He paid a perfunctory visit on the third day of the holiday, the day for visiting friends. The second day was the day for visiting one's wife's family. When he made excuses to leave after fifteen minutes, Hai Bao could say nothing. She could not even apologize because she had not actually criticized him. She went visiting herself, to *Xiao* Wang. "Don't play games of indirection with Ningbonese," her friend advised. "You can't win. We're masters at that. If you want to get anywhere, remember what I said before: shout out your grievances."

She wrote him a letter reminding him that he would leave in two weeks, telling him she was sad, speaking only about herself, for she found she could not shout out her grievances about his family. Hinting at them had put her in the wrong and left her reeling that the balance between them was so delicate. She felt as she sometimes did in the new free markets, knowing the wobbly scale dangling from the merchant's hand was being manipulated to give unfair weights but afraid of the stares an objection would attract, afraid of the act of injured innocence the vendor would put on.

When they met he was sympathetic toward her and sad himself at their forced parting. Certainly he did not want to leave Shanghai. They consoled each other for two hours and said nothing about his family. That was also the tone of their other two meetings before he left. And once he was gone it was as if he had taken flight without wings. Not a single letter from him arrived.

She was shocked by this and then surprised when she heard a strange whistle outside her window one evening around the May Day holiday, peered out and saw Huang signalling for her to come out. *The fool. He didn't want to enter the house. He couldn't see behind the shabby facade into the cubbyhole palace over which the princess reigned at her ease. He wouldn't step through the rotting doorway which frames some of my most precious memories.* She rushed down and he greeted her happily, almost kissed her then thought better of it in the narrow passageway surrounded by doors and windows. As they walked he told her, "I've got good news," and her heart jumped. "An American teacher in Nanjing has agreed to teach me English. I'm sure to pass the exam and come back to Shanghai next year or the year after."

The letdown made her lose control. "Don't sneak around here like a ghost to kiss me. If your English teacher is so wonderful, go back to Nanjing and kiss her."

It was the first time she had spoken angrily to him. He jumped back in surprise. "But my English teacher is a man," he tried to protest while looking around, as if for an escape route. The angrier Hai Bao grew the more observant she became of details.

"No way out. Maybe the ground will open for you. Do you think I'm a marionette dangling from your thread that you can pop up after three months and expect me to dance for joy over some big nosed foreigner when you won't say a word about your own family?"

"It was only two months and eighteen days. But I've been thinking about you all the time. I don't like to write letters. My calligraphy is poor. And what if someone at school reads your letters to me? Besides I've been really busy. This is my first teaching job. I've got a lot to learn. Why, in my first year course...."

He was engineering words hydraulically now, sliding around the topic of his parents. Ningbo *ren* had a reputation for worldly wisdom, for always playing safe, for being able to use round and smooth words to slide out of or around difficulties. She had always liked him because he wasn't glib, didn't say much. She interrupted him: "I don't want to hear your nonsense words. I don't want to hear anything from you until your parents are willing to meet me." She was starting to cry. "Let your mother find some stubby, ugly Ningbo woman to marry you." She turned and ran.

He ran after her. She was grateful for that and gradually calmed down when he said nice things to her. She didn't care what he said now so long as he was nice. She was too upset to speak anymore, but she let him lead her away. Nevertheless, by making her yell at him in public, he had humiliated her. Everyone in *Pushan Lu Yi Cun* would soon know of their argument, and she would not forget that. As a Chinese person she knew how to wait, and as a Shanghai woman she knew how to get the last word. Shanghai women were famous for lips that could stab like spears, tongues that could cut like swords.

He saw her every day of the three he was in Shanghai. He said there wasn't time now but promised to bring her to his family during the summer. Then he returned to Nanjing and she did not hear from him for over two months. At least this time she was not caught off guard by his uncommunicativeness. One day in July he was back, whistling under her window as if he had never gone away, as if letters were written in blood and her opening his letter would be equivalent to opening his artery. *It took me hours to find the place the first time I tried. I'd rather be lost in a B.C. forest in a blizzard than in Shanghai's back alleys on a blazing summer day. At every turn I was surrounded by children pointing and calling "na guo ning, na guo ning" (foreigner, foreigner) or "hello, bye bye." When I finally found the house, her mother's bemused incomprehension – she couldn't even make out my pronunciation of her daughter's name – flustered me all the more. Then a bare foot appeared on the stair below the hole to the second floor. One didn't come fast down those rickety stairs, and I still delight in playing back that memorable descent step by step. The afternoon sunlight was behind her, so on the next step I could clearly see the outline of her dancer's calf through the flimsy material of her dark summer skirt. On the next step her entire legs became visible. She hesitated there for a second, as if to allow me to admire those beautiful legs, which seemed to glow within a circle of gloom, luminous shadows in one of those x-ray boxes Chinese doctors use in place of film.... In fact she was asking her mother a question. The one word I caught was "ma," but I still don't know if it meant mother or was the interrogative which turns a Chinese sentence into a question. When she resumed her descent, she was moving more quickly. The next step revealed her midsection and the next her upper body clad in a cheap, checkered cotton blouse. Not long ago I caught her stuffing that blouse into a bag for the Salvation Army and refused to let her give it away. Despite my overwhelming desire for her, hearing her voice without comprehending her words had momentarily made me apprehensive, for when she had given me her address she had warned me to use it only to write to her. I knew she considered her home too poor for me to see. But when her head appeared, the hair in gloriously wild disarray, sticking out and in and every which way, the transparent joy on her face that I had found her, that I cared for her and couldn't care less for her surroundings, would have summoned me back again and again even if I had to make my way blindfolded through the labyrinth of lanes which separated us.* Yet Huang seemed to have missed her, seemed genuinely happy to see her, raised the question of his family without prompting, said he would force the issue.

Two weeks later Hai Bao received a letter from him – in Chinese. He told her to meet him on Sunday and go to his house. But when she met him he told her his mother had led his father out of the house to avoid meeting her.

"She thinks she just has to stall again until September," Hai Bao sighed.

"But she's wrong. If we don't give up, she'll have to give in. She wants me to be happy. She wants me to marry. She wants me to have a son. She's my mother."

"Yes, she's your mother," repeated Hai Bao dejectedly. She was not thinking what a Westerner would, that she would have to live with this woman, that perhaps it wasn't worth the torment both now and later. She was thinking that she was committed to this man and that meant she was committed to his family, that she had given him two years of her past and had tied her future to his, that she would be a laughing stock in the neighborhood and among her friends if she did not marry him now, that she was getting too old to find another man. She knew that everyone would say she had aimed too high, that she should have been content with one of the neighborhood boys who would have gladly married her, that a poor Subei factory worker should not be trying to marry a rich Ningbo scholar.

The next time they met she waited for him to say something about his mother. He said nothing, so she asked him. He replied vaguely and changed the subject. That summer they met less frequently than the previous one. They did not make regular dates. He would send her a note asking to meet her that night or the next, or he would just show up under her window, whistling for her to come out. He never came in or greeted her parents. *Whenever I came to that wonderful house she always led me upstairs, where we could have privacy. It got awfully stuffy in that attic and she knew how I suffered in heat. She had a white feather fan of the sort favored by Zhuge Liang on the opera stage. The first time she pulled it out and began fanning me, I leaped up in protest, forgetting how low the slanting ceiling above us was, and banged my head so hard I almost knocked myself out. But when she took my head onto her lap and caressed and caressed it, I would have felt privileged to butt my head against that rafter every day for the rest of my life.* But he remained affectionate to Hai Bao. Usually they walked in a park and he could be relied upon for a somber kiss in dark corners. If they sat on a bench he first wiped it meticulously, then kept a space between them the width of a sword. There seemed to be no way to make Huang talk about his mother, let alone act, and Hai Bao drifted through the thick summer air trusting, hoping, waiting for something to happen before he left for Nanjing.

Nothing did. He came by two nights before he was to leave, walked with her on the street (in her neighborhood, always in her neighborhood, never in his), did not go to the park, did not kiss her, assured her everything would work out. Then he was gone again. He did not write from Nanjing, but he showed up under her window on National Day and took her into the river of people flowing along the Bund, whose banks were lit like blazing trees and silvery flowers. Then he returned to Nanjing and Shanghai returned to darkness. She sent him a letter with two poems she wrote. One began (freely translated) "The light gleams and is gone." The other ended, "The highest mountains are obscured in fog; To climb them risks a fall." He did not reply.

She was working on the great machine now and using the idle time this left her to read and write. She had completed her middle school diploma and was considering taking classes at the Workers' College or even taking the exam to get into a part time degree program. There were several of these now to compensate those who had missed the chance to study during the Cultural Revolution. Every level of education completed enabled one to get higher pay and often a better job. The new purpose of education was profit, a concept which could not even be discussed a few years ago. Profit was becoming the key to everything, knowledge and culture as well as production. And marriage: although the changes brought some advantages to her, she knew they could only strengthen Huang's mother's resolve. Under the present conditions her poverty was as great a crime as her origins.

Spring Festival approached pushing Huang before it. He said it was too cold for the parks they had frequented in previous winters, so they went to movies together. He wiped their seats at the theater as carefully as he did park benches. He said nothing about his family and she knew she should not either, but she could not prevent herself from asking if she could visit during the holidays. She said she could come with friends and pretend to be students of his. He replied that trying to trick his mother was out of the question. She would have to be patient and leave things to him. She did not mention how many years she had been doing that without result.

When Huang returned to Nanjing, Hai Bao decided to act on her own. She was twenty nine by Chinese reckoning although by Western calculations she was not yet twenty eight. She was getting too old to leave her future so uncertain. She wanted to settle in to the rest of her life, to cease being treated as a child. She had not grown ugly, but she felt she was not as good looking as she had been. Without the dance troupe she got little exercise and felt less trim, less comfortable with her body. She started *tai chi quan* lessons. One of the boys in her class was her own age and handsome. They began chatting before and after class and rode their bikes together until their routes diverged. He asked for her address but never came to her house, then became cool toward her in class. She knew he must have checked the place out, seen how poor it was and changed his opinion of her. Modernization had added a new layer of ugliness to *Pushan Lu Yi Cun*. Running water had been installed into concrete sinks outside each residence. Then wood had become available from shacks torn down to build concrete five story apartment buildings a block away and everyone had hammered on a kitchen a meter and a half wide to enclose the sinks. Everyone except Hai Bao's family, that is. Their small family did not need the room and ma much preferred doing kitchen work outside. But the passageways between the rows had shrunk by three quarters, the playing children had to run in single file instead of groups, and the "village" had been upgraded to a city tenement.

Her mentor at the factory offered to seek a man for her. Of course Hai Bao could not accept such an offer: it would be too humiliating. But she carefully refrained from explicitly forbidding the woman to search although she doubted that men she would be willing to consider would be willing to consider her. The society had changed while she was dating Huang: family wealth and position were now the criteria for choosing a spouse and she did not measure up. She did not even measure up for one family which did not require wealth. A couple with one son and a large apartment rejected her because she was an only child. They required someone strong and capable who would do the housework and care for them in their old age, and they assumed an only child would be too spoiled, a princess, not a worker.

When Huang returned from Nanjing that summer, she urged him to confront his parents and settle everything one way or another. He agreed. She did not see him again until shortly before he was to return to school. He said his mother had been sick. He said it was because he had been pressing her too hard. She had been in the hospital. He had stayed with her much of the time and had become sick himself. He looked as if he had been sick, looked gaunt, wan, preoccupied. Talking seemed even more of an effort than usual, but he made the effort. He invited Hai Bao to visit him in Nanjing over the October first holiday. Many students would return home and he could get her sleeping space in a dormitory, he said.

"I wish I didn't need to write up your big romance," I told Hai Bao. "It's boring."

"A Chinese woman's life is supposed to be boring," she replied. "Boring and moral. That is one reason why Chinese culture has lasted so long."

"But my novel isn't supposed to be boring."

"Oh, writing is different. You can liven it up. Tang Xianzhu took Du Li Niang to hell and back to make her life interesting."

"Do you think you went through hell for Huang?"

"Hell came later. But I did go to Nanjing."

Huang treated her like an empress in Nanjing. He met her at the train, took her all the way out to the Sun Zhong Shan (Sun Yat Sen) Memorial and then out to eat. It was the first time in three years of dating he had taken her to a restaurant. The next morning they set off early to tour museums, palaces and tombs. They got back to campus in time for dinner, briefly strolled around the lit up streets packed with holiday celebrators, then returned to the school. He showed her his laboratory. The building was deserted and they went into an office. Never had they been alone together like this. They sat on a small sofa and hugged and kissed. They didn't speak. They didn't have to. For the first time they could communicate through their bodies, and the news was good. They kissed hard, leaned into each other. He rubbed her legs, then her breasts. Her body was feeling feelings she had not known it possessed and he moaned with feelings which must have been similar to her own. Sometimes when their bodies met she could feel a pressure against her hip which did not come from his hand. He unbuttoned her blouse. She waited. She had been waiting for this all her life and had not even known it before. He shuddered, gave a small cry, sank back in the sofa for a moment, then leaped up. "I think I heard someone." He went to the door, then out. In a few minutes he was back, wiping his hands with a white cloth. "I think there might be someone in the building. It isn't safe."

They straightened their clothes and walked hand in hand to his dormitory. There had been a foulup and he had failed to get her a bed in a student dormitory, but his own roommate was gone and she was sleeping in the roommate's bed. The previous night she had lain awake a long time wondering if anything would happen, but nothing did. His breathing lulled her to sleep much as her mother's did at home. Tonight she knew it would be different. Even before they washed they kissed long and hard and he lifted her skirt and slid his hand up and down the back of her legs. "When we're married," he began, and she kissed his mouth. It was the first time in years she believed they really would be married.

Yet he was circumspect when they went to bed. They undressed under their own quilts, and she lay in her bed listening to him in his. He tossed around and around as if in a wrestling match, wrestling with himself. Finally he got up, padded softly to her bed and stood looking down on her in the near dark. She lay quietly, curious, expectant, awaiting the feeling, awaiting the knowledge, awaiting the commitment. Although he was no longer moving, she could feel him still wrestling with himself. He seemed hardly aware of her beneath him although several times he reached out as if to touch her, then retracted his hand. Then he did touch her, or touched the quilt which covered her. When she did not react he lifted the edge of the quilt, sat down on the bed beside her, then drew back the quilt, slowly to give her opportunity to object. She lay still and he looked down on her. She wore underpants and a thin blouse. He placed his hand on her shoulder, then slowly and softly slid it down her body, over her breasts, her stomach, her vulva, her legs, her feet. Then he undid the top button of her blouse, waited, then the rest of the buttons. He ran his hand over each breast, then down her stomach to her underpants. He fingered these and when he began to tug lightly on them she raised up slightly so he could pull them off. He sat in the dim light looking down on her body, taking it in or trying to make it out, she was not sure which. Then he kissed her navel, kissed each breast, kissed her neck and finally her lips. He seemed unable either to tear himself away or to tear into her as he had earlier. He kissed her lips again and she turned onto her side facing his body. The movement, her first, seemed to alarm him and he stood up. He was wearing only underpants and she could see a bulge in them. She stretched out her hand and took his and he knelt on the floor beside the bed and kissed her lips, harder this time. They kissed that way while he ran one smooth hand, nervously now, over the side of her body. She squeezed the other. He was struggling with himself again, she could feel it. Then he broke loose and stood up, and she knew he was going to leave. "Wait," she whispered, and while he stood indecisively she reached out quickly and jerked down his underpants. It was not fair that he should see and feel her but she not do the same for him. His penis stuck straight out and she grabbed it. He jumped back in surprise, but that was not a wise move with her holding him tightly and he jumped forward almost before he landed. The hard flesh grew softer in her hand. It shrank until it felt like a raw *jiaozi* and then she let it go and he ran back to his bed. She redressed herself, pulled the quilt back up and lay quietly listening to him wrestling again. Then she fell asleep and dreamed of Du Li Niang, who died because her life allowed no outlet for her passion but whose passion was too great for death and gave her a new life, a love life. She woke up remembering the dream, wondering.... She had not dreamed like that in years.

The next day they went to the movie *The Liberation of Nanjing*, the story of the Red Army's crossing the Yangtze and victory at Nanjing. They sat in the back, held hands, touched each other tenderly. Then he took her to the train station.

On the way to the station he had promised to write his mother and inform her that at Spring Festival he was bringing Hai Bao to meet her, but when he came back to Shanghai he said nothing about it and she knew his mother was not backing down. She waited until they were about to part, hoping he would bring up the subject himself. He didn't. She had known he wouldn't as soon as she saw him. She could feel his gloom and reticence, knew she should not violate it, could not control herself. "What about your mother?" He simply shook his head. She kept herself from crying but could not prevent a tear from slipping down her cheek.

"She'll come around, Hai Bao. She has to. I'm already thirty three." It was true. His mother was destroying his prospects for a happy life as surely as hers. When she finally did cry, it was for him as much as for herself, but he had no comfort for her. When a bus came, he did not try to keep her from getting on. When she reached her home she had to keep walking the cold streets, for if she went to bed crying ma would surely wake up alarmed.

They saw each other only twice more during his vacation. They were both sad and subdued, did not want to talk about their situation. When they did he merely repeated his refrain: "She'll come around. She has to." Once he added, "When she sees I'm not going to change, she'll have to." He said it so softly she decided he was telling himself more than her.

She was taking a writing course. The students were all of an age, physically and mentally. All had lost the chance for education during the Cultural Revolution; all were ambitious and knew they needed education to advance. But this class was different from others she had taken in that many of the students' goals were more artistic than financial or social. The end of the Cultural Revolution had released a surge of creativity, especially in literature, because young people had been flung into new worlds, seen and experienced dramatic events which challenged their minds and demanded resolution. The teacher was a cheerful old cynic whose pockets were full of little boxes containing singing insects. When class got dull, he would pull out a box and open it enough for everyone to hear the chirps. He had given up on the society and so encouraged the students to experiment. Yet he had been well trained in the old forms and appreciated them as well. Hai Bao liked this eccentric old man and several of the students. In the new semester she plunged deeper into the class discussions and took her writing more seriously. She lacked the wide range of experience of the others and turned out sad, intricate miniatures in a poetic prose rather than sweeping, tragic epics. The teacher singled out for special praise her story "Cold Mountain," which froze a brief memory of love in an escaped prisoner dying in Xinjiang's cold Mountains of Heaven, and advised other students to learn from her and write less but write it more carefully.

The teacher liked to hold informal Sunday afternoon gatherings in his big, old apartment and she began attending these. It made her sad to be the only single person there – the others brought spouses or fiancees – but they were impressed when she told them she had a fiancee teaching at Nanjing University, and she joined in their fun. They liked to sing operatic arias and her training in the song and dance troupe made her the best singer in the group. Soon Qiu, an artist who wanted to write philosophical novels and paint huge abstracts, and Peng, an ironic poet who was the daughter of a high ranking cadre, became her best friends. They seemed more interesting and deep than her friends at the factory. Besides, the other members of the little gang of four were all married and had no time for her now. She liked the way her writer friends treated each other as equals regardless of sex. Qiu would bubble with enthusiasm until Peng pricked his bubble with a sharp observation and then all, including the deflated artist, would roar with laughter. Or Qiu would draw caricatures of each of them. Peng's family had a piano and they would sing away many an evening around it. Or they would discuss the latest novels. Hai Bao needed the diversion although Huang actually wrote to her, a note inviting her to come to Nanjing for May Day. She declined and went to Suzhou with a group from her class.

When she returned from Suzhou her mother informed her that Huang had been by. She gasped. Could his mother have relented and she not been there to take advantage? But he had left no message, as surely he would have if that were the case. And no letter arrived for over two months. He did not get in touch until he whistled under her window shortly before her birthday, her thirtieth birthday by Chinese reckoning and no marriage in sight. As she looked at him summoning her down, a new bitterness rose up in her. How she wanted to shout out her grievances at him. She didn't; she wouldn't let him make her lose face that way a second time, but for the first time she allowed herself to feel hatred for Huang. *Probably he was lucky he didn't marry her and so slid out of the bride price she was planning to exact. Given the chance, a Shanghi woman always gets the last word – and, usually, deed. I hope being able to shout at me helped. Now. I made her lose face too. She couldn't take it out on Huang as she did on me because they had no private place. And because Huang didn't raise his voice in public. Whatever his other faults he was Chinese enough to know that. I wasn't: we were on our bikes and she stopped to window shop. From the street I called to her to hurry. When she did come, she said not a word. Until we got home. Then she said plenty and not softly either. I couldn't take it in. What had I done wrong? I had even spoken in English so passersby couldn't understand. What I couldn't understand was that that made it worse, attracted more attention and turned innocuous words into a tone of voice that was not innocuous. She was being shouted at on the street by a foreigner, and that made her lose face. So that night I lost her face and had to kiss her feet. I still didn't understand. I was merely confronted by a new inscrutability. I needed Huang to teach me the lesson. God, do other writers write simply because they are slow learners?* They walked out briefly and he invited her to an opera for her birthday. At least he remembered. And knew what she would like. But he knew so little about opera that he did not realize the one he had selected was about a woman who dies waiting for her scholar-lover to return home. All during the performance she cast quick glances at him, but he kept his head rigidly forward, his face emotionless.

At the opera they met Hai Bao's writing teacher, who invited them to come to his house next week, said he was intending to get in touch with his students anyway. Huang tried to claim he was busy, but the teacher's wife (another teacher) insisted and finally made Huang choose an evening. Hai Bao wanted to go but was not sure she wanted to bring Huang: there had been a scandal. Qiu had thrown over his girlfriend for a new one. The old girlfriend was protesting loudly and all over. She had gone to the man's work unit to get his leaders to force him to honor his commitment. She had gone so far as to declare publicly they were already married. They had indeed applied for the license so as to obtain a higher place on the waiting list for new apartments, but everyone understood her words had an uglier meaning: they had had sex. To have sex was not unheard of, but for the woman to admit it was. It would ruin her chances of finding another husband. Hai Bao was not sure she wanted Huang to hear this story. On the other hand, she had to feel grateful he had not attempted to have sex with her in Nanjing. If she could not marry him, being a virgin gave her at least some chance of marrying someone else. He knew this and must have held back out of consideration for her. It was the first positive feeling she had felt towards him in a long time. Or had he held back because he knew sex would commit him to marriage? She tried to puzzle out which it was, then gave up and told him about Qiu. She wanted to go and the story would rouse his interest in coming.

Everyone except Qiu and the new girlfriend arrived early. That was because the others all wanted to gossip about him. Hai Bao knew she would have to denounce him because Huang was there, but she was surprised that all the other young people also opposed what he had done. If anything the men judged him more harshly than the women. Finally their teacher chuckled and said, "You mean an old fogey like me is the only one here with liberal views?"

"Two old fogeys," chimed in Huang, who liked to think of himself as modern.

"Don't you see the reason?" the teacher's wife asked her husband. "All the young people here are either just married or about to marry. If they value their own marriages, they have to oppose what Qiu did. Five years ago or five years from now their opinions may be quite different. Hai Bao, watching Huang, saw him turn red. He did not say anything the rest of the evening.

Qiu arrived with the new woman, whom he introduced as his fiancee. "They've only known each other a few weeks," Peng whispered to Hai Bao as Qiu was listing her many accomplishments.

"Perhaps you'll favor us with the 'Mongolian Shepherd's Love Song,'" Hai Bao put in when folksinging was added to the list.

"I'm not sure I know it," she replied, too happy to see she was being mocked. In fact she spoke perfect *Shanghaihua*. She had seemed so young and pure Hai Bao had guessed she must be from the country. Once I was like that too, Hai Bao reflected bitterly. Now all I can do is envy her. Huang was watching the young woman out of the corner of his eye. "Do you wish you found her first?" Hai Bao whispered to him. He turned red again. "You look like a *longxiapian* tonight," she told him, but when she saw how angry he was getting she added, "I'll stop frying you" and took him up to meet Qiu and friend.

"Ah, so this is the famous scientist," Qiu exclaimed. "Maybe you can tutor me in math." Qiu had failed his middle school graduation exam.

"Are you really a scientist?" Mei, the fiancee, asked admiringly. Huang could only nod in reply. He really is a *longxiapian*, Hai Bao thought, pink and fat and wriggling in the oil. She brought him some candies as a peace offering, but she knew he was seeing in Mei what he once saw in her and the fact that he was seeing it meant he no longer saw it in her.

Huang wanted to leave early. Outside he told her he did not like that kind of people. "Yes, they're not like you," she told him. After he rode off on his bike, she returned to her teacher's house.

By the time he whistled under her window again, it was almost time for him to return to Nanjing. She would begin teaching in her factory school and studying history at East China Normal University in a program designed for workers like herself who had missed their chance at education as a result of the Cultural Revolution. She would attend classes three days a week and work the other three. She had wanted to study Chinese, but there had been no openings in that program. She took what she could get, history. Now she and Huang talked about school. As usual they avoided discussing what was central in both their minds. He invited her to Nanjing for National Day. She didn't reply immediately and they walked silently a few paces remembering last year. Then she declined, saying she would need to study. That was the proper attitude, he told her. She was out of the habit of serious study and should devote all her free time to it. He shouldn't have asked her. Just before they said good bye he muttered, "I think Tongji will let me into graduate school next year. I'll be thirty five the year after next." Thirty five was the cut off age for graduate students in China. "Once I'm back in Shanghai she'll give in. I know she will." I'll be thirty one, she thought. It would still be acceptable if they married next summer, but she had no great hope. Her best hope was that she might meet a new man at her new university.

For the National Day holiday he came back to Shanghai, but she did not see him. She knew he had come back because one of her neighbors saw him standing in the passageway looking up at her lighted window. She was home studying, but he did not whistle for her.

She wondered if she would see him at Spring Festival. Every Spring Festival hope sprang in her breast that his mother might relent. His mother did not relent, but he came, more out of duty than devotion, it seemed to Hai Bao. He even visited briefly but politely with her parents on the third day of the new year. He left shortly after Qiu and Peng and their fiancees arrived. Qiu and Peng were both two years younger than Hai Bao and would both marry this year, Qiu at May Day, Peng at National Day. "What's wrong?" Peng asked after Huang left. It's obvious then, Hai Bao thought. She had liked to believe she was concealing her pain.

She had looked forward to teaching, but there was nothing glamorous or even interesting about the factory school. The purpose of the school was to force a bit of knowledge into the heads of children of the Cultural Revolution. Her students were a few years younger than herself and appalling in their ignorance and lack of desire to correct it. Teaching them was more unpleasant than operating a machine. At least the machine followed orders when you pushed the right button. Still, the work was easy. She taught only a few hours a day. The rest of the day she sat around drinking tea with the other teachers and reading newspapers. She would have liked to bring her own books to read, but that was not permitted on *danwei* time.

Studying was better than teaching, but the university was also a letdown. She had begun university the same year the urban reforms began, and all the students were more interested in financial than intellectual advancement. She preferred Peng and Qiu and the students who had been in her writing class. Her teacher held a reunion of that class, and it was the most pleasant day she spent that year.

Summer came, but before Huang whistled she decided she had to get away. Everyone was talking. Neighbors and fellow workers asked her why she didn't get married, offered her men she would have died before considering, gossiped behind her back. She wrote Jie, now living in Qingdao, China's most famous beach city. She would take a two week vacation, visit Jie, tour Taishan, the sacred mountain, and Qufu, the birthplace of Confucius.

She took the boat to Qingdao. Coming back she would take the train so she could stop and be a tourist. Before leaving she had her hair cut and permed. She looked like a new person even if she felt like a very old one. Perms had become too commonplace in Shanghai for anyone to notice her natural curl, but probably her perm would stand out in Qingdao and certainly it made her feel better, newer. If only she could renew the rest of her body as easily as her hair.

The boat gave her time to think. Not about Huang. She refused to let herself think about him. But was she willing to accept the men who might consider marrying an old maid in her thirties from a poor family? Her teacher at the factory and several friends were searching for her, trying to thread the needle of matrimony. They would bring her photos and give her biographies. But the thread was too thick: the men she thought promising balked even at meeting her. She was told they all said the same thing, that she looked good but her family was too poor. They demanded silk thread, were not about to marry a woman in her thirties unless it paid well. These days money was everyone's first priority. It had not been that way before. How could she have imagined when she was in her twenties that a day would come when good looks, intelligence and a good family background would not be enough to assure her of a husband? Now her family background actually made finding a good man impossible. Girls from bourgeois families were what men were looking for today. She found she could not stand at the ship's railing and look out at the vast grey sea: the temptation to throw herself in was too great. What did she have to live for? Ma and Ba perhaps. Certainly they were the only ones who would miss her. They were both over seventy. They could only grow more dependent on her help. And prices were beginning to rise. If that continued their pensions might not be adequate to live on. It wasn't much of a reason for living, and the idea of living merely as a caretaker to elderly parents, however praiseworthy in Chinese tradition, could almost become another reason for suicide. But it would be a selfish reason, and although times might have changed, she was still strongly influenced by her training never to be selfish. She remembered learning to do up buttons by helping button the backs of other girls' blouses in nursery school and how the teacher had carefully explained that helping others was life's most noble accomplishment. She even remembered Lei Feng, whom everyone today, herself included, ridiculed. Probably he never existed and certainly he was an obsequious fool, but the philosophy of helping others was not foolish. Perhaps it had not been of much use to the carters, but she was proud of having used her childish lack of strength to help push carts up the bridge on Gonghe Xin Lu. No, helping her parents was a reason for living, not dying. She only wished she could have someone else to live for too.

Jie had transformed herself again, but her changes no longer surprised Hai Bao, who was now old enough to see that all her sister's glitter simply reflected the times. Now Jie was beginning to grey and had grown plump and prosperous. She had given up doctoring to act as a dietician in her husband's school's day care center, a job which took little time and less effort. Mainly she had become a bourgeois housewife and was basking in the role. She had attained the goals she had set out for her life. Jiefu, even more plump, was vice president of his university, head of his department, an internationally renowned scholar and a delegate to a prestigious albeit powerless provincial legislature. They lived on a hill overlooking the ocean in an apartment which was immense by Shanghai standards. Hai Bao swam in the ocean every day and went for walks along the beach and a hike up nearby Laoshan with her seven year old nephew. Jie had managed to get pregnant soon after losing her first son, and now Hai Bao enjoyed getting to know the boy. Mainly it was a relaxing and pleasurable time.

But not entirely. One night after the child was packed off to bed, Jie and Jiefu sat down to serious business with Hai Bao. Chinese intellectuals are universally noted for the circuity and impenetrability of their subtlety. "Why don't you get married?" Jiefu began.

Hai Bao wept. Jie comforted her. Jiefu scratched his head. He wondered why so little progress had been made in their relationship during the fifteen years since he met Hai Bao.

Eventually Jie drew out from Hai Bao the tale of her relationship with Huang. "How about Wang You Zi?" suggested Jiefu. "He'll soon be a full professor."

"He'll soon be fifty too," Jie countered.

They proceeded to make their way through every unmarried teacher and graduate student Jiefu knew in Qingdao. Jie found a fault with each of them. "I don't want to get married," Hai Bao finally cried in exasperation. "I want to stay home and take care of ma and ba."

"That's very noble," said Jiefu, "but it's too old fashioned. It's not what people do these days. People will talk."

"Yes," proclaimed Jie, rising like the empress dowager condescending to instruct her wayward child. "It is your duty to marry. Ma and ba will never be happy until you do. Come with me," she commanded. She led Hai Bao to the bedroom and rummaged in a trunk until she uncovered a silk *qipao*. "Put this on." Jie made a few adjustments, pulled a curl onto Hai Bao's forehead, gave her a pair of leather shoes to wear, straightened her shoulders and stood her before the rosewood framed full length mirror which had accompanied Jie from Shanghai to Hefei to Jilin to Qingdao. She said nothing. She didn't have to.

Hai Bao hardly believed what she saw. She was still beautiful. She preened and posed in front of the mirror. In her head she heard stately ancient music and moved gracefully to it, imagining a long, slow, sensual dance before the emperor. She had hated Jie a moment ago in the other room; now she wished she could hug her for showing her this. "Oh Jie...," she began.

But Jie wasn't done yet. "Watch Jiefu's face when we go in the other room," Jie ordered. "Walk tall." She pushed Hai Bao through the door. Jiefu's jaw dropped and his eyes bulged. The look lasted only a second, but Hai Bao had seen the lust.

"I'll give you my *qipao*," Jie told her. "They'll never fit me again anyhow. Wear a different one to school every day. You're looking for a bourgeois intellectual, someone who was slow finding a wife because of his class background in the early Sixties, then was arrested or criticized at the start of the Cultural Revolution. Maybe he was married, but his wife divorced him because he was a class enemy. That means he'll be forty, maybe forty five. That's not too old. He'll think he's too old – that's why he didn't get married right after the Cultural Revolution – but you'll teach him otherwise. You'll inspire him to regain his youth." She looked at Jiefu. "Right, dear?"

"Right," Jiefu replied automatically. Then he looked at Hai Bao again and said with conviction, "Certainly."

Hai Bao shuddered. She had always feared Jie a man like that. On the other hand she knew her negative feelings about Jiefu were mainly the result of the circumstances under which she had met him. Jie lived a very comfortable life with him. Hai Bao would love such a life. And forty wasn't really old. Huang was already thirty four. Even forty five, almost Jiefu's age, wouldn't be bad if the man looked and acted a little nicer than Jiefu. But the look in Jiefu's eyes had told Hai Bao something else. She knew she couldn't wear the *qipao*. Ten, even five years ago, she would have relished doing it. But now everyone would laugh and talk behind her back, say she was a prostitute, say she was offering her body to any man who wanted it. Young girls could show off their bodies; old maids couldn't. However good it had made her feel, the lesson Jie had just taught was not one she could use.

Jie interrupted her reverie. "*Mei mei*, you know Jiefu and I really admire the way you take care of Ma and Ba. It's very convenient for everyone. We would be glad to take them in, of course, but they like it much better living in Shanghai. If you really want to take care of them, it doesn't matter whether you decide to get married or not so long as you live in Shanghai. We can send money sometimes."

Back in the room she shared with her nephew Hai Bao planned the rest of her trip. She had better buy tickets tomorrow. This might be the only chance she would get to see some of China's historical sights. Once Ma and Ba got old, she wouldn't be able to leave them alone.

Chapter Sixteen

I revel in contrasts. For that reason alone I could have loved Shanghai. After eight years of isolation among the mountains I found myself amidst the masses as soon as we left the airport: pedestrians and bicyclists, people pulling and pushing assorted homemade carts and towing them behind cycles, children running in and out and plodding alongside huge water buffalo, adults bearing loads of produce on sagging shoulder poles and hauling heavier loads in truckbeds pulled by hard chugging, slow moving, pint sized tractors. They were all there, all over the road, and our car was weaving through them at high speed. Fortunately we couldn't see much because it was growing dark and the car was driving without headlights. The driver apparently needed to conserve the battery so he could constantly lean on the horn as he zigzagged from one side of the road to the other seeking openings through the mobile masses. I attempted nonchalance and nudged Ruby: "Do you notice that the main crop being hauled is garlic?" We had harvested our garlic and given it to friends shortly before leaving British Columbia. Ruby cowered unresponsively beside me. Another headlightless car approached from the opposite direction and the two autos winked headlights conspiratorially as if to say, "You mow 'em down on that side while I run 'em over on this." In the nightmarish flash we got to see the whole scene. A cyclist swerved into the ditch to avoid us. "The driver must know what he's doing," I whispered to reassure Ruby, but I, an ex Chicago taxi hack accustomed to cutting fearlessly through rush hour traffic, was scared stiff too.

The next day, our first in Shanghai, we hurried out to get to know the new city. Ruby learned all she needed to know and was ready to return to our air conditioned hotel in two minutes: Shanghai was too hot and humid for human habitation despite overwhelming evidence that more people inhabited it than she had ever before seen in her life. But Ruby had not spent a third of her life dreaming of China. To me Shanghai was a dream, but much more than a dream, come true. A scene more crowded than my most crowded butterfly dream opened up, opened out, opened colorful, fluttering wings before me, butterflies and people interchanging, floating by like clouds, then solidifying, people, solid yet light, so many, so much motion as they skimmed along, as if caught up in drafts which moved them by, moved them together, moved them apart, moved me, so many, I had not thought life could do so many so proudly, had forgotten my first sight of Bissel Street, forgotten that life could be so varied, so flowing, so fleeting, so permanent, so concentrated, so alive. Yet there was a uniformity, a uniformity I could not place until Ruby said, "They're so thin." There was no fat. All these beautiful, moving people were slim, even the old ones limber, lithe, desirable, an orgy of clean bodies, yet no sex in the orgy, people clothed to be comfortable, not to show off their bodies, no need to show off because their bodies were what bodies should be, trim, alive, unselfconscious. Moving.

Ruby was moaning about the heat, fearful of the crowds, but I was too excited to be deterred and insisted we push on. Holding Ruby's hand, we two one island amid the river of people flooding down Huai Hai Lu, I practiced Chinese by asking directions to Huai Hai Lu. The hordes of passersby practiced stares of incomprehension. Finally a woman pointed us toward Wei Hai Lu, a mile away. On and on we trudged until we reached an arm of People's Park where old folks sat in the shade, sawed away on strange, scratchy stringed instruments (erhus) and screeched stranger songs (Beijing Opera). The sounds were so peculiar that had we not been too hot and tired to move we might have run away. As it was we sat a long time, rested and listened. No one spoke to us, for they knew we did not understand their words, but many people smiled at us, a man with a beard thicker and longer than anything any of them had seen off the opera stage and an eleven year old child with hair blonder than any of them had seen outside the movies. I felt they were performing for us. (They weren't; I often returned and always found music in that park.) Soon I became perfectly comfortable with my discomfort. I was exhausted, wet with sweat, and a shrill ringing was assaulting my ears. It was wonderful. I don't know how or why, but I felt at peace with the world. I fell in love with Shanghai and China right then. Later I even came to love the music.

I had expected Shanghai to feel strange. I had not expected it to feel familiar. Jet lag and excitement did not permit much sleep those first nights in Shanghai, and the night noises took me home. I lay in bed listening, awake, alert, a boy. At the first glimmer of light in the sky I crept out of bed, careful not to wake Ruby, and ran into the streets of Shanghai, streets my nose remembered. I suffered from a sinus condition as a child. As a result I am a mouth breather and have a poor sense of smell. I thought I had never smelled much until my nose told me that Shanghai shared with World War II Chicago a rudimentary system of refrigeration. Ten days later I met my students. They were middle school teachers of English, most of them much the same age as I. We hit it off from the start, and soon they had me writing for them as much as I had them writing for me. The first thing I wrote for them were impressions cribbed from my journal of my first days in Shanghai:

Shanghai must be the most sensuous city in the world. The only place I have ever experienced like it was the Chicago of my boyhood. Not that Chicago really was that sensuous, only that I was young and my senses were alert enough to perceive much they no longer can. They magnified sights, sounds, smells and tastes which need not be magnified in Shanghai. They made my home village seem the great city Mayor Daley always called it. They made Chicago seem what I now see Shanghai is.

Now the sensuousness of Shanghai has reawakened city senses which I had forgotten in British Columbia, childhood vividness I thought age had dimmed. I can once again respond to a flat, crowded, concrete landscape. So I awake in the middle of the night to the bass of foghorns, the tenor of train whistles, the soprano of crickets, the night sounds which sang to a boy in long ago Chicago and haven't sung to me in Chicago or any other American city since. I peer out the window, and it is as dark as night once was but no longer is in Western cities where fear and mercury vapor streetlights have chased it away.

And about 5:00 a.m. I run from the West of memory into the streets of Shanghai. Except it's more like swimming through a sea of smells. Almost every stride brings new odors, some so strong they wash over and overwhelm me as waves do a child. I summon up my adult strength, and they part before me only to reform around, new and wondrous as smells are to the recently born. Then one fragrance pursues me like a monster, neither new nor wondrous, out of an adolescent nightmare inspired by a trip through Chicago's stockyards. But fear is as foreign to Shanghai as to a boy. I dodge merrily through traffic which should be more frightening than any smell. In Shanghai the streets belong to the people – as we used to chant marching through Chicago during the Sixties, lying to revive spirits as dull as senses in a place where the primary sight and only smell is the smog of tear gas. To a boy during the Forties Chicago's streets also seemed to belong to the people. I loved dodging through crowds, racing straight at a startled adult, then twisting sideways to avoid him into a position in which I imagined myself so thin as to be invisible, a pane of clear glass. I had forgotten those crowds until I rediscovered them in Shanghai. Perhaps the Sixties slogan was more than propaganda. There were few automobiles in the Chicago of the Forties, as in Shanghai now. When people don't own cars they walk, sidewalks crowd up, folks spill into the streets and fill with confidence to challenge motorized intruders in their domain. So I run on into the past, again a boy skittering through crowds, following his nose, doing combat with traffic, and into the immediate, sensuous future, Shanghai, far from present day Chicago and farther still from British Columbia, where a tiny few pedestrians huddle together waiting for a green light to cross a street on which there isn't a car – or a bicycle – in sight.

My early impressions of Shanghai were all powerful, even the many that were all wrong. Eyes were far slower to see than ears to hear or nose to smell. It may be that the eyes work more closely with the brain so we think we rely on them, but we rely on them mainly to think and the other senses have deeper, stronger roots. More memorable roots. Sensation far outstripped understanding. Until one day I looked at a pile of garbage blighting a campus lawn and saw that the garbage was not the same garbage that had been there the day before. I watched that trash change daily until I figured out it was being burned to boil the copious quantities of water needed for tea. Similar piles were all over the otherwise spotless city, whose streets and sidewalks were constantly swept with big rice straw brooms. Understanding began: I was seeing recycling at its environmental and economic, if not aesthetic, best. My students helped me understand much. They had to be cautious, for until very recently consorting with foreigners had been very dangerous, but the presence of a child made consorting look more innocent. None dared let themselves get too close, but warily at first, later a little more boldly, they visited, then invited us to visit them, then began to show us the sights, take us to movies, concerts, operas. At first I understood little, appreciated less. *Years later Hai Bao and I watched on television one of the operas I had seen in those early days. To my surprise I discovered it was about Zhuangzi. In the opera Da Pi Guan [Splitting Open the Coffin], written by Confucianist opponents of Daoism, the ethereal, lepidopteral Zhuangzi is portrayed as an earthy, middle aged magician married to a young, beautiful wife. He is so earthy he even contrives to be buried to test his wife. His jealousy does in his marriage and his wife. Another anomaly Zhaungzi would have enjoyed.* As she did in Marquette Park, Ruby helped just by being there, winning over people who might have been skeptical of someone who looked like me. And while she was there she was also ingesting two dialects of Chinese. I studied the language constantly and learned little. She seemed not to study it at all, but one day, three months after our arrival, a woman in a store asked her a question and Ruby began speaking to her, then to the crowd that quickly gathered. "I didn't know you could speak Chinese," I told her when we finally got out of the store. "Neither did I," she replied. With her as my translator I could go many places and ask many questions I could not have without her. And answer many of the endless questions asked about my own native country.

Love for the mountains of Canada had completed a cycle of estrangement from the land of my birth. Love for Shanghai started a cycle of reconciliation.

Once Shanghai had given me back my childhood and the city of my childhood, I could proceed to my youth, the years before Bissel Street, which had seemed to me wasted. The study of literature had led to the deadend of the penultimate chapter of *Hydriotaphia*, but now that study had got me to China. I was hired to teach literature, something I had not done in fifteen years, not since I left Greensboro in 1968. I was teaching American literature to students with no knowledge of its cultural context. I had constantly to explain both the words and their context. And not only explain: I was determined to make the students feel and appreciate American literature. Even love it. Why not? The strangeness and strange familiarity of their native city had given me back my own childhood and native city. Why not return the gift to them, who so wished to understand American ways, whose respect for and courtesy toward their teacher so overwhelmed their teacher? It was not a conscious decision, but teaching the literature and culture of my homeland to strangers to that land inevitably began to reconcile me to it. In the Chicago of the Sixties and Seventies I had dealt with America at its worst and been defeated by it. In teaching its literature I was dealing with America at its best and was, to my students at least, the master of it.

I followed what seemed to be Chinese custom and wrote brief introductions to authors. Overworked secretaries then typed onto mimeograph stencils my introductions plus full length stories or chapters from the authors' novels. It was the first time many of the students had seen real English language literature. Previously economics and politics had limited them to abridged, simplified versions. I don't suppose any of my students ever read one of Henry James later novels because of my introduction, but you can be sure I understand more about James, why he wrote as he did, why he fled his and my native land, than I did before I made that introduction. So it was with many authors, even Hemingway, who grew up a mile or two from where I grew up and whom I had never liked. My students liked Hemingway because his words were simple and because unspoken understandings, the essence of Hemingway's art, are essential to Chinese culture. Watching their enjoyment enabled me to ignore Hemingway's boring heroes and recognize the intuition which drove him from his home country before his machismo took him back. I would not go home – I still prefer old lady James to old man Hemingway – but I learned that one cannot completely deny one's home without losing one's self. Being high in the mountains of the Kootenays had let me look down on the land of my birth; was being far away in Shanghai giving me perspective? To my surprise I found I could settle for less than I had once demanded – of myself and my country – and laugh instead of shout at America's inanities, vent analysis rather than rage at its asininities, relax. I could have loved Shanghai for that alone. In point of fact I already did love it – even before it gave me back myself, even before it gave me Hai Bao. In Shanghai my loves came one by one by one.

In Shanghai my loves came together.

"Six hearts," bid my partner.

"Double" on my right.

I knew my partner had bid the slam to induce our opponents to sacrifice, but I also knew I could make the contract no matter how badly suits were breaking because my trumps were solid and I had been underbidding shamelessly, trying merely to buy the contract in a competitive auction at unfavorable vulnerability. I knew just what right hand opponent must have and that he had miscalculated. The only question was whether a redouble might scare his partner into running. But I knew my opponents even if I understood nothing of the Shanghai dialect they spoke between hands. My partner and I had been wiping the floor with them. Although they had never ceased smiling and their incomprehensible words sounded pleasant, I could feel them hating their humiliation. Nothing I could do was about to make left hand opponent run when his partner said he could set us. I reached for the pen and paper.

I had not played bridge for sixteen years when I came to Shanghai and had no particular desire to begin again. But when a student invited me to his home for a game, I accepted, hoping this might be what I had not yet found, an opportunity to meet Chinese on an equal basis. Surely even Chinese courtesy would not extend to deliberately allowing me to make an unmakable contract or failing to double seven no trump on lead with an ace. In everything else Chinese deference to me made anything resembling equality impossible. I earned ten times their salary, but when I was with Chinese friends I was not allowed to pay even a four *fen* bus fare. And I had stopped accepting dinner invitations because my host invariably spent a month's wages on a banquet (inevitably called a "simple meal") for Ruby and me. Playing bridge did prove different. My student and his friends quickly saw I was much above their level and arranged a game with more skilful players. In this way I was gradually introduced to better and better players until I reached the best in Shanghai. The present game was the culmination of that process. Partnered by the best player in the city – he was better than I and we got along splendidly because I recognized his brash style: he played as I had in my youth – we were putting on an exhibition before scores of spectators.

Having assured myself that redouble was the winning call, I reached for the pen and paper. Playing at high levels was no problem despite the language barrier because all bidding was done on paper, using standard English abbreviations no less. "P," I wrote. Pass. The hand was exactly as I had envisioned and I quickly wrapped up the doubled slam. My frustrated opponents resigned and led a new pair to the slaughter. They did it graciously, without recrimination, in a manner which amply recompensed me for not rubbing in our superiority with a redouble. "Friendship first, competition second," or something like that, went the Cultural Revolution slogan. I chuckled inwardly at the thought of telling that to a North American bridge expert.

I knew I had learned a lot in my year in China. *As I write this novel I sometimes fear I learned too much. Unbolting the gates of memory, writing to remember, not forget, trying to imagine Hai Bao and second sister and* Xiao Tuzi *and the* Tiananmen Massacre, *has taken the romance out of New China. Yet the love remains. China gave up the opium Westerners had forced upon it and itself became opium to Westerners like me. When I began writing my great fear was of letting out memories of Chicago. Now I know that if my novel fails it is because I tried to make Chicago my symbol of blood. New China was born — is still laboring to be born? — in a bloodbath as vast as the ocean it lured me across. Maybe I got it wrong and Mao was right after all: "War is politics with bloodshed." Chicago's lake, the one which gave me years of nightmares, barely qualifies as a blood puddle. My own mind dammed it into a lake. I am a damned dam builder when I want to be a bridge builder. Yet in British Columbia, where dams transform the natural flow of our wild rivers, turn beautiful waterfalls to bare rocks to turn our power to the United States' dawn, the dams also serve as bridges across the rivers. If my damn novel has indeed bridged two cultures, blood has not flowed and coagulated in vain.* If I had learned courtesy at the bridge table, I had learned even more than I thought. I needed to flit back to my mountains and write the breakup of my relationship with Peg out of me. I gave myself a year. Then I vowed to return to China and try for a grand slam.

Chapter Seventeen

It was only a three day breather, but during those days in rural Shandong Hai Bao felt she was exhaling five years of constriction. It was not the setting, although the scenery and history she labored up and meandered through were superb, but that she was alone. No, not alone; that would have frightened her. She was among strangers to whom she owed no explanations of actions, thoughts or feelings, past or present. She sucked in the air of freedom, of being able not to care, not give a good goddamn about anyone or anything. Occasionally this made her conscience stricken, like a thief plying his trade: it was antisocial and decadent individualism, spiritual pollution she knew she would be punished for. But feel that way she did and more than once almost shouted out loud for joy. She mounted the six thousand stone steps of Taishan in the dark, a feat emphasized by Qiu when he first told me about her and which instantly turned her into a romantic figure in my mind. *"I too like to climb high mountains in the dark. But the mountains I want to scale have no steps. I seek a fellow traveller,"* I pontificated in my first letter to her. The reality was more simple and practical. The train let her off at Tai'an in the evening. By checking her suitcase and climbing at night she could save hotel money and reach the summit in time to see the sunrise. Needless to say, climbing alone at night was also a first expression of the inrush of freedom and the outrush of exhilaration she was breathing.

Even in the middle of the night she was not alone on the mountainside. Others had the same plan. Some zipped past her as she climbed while others she passed easily and left behind. Most of the way up she kept pace with a well dressed man of about forty. She passed him a few times as he rested, but whenever she arrived at a particularly dark area she halted so she could follow him because he carried a flashlight. After a while they smiled in greeting whenever one passed the other. She had to suppress an urge to giggle and call out, "Are you a bourgeois intellectual?" On the final straightaway toward the top she passed him and did not stop because it was too cold when she wasn't moving. She reached the summit before dawn but couldn't see the sunrise for the clouds. She stood, shivering and stamping her feet, in shorts amid a crowd clad in winter greatcoats like her father's, everyone watching the east anxiously, hoping for a break in the cloud cover, but all they saw was the black grow grey and the grey grow lighter until it was day. Her life was like that too, she reflected, grey, contrastless, cheerless. Then she spotted a charming temple amidst the misty clouds and forgot all the ill will she had conceived for those clouds. She even forgot temporarily how chilled she was and wandered through a fairyland forest of pines filled with the melodies of birds and breezes. If she had had a coat, she would have stayed longer at the top instead of hurrying down toward warmer climes.

I was there. Indeed, for once I was there before her. Ruby and I climbed Taishan the previous summer. And we knew enough about mountains to carry warm clothing in a knapsack although it turned out we didn't need it since the hotel at the top provides long, bulky Russian greatcoats for its patrons. We did see the sunrise, we and a hundred or more other fans. Sunrises atop Taishan are spectator spectacles far more spectacular than those Shanghai's air pollution begets. There were enough clouds to intensify the colors and give a veiled effect but not too many to obscure the sun, which received a round of applause as it cleared the ridge to the east.

Hai Bao slept on the bus to Qufu. She wouldn't have been much interested in the lessons in mechanized agriculture she could have learned on the way.

Again I was there and saw more than she. My journal records in detail the way the local peasants thresh their grain by placing it on the road for cars, trucks and busses to drive over, then winnow it on the side of the road. It occurs to me that I no longer have an excuse. From this point on I was everywhere Hai Bao was, first Shandong, then Shanghai. I arrived back there from Canada only a few weeks after Hai Bao did. I stayed awake all my first night back, listening to the tumult of a typhoon outside, writing to allay the tumult inside. I can no longer say I was not present, no longer play the attached Western observer detranslating then retranslating Hai Bao's stories.

Qufu filled Hai Bao with peace. She stayed two days instead of one although this meant she would be a day late reporting back to work. It was the natural beauty, the wild old forests, the birds singing everywhere, which surprised her and which she loved. She did spend a day visiting temples and reading ancient steles as planned. Many of the steles were borne on the backs of stone tortoises. Ma, to whom turtles meant cuckolds or bastards, would have laughed to learn they were also symbols of longevity. The temples looked impressive, but she knew they would. She also knew there was little left of the historical structures. Red Guards had seen to that. She was viewing recent renovations. The cypress and pine

forest was genuinely ancient. She wandered in it for a whole day, meditating at the
tomb of the sage, bowing to old stone statues of animals which crept up on her in
unexpected places, and whistling back at birds who piped songs as clear and tuneful
as if they were using a bamboo flute.

*As usual I saw more than she. She merely saw what existed, contemporary
reconstructions necessitated by the Cultural Revolution's sacking of Chinese culture; I
saw what I wanted to see, ancient temples and artifacts. How imaginative of me.... Well,
maybe this mistake is ignorance, not imagination, but maybe it's also time I quit making
that excuse too. I've been making it most of my life, using lack of imagination as an excuse
to write badly. Maybe it's time I prove that I am a novelist, not a biographer, that I can
do more than play with words to disguise the fact that I am retelling Hai Bao's stories,
not telling my own, that I have a novelist's empathy and can use it to get into my heroine,
slip into her mind and build with my words that bridge across the Pacific. I have learned
much living with Hai Bao, watching her grow up, the child I married become a woman,
watching her grow tough like her mother, like her motherland. I am learning even more
writing about her. I am, in fact, learning to write as I always wanted to but never thought
I could. Before this I wrote to purge shit from my system. As I might have guessed, writing
a Chinese novel is a didactic, not a purgative, experience. But who would have guessed
that the main lesson I am learning is that I have imagination? Even if I am but imagining
I have learned that, doesn't that show I have imagination?*

*Trust a Chinese to teach a lesson even when she is not lecturing, is not even
present. Because she is present, even when she is not here, present in me, forcing me to use
words to make her present to others, luring me ever farther into the realm of imagination.
Once I stop making excuses, I can see how she has led me to this point. Her presence in
me is another of her presents to me, her stories, her past, for I have been enabled to recreate
her past without fear – at least until she reads all I wrote – of rubbing her the wrong way,
to create her as I love her, more silk than abrasion, as I wanted her to be when I first
peered over a mental wall and saw her. I wanted her to be like the statues in the newly
rebuilt temples of Qufu, ancient in culture but glossy in texture. Well, she has become far
more, has become more real to me than any shiny work of art. For by writing about her
I've become part of her past as surely as by marrying her I've made her part of my present.
Now she is leading me farther, into her mind, not her body. Now I must become present
in her, and if I do that, I may not only become a novelist but build a new foundation
for our marriage, a true foundation as opposed to the misconceptions and inscrutability
I originally loved in her culture and her. Except that by writing I've also rediscovered
how beautiful many of those inscrutable misconceptions and misconceived inscrutabilities
were. That's China all over. China does not permit truths divorced from history. Can I
love Hai Bao for what she is by becoming what she was? Can I make my novel in which
the lovers never meet a true story in which the lovers become one? If I can, it will be a true
novel which not only combines old and new as China does but links East and West, Hai
Bao and me, as only a work of imagination can do.*

So when the crisis comes, I'll slip quietly into her mind. I don't really have much choice. She has led me in by not telling me one story. She tried to once, early on, when it still affected her powerfully, before she could be sure we would marry, before she discovered she didn't have to relive it. Neither of our language skills were up to it and it was connected to too many other stories she hadn't yet told. I remember eventually figuring out that she was talking about two boyfriends, not just the one she was angry at, and that one had written a story which had something to do with the crisis she was experiencing with the other, but since I knew little about the recent boyfriend and nothing about the earlier one, I couldn't grasp what she was trying to tell me. It reminded me of something in Peg's breakdown, so I brought that up and pushed us into total confusion. We were both flipping frantically through the dictionaries in our laps when we suddenly looked at each other and broke out laughing. "Mei guanxi" (it doesn't matter), she said. The moment had finally come. I kissed her as gently as I could.

She arrived home exhausted but feeling more optimistic than she had in a long time, washed clean, ready to seek a new future, a poetic future. She slept right through the dinnertime din of Pushan Lu, from early afternoon until the next morning, and rose refreshed. But at work nothing had changed; the prosaic past overcame her and she felt ill. She was running a fever which recurred every afternoon for two weeks and puzzled the factory doctor. He would have liked to examine her, but she had long drawn a line at discussions – of literature, opera, art and history as well as her symptoms – with him. Besides, she felt no pain so what was there to examine?

The pain was saving itself for a rainy night. On that night it hit her full force in the belly. Her father threw one poncho over her, another over himself, sat her on her bicycle and pushed her through a typhoon to the local hospital, where a doctor examined her, asked if she was married or had ever suffered from uterine problems, and sent her back into the typhoon with pain pills when she answered no to both questions. By the next night she was sure she was dying. This time her poor old father pushed her to the bus stop, where she screamed in pain waiting for a bus to get her to a decent hospital. At least it wasn't raining as hard as the previous night. At the district hospital the doctors took one look and scheduled her for surgery in the morning. They said she had a ruptured appendix. She didn't think she would live until morning.

She spent the next two days in *Mudan Ting*, Du Li Niang's Peony Pavilion, dying and reviving, heated by sunbright fevers and cooled in showers of clouds and rain. Her passion was scattered by a sudden and callous west wind. The midautumn moon set. When it rose it was spring again in the garden and the thick musk of the flowers overpowered her. How she hated to leave. How reluctantly she returned, awoke to find that what she was smelling was not the scent of those bright flowers but the stench of a grey hospital ward.

She was fed a few sips of her mother's chicken soup by her faithful old father, who had been sleeping in a chair to nurse her. A squat but efficient doctor materialized to inform her she had almost died, that her badly infected right ovary had been removed. He chastised her for swimming in the ocean, where she must have caught the infection, and for not coming to the hospital earlier. He advised her to have a baby soon since she had but one ovary left. Then he faded away, leaving her in tears. But the woman in the bed to her left dismissed his scolding with a laugh and told her she had confounded him and the other doctors by surviving. "I knew all along that anyone who sings Kun opera when she is unconscious will live to dance and sing in a time of peace," the woman assured her. "I wish you could teach me to sing." This woman had recently had a leg amputated and was dying of cancer.

The hospital ward was the gloomiest place she had ever been. Patients died in the night with eyes unshut and were not discovered until morning. Others cursed the doctors and their fate night and day and called in relatives to curse when they felt too weak to do it alone. Only the dying woman in the next bed attempted to be cheerful – when her pain was not too great. Hai Bao lay in bed too weak to move, wanting Huang to come, waiting for him. She hadn't seen him all summer, but he was in the city, he was around. Before she entered the hospital a neighbor had informed her he had been seen skulking about at night. She felt certain that he knew she was ill, that she had been near death, certain that he knew everything about her, that he spied on her. He was a clever one. So why didn't he come? She felt awful and everything about the hospital ward depressed her. She felt lonely and alone. The doctors came once in a while and looked at her, strangers looked at her, her father looked at her and muttered a few stock phrases about home. Everyone looked but no one talked to her. Why didn't Huang come? Why, why, why? The clever, like the rich, are not benevolent. Come, come, come. I need you. Remember me with coal during a snowstorm.

At the end of a week she prevailed on her father to recruit a friend and carry her home in the back of a cycle cart. At home she lay in bed neither thinking nor dreaming. Only Mrs. Ling visited her. Huang didn't care if she died; therefore, she didn't care if he lived. If he showed his face, she would summon up the last of her strength to spit in it. *Pei.* The rat. But the coward didn't show. No doubt he knew how she was feeling about him. *Pei.* The mouse.

Qiu, who did not know she had been sick, sent her a letter inviting her to a party at his house on Sunday. Teacher Jiang and many of the students from the writing class would be there to meet a foreign writer who wanted to meet Chinese writers. Qiu described him as an interesting person, a big man with a huge beard like Marx. Immediately she pictured him as Cao Cao on the opera stage with a pure white, evil face to go with the beard. She had never met a big nose, never been close to one. They were said to smell bad. She did not particularly want to meet this fearsome sounding foreigner, but she badly wanted to get out of bed, out of the house, see some friends, cheer herself up. It had only been three weeks since her surgery and she was supposed to stay in bed at least a month, but on Friday and Saturday she forced herself to walk around. She thought she could manage going to the party.

Qiu and Mei lived with Qiu's family on the south side. It took her almost an hour on three busses to get there and she arrived late. When she pushed her way off the last bus she discovered she had forgotten the letter with Qiu's address. She remembered the name of the street and paced up and down it, forcing herself to ask strangers if they knew the family, hoping to spot someone from the class, wanting to shout Qiu's name to the skies, growing more and more tired, hot, desperate. Finally, fighting an urge to throw herself under a bus, she forced herself to board one. The trip home was a blank. The only good feature of Shanghai busses was that passengers could not collapse. They were packed in too tightly to fall. She staggered home, dropped onto the bed and bawled. Ma tried to comfort her, but she couldn't stop crying. She spent the next week teetering between suicide and hysteria, tottering on the brink of breakdown, keeping herself from plunging to the bottom in true Chinese fashion: by descending cautiously along the side of her depression.

I spent an educational afternoon observing Chinese deference toward a teacher who was not me, learning in the process that much of the deference toward me was because I was a teacher, not a foreigner. Indeed, I witnessed two generations of deference, for the teacher, a writer himself, had brought copies of his own teacher's recently published volume of poems, which he proceeded to autograph before passing out to his students. Talk about identifying with one's teacher! I was offered a copy but managed to decline on the grounds that it would be years before I would be capable of even attempting to read Chinese poetry. I should have taken it and saved it for Hai Bao. The reason there was an extra copy was that one student had not turned up. How lovely it would have been to give her a first gift. Their long history has developed in Chinese an instinct to anticipate the giving of gifts. They always want to be owed, not owing. Call it their culture's insurance (but so much nicer than purchasing a policy). It insures that asking for a favor carries no risk of losing face, and in event of catastrophe there is no need to ask. Even this novel, which I set out to write for her and our relationship, turns out to be her gift to me. The more I write, the more I learn of my debt. Not only did I unwittingly cause a crisis for her by inciting the literary gathering which precipitated it, but when she leads me into her mind to examine its crisis, she will complete her lesson that I can get out of my own mind, that I do have imagination. Fancy that: in China didacticism and imagination are complements, not contradictions.

At the party the book was the only thing I was able to decline all day, but this was one occasion on which Chinese courtesy genuinely touched me. At one point I was embarrassed to realize no one had eaten any plums because I had not yet tasted them. Such surfeits of courtesy usually discourage me, but after I took a plum and everyone dug into the bowl, the teacher recited an ancient poem extolling the winter plum for its hardiness in standing up to snow and frost. After Mei translated the poem for me, Qiu recited another one on the same subject by Mao and explained that he bought dried plums along with the more appealing fresh fare because it seemed a particularly Canadian fruit. This brought tears to my eyes, which told me in a new way how I was changing, how I, who had always prided myself on directness and lack of politeness, was falling in love with China in large measure for its people's politeness toward me. I was won over by the funny old writer-teacher, who kept producing singing insects from boxes in various pockets, and his earnest students, who respected him and flattered me. I became especially friendly with Qiu, the new husband of my old friend Mei, an English teacher. She had given the party because she knew I was interested in meeting writers.

All night Hai Bao was pursued by Cao Cao, huge, white and horrific, spurred on by those she thought were her friends: Qiu, who sketched her in Cao Cao's hairy arms; Peng, who wrote them a love poem; Mei, innocent Mei, who serenaded Cao Cao with the Mongolian shepherdess' love song to her swain. Even Teacher Jiang joined the nightmare, writing an essay lauding international love relations as a means of promoting international peace relations. Ma and Ba paraded by bearing placards which read "over thirty, not yet engaged," and Jie and Jiefu followed carrying posters with Cao Cao's photograph and the caption "Genuine Bourgeois Intellectual." In the background a chorus of neighbors and workers from her factory sang a song of farewell while her history professors lectured about how ancient emperors sent concubines who had grown old and fallen from favor as gifts to foreign potentates.

What was happening to her? Was every male she might meet, even a foreigner she had never met and about whom she knew nothing, not even if he was married, to be viewed only as a potential mate? Was she to be permitted no thought that did not lead toward marriage? It was bad enough that friends, family and near strangers were dropping hints and making comments. Was she to be tortured by her own dreams as well? Her whole body ached. She felt as if she was being crushed. She felt she was in a grip as ancient as the earliest ancestor of the Chinese race, as final as its last descendant. The wife of one of Mrs. Ling's sons had recently given birth and she had seen the tiny creature wrapped in its swaddling bands, immobile, lifeless except for staring brown eyes. She too had been bound that way as a baby, but only now was she beginning to comprehend that she had never been unbound, that the bands were part of her, were culture. And biology. Maybe politics and economics as well. And who knows what else under heaven? They bound all Chinese, especially women. They bound all women, especially Chinese. Probably they bound all human beings, especially Chinese women. How could her bands disappear? They were fate, they were China. As soon as she realized this, all the pain she had been feeling seemed to concentrate itself in her neck. At first she thought she had been lying too long in one position. Then she knew: the bands had become a cangue. She was being marched to madness in the pillory of her own culture. Once she knew that the cangue was there, she knew it had always been there, would always be there. If she had not felt it before, that was only because she had grown up wearing it, had grown accustomed, had been too young and thoughtfree to understand that the disaster going on around her, the calamity that was her country, was going on inside her as well. Inevitably.

And the terrible thing about a cangue was that although it tortured endlessly it did not end life. Only she could do that, and the cangue would actually immobilize her in ways that would prevent her. Look at her now: lying in bed, her neck aching, her body numb, her mind overactive. She was thinking about death and couldn't stop herself, yet she knew she could not die because the same culture which declared her useless for not giving herself to a man and his family demanded she give herself to her own parents and family. The same knowledge that screamed against that culture's feudal restrictions and her own sacrifice on the altar of family whispered of the need for kindness, self sacrifice and humanity in the modern world. The same humanity that sought to make the modern world better made it worse by accepting a feudal culture like China's. Yet that same modern world insisted she possessed the power of passion within her to remake her life, not take it as was the feudal custom, while all her passion cried out to escape a life which left it no outlet. But it loved life too passionately to leave it.

She was sobbing – softly so her mother, who was already up and downstairs, would not hear. She refused food and did not budge from bed all day. She would die. If she could not act, she would lie there suffering until she starved to death. But in the evening Ma carried up a steaming bowl of *hun dun*. She had made them specially for Hai Bao, whose sickness she thought was still physical, and had brought along a large dollop of homemade hot sauce which she guaranteed would heat Hai Bao's innards, drive out the chill, stimulate her vital ethers to flow smoothly and thus enable her heart once again to regulate her stomach, liver, kidneys and lungs. Hai Bao could not resist the plump dumplings filled with love and folk wisdom. They smelled too good, reeked of garlic. Her mouth felt dry and she thought anything put in it would taste like dust. But the first dumpling was smooth. She rolled the whole thing around in her mouth, savoring the gloss her tongue could feel, enjoying even the way it burned. She had thought she would spit it out, but it was too hot, too smooth, too fully packed. She rolled and rolled it. Then she bit into it, felt the delectable juices squirt out and scorch her mouth. She chewed and swallowed it. Ma hobbled back downstairs so silently she might have been tiptoeing. Hai Bao ate half the huge bowl without hot sauce, swilling each bite around and around in her mouth, savoring before swallowing. Then she added the hot sauce and ate the rest with greater zest, greedily relishing the way the spices heated her mouth, throat and innards, just as Ma had predicted.

Ta ma de! Damn! Why do *hun dun* have to taste so great just when I want to kill myself? I could laugh out loud. Except once I begin I'll never stop; I'll become hysterical and scare my poor parents to death. Society already has me in a straightjacket. Going crazy can't change a thing. The *hun dun* already told me I can't commit it, but I'm going to lie in bed and plot suicide anyway. The traditional method is throwing myself down a well. That's out. The only pit resembling a well around Pushan Lu is the bin where we dump our chamber pots. Probably I could sneak into it late at night and I'm sure it would kill me, but I don't deserve to die that way. I want to die to escape suffering, not make it worse. Water is out. I'm too good a swimmer. No way I'd drown easy like Bianji's heroine did. The pollution in Suzhou Creek might kill me without drowning, but that wouldn't be much better than the night soil pit. No, Bianji. Death is too easy for you. Just like life is. What about slashing my wrists? Too messy. And it would leave me scarred if I didn't succeed. Huang would do it more neatly. Very neatly. He'd use gas. If only I could sneak into Huang's house and do it there. That would teach you, you turtle. You genetically diseased, short lived turtle. There are no gas lines, not even any propane stoves, on Pushan Lu. I wonder if fumes from the little coal grill we cook on would kill me. Maybe if I bring the stove inside and close all the windows.... But how would I find a time when Ma and Ba are both out and not going to return for several hours? That almost never happens. And even when it does, I never know in advance. Sleeping pills. But Chinese sleeping pills are no good. When I worked shifts, they never kept me asleep. That good old impotent lecher, the factory doctor, would supply me, but I don't think I can swallow enough to kill myself. Poison is surer and there's plenty of rat poison around. Mrs. Han always keeps a supply for the periodic pest extermination campaigns. But am I a rat? What a horrible, painful way to die. And what pleasure it would give you, Mrs. Han. So sorry to spoil your fun, Mrs. Zookeeper. The ceilings in the house are too low for hanging. I might manage it through the hole where the steps go up. But my foot would automatically seek the steps and likely find them. I could tie the rope round the upstairs window post and jump off the roof. *Aiya.* The whole neighborhood would rush out to gawk at me dangling above the passageway. That would be worse than death. The more I plan the less feasible the idea becomes. The big machines at work. But someone is always around to switch them off. What if I get mutilated but not killed? The train tracks are nearby, but I could never get onto them without being seen. Some hero would be bound to rescue me. Maybe I could go out to the country and do it. Shanghai is simply too inconvenient a place to commit suicide. And who would take care of Ma and Ba? I would never want to inconvenience your life in Qingdao, dear Jie.

Yet there were times she knew she could do it if she could do it without planning. After she was up and around, she found she was incapable of walking across a bridge and not peering over the edge to see if it was suitable. She was storing up information. One time perhaps she would leap without peeking. She tried to cheer herself by window shopping on Nanjing Lu and found herself staring up at the International Hotel. How tall it was, and many of its upper floor windows were open. She turned automatically toward the door, but the doorman prevented her from entering the building. Thwarted again. Such places were for foreigners and high officials only. Of course there were tall buildings she could get into, some of the new highrise apartment buildings perhaps, but that meant planning, deciding to do it, and she knew she could not do that. Maybe if she kept thinking about it, she would get frustrated enough to really do it. Maybe if she didn't stop laughing at herself when she wanted to cry, she would go crazy.

On October first she dragged herself to the Bund. Once she and Huang had strolled there, been happy together. National Day had always been a good time for them. She remembered the one she had spent with him in Nanjing. Then she stopped letting herself remember and just let herself be carried along in the overwhelming current of the crowd. So many people on the Bund, so many people in Shanghai, so many people in China. Mao had declared every person precious. Could she be the only one who wasn't? So much happiness, so much light. Surely there were enough people, happiness and light to fill and brighten all the dark, empty spaces of the world. Except the one inside her. She was the only one alone. She sought among the faces of the crowd for another which looked lonely. If she found one she felt miserable enough to grab him, to cry I'm lonely too, I hate all these laughing faces too, to pull him out of the glowing crowd into the glowering shadow cast by their loneliness, to do with him she knew not what, then go with him she cared not where so long as only they two were there. She would forget her family and never inquire about his family or even his name. But she saw no one who looked lonely. Everyone was in couples or groups, mainly family groups but single generation groups as well. The children wore their most brilliantly colored clothes and had their lips painted and dots of joy on their foreheads. How different everything was from the Cultural Revolution, how much livelier. How much sadder she felt.

I was there too, promenading up and down the Bund with Mei and Qiu. The crowd was amazing, bigger than any I saw in the marches on Washington of the Sixties, more people than lightbulbs and there were lightbulbs, ordinary, clear, nonflashing ones, strung up and down every skyscraper, tree and bush and from pillar to lamppost and back. I was fascinated by the people, both the number and the bright faces. I guess I didn't see her either because in my journal I wrote of a million people, all happy, all together.

Would she have recognized my unhappiness if she had seen us? Qiu and Mei got me talking about the novel I had written before I returned to Shanghai, then about its topic, my breakup with Peg. Why I told them the story I didn't know at the time. I had written the novel so I wouldn't have to tell it again, and looking at the million happy faces around me I didn't believe any Chinese could understand planning to go crazy the way Peg did or trying to follow her the way I did. (Yet had I not followed Peg's planning then, could I follow Hai Bao's planning now? Could I understand why planning suicide to stave off insanity worked while planning insanity to stave off suicide failed? Hai Bao stayed rational: no great romantic leaps into the unknown.) In fact Chinese understand stories like mine much the same way Jews do. By the end of it Mei and Qiu were doing exactly what my parents would have done, offering to find me a nice girl to marry. At that time, at least, they did not actually offer me a woman as other Chinese have – from a young rake who brought round his girlfriend and told me (in English, which she did not know) he did not intend to marry her and I could have her if I wished to a seventy five year old grandfather who did everything short of going down on one knee to propose for the girl of his choice. If Hai Bao had stepped out of the crowd, would they have offered her then? Probably not. Chinese can be as sentimental as the most sentimental Jews, but they are usually more cautious. Qiu and Mei waited more than half a year, until her mental state had improved. At that time I recognized her at first sight. Would I have recognized her – and her mental state – eight months earlier? Likely I would have recognized her – she was beautiful and I was needy, or I wouldn't have been telling my story – precisely because I wouldn't have recognized her mental state. I didn't recognize Peg's until I wrote everything out of me three years after we split up. If I had recognized Hai Bao's mental state, would I have followed her? Never again! And coming back to the original question, would she have recognized me? In that beard?

As my mother used to say – and how I hated it when she did – things work out for the best. Had we met amid the gaiety of the Bund, I can imagine what would have happened: there would have been a round of polite introductions and I would never again have heard of Zhang Hai Bao. Chinese are much better at concealing their emotions than I am at understanding or expressing mine. At the time I was groaning inwardly for having opened my mouth. In answer to the offer to search out a wife for me I used my usual dodge, insisted I would only consider marrying a writer. Writing had ceased being a prestigious profession in China, and I doubted there was an unmarried female writer among all the million promenaders on the Bund. Being a Jew and knowing a bit about the Chinese, I knew my two friends would not believe an outright refusal. Being me I did not know I did not want to give one.

She was back at work, bearing her cangue, trying to smile at coworkers and not notice the looks they gave her, not hear the whispers behind her back. Thank heaven she was off the factory floor. Even before she turned thirty the coarser men there used to wink at her and tease, "Better hurry up." Then one day the boyfriend of another teacher came into their office. His girlfriend was knitting him a sweater and complained of its difficulty. The boy replied, "Don't complain. There are some girls who wish they could be knitting that sweater." He said it loudly so Hai Bao would be sure to hear. She disliked her students more than ever and felt she had nothing to say to the other teachers, but wandering into the factory to see old friends was even more dispiriting. The little gang of four was no more. The others all had children. She had recently encountered Xiao Xiang and been forced to listen to a long, proud narrative of her naughty son's most recent exploits.

She was back at school, discussing missed work with professors, borrowing notes from classmates, not letting herself wonder if any of the men were unmarried. Not that it mattered: since the operation she had lost weight, felt dark, ugly and listless, felt she could never be interested in a man even if one could be interested in her, which was impossible. She liked to walk around the campus, for there she was anonymous, but the students were so young, so carefree.

Living at home was where the cangue around her neck dug deepest. It held her prisoner and singled her out as a target for insults and innuendos but gave her no guard who might pity her or would at least lead her along the road to new places. Several times she caught snatches of conversations as neighbors passed beneath her window: "well over thirty." "no boyfriend in sight," "used to come around whistling." One day when she was downstairs a neighborhood leader and his wife came by to check the electricity meter. The man took one look at her and declared in his bossiest tone, "You should get married." "Not her," his wife interjected. "She wants to choose a great man before she'll get married."

As neighborhood leaders they were friends of the Hans, who loved to make sarcastic remarks and drop loud hints about her when she was within earshot, but Xiao Han, the horseface, had never been rude. He was married now and managing the family restaurant. One day she encountered him in the passageway. He was carrying his precious son so she stepped aside and turned her body to give him room to pass. He did not acknowledge her, but as he passed his hand shot out and brushed her breast. Had he done it intentionally? He had never been anything but respectful toward her. Perhaps the child had jogged his arm.

Another time a cousin dropped by to visit her mother. Hai Bao stayed upstairs studying because she did not like this woman, the daughter of her mother's oldest sister, but the house was too small for her not to hear every word spoken and the cousin was not one who would leave before she had uttered every cliche the Chinese language contained on her subject. Today's topic was avoiding trouble, perhaps the language's most bountiful source of cliches. The cousin had a daughter a few years younger than Hai Bao and the kinswoman boasted to ma about the girl's fiancee, a bona fide Communist Party member who would be able to aid the family in times of trouble. Only a fool asks for trouble. Number one sister had married a landlord; as a result her entire family had suffered during the Cultural Revolution. Now a whiff of wind or a stir in the grass foretold problems. Once burned always afraid of fire, and a single spark could light a prairie fire. Before one trouble goes away another arises, the cousin warned, and confided the secret of her daughter's success in finding the perfect man: the girl always listened to her mother, always followed her mother's directions. The instructions had been to marry a man who could protect the family, and the filial child had obeyed them to the character.

When Hai Bao came down to dinner the cousin was gone, but ma was still upset. Hai Bao didn't know whether to comfort her by criticizing their relative for being stupid or for being out of date. Her proverb loving cousin was like a blind person at the opera (*a Chinese saying illustrating the difference between Chinese and Western opera*): she tried to laugh with everyone else but was always a little late. Imagine still thinking it was desirable to marry a Party cadre! But before Hai Bao could say anything, the wife of a neighbor's son passed by the open door carrying her baby. The woman was pretty but slow of speech and thought. "Even an imbecile like that can get married and give her parents a grandchild," Ma burst out. "Hai Bao is just too fussy," chimed in Ba. Hai Bao ran back upstairs and refused to eat dinner.

Huang failed to turn up for Spring Festival for the first time in six years. She decided she was glad because she both hated him and knew that if he came and showed her any affection she would take him back. Then she might hate herself as well as him. For she did not hate herself, at least not all the time. Before the holiday she had been feeling a little better, had even planned to use her vacation to write, a diatribe against Huang if nothing else, but the firecrackers and boisterous family celebrations everywhere depressed her again. She wished she could get away – from home and from the crushing tangle of dreams which gave her no rest at night. Cao Cao was now leading the Japanese army, her traditional pursuer in nightmares, and had recruited other followers, human, part human and animal. She woke many times at night begging what do you want from me? but she never found out and they never ceased pursuing.

I spent my winter vacation touring southern China as a sort of chaperon to a pair of student lovers who acted as my guide and translator. Ah, the innocence of young love in a land where it is truly innocent. I tried to give the lovers time together, but they seldom grabbed it and never, in my presence, grabbed each other. The girl, Little Feng, tiny and brilliant, had just turned twenty and just begun graduate school, so the couple knew marriage was several years away and were not rushing matters, not pushing for sexual experimentation as a Western couple would. Or were pretty good at concealing it from my old eyes.

I fell more in love with China watching them and watching the scenery. I got to indulge in one of my favorite occupations, comparing mountains, Huangshan, where many emperors have trod, and Jinggangshan, where the original Red Army trod. Huangshan is the ultimate Chinese mountain, the one seen in painting after painting, unlike any mountain outside China, covered in shifting mists and odd shaped flat topped pines sticking out of bare rock at odd angles. Had I seen these dreamscapes in my own dreams or was I simply remembering paintings? Jinggangshan is more universal, conventional, solid in its beauty. I knew where I had seen it: get rid of the bamboos and other southern vegetation, drop some snow on the peaks and it could have passed for the Kootenays. Except for the history. The Place Zhu De Rested, for instance. Listening to our guides no one would guess The Place had any use except to let Zhu De rest, but anyone walking up that mountain, with or without a load of grain for his soldiers, would have rested there. It looks out over magnificent mountain scenery, is simply the most beautiful view of the climb. Yet the story and the knowledge of the mountain's revolutionary past add a dimension to the beauty just as the more ancient imperial tales did to Huangshan. As I concluded in my journal, in China beauty is history, history beauty.

I made my own kind of history when I lived a week in Little Feng's peasant hovel in an area closed to foreigners. As Little Feng led me toward this fifteen room brick hovel, her mother came rushing out. To embrace the daughter she had not seen in many months, I assumed. But she ran past the heavily laden girl without a word to take the suitcase from my hand.

As I trod the socialist roads of eastern Hunan, Mao country, the place he recruited his first Red Army, I could hear people who had never seen a Westerner except in pictures whispering "Ma Ke Se, Ma Ke Se" (Marx, Marx) behind my back. Heady stuff for a guy whose Marxism was denied by every Marxist he knew in the Sixties, but headier still was the knowledge that a girl from that out of the way spot, the daughter of loving but illiterate peasants, was attending graduate school in Shanghai. I pumped her for stories of her childhood. She told me that when she was in primary school (during the Cultural Revolution, when traditional literature was being confiscated and burned in the cities) all the neighbors, adults and children, would gather round her while she read The Romance of Three Kingdoms aloud. Few of them could read and the stories are wonderful. She got out the book and translated some for me. To see what she would say, I asked her if she thought I was like Zhuge Liang, the wise hero. She replied a polite yes, hesitated, then laughed shyly and told me I looked more like Cao Cao. To prove it she took me to an outdoor opera based on a story in the book. It was my first full length Chinese opera. In Shanghai, where I had seen excerpts played and explained for foreigners, I had been put off by the strange sounds. Here, among folks who enjoyed every sound, gesture and word and showed it by laughing, calling out and commenting to their neighbors, I hardly noticed the strangeness. I was laughing too. Zhuge Liang was a little guy with an unpainted face and a wispy Chinese beard. He invariably outwitted Cao Cao, a hulking brute in whiteface (the symbol of villainy) and a big, full black beard. That was how I looked to Little Feng.

Whose shy laughter gave me a glimpse beneath the mask of Chinese courtesy, was a first draft of Hai Bao's honest laughter, a penultimate step on the road that leads home to Pushan Lu. A novel begins with the next step.

I walk free at last. The key word in this penultimate chapter is imagination. I have learned that imagination bestows perspective as well as creativity. Imagination obviously *quickens the current of creativity, but it also enables one to escape the current instead of being swept away with it, to see people and events through other eyes than one's own, from other places than their midst, from other times than the present, to be free of the bounds of time, space, self. When I first contemplated slipping into Hai Bao's mind, I was nervous and excited. It was not the sort of thing I had ever believed I could do. Yet suddenly I felt confident I could pull it off. And I did. It wasn't hard after all. I was amazed at how comfortable I felt in there. How spacious a mind is. Or, at least, how spacious Hai Bao's mind was. I couldn't resist rooting around. So I created some dreams. Hai Bao really does have incredibly lucid dreams. She tells them to me all the time. I am always astonished how clear they are and how fully she can remember them long after she has waked up. The dreams I created are like her dreams, but they are not dreams she ever told me about. I imagined them there inside her mind. It seemed like I should do more than relive her crisis while I was there, and they ended my novel so neatly. I couldn't resist. I didn't want to: they made me a real novelist.*

    In the spring she got her chance to get away. She was chosen to spend two weeks at a worker's health spa in the country. Exemplary workers were periodically given such rewards. Hai Bao did not really qualify, but none of the other teachers wanted to go because this resort was near Shanghai. The better ones were out Hangzhou way, in the Zhejiang mountains. Other workers were willing to wait for them, but Hai Bao didn't care. Any change of scenery would feel good to her. Perhaps it would lighten the load around her neck. Every morning she awoke with a stiff neck.

    She travelled with half a dozen others from her factory, all older. She and the only other woman in her group shared a room with a young worker they did not know, but the woman from Hai Bao's factory, who was in her fifties, quickly snared herself a lover and was seldom in the room. The young roommate had many boyfriends, none of whom she took seriously. Every evening a new one paid a call and Hai Bao felt obliged to take herself and her book elsewhere. One such evening she looked in on the men from her *danwei*, who were playing cards. They asked what brought her, and when she told them and joked about her young roommate's habits, one of the men, a man who was usually sensitive, commented without thinking, "It must make you sad to see how many boyfriends an immoral girl like that has." Hai Bao felt tears start to come and ran from the room onto the spacious grounds of the spa. The men ran after her calling her name but she hid from them. She was not about to give them the satisfaction of seeing her cry. When she returned to her room to sleep, the older woman found her, sighed with relief and dragged her off to see the men, who, she said, felt very bad and even feared she might commit suicide. She couldn't help remembering that after her illness, when she was at her lowest and had really contemplated suicide, she wanted to do it in the country. However, there were no train tracks near the spa.

Back at home the cangue felt heavier than ever, and now there was a new problem: Qiu really did want her to marry the big bearded foreigner. He and Mei had both written singing the man's praises and inviting her to their house to meet him. Mei had originally met him through her old English teacher, a Canadian. Qiu effused about the foreigner being a novelist and a philosopher, good, kind, generous, loyal, in love with China, lonely, wanting to meet Chinese writers, wanting to marry a Chinese writer, etc., etc. He effused about North America, the gold mountain of Chinese legend, but when Hai Bao checked her map and saw how far north Canada was, it made her shiver. The whole country was farther north than Harbin. It was the cold mountain, not the gold mountain. That path she did not need to climb. She remembered the story she had written of *Xiao Tuzi*, freezing to death in Xinjiang's cold mountains, remembered the chill she had felt writing it and for weeks after writing it. She liked Qiu, but she knew him too well to trust his effusions, knew that once an idea captured him he would say and do anything to further it. She remembered how his old girlfriend had been hurt when he threw her over in his enthusiasm for Mei. He was perpetually enthusiastic about something, and she did not intend to become the latest victim of his fervor. Besides, one can never trust a matchmaker. Still, she couldn't help being curious and she was bored and frustrated with her life. Meeting this foreigner would be an adventure. *Aiya*, that she surely knew better than to seek. Did she need another disappointment? Still.... Mei was expecting a baby soon; it would be appropriate to visit her. Hai Bao did not reply to the letter. She knew Qiu would take this as an acceptance of his invitation, but she had not actually accepted and could wait until the day to decide.

The night before the scheduled meeting Du Li Niang met Cao Cao. It was in the autumn garden amidst fading flowers and yellowing weeping willows. He jumped out from behind a tree. "Lady, I am dying of love for you. I am the partner for whom you wait as the river of years rolls past." He was speaking the willow lover's words, but he spoke in a barbarian dialect she would not have recognized if she did not already know the lines. He was Cao Cao all right. He looked as he always did in operas. Everything about him was huge: his black beard, his white painted face, his beak nose, his eyes which leered and lusted at her like a tiger, his elephantine body which desired to crush hers. In his hand he held not the willow bough but the whip used in opera to symbolize riding a horse. He was planning to mount her.

"Sir, I do not know you," she lied.

He laughed the evil laugh Cao Cao always laughed on the stage. "But you will. In some future time you and I will meet." He laughed his terrible laugh again, grew even larger, more menacing. She tried to run from him, but her feet were rooted to the ground. "You will need your power to die and return to life.

Ha, ha, ha."

He reached for her. She screamed. He touched her shoulder. She screamed louder. He began to shake her. "*Xiao Mao, Xiao Mao.*" How did he know that name?

"*Xiao Mao, Xiao Mao,* wake up." It was her mother shaking and calling her. "*Xiao Mao,* wake up. It's just a dream."

Thank heaven for that. She struggled out of bed, sat on the chamber pot and let the cold fear flow out of her. The hell if she would go to meet Qiu's foreigner. She still had some pride left. Better a caged pigeon than a wild chicken. Better ten thousand times to live out life caring for aged parents on Pushan Lu than to be the whore of some big, lewd, hairy barbarian who would tear her from her country, her culture, her family, her self.

In the morning she wrote a note to Qiu and Mei telling them she was too busy studying to come to their house.

She had done the right thing. Her dream that night told her so. In it Du Li Niang's willow lover finally appeared. "I have never seen you before, sir," she told him courteously. But she knew him. He was smooth faced, tall, pale from study but vigorous. His big eyes knew her too and were full of joy at the recognition. "Somewhere at some past time you and I met. Now we behold each other in solemn awe." Where was it they had met? He spoke the lines of the willow lover strangely, looked strange too yet somehow vaguely familiar. He took her hand and led her into the garden. At the Peony Pavilion the spring flowers were at their peak, the mist laden air heavy with their fragrance, overpowering.

Play of clouds, showers of rain,
Rising from shrouds, passionate pain.

Softly come, softly go,
River run, gently flow.

She wrote down the lines upon awakening. They were the first she had written since her trip to Shandong. All that day she did not feel the weight of the cangue. At the factory she felt light hearted, in class almost light headed. She even demonstrated a few light footed steps from a folk dance, a performance which earned approving calls of "*hao, hao*" (bravo) from some of her students. Going to bed she felt none of the dread of dreaming which had been tormenting her recently. Which will it be tonight, Cao Cao or the willow lover? she wondered as she lay down. It didn't matter. Whichever appeared or if they both appeared hand in hand, she would laugh at them.

Everyone who knew me in Shanghai assumed I shaved my sixteen year old beard because I fell in love with Hai Bao. I let them think so. It added time to our too hasty courtship. In fact I shaved several weeks before I met her and did so for the most practical, unromantic of reasons: summer was looming, the annual steam bath which overwhelms the Changjiang Valley and most of eastern China. I had experienced enough of it to know I could not endure a summer in Shanghai with a full beard. At the first hot weather in May, the first misery of moisture trickling down my neck, off came the hairy foreign devil's facial hair. The beard had been splotched with grey, so the result of shaving was that Hai Bao met a younger, cleaner looking devil.

On the other hand I had heard tell of a young woman writer before I shaved, knew a meeting was in the works, had even been told I could marry her. Leave it to the Chinese to say something like that. Consciously I was interested in her only as a fellow writer and was scoffing at the notion of marriage and chuckling at the bald way it had been presented, but my unconscious mind may have had different notions, may have been preparing and adorning me.

In my journal I wrote:

May 18, 1986

Spent the day with Qiu and Mei. Their reaction to my new face the most spectacular yet. Qiu opened the door and obviously did not recognize me for a second or two. Then he leapt up and down and cavorted in a dance which would have served a mating bull moose well, all the while bellowing for Mei, who hurried over in alarm to see what the matter was, took one look and joined the dance despite her advanced pregnancy, stomping about and heehawing like his mooing cow moose.

They've actually found me a writer to marry. You can't win in this country: I used the ruse of wanting to marry a writer because no one would believe me when I simply said I was not interested in marriage. Chinese constantly refuse things they want out of courtesy, so no one believes denials. Today was the day I was supposed to meet their young writer, and Qiu would speak of nothing but her. I kept trying at least to get him to talk about her writing, especially after the first thing he told me about her was that she was "chaste." That word took a dictionary to work out and did not, I'm afraid, elicit the proper response from me. (I laughed and said I was a bit old for chastity.) Qiu never did say much about her writing, but he seemed to learn from his initial false step and started saying the right things about her. In fact he seemed to know just what buttons to push. I am far more likely to be attracted by misuse than lack of use, and she has been discriminated against in all the ways I hate. I did not realize such discrimination existed in China. Although she was born and raised in Shanghai, her family is from northern Jiangsu, an area of poverty and one looked down on by many Shanghainese. Because of this she was actually not permitted to marry a man she loved and who loved her. His parents prevented the match. When I referred to the marriage law and asked how, Qiu and Mei both laughed and assured me there was much I did not understand about China. I guess they are right. There is also economic and class discrimination. This

I thought I knew but was stung to discover the victims are no longer the rich and upper classes as they were during the Cultural Revolution but the poor and lower classes. Is this what I came to a socialist country for? They related story after story about how men approve of the woman's photograph yet refuse even to meet her because she is poor and working class. Yet although her education was cut off by the Cultural Revolution and she did not even finish high school, she has studied on her own and even managed to get into university. Before long they had me eager to meet her and angry at China in a way no one else has been able to make me. That is because I know them, know they have no axe to grind, know they love their country and appreciate its culture. They have never denigrated China before and were doing so today only in specific, limited ways, only for the failures of socialism to wipe out the prejudices and injustices of the past.

After they had built me up for the meeting the woman failed to show. When she was about an hour late, Qiu thought to go downstairs and check his mailbox. There was a letter from her saying she had to study and could not come. In retrospect I think I'm glad. It would have broken my heart to meet some scrawny, shy, faded damsel after Qiu's description of this working class heroine.

AFTERWORD

by Zhang Hai Bao
(Polished by Jack Freidman)

Afterword: After Words

Words, words, words. I just finished swallowing Jack's. Now I'm going to make him eat mine. Without sugar. Americans love sugar, but we Chinese prefer vinegar. Sometimes we use sugar and vinegar, sweet and sour. But I'll make Jack eat my words with just vinegar. Black Chinese vinegar, not Western vinegar that looks like water. Or the yellow apple vinegar that looks like.... I won't say that ugly word. I don't think even Jack says that one. But he does say lots of ugly words. That's how I'll get even. I'll serve him a dish of *bao chou* using his own words. And he'll think it's delicious because it's Chinese food.

His appetizer will be the same disgusting word he starts with: Damned if I know how anyone who understands so little can write so much about what he doesn't understand. I know I shouldn't swear. We never do. But I'll be damned if I'll let Jack get away with anything I can't do. My words will flow like a flood in reply to his. He swears so I'll swear back.

Bao chou! It means revenge. Sometimes I let Jack insult me just like sometimes I eat bread. You get used to some bad things when you are married. Jack insults me all the time. Just yesterday I asked him, "Should I say I very happy to know that or I very happy to learn that?" He didn't answer my question. He said, "You can't say 'I very happy,' of course. You should know that, and if you don't know it you should learn it." Then he laughed. At least he wanted to laugh. He caught himself just in time. I almost laughed when I saw that. He's learned not to laugh at me. But he still thought his answer was very clever. "Of course!" Every fool knows you have to stick in useless words in English. Of course. He thinks we Chinese are too stupid to learn that. Well, I learned that and I know that. I just forget sometimes because English is so silly or simple or whatever the right word is for a language too young to be complex like Chinese.

I'll show you what I mean. Maybe you noticed *"bao"* in my name, *Hai Bao*, and in "revenge," *bao chou*. Maybe you think my name has something to do with revenge. It doesn't. The word *bao* only looks the same in English. English can't show differences the way Chinese can. The two Chinese words have nothing to do with each other. They are completely different in the way you write the characters and the way you pronounce the sounds. The *bao* in my name means treasure. It is written 宝. It is pronounced in the third tone, falling then rising: *bǎo*. *Hǎi Bǎo*. The *bao* in revenge is written 报. It is pronounced in the fourth tone, falling: *bào*. *Bào chóu*. Maybe you couldn't hear the difference. Jack can't. Any Chinese two year old can, but Jack can't. You'd think someone who can't hear wouldn't talk so much and write so much about what he can't hear. Would someone who can't taste try to write a cookbook? But Jack thinks he can write or say anything. It's his right, he says. It's in the Constitution. Well, it's in the Chinese Constitution too. But we Chinese have learned enough to know when not to use our rights. Of course. Even though Jack knew he better not laugh, he'll never learn not to insult me with his of courses. Americans never pay attention to others. They're never careful about what they say. They're selfish. I'm used to it. I'm used to being insulted, but he's lucky he didn't laugh at me. I won't take that and he knows it. So he controlled himself. Almost like a Chinese, but a Chinese wouldn't be so obvious about it. I controlled myself too, but he couldn't notice that. The reason I controlled myself is that I have a better way to get revenge. Living with Jack for twelve years has taught me how hard it is for Americans to learn anything. But living with myself for forty-three years has taught me it is even harder for Chinese not to teach. So I'm going to teach Jack a lesson. Even if I know he won't learn it.

Insulting my family and my country is different from insulting me. I can criticize my family because it is my family. That's why I let him insult me. I'm his family. But my family isn't his. Even though it is me. It's part of the part of me I won't let him insult. He's learned about that part. Not much, but a little. That's why he knows not to laugh even if he doesn't know not to write. I'm part of my mother and father and they're the best part of me. They gave me life. They raised me up. They fed me. I must respect them and help feed them while they're alive and remember them when they're dead. In Chinese tradition we even give food to our dead ancestors by putting it on their graves or in front of their pictures. That's a superstition, but it shows filial piety, and filial piety is part of the best part of our Chinese culture. Jack acts like a child, but he doesn't know anything about the duties of a child. His Jewish mother was a little like a Chinese mother. Although she fed him bread, not rice, she also gave him lots of good advice. Jack never listened to her. In his novel he even makes fun of her. He doesn't know his duty to his own parents, so how can he know his duty to mine? If my parents argued sometimes, his duty is to hide that. If my parents were silly sometimes, his duty is to hide that. Jack hides nothing because he respects nothing. He admits he has no filial piety. He's a typical American. Lots of time in China can't change him even though he always brags about his changes. So how can I let a man without filial piety criticize my parents?

My parents have to suffer enough criticism from *danwei* and neighbourhood leaders. The Party treats them like children, and Jack treats them like caricatures. He thinks he's the great writer, but he can't understand anyone who is not like him. The characters in his novel are all alike. They all talk alike. They all have to fit Jack's American ideas of what is Chinese. I watched my mother, the landlord's daughter, the rich merchant's boundfooted wife, work like a peasant. She worked at a factory six days a week. She took care of me and did all the housework and cooking. Her hands swelled up and turned red every winter. She did most of the shopping on her tiny feet. The only time she wasn't working was when she was sleeping. My father, the peasant, lived more like an intellectual. He read a lot. He recited poetry. He taught me about politics and philosophy. At his factory he worked with his brains, not his muscles. He was an accountant, and his fingers flew on an abacus. My parents talked very differently because they were very different. And even when they argued, my father never talked back to my mother. He wouldn't dare treat her like Jack treats me. He only does it in Jack's novel. All Jack's characters are like Jack. They're all shallow. He doesn't know how my parents suffer because of him. Neighbours laugh at them because their daughter married the only foreigner anyone in China ever heard of who doesn't have money. He thinks he is acting very Chinese, but he never learned anything about the Chinese in all the time he lived in China. Everyone laughs at him because he lives on Pushan Lu, not a fancy hotel, when he visits Shanghai. And my parents always welcome him into their apartment which is not much bigger than a sparrow's nest. What a disgrace. Everywhere he goes he makes me lose face. A man who can't understand anything he sees isn't ashamed to write about everything. He misunderstands everything I ever told him. He makes my family look stupid and selfish. In other words he writes them like Americans, who are the only people he can understand. My sister and brother-in-law are good people. They suffered a lot and sacrificed a lot to feed and raise up their good son. In Jack's novel they are like typical selfish Americans. It wouldn't be so bad if he just wrote for himself. He might learn something. But he shows what he writes to all our friends, and he even wants to publish it for the whole world to see. He doesn't care if everyone thinks my family is terrible. What can you expect of a man who grew up eating bread, not rice?

And my country, China. Good heavens, what will people think of my country when they read what he wrote? It's not like he's criticising the government for massacring its own people. Everyone does that and the people and governments who criticise the loudest are just the ones who invest in China. So the criticism doesn't even affect business, which is the most unimportant part of Chinese culture. I don't care about the government. China has a very long history of very bad governments. Kongzi said lots about that 2500 years ago. He said it was worth facing a man eating tiger to live under a good government. At least I've never had to face a cougar. Kongzi never found a good government he could serve. But Chinese culture has survived all its bad governments and defeated all its invaders. Chinese culture must not be insulted even though some parts of it need to be changed. No Westerner could criticise Chinese culture more critically than Lu Xun did. But Lu Xun understood and loved Chinese culture. Jack thinks he loves Chinese culture, but he can't understand it. Love is Americans' Chairman Mao. They think they can do anything in the name of love. We Chinese know that love without understanding is like stir frying without oil. The food gets cooked, but no one can eat it. Everything gets burned in Jack's novel. No one can read it. And I'm writing this just in case anyone does. I'm using his own weapon, his own language, to get revenge. And the sauciest part of my revenge will be making him polish what I write. "Polishing" is a tradition in China. Few Chinese could study in English speaking countries. Scholars learned English from books. They could translate English into Chinese well, but when they translated Chinese into English, they had problems. The language often sounded like the "Chinglish" Jack and I used to speak. So they gave their translations to native speakers of English in China to polish their rough words into smooth English. How Jack ridicules these "writers" who are not allowed to write for themselves, who are not allowed the elation of creation, who are not even allowed to think for themselves, who are only allowed to rub the words of others until they shine. (I allowed Jack to use a fancy sentence here. I wanted readers to be impressed by what he hates. So I did not cut any of his fancy words or chop them into shorter sentences.) This is the job I will give Jack. The great writer will be reduced to polisher. The great writer will be forced to turn my weak Chinglish insults of his great writing into effective English insults. He says he figures things out by writing. I'll give him a chance. We'll see what he figures out by writing over what I write here.

Maybe that doesn't seem like revenge to you. That's because you don't know Jack. He tried to escape all his American failures. He isolated himself in the mountains of British Columbia. But that wasn't far enough away. He came to China. He thinks China is his big success. He was respected and flattered by his students. He made friends with some Chinese teachers of English. He even found a Chinese wife. Me. He thinks I'm part of his success. Except that by writing me, he shows everyone that his great success is another failure. He doesn't understand China or me or anything. As usual. Of course. He came to China at just the right time. For the first time in my life we Chinese were seeing foreigners and finding out the truth about foreign countries. After liberation almost all the foreigners left and we only heard propaganda about how terrible life was in capitalist countries. Then Chairman Mao died, the Cultural Revolution ended and China opened to the outside. We found out that the capitalist countries were really much richer than China. So we were impressed by foreigners like Jack. We thought they were sacrificing to help a poor country like China. We were used to equality. We didn't believe there were poor people in rich countries. It seemed like a contradiction. We thought it was more of the propaganda we didn't believe anymore. And respect for teachers and flattery of foreigners are part of Chinese culture. So Jack was impressed by China. All the good impressions, all the false impressions fooled Jack about China and fooled me about him. I thought he was a scholar and a great writer. I was happy when he was inspired to write again. Then he isolated us in these lonely mountains full of bears and cougars so he can write and rewrite forever. Every year he rewrites his novel. The sentences and paragraphs and chapters get longer and more complicated and harder to read. All he wants to do is write and garden. Dealing with my English is a waste of his precious time. He thinks living in an English speaking place should teach me all I need to know. He forgets that trees and bears and cougars don't speak English. How can a Shanghai person stand being surrounded by trees and wild animals, not people? Who am I supposed to speak to but him? But every time I ask him to correct my grammar he throws one of his of courses at me and tells me how many times he has told me you can't say that or this in English. He sounds like my father did when he was trying to teach my mother to read. And my real revenge will come from making him write simply and clearly. He always has to be the great writer. He has to write everything fancy and complicated. I'll count the words in every sentence. I'll make him shorten all the sentences and take out all the long words. I'll even change his corrections if I don't like them. When he finishes he'll know what being in a cangue really feels like. So don't worry about my revenge. I know what I know. I've learned a lot since I married him. O.K., maybe it's not *bao chou*. If you know Chinese, you know I did what Americans always do. I *kuadale* (exaggerated). I left that last word for Jack to translate. It's part of my revenge even if it's not *bao chou*. It's only *bao fu*. *Bao chou* is much stronger, killing or something violent like that. *Bao fu* isn't so strong. I can do it using words as my weapon. But both Chinese words get translated as "revenge" in English. English can only make useless distinctions, not subtle ones. Of course.

You might think that if I'm going to make him correct my writing, it isn't clever to talk about revenge. You're wrong, if you'll forgive me for saying so. I have to say it. If I didn't he might not know I was insulting him. Jack is always running away and criticising his birth country, but he's a typical American. Americans are like their language. They are the opposite of subtle, whatever word that is. It's almost as hard to insult an American as to teach him something. Americans are so self centered they can't imagine anyone could possibly disagree with them. The whole world disagrees with them and they don't even notice. You might say that's because the whole world wants their money and wants to make money like them. You'd be right, but you'd also be wrong. Excuse me for saying that too, but Americans never notice what the rest of the world wants. They think the whole world is greedy because they are. When Chairman Mao was alive and China was not greedy, did Americans listen to China's criticisms? Only a few hippies like Jack did. Only the Americans who wanted to be unamerican. And failed. Of course.

Jack failed in everything he tried to do. His novel, his Chinese novel he calls it, is his biggest failure. What could be more American than this "Chinese" novel? The characters all come from Chinese stories I told him, but they're all American. My second aunt got murdered twice, once in life, once by Jack in his novel. In Chinese history Second Sister got murdered because she was strong and independent. In Jack's novel she gets murdered like an oppressed Negro slave woman from American history. Chairman Mao talks like an American lawyer. My parents, who are so different, talk just like each other and argue like low class American peasants. And me, poor needing a man me? I'm now an independent Canadian businesswoman. I earn the money in our family. Jack sits around the house canning and freezing food from his garden, writing novels no one will ever publish and correcting my grammar when I order him to. I bring home the cash. But in Jack's novel I'm the helpless country girl who has to sell her body to survive in the big city. I read the story during the Cultural Revolution in an American novel named *Sister Carrie*. See how much Jack knows? We could get foreign books during the Cultural Revolution, and I did read some. Maybe our *Sister Carrie* was cut. We cut our food too. Americans eat big slabs of bloody meat, but Chinese chop food and fry it well. My Chinese *Sister Carrie* was much shorter than Jack's English one, but at least it finished the story. Jack can't do that. You probably think he's told me lots of stories about his life just like I told him stories of mine. No. He starts lots of stories, but he doesn't know that when there's a beginning there should be an end. He always gets distracted and goes off about something else. If you read his novel, you know what I mean. And in my story the only good part comes at the end, the part Jack doesn't get to. Of course. Listening to Jack trying to tell a story is the most frustrating experience in the world. I always get impatient and tell him to get to the point. He never does. So I usually end up saying "*Suanle.*" Forget it. Then I tell him a story. That's why he knows so much about my life. Only an American could know so much, learn so little, understand nothing. (Kongzi said something like that. I hope Jack has lots of trouble saying it in English.)

Americans are like their language, simple. Jack actually thought his novel would make me happy. He thought I would be proud of him for telling my stories. He loves me because I'm Chinese, but he treats me like I'm an American who wants to show off every piece of my private life. He probably believes what I once heard an American professor say. The professor said Chinese don't believe in privacy! Another amazing American. Just because we don't have room for privacy in our crowded cities and lives, he says we don't believe in it. A Canadian might be wrong, but he would never be so rude. After the lecture I heard, the professor probably went to a wine bar and told anyone who would listen about all his girlfriends and what they did in bed. But it's Chinese who don't believe in privacy! And Chinese whose scholarship led them to a dead end. Whatever that means. The professor said that too. He must have thought Chinese scholars were like him. No wonder I got tricked by Jack. I thought he was a scholar. He was a professor of English and he was so proud of being a writer. If only I could have read something he wrote. Then I would have known. I would have learned that American professors are at a lower level than Chinese middle school teachers during the Cultural Revolution.

I don't blame Jack for not understanding Chinese culture. I blame him for not understanding his own culture. When he told me he would name his novel about us "Butterflies," naturally I thought he meant the butterfly lovers. It's China's most beautiful love story. It was told in a Shaoxing opera, 梁山伯与祝英台, *Liang Shan Bo Yu Zhu Ying Tai.* Zhu Ying Tai, a girl from a rich family, wants to study. Girls are not allowed to go to school, but she persuades her father to let her disguise herself as a boy and study. She studies well for many years, living in a boy's dormitory. No one can guess her secret. She becomes close friends with a classmate, Liang Shan Bo. She tests his love in many ways but never reveals that she is a girl. After their graduation she tells him she will arrange a marriage for him with her sister. She sets a date for him to come to her family's home to meet her sister. Herself really. When he comes she will reveal her secret. But he doesn't come on the arranged date, and Ying Tai's father pressures her to marry a much richer man. For a long time she refuses, but Shan Bo still doesn't come. Finally she can't refuse any longer. A few days before the marriage he finally comes. His mother has been sick or something. When he realises his friend is a woman he is overjoyed, but when he finds out she must marry someone else they both cry and cry. He leaves and soon dies of a broken heart. On her wedding day she insists the *jiaozi* (sedan chair in English) must stop at Shan Bo's grave. Here she kills herself or maybe just dies of a broken heart too. From the grave two butterflies rise, circling together, dancing together. The two lovers. How touching, I thought. Despite all the difficulties of our marriage, he still thinks our love is eternal. Americans may not be able to learn everything about Chinese culture. They may not know that rice is better than bread, but they know about love. Imagine what I felt when I found out the butterfly he used was from that silly old story of Zhuangzi. He was an ancient Chinese philosopher who dreamed he was a butterfly. When he woke up he didn't know whether he was a man who had dreamed he was a butterfly or a butterfly who was dreaming he was a man. Now you see why Jack fails at everything he does. He can't choose the right butterfly from Chinese culture. He can't understand the meaning of love, his own culture's favorite idea, America's Chairman Mao.

And since he can't end a story either, I'll have to do that for him too. *Suanle*. I always do. Let me tell you how he tricked me. Why do we Chinese always get tricked by Westerners? Maybe it's because their culture is so young. They seem so innocent and childlike. We don't think they could trick us. Until we're caught like fish in a net. Like they caught us with opium. In China Jack always looked so clean and pretty. In movies Americans look clean and pretty like Jack did. I had never been out of China. How could I know that at home Americans dress in sloppy jeans and oversized sweatshirts? And that Canadians, who usually are better than Americans, dress just as ugly? And that at home Jack's clothes all have holes? He didn't bring his garbage clothes to China. I remember the first time I met Jack. He was wearing tight yellow pants and a purple Nehru shirt with a flowered border. Except in American movies I had never seen a man look so pretty. In those days, in 1986, Chinese women were starting to wear pretty clothes, but Chinese men all wore dark, plain, bulky clothes. Jack looked so pretty and acted so polite.

What he says about our first meeting is true. I laughed at his Chinese. I couldn't help it. I thought he was speaking English. I kept waiting for Mei to translate. Finally I caught Mei's eye and mouthed "*fanyi*." Translate. She mouthed back that he was speaking Chinese. How could I keep from laughing? He didn't get angry or upset. When I told him why I laughed, he apologised. "*Dui bu qi*," he said. They were his first Chinese words I understood. They made me feel ashamed. He apologised for my rudeness. How Chinese, I thought, even though he looked so foreign. He had tricked me already. I thought he had all the good points of a Chinese without their bad points. And he kept looking at me like I was a dish of *ma la dofu*. No Chinese man had looked at me like that in years. Later he wrote me letters I couldn't read, but Mei told me they sounded very poetic in

English. I should have known not to trust a matchmaker. Jack even cooked for me. The second time we met he cooked a big pot of spaghetti sauce. And spilled it on his pretty clothes bringing it. It was another example of his childishness. How could anyone try to carry sauce in a pot with a loose lid on a Shanghai bus? He looked so silly with that big red stain, but he acted happy, not like a man who had lost face. Now I know Americans have no face to lose, but then I thought he must be as brave as Guan Yu. Just like I thought he must be as scholarly as Mengzi.

I let Qiu persuade me to let him ride the bus home with me. We were way out at Bao Shan, at Mei's sister's apartment. It was late at night, when you could actually sit on a bus. As we sat down our bodies touched. He jumped away like a *xiaojie* in an opera. He's shy too, I thought. How sweet. Like a lovely child. Then I noticed that everyone on the bus was looking at us. One man got out of his seat so he could stand next to us. I whispered to Jack to speak English. He acted confused, innocent. Finally he spoke English, but then I couldn't understand him. Besides, I was sure the man could understand English. Much better than I could. That's why he stood next to us. I stopped talking. Soon Jack started worrying. "What's the matter? *Shenma shi?*" he kept asking in both languages. "*Mei shenma,*" I answered. Nothing. "I don't talk," I told him. He was so sad, so worried. I didn't know whether to hate him for being so stupid, not knowing what was going on around him. Or love him for being so concerned about me.

The next day I wrote Qiu and told him to stop arranging meetings. He did just what I knew he'd do. He arranged another meeting. This time Jack rode his bike all the way to Bao Shan. He learned about busses, I thought when they told me. He's strong and willing to make sacrifices for me, I thought. Tricked again. Since then I've learned a few things. Now I know that Americans like to work up a sweat when they're emotional. In Canada he splits wood when he gets upset. Another childish characteristic. But Jack's bike ride impressed Qiu too. So far as Qiu was concerned, Jack passed the love test when he arrived in Bao Shan looking like a chicken after the boiling water but before the plucking. He telephoned me at work. He told me about Jack's heroism and said I should come to Bao Shan. It was easy to get off work because the *danwei* leaders thought something terrible must have happened in my family. Why else would anyone telephone? Lucky for Jack I got to hear about his heroism without seeing or smelling him. By the time I got there they had given him a bath and found him clean clothes. So he looked clean but not as pretty as the first two times I saw him, more like an ordinary man, more attainable. His appearance gave me courage to test him too. On the phone I told Qiu again that Jack and I shouldn't meet, but Qiu knew I wouldn't come to Bao Shan if I meant that. So Qiu and I did a verbal dance. Like a Mongolian folk dance in which the dancers take turns pulling each other. We argued in *Shanghaihua*. Jack couldn't understand a word, but he kept defending my right not to see him. Maybe he doesn't care about me, I thought, but his big eyes told me that wasn't true. He loves me so much he's willing to sacrifice his love for me, I thought next. Maybe he did love me, but now I know he would have defended me the same way even if he hated me. Americans spend half their time robbing people and the other half defending people's right not to be robbed. So he tricked me again. At least this time he didn't do it on purpose. Qiu arranged for his brother-in-law to ride Jack's bike into town the next day so Jack and I could take the bus home again. People stared again, but this time I talked to him all the way.

From then on we met each other alone. We didn't need matchmakers anymore. Without Mei we couldn't say much to each other, but I didn't think we had to. I had fallen for his tricks. I thought I knew he was a prince and a scholar. The language barrier kept me from learning what he really was. He sang me "The Spring Snow" (which is an ancient song only scholars can understand). He promised me we'd live in China. But what does a Shanghai person know about snow? He took me to Canada. At first I felt like Dou E. When she was unjustly executed, it snowed in summer. In China that is unbelievable, but in the mountains of Canada it can happen. Yet Canada is not an unjust country. I am far from my family, my culture, my country, but better snow in July than blood in June. So now I'm tricking Jack. I'm becoming Canadian. Too bad Jack can't become Canadian. He tries hard, but he has a bad cultural background. As soon as he starts to write, he ends up back in the American womb he came out of. Still, I guess he loves me. Although Jack's book sometimes makes me too hot, usually his love keeps me warm. That's important in Canada. I married a lie, but a beautiful lie is better than an ugly truth. Maybe that's the moral of Jack's novel: living a lie devotedly can turn it into a fiction. A work of art.

In our beautiful Shanghai summer lie we met almost every day. In a few weeks I saw more of Jack than I saw of Huang in six years. Almost always we were alone together. We went to his room in the Jin Jiang Hotel. It was safer there. On the streets people insulted me. They called me a prostitute. I felt like a princess walking with her prince, but I also felt afraid. Walking with Jack was the only time I ever felt afraid on the streets of Shanghai. He was the first person I ever knew with a private room. Why not use it? We could do anything there.

All we did was talk. I was getting impatient, restless. Maybe my impatience and restlessness is what lets me become Canadian. Maybe I was never a good Chinese. One night when he was talking so nobly I called him my *jiushizhu*. He thought I was saying ninety nine, which is *jiushijiu*. Listening to Jack speaking Chinese is like trying to eat when you can't see the food. You never know what to expect and are always guessing about what he is trying to say. This time he paused after the second character. *Jiushi* means "ninety," but it can also mean "food and drink." So I started thinking about eating as I looked my word up in the Chinese-English dictionary. "Messiah," I read him. "Huh?" he said. I thought I had mispronounced the word. I went over to his chair to show him. He was looking for his own words in the English-Chinese dictionary. Seeing him looking so hard for the right words to understand me and help me understand his foreign ideas made me feel good, and feeling good always makes us Chinese think of eating anyway. He was wearing a dark orange shirt the color of one of the sour fruits I love to snack on. I was drooling. All over. He looked good enough to eat and I felt juicy enough to be eaten. When I pointed to "*jiushizhu*" in my dictionary and he saw I was calling him my saviour, he looked confused. He was thinking about Jesus, but I was thinking about food. "Skinny old me feels like one of ma's fat *hun dun*," I thought to myself and laughed. He thought I was laughing at his foreign ideas and laughed too. We laughed and laughed because in the middle of our laughter we both figured out we were laughing at different things, and that was funnier than what we started out laughing at. It revealed that love was more important than understanding. So when we stopped laughing, he stood up and finally kissed me. It was a silly little foreign kiss meant to be sweet, but I was revolving around like that *hun dun* in ma's hot sauce. Even the stink of his sweat, which I smelled when he came close, couldn't slow me. So I kissed him back. He can call that the meeting of revelation and revolution if he wants; I just had to teach him how to do it. Of course.

Silkworms

By Zhang Hai Bao

If you worship change, love a butterfly. But maybe you prefer a more Chinese virtue, stability. Then choose a silkworm. Chinese, who love food and silk, have loved silkworms for thousands of years. They are larvae of a small, plain, ash colored moth. Butterflies and moths are all change artists, but silkworms ("can bao bao," the peasants call them, "little darling worms") only do two things, eat lots of mulberry leaves and spin the finest, strongest thread in nature. The artistry is in the process, not the product, in the cocoon, not the butterfly.

Brief introduction

Call me angry. Well, maybe call me fool. I should know you can not teach Jack. He can not learn, so why did I try to teach him? Maybe I can not learn too. If I did not try to teach him, maybe I will not have to do what I have to do now. After I taught him to polish in my Afterwords, he polished his novel for two years. He should not polish it. It is no jewel. It is paper. He should burn it. But he polished it again, and now he is trying to publish it again. So now I must finish what I started. I must finish what Jack started. A Chinese proverb says that even a ditch is not complete without water. At least I have time. It snowed last night. Canada winter started too. I hate it, but it gives me time. My son and husband are cross country skiing. A *cun* (that is a Chinese measurement word that means 3.3 centimetres) of time is worth a *cun* of gold. Canada winter and Chinese proverbs all tell me what to do. A Chinese woman who lives in Canada should listen. When the melon is ripe, the stalk falls off. In Canada the melon is ripe in winter. The time is ripe now. The year is 2000. I will write.

What is wrong with a brief introduction? Jack always makes fun of us Chinese people for liking them, but where else should a writer start? I do not understand why Westerners are afraid of learning some thing when they read. They always want enjoyment. Or is it entertainment? I get the words confused, but they probably mean the same thing any way. It is amazing how many extra words the English language has. No wonder English speakers can not figure out how enjoyable learning is. They are too busy entertaining themselfs with their words like children playing with toys. I never had toys when I was a child, and the Chinese language does not have room for too many characters. When every character has its own strokes and shape, it becomes a individual to remember and practice. Then words become precious. That is what is wrong with a alphabet. You can stick the letters together any way you want and make as many words as you want. I heard that English has hundreds of thousands of words.

Why? The *Ci Hai* (it literally means word sea), the biggest Chinese dictionary, has fewer than 15,000 characters. English is a language of quantity, Chinese is a language of quality. The good thing is to put characters or words together. You create new ideas by putting old words together, not by making new ones. The new should grow out of the old like a meal grows out of good ingredients. When you build a building, you start from the bottom, not the top. When you write a book, you start from the beginning, not the end the way Jack does and not in the middle the way the Greeks did and Westerners still imitate. You begin at the beginning with a brief introduction and end at the ending with a good moral. Because it is important to learn from a book. Since I am writing this book, I will start by introducing myself. I am Hai Bao. And although Westerners think we Chinese are all alike, but I am unique.

When I was a child, I did not like being unique. I was unique then because I was the only child in my family. My half sister and brother were much older, and they did not live in Shanghai. All my friends had many brothers and sisters. How I wished I had one at least. How I wished to be like my friends. The one girl in Chinese families today does not feel unique because her friends are just like her. I had to leave my beloved Shanghai to find out that we were all unique. Not just me. Shanghai women. We are not like women in the rest of China and the rest of the world. In my opinion this is because of our ancestry. I am a historian, and I studied this subject. Our grandmothers were the "flowers" of Shanghai. In the late nineteenth century and the early twentieth century Shanghai, "flower" was a name given to courtesans. Courtesan society was called "Flower Country," and there were competitions in which scholars made "flower lists," then "judged the flowers." At this time there were more prostitutes in Shanghai than any other city in the world. There were hundreds of thousands of prostitutes in old Shanghai but only hundreds of flowers. Maybe you saw pictures of them. Silky women in silk *qipao* with perfect hair winding all over their perfect heads like snacks. They were famous for more than beauty. They were artists, poets, calligraphers, musicians, dancers. Their ancestor grandmothers drank wine and wrote poetry with Li Bai and other great Tang Dynasty poets and scholars. The thousand year old tradition of educated, talented courtesans died out in the rest of China when the Qing Dynasty forbid officials to contact them, but Shanghai was a international city, and the flowers kept blooming there. The best ones seldom had sex with their customers. They accompanied those who could afford them to "flower banquets," where they played music, sang, danced and wrote poetry.

When they did agree to sex, it was on their terms. And their terms were not only money. There are many stories of men who spent a fortune on a flower but never had sex with her. The flowers had much more power over their admirers than a Chinese wife had over her husband. Families chose wifes. The men themselfs chose the flowers they loved.

In 1949 liberation ended prostitution in Shanghai but not the tradition of powerful women. Today a Shanghai woman controls her family. Specially her husband. It is easy in Shanghai. Shanghai men make jokes about being hen pickled, but they expect this. They choose their wifes, and they expect their wifes to control them. They know the family will be better off with the woman in control. When a Shanghai man gets paid, he brings the money home to his wife. She decides how to spend it. And she spends it wisely. Ask any Shanghai man. When important decisions are made outside home, the man seems to make them. But you can be sure he asked his wife first and took her advice.

It is not so easy when you are not married to a Shanghai man and you do not live in Shanghai. I have to write a book. This book. It is funny. Jack fell in love with me because he thought I was a writer, and I fell in love with him because I thought he was a writer. We all thought wrong. I mean I could write, but I was not planning to, and he planned to, but he could not. Now I am going to prove he was right because he proved I was wrong. I mean if he wrote us well, I would not have to do it. But he did not, so I have to. And I have to do it in English, which maybe I can not do. Because I will not let Jack correct my English this time. I gave him a chance. I wrote what was wrong with his "novel." I gave it to him to correct. He polished my English, and he polished his novel. But he did not correct what he wrote. He still mails his novel to publishers. He learned nothing by reading. He thought I only wrote to entertain him. How characteristic. Jack has the eyesight of a rat. He can only see the food in front of his nose. When you say one thing to a Chinese, she understands three more. A American never goes past the one thing you tell him. Maybe I can not write a whole book in English, but maybe I can because Jack showed me with all his fancy writing that it is better to write simply, and for sure I will have to do that if I write in English. That is funny too. Because when I wrote in Chinese, I used to try to be fancy like Jack does in English. Maybe if he wrote in Chinese, he could write well. Except he can not because Chinese is too complicated for him to learn. But English is a more simple language even though it has more words, so maybe I can write simply in it. At least I will try. The spell cheque on my computer will help a lot, and so will all my dictionaries. But I will have to do the work. Successful things depend on the person. Or as that Chinese proverb gets translated into English, where there is a will there is a way. And I will try to make sense, which is more than Jack could do. Which also is funny because I will make him happy by making him unhappy. I mean I will make him happy because I will be writing, which is what he wanted me to do. But I will be writing because he could not, which will make him very unhappy when I prove that.

By writing so lousy Jack forced me to do what he could not do. Probably I should not write "lousy." Jack says it all the time. It is one of his favourite words, but he would never write it. It is not fancy. That is why I write it. But I think I am wrong. I think I should write "lousily." Except I never heard any one say that.

But my spell cheque says "lousily" is a word, so probably I should change it....
No. I will leave it. If I start out worrying about every word, I will end up writing
like Jack. So by using one of his favourite words, I am writing different from
him. That is one of the things he does not understand that writing can be fun if
you do not worry about every word. So I will use "lousy" and laugh at him and
his fancy words.

It looks like my writing is going to be full of contradictions. Chairman Mao
loved contradictions too. That is another contradiction. When I was in China,
I would never dare compare myself with Chairman Mao. But Chairman Mao is
gone long, and I am in Canada. I can do any thing. But I will not because I am
Chinese. Like Chairman Mao was. Maybe that is why we all like contradictions.
And maybe it is time I thought of Chairman Mao like a person, not a god. A
Chinese person. We do not believe in gods. Yet we believed Chairman Mao
was a god. Maybe Jack was right. Maybe you do learn by writing. So I will stop
laughing at him and get to it.

After all, one reason I can get it is because even though Jack can not write,
he did a lot of it. I can write a brief introduction because Jack wrote such a long
one. That is all his "novel" is. He never gets to the story. He does not think a
novel needs to tell a story. He started out saying Bissel Street and Pushan Lu
were intersected, but at the end of his novel they are still separate. We are still
separate. Maybe that is the story. Maybe not. I will tell it and you decide. I know
I should just tell the story, but I know I can not. In his writing Jack always misses
the sharp point. He can not get past himself, and I can not stand that. I have to
correct him. Almost the first thing Qiu told him about me was that I was chaste.
Once Jack figured out what *zhenjie* meant, he laughed and replied he was too old
for chastity. The point is so was I.

The point is that if our story must be told, it must be told fully. Jack taught
me a lot by taking me around China and North America even if he did not learn
himself. I do not know if he did not learn because he is a man or because he is a
American. Maybe all of them. But travelling is useful. He took me to many places
I would not go to without him. Shanghai people usually do not like to travel.
We like our own city too much. We know that travelling is uncomfortable, and
we do not like to be uncomfortable. We know that what we will learn by going
to other places is that Shanghai is the best place. I learned that by travelling, but
I learned other things too. So I will write them too, and Jack will help me write
true. When we were travelling, he wrote all the time. His novel proves that Jack
can not write, but his diaries will help me remember. And using them means I
will not have to write so much myself. Even when Jack is wrong or writes badly,
what he wrote will let me tell well. Tell like it was. Maybe some times I can say my
words into a tape recorder. Then write them down. Because I say better than I
write. But I write not bad now. Even in English. I am sorry if it sounds like I am
bragging, but it is true. Do not believe the mistakes Jack put in my mouth in his

novel. Since many years I do not talk like that. When we first married, Jack and I talked in our own language, Chinglish. It was not beautiful, but it worked. It was funny. We laughed. Jack wanted us to write a Chinglish book together, but how can you write in a language of mistakes? Now we speak English because I learned his language much better than he learned mine. Oh, once in a while I still mix up words. Yesterday I told Jack the buffalo was broken. "What?" he asked. "The buffalo," I repeated. He still could not figure it out. "On the car," I told him. "The buffalo on the car?" I had to take him out and show him. It turned out it was the muffler. He should be able to figure that out. It is a obvious mistake to make. The words all have a lot of fs and a l in the middle, and that is unusual. And you can see why I would say "buffalo." You can not eat a muffler. So maybe I will make a few mistakes when I write. They will be the soy source that adds spice to the writing. Because I am going to write the book Jack should write. In English.

Shanghai

Two women pushed into an artist's studio where two men and a woman awaited them. It was a tight squeeze. The room must have been crowded when the artist worked alone in it. An easel was jammed behind the desk, but where would it fit when the artist wanted to paint at it? Yet paint he obviously did since the room was strewn with artwork: stylized Chinese folk drawings of oversimple trees, oversimple houses, oversimple people wedged between huge, pretentious Western inspired abstract paintings. No middle ground in this mini middle kingdom, nothing combining styles.

Two women squeezed into a tiny studio. Two cultures met alongside paintings in which cultures did not meet. The first woman was striking – tall, expensively dressed and made up – while the second woman was of average height and wore simple cotton dungarees, a checked cotton blouse and no make up. She might have been any ordinary worker, but she was so extraordinary to me that I missed the introductions and spent the first minutes assuming I had fallen in love with the wrong woman, for surely the woman who had dressed up to meet me was the one intended for me. Then the unstriking woman, the one I had been struck by, laughed. She laughed at my Chinese, and I knew that she had been told about me as I had been about her. Mao was in his Marxist heaven, and all was right in the world.

Jack wrote that on June 10, 1986. Three days after we met for the first time. He was already making me myth. On June 8 he wrote facts, but by June 10 he was starting his novel. And as usual he wrote it wrong. Qiu's studio was not a mini middle kingdom. A foreigner would not be there if it was. It was a mini Shanghai. I saw it right away. The tiny room, the squeezed people, the contrast of poor and rich, the mixture of cultures that do not mix. That is what Shanghai is. That is why Jack fell in love with Shanghai. That is why he fell in love with me.

I did not know he fell in love with me, and I certainly did not expect to fall in love with him. For weeks before we met my friend Qiu and his wife Mei flattered him to me. *Pai mapi*, we say in Chinese, pat the horse's ass. But I did not want to pat a horse's ass or a foreigner's, and I did not want him to pat mine. Why should a foreigner be interested in me? And why should I be interested in a foreigner? I did not come the first time they wanted me to meet him, so this time they sent Peng to drag me down into the water. They did not need to. Meeting him seemed silly, but asking me the second time showed they were serious. Peng and I walked up *Gonghe Xin Lu*, New Republic Road, the main street in our neighbourhood, to Qiu's school. But I walked home alone down the little lanes. Later Jack told me he looked for me after I left Qiu's school. He could not find me. Without me he could not find the real Shanghai either because he only knew the streets, not the little lanes. That is where I live. That is where Shanghai lives. In narrow back ways that curl like snacks. They are older than the streets and not made for cars. Some of them are even made of hobble stones like they used to use when there were horses. In a few weeks the lanes would be crowded with people sleeping outside, some breathing deeply or snoring, some chattering from bamboo bed to bamboo bed. But now was before the seasons of heat, and the lanes were quiet. Only a few walkers like me. It was the season when the grain fills, a time of small rains. Every thing was damp, and the air was misty and kind of glowing. I looked up and saw the reason for the glow, a crescent moon squeaking between the clouds. All of a sudden I was not sure of myself. I felt misty too. The crescent moon does not have a good reputation in China. Lao She wrote a story about a woman who has a disaster every time she sees the crescent moon. She becomes a prostitute and ends up in jail. But the world seemed *weiguang,* "glistening" says my dictionary. The walls around me, the stones in the lane, the buildings which looked so lousy in the daylight were all glistening. Shanghai was glistening. I did not want to be like the woman in Lao She's story, but I did not want to be like Du Li Niang either. In the opera *Mudan Ting* (Peony Pavilion) she watched the moon set and died. She had to go through hell to find love. I followed the moon home singing one of her songs from when she was young and her world was misty like mine.

I did not think about the foreigner as I walked home singing through those glistening lanes underneath that crescent moon. I thought about Shanghai and how I loved it. Every one has ideas about what makes Shanghai unique. To foreigners I think Shanghai is mainly a idea, a thing to use for some purpose, not live in. The British had the first idea. They wanted to use it as a port at the end of China's Long River. At that time, right after the first Opium War, it was just a fishing village. We Chinese did not need a port. We did not need to trade with countries on the other side of the ocean. Soon European capitalists arrived. Their idea was to use Shanghai to get rich. That was a popular idea. Chinese merchants wanted to get rich too. They came from Ningbo and other near places to open factories and stores. Peasants left the countryside to come to the new city to get rich. Once lots of new people got to Shanghai, new ideas started from extraterritoriality to extra brothels which made Shanghai a extraordinary

mixture of extravagant ideas and cultures and people. I could not find any more
"extra" words in the dictionary, but that last sentence is one Jack would be proud
of. It shows I can write fancy in English if I want to. But I do not want to. The
sharp point I am trying to make is that Shanghai grew up too fast for any idea.
So many people came so fast from so many places that no idea or person could
control it. Any thing could happen in Shanghai. It grew up in seven disorders,
eight messes. It grew up in a confusion of people and cultures, prostitutes and
princesses, busy streets and narrow lanes, ancient walls and modern skyscrapers.
Its contradictions gave it its life. The mixture that did not mix made it a unique
place. That is what I thought then. Now I would say a unique place full of
unique women.

Some times I wonder now if I thought about Shanghai then because I
knew I would have to leave it if I married a foreigner. Usually you do not think
about what you take for granted, and I lived in Shanghai all my life. I never
expected to live any where else. At that time Canada seemed farther away than
the crescent moon. I could see the moon. I could not even imagine Canada.
How could I imagine a completely white world of snow like the one outside
my window now? The only thing I knew about Canada was Beiquan, the most
famous Canada person in China. I think just meeting a foreigner and talking
about foreign places made me think about my place, Shanghai. How could I take
the foreigner seriously? How can you be serious about some one you can not talk
to? I could not understand what he said in English or Chinese. Once he tried to
answer one of my questions, but Mei shook her head and explained in English
what I said. From then on Mei translated for us. You would know I did not take
the foreigner seriously if you could hear the questions I asked him. I asked him
every silly question about every silly story or propaganda about foreigners I ever
heard. I did not expect to see him again. Why not open some of his holes to fill
in the holes in my knowledge of foreigners? I asked him about foreigners' eyes
and noses and body hairs. I asked him if it was true that foreigners went out in
the sun and showed him that the skin on my arm was whiter than the skin on his
arm. I was proud of that. I asked him if dogs really were allowed in foreign cities.
When he said yes, I asked Peng if she thought that was why Chinese capitalists
used to be called running dogs. Qiu said he was very generous, so I asked him
why he was not greedy like most foreigners. The only questions I did not ask
him were about sex. Foreigners were supposed to be very strong in bed. And you
can be sure that I smelled him. Maybe he took a shower before he came, and
the weather was not hot because he did not stink. Or maybe I was afraid to get
close enough to get a good sniffle. The funny thing is that all my silly questions,
which should make it impossible for any one to take me seriously, were just what
impressed him. In his diary he says I was very lively and funny. Maybe I was.
Maybe before he was so bored by Chinese seriousness that he fell in love with me
because I was not serious. But why was he serious then? Love is not a joke. Can

you be serious about not being serious? The answer is yes. If you are American.

May 24, 1986

Walking the streets of Shanghai makes me sad. The people exude life and look good without all the layers of winter clothes, but the effect is not so wonderful as two years ago. The reason is simple: all the makeup and attempts at "fashion." People are well on the road to becoming as stupid and ugly looking as Westerners. Why? The question could be asked about so many things. This was a wonderfully sensible society two years ago. With every day it becomes less so. The authorities have decided to take the capitalist road into the consumer society. Everywhere people are exhorted to consume and units to make profits. It isn't as bad as the West yet, but no doubt it soon will be because ordinary people are following the new mandate of heaven as unthinkingly as they once followed Mao's opposite mandates. Damn. Mandates are supposed to come "from the people to the people," not from heaven to the government to the people for the government. Even now the mandate of government is disguised under the all embracing word "reform." Can this society still be called socialist? Usually I think so, but I keep having more and more doubts. Am I falling out of love with China? I fear I may as Chinese become more and more avid to become unchinese, Western.

I think "avid" means serious. You see. The foreigner could take me seriously when I was not serious because I was a Chinese who was not avid to become unchinese. I did not wear the Western fashion clothes like Peng that he hated. He could take me away from Shanghai because I loved Shanghai and he loved Shanghai and he loved me because I was Shanghai. He could take me to the West because I was unwestern. The amazing thing is that I came to take such a unserious man seriously. I told you I liked contradictions. And apparently I was as contradictory as he was. According to Jack's diary when he asked me why I write, I replied, "To show up the backwardness of China compared to the more advanced countries." Did I really say that? Did I really think that the foreigner's land of ice and snow was more advanced than my beloved Shanghai, my land of fish and rice? Showing up the backwardness of China was the very fashionable idea at that time. Among writers it replaced Mao's idea that literature should educate and unify the masses. Mao wanted to make the masses one mass, but after he died, writers wrote about a mess. They did not dare to say that Mao made the mess, but they showed what a mess the masses were in. I was not a real writer, and I did not really believe every thing the writers wrote, but probably I did not know how to answer the foreigner's question. I maybe said what I said because I thought the foreigner would like it. He did not and Qiu knew that he did not. I got a long lecture from Qiu about how the foreigner loved China and I must not say things like that to him. Qiu loved to explain the foreigner's ideas to me. He did it in *Shanghaihua*, so the foreigner could not understand what mistakes he was saying.

Jack often thought about me after our first meeting. He thought about me at strange times when he should not think about me. I know that from reading his diaries. He wrote about me six times in ten days between our first and second meeting.

June 15

Last night I went to a new old Chinese opera gala, Kun opera, four 400 year old excerpts performed for the first time in many years, perhaps since Liberation, certainly since before the Cultural Revolution. My favorite excerpt dealt with a prostitute luring a student into marriage. As could have been predicted I turned it into a soap opera. I pictured myself as the naive student. If only I could figure out how to lure Z into luring me into marriage. The proper technique, according to the opera, is to act as rich and unknowing as possible. Well, I should be able to handle the unknowing part. The problem is that Z really is the innocent the prostitute pretended to be. The blind leading the blind, the unknowing lured by the unknowing. In the least innocent city of the least innocent country I know. I had a lesson in Chinese lack of innocence going to the opera. The student who had invited me to the opera insisted that I bike to the theatre (at Ruijin and Yanan Lu, easy walking distance) while she took the bus. However, her younger colleague (about Z's age, I hope) rode with me and laughed at her friend's fears. I'm still not sure of the reasons for either the one's caution or the other's lack of it.

I was from a different generation from the Shanghai people who grew up with foreigners around them. By the time I was born, most of the foreigners were gone. Even the White Russians, who grew up in Shanghai. They spoke perfect *Shanghaihua* and were Shanghai people in every way but the shape of their eyes and nose and the colour of their skin and hairs. They were gone too before I could remember seeing one. But I heard many stories about foreigners, and I encountered them. Twice. Once was at Number One Department Store. A American basketball team was visiting Shanghai. They came as a group to shop. I did not get close to them. I could not get close to them if I wanted to. I did not want to. They were surrounded by ass patters and starers. No wonder. I stared too. They were giants, not men. Some of them were wearing sandals, and a woman in front of me said to her friend, "Look, their toes are the same as ours." I was amazed to hear that. I remember thinking that if the valleys of their minds were as broad as the mountains of their bodies were high, maybe they really were the future. Many Shanghai people thought they were. The ass patters thought they were. But I did not believe that. Most of them were black, and I already had another encounter with a black foreigner. It happened at Tongzhi, Huang's school, which had many African students. I went with Huang to a movie. During the movie I needed to pee, so I went outside to the women's toilet. It was a typical Chinese toilet. No seats or bowls. You put one foot on each side of a concrete channel and squatted. There were wood petitions all along the long channel so you could not see who was squatting there, but the wood did not go down to the floor. That was to let the smell out. The channels were not often flushed, and they stanked. Without the opening the smell would have been unbearable. Even after more than ten years in Canada I still have bad dreams about the smell of Chinese toilets. And the long lines of bare bottoms sticking out under the wood when the toilets were crowded. But tonight every one was watching the movie. I was alone. Some one came in after I squatted, but I could not see who. I just finished peeing when a hand reached under me and grabbed my vagina. I screamed and jumped up. The hand pulled back, but I saw it. It was black. By the time I got to the door of the toilet, the man it belonged to was far off and running. I am sure it was a African.

So I did not think foreigners were the future. But I was worried about becoming the past. I was thirty two years old. Shanghai women may be unique, but the flowers were all picked. We are Chinese too. A Chinese woman can not live a full life if she is not married. So I let Qiu and Mei talk me into meeting the foreigner again.

June 14

Too long. It's now a week since I've seen Z. Immediately afterwards I had no doubts. Now I am beset with them. Inevitable under the circumstances. After my run around her neighborhood on Sunday (the day after I met her), I resolved to return often, by bike when I could not run. Altho I didn't find her on Sunday and didn't expect to find her subsequently, returning was an act of faith in her, one I have been unable to keep. Now that I want to be alone with my fantasies, I have suddenly become busy: Mon. and Tues. nights students, Wed. the afternoon discussion group stayed on into evening, Thurs. pouring rain, Fri. a student invited me to his house, Sat. (tonight) other students have invited me to a Kun opera. Also Qiu keeps changing the time and place of the next meeting. Now it has been put off until Mon. in some out of the way industrial suburb famous only for its steel mill. How romantic. I am worried that it may not come off at all. No Kun operas, only soap operas in my head. Are any of them real?

No, I would want to answer then. I would want to burst his soap bubbles. But a few days later the soap opera became a real opera. He loaned me his umbrella.

We met at Mei's sister's home in Baoshan, north of Shanghai. It took me a hour to get there, and I lived on the north side of the city. The foreigner lived farther south. I only had to change busses once. He had to change twice. He wanted to impress me with his cooking, but it was not clever of him to carry a full pot of spaghetti source on three crowded busses. The pot had a loose lid. He arrived in Baoshan, his precious pot in one hand, his umbrella in the other hand, a big red stain in his middle. In the worst possible place on his light yellow pants. He looked like his period came suddenly. And his shirt. He was wearing a bright shirt whose whole front was a huge wild cat face. Mei's seven year old niece took one look and hid behind her mother. I wanted to laugh and cry at the same time. But I did not. I could not laugh like I did the first time we met. I had to be polite. The man I could not take seriously was serious now because he came to see me the second time. I stalled and did a lot to make his second coming difficult, but he came over my obstacles. He came a long way. He was serious. The unserious way he looked and the unserious way he talked could not change that. Besides, the more I looked at him and the more I listened to him, the more I started to understand that Americans could be serious when they were not serious. At least when they did not seem serious to a Chinese.

Stared at by ten pairs of eyes and pointed at by the fingers of ten people, the foreigner pointed at the mulberry while attacking the locust. He concentrated himself on the little girl. She told her mother it was a *meng lao hu*, a fierce tiger. He said clearly enough for every one to understand, *"Bu shi lao hu, shi qing bao"* (is not tiger, is green leopard). *"Qing bao?"* several people asked. His words made no sense. The spotted cat on his shirt was yellow and brown. He tried to explain in Chinese, but no one could figure out what he meant. Finally he told Mei in English. *Qing bao,* she explained to us laughing, was supposed to be the opposite of *lao hu.* In Chinese a tiger is called a *lao hu,* and *lao* usually does mean old. But *lao hu* does not mean old tiger. It just means tiger. And *qing bao* does not mean young leopard, I explained when I figured out what he was trying to say. You would have to say *qingnian de bao.* *"Bu yao shuo qingnian de bao,"* he insisted, *"tai* clumsy." *"Benzhuo,"* Mei quickly translated. She and the foreigner talked and she consulted her English-Chinese dictionary. That would destroy the parallelism of the words, she announced, laughing harder. He demands *qing bao.* You just could not do what he wanted to do in Chinese. Most of us tried to tell him that. Why not? Qiu asked suddenly. Qiu always took the foreigner's side. Qiu was in my writing class for a year and never wrote any thing. He talked about writing great philosophical novels, but he never produced even one unphilosophical sentence. He had talent as a painter but no knowledge of language. He was willing to turn Chinese into English if the foreigner wanted to. Not knowing what he was talking about never slowed Qiu down. He was talking away and the rest of us were arguing with him and Mei was translating to the foreigner and for him and the foreigner was telling her things that were different from what Qiu was saying he was saying and she was trying not to laugh and to tell him and to tell us. Six players were trying to play ping pong at the same table with another player who had to keep switching sides and bumping into all the others. The only watcher, the little girl, was jumping up and down with excitement. The foreigner kept making funny faces to attract her.

The crazy ping pong match went on for a long time. After a while I stopped playing and started listening. Comparing what the foreigner was saying with what Qiu was saying made me realize that the foreigner understood language even if he did not understand Chinese. You could not take what he was saying seriously, and he did not seem to take it or himself seriously. Yet we ended up having a serious talk about what you could and could not say and should and should not be able to say in Chinese and English. The match ended when Mei, who was very pregnant, collided into a chair with laughter. Soon every one was laughing and sitting down. And the little girl was sitting in the foreigner's lap, touching his cat shirt with careful fingers. I was told that the other time they met, she touched his beard the same way.

This is when we had the serious discussion. I had to admit that classical Chinese, which was more concise and poetic than modern Chinese, was closer to the foreigner's ideas of what Chinese should be. You still could not say *qing bao*, but you could leave out the *de* in *qingnian de bao*. The foreigner said that in English there were more words. You could use them to make phrases parallel and lines rhythmical. I realized that rhythm was built into Chinese and told him about classical poems composed entirely of one syllabus. By always changing that syllabus's tones, meaning was created. So meaning grows more out of rhythm in Chinese and more out of words in English. We reached this conclusion at the same time in different languages. By this time the foreigner and I were talking with Mei translating and the others listening. Until Mei's sister asked what was supposed to be done with the foreigner's pot. He and the little girl went to the kitchen to help prepare the food. Unsubtle Qiu said to me I told you you would like him.

But I did not like his spaghetti. Which is strange because now spaghetti is my favourite Western food. Maybe it was too strange the first time. Maybe every thing was too strange. Maybe I still could not stomach the foreigner's strange appearance and stranger ideas. Because it was his food and not like Chinese food, I could not stomach his spaghetti either. The foreigner tried to make his food less strange by telling a story about how Make Poluo brought the noodles from China to Italy and now he was bringing the source to China. I was the one who figured out that the man he was calling Marco Polo was Make Poluo. Maybe that was because I studied history. But some thing really happened between the first and second time we met. I was beginning to understand the foreigner's Chinese. Mei still translated my Chinese into English and his Chinese into Chinese, but some times I understood him before she translated.

June 17

Yesterday a lovely day with Z at Baoshan, but at the end something happened. We took the bus back together and were alone for the first time. Alone on a Shanghai bus: ha! I think that is mainly what happened, Z's sudden realization of others. Yet late at night busses are less crowded and we actually got seats, the little single seats. I sat behind and Z sat in front of me, turned sideways so we could converse. It was a good arrangement: I could feast my eyes on her profile, and she didn't have to look at me. At first we chatted quite freely, full of mistakes and misunderstandings but laughing at them as we must.

Then suddenly she grew quiet and I felt her near tears. I don't think it was anything I said, but who knows? I might easily have said something which had the wrong connotations in Chinese. When she grew silent her face grew puffy and I felt fear in her. It happened right after a man standing beside us addressed me in English, asking the usual "practicing my English" questions, I think two, where am I from and where was I going. I answered in Chinese, as curtly as possible. I think he got the idea that I didn't want to talk to him, but surely standing there listening he must have known this before he spoke. Was his speaking intended as a warning to Z? I have no idea, but perhaps she took it as one or perhaps it simply reminded her of her circumstances, crashed her back to earth. (I am assuming she had been in heaven with me.) I whispered to her "bie zhaozhi" and she laughed, but her laugh was no longer carefree. I then felt a lengthy (a couple of minutes) struggle to master her emotions, a struggle she mainly won. But things were not the same thereafter. I wanted excruciatingly to put my arm around her or at least touch her, offer her some kind of physical reassurance, but I thought – and still do – that would probably have been the worst thing I could do. She might even have jumped. We did touch getting on the bus, and she did jump altho later, on the second bus, on which we sat side by side, we were inevitably thrown together occasionally by the lurchings of the bus and she handled that.

I was proud of the way she struggled with herself, but I suspect things will never be innocent again. Doubtless this was inevitable at some point, and perhaps it will lead to a deepening of whatever is between us – if it does not end it. On the bus she tried to switch to English, pulled out her textbook and tried to find words in the dark bus. She has only studied English a year and so had insurmountable difficulties, but how she tried! Again it made me proud of her even if it was not a fully rational effort: one man had already shown he could understand English better than she, and even without knowing English anyone with brains who looked at us – and needless to say everyone stared – could surely tell more or less what was going on. It goes without saying that the conversation became even more disjointed once she decided to use English. At first I continued mainly in Chinese. I didn't fully comprehend what was going on. Eventually she told me to speak English and why, but for us to function in English is even more difficult than in Chinese. We did manage a few laughs over our predicament but not so many as before. She told me her family and home were very poor and I tried to tell her I couldn't care less, that writers were supposed to be poor and live in garrets if they were serious about writing. I wanted to say so much and was able to say so little. For her, speaking English doubtless for the first time in her life, it must have been even more frustrating. Both the strength of her efforts and the depth of her problems were clear even if I couldn't understand well the sources of her strength or of her problems. Are they just the inescapable problems of a 34 year old Chinese virgin or do they go deeper? Time will tell, but I am willing to do my part fighting them, whether they be cultural, familial or mental. She wavered long and waveringly on whether we should meet alone. Some of the difficulties may have been language difficulties but surely not all. In the end she agreed. Hooray!!!

Maybe she only agreed to meet me to return my umbrella. Qiu had told me to walk her home, which seemed an excellent idea as it was raining and I had the only umbrella;

however, she said clearly that she did not want her "friends" (the word she knew and therefore used; no doubt she meant her neighbors and people in general) to see us together. Given the reality of Chinese gossip, I certainly did not blame her, but if we go on the gossip is inevitable, and she is the one who will have to bear it, not me. I wanted to see her home, she wanted me to stay on the bus. In the end I had to get off with her at her stop before she would even accept a compromise, my umbrella. Waiting at her busstop for the next bus and walking home in the rain from my busstop did nothing to cool my ardor.

In his diary Jack says no thing about the long, nice day we had at Baoshan. But he says even more than this about the bus ride home. I cut out a lot of what he wrote. Maybe I will let him write mostly about the bad parts and I will write mostly about the good parts. That would be funny. In our marriage he always jumps happily into new messes and I try to be careful. But this time was different. Jack already jumped. (Just like he jumped on the bus. He jumped when we touched, not me like he says.) He wanted to marry me. So he only worried about problems. I still did not believe it was possible. So maybe I looked for good things that might make it possible.

I was feeling happy when we got on the bus in Baoshan. We continued our discussion about language and about differences between Chinese and English. He had a theory about Chinese, but all I could figure out was that he wanted Chinese to be English. He thought Chinese needed many new words. He wanted to make them by combining *zi*. *Zi* are Chinese characters, one syllabus each. Most words are made up from two or more *zi*, but many *zi* can stand alone. I asked him why he wanted to create so many new words. We Chinese do fine with the words we have. He had to think a long time, searching for a few words he knew. I told him that the more words we had the more he would have to learn. His theory was against his interest. At first he did not get my joke. It was the first time I tried to make one. Then he laughed. And I laughed with him. Then he said what he could say with the words he could think of. He said that words are gifts from heaven for writers. New words create new ideas and new ideas create new words. It is a circle that keeps growing bigger. He did not know the word for circle, but he made the shape with his hand and I told him. We laughed again. Chinese like circles, he told me. He said that because he wanted to use his new word again. I told him that Chinese liked cycles, not circles. That confused him. I tried to explain, but he never did figure it out. We laughed at that too. We laughed at what we understood, and we laughed at what we did not understand. I was really starting to like him. It was nice to be able to laugh when you were being serious. I asked him how he would create the new words and he gave me a example. He told me a story about buying gloves and calling them *shougai*. I told him there was no such word. Gloves are *shoutao*. He said he knew that now, but when he asked for *shougai* the shop assistant knew what he meant. We laughed, but he was laughing because he thought he succeeded.

I was laughing because I knew the shop assistant only understood because he was a foreigner, and I knew she was surely laughing at him and would tell all her friends about his mistake. I did not tell him he lost his face. I wondered if he would care. I was glad it was dark and no one could see the stain on his pants. But he never seemed to care that he lost his face about that. I explained that *gai* and *tao* all meant cover, but *gai* was only for hard covers like pot lids or turtle shells. He was not interested in my explanations. He said it did not matter that his word was wrong. What mattered was that he was understood. That proved that his idea would work. People would recognize the new words. The Chinese language worked the way he said it did. He was becoming excited. He said that being a foreigner gave him prospective on Chinese that native speakers did not have. Of course he did not know the Chinese word for "prospective." He struggled with many words and made many gestures with his hands. Maybe that is what attracted attention, but probably it was just that he was a foreigner and I was not. A man got out of his seat and came to stand by us. He wanted to hear what we were saying. I quickly told the foreigner to speak English. At first he did not want to, but when he did, I could not understand him. I was trying to read my English text in the dark bus to find words when the man asked the foreigner a question. In English. He knew English better than I did. It was hopeless. The whole idea of the foreigner and me was hopeless. I wanted to cry. Even before the man asked me if the foreigner understood *Shanghaihua*. I did not answer. Then he gave me a lecture. Why does not Jack mention the lecture in his diary? Could I imagine it? Could it be my own mind that was lecturing me? Every one who saw me with the foreigner wanted to give me the same lecture. The man on the bus spoke very soft and fast to make it hard for the foreigner to understand even if he did know a little *Shanghaihua*. He told me to be very careful. He told me I should not be alone with a foreigner, specially at night. He told me not to trust foreigners. He told me that with Deng Xiao Ping's opening policy there would be more and more foreigners in China. He told me they had no morals. He told me he knew several women who were ruined by foreigners. I did not say any thing. After I heard the lecture a few times, I was amazed how many people knew women who were ruined by foreigners. Until I met Mei I do not think I ever met any one who ever met a foreigner.

As Jack said, Qiu told him to walk me home from the bus stop. Qiu knew that if we were seen together by my neighbours, I would almost have to marry him. I could not allow that. I did not want his umbrella, but it was much better than him. When he first tried to give me the umbrella, I looked at him in the dark bus. Any Chinese man would know the symbolism of loaning a umbrella. In a famous scene in *The White Snack* Xu Xian loans Bai Suzhen his umbrella and they fall in love. The foreigner did not know what he was doing. But he did it, and *The White Snack* is my favourite Beijing opera. When I got home, my face which was protected from the rain by his umbrella was wet. I was singing the song where Bai Suzhen's sings of her love. It is very sentimental. She and her sister, the green snack, are immortals and know that marrying a mortal man will lead to disaster. But she does it.

June 20

Big rain. Area north of Jin Jiang awash, courtyards flooded. Impossible to walk to my usual restaurants: even four hours after the rain stopped Changle Lu and Rui Jin Lu impassable without hip waders.

Supposed to meet Z tonight. Will get there even if I have to hire a boat. Received a chain letter – is nothing sacred to be left in China? – telling me I would have good luck if I mailed out twenty copies and bad luck if not. I must be in love because I was tempted. But in the end I didn't send it, so I know who to blame if everything kaput.

We met at the People's Park. It was a good place to meet, it was a bad place to meet. You pay five *fen* to enter. That is almost nothing, but it is very enough to keep many crowds out. You enter off Nanjing Lu, the busy city's busiest, noisiest street. You enter and you are in peace. Peaceful beauty, not wild beauty like in Canada. Trees but no forests, flowers but no thorns, grass without weeds, people, not animals. The beautiful park always seemed like the safest place in my safe city, yet I was never attacked by a animal in Canada. The people in the People's Park all looked at the foreigner and me. First a glance, then a stare. People were staring at me the way I once stared at the basketball players in Number One Department Store on Nanjing Lu. But they were mountains with legs. They were used to being stared at. I was not. Some people were just curious, but some did not want to live under the same sky as me. These ones made soft comments like claws to me or loud comments with teeth to the person they were talking to. It was terrible. The foreigner walked next to me, happy in the peaceful park. He noticed no thing. He was used to being stared at too. He wanted to sit down. At first I did not. Sitting would make it too easy for people to stare. A moving couple could only gather glances. But as we walked, I began to see that the more we walked the more people could see us. They did not need more than one glance.

As we walked, we talked of what was becoming our one subject, our two languages. I tried to talk in English, and the foreigner tried to talk in Chinese. I had my English text to help me, and he had two big dictionaries, one English-Chinese, one Chinese-English. I felt sorry for him. The dictionaries looked very heavy, and he could not use them while we were walking. We talked and laughed when we did not understand each other. Until I noticed that laughing made people notice us and comment more. Since we met the last time, the foreigner was thinking about what we said at Baoshan and in the bus. He also went to a Kun opera. At Chinese operas the words are flashed on the side with a magic lantern. The foreigner thought that showed how important words were to Chinese. He said that at Western opera most people did not try to follow the words. They came for the music, not the massage. I said that the music was in the massage. It grew out of the words. He said that in the West words were usually written for music, not music for words. Trying to say that was too complicated for his Chinese. Say that again, I asked. We laughed. Did you hear that prostitution started up again? a man passing by remarked to his friend. It does not matter, the foreigner said when I did not reply to his explanation. I do not think much about opera, I told him. I just like it and I like to sing it. He asked if I could sing Kun opera. Of course, I told him. Although of course I can not sing it well. That takes years of study. I can not sing at all, he told me. But you always think about it, I said. I am a singer, you are a thinker, I said, and we laughed. Probably he was laughing because probably what I said was "I sing person, you think person." But he understood me, and I laughed with him. Japanese pay prostitutes more than Europeans, another passing man remarked. Let us sit down, I said.

We sat at one of the little stone tables usually used by chess players. I chose a table where a man and a woman were already sitting. I did not want to sit with others, but I also did not want people to think we were trying to be alone. The two at our table were young lovers. They were not interested in us. In his diary Jack says I was nervous. He thought I was nervous of him. No, it was all the people staring. I kept trying not to see them, but I could not. I could not not see them looking at me or I did see them or whatever you are supposed to say in English. *"Nande hutu,"* I thought. What does that mean? the foreigner asked. Accidentally I said it out loud. I chequed my text, but I could not find it. I asked to use his dictionary. That is when I realized he brought the Chinese-English dictionary for me. How polite. "It is hard to be stupid," I told him. It seems easy to me, he said and laughed. I did not. "A Qing Dynasty poet said that," I told him. I was understanding it for the first time. It is hard when you do not know some thing. But it is even harder to act stupid when you already know some thing. I could not pretend that heaven and earth did not turn over. I knew I was not nervous of the foreigner. I was nervous of the Chinese.

Slowly the sky we were all under grew darker. It became harder for people to see us and for me to see them. Slowly I became less nervous. Maybe the foreigner did too. For sure he became more comfortable because he could put his heavy dictionaries on the table.

I wanted to keep talking about language and opera. How nice to talk like scholars relaxing after the imperial examination. How long since I could talk that way. It seemed like we could not go deep because of the language problem, but in a way that dug us deeper. I mean our problems showed differences in our languages, and that was what we were trying to understand. And maybe the way we solved our problems would lead us toward answers. But that way was undirect, and undirect is unamerican, I know now. After we sat down, the foreigner wanted to tell me about himself. Westerners love to confess. No Chinese man would ever want to tell the things Jack wanted to tell me. I wonder if that is one reason why Westerners need so many words in their language and so many melodies in their operas. They need to say and sing what we Chinese only hint. They need to make themselfs different. Why? We know every person is different. That is why we try to act similar.

The foreigner asked me if I knew he was from Chicago. "What is that?" I asked him. He told me it was a American city, but I still did not understand. He looked in the dictionary, but before he found the word, I figured it out. "I know," I said happily, "Zhijiage." He found the word and showed me the dictionary. "Yes. I was right," I told him. He said he was born and raised up in Chicago. "Ah," I said. I thought he was from Canada. He asked if that scared me. "Why?" I asked him. Very many people are afraid of Chicago, he told me. "Why?" I asked again. I was feeling proud. I was talking in English without having to use a book. He told me about a Japanese friend he had when he was a student. He invited his friend to his house, but the Japanese did not want to go to Chicago because he was afraid he would be killed by gangsters. We had trouble with that word. "Bang, bang," he said, pronouncing the American way, then *"bang,"* the Chinese way. He was trying to combine the sound a gun makes with *bang*, the Chinese word for gang, which he knew because he knew *si ren bang*, the Gang of Four. I laughed and laughed when he looked up "gangster" in the dictionary and I found out he meant *liumang*. I am not afraid of Zhijiage or gangsters, I told him. I am afraid of Japanese. In China we did not hear that Zhijiage was worse than other American cities. We were taught that all American cities were bad, violent places, but we knew this was propaganda. The Japanese invaded China. The terrible things they did were much more than propaganda. All my life I have nightmares about being chased by Japanese soldiers. We all hated the Japanese, not the Americans who fought them too. When I figured out that the foreigner thought I might be afraid of him because he was from Zhijiage, I laughed more. Foreigners are like children, I thought. They do not know much, but they say funny things.

So he told me about Chicago in the 1960s. I was surprised. I did not know much too. "Zhijiage too had *wenhua da geming?*" I asked after a while. It sounded as bad as China. We did not call it a cultural revolution, he told me, but maybe that is what it was. He told me that in Chicago he and his friends thought China's Cultural Revolution was good. They thought Chicago was much worse than China. I was so surprised I stopped talking English. I thought we were misunderstanding each other. How can a advanced country like America have a cultural revolution? I asked. He did not know *xianjinde*, so I said *zibenjia*, capitalist, instead of advanced. "*Zibenzhuyi?*" (capitalism), he asked. He knew that word. Capitalism is the cause of it, he said. He looked in his dictionary. Capitalism is the problem, not the solution, he said. He sounded like a Party secretary.

Communism is a problem too, I told him. I was still talking in Chinese, but suddenly I remembered a sentence I practised with Mei. Yesterday I went to see Qiu and Mei. "The Communist Party wants to be feudal father to the country," I said. He looked at me. Then English words flowed out like a flood. Then he saw I could not understand. We all laughed, and he changed back to Chinese. He asked me to explain, so I told him about feudalicism and the family in China. It was difficult. We had to look up many words. In the almost dark. I looked in the Chinese-English dictionary, and he looked in the English-Chinese dictionary. Since then that is the way we talked. He was interested in Chinese history and culture. I liked that. But I also liked to hear about Zhijiage's cultural revolution. That was new and interesting. I knew that if I was younger, maybe I would not risk being interested. Interesting people are like interesting times. They can be a curse. China just came out from the curse of a interesting time. If my future did not look so dull, would I be interested in this interesting foreigner?

By now it was dark, and I forgot about the people staring. Well, maybe I never completely forgot about them. Maybe one of the things wrong with us Chinese is that we never can forget about others. Maybe it comes from living too close to too many people for too long. In fact that is one of the things I was trying to explain to the foreigner, what it was like to live in such a crowded country with such a crowded history. That is a nice sentence, is not it? I can feel my English writing improving. But maybe I am wrong. I thought my English speaking was improving in the People's Park too. We talked a lot about history. He told me the United States and Canada were only two hundred years old. I told him that was why Americans did not understand history well. They had so little. He said some times that was a good thing. Maybe Chinese some times had trouble understanding the modern world because they thought too much about ancient history. That is how I found out about his age. He said he knew more about today's world because he lived longer in it. I asked how old he was, and he said forty seven, fifteen years older than me. I was surprised. He did not look that old.

Suddenly I felt very tired. He saw right away. He understood. He said the same thing happened to him when he had to speak Chinese all the time. He said he was not tired yet because he was more used to talking in a foreign language. He said the first times he had to speak Chinese he got tired much sooner than I did. He said it was late and I should not try to talk English any more. He said he would walk me to my bus stop. He stood up and offered his hand to help me up. I stood up without taking his hand. My mind is tired, not my body, I told him. We laughed. "Prostitute," a passing man said softly. And he did not say *hua*, the word for "flower."

I did not speak any thing all the way to the bus stop. The foreigner was quiet too, but I was sure it was not because he understood the man. Just as my bus was coming, I remembered. "Aiya, I forgot your umbrella." I could feel tears in my voice. It was why I did not want to talk. It does not matter, he said. But Bai Suzhen, the white snack, also did not return Xu Xian's umbrella the next time she saw him. She knew that as long as she kept it, she was connected to him. He would keep coming back to get it.

June 21
Dear Hai Bao,

    I hope you will laugh at the pomposity of the think person who cannot sing writing three drafts of a letter to make it sing to the sing person who cannot read it. Although its rhythms may never sing to you, I will be well rewarded if you laugh. I like you best when you are laughing. I like us best when we are laughing. I have tried to make my heart laugh and sing as I write, to keep myself from becoming too serious over a letter whose length proves I have become too serious in a situation too laughable for words. At least for English words. Laugh now; keep the letter as a memento; use it when you understand it.

    This is entirely my idea, so I wanted it to be my words. I feel certain that if I had asked for advice, I would have been told not to write anything like this. However, I feel that I must write because last night (Friday) made me understand that the process which has been taking place is unfair to you. I hope this letter, this laughable letter, will make the situation and some of my feelings clear although I fear – or would fear if I did not also fear you cannot understand it – it may make them too clear, seem to you too direct. For me China is still a strange combination of a directness which often shocks me but which I like very much and an indirectness which utterly baffles me. The way we met was just such a combination, and I want to be frank about it. You were presented to me as a possible wife. No Westerner would have been so blunt. I assume I was presented to you as a potential husband, yet apparently you were not told my greatest disadvantage, my age, lest it discourage you. Well, it should. You are still young and beautiful. You need not saddle yourself with a man of my age. Do not consider doing so unless you feel something deep for me in spite of my age. In my defense I want to say that I have one (and only one) advantage worth considering: I am a writer, and writers are a fairly rare species in any country. If you want to get married – and unlike every Chinese I know I see little reason why you should – might there be advantages to marrying an old writer rather than a young buck?

    Let me talk briefly about something which may seem important but probably is not, the tiredness you felt with me. I know the feeling well. Qiu and Mei can tell you that it used to come over me whenever I spent much time with them. It comes on suddenly and overwhelmingly. It is caused by having to function in a foreign language. We are creatures of habit. Even the best of us, people like you (and me too: although I am not one of "the best," I feel a strong bond with you because I too desire, desperately need, change in the terrible world I see around me, a world I have tried to escape by coming to China, from which I have tried to exempt China, of which, you showed me last night when you spoke of the feudal father, China is very much a part) who want change for all the right reasons, unconsciously resist change. So our minds simply refuse to function in the foreign language. They revolt. The tiredness you felt was your mind's method of revolting. This is one revolution of which even Chairman Mao would not approve. Even he would sanction counterrevolutionary torture: the mind is placed on the rack of the new language and stretched until it becomes compliant. With good old Confucian patience the tiredness vanishes – in a few months. They may be torture, but our confrontations over the language barrier are the best possible way to learn a foreign language.

But they may not be the best possible way – and certainly they are not the quickest – for us to learn about each other. I have many feelings about you, almost all good, but little knowledge. Your situation in regard to me must be even worse. Only by talking can we learn, but talking is too difficult. We both know that by talking we will gradually learn each other's language and then be able to learn about each other more quickly. But such a process is slow, and I must leave Shanghai before it can advance very far. I wish I could stay. I would have stayed if I had met you earlier. Such regrets are useless. If I were Chinese, I would regret but be patient and let whatever develops develop – in its own slow and natural cycle (not circle). I am not Chinese. That is why I am writing this letter. However, this letter is also an attempt to be fair to you. I have a long past (not only on account of my great age), and you have a right to know everything about that past. You will learn more faster talking to Qiu (and Mei if she is up to it). I have told them much about myself. I will instruct them to tell you everything, including things I once asked them not to repeat. Don't be shy. Ask anything. Of course, they won't be able to answer everything. If after talking to them, you are interested in more, we should talk with a translator. If Mei is too far away and/or not up to it, I have another friend who may be available and is completely trustworthy. She could probably meet us at a more convenient place than Baoshan.

My point is that we should quit pretending we can proceed in the way we could if we were both Chinese. We aren't so we can't. If I seem too direct on a topic about which I should be more delicate, I apologize. If you have a way you would prefer, I will try it. But I feel that by pretending and being indirect, I have been unfair to you. I also feel that the part of you that you like best demands knowledge, that refusing to allow women to discuss delicate subjects is part of the feudalism you hate. So cut me open and examine my insides. They're not pretty. I've been a gambler. I've been in jail. I've been close to crazy if not actually crazy. I've failed in most of the things I've tried. But that's partly because I've never tried anything easy or conventional. What we are attempting continues that tradition, I hope with justification since I sense a similar spirit in you. If I am right, perhaps we can overcome the many obstacles between us. The first decision should be yours. If after learning as much as possible about me, you wish to go on, I will then ask about you. I will be less rigorous than you should be because it is easier for an old man to love a beautiful young woman than the reverse. Besides, Americans are a hasty people, and I am often downright precipitous. I am quite unchinese in most of my ways, yet I love China. Not all of China by any means. But at least two parts, one of which is very old, one of which, like you, is young and new.

I too like to climb high mountains in the dark. But the mountains I seek to scale have no steps. Perhaps they can only be climbed alone. Perhaps I am simply growing too old to keep trying alone, but I feel I need others. At least one special partner I can trust roped to me. Making friends across the language barrier has given me a great love for China. If I can find the partner, I think I would settle in China and try to write with her of our gropings in the dark and – I hope, I hope, I hope – of the sunrise at the top of the mountain. From our two very different points of view which we will have to work out together how to combine.

What was I supposed to do when I got that letter? The address on the envelope was printed like a child writes, and the inside was English. At first I got out my dictionary and actually tried to read it. I spent a hour looking up words, but after that hour I knew the same thing that I knew before it. I knew that the whole thing was hopeless, crazy. I went to see Qiu and Mei. I did not tell them about the letter. It was not the problem. I knew the foreigner was trying to be nice in his letter. The foreigner was not even the problem. I knew he was serious. I knew he was a good person. Probably he stayed up all night writing the letter. It was not his fault he could not write what I could read. If I studied harder, maybe I could be able to read what he could write. But how could I know he was going to write it? Crazy.

Qiu and Mei lived with Qiu's parents in the Nan Shi District, a area with little history, south of the old city. As Shanghai grew the area gradually filled up with workers from the factories. My neighbourhood, Zha Bei, was also a workers' neighbourhood, but a older one, one with history. I was thinking about history because riding the bus from my house to Qiu and Mei's I was seeing Western buildings. Of course I saw them many times before, but before I just thought how beautiful and felt proud of the great city I lived in. Now I thought of the foreigner and I thought of history. Shanghai's history is not long, but it is like my city, unique. The fancy, central parts were originally built for foreigners. Nanjing Lu was once the main street of the "International Concession." Huai Hai Lu, where the foreigner lived and taught, was the main street of the "French Concession." There was also a "Japanese Concession." All these "concessions" were conceded at the point of guns. That is why Zha Bei had history. It was not conceded. It fought the Japanese in 1937. For three months a poorly armed Chinese army resisted the powerful Japanese army in Zha Bei. Although Zha Bei was destroyed, but the memory of the way it fought instead of conceding inspired all Chinese all during the war against the Japanese invaders. To get from Zha Bei in the north to Nan Shi in the south my bus had to go through the "concessions" in the middle of the city. The signs and burped wire fences which kept Chinese out of their own city were gone, but the factory districts of Shanghai were still separated by a line of fancy, foreign buildings and parks as clear as the line between true and false. The foreigner lived there, between us, separate from us. His ancestors kept out dogs and Chinese. Now Chinese would keep him out. The cycle of history.

The building Qiu lived in did not look fancy. It did not look Western or Chinese. It looked like a cube. Later Jack told me he called it a concrete box. He thought it looked old and dirty, but then it seemed luxury to me. It was built after the Cultural Revolution. The apartments had their own kitchen and bathroom. No buildings built before about 1980 had those. The apartment was much bigger than mine, but most of it was one long room with a sofa that changed into a bed at one end and a table for eating at the other end. There was also a bedroom as well as the kitchen and bathroom. When I came, Qiu's parents took the television into the bedroom. Although they said hello to me, but I knew they were not happy I was there. Qiu already told me they wanted him to arrange a match for his young sister, not me. After they left, Qiu and I sat on the sofa. Mei, who was too big to sit between us, sat in a arm chair. Later Mei wanted to sleep, so Qiu's parents brought the television back into the big room and Qiu and I moved to the table end so they could sit on the sofa.

It was a good thing Qiu's parents were there. I was sure they did not like me, and I did not want to give them a reason they could use to criticise me. Shanghai's crowded conditions often made people control themselfs. If we were alone, I would yell at Qiu right away. I wanted to yell at some one. One reason I came was because I did not want to yell at ma, and I knew I would if I stayed at home. I tried to be calm. I told Qiu about the People's Park. I told him what people called me. I told him it was his fault. I told him he began it and he had to end it.

Qiu deserved to be yelled at. For weeks he was leading me like a horse. Now I came to a wall, and he kept pushing me straight forward. He was not at all sorry for me. He was very happy. He said things were going very well and the people in the park were jealous. He said the ones who called me names all wished they could marry a foreigner. He said they all wanted to get out of China. He was proud of his matchmaking. He said his little spark lit a prairie fire. That sounds funny now because now I know that in English a match really does start a fire. It was not funny then. I pointed out that I was the one getting burned.

We did not say all this as fast as I wrote it. I tried to be calm, but I was angry. And Qiu was enthusiastic. We repeated ourselfs a lot. Qiu could not understand why I was not quacking like a happy duck. I think he loved the foreigner more than I did. Maybe Mei thought so too and that is why she jumped in. At first she sat quietly. Her head did not follow as Qiu and I batted the ball back and forth. I thought she was more interested in what was happening inside her than in what we were saying. Suddenly she agreed with me. It was the first time I ever heard her disagree with her husband. Hai Bao is right. She is suffering, and it is your fault, not Jack's, she told him. He does not know what is going on. He can not. You must find out if he is serious. None of us knows how a foreigner thinks.

I should be grateful she said that, but I was not. I wanted the storm to be over. I did not want to be insulted by my own people in my own city. I like to think now that I knew what was happening then, but I did not. Being with the foreigner was like walking in a typhoon. You do not think, how exciting. You just want to find shelter. And what if my friends and family found out? The sky would never clear up, the rain would never end. I do not care what the foreigner thinks, I said. He is not the problem.

Right. You are, Qiu said to me. He did not dare to reply to Mei, whose baby was due on any day. The man you were looking for all your life has come into your presence, and you are afraid to know him.

I was *cuiruode*, brittle, my dictionary says, with anger. Like the hard candies shaped like animals a old, monkey faced peddler with sharp eyes and quick hands used to make when I was a child. No, I shouted at Qiu. At first I shouted softly, if you can say that in English. The man you were looking for has come into my presence, and you want me to know him so you can use him. You are the one who wants to get out of China. You hate China because Chinese do not like your painting. You think you can be a great artist in the West. You want to find the foreigner a wife so he will help you get out. You do not care about me. I love Shanghai. I love my family. I want to stay here.

So does Jack, said Mei.

That surprised Qiu more than it did me. He knew the foreigner loved Shanghai and China, but he did not think he could love it that much. I think maybe I was beginning to guess that even though the foreigner was going to Wuhan. But Mei knew. She was the only one of us who spoke English, and she knew the foreigner much longer than Qiu and I. She knew him before she met Qiu.

Qiu actually paused, but even being wrong could not slow him down long. See, you do not have to leave, he told me, and went on about all the ways I could help my family living in Shanghai with the foreigner.

It was too much. I was brittle. Now I broke. I used to try to save the old peddler's lovely candies, but they always broke too. I shouted and not softly any more. For a few minutes I did not care about Qiu's parents. I did not care who knew I was meeting a foreign man. I do not want to live in Shanghai, I shouted. I meant I do not want to live with the foreigner, but that is not what I said. I could not control what I was saying, but I can still remember every word. I do not care about Shanghai, I shouted. I do not care about my family. I am ashamed I said that, but I did. You have to be honest when you write. I would never say that about my family when I had control of myself, and I would never admit I said it if I was telling the story to friends. But writing is different. If I am not honest when I am writing, why waste all this time? It is that line I saw crossing the concessions. It is a clear line. Truth on one side, falseness on the other. On paper you see it. It does not go away like words you speak. You can hide your bad points and praise your good points, but the words remain on the paper to laugh at you. If the outside is not the same as the inside, you will have to eat your words. After the candies broke, I used to eat them. But they never tasted as good as they looked.

Qiu laughed at me. If you do not care about leaving Shanghai and your parents, why are we arguing? he said.

There is nothing worse than being laughed at. I hate people to laugh at me. I swore at him. Your mother's, I yelled. You are the one I do not care about. You are the one I want to run away from. You and your great ideas. You and your little plans. You and your wonderful matches. You and your selfishness. You and your fake enthusiasm. You and your fake knowledge. You are a very stupid, very stupid man. I was standing over him and shouting. I had lots more things I wanted to call him, but Mei stood up too. At first I thought she was trying to protect her husband, and when she came towards me I almost hit her. She saw me raise my arm and covered her stomach. I realized what I almost did. I put my hand down. I started to cry. Then she came forward and hugged me. I was crying on her shoulder, feeling her huge belly. I cried like that a long time. Her belly against mine comfortabled me. You are a very good person, I whispered in her ear after I started to stop crying. I whispered so Qiu would not hear. I was still mad at him.

When we sat down again, Mei made Qiu sit on the armchair so she could sit with me on the sofa. Qiu still talked for them. He was used to that. But Mei held my hand, and that made it easier for me to talk. I talked a lot. I told them about Huang. They knew a little, but I told them every thing. I told them things no one else knew. I even told them how I thought about suiciding. Even Qiu had sympathy when I told them that. I am glad you did not, he said. Then he smiled a little smile and became Qiu again. Why not? he asked. To him it was a philosophical question. He was disappointed at my practical answer. Who would take care of Ma and Ba if I died? I asked him. So then I talked about my family, how Ma and Ba were getting old and difficult to deal with. They were much older than Qiu's parents. My sister and brother lived far away, so I was the one who had to take care of Ma and Ba. Qiu did not think so. He said they could still take care of themselfs now, and when they were too old they should take turns staying with all three children. I never thought of that before. I almost laughed because I suddenly saw a flash of Jie's face when I told her. To my surprise even Qiu was beginning to make sense.

We talked a long time about me. The foreigner was not even mentioned. When we did come back to him, I could explain more calmly why the idea was crazy. We could not even talk to each other, but every one who saw us together talked about us. And so far these were only people who did not know me and my family. What would happen when neighbours and friends found out? What would Ma and Ba say?

What would they say? Qiu asked. At first I did not think I knew, but then I did. Ma and Ba were difficult to deal with when they often disagreed. But they never disagreed about me. They always helped me. They always let me do what I wanted to do. They would support me. But I still did not want them to find out. That is why it had to be ended quickly. What could they do against the rumours and lies that would be all around me? It was hopeless, crazy. And the foreigner would leave for Wuhan soon. I was experienced with that. I knew what it was like to be alone with a man far away. And this one was a foreigner. Every one knew foreigners were like children. Women were toys to them. Specially Asian women. I knew about the opera *Madam Butterfly*, and I knew many stories about Chinese women who were divorced by Western men. Foreigners changed women as fast as children grew tired of toys.

Not all foreigners are alike, said Qiu, but his voice did not have enthusiasm like it usually did when he talked about him. He heard the same stories I heard.

Mei was getting tired. I could feel that. She got up to go to the bathroom. She often did that. You have to when you are pregnant. I looked at the clock. It was late. We were talking for four hours. You should go to bed, I told her. Right, she agreed. I have to. Qiu went to tell his parents. They came into the living room with the television, and we went to the bedroom to wait for Mei. She came in and lay on the bed. Qiu put a thin, white blanket over her. She looked like a hump backed stone bridge covered with snow. I hugged her gently. He is a good person, she whispered in my ear.

Qiu and I went back to the living room, but there was not much more to say, and he needed to be with Mei. The last thing I said to him was remember what I told you. You have got to end it. I waited a long time at the bus stop, and after I got off the bus I walked around in the small lanes. I was relieved it was over. I really thought it was. But there are many dreams in a long night, and they may be as different as heaven and earth.

June 23

They are knocking down the wall outside my window. Symbolic but noisy. And the Café Rev, a Western style nightclub (I guess: haven't been and don't intend to go), has opened. Also symbolic but noisy.

It seems typical of this place that I may have become engaged yesterday, but damned if I know. Whatever happened it was a long, eventful and fascinating day. Qiu called (and woke me up: I hadn't slept much the night before) about 7:30. He asked me to meet him and Mei at Baoshan. Said it was important. I rode my bike there because he said Z would not be there. When he said that, I was sure it was bad news and wanted physical exercise. I left feeling dejected, but the exertion of riding more than an hour on a hot, humid day had the desired effect and I arrived feeling more hopeful. I rested only once, over a waterway. Was this the one? I remembered my peasant student's description of a river he helped construct: 30 miles long and deep enough for ocean going ships. Its purpose was to link the huge new steel mill (Baoshan's glory altho I have heard it was too huge, had technical problems) to the outside world. Half a million people, one of them my student, worked together to dig the channel. By hand! Machines couldn't work in the muck. Line after line of workers, thirty miles of bucket brigades. At the bottom of a deep cleft diggers with shovels. They filled buckets with mud. Then the buckets were passed by hundreds of hands up the steep incline to waiting trucks. This went on for months until the channel was completed. The China that built the Great Wall lives! I want to become a part of it.

Later Z, my hope for becoming a part of it, came after all. I had done a quick wash – no muck, only sweat – and they had found me some clothes that almost fit. I didn't look pretty, but Z said she preferred me that way because I am less conspicuous than in the fancy clothes I have been wearing.

But I'm jumping ahead. At Baoshan I learned that Z had gone to Qiu and Mei Sat. night and had a long talk with them. It sounded as if she bared her soul more than asked about me, but the fact she went on her own (at the time I thought she had not received my letter since they made no mention of it) impressed me. She cried, told about her miserable life (taking care of parents of 80 and senile) and a previous romance (in which her boyfriend's mother refused to permit him to marry her because she is from Jiangsu and Shanghai ren look down on Jiangsu ren; he begged on his knees and tried for years but failed to persuade his mother and would not marry without her permission. Mei said only "mother," but surely the father must also have been instrumental: thus Z's strong opposition to the feudal father). She had contemplated suicide but never committed it because she had to care for her parents. (How perfectly Chinese!)

Her fears about me were three: 1) language, 2) gossip, 3) will I desert her? She did not object to my age – the insurmountable objection. I felt relieved, felt her objections were not the ones I feared and could be dealt with. So Qiu called her and she took off work and came to Baoshan. Almost immediately I was out of it. There was a long discussion, all in Shanghaihua, which I couldn't follow. Qiu was obviously exhorting her, and I did catch the words Wuhan and Xinjiang. Obviously he was playing on her desire to escape her present life. In the end she agreed to something, what I have no idea. To marry me? To see me again? To talk more to Qiu? It might have been anything. I was told nothing. But she rode the bus home with me again. Mei's brother-in-law will ride my bike back to me.

Whatever decision she made she cannot be held to because of the pressure she was put under, but once such a decision is pressed from her, she is likely to affirm it later (also likely to bounce back and forth, as people under pressure do). I need to know if she has feelings for me, not simply a need to escape. I think she does, but it is becoming harder, not easier, for me to tell. As the possibility of marriage becomes real, her feelings are retreating into a shell. They seemed most clear to me at our first meeting. Of course, I am here perhaps also expressing my own doubts. If I am to take the leap, there must be love, not gratitude, in both of us.

I gave a brief account of my life, which I realized must have sounded incredibly romantic to her. She said her life never changes and obviously wants to escape it badly. She jumped twice, once in Baoshan when I began a sentence with "jie hun" (marriage).

My sentence was "jie hun huodze bu jie hun, women hai pengyou" (whether or not we marry, we should still be friends). When I finished the sentence she agreed heartily, but the start at the first word was pronounced. The second jump was on the dark bus when we were alone except for the driver and conductor. I put my hand on her shoulder as a gesture of reassurance after the tough day she had been thru. She jumped and removed the hand. I'm sure she misunderstood my intention, but the fear of being touched is disturbing, albeit not surprising. She constantly deprecated herself in a way I felt well beyond traditional Chinese modesty, saying that she will bring me trouble and that her health is bad. She clearly needs to be filled with the kind of confidence love can bring. On the other hand, will she be too delicate? Will the doubts return at any problem between us? Important questions. One thing I like: she says "NO" (in public, at least, her idea is that she should speak English while I speak Chinese – which she no doubt assumes no casual listener will recognize as Chinese) quite firmly, not in the tone of a weak person. I usually feel confident that she is strong and that weakness has been foisted on her. All is not settled, and I remain unsettled. I will see her this evening. I'm not sure what to expect.

Poor Jack. I was insulted, but he was confused. All I agreed was to meet him again. But that was a lot, and Qiu and I all knew it. Unmarried Chinese men and women only meet alone for one reason. Well, two reasons. I did not want to meet the foreigner again. Not alone. The comments were too terrible.

I left in Jack's description of the river digging because it shows his view of China. I was part of that view. Probably Qiu was a bigger part. It was why Jack linked with him. They shared enthusiasm, and Jack thought any enthusiasm must be revolutionary like his. In fact unless Jack made a wrong turn some where, he did not ride over the river his student helped build. And I do not think it was thirty miles long. Thirty *li* (ten miles) maybe. Even that seems too long. Maybe only three *li*.

You can see from Jack's diary what Qiu was doing to him. It makes me mad when I see it now, but it was what matchmakers always did. Ma and Ba were not eighty and certainly not senile. Qiu figured out that the more bad he made my life sound the more the foreigner would like me. All the things that made Chinese men run away from me made the foreigner run toward me. But pity was not what I was looking for. Just like Jack was not looking for gratitude.

Qiu did put pressure under me. But he did not make me do any thing I did not want to do. I did want to see the foreigner. I just could not stand to be insulted for seeing him. That was why I agreed right away to come to Baoshan. Baoshan was a long way, but it was worth it. No one I knew would see us there, and no one would insult me. Mei's sister's family was very nice to us. The grownups liked helping a secret match. All Chinese do. A few years earlier helping a foreigner would get them in trouble, but now China opened its door and they could not be blamed. The little girl liked the foreigner a lot. She wrote letters to him, and he replied. It was good practice for them. They were all learning to write Chinese. Except I was not learning to read English. I did not know what to do with the foreigner's letter. I did not want to show it to Mei because I did not know what it said and I was afraid for others to find out. Specially Qiu. On the bus I told the foreigner I could not read it. It does not matter, he told me. It is already too old. He did not know how to say out of date. After we married, I made him use it as a text for my English lessons. He said the letter was silly, but it was not. He said he wrote it for himself, not me, but it helped show me how serious he was even though I could not read it. He said he wrote it because he thought I would not marry him because he was too old, but I think it shows he was still young. Using it as a text made us both remember that time and how things changed so fast that what we said was out of date before we understood what we were saying. The lessons were cry eyed, and usually we did not finish them.

Most of the time in Baoshan was Qiu lecturing at me. He was playing the matchmaker role in front of the reluctant *xiaojie* (young lady). Only I was not a *xiaojie*. A *laochunu* (old maid) like me did not need his lectures. I got too many lectures for too many years. He knew I liked to travel, so he was trying to tempt me with distant lands and distant cities and distant provinces. Canada, Wuhan, Xinjiang. Canada seemed very romantic then. I did not know what Canada winter was like. But he thought I liked Xinjiang because of a story I wrote about it. Which shows how much he knew about literature. It was the character in my story, not me, who liked it, and he only liked it because it was better than jail. Qiu liked it too. He wanted to go there to paint the scenery. That was Qiu. He thought I wanted to go because he did. At first I tried to argue. Why did not I know better? The only way to stop some one like Qiu is to agree with him. Later you can do what you want. Qiu wanted me to be a hero, a Mao Ze Dong. That is the way he thought of himself although the bravest thing he ever did was running away from his first girl friend when he found Mei. I am not a hero and I did not want to be, but I could not say that. Chinese of our generation were raised up on that idea. We had to pretend to be heroes even when we were not. We could not even admit to ourselfs that we did not want to be. So Qiu won the argument. He had to. Although I was not a hero, but I did want to meet the foreigner again. Then Qiu and I had to argue about where to meet. Neither of us could win this argument because neither of us could think of a good place, a place I would not be insulted. So I agreed to meet the foreigner again, but I still did not have any hope.

I got to Baoshan late, and with all Qiu's lectures and pressures and arguments I did not get to talk much with the foreigner. But we had a good dinner. No strange foreign foods I had to pretend to like. Good food makes people feel good, and I felt better about the foreigner because the people were friendly and because several times he tried to rescue me from Qiu, but Qiu was too enthused by his own enthusiasm to pay attention to the man he was enthusiastic about. Wow. That last sentence is great, and it is just what the foreigner was talking about on the bus. I am learning from writing now what the foreigner was trying to teach me then. He said Chinese was hard to learn because when you saw a new zi, you had no idea what it meant or how to pronounce it. In English you could see from the spelling how to say the word. I told him he needed to learn more characters and he would start to recognize meanings because often a radical told you what sort of thing a new zi was. For example, a *wang* radical usually meant some thing was made of jade or had some thing to do with jade. And a component of a zi often told you either the pronunciation or the meaning of a zi. For example, if one component of a zi was the character "zi," you could guess it was either pronounced zi or had some thing to do with words. He said you could change English words too by sticking different zi before or after the main word. Like I just did with "enthuse." I had to cheque a dictionary, but it worked. When we were talking on the bus, I did not know enough English words to see that, and he did not know enough Chinese zi to see what I meant. But we saw enough to see that maybe our two languages were not as different as we thought. I thought to myself maybe we two people were not as different as I thought too. I was sure he was thinking the same thing.

We were lucky that night. Two busses came together, and by taking the second one we were almost alone. No one bothered us or insulted me. But I still told him, "No," when he put his hand on my shoulder. That was too high up. If he touched me lower, where no one could see it, that would be ok. He did not understand things like that. He did not touch me any where again. Still it was much better than our first bus ride together. I could relax a little. Even when we changed busses and the new one was more crowded, no one bothered us. Maybe because I was more relaxed, I hardly noticed people staring at us. We agreed to meet the next evening at the south end of the People's Park. A more quiet, less crowded place than Nanjing Lu, where we met the first time. The foreigner did not try to get off the bus with me at my stop this night. He is learning, I thought.

June 24

Yes! I feel affirmative, feel for perhaps the first time that the marriage may in fact be one of true minds (bodies are still out of the question) and, especially, that it may take place in reality, not only in my dreams. Yesterday a quiet, pleasant evening. In my room! The weather cooperated by being uncooperative: it started to rain just before we met. Picture: Z across the street under an umbrella, wearing a wide skirt, standing legs apart as no Western woman would, making some undecipherable sound to attract my attention. An attempt to be simultaneously noticeable and sedate, I think. The sight was lovely and compelling, and the umbrella she was standing under was mine. It seemed symbolic. I wish I knew of what. We obviously needed an indoor meeting place, so with much trepidation, fearing, perhaps, a swat with my own umbrella, I suggested my room.

The idea apparently does not have the connotations it does in the West. She accepted with only a brief hesitation.

It turned out to be exactly what we needed, a place where others cannot see us. She still worried, especially at first, and asked me to speak softly. I played music to help that problem. She even liked Bach. The time was relaxed and passed so pleasantly that we were both astonished to find it 10:00. (We arrived about 6:45.) Nothing profound. She looked at all my pictures and slides (no etchings), listened to music from Bach to Bartok (whom she also liked) to The Who (no comment). We exchanged fairly lengthy language lessons (she has a test coming up). She, in fact, was able to give me a surprising amount of help. Altho she didn't know English translations, she (with my assistance: she told me how a character is pronounced, and I located it in the Chinese-English dictionary; she is no more proficient at alphabetical order than I am at stroke order) was able to locate hanzi in the dictionary, something I am unable to do. And we did talk and at least attempted some difficult topics – a comparison between socialism (Western European), Chinese communism and capitalism, e.g. We still didn't always understand each other – I caught several of her subsidiary points in the social system discussion but never got her main point – but we laughed quite nicely at ourselves when we failed to understand. For the first time we began to feel at home with each other, and at the end she was much more willing to meet frequently (but not every day, as I had suggested at Baoshan in the flush of her agreement to meet at all; it was she who brought that up, and her "NO" for the first time had a laugh after it). We will do it again in two days. I'd better clean up the room, which was a mess. We had the meeting again discussion waiting for her bus. We let several busses pass because we were not at all in a hurry to part. Once on her bus, however, Z did not look back at me.

I had feared a reaction. On her own she confirmed my suspicion that Qiu had pressed her hard the previous day and went farther, saying he tended to give her too many lessons and not respect her ideas. I made it clear that I didn't approve, that she is not bound by decisions made under pressure and that I would always try to respect her views and her way of writing, which, I gather, is more realistic than Qiu's and mine. (I must laugh at the first four words of the previous sentence: I have no way of being sure how clear I made anything; such phrases flow automatically from the pen, and my use of that one proves how meaningless they are.) The important thing is that there was no inclination to retract anything. I'm still uncertain what she agreed to, but there certainly is an agreement of some sort between us and that is great. Exactly what it is is not important since no final decision can be made until we know each other better.

I felt a strong physical desire for her which I had to work to control. I made no attempt to touch her, but we sat close together (on two chairs) and inevitably brushed several times. She did not jump or pull away, an excellent sign. I love the way she hikes up her skirt in the back just before sitting so she does not sit on it but lets it flow around her. Not only does it look lovely and avoid wrinkling the skirt, it seems to me it must be more comfortable than sitting on the skirt. Why don't Western women sit that way? There is so much about her I have never seen in a Western woman. In fact for all my vast experience

I know nothing about how one should act with a thirty four year old Chinese virgin. But last night I had the feeling it may not be as difficult a problem as I have feared. She expressed concern over her physical beauty, said she is not as beautiful as she once was, but perhaps she feels this because she has been so often rejected. I find her very beautiful, but on reflection I realize that, utterly Chinese as she is, her beauty is closer to the Western style than the Chinese. Each time I see her she seems bigger: thin but tall and not small boned. Her legs must be fine and her breasts larger than is common in China. Her eyes too are big and deep. When we eventually look into each other's eyes, I expect to see a lot. Now I know I cannot keep my eyes off her as I know I should, but I can't tell how she takes that. There is much emotion and perhaps passion beneath her surface, but she controls it and I am not certain of its content. I'm pretty sure she is coming to like me but slowly. Too slowly for me, but, after all, I am the first Westerner she has ever met. She said she used to consider them all terrible, and her comment about me with my beard (in photos) was "hen kepa" (very terrible).

Her most emotional moment came when she described having to go to work in her factory at age 17 (no doubt 16 the way Westerners reckon age) with no chance for further education. She has a powerful drive for education and has been educating herself for years. My reaction to this surprised her and probably was not the proper one: I told her I consider most of my education wasted and consider self education preferable to formal education. At first she seemed skeptical, but when I explained in terms of my writing being too complicated, she understood.

I'm back: I keep stopping, then think of something more to add. The more I think the angrier I become with myself for deprecating my education to someone who was denied my opportunities. I would have been mad as hell – she is sad, not angry – if I had been denied the chance at the education I now reject so casually. My unconscious mind must also have been dissatisfied with this part of the tete-a-tete. I didn't sleep well last night, woke up full of thoughts of Z. I tossed and turned with them, tossed them around my mind until they turned into a new opening for the new novel, the first time I've been able to figure out a way to do the opening scene relatively simply and straightforwardly. I'm sure this derives in part from my complaints to Z about being unable to write simply, so I feel she is somehow responsible for what I worked out last night. The new opening also addresses madness more directly than I have up til now. I suspect I am (mainly unconsciously, but occasionally consciously as well or I wouldn't be writing this) busily assessing the chances of the depth I feel in Z turning to madness, for of course such depth is full of that potential. Can we explore the depth without the consequences it had in P? Z is less capable of dealing with madness than P was, but perhaps I am more capable of helping because of the experience with P? Can I talk to Z about my experiences with P without putting the suggestion of a similar course in her mind? But no doubt Z has already considered the possibility. The worst thought is that she might consider marriage to me as a way of avoiding the possibility and I may lead her into everything she feared and more. How do we discuss that over the language barrier? But for now she has done an extra wonderful thing for me if she has indeed led me into the right opening for the novel.

I must tell and thank her. It can be a way of apologizing for last night's insensitivity. That's a much nicer thought than the ones about madness. Perhaps all other thoughts are a comment on me, not her.

Up to now I am surprised by Jack's diary. It is not as bad as I thought it would be. It is much better than his novel. Maybe he is right about his education. Maybe the more he thinks, the worse he writes. He changes things in his novel, his "China novel," not the one he talks about here. He makes every thing complicated. In his diary he usually does not do that. He does not have time to think so much. Too much was happening. In the ten days between our first and second meeting he had time to fictionise, so he did. After that he did not. He did not have time, he did not make me myth, he did not try to write a novel. His words are complicated, but his thinking is not. In his diary the mistakes he makes come from what he does not know, not from what he thinks he does know. That is much easier to stand. I can correct those mistakes. That is why I am using his diary more than I planned to when I started. I changed a lot of my plans since I started writing. Not all change is bad. This was a time of great change for me, and it was a very good time. Jack's novel made me forget a little how good this time was. His diary is making me remember. It is hard to plan a long writing. Things do not work the way you thought they would before you started. In his novel Jack wanted to make me better than I am, and he made me worse. I wanted to make him worse than he is and maybe I am making him better. Maybe my history will have the affect he wanted in his novel. I am writing more than I planned to too. Maybe that is because this was such a good time. But I should explain that I still cut a lot out of Jack's diary. I would never finish if I used every thing he wrote about us. I cut a lot out of what he wrote about this night. It was the longest he wrote so far. Which is not a surprise because it was the longest time we were alone together. Maybe the best too because it was the first time we were completely alone.

I had to look up "connotations" in my dictionary. I thought it was something foreigners put on sandwiches. They put every thing on bread, but it is still too dry. But sandwich or sex does not matter. I did not have to look the word up to know that the idea of going to some one's room did not have connotations. The idea did not even exist in Shanghai at that time. No one had a private room. At least no ordinary people did. We heard stories about high officials' sons who did, but I did not know any one who knew any one like that. If I hesitated before I agreed, it was not because of any connotation. It was because I could not believe it. What I was hearing was too far from what I saw in my life. Qiu and I wasted half a hour trying to think of a private place to meet. We never saw the simple solution in front of our eyes because our eyes never saw such a simple solution before. The foreigner's room was the sauce of our marriage. The little stream that grew into a river of love started there. Although

I before agreed to meet him again, but I knew I could not keep meeting him in the public. I could never do on a park bench with a foreigner what I might force myself to do with a Chinese. Even when I got to his room, I could not believe it. I kept expecting people to break in the way workers broke in when they thought a woman and a man were alone together at my factory.

Much changed since those days. China's face and mine are totally different. Chinese people can go into the foreign hotels and shops now, and I some times use makeup. Just a little. Forget principles, make money is the now principle in China, but then socialist principles and uniformed guards protected us from bourgeois greed and spiritual pollution. You should see the looks the guards at the gate of the Jin Jiang Hotel gave a Chinese woman going in with a foreign man. But they did not stop me. I was in. They were guarding me now. We Chinese people were always told that the gardens of the Jin Jiang grew nothing but poisonous weeds, but why did not the Party root them out then? Instead more shops were being built, new poisonous weeds. The construction made a big mess, but to me this was the Jade Emperor's Peach Garden. I wanted to test forbidden fruits. Although no one I knew ever went into them, but the shops of the Jin Jiang were famous in Shanghai. I wanted to see them, but I did not dare to ask that first time. Later I did. I had to. If I did not ask, Jack would never think to take me. Those shops were like his education. He could reject them because he took them for granted.

It was what Jack said, a quiet, pleasant evening. "*Fangshou*," he said when we got to his room. This meant guard or defend. It took me a few seconds to figure out he probably meant *fangsong*, relax. He saw he said wrong. "Make yourself comfortable," he said. I did not understand that either. He explained "comfortable" to me by insisting I sit in the soft chair, not the hard one I was going to sit in. I was too confused to be polite and tell him he should sit in that one. I hiked my skirt and sat on the edge. He pulled the hard chair next to me and sat down too. At first we did not know what to say. I could feel him looking at me. I knew I should not look back, but then I did and we laughed. We laughed a long time, and when we finished I let myself look around his room. It was big but messy. Usually I would not like that, but this time it was good. If his room was very fancy and beautiful and clean and neat, I would be too nervous to relax. I sat back in the chair. I learned the meaning of "comfortable."

I learned many new words that evening. I learned to call the foreigner Jack. "Jiake," I really said. It is not possible to say "Jack" in Chinese. He became a man, not a foreigner. I learned a lot about him. I learned a lot. We all learned a lot. No, both. "Both" was another word I learned that night, but I did not learn it as well as I learned "comfortable." I still usually forget it when I write or speak. "Both" is a word of intimacy. It does not exist in the Chinese language because Chinese culture does not like intimacy. "Both" is unchinese. It makes two a special number. It is only necessary in a culture where the most important relationships are between two individuals, not one person and a family or one person and a society. Individualism is unchinese too. It is very American. In the West if two individuals both agree, that is very good enough. Jack taught me what the word "both" meant in his English lesson. Later he taught me what the idea meant in life. It meant both of us could decide together. We did not need "all." All the people in our families, all the people in our governments, all the people in our units, all the people in our societies.

That is the most political thing I remember from that night. I do not remember what we said about socialism and communism and capitalism. Jack was always trying to talk about politics. Lucky my English and his Chinese were so bad that I usually did not understand what he was saying. I thought he loved communism because it was Chinese. That made sense. He loved me because I was Chinese. I never thought that he might love China because it was communist. He always said it was not.

I wonder if Jack thought the "thirty four year old Chinese virgin" was too innocent to know he felt physical desire for me. I should explain about the ages. The way Chinese figure ages I was thirty two. The way Westerners figure I was only thirty. My birthday is in July, and it was still June. Jack thought I was thirty four because Qiu lied to him. He knew Jack worried about the difference in our age, so Qiu added some years to mine. To me he pretended he did not know Jack's age. Maybe almost forty, he told me. In China matchmakers always tell lies. I do not think Jack and I figured out our right ages until we filled out the marriage application and saw the years of our births. By then it did not matter that he is sixteen years older. Getting back to physical desire, I think all women know when a man has that for them. Age and culture do not matter about this. That night was the first time I felt happy Jack desired for me. Maybe I began to desire for him too, but I was glad he controlled himself. Later I got impatient with his control and I had to control myself, but that night I was happy. It made him seem Chinese. I remembered the black hand in the toilet. I did not think foreigners ever controlled themselfs.

Another surprise is that Jack noticed the way I hiked my skirt. He likes to talk about his writer's eye, but usually he does not see small things. That is a funny word, "hike." I thought it meant a long walk. You just sort of flip (flap? flop?) your skirt up when you are starting to sit down. Chinese women all sit that way, but I do not do it anymore. When I came to Canada, I saw that Canadian women do not do that, so I stopped too. I think they do not do it because they usually wear tight skirts. It only works with a loose skirt. If I knew Jack liked it, maybe then I would not stop. But I do not worry about him the way I used to. Maybe I should. Not worry, remember. Remember the good things, the first things. I guess that is what I am doing.

Jack does not say what happened to his umbrella in the end. He did not understand about the *White Snack*, but he still acted Chinese. He understood that so long as I had his umbrella, we were connected. I had to contact him to give it back. It was not raining when we left his room, but he took the umbrella along in case it started. At the bus stop he told me to take it. He said it might rain again before I got home. I said he should not worry about me so much. He said he was not as worried as he used to be. We laughed and went on about the umbrella. He said take it, and I said no. It was a typical Chinese argument. Both of us were arguing for the other person. That is why we let three busses go past. In the end I took the umbrella again because I was feeling like Bai Suzhen. We were in act one of *The White Snack*.

June 26

She's better <u>and deeper</u> than I dared dream. And she really has agreed to marry me. I think, I think, I think. I'm almost sure. It has something to do with my umbrella, but I don't think I'll ever figure out what. Little time to write. If I had time I'd fill the rest of this journal. It's 6:30 a.m., but this is final exam day. God, how am I going to grade exams the way I feel?

I'd better try to be chronological about last night. It began with the worst twenty minutes of my life. She was late and, unlike Westerners, Chinese are never late and she had never been late before, had been waiting for me every time we met even when I arrived early. I became increasingly distraught, concluded she had backed out, alternated between trying to hold back tears and keep myself from banging my head against the wall I was backed against, kept trying unsuccessfully to figure out why, what I had done to drive her away. I had half expected it last time because of the way she had been pressured in Baoshan, but I could see no reason for it after the lovely evening Mon.

Picture: Z running toward me thru the crowds on the sidewalk of Yanan Lu, a dainty white and purple umbrella over her head (on a sunny day), my ugly black one sticking out of her other hand like a spear. A dancer she may be but an athlete she is not, and she was wearing inclined sandals which were not made for running, but running she was, clumsily but full tilt to me, and my heart rebounded full tilt from despair to ecstasy. A bus had been late. She has a long way to come. But she comes full tilt and promises to come all the way. I wanted to open my arms for her to run into and lift her into heaven, where I already was. But I didn't dare. Yet.

It's hot out, the dreaded Shanghai summer coming on full tilt too. She was all in a sweat, said all kinds of wonderful things about how worried she had been that I might not wait for her. I was too elated to have my Chinese vocabulary in gear, or I would have said something corny about waiting forever. Once in my room she headed straight for the bathroom as if she lived here already. She came out utterly beautiful and glowing. Again I wanted to take her into my arms but didn't dare. She tried to explain about the umbrella. I couldn't understand, and we laughed as we've become accustomed to doing when we don't understand, but somewhere imbedded in the welter of words was "agreed to marry." I sprang to attention at that, and she laughed and laughed. That's when I really should have taken her in my arms, but we were both too busy laughing.

We talked about exams, I giving, she taking them. She seemed worried about hers, so I offered to help her in English and world (Western) history. Out of the blue she declared, "I am not a child." Was this in response to my offer of help, or was it, as I suspect, a sentence she had rehearsed and was inserting here? I think she often does this – as do I; it's natural when you must speak in a foreign tongue. The strange thing was that at the moment she said it I had been thinking of her as a child. I was imagining her carrying a bundle of books, as I saw Ruby's classmates do, into the school to take an exam at age ten or eleven, black hair in pigtails, red neckerchief and sleeve patch, her face both eager and tense. I was dumbfounded. It was as if she had picked my mind. "You think I'm a child," she insisted. Did she mean what was happening in my mind right then or the way I treated her generally? Because I am so much older and more experienced, I do think of her as young, occasionally as childlike, but I don't think I had ever before thought of her as an actual child, as I was doing at the moment she accused me. Instead of replying I wanted to describe the picture in my mind, but I didn't know any of the words – pigtails, neckerchief, sleeve patch – so I stammered around until I felt like a child too and said so. She caught my mood effortlessly and became a child with me. We described childlike feelings in our childlike vocabularies. I told her some of my childhood experiences, how they flooded our school playground in winter and I broke my arm on the ice, and she told what it was like when the Cultural Revolution came to her school, big signs, big Mao badges, big meetings, big excitement, little learning. If there was antagonism in her original assertion, it vanished completely. I felt uncanny empathy: I was in her childhood and she in mine. I felt she understood me better than I do myself (not all that difficult, but that's my shortcoming and does not diminish her insight). I love her.

Must depth always lead into pitfalls? There was one bad spell when she kept repeating, "Wo bu hao" (I am not good). I did not know – I never do, never did when P said it either – what to say, kept assuring her she was very, very good until the spell passed. It scared me at the time, yet I have a suspicion that such self deprecation may be expected of a Chinese woman in Z's position and that it may even have been a test of me and my sincerity. For she went on to say I would regret my decision and ask if I would leave her two or five or ten years later if I met a more beautiful woman. I tried to reassure her, told her that I certainly would not leave her for a woman more physically attractive and talked about beauty as depth, but the language barrier got in the way of eloquence. I think I did better when I was just telling her she is good. I refused to lie by claiming I could predict my reactions in ten years time, but I suspect she wanted such a declaration. Must stop here and prepare for class.

Returned from class loaded with exam papers and love for and from my students, then promptly conked out. How can I grade papers the way I feel? I can't look at the exams for more than five minutes without my thoughts running to Z. She gave me a short writing lesson last night and wrote 你真好 (ni zhen hao, you are really good) for me and to me. I tried to write that together we were really good, but I failed to communicate what I wanted to say because I didn't know how to phrase it. She said I couldn't say that in Chinese and changed it to together we are really industrious. Industrious?! With this stack of exams unlooked at? Anyhow she does like me. She wanted to visit today since she has the afternoon free. I don't know how I resisted, but I did. We settled on tomorrow afternoon, when, hopefully, my exams will be graded and F can come to meet her. She also asked me to take the 71 bus with her, a great leap forward. A student knocked on the door while we were talking and I rushed into the hall to talk to him, certain she would not want to be seen. When I returned she said I should have invited him in, which surprised but overjoyed me. That was when I decided she really has agreed to marry me. She also asked my permission to tell her jie jie (in Qingdao), saying she must tell her family. She does not want to tell her mother yet (because the mother is senile?). I asked her if she was close to her sister, but she said no. I hope that means there will be no difficulties with the family, which there might have been if the family were a close one. Must grade exams. But every time we see each other is much better than the previous time, and it is all wonderful and exciting. The language barrier is even a help: it insures we are always paying full attention to one another. She has not tired as she first did from the strain of speaking English. She now calls me Jia-ke, two syllables the way the Chinese do, and it sounds like the Hallelujah Chorus to my ears.

I keep putting this down and coming back to it. She says she doesn't want my money (at least in China I have plenty). I talked about sharing. She will cook dinner for us tomorrow and insisted that she buy the food. I cooked ratatouille for my own dinner and fed some to her just before we left altho she had eaten dinner. We may have some food problems. She doesn't like eggplant and doesn't eat onions or garlic because of the effect on breath odor. We laughed about our different tastes.

You forget how much you change. When I was a girl, maybe I was more like a butterfly than I thought. Now I like eggplant, and I use garlic and onions in almost every thing I cook. It is hard to believe I once said I did not like them. I did not always know I was unique. I used to try to be like all the other butterflies in Shanghai. I wanted to look and smell pretty. I even tried not to use soy source because it might make my skin dark. But my words and my eating were not connected. I said I did not like onions and garlic, but I ate them all the time. Ma did the cooking in our house, and she always used them. She used lots of soy source too. When I complained about any food, she told me I would eat every thing after I married. She was right. She was always right. As soon as I got married and started cooking, I cooked every thing. My mouth had to test, not talk. It is funny. I did the opposite of nature. When I was young, I was a butterfly, but when I grew up, I changed into a silkworm. I learned that eating is more important than looking. I started using lots of garlics and red peppers. I started using yellow onions, not just the green ones we use in Shanghai. We call the big yellow onions yangzhong, which means foreign onion. I love fresh vegetables. Jack's talk of food reminded me at just the right time because the season was changing as fast as I was. The markets were filling with colour, bright

red tomatoes and light red amaranth leaves and bright green peppers and thin
purple eggplants and dark green cucumbers and light green long beans and
violet lined flat beans and light brown east squashes and the first striped west
watermelons. Not mainly leaves and greens like before. The real silkworms were
finished their eating and all their spinning work. Poor little darlings. If they
lived longer, they could find better things to eat than mulberry leaves.

In Shanghai we got fresh vegetables all year. All through the winter, when
Canada is covered with snow, there was *mei qing cai* and *ta cai* and Chinese
cabbage and the little Chinese celeries and spinach and white daikon and green
daikon and other roots like lotus and turnips and carrots (although we seldom ate
them, but mainly used them to add colour), and in late winter the winter bamboo
shoots (my favourites, the small, delicate ones). Then it was spring and there
were broad beans and peas and snow peas and spring cabbages and cauliflowers
and *jiu cai* and *jiu ya* (green and yellow garlic chives) and green garlics and spring
bamboo shoots (the medium sized ones) and all kinds of small wild vegetables.
At the end of spring long beans (almost half a metre long and so tender) and
flat beans and fresh green soybeans and small peppers, then all the summer
vegetables, tomatoes, large sweet peppers and little hot peppers, beans, eggplants,
the big summer bamboos and all the *gua* (squashes and melons), cucumbers
and big east squashes for soups and south pumpkins and west watermelons and
Hami melons from Xinjiang and little potatoes that you did not peel and hardly
had to cook they were so tender, and corns, little chewy ones, not the big watery
ones you get in the West. In early fall there were still many summer vegetables
and later the roots started and onions, little green ones (we got those all year) and
the big foreign ones, and the late cabbages and Chinese cabbages and celeries
were starting that would run all through the cool weather. How wonderful to live
where the seasons were always changing and the markets had new vegetables all
the time. In the West super markets always look the same, the same vegetables
every season and none of them fresh. Even with a big garden like Jack's we only
get fresh vegetables half of the year. The other half of the year we have to get
them from the root cellar or the freezer or buy the super market vegetables that
look good but do not test. What a difference between a Western super market
and the open air free markets of Shanghai, where peasants bring fresh harvested
crops or still alive fish and shellfish every morning, where you know the food will
be great. You do not need all the spices Westerners use. They have to use so many
because their food does not test. All you need is fresh vegetables grown without
chemicals. A little meat and lots of garlics and onions for the best flavour. And
I make sources that would even make mulberry leaves delicious. Brushing your
teeth after you eat is a small price for a feast.

When I got off the bus on Yanan Lu, Jack was happy to see me, and I was
so happy he waited. Except for that I was not so happy. Although I am Chinese
and Chinese are often late, but I do not like to be late. I worried on the bus. We

always heard how on time and efficient foreigners were. If Jack did not wait for
me, what would I do? Would I dare to ask at the Jin Jiang gate for him? I was so
happy to see him that I ran to him, but that made me sweat, and I do not like
to sweat either. I was still tense and sweating as we walked from the bus stop to
the hotel. Then Jack told me Ruby will arrive in one week. Then he told me
he hoped his and Ruby's little friend Xiao Feng could come to meet me. He
showed me pictures of her before. Although she was in graduate school, but
she looked like a child and was only twenty one years old. Nineteen or twenty
the way Westerners count. Another child. I remembered Mei's little niece in
Baoshan. How Jack liked her and she liked him. It seemed like all his best friends
were children. It was not fair to think that way because Qiu and Mei were not
children, but I was hot and tired from being late, so I was not thinking clearly.
Ruby's coming really worried me. Chinese children hate when their parents
remarry again, and I was sure Ruby would hate me. When Jack started giving me
lessons about history, I thought he thought I was another child. English lessons
were fine, but history was my subject. We Chinese have so much history, and we
love to use history. We learn how to act in the present from the past. Every time
I talked about history with Jack, I felt how little history he and his country had.
How could he teach me about history, even the history of North America? So
I told him, "I am not a child." Maybe I rehearsed saying those words when we
were walking and he was talking about Ruby and Xiao Feng. Maybe I thought
them in Chinese, then thought how to say them in English. I am not sure, but
I am sure I was trying to tell him I was not like all those children who followed
him. Then he became a child and I followed him. A wise man looks like a fool.
Or a child. I was a child and he was a child. He even said me a poem about that.
I think it was named "Isabelle Lee." He was always saying English poems. In
English he could remember what he red once, but in Chinese he forgot poems
when I taught him twenty times.

 I am used to Jack now, and he seems very ordinary, but in those days
every thing he said and did surprised me. The differences between our cultures
made small things big, and turned misunderstandings to love. He let himself
turn into a child like no Chinese who was not starving to death would ever
do, and instead of looking down on him the way I would if he was Chinese, I
followed him. I was not starving to death, and I became a child. We chattered
like children. Then all of a sudden we both felt surprised at the way we were
talking. I did not know what to say and he did not know what to say. I wanted to
take him in my arms because he was a child. I wanted him to take me in his arms
because I was a child. I wanted us to take each other in our arms because we were
children. Shy children feeling adult feelings. So we did not take each other into
our arms. The differences which made us the same were real differences.

 I do not blame Jack for thinking I said I was bad because I followed him
and became a child. It sounds like some thing a child says. It is hard to remember,

but I do not think it was that way. Jack thought it was good that I became a child but bad when I said I was bad even though he thought I was talking like a child then. I do not think it was good to become a child even though it was good because we came together doing it. We were so different, but suddenly we were so together. But I was tired of being treated like a child. That was why I told Jack I was not a child. All the Chinese people treated me like a child because I was not married. I did not want Jack, a man I might marry, to treat me the same way too. But he was so nice to me, so polite, so gentleman although he was so big and his voice so funny and some times loud. That made me feel bad compared to him even though we were together. So I said it. I felt sorry for him. He wanted to marry a Chinese woman that no Chinese men wanted. I wanted to tell him he should not want me either, that I was bad and that later he would feel bad. I was very emotional, but he kept telling me I was very good. The reason I felt bad was that I felt good because he was so good. So if I was not that bad, maybe he was really not that good. All the stories about foreigners were that their goodness did not last. Maybe he would find another woman in a few years. This was even before I knew how many women he already found. Since then I learned that the stories about foreign men changing were true, and Jack was a typical one. Yet he was always true to me, and he still is. Like Chairman Mao said, everything is contradiction.

I think this sounds very confused. Or very philosophical. In China philosophy is usually confusing, but in the West I think confusion is often considered philosophical. But philosophical is just what this time was not. We were both feeling so much, not thinking. I kept trying to think, but I felt too good to do it. I tried to remember how I felt with Bianji and Huang. I knew it was not the same, but I thought maybe that was because Jack was a foreigner. How silly I was, but I was feeling too much to think clearly. The little stream was turning into the river. First it carried Jack away. Now it was carrying me.

I tried very hard to explain about the umbrella and the *White Snack* to Jack. It is used through the whole opera as a symbol of their love. He could not understand then. A year later I took him to see the opera. Finally I could explain. I was trying to tell him that Bai Suzhen did not return Xu Xian's umbrella until they agreed to marry. He said I jumped when he used the word for marriage at Baoshan, but you should have seen him jump when I used it talking about the *White Snack*. As usual our language misunderstandings made us laugh and our laughing brought us together. But even if he understood the *White Snack*, Jack could not understand what I was trying to tell him. Bai Suzhen and Xu Xian married very quickly. Real life is not like opera. In China people usually agree to marry years before they do it. That was a lesson I knew very well. But it turned out he was not the only one who did not understand. We married less than two months after we met.

Our language lesson was like another Chinese opera. I was trying to teach him to write, and he was trying to write I love you in Chinese without saying it.

A Chinese man would know a hundred ways to do it, but expecting a American to be subtle is like asking a tiger for its skin. I kept correcting his grammar instead of catching his meaning. It was like the famous opera scene in which Wu Song and Sun Erniang battle in a dark room. Except I was only pretending I could not see. It was not really a lie. Just like it would not be a lie if he told me he would never leave me. So far he never did.

Jack's diary gets a little confused the next day. I will not use it. I want to write true. It took me a while to remember because Jack keeps writing about me like I was there. But I was not. We did not meet that day. He was trying to grade exams. I did not understand how difficult that was until I saw the exams. He makes his students write long stories and essays in English. Up to then the only exams I heard of like that were the ancient imperial examinations. Modern Chinese exams are always multiple choice. Jack calls them multiple guess. He hates them, but he said he wished he gave them because they are so quick and easy to grade. I think maybe he wrote in his diary in between exams. He still wrote about our same meeting, but some times it changed in his mind. At least it did not change into his novel. Some times he wrote about what he wanted to do and what he wanted to happen, not what did happen. Poor guy. I knew I should not leave him alone. I know he had no time. I remember the high pile of exam papers he had to grade. But he wasted time dreaming. At least he was dreaming about me.

We agreed not to meet that day, but when I finished my classes, I changed my mind. He had a telephone. How convenient. I called and asked if I could come. "Dang rang" (of course), he agreed enthusiastically. It was the first time we tried to talk on the telephone. I was surprised we could do it because talking in a foreign language is much harder when you can not see the other person's face. Jack was surprised too. "Love is the best linguist," he told me in English. I told him he had to teach me that word, and he promised he would. Jack told me he could not grade exams. That made me glad, but then it made me mad at myself for being glad because it was his duty to grade them. Then Jack said Qiu was already on the way to see him. I did not like to hear that. I did not want to see Qiu. I did not want Qiu to see me with Jack. I knew he would see too much. I tried to tell Jack not to tell him too much, but I knew he would not do it. I knew he would do it. Which is right? I don't know. I was confused then too and not only about language. I said I would not come. He said I should, so I told him how I felt about Qiu. He said he would try to get rid of Qiu quickly, but I knew he would not be able to. I knew Qiu better than he did.

The summer solstice was past, and although the season of small heat was not yet begun, but it was hot and not rainy, the first fine day of summer. I walked in Changfeng Park near my school. Every thing was green and growing like bamboo shoots after the spring rains. Frogs were calling each other from the water, dragonflies were mating in the air, and lovers were knotted on every bench. How jealous they would be of our private room, yet I was the one who felt jealous. I even felt jealous of Qiu. He already had a wife, and soon he would have a child. He would not go to Jack's room if he did not hear that I was going there, but now he was there with Jack, and I was not. Behind the fresh, pregnant air of the park I could smell the nearby factories.

I left the park and took busses into the city. First number 67, then number 20 down Nanjing Lu. The number 20 bus was even more crowded than usual, but I got on early, so I did not have to stand near the door, where people were packed like fish scales. At one crowded stop I saw a woman push her boyfriend on to the bus. But there was no one to push her, and she got left behind. Jack would not let me push him, I thought. He would push me. At Xizang Lu I got off the crowded bus on to the crowded sidewalk. Usually I always like being one of the crowds on Nanjing Lu, but this day the shop windows bored me. Even the big silk shop, my favourite, seemed boring. I thought the shops in the Jin Jiang must be much better. I walked south and took the number 26 bus on Huai Hai Lu. I guess I wasted time dreaming too because I missed my stop and had to get off one stop later. I was by Shenyang Park, across the street from the Jiaoyu Xueyuan, where Jack taught. Students were coming out the gate. I wondered if some of them were Jack's. I wanted to cross and ask them about Jack, but I felt shy. Maybe they would ask me why I wanted to know. Maybe they would guess. I walked slowly back on Huai Hai Lu, hardly looking in the shop windows. The ones I wanted to see were inside the Jin Jiang walls. I came to one window where a ugly man in a dirty white apron was shaking a huge, black iron wok of *shengjian mantou* over a big fire. You could smell the *mantou* and hear them burning. This must be the restaurant Jack likes, I thought. I did not know why he liked burned food, but many Shanghai people did too. The restaurant was dirty and crowded. Every one sitting at a table eating had some one standing behind waiting greedily for the chair. Some people were eating standing up. Jack was not there. I wondered if some times he ate standing up. I wondered if people stood up to let a foreigner sit in their chair.

I turned up Maoming Lu and walked next to the hotel. A crowd was trying to peek into the Cafe Rev, to see where they could not go. There was always a crowd there. Chinese people are like other people. They always want what they are not allowed to have. That is why every thing Western was becoming so popular. We were denied it for too long. I tried to tell myself that was not why I liked Jack, but I was not sure. I was denied for too long too. But not of any thing in the Cafe Rev.

I stood quietly north of the second gate. If Qiu came out, he would go south to the Huai Hai Lu busses. But I was not patient. I walked to the first gate and back to the second gate several times. Then I walked away. I found a small lane and got lost in the forest. Shanghai has forests too, forests of poles and sticks like trees trying to reach the sun. Except the many coloured leaves hanging from Shanghai's woods are clothes. On a sunny day after several rainy ones, lines of drying clothes were every where. And while Canada's forests are brightest and most colourful in the autumn, Shanghai's are most colourful in the summer. I noticed that more in this fancy neighbourhood than I would in Zhabei, but the big contradiction was with the Cultural Revolution. Then the only bright clothes were underclothes. Then Shanghai people were afraid to show the bright colours they loved. Now those colours that the "flowers" of Shanghai once wore were returning. But the styles were new, foreign. My clothes were not as bright, but my boy friend was ahead of the style. I think I laughed out loud because people were staring at me. That made me laugh more. I did not know if I was laughing because I was happy or sad or crazy. Or maybe I only think maybe I was crazy then because of what Jack wrote in his diary.

The houses around me were as colourful as the clothes, and they looked even less like Zhabei than the clothes did. They were old European style houses the French built, with straight lines and pointy shapes where there should be curves and colourful foreign paint on the doors and around the windows. The paint was old and cracking when you looked closely, so I tried not to look closely, just feel the colour filling me up. The colour, the plenty, the madness, the heat, the passion of summer. Summer in Shanghai. How nice. Writing let me forget for a while that it is winter in Canada now.

June 28

Yesterday I learned what I have suspected – clever me – all along, namely that Z is human. All too human. Deliciously human. Horribly human. I learned that the physical aspects will not be the problem I feared they might, that she is not coy and that she has real love for me. Enough love to be jealous, and there's the rub. The combination of love and jealousy is not one I like, but it may be unavoidable, at least for the present.

The day falls into three stages (omitting such trivialities as the exam I gave in the morning and the futile attempts to grade the mountain on my desk): before, during and after F. Z came early so we could have an hour together before F arrived. We spent the hour talking (altho I was wanting to do better things) in our accustomed positions, she in the soft chair, I in the hard one alongside her. Everything seemed normal until suddenly she said, apropos of what I can't for the life of me remember, that I wanted to be a.... Then it was dictionary time and a long quest for the word, which eventually turned out to be "jiushizhu," which the dictionary defines as "the Savior, the Redeemer." I assume it refers to Christ. I failed to comprehend at first, thought there must be a language mistake (and perhaps there is, but if so it is a small one having to do with her lack of knowledge of Christianity, not her lack of knowledge of me). She repeated that I wanted to be her savior. At first I was embarrassed and denied it, for surely this is not a role I am eager to admit, but she insisted and I was forced to admit, to myself even more than to her, that many of my dreams of her cast me in that role. (Last night's did not: for the first time the sleeping dream was pure physical desire, so powerful it woke me up. I got almost no sleep.) Again

I was stunned at the depth of her understanding. She may not understand my language, but she sure understands me. Perhaps she'll end up being my savior.

Z and F seemed to get on OK. We indulged in that favorite occupation of Chinese, taking photos, and generally stayed at a superficial level. Z cooked a lovely Shanghai style dinner on my hot plate, but while she was cooking a student arrived, a woman who does insurance business and who is probably the only student in all my classes I really don't like. She is in the class that had a take home exam and was the only student who took advantage and brought in her exam late– disgusting but she didn't cheat: the paper is too poor for that. She claimed she had to go to Suzhou on business. She asked to use my phone, couldn't reach her party and stayed a long time, trying repeatedly and between tries regaling F and me with her business adventures, speaking English, ignoring Z completely. I was vaguely aware that Z wasn't happy and tried to smile and wink at her once or twice. Eventually the student left and we ate and walked F to the bus. On the way back Z complained of stomach pains. (Probably she had them earlier but didn't want to say when F was there.) She ascribed them to not eating breakfast, having little lunch and then our big dinner. Back at the room she lay down. I started cleaning up, but she soon forced herself off the bed to help. Over my objections, of course, but I know too well how efficacious such objections are with Chinese. After we finished cleaning she said she didn't want to come back to my place. The reason was because she was very unhappy when my student was here. She had good reason for that and I don't blame her, but it quickly came out that she was jealous of the student and the women in my past and is likely to be jealous almost any time I talk to another woman. Our first embrace came from my efforts to console her and assure her of my love. I said "I love you" (using English: I did not want to mispronounce my first profession of love). She did not speak of love but showed it: she kissed me back. Bliss.

We talked long and hard about my past and our future. She wanted to make sure I had no bad Western habits. The three she named were smoking cigarettes, smoking opium and homosexuality. I refrained from mentioning that far more Chinese males than Western smoked cigarettes. And what could I have said about smoking opium? I just assured her I had none of the above habits altho long ago I used to smoke cigarettes. I tried to tell her I had been known to toke pot, but she had never even heard of that and had no concern. She was quite interested in homosexuality, thought of it as a sickness, wanted to know more, especially about lesbians (altho of course she didn't know the word) but was dissatisfied with my attempts to explain. She was obviously upset by the other women in my past and even accused me of lying about my sexual experience. Enough. I must grade papers. She will come again tonight, and no doubt the discussion will continue.

When Z and F met I introduced them with full names, but later neither of them knew the other's name. Obviously my pronunciation is so bad the Chinese often have no idea what I'm saying and don't tell me either out of politeness or because it is too much bother to correct me constantly. On the other hand Z and I are able to talk together better than I thought, better than it seemed at first. As I told her over the phone two days ago,

"Love is a linguist." I explained last night, pretending the difficult word was love. (Well, it is, isn't it?) Back to the exams.

I graded two, which is twice as many as I graded the first time I stopped. We have begun reminiscing, as lovers should. She said that at our first meeting she had what she first called a sixth sense (liu ganjiu) and later a word which translated as "intuition" about me. I thought I had detected a response in her at the time but was glad to have my suspicions confirmed. She also said she thought we had many similar ideas and could write together. Such a future prospect makes me even happier than the present joy of being able to talk together. If that can happen so fast, everything is possible. I am very happy altho some of our problems are now coming out. I hope I can show her that jealousy is a feudal idea – she hates feudal ideas – and so talk her out of it, but that may still be beyond our language abilities. It will not be easy for me to live with a jealous woman (but I sure hope I get to try with her). Besides, she is 31, not 34. An old man should be jealous of a beautiful young wife, not the reverse.

11:45 p.m. Just returned from what is becoming my nightly bus ride: two stops on the 71 bus down Yanan Lu. Every night it becomes later. Every night it becomes hotter (inside and out). The late night streets are still crowded with people, playing cards and chess, chatting, holding animated discussions, pairs of lovers (and now Z and I are one of them, touching surreptitiously and even holding hands when we think we are not being watched). And, mainly, sleepers. People are sprawled in incredibly uncomfortable looking positions on flimsy deck chairs and other lawn and bamboo furniture, asleep on the sidewalks and streets amidst the noise, bustle and sweltering heat. But obviously it is even more hot inside. (The weather forecast: high 34, low 27!!, rain.)

Aiya! There is a insect in my soap. A Chinese idiom is, To review the old is to learn something new. But what if you review about a kiss and learn about a insect? In his novel Jack remembered our first kiss one way, and I remembered it another way. And here in Jack's diary, which he wrote at the time, it is a third way. The diary is different from any of our memories. Maybe some times the line between true and false is not as clear as I think. As we Chinese think. Jack often asks, "What is truth?" It is a quotation, I think. There is another line that I always forget. I get mad at Jack when he says it. He says it to sarcastic me and the clear way we Chinese think. He is like some Daoist philosophers like Zhuangzi who do not think you can know the truth. I wish he is not right, but maybe the truth is not as clear as I always thought. Maybe my memory is wrong. I red the diary again, counting. It seems like we kissed the third time we were together in Jack's room. My memory says we were in his room many times before we kissed. I kept waiting for him to kiss me and he kept not kissing me. It does not seem possible it was only the third time. And the first time does not even count. I was not impatient yet. I was not ready yet. Jack and I agree on this memory too. In his novel he says it took forever before we kissed. Can the diary be wrong? Can truth be false? After the insect is removed, the soap must be boiled again before you can drink it.

Last night I dreamed Japanese soldiers were chasing me. I had dreams like that all my life. I had so many that memories of the dreams seem like memories of reality. Yet I was born ten years after the Japanese were driven out of China. I do not have the dreams because I ever saw a Japanese soldier. I have the dreams because when I was growing up I heard many terrible stories about Japanese soldiers. My mind turned stories into dreams and dreams into memories. When I write, I think I am turning memories into stories. But what if the memories are dreams? What if the memories are false? What if my dreams and the romance stories Jack and I told each other when we were teaching each other to speak a foreign language became the memories I am now turning back into stories? What if I am telling stories about stories, not realities? What if I am writing fiction, not truth? "What is truth?" Jack asks. I thought I knew, but what if by becoming a writer, I am becoming like Jack? What if this history I am writing to correct Jack's novel is becoming a novel? What if it is becoming Jack's novel? What if I ate that insect and only told myself I took it out and boiled the soap again to keep myself from having a stomach ache in my head? *Aiya!*

Jealousy is better than philosophy. I almost wrote "bitter" instead of "better." Some times I mix up English words. When I figure out the right word, I am happy and I want to play games with the words. Now I want to say philosophy is bitterer than jealousy. I wonder if that is true. If it is, it is because jealousy is based on morality. You do not have to think about it. I wonder why I am playing games like Jack. Am I really becoming like him? We Chinese do not like games. We like clearness. Jealousy is better than philosophy and philosophy is bitterer than jealousy because jealousy is so clear and philosophy is so confusing. You know exactly who you are jealous of and why you are jealous. Maybe that is why we Chinese are often jealous.

Jack's insect is jealousy. Mine is being wrong. When you are wrong, you are criticised, you lose face. Jack wants to kill his insect. That is not hard. The problem is that there are so many. You kill one and another one bites you. In China Jack always searched the room for mosquitos to kill before he went to bed. The Chinese way is easier. We sleep inside mosquito nets. I just do not want to eat my insect. In life maybe you can not not eat insects. They are too small and too every where. I am sure I ate some, but as long as I did not know I ate them, it did not bother me. I try to keep my life like my food, clean. Please do not tell me about the insects I ate. If Jack did not tell me about all his other women, maybe I did not have to be jealous.

I know jealousy is not good, but I had good reasons to be jealous of Jack. It was not that stupid business woman. She would love to catch a foreigner like Jack. I knew that right away, but I also knew Jack was not interested. In this one. She was not very beautiful. But her interest showed me what it would be like living in China with Jack. It showed me how in fashion foreigners were. Many women would try to catch him, and I was getting older and uglier. If he left me when a younger, prettier woman caught him, I would be trapped inside my own cocoon. People always told me about many Chinese women who foreigners married, then left. So I asked Jack about women he loved before. When I found out he loved many other women, not just his first wife, I was very unhappy. I cried. I showed him "*bu ke su yi*" (inconceivable) in the dictionary. In China people do not have sex except with the person they are married to. Some times people have sex before they get married, but that is only because they had to wait too long to get married. We do not criticise them because they plan to get married as soon as possible. Jack was not like that. He was not moral. How could I trust such a man? How could I not feel jealous? He loved many women and got lots of sex. All I got was suffering.

And if the diary is right, this must be when he kissed me, when I was crying because I was jealous of him. That is *bu ke su yi* too. I can understand why he felt bad and wanted to kiss me to show his sympathy. I can understand why I might let him kiss me. I can not understand how I could kiss him back. Not at that time. And I know I did it. I remember and he remembers and the diary says so too. That is why I think maybe his diary is wrong about the first kiss. Maybe my memory is not wrong. Maybe Jack was writing one of his dreams, not a memory of reality. Maybe the kiss really did come later like I remember. Maybe I did not eat the insect. I do not know what to think. This is not the kind of contradiction I like. I will think about it later. If I keep thinking about it now, I will not be able to write.

It is strange that when I worried about Western bad habits, I did not worry about this one, about immorality. Maybe I asked him about the other habits because I was curious. Maybe I asked to make myself forget jealousy or to find out if he was completely bad, if I was completely wrong about him. I knew he was married before and that his wife went crazy. I did not like that. I always expected to marry a man who was like me, a man who did not have sex before. We would start out being equal, and we would learn from each other. A little like the way Jack and I were learning language from each other. But I could not blame Jack for marrying, and I could not blame him for divorcing if his wife was crazy. He was forty seven years old, and he was a good man. At least that is what I thought until I heard about all the other women. Then I knew that all the bad stories we heard about Western immorality were true and that Jack was a typical immoral Westerner. That made me sad more than jealous. Before that I fooled myself into thinking Jack was different. I needed to find out if he was typical in other bad ways. Thank heaven and earth he was not. If he kissed me after this, maybe I might kiss him back. But the diary says we kissed before this.

From the diary it seems like we talked about *jiushizhu* before Xiao Feng came, and the kiss came after she left. That is not the way I remember. I remember he kissed me right after we laughed about *jiushizhu*. That is when we should kiss. We were laughing at our differences and feeling our similarities. At least my memory is right that we kissed the time we talked about *jiushizhu*. In his novel Jack does not mention *jiushizhu*. In his novel I think we kiss at a later meeting. But I think we kissed later too. I remember the *jiushizhu* and the kiss coming later. Our both memories are confused. But we should not kiss because of jealousy. That would be unromantic, and it was such a romantic kiss. If this was our sixth or seventh time in his room, which is what I remembered, maybe I might think about using jealousy to get him to kiss me. But it was the third time. And I was really shocked and upset by his immorality.

I did not have any of these doubts then. The short kisses kept burning inside me. I let Jack ride the number 71 bus with me. I thought I still wanted to be with him. In fact I felt too wonderful, and I could not show that on the bus. So I told him to get off after 2 stops. I got off after 3 stops and walked alone to my number 46 bus start. Yanan Lu was a blaze of lights. I had to search very hard in the dictionary to find the right word, but I think that is the right one. A blaze of lights. It seemed like Shanghai was on fire. The fire was really inside of me. It came from those kisses. I was seeing what was inside of me outside of me. There seemed to be so many lights on Yanan Lu. There were so many colours, even at night. Except there were not. Maybe it seemed like that because there were more lights than in Zha Bei, where I lived. But there were not many lights and colours even compared to Nelson, the little town in Canada I live near, and nothing compared to Shanghai now. The fire and the colours inside me made my city more beautiful than it ever was before. I did not know if I loved Shanghai or Jack more.

June 29

A fun and funny meeting. It began with a wonderfully comic incident that set the tone for most of last night. It is hot outside, so on coming inside Z always insists we both have a quick wash. Last night I showed her how to use the shower and persuaded her to take one. Soon after she jumped in, in trooped S, a beginning English student, not even mine, who has adopted me as his advisor on matters of English. With him came a group of his friends. No doubt S was enhancing his prestige by showing his friends he was intimate with foreigners. He must know a guard who lets him thru the gate. The bathroom door was locked, of course, but the water was running loudly. I kept telling S that I was busy and that he should go, but he is amazingly dense. He was given an assignment and didn't understand the essay he was supposed to analyze. Finally, seeing no other way and that his friends at least must have figured something out, I read his silly essay about the days of the week, told him what he needed to know and got rid of the bunch, but they were here about fifteen minutes. As I listened to the sounds of water turning on and off in the bathroom, I almost burst with laughter and it was all I could do to pay any attention to S's essay and questions. Not only that, as soon as they left I noticed that Z had left her handkerchief and ID (she didn't carry a purse) on the windowsill around which S's friends had been milling. I didn't see anyone pick her things up, but I've never seen any Chinese who didn't pick up and look at everything pickupable and lookatable around them, so I would be surprised if someone didn't look her ID over while S and I discussed the essay. I'd give anything to have heard the conversation which must have ensued after the group left. The one between Z and me was good enough. When the coast was clear and she emerged, we simply roared with laughter for several minutes. Then I tried to describe my feelings outside and she tried to describe hers inside. The rest of the evening we made jokes about people coming – there are always sounds from the corridor and the other rooms – and her hiding in the bathroom. It would be easier if we simply let out the news, but Z isn't yet ready for that. I'm sure she wants as short a time as possible in Shanghai after the news comes out. She says she will make a final decision after I return from travels in August. Do I really want to go on travels without her? There are plans to rethink.

Given that beginning, most of the evening was light, simple and lovely, but near the end we got into the whole jealousy then love syndrome. I tried to tell her how much I dislike jealousy and why while she told me how much she disapproved of my past and got me to make lots of promises about being faithful in the future. Some of the edge has gone off my physical desire, perhaps because I now know there will not be physical problems, perhaps because of the way she uses jealousy. It means I must always take the lead to console her. On the other hand, there was humor in last night's scene and I was aware that she was becoming aware it was silly. In the joking she called me a huai dan (bad egg) and said she was good and I was bad. The jealousy shtick was worth it to have her say that instead of the opposite, which she has been saying up 'til now. How sane she felt and how I enjoyed it: it is a long time since I was with someone so young and innocent in such matters. I have to go back to my teenage years to find such love play. I have to work hard to stay in the Chinese pattern and keep things – at least physical things – from getting too serious. In the West we would have made love last night. I told her that I would try to follow the Chinese traditions of sexual morality with her. I suppose that is an attempt to atone for past indiscretions.

I also told her that I have always had female friends because women's ideas are generally more interesting and stimulating than men's. Oppressed people are more interesting than oppressors, and contrast is more stimulating than similitude. I told her we should have friends, female and male, whose ideas are profound. Her reaction explained to me the attitude of many Chinese, especially unmarried ones, towards friends. Unmarried women, especially, call friends false, as she did. She says she doesn't want friends, i.e., that husband and wife (and family traditionally, no doubt) should be all in all to each other. Obviously such an attitude means that friends before marriage are dropped after marriage in China and this explains the bitterness toward friends of so many (usually unmarried) Chinese I have met. Certainly her idea is opposed to all mine, yet I also feel that Z alone is enough to satisfy me fully for a long time. As long as I can feel the depth of her ideas and as long as we can write of our ideas and feelings together, I can be content, happy with just her. And I will have a far better chance to change her mind if I don't make an issue of it, go her way and gradually discuss my ideas. I'm very happy. And confident our relationship will be a good one even if it turns out *different from my ideas of what it should be. Isn't it lovely to be young and in love again. (How she will dislike that last word when she reads this.) Back to exam grading, which, needless to say, is going wretchedly slowly.*

Z gives me instructions on all sorts of little things: e.g., the proper way to hold a glass of hot liquid to avoid getting germs on the rim. Like all Chinese she is much concerned with dirt and germs and expressed horror when I told her I used to bite my nails. She says I should even stop my nervous habit of scratching my thumbnail with other fingers of the same hand. However, she has nervous habits of her own, is restless and constantly pulling up her skirt with her fidgeting then readjusting it with her hands. At one point she had a pencil in hand and was unconsciously lightly scratching parallel lines on the wall. Back to exams.

The bit about friends is a strong indication why one so often sees unmarried people of the same sex so obviously expressing friendship hand in hand, arm in arm, arm over friend's shoulder etc. but virtually never sees anything like this in older, married people. Z says that even people I now tell about our relationship (F, Q, M, Ruby) I must not tell about her ideas, that these are only for discussion between ourselves. I pointed out that this is an odd attitude for a writer who wants to be published one day, but she persisted.

I didn't even finish grading one paper this time. I suddenly feel even better because I have decided to try to do things Z's way. My heart is lighter and I am suddenly filled with joy. As I wrote before I hadn't understood the implications of my decision. Now that I do understand, a load has been lifted from my mind, so I am suffused with happiness and feel a great desire for Z in the pit of my stomach, a strange place it seems to me. But quite in line with D.H. Lawrence's psychology. I also realize that our argument is the one between Ursula and Birkin in Women In Love. *Birkin also lost.*

One interesting thing is my previous reluctance to admit to myself that my feelings for Z had diminished, albeit very slightly, when I was thinking of her views as wrong, as showing she wasn't as deep as I previously thought. Understanding their validity, putting them in the context of D.H. Lawrence – Women In Love *is the book I want us to translate together: that will go far towards eliminating the language barrier, which is largely responsible for my previous mental belittling of Z's ideas – has brought the love back stronger than ever. How I wish she were here so I could embrace her. (And never grade exams. I doubt I have graded a dozen all day. After every paragraph here I have tried to grade some. And failed miserably.)*

Z wore perfume for the first time last night.

Jack is right. It was a funny night. Once I got a wiffle of the stink of Jack's sweat. After that I always made him wash when we came to his room. I do not sweat, but his bathroom was so nice so I always used it too. Being trapped in the bathroom was the funniest thing that ever happened to me. But if it happened the first or second time I was in Jack's room, it would be one of the scariest. I would never go back. That shows how fast things changed. Another funny thing I can see now is that I thought we were always doing things Jack's way. At the same time he thought we were doing them my way. Did we say? Did we not understand each other's language? I think maybe this was not a language problem. I think maybe we did say. But we did not hear. Our minds and hearts were on other things. Not our every mistake was because of language. Some times the two languages are similar. You can use the word "funny" to mean ha ha or strange. We figured out that you can say that in English and Chinese too. The two languages are so different, it always seems funny to me when they are the same.

Only a man, probably only a American man, could blame at me for being jealous. I should get mad at Jack, but when I write, I get in the mood of the time I am writing about. Now I can not get mad after that funny time in the shower. That is what happened then too. That is why I joked with Jack about my jealousy. That is why I called him a *huai dan.* If I was not in such a good mood, I might call him other things. How could I, a Chinese woman who was always a slave to her culture's morality and suffered, not be jealous of a man who never worried about morality? He always lived a life of sexual freedom without any bad results. Now he was getting a bad result, and he did not like it. Now a Chinese woman dared to be jealous of his easy life and his easy women. Jack deserved to be worried about jealousy. He had a lot to worry about, his past and his culture's present. Both of them seemed very immoral to me. Maybe Jack was not immoral. I did feel that, but I could not know it. Not yet. I had to live with him and in his culture for many years before I could be sure. Finally I learned I did not have to be jealous. Even some times when we argued, and even when he stopped loving me in Xinjiang, it never was because he loved another woman. Now I can figure out that there were bad results from Jack's easy life. Bad results for him that were good for me. Because he never fully gave himself to a woman before, he still could give a lot to me. Because he tried to fill himself without knowing how, there was a hollow space inside him. I fit in the space like the Red Army fit in the caves at Yanan. I know that now because I lived there longer than the Red Army lived in Yanan, but how could I know that then? How could I not be jealous? Besides, instead of sharing his freedom with me, he insisted on sharing my slavery. That was a very Chinese thing to do, but I was too impatient to admire that then. I was trying to escape my past too. Jack was running east, and China was turning me west. I could meet him, but I could not not be jealous of him.

How did we talk about so many serious things on such a funny night? We talked about friends, but we did not talk about D.H. Lawrence. For the first time we did not talk much about language. We figured out that "funny" was used the same way in Chinese and English, but maybe that was all. We were agreed to marry, so we talked about ourselfs and our future. Jack never asked me to marry him, and I never asked him to marry me. He thought I agreed to marry him at Baoshan, but I did not really. I really agreed when I finally returned his umbrella, but I knew he did not understand that. When we both agreed was when he kissed me and I kissed him back. Words confused us, but those kisses were clear. If we were both Americans or even if we were both Chinese, two kisses could not have that one clear meaning. We did not need language. We did not need friends. We had each other. So if those kisses were so important, I really need to figure out when and why we kissed. What if his kiss proposed marriage out of pity and my kiss accepted out of desperation? But I do not believe that. I will not believe that. How can I be who I am if I did that?

June 30

Last night very wonderful, much more calm than the previous two nights. We were able to be loving without the necessity of leading into it with jealousy, so we could be more tender than previously. Z almost instinctively attempted some small jealousy ploys, but they were halfhearted and I managed to deflect them. The reason they were halfhearted and the reason we were able to be so tender, I think, was that I began the evening by telling her I would try to live her way: few friends, mainly relying on each other, etc. Interestingly, she replied that I had misunderstood what she said on this topic, that all she had said was that in China friends are often false. Apparently I had inferred far more than she intended. She said we would have to discuss this more. Nevertheless, she was obviously pleased that I had conceded to her, and that surely had much to do with the subsequent calm and tenderness.

She is very wonderful and my feelings for her keep growing. My desire also. I want excruciatingly to make love to her and I think I could probably lead her into it. But I must not. I must play it the Chinese way. So mainly we talked. One good aspect of the language barrier is that it takes so long to discuss everything (and even when we finish we are still not fully sure of much and often later end up reopening topics) that, given how much we have to say to each other, it will be years before we even begin to exhaust our initial fount of discussion. And since every conversation generates more things to talk about than it concludes, I can't envisage the silences and perpetual small talk that usually overtake married couples. I want to be with her all the time, hate seeing her off. When I told her this – we walked to her second bus near People's Square for the first time last night – she was very happy. We talked about having a child. Mainly she sounded me out and I tried to take a balanced approach, stressing both the joy of raising a child and the work. At first she thought I was opposed, but I assured her I would like and support any decision she came to. My feeling is that she wants a child, but she did not actually say that. She is obviously still resolving many doubts about me. She volunteered the information that she intentionally did not come to our first scheduled meeting because she did not want to meet a foreigner. I was not surprised but appreciated her openness in telling me. We are coming to trust each other more and more. But shows of affection are still strictly private. On the street I automatically patted her back to reassure her and she said I mustn't, said it would be ok if I were Chinese and is ok in the room but not in public. Of course when we stand making plans in the shadows near the busstop, I think anyone who isn't a fool must be able to tell what is going on. But that is because my own feelings are so strong, I assume they must ring an alarm to anyone in the vicinity.

When she first came to the hotel I took her to all the fancy shops. She entered with great trepidation but was sensitive to everything, noticed small things that are second nature to me, like the little bow shop assistants gave us as we entered. In the bookshop she pored over a fine, huge, expensive color plate book of ancient Chinese clothing with obvious fascination, the fascination of a historian. It was nice that she was interested in that book, not the fancy modern clothing, jewelry etc., but how much of that was my fault I don't know since I started our tour by stating my dislike for the shops and the things in them. It is natural for a woman who has been poor all her life and discriminated against because she has no fancy clothes to want some, and I must not begrudge her (and don't want to, but I also don't want them to be important to her). If I can take or send her shopping with Ruby, that should make her happy and serve the additional purpose of bringing them closer together. I brought up the possibility of her not working, just writing in Wuhan. She would like that but feels strongly that if she does not work she has no right to eat my food. I did not press her, simply planted a seed. I wonder if it will grow. On her own she told me she did not want to write with me concerning our relationship. Must grade exams! This is preposterous.

Graded three papers and I'm back. (Briefly, damn it!) We examined each other's skin hair. Or lack of it in her case. She seems to have no hair on her arms and legs as Westerners do, is amazingly, wonderfully smooth. She was fascinated by all of mine, laughed at it, pulled at it. We also compared the thickness of our limbs. She is really slender. She played with the fat of my calf – of course I'm wearing shorts these days – and laughed good naturedly at it. She did not say I was "strong" (a euphemism for "fat") as most Chinese do; perhaps she lacks the vocabulary. But when we arm wrestled, I could defeat her even when she used two hands.

The understanding in myself which I reached two days ago is obviously based on love. The more I love her, the more I am willing to concentrate wholly on her. She has given me back my youth, restored the power I thought was long gone, the power to love fully. Naturally I am grateful and want to exercise that full power fully, but beyond that we share a creative interest (or an interest in creativity) which should be able to perpetuate the high of love I feel beyond the usual limits. On the other hand, such hopes may well be mainly an old man's fantasies. Time will tell.

Jack's diary is changed now. Before he wrote about many things. Now he writes only about one thing. Us. If I use more of his diary, I will not have to write so much myself. And maybe I can do that because at this time it seemed like we had lots of similarity and not much difference. Although our languages and cultures and habits and classes and sexes and ages were very different, but some times in his room I felt like we were one person, and some times like Jack was my brother, the big brother I always wanted but never had. Maybe this is when I started to get impatient. Maybe it really started after the kiss, not before. Maybe that is why I got impatient. We kissed, and we became like one.

It seemed like we should do more than talk. Even though the talk was very wonderful. Outside it was different. Outside I could never forget that he was a foreigner. Even today I can not do that in China. Just like it is still hard to forget that I am a foreigner in Canada.

I keep thinking about that first kiss. I keep asking myself how can there be three different memories of some thing that only happened once? I still do not know when and how it happened, but I have a idea about why we write about it so many different ways. We like to think that love makes lovers equal, but maybe we are not so democratic. A Canadian once said to me, "The heart is generous, but the mind is selfish." Chinese do not split people in half this way. Our word xin means mind and heart. There is only one xin, but it can be divided. One part can want one thing, and another part can want some other thing. Maybe both of us wanted two things at once. Both of us wanted to be equal, and both of us wanted to be the leader. Maybe memory is a toy of our wants, and writing is the way we play with that toy? So in his diary Jack wanted the kiss to come when he was above me. His heart could be generous, while his mind could look down on me because I was jealous and he was not. I wanted the kiss that brought us together to come when I was above him. I called him jiushizhu because I suddenly understood him. I understood a foreigner better than he understood himself. I was standing above him. He had to come up to me for us to be equal. Later, when Jack wrote his novel, he did not want to be above me any more. He was trying to find a new and equal relationship, so he writes us laughing together. No one is above and no one is below when we kiss. Maybe Jack's novel plays more fair than both of our minds. It gives the traditional Chinese way, the middle way. But that does not mean the kisses really happened that way. It does not mean that way is true and the other ways are false. Does it mean that the line we younger Chinese were taught always to draw between true and false comes right in the middle? We can not know what is true and what is false, so we take the middle way? That is a contradiction that even Chairman Mao would not like. Chairman Mao always knew what was the right way and what was the wrong way to solve a contradiction. He never took the Chinese middle way just like he never took the capitalist road.

July 1
    Last night we advanced to the stage of "bolande ganqing," which the dictionary defines as "great waves of emotion," but "passion" is the appropriate word, not "emotion:" great waves of passion. Who would have expected Chinese to have an expression for such things? It proves my contention that you can make anything in Chinese by combining zi. But I no longer care about Chinese zi, only Chinese Z. She has more passion than I have ever experienced in a woman. How has she survived alone? No wonder she has been unhappy. And how wonderful that all that passion has been stored up for me. And how wonderful to discover that I still have so much left to give her in return. How we

managed to keep all we felt from leading to sex I'll never know, but I do know we had better get married soon if we are really to do this the Chinese way. As one of our great waves broke against a rocky headland, she asked me whether I "neng bu neng?" (able or not?) Obviously Z had unexpressed doubts about my advanced age. Even riding the great wave we were able to laugh a little over those doubts – I placed her hand where she could feel my ability – but she still wanted to know about the future. I said "always" a lot more times than my mind now informs me is possible, but even now, in the calm, unwavy light of morning, I feel that my mind is wrong and that what my heart told her last night is true: when I am dead "cai meiyoule" (only then no more). I am young again and our love is far greater than anything I ever dared hope for. The longing for her I now feel in the pit of my stomach makes it almost impossible to write. This is what I have dreamed of all my life, a love which encompasses ideas, emotions and action together, and I understand that all my previous theories were simply attempts to find substitutes for that dream, this reality.

She feels astonishingly thin, fragile, but so full of life and passion. Even on the street (we walked far and slowly) we couldn't help touching surreptitiously.

"Great waves of passion, a flower floating on a boundless sea." I wrote that on the bus on my way home. I wrote it in Chinese, of course. The idea came from "*bolande ganqing,*" which I showed Jack in the dictionary, but by the time I got home I figured out where else it came from. I took my copy of *Hai Shang Hua Lie Zhuan* (usually translated Sing-Song Girls of Shanghai, but the literal translation is Lives of the Flowers of Shanghai) downstairs to read so I would not disturb my mother, who was sleeping upstairs. Early in the novel the narrator dreams he is on top of a sea of flowers. Flowers Too Feel For Me is a literal translation of the narrator's name. Let me quote a little from a translation of his dream. "With no water visible, Flowers Too Feel For Me saw only the flowers and danced for joy. Ignoring the sea's vast area and fathomless depth, he lingered and loitered, unwilling to depart, as though he were on dry land. But although the flowers had their complements of leaves and branches, they were all rootless. Once the sea water beneath them started to surge violently, the flowers could only follow the waves wherever their destiny might take them."

The flowers in the dream are courtesans of Shanghai in the late Qing Dynasty. They were my ancestors. My experiences with Jack were strange. None of my friends ever talked about experiences like that. But flowers would have experiences like mine. They would experience passion with a man from another world, for they really had no roots. Most of them were bought as young children and raised up in their own world, the world of the Shanghai brothels, a world of women. Men had to pay to get in. All men were foreigners to the flowers. Foreigners who could take them to a new world. A new world of body, a new world of mind, a new world of place. I am sure some of them dreamed what

I was dreaming. But they had what I did not, sister flowers. They could meet with each other and talk about their experiences of passion. Maybe some of them tried to recreate with each other their own feelings and even their lovers' feelings. Maybe some of them wrote poems for each other or they wrote together, poems of passion in their own dialect, poems that only flowers could really understand. For their dialect was *Suzhouhua*, a *wu* dialect like *Shanghaihua* but not the same, and probably after generations in the brothels of Shanghai their *Suzhouhua* changed from the dialect spoken in the city of Suzhou, a ancient city of canals ninety kilometres westnorth of Shanghai. Traditionally Suzhou was famous as one of two Chinese paradises on earth. "Above there is heaven, below there are Suzhou and Hangzhou," is a famous saying. In Shanghai the flowers created another kind of earthy paradise. They could not write about it in ordinary Chinese, for such writing would be considered yellow, very immoral. But they were trained as poets, so they could figure out how to write in their own dialect, in *huahua*. The name sounds funny in English. Although the two *zi* do not look like each other and are pronounced in different tones, but in English they both come out "hua." The *hua* flowers certainly had such a *hua* dialect. Every small community in old China had its local variation of a wider dialect, but the flowers were unique because they were all women, all educated, all artists, all poets. Not many dialects had a written as well as a spoken dialect, but Han Bangqing, the author of *Hai Shang Hua Lie Zhuan*, wrote all his conversations in *Suzhouhua*. He spent all his free time in the brothels, so probably he learned to write in dialect from the flowers. He hints that the flowers experimented with their bodies as well as their words. They could do that in ways only they could understand too. Their own world was very separated from the rest of China, so that would be safe. And they would need to do it. I knew. I needed to do it too. I loved *Hai Shang Hua Lie Zhuan*, but it was written by a man. How unique the flowers' own lost poems and novels would be, unique in their language, unique in describing passions forbidden in China, illegal passions with men foreign to them, illegal passions which maybe led to illegal passions with women, with each other, with the only ones who could understand. The only ones who could understand the passions and the words.

I had no sister flower. I went to my factory floor and found Xiao Wang. She was the only person I could think of who might understand a little of what I was feeling and thinking. We had no *huahua*, but at least we could talk in *Shanghaihua*. Talking to Jack was double difficult. I had to talk like a child, and I had to talk in English, which I thought I could never learn, or Mandarin, which is a dialect I learned and spoke only in school. Shanghai people always want to talk in *Shanghaihua*, but even in our own dialect Xiao Wang could not understand what I was trying to tell her. No, she could understand. I felt that. She would not let herself understand. She had a husband, a mother-in-law, a baby. Her life was now in her family. The Xiao Wang I knew two or three years ago would try to talk to me like the flowers could talk to each other. Not now. It was what I was trying to tell Jack when I told him that in China friends usually are false after they marry.

Friends are false, but ancestors are true. They can not change because they are dead. I went home and tried to write like the flowers maybe wrote for their sisters' sharp eyes, writings their nimble hands could destroy or Chinese society would destroy if the flowers themselfs did not. I had to create my own sister flower. I needed her. I needed to say many things I could not say to any person. I could say them to the paper. Then I could tear the paper into little tiny pieces. My sister flower's name was easy. I would call her Erbao (Second Treasure) after Zhao Erbao, a character in *Hai Shang Hua Lie Zhuan*, a beautiful country girl who chooses voluntarily to become a courtesan at the age of fifteen. She was more like me than the other courtesans in the novel. She had roots. She had a family. The novel is based on real courtesans the author knew, and my mother told me that when I was a child, I met a very old woman from the Subei who once was a famous courtesan. "You found her when she needed help," Ma always told me. The funny thing is that I kept finding her. When I needed help.

The year is 1890. Erbao stands in front of her mirror. Here in Canada I have a big mirror. I can see my whole body in it. When I was growing up in Shanghai, we only had small mirrors in my house. But my sister had a big one with a rosewood frame. She bought it at a store that sold old things, so maybe it was made around 1890. The mirror I see Erbao looking at looks like my sister's, not mine. When I was a teenager, I visited my sister in Hefei. Once when I was alone in her apartment, I took off my clothes and looked at myself in her mirror. It was the first time I could really look at my whole body. Too bad it was winter. It was too cold to look as long as I wanted to. Now it is winter in Canada, but it is not winter in my writing.

Erbao stands in front of her mirror. She will do everything for herself tonight. She will not let Ahu, her maid, touch her. When she told Ahu, the woman laughed. What a child you are, Ahu told her. What a child she is. Long, lithe limbs, slender legs and hips. And breasts. She touches them, squeezes them gently. They were her body's way of rejecting childhood. Nothing is childish about her breasts. In the countryside she was ashamed of them, but here in Shanghai they are what makes her a woman, a woman to be desired. Shi loves to rub against them, accidentally of course. And when he rubs, Erbao knows just how to lean so he can guess what is there. Tonight the guessing will end for both of them. Erbao laughs out loud. Then she deals with her hair. She knows her hair is too short. It does not yet reach her waist. She can not wind it into as many snacks and serpents as some of her sister flowers, but it has some thing none of their hair has, its own curl. She brushes it many times. She likes to let Shi see her brush it, likes to let him see that she needs no heat to make it curl. Now she lets it frame her hairless body. How Shi will love her body. How will her body feel?

She wonders. She examines it more closely. One, two, three body hairs. Should she pull them out? No, she will let Shi. How he will enjoy that, and he will keep them to help him remember this night, this perfect night. How he will want her body, her silk body. And how she wants his although his is heavy wool, not fine silk, wool to keep her warm. She places all the combs just right and turns to her face. It is too long, not the traditional full moon considered most beautiful. Even before she became a courtesan, she decided she would emphasize its length instead of trying to hide it. Hers would be a crescent moon face, not a full moon. That shape suits her long body. She always arranges her hair in a curve which makes her face seem to curve too. The curve of her face matches the curve of her breasts. It is not the traditional beauty, but Shanghai is not a traditional city. Its foreign women are often tall and long faced. If only she had their full bodies instead of her own half starved one. Still, she knows that her slim body makes her breasts more desirable. Although her beauty is neither Chinese nor foreign, but it is her beauty, and Shi approves. His eyes are big when he looks at her. Her eyes are big too. Not as big as those of the foreign devils she has seen on the streets of Shanghai, but big for Chinese eyes. They make her look innocent. She does not like that, but she knows men do. No one likes her eyebrows. They are too much like the rest of her body, almost hairless. She puts on colouring, deep black with just a little purple, a long, thin line curved like her face and body, unlike the flying moths eyebrows should resemble but emphasizing her big eyes like her thin body emphasizes her breasts. How Shi will love her breasts. Now she works on her lips. Not too much paint, not too red, just enough to make him desire them, to desire her, not her paint. The middle way. No thing too much. But every thing perfect. Her face is too red, too healthy from too many years in the countryside. How could she live so many years without even knowing this Shanghai life, this pleasure life, was here? Why did she not find it for fifteen long years? Her powder makes her face whiter, but not too white just as her lips should not be too red. Every thing must fit. Beauty must bend but not too much to either side. To sway gently as a woman learns to do on bound feet. Erbao looks down at her feet, her three *cun* golden lillies. They are the only part of her body which is covered. By the new red silk slippers she embroidered for herself. Red symbolizing marriage, the mandarin duck pattern, symbolizing beauty and constant love. Shi will kiss those slippers tonight. She wonders if he will want to unbind her feet before kissing them. Shaungbao told her that some men do. This shows great love, for the only time Erbao unbinds her feet is when she wants to punish herself. Then she unbinds a foot and holds it under her nose. The stink is her punishment.

Erbao remembers. She dreams. She plans. Shi already fulfilled all the traditional rituals of courtship. He gave her many gifts, and tonight she will give the gift a woman only gives once. The mirror she is looking in with its carved rosewood frame is his gift she likes best. The pearl combs she used to style her hair also come from him as do all the clothes, except the slippers, she will wear tonight. Red embroidered silk, the colour of brides, the colour of blood. She will bleed tonight. The fine perfume she will wear is also from him. A flower must smell like a flower. Four times he took her and Ahu in a horse cart to the Ming Gardens, feeding her delicious purple plums which made her white skin look even whiter, showing her off to the city and the other flowers in the Gardens. Three times he took her to the opera, always sending a boy ahead to wave the tickets and announce loudly, "Inviting guest." Then he picked her up and they drove together in a horse cart for all to see. But Shi went past tradition. He is modern too. Twice he took her to the strange, new, foreign photography studio, the first time to pose alone, the second time with him. In the photograph the peacock feathers he gave her float over his head as well as hers. Three nights ago he took her to a Western style restaurant. The food was not as good as the Chinese restaurants, but they ate alone, not at a banquet with many other men and their flowers. She wore the moon white silk blouse with cloud patterns and sky blue slippers, but tonight she will wear red. He will offer far more than the usual price for a virgin courtesan, but she will refuse any payment. Shi considers her a *changsan* (long three) and always pays her a extra dollar when she accompanies him. He calls her *xiansheng*, not *xiaojie*, as others call her. *Xiansheng* means sir and is the name for *changsan* courtesans. *Xiaojie* means miss and is the name for *yao'er* (one, two) courtesans, a lower class. By refusing payment tonight, she will show Shi he is right. Shi deserves this. He always praises her singing and her poems although she knows her art is not the highest. How could it be? She studied months, her sister flowers studied years. But Shi praises her and was patient through all the rituals. More patient than she. Waiting patiently is another talent her sister flowers were trained in from childhood. Shi will be surprised tonight. How she enjoys knowing what he does not. This is to be the night she will grant him what he wants. What they both want. She knows just how she will do it. He will kiss her, gently as he always does, but she will lean against him, let him become passionate, touch her. Then she will touch him. "*Neng bu neng?*" she will ask. As if she does not know.

Erbao finishes her work at the big mirror. She takes her small hand mirror, sits on her bed and examines herself. She looks long and carefully so she can remember. Will it look different tomorrow? "I can not wait to see." She says it out loud, and Ahu laughs. Erbao jumps up. "You were spying on me," she accuses angrily. Then she laughs. She and Ahu both laugh and laugh together. Then Erbao says, "Come. Hold the mirror. Maybe I can see more if I stand on my head." How nice to have a servant. It is hard to see if you are alone even if you do it against a wall.

July 2

　　The reaction which came last night caught me completely off guard. It was a reaction against my past and a powerful one. That I didn't expect it – or didn't expect it in the way it came – shows my ignorance of China. Love is indeed blind. It's hard to believe I can love so much yet know so little about the woman and culture I love. Z asked me about and – since to me being fully honest is vital to our relationship – I told her about my past sexual experience. Only in a general way, for her hurt immediately became so great I had to spend the rest of the evening comforting her. I'm afraid I understated the number of women I have slept with: I admitted to eight to ten. Z was hurt to tears, which she several times suppressed. There was so much I needed to say to comfort her, and, it goes without saying, my Chinese failed me utterly as her English did her. How the hell do you say in Chinese that virtue is rewarded, or that it is its own reward? I went for the English-Chinese dictionary: sometimes English proverbs have a Chinese equivalent. No dice. She found something in the Chinese-English dictionary first: "bu ke su yi," inconceivable. A Chinese cannot conceive of our Western attitude toward sex. In China, Z chokingly informed me, it is assumed that a man will have one woman, a woman one man for life. (Multiple wives and the double standard were conveniences of the old society and its upper class only.) I suddenly realized how profound is the influence of Freud in the West, for the Chinese view of sex (purely as an adjunct to marriage) is as inconceivable to a modern educated Westerner as my view (of marriage as, at best, as it is with her, an adjunct to sex) is to Z. So when I listed all my faults which didn't faze her that Sunday in Baoshan, it didn't even occur to me to list my sexual "exploits." Because I know that compared to most Westerners of my age and background I have had few. Because I have never slept around. Because I don't think of myself as immoral in any sense.

So much to say and no time to say it, so I'll summarize briefly. All's well that ends well, and this eventually did. Z's love conquered her hate of my past and we reconciled. With a deeper understanding of our differences. But Z was shivering and spent most of the evening wrapped in my sweater. Even walking outside she felt cold. (The weather has taken an unexpected but, to those of us who have not suffered bone chilling disillusion, lovely cool turn.) We certainly did not conclude this subject, but I think (hope) we were mauled by it enough to keep us away from it for several months.

My memory really is wrong. "Bu ke su yi" came here, not earlier, like I thought. Not right before the first kiss. This is when I was feeling those terrible jealousy emotions. So maybe the first kiss probably came where the diary says too. At least I was not feeling terrible like I thought. Probably I could kiss Jack back.

I wonder if Erbao would worry so much. Would she care how the kiss came? I was too upset to ask myself theory questions when Jack left me at the bus stop, but I asked them a few days later when I red more of Hai Shang Hua Lie Zhuan. Am I loving from desperation? I asked myself. Am I loving to despair? Like Erbao, my sister-grandmother did?

Erbao was worried. It was more than a month since Shi left, promising to return and marry her in a month. As soon as he left, she removed her nameplate and locked her door. She put on the dress of a housewife and borrowed more than three thousand *yuan* to buy her trousseau. She ignored Shi's promise to buy everything she needed when he returned just like she refused his offer of a thousand *yuan* to pay for the wonderful month he booked her for before he left. Now he was late. He was never late before. He never failed to keep a promise. What should she do? She sent Ahu with a note asking her friend Shuangbao (Twin Treasure) to visit when she had time.

Shuangbao came at once. She bounced into Erbao's room in her brightest, lightest green *qipao*. Even before she took off her hat, she was asking, "Mei, mei, what thing is happening? What clothes are you wearing? Why is there a light patch where your nameplate was?" Although Shuangbao was only two years older than Erbao, but she had been raised in a brothel. She knew the signs immediately. "Shi deserted you," she concluded before Erbao answered her questions.

"No.... I do not know.... He is a good person. He loves me."

"Tell me," Shuangbao told her.

Slowly, pausing often, Erbao told her story. When she finished, Shuangbao said nothing. She took Erbao in her arms and kissed her gently. Erbao looked up at her in surprise. Shuangbao sighed. "A woman in our profession can not afford to know too little, love too much." There were tears in her eyes. "Ah, *mei mei*, if you want to become a wife, you should stay in the countryside and let your family choose you a husband."

"But my family could never choose Shi. He is so gentle."

"He is so rich. I know. Unfortunately you can not choose Shi either. Because Shi's family can not choose you. Do you think his family will ever accept a flower?"

"But Shi...."

"Do not tell me about Shi. Shi can choose a flower. Only his family can choose a wife. Let me tell you about Shi. He is from Nanjing, right?" Erbao nodded. "I will send someone to Nanjing to inquire, but even before I do I will tell you what he will learn. Your Third Young Master is preparing to marry as he told you." Erbao's face caught fire. Shuangbao held her tightly. She kissed her again and whispered, "He is not preparing to marry you." Erbao tried to pull free, but Shuangbao held her too tight. "Listen. The wedding was probably arranged when he was a child. Maybe at his birth. His family let him come to Shanghai to play before his marriage."

There were tears in Erbao's eyes too. "But he will take three wifes," she tried to protest.

"None of them will be flowers," Shuangbao told her. "When he is old and his father, mother are dead, then perhaps he will take a flower as a concubine. But by then you will be too old. He will take a young girl like you are now. He will tell himself, 'She is lovely. She is just like Erbao was.' He will remember you, but what good will that do you?"

Erbao cried. Shuangbao held her for a long time. Then slowly, between sobs, Erbao began to talk. She told Shuangbao about her life in the countryside. She told about coming to Shanghai to help look for her brother. She told about seeing a world she heard of in stories but never believed existed. She told why she became a courtesan. She told her dreams. She was talking freely by the time she got to Shi, no longer crying. Shuangbao said nothing, just held her. When her words began to slow again, her elder sister sighed. "Ah, the new born calf does not fear the tiger." Then Shuangbao laughed. "Chinese has many proverbs, but only flowers know the one you need. Families like Shi's demand virtue, but flowers know: work is virtue. If we study what we do and do it well, we become artists. If we do it badly, we become whores. Work, *mei mei*. We can know more and live better than most women who marry." She began unbuttoning Erbao's housedress. "Come. Take off these rags. Your *jie jie* will give you a bath and message."

That evening Erbao put back her nameplate and reopened her door.

July 3

I'm sure my revelations of the previous night influenced Z's of last night tho I know she has wanted to speak of herself and tell me why she thinks she isn't good enough for me. Hopefully understanding at least one way in which I'm not good enough for her has helped her. Last night we set the stage by watching Pavoratti in La Boehme *on TV from Beijing. From that tragic and sentimental mood flowed her story and great distress. She cried lots and I'm sure she needed to. I have felt her overcome a need to cry on several previous occasions, and the night before it was overwhelming, so this time I encouraged her to let the tears out and she did. If I had cried as I should have the night before, we could have done it together. Mainly she talked about her six year (1979-1985) romance which failed. For six years she and her boyfriend met once a week (as F and her boyfriend do now). For six years her boyfriend wouldn't shit or get off the pot while she went nuts. Near the end, she said, she was twice near suicide. I knew from Mei and Qiu that the boyfriend's parents refused the match, but what she added to that was that he then would neither defy them nor break off with her, left her dangling. For six years. The gutless bastard wanted to have his cake and eat it too. She expressed, I'm sure for the first time, real hatred of him, enumerated and elaborated about the ways he destroyed her spirit and how, as a result, she now feels sick, experiences frequent headaches, feels reduced from what she was. I felt hatred both for him and for this society in which feudal ethics still control so much, in which women are pawns of male egos and feudal familial customs. This is the other side of the coin of what is bad about Western ethics which I understood the previous night, how Freud has incapacitated us when we encounter innocence and purity. (How I hate myself for laughing when I was told she was "chaste.") We didn't – couldn't – say this, but I hope together Z and I can evolve an ethic far superior to both my previous pontificating in the West and her victimization here.*

Walking to her bus – last night it was 1:00 a.m. when I returned, by far the latest so far; after midnight busses are few and far between, so we had a time in the shadows

(I wonder when we will be able to have a time in the sun?) – she talked of hardly being able to write at all because her spirit had been so low. In the room she had talked of perhaps being able to write now, even outlined a story which would express her hatred for what her Chinese boyfriend did to her. She said it will take place in a turn of the century brothel. We had trouble with that word, and she blushed beautifully explaining it and "prostitute," which apparently goes by the euphemism "flower" in Chinese. *(She spoke obliquely, and I couldn't help remembering how, when I was a child, I told my mother some place that I did not want to go into with her "looks like a whore house," and she, surprised by my vocabulary, asked me if I knew what a whore house was. "A place where men go to fuck women," I told her. That was the extent of my nine year old schoolyard vocabulary and I did not know what the words meant, but my mother was even more shocked than I had hoped she would be. Yet maybe the Chinese know more about using words than I give them credit for: I swear that Z's vague explanation impressed me even more than my succinct one did mom.)* I did not understand how her story related to her and her boyfriend, but I encouraged her to write it. She said it was due to me she now felt she could write: heavenly music to my ears. If I have this effect on her, I thought, I can ask no more. And I told her what I think is true, that she will have a similar effect on me. She will free me from the necessity to write as therapy. If my life is not full of shit, I won't have to write to get the shit out. When I told her this (not in those words, of course), she seemed to accept it, but I felt she had not really understood what I meant. This happens all the time because of the language barrier, but this time was different. The notion apparently stayed in her mind, revolved until, when we were beginning to talk about something else, it came around again and she suddenly asked, "If not learn write, why write?" Or something like that. I managed to figure out she was asking, "If you don't learn by writing, why write?" What a perfect example of Chinese didacticism. Writing is worthwhile only if it teaches a lesson. So is life. I talked about revising my novels to make them readable for other people, but I don't think I ever answered her question. I'm sure she took what I said as meaning I want to teach other people lessons. I tried to talk about creativity, but that is well beyond the limits of the language barrier. I fear it may be so alien to Chinese thought that even when the language barrier is overcome I may not be able to explain it cogently. But perhaps life – living with me – will teach her that lesson. Hmm. Does that last sentence mean that life – being with Z – is teaching me the lesson that didacticism is not such an alien concept to me?

　　Last night she began saying "I love you" – I have been saying "wo ai ni" for several nights – but she always added a "keshi" *(I always say "danshi" for "but"; I wonder if "keshi" is stronger)* after it that she wasn't good enough for me, that I should choose (she asked me for this word in English) another woman. Her idea is that while I travel (can I really contemplate travelling without her?) I should be on the lookout for another woman and we will decide nothing definitely until I return. In a way this is a proper idea since it will give us a short chance for perspective – how incredible it seems that we met less than a month ago – but we both know that the die has been cast and the decision is irreversible on both sides. In any case I'm sure we can't really do anything until I come back to

Shanghai in August, so I'm willing to go along with that plan (if I can tear myself away).
How the hell do I find out the official procedures for marriage when I am not allowed
to tell anyone? Most perplexing. She still will not meet my students or friends who could
help us work out such matters. She does not even want to meet Qiu. Yet I'm sure plenty of
people know. X dropped in for a visit day before yesterday when she was here. He is much
too smart to fall for stories about mutual Chinese-English lessons. He had a big grin on
his face the whole time he was here altho of course he was too polite to say anything.

In any case two nights of travail have greatly deepened our love. Even on the streets
we are touching both casually and deliberately and she is as often the instigator as I. It is
utterly mutual, impossible to stop. Yet a few steps later she will ask me to "choose again."
I still look around to make sure there are no people looking before patting her back, but
she seems to take no precaution before poking me back. Then she remembers. "You can't,"
she tells me. "Choose again, Jiake," she implores and retreats a few steps away from me.
"Choose again." I go back to her and take her hand. "You can't." She squeezes mine.
"Choose again." We resume walking. I lean against her. "You can't." She dexterously runs
her leg up along mine. "Choose again." By the time we approach her busstop and I take
her into the shadows and kiss her and she turns it into a French kiss before telling me to
"choose again," her plea has become our joke.

She considers herself bad for coming to my room every night. Another thing immoral
in China, but I have been very careful (it's bu ke su yi how difficult that is becoming)
to insure that nothing genuinely immoral occurs – altho I have no doubt that necking is
considered immoral in China too. Anyhow we won't see each other for three whole days
because students will be coming constantly to say goodbye. I might even be able to finish
grading their exams and get their grades in. Can I stand not seeing her? I suppose I'll have
to, but I wish I didn't.

I wonder what might flow if the opera we watched then was Madam
Butterfly, not La Boehme? Probably the same thing. We were too much in love
for a opera to teach us or change us. But maybe it might make our love a little
bit less sentimental? And maybe I might not think so much about Erbao at that
time. You see, the Paris of Puccini was like the Shanghai of Han Ban Qing.
They both had a section where people did not live by the morality of the rest of
society. Puccini wrote a opera about China and a opera about Japan. Why did he
not know that Paris at the end of the nineteenth century was more like Shanghai
than Bohemia?

I am surprised that I told Jack what I was writing then. Very surprised.
Because I even forgot I wrote it then too. I am learning how funny memory really
is. It seems like just remembering that time now made me do the same thing I
did then. It made me write like I did then. But then I did not tell Jack the most
important thing. I did not tell him that I was tearing up what I wrote as soon
as I wrote it. I could not even read it myself. It was too yellow. But I had to talk.
There was no person I could talk my strange new feelings to, so I talked to the

paper. The need to get things out of you is a strong need. It is a natural need. Jack, with his as usual bad language, calls it getting the shit out. He says it is why he wrote his first three novels. I understand that now. I also understand that I did the right thing then. I tore up what I wrote as soon as I wrote it. Such writing is not literature. It needs to be written, but it does not need to be red. It is not even worth remembering. That is why I forgot it until now.

After living so many years in North America, maybe I can write it again. It will not be the same as what I wrote then. I wish it will be better. I wish it will be literature. I know much more than I knew then. But maybe it might be worse. I feel much less than I did then. I maybe can even become more Canadian by writing Erbao's Shanghai story that I had to tear up in China. Canadians are not afraid to write such things. After Liberation Erbao had the same problem of yellow writing. She solved her problem by writing in dialect. So she did not have to tear up what she wrote, but writing in *huahua* meant that no one could read it. The only people who might read *huahua* were *hua*, and almost all the old flowers were dead, and the younger flowers were very busy pretending they were not flowers. In the new revolutionary society flowers were called poisonous weeds. Flowers who wanted to grow had to pretend to be gardeners. Even the old Emperor did that too. The dialect I have to write in is English, but even in China many people can read English now. I think I do not care. In Canada I red yellower novels than what I want to write. I wonder if I can write a whole novel. Not in English. No, in Chinese. But what I write in English might be a outline for that novel. I can write my English outline to say some of the things I do not think I can say yet in a language that has deep meaning for me. I can write it to see if I want to write a real novel, a Chinese novel.

You win, Jack. You won then and you are winning now. That should make you happy. Americans always worry about winning. Just thinking about winning and losing tells me how American I am becoming. I am afraid the whole world is becoming American. Canadians and Chinese too. You win, Jack, because I am becoming American. But you lost when you tried to become Chinese. Americans are winning now, but maybe they will lose at the end. They can not change. They can never be any thing but American. They are too like children to understand that there is more in the world than winners and losers. I might be becoming more American, but I will still be Chinese too.

You win, Jack. We are writing together just like you always wanted. And this time I will not tear the paper up. Feeling the same now as I did then shows me how different I am. You wrote your Chinese novel to try to bring us together. When I started writing this history, I thought I was writing to show how not together we were. We are. But we were together then, and we are together now. I thought I was attacking your fiction with facts. Now I see that I am not even sure I know the facts. And I am talking about writing a novel, a Chinese novel. If you were me, you would say "damn." But I do not say "damn," and it is not only because I do not like to curse. Suddenly I just figured out that I am happy. It is worth losing to relive the love we lived. The love that brought together two streets, two cities, two cultures, two people. It made them all both.

I was fooling myself. I can not write about this time like I wrote about Jack's novel. I need this time. If this time was not beautiful, if it was just a misunderstanding like many of our words, I wasted the rest of my life. If my past was a misunderstanding, then every thing since then is a mistake. What am I doing in the Canada countryside when Shanghai is the only place I love? Except my Shanghai is not there any more. I keep going back to look for it, and I can not find it. The past is a dream whether we understand it or not. And dreams are the stuff we turn into novels. What I am doing in the Canadian countryside is writing a dream.

Kongzi (Confucius) said, To know that we know what we know and we do not know what we do not know, that is knowledge. (The classical language did not waste words like modern English and Chinese do. A very literal translation of his words is, Know know not know not know is know.) Now that I know I do not know all the truth. Now that I know I am not writing a history. Now that I know I am creating a fiction just like Jack did, it is important that I create my own fiction. From now on I will let Jack be the main historian of our love, and I will become the novelist. His diaries are probably closer to the truth than my memories, which are almost the same age as Erbao. Erbao, who made me remember literature as well as history. I first met her at this time. I finished reading *Hai Shang Hua Lie Zhuan* at this time. For three days I could not see the man who I suddenly loved, who loved me but who was not yet my lover. He had to grade exams, say goodbye to his students, welcome his daughter. How jealous I was of his students and daughter. I red to keep from thinking of my jealousy. I started *Hai Shang Hua Lie Zhuan* just before I met Jack, but I stopped after I met him. Now I started again. I became tangled in the demimonde of 1890 Shanghai. Are you surprised I know a fancy word like "demimonde?" Maybe you will be more surprised to hear I have a Master of Arts degree. And my thesis was on *Hai Shang Hua Lie Zhuan*. Jack and my thesis advisor revised my English and taught me fancy English words like demimonde. But the ideas were mine. Mine and Erbao's. I know what I know, and I can use what I know to make my own novel just like I made my own thesis. I know it is not modest to mention my degree, but it seems necessary because it is in Chinese history and literature. Both. So maybe it is natural for my history to turn into a novel. Maybe I can not write all of the novel now. I still want to finish the history. But maybe it is also natural for my novel to turn into a history. Jack has a book named *The Outline of History*. The outline of my novel can be like the outline of the history of the city that made me what I am. The city that caught Jack and brought him to me. The name of my city even gets used that way in English. Shanghai shanghaied Jack.

Writing a novel, even a novel that acts like a history, I feel free. I am not

tied down by time, by history. To you, Erbao, sister who got me through hard
nights then and now, I can talk about bees and butterflies and food and silk and
poetry and all the secret things flowers love. I can sympathize when Lai breaks
up your house and listen when you tell dreams of Shi. And I can tell you what
I dream. Dreams may come and change and go before a dish of millet can be
steamed. They do not always come true, but they never die. Your dreams live in
me, sister. My dreams once lived in you.

Erbao, sister, grandmother, how much could you tell Shaungbao about
Shi? Did you have words? Did she really understand? I told Jack about Huang,
and he did. He understood. He had no words, but he really understood. He
understood with his body. My words flowed like a river, and he understood
the way a body understands water when it is swimming. When it is drowning.
He was drowning in the river of my words, but I was the one who was saved. I
told Mei and Qiu about Huang, but they felt sympathy for me. I did not want
sympathy. I wanted understanding. To know that some one knew what I knew.
Almost as soon as my words began to flow, I felt that Jack knew. Suddenly I
knew I was feeling what Jack was feeling, and it was what I needed some one to
feel. I was feeling understood. By a man who could not understand most of my
words. For although my river of words began flowing in English, but as it gained
speed it was more and more in Chinese, and by the time it reached the waterfall,
I lost control and the words were breaking into *Shanghaihua* and I knew that
Jack, who could not possibly understand my words, understood every thing I
felt and so the words kept flowing and his hands were understanding and his
legs and his what ever understood and my words flowed faster and faster, flowed
into a great waterfall of understanding and I was the water falling, falling and
being understood in my falling and never wondering how can a waterfall be
understood because his whole body understood my whole body and for the first
time I was free, free of Huang, free of fear, free of morality, free of history, free
of China, free of me, free, free, free. It was amazing because when the waterfall
finished falling, I was crying and he was holding me, and I was amazed because
we both had all our clothes on.

Erbao, sister, grandmother, did you take night walks after you finished
your business? I guess not. You would be tired after work, and bound feet were
not made for walking. Why would you want to walk any how? The streets of your
Shanghai were not the streets I loved. In the Chinese city many people died on
your streets. Wagons went around picking up dead bodies every morning. In
the foreign concessions Chinese women might be insulted by drunk foreigners
protected in our country by their foreign laws and courts. I was tired too after a
evening talking in English, and this night I was most tired because I went over
that waterfall. But the walks were my favourite time. The streets of my Shanghai
were safe. Looking back now I can see that those safe streets that seemed so
normal to me were not normal to Shanghai. The streets of your Shanghai, the

Shanghai of Foreign Concessions, the Shanghai where people died and got shanghaied, lasted more than fifty years and were replaced by the far more dangerous streets of Japanese rule. Even in my time the early and middle 1980s were a safe period between the crazy Cultural Revolution years and the greedy Reform years. And Jack was not like your clients. (It took me a while to remember that word. I learned it writing my thesis, but I did not use it for a long time.) He was proud to be on the streets with me, and that made me proud to be with him. At first I worried a lot about what other people thought, but this night I said *suanle*. Forget it. Maybe I was some times crazy. Often I did not care what people thought. Then I would notice that Jack's hand was on my shoulder or back or even my *pigu*, and I would remember and tell Jack, "You can't." Those were two English words I learned well. The other two I learned well were "choose again." I said them when I remembered myself. When I remembered I was crazy. When I remembered what happened with Huang. When I remembered all the women Jack was not true to. When you get deep enough under a word or phrase, it has a lesson to teach. Or a joke to tell. Or both. "Both" was once such a word for me. Now "choose again" became one too. Or two too.

I love Shanghai at night, and I learned to love it even more at this time. I learned that at night Shanghai was one world. In the daytime Huaihai Lu and Yanan Lu seemed like a different world from Pushan Lu, but at night you did not see the fancy shops and the fancy cars and the people in fancy clothes. The sidewalks were just as crowded with people sleeping on the same kinds of bamboo beds they slept on in Zhabei. Some times we had to walk one by one between them. I held his hand and pushed him first. I liked to see him from behind. He looked even bigger. Once he bumped into a bed because he was looking back at me. I laughed. "Look where you go," I told him. "*Ni shi zai nar wo qu,*" he said. By translating his words one by one into English, I figured out he meant, "You are where I go." My face felt hot. I quickly changed the subject. "What word means that noise?" I whispered. "Snore," he told me. People in Luwan snored the same snores people in Zhabei snored. "Do foreigners snore?" I asked Jack. He laughed his funny laugh. "Of course," he said. "Do you snore?" He laughed his snakiest laugh. "Of course not." Despite the snaky laugh, usually that is true. Usually he only snores when he sleeps on his back. Then I have to push him until he rolls on his side. Even when I push him away, usually he still rolls toward me. That is a good sign.

July 4

    Down with Independence Day. Give me Z or give me death. She called shortly after I had mailed her a letter (two sentences, one hour). Very frustrating: I couldn't say any of the things I wanted to say because there was a student in the room. She told me she couldn't come Sunday – and told me before I could ask her. The plea to come Sunday was what my letter was mainly about. Could she have received it already, I thought, but even the Shanghai mails are not delivered in fifteen minutes. It was funny trying to talk thru three barriers: language, telephone and student. I had to sift everything I thought thru those three meshes. Like a flour sifter. And in this ovenless land Z proved herself a baker. She caught on immediately that there was a student in the room which prevented me from speaking openly. Understanding without words is a piece of cake to her.

July 5

Ruby arrives tonight. Really missing Z. After the daily intensity of our contact I thought it might be something of a relief to have a few days off. The first day it almost seemed so – I actually got the exams graded and most of the final grades finished – but by the second day I was feeling her lack, and now I have a constant desire in the pit of my stomach. Last night I woke up every hour wanting her. I study Chinese continually in my mind by making up conversations with her. There is still so much we have to say to each other, from plans for the little, quotidian details of living together to the biggies, ideas for writing together, for living with and within each other on the kind of spiritual scale we both envisage but perhaps not in exactly the same way. Meanwhile I've got a slew of letters to answer, recommendations to write, all the stuff I should have been doing the last month but have not. I want to spend many hours each day studying Chinese but lack time. Z and I certainly should talk with Mei or another translator, especially regarding practical details – like how the hell we go about getting married – but Mei is due any day now and Z will be reluctant to deal with anyone else. Qiu hasn't called now for at least a week. Is this because he knows or because he doesn't? Probably he's just too busy with Mei.

Last night a lovely interlude seeing the Kun Opera (kunju) version of Macbeth. I only wish it played one day longer so Ruby could see it. And Z. How she would have loved seeing it, but I couldn't take her because my student C and her husband were taking me, and they are not allowed to know about Z. The opera was pure spectacle. It had little to do with Shakespeare altho the plot was borrowed from Macbeth. Kun and Beijing Opera, especially, are spectacles, not drama. (All opera, Western as well as Chinese, are to some extent, but these two are to a greater extent than others.) But it was a great spectacle, a spectacular spectacle. Why does it last only two nights? The answer, it suddenly occurs to me, is that Shakespeare is unknown to Chinese audiences. Were it Cao Cao and Zhuge Liang it would have played for weeks. Great preparation went into it: it was long and carefully rehearsed, yet the house was half empty (because, I was told, all the tickets were freebies sent to politicians etc. who have little interest). But the sparse audience was full of celebrities like Cao Yu (how neat that a classic like him is alive and well and living in Shanghai) and was warm and appreciative, far more attentive than most Chinese audiences. The costumes were magnificent, the acrobatics spectacular, every movement practiced to a perfection of coordination. There was a minimum of singing, the last half especially closer to dance than drama. Altho it wasn't really Shakespeare, it was real. Some of the other adaptations (especially Othello) in this "Shakespeare Festival" attempted to be Shakespeare but weren't real. This one had become genuinely Chinese. Some of the Chinese touches which were translated for me: the doctor (acting as prologue and explaining omissions since altho the version we saw lasted well over three hours, it contained only seven of nine scenes) says Macbeth and Lady Macbeth cry over Duncan's murder "like cats crying for a dead rat;" as a favor Macbeth does Lady Macbeth's maid the great honor of loaning her his sword and allowing her to commit suicide next to her dead mistress; there is lots of talk about god's will, Macbeth constantly saying that if it is god's will everything will be OK, Lady Macbeth saying her dream (of the tiger lying in the dragon's bed) and Macbeth's encounter with the witches match and therefore prove that it is god's will they act and become king and queen; and lots of unshakespearian supernatural, firebreathing, dancing ghosts etc., all of which were forbidden on the Chinese stage for many years and only permitted again recently. The Chinese can't resist adding morals (it is amazing how unsubtle this amazingly subtle people can be): e.g., at the banquet Macbeth says to Banquo's ghost: "The one I murdered is in much higher position than you." And Lady Macbeth is actually driven to death by four ghosts altho her clothing and general disarray in that scene – the difference was striking – also symbolized madness. I loved the many and various shivering motions. All in all a great performance, but it angers me that tickets weren't sold publicly. Surely there are enough people in Shanghai who would buy tickets to give such a play a week's run. I was really lucky to have knowledgeable friends who provided me with tickets, explanations and translations (the expert knew no English, so he explained to his wife, my student, who then told me: I was glad our tickets were in the balcony – first row, center – which was almost deserted, so our explanations and translations weren't disturbing others). Altogether it was a lovely evening of very modern opera – have I mentioned that everyone knew that Lady Macbeth was Jiang Qing? – which combined the best of Western classical art with the best of Chinese classical art. In the best Chinese tradition I cannot resist adding that I hope to spend the rest of my life adding to that new tradition with Z.

If Lady Macbeth is Jiang Qing, maybe Duncan is Chen Du Xiu. Chen Du Xiu was the first leader of the Communist Party in China. He was a intellectual who was a professor at Beijing University, but it was also well known that he always went to the brothels when he was in Shanghai. Maybe he knew Erbao.

The year is 1900. In the north the Yi He Tuan (literally glorious fists, called Boxers in English) are trying to beat China back into the seventeenth century. Only Shanghai is ready for the twentieth century. Han Bangqing is dead, so it is up to me to imagine the rest of Erbao's life. She is twenty five now, and she is one of the most famous courtesans in Shanghai. She is judged number three in the judging competition to choose the best flowers for the start of the new century, but maybe she would be number one if she was from Suzhou or Hangzhou. The best flowers were always supposed to be from there. Many people were prejudiced against Subei ren. Just like now. Erbao is clever as well as beautiful. At the competition she gained many new admirers, but she did not need new clients, specially a big, clumsy, young bumpkin from Anhui Province. I do not know why she agreed to meet him. But it changed Chinese history. And

Erbao's herstory that maybe I will write.

Do you like that word, "herstory?" I learned it from some Canadian feminists. They are trying to make a woman's language like maybe Erbao and her sister flowers did. But in Chinese we would not have to change the pronunciation. We could just change the zi so it sounded the same but meaned different. The joke would be much more subtle. But that means we could only do it in writing. If we wanted to say the joke we would have to write the zi in the air when we said it. Maybe only intellectuals would understand it. Chinese was always a intellectuals' language. The May Fourth Movement tried to change that. But I am getting ahead of my herstory.

The boy from Anhui was skinny and moved like a bumpkin although he wore a expensive silk gown. He came very early, before noon. Later Erbao would always say that she had a sixth sense about him, but maybe she told Ahu to let him in just because he came so early. Maybe she was bored and wanted a change. It was safe to let him in because no one important would see him there at that hour.

The boy had long legs and arms but a square chin and proud eyes. When you saw his eyes. He spent more time looking down than a hungry bird looking for worms. His fancy clothes and courteous manners showed he was from a rich, upper class family. But he wore his gown so loosely that the clothes underneath showed, and he moved like a clumsy boy of ten, not one twice that age. He bowed to Ahu at the door, but he was scratching and rubbing his nose while he did it. Ahu was laughing at him when she told Erbao who was there. She also laughed at his hat. Although he dressed in Chinese style, but he wore a Western style hat. Except for officials, Chinese men did not usually wear big hats. In the north his foreign hat might get him killed, but Shanghai people like to show off that they are independent, and Western clothes were starting to be in fashion. But not on him. He was not a Shanghai person. His accent was from Anhui, and his manners were like a country person, not a city person. Maybe all these contradictions attracted Erbao. She liked contradictions.

"Please sit down, take off your hat," Erao told him. "Serve tea," she told Ahu. The boy did not know how much serving tea cost. Erbao would decide later if she would charge him. The boy sat down, but he did not take off his hat. Erbao smiled to invite at him, but she said no thing. She would let him start the talking.

Except he did not. He stared like a tiger. At the rug. It was a fine silk rug with a mountain and water pattern, but it was not worth studying like a essay by Mencius. The boy sat like a stone and did not open his mouth. How lovely, thought Erbao. So rich, so shy.

So boring too. She almost decided to end his visit when a petal from a vase of last night's roses fell slowly and softly to the floor. No Chinese can see a petal fall and not think of many famous poems and specially of the wonderful chapter in *Hong Lou Meng* (A Dream of Red Mansions) where Lin Dai Yu and

Jia Bao Yu make a grave to bury fallen petals. "Red petals fall in drifts," Erbao quoted automatically. Just as automatically the boy replied, "For you are fair as a flower and youth is slipping away like flowing water." For the first time Erbao's smile was not the one she gave clients. "Water flows and flowers fall, knowing no pity." "Spring departs with the flowing water and fallen blossoms." "Flowers fall, the water flows red, grief is infinite." They were out of poetry at the end of the chapter, but he did not hesitate. He went back to earlier in the chapter. "Yours is the beauty which caused cities and kingdoms to fall." She did not turn red and cry, as Lin Dai Yu did. She laughed. "And you are sick with longing, no doubt." He was proud, and he thought she was making fun of him. He quit *Hong Lou Meng* and quoted a much earlier poem by Du Mu of the Tang Dynasty. "The singing girl does not know the bitterness of a nation ruined. Across the river she still sings 'Flowers of the Inner Court.'" "The nation has been destroyed, mountains and flowers remain." "Moved by the times, flowers blooming make me weep." These were the next lines of the poem she quoted. It was logical for him to say them, but as soon as he did, his face turned so red it looked like some thing hotter than tears might explode in it.

"Do I make you weep or the times?" she asked, breaking the game they were playing. Fast moving conversation by quoting ancient poetry was a favourite game of Chinese intellectuals, but the last quotations were more than a game in a time when war was being fought in the capitol. And his red face made her pity him.

"All," he replied. Then he stopped. He was afraid he might have insulted her again. After a while he corrected himself. "In such times every thing makes the man of virtue weep."

"Junzi," the man of virtue, is a word from Kongzi. It surprised her. "I did not think you were so traditional," she laughed.

For the first time he looked up from the rug. For a second his eyes met hers. "Excuse me," he said sincerely.

"Did you say such a terrible thing?" He apologized as if he did a great crime. She thought he must be apologizing because he thought he insulted her before. Inside herself she laughed. At the same time she admired his innocence.

"I hate every thing traditional." He tried to say it proudly, but he did not look up again, and she felt that he expected to be punished for what he said. It was the key moment of their talking.

"Ah," she said slowly and with sympathy, "If you were a woman you would become a flower."

Now he did look at her again. "Yes," he said. The idea was new. He thought it over. "Yes," he repeated. The idea was true. "Some times I wish I was a woman."

It was a shameful thing for a Chinese man, a man who was raised up reading Kongzi, to admit. As soon as he said it, he looked ashamed. But she was won over by his honesty. "That is not terrible too," she told him. "Please. Always speak so honestly with me. You can be comfortable here."

He looked down again. "I think maybe I am too comfortable here," he said slowly. "Feeling so comfortable makes me uncomfortable." He looked up at her, stared deeply at her. Suddenly he raised up his hand, hesitated a second, then grabbed off his hat.

"*Aiya*," Erbao cried out. She suspected it, but seeing it still shocked her. He had the head of a foreigner. Hair grew all over it. No queue. No top knot. A saying from the early Qing Dynasty was "lose your hair or lose your head." It was a revolutionary action and a great crime for a man to cut his queue and grow his hair. Maybe lately no one was executed for such a crime, but in a time of war, who knew what might happen? Certainly he would be in great trouble if it was known. Yet he trusted her and revealed it.

How write the rest? There is a big irony here. At this time no one thinks there is any thing wrong with Erbao. Her crushed and broken feet are normal. They are considered very beautiful. They are called "golden lilies." But every one would be shocked because Chen let his hair grow and cut his pigtail. Erbao might even start to love him because he was so brave and because he trusted her and showed her. Yet Chen could usually wear a false pigtail like the imitation foreign devil in Lu Xun's famous story of Ah Q. He could shave his head if he had to, but bound feet could never be fixed. It is a comment on Chinese society. I wish I can become a good enough writer to know the best way to make it. I must work hard. Practice makes better.

July 6

    Ruby here and lovely. At the airport I managed to use my big nose to get admitted to customs and stood quietly beside her as she made her declaration. She had never seen me without a beard. She did not realize the clean shaven youth next to her was her old father until I spoke.

    A letter from Z:

Dear Jiake,

    While you spoke "Many year, I look for you." While you spoke "I love you," I how think have a good cry bend at your side.

    I thirst for love people, I also thirst love, Like Jane Eyre spoke: woman of ugly with woman of beautiful identical on emotion.

    Jiake, My before this boy friend, He with you contrast, How paltry and petty and low his spirit!

    Jiake, I love you, I love you.

    But you can don't love me, you can choose again.

Surely the most wonderful letter I have ever received. Being without her these few days has been terrible, tears in my eyes now as I think of her and need for her in the pit of my stomach. We must acknowledge our love openly. If we don't tomorrow will be a mess. I forgot that some students had invited me to lunch tomorrow just when Z will come.

How characteristic of Jack. Just when I feel better about him, he does some thing that makes me feel bitter again. He sarcastics me by writing my bad English at this time. I wish this is the only time I wrote English to him. I think it is, thank heaven and earth. His letters to me in Chinese were just as bad, but I did not keep them or copy them. He wrote mine down because he wanted to use it in his writing. I would not do that to him although I could do it much better because I learned English. He still can not write a sentence in Chinese. He is older, but I am smarter. Maybe you will say he only wrote it in his diary. He did not use it in his novel. But he planned to use it. He wrote his diary so he could write a novel later. The only reason he did not use it was because he could not finish his story. That is what is bitter. I am finishing his story, so I have to use it. How I wanted to leave it out. I almost did, but saying the truth is my characteristic. If I leave out any true thing, my whole history will be false. That is why I want to write my herstory. In it I can make things turn out right. The smart will live longer than the old. At first Shuangbao seems smarter than Erbao because she is older. But do not worry about my sister, grandmother Erbao. Wait and watch.

"Shaungbao, *jie jie*, my little flower is blooming."
"Ah, the flower's flower."
"It is very lovely."
"But not so lovely as the vase."
"That is the difference between us, *jei jei*. You prefer the vases, I prefer the flowers."
"Yet you live as a vase. The vase is art. The flower is only nature. The vase lasts. The flower must die."
"That is why I will cultivate this flower, not cut it. It has thorns."
"Ah, a little yellow rose."
"No, a red one. It will draw blood. It will scratch even a empress. It will leave scars. Only she who loves it and cultivates it will be spared."
"Be careful. In the end it will still die."
"*Aiyo*, the best cultivated flowers often die the slowest, most painful deaths. I can only do what I can do. And grow with my flower even when I can not see it."
"Ah. We know how quickly a flower can grow, but a vase?"
"It appears he thinks I am more than a vase. Look, he has written me a love letter."
"How romantic. Ha, you are teaching the little scholar *bai hua*. But he

needs much practice. He makes many mistakes."

"The words are as unfamiliar as the feelings, but could I let my little lover of the new write in the old classical language he studied? I might as well let him make love to me as he does to his wife. I will make him a master of new words and new feelings. I showed you his first letter so you can follow his progress."

"He has a wife?"

"And a son. He was shy of me, not of women. Is not that lovely? Now he tells me every thing. He calls the wife his monument to filial piety. He says her conversation is as fascinating as a monument's."

"And her body?"

"Sister who knows me, need I fear that?"

They laugh together. Then Shuangbao becomes serious again. "Do not teach him too much, *mei mei.*"

"I will learn as much as I teach. You and I are women. We know where we want to go and like being taken there. He only knows that he does not know, so he lets me take him where I want. I like that. And I like the strange places where we end up."

"Better than my places?"

"Different. But do not fear. I will not teach him *huahua.* He is lovely, but he is not our kind of flower."

"Of course not. He has no vase. Come, let us decorate ours."

July 8

At long last a day with Z again. Sort of messy, but any day with Z is a fine day. The day was messy because there were too many other people, too much food: two banquets. When Z first arrived we took a short walk to get Ruby's passport copied. Z and Ruby hit it off immediately, a joy to behold, but my student was already waiting when we returned (about 10:30). I had persuaded Z to come to this banquet. It was acceptable because it was at a home, the student's jie jie's apartment, off Nanjing Lu yet surprisingly quiet. Needless to say the Chinese have a saying for a quiet spot amidst the bustle of life, a still point of a turning world. Needless to say I have forgotten it already.

We had an hour between banquets, then off to the school for number two. Z refused to come to this one but stayed in my room writing a long letter to her family about me, about us. She said it was a hard one to write, but with luck it will get her father back home so Ruby and I can visit her family next week. She warned me to be prepared, that her house was hot and poor. She also warned me that I was going too fast, that Chinese normally know each other at least a year or two before marrying, that her family needed time. Of course she is right and I know it, but I also know we are right for each other, etc., etc., etc. I would like very much for Z to come travelling with Ruby and me, a honeymoon trip even if we can't actually get married until after it. She has done little travelling and would like to do much. Another of my ideas, one she agreed to – the travelling I have only hinted at: imagine trying to hint given the level of our verbal communication – is that we will cohabit in different places the next few years at least before settling down.

Our best time together was on the night bus going back to her bus and after. On the afternoon bus (returning from banquet number one) I had whispered "wo ai ni" in her ear, and she had whispered loudly "you can't" then relented and said "I love you" would be better in public. But when I whispered "I love you" on the night bus, she was back to "you can't." I wiped a fake tear from my eye. (I'm becoming an accomplished mime.) Then we got off the bus and into one of our prize conversations. It was about the official nonsense involved in getting married. I think what she was trying to tell me was that altho the government says it's OK for us to marry, her unit leaders may demur and attempt to dissuade her, so she will attempt an end run around them. She tried about eight times to explain this and I couldn't make it out. Finally we looked at each other and just laughed for several minutes. At any other time our raucous merriment would have attracted a crowd, but in the late watches of the night people are still. And lovers more free. But the funniest thing is that after our laughing jag, when she explained it again, I got it. At least I think I got it. Altho we didn't get far in our discussion we parted happy, I running after her to whisper one last "I love you," over which we both roared again.

A real problem for her will be finding work. She wants to keep working, but her unit has no jurisdiction outside Shanghai and jobhunting is not something familiar to Chinese. It is obviously important to her: she says that if she is not working and contributing, she can't eat my food. I can't see the problem since my salary is so high (at least in China), but it is a big one to her, is perhaps a matter of face. I wonder how many other problems I am causing her of which I am ignorant.

Our time from 8:00 to 10:00 (after the evening banquet) was spent with Ruby sound asleep in bed. Jet lag: she was exhausted and conked out as soon as we got back. On the street earlier she and Z were holding hands in the wonderful, innocent way the Chinese do.

The saying Jack forgot is nao zhong qu jin. It means to have quiet in the middle of busyness. At that time I did not appreciate even one of those quiet days when we did not see each other in the middle of our busy falling in love. I missed Jack. I wanted to be with him all the time. I never felt like that before. I never was in love like that before. But now I can see that it was good to have that quiet time. While Jack was finishing grading his exams, I was finishing reading Hai Shang Hua Lie Zhuan. It was my introduction to Shanghai's demimonde. I met many flowers, many unique women. While Jack was meeting Ruby, I was meeting Erbao. "That is only fair," Ruby would say. Western children are taught fairness, not filial piety. So usually Ruby was on my side, not her father's, when we talked. How unexpected. How nice. How strange. It was even stranger to think that Ruby was the same age as Erbao (in 1890, in Hai Shang Hua Lie Zhuan, not in my imagines after the novel ends). And maybe she loved Shanghai the same way Erbao did. The demimonde was gone, but Ruby loved all the shops, all the people on the streets, all the mixture of people and things and ideas that did not quite mix, all the life. Ruby was raised up in a small countryside place just like Erbao was. She was full of childish life, covered with fluffy feathers, not thick, slick ones. I think maybe Erbao was just like that when she first came to Shanghai. Yet Erbao voluntarily chose to become a flower, and Ruby stayed a bud, a child. How different a young, innocent culture like Canada's is from a old, sophisticated culture like China's. You can not change that even if you destroy the demimonde. In my Shanghai girls were not even supposed to think about boys until they were more than twenty years old. Of course we all did. They could keep us from showing our thoughts, but they could not keep us from having them. Ruby did not know how to hide her thoughts. She never had to in her whole life. She often talked about boys. But she was a Canada person, so she stayed a child, and Erbao became a courtesan.

A saying that I forgot is *geng shen ren jing*. Jack does not say it in Chinese, but it is there. I taught him the saying. He taught me the translation. When he speaks of the "late watches of the night," he is using that saying. In ancient China there were watchmen who beat gongs to tell people what part of the night it was. People who liked the night, or people who could not sleep, or people who needed a sound to make their dreams more real. Or lovers. "In the late watches of the night people are still" is the literal translation of *geng shen ren jing*. How nice to rediscover it in Jack's diary. How more nice what he added to it. One reason I did not appreciate the quiet days is that I did not know how busy our later days would become. After Ruby stopped jet lagging, Jack and I could not have so much time alone together. And soon we had to use up our days trying to get married. It was very hard, and we had to spend a lot of time to do it. Our only long times alone together were in the late watches of the night. How we both loved those late watches. I think this was the last time we took the bus on Yanan Lu. Later we walked all the way to People's Square, where I could get on my 46 bus. We stretched out our time alone together like a candy maker stretches out his candy before he shapes it. How sweet the candy is. How sweet those long night walks were.

Alone together was wonderful. Others were the problem. Even my own family. In my letter I did not even tell them about Ruby. A foreign boyfriend was enough to tell the first time. A divorced one with a child would be too much even though that is what my mother was when she married my father. So maybe my family would understand more than most Chinese families. I wished so. I wished I could marry Jack without any one knowing, but I could not. Every one would know. I thought every one would laugh at me and criticise me. I still did not believe I was doing a fashionable thing marrying a foreigner. Zhabei and Luwan might be alike at night, but the day time fashions of Luwan did not yet reach to Zhabei. Really I was out of the fashion even when I was in it. The different places Jack and I were talking about living were all in China. The fashionable people all wanted to marry foreigners to get out of China. Jack wanted to stay. That was one of the reasons I loved him. I did not want to leave China. I thought people would think I did and criticise me for this. I was happy, but I was also confused. Maybe this is when I started liking contradictions. New worlds were opening in front of me, and I wanted the old and the new at the same time.

Sister Erbao, did you have that kind of problem? You were not hesitant like me. Usually you were sure of yourself. You loved your family without being afraid of them. You did worse things than I did without trying to hide them from your family. When your brother and mother tried to take you back to your hometown after Lai wrecked your house, you refused. At least that is the way I imagine you. Han Bangqing's novel, *Hai Shang Hua Lie Zhuan*, ends with the scene where Lai wrecks your house. That was 1890, when you were fifteen years old. The rest of your life is mine to finish.

This is the way I will start to finish it. Lai wrecking your house turned out to be good fortune that just looked bad. It forced you to choose. You could quit the profession or you could take it seriously. You chose to take it seriously. You sent your mother and brother back to the countryside where they belonged. No more thoughts of marriage. No more amateur. You became a real courtesan, a professional. Because you were beautiful, because you were independent, because you had a genuine innocence and a genuine eagerness which no courtesan raised in a brothel could have, you became one of the most popular courtesans in Shanghai. At first maybe you were not one of the most skilful ones, but your popularity let you develop your skills.

The year is 1910. The old empress is dead, the old empire is sick and about to die. Erbao now runs her own brothel. She plays teacher, manager, mother to younger women. Her own activity is limited to a few old clients who became friends. Xiao Chen is one. He studied in France and Japan and fattened in body and mind. He is no longer small, but Erbao still calls him *xiao*. He calls her Lao Bao (old treasure). Because Erbao lives outside the traditional Chinese morality and the traditional Chinese family, she is a refuge to Chen from these prisons. They can have the honest, joking relationship almost impossible inside the walls. Inside the walls is Confucianism, unsmiling. Unlike Confucius, who sometimes made jokes and liked to play with words.

"I fight for everything new," Chen tells Erbao. "All over the world the new will beat down the old. The dynasty will die. Science and democracy will grow from its dust. In the new world, Lao Bao, you and I can live together."

"Slow go, *Xiao*. You are breaking our rule. No talk of politics with clothes on....

I am not sure I can write this scene, even in English. A Chinese idea about sex comes from Daoism. Daoists believe that sex is a contest in which women and men both try not to spill their juices. You live a long life if you do not spill your juices but get lots of your partner's juices into your body. Erbao and Chen do not believe this. Maybe that is because Chen has been to foreign countries and learned foreign ideas. Maybe it is because Erbao knows that pleasure can be guided but not be controlled. Together they try to cooperate when they make love. They try to make it last a long time before they both spill their juices. One way to do this is to have a political discussion while they make love. I will write the political discussion. That is not hard. But I want the reader to guess about the sex. That is hard. Because the other part of their rule is no talk of love with clothes off.

"Ah, better. Slow, *Xiao*, slow. Long, slow strokes. To help the memory. I was your first follower even when you were following me. You knocked on my door, but I opened yours. You came out of your thatched hut, and now you want to conquer the world. Measure your strength, and save some of it, my big calf. The world is full of tigers."

"The youth of China will risk the tigers to make the new world. They will beat down the tigers. We must be aggressive, not passive."

"Teach aggression to the youth. Make old people like me comfortable."

"*Aiya*, when you are so comfortable, it makes me more aggressive."

"You see, aggression makes the young too hot and the old too comfortable. Change." They roll over so she is on top. "The youth must learn when to be aggressive and how to use their aggression. Be patient and prepare. The emperor is still in the Northern Capitol even if he is a baby. You have a family, and I have no desire to be a concubine."

"A companion, not a concubine. In the new China there will be no emperors. The phoenix will chatter like a magpie. Men and women will be equal. You will be able to unbind your feet and walk at my side."

"The sky might fall and the earth might sink, but my feet will never grow. Where would I want to walk to?"

"Everywhere. In the new China there will be no more walls. The emperor's palace will be no more forbidden than your palace is to me now. In the new Shanghai the streets will be full of life, not death, safe, not dangerous. And walking is good for you. Science tells us exercise helps the body.... Oh, you are exercising too well. Let me exercise more. Change." They roll over again.

"Who is this Science *Xiansheng* who is always telling you things? Another one of your foreign friends? Why do not you bring him to meet me?"

"Ha ha. Science Mr. Too good. I like that. Oh, very much." He laughs and groans at the same time. "Lao Bao, in the middle of our political discussions you always say some thing that makes me want to put on my clothes exactly when I do not want to put on my clothes. I love... the way you translate my foreign ideas into Chinese.... Science is...." It is easier to feel than to explain. He feels first. Then he tries to explain. "Mr. Science is a foreigner, but I want him to live in China. He is the most clever person in the world. *Aiya*.... The second most clever. He uses new ideas to tear down old superstitions and build a new world.

Ah, such a beautiful world."

"Every time you get on top, you get impatient. Learn to go with others, not try to lead always. Slow. Half change." They roll on to their sides. "Now use your impatience to polish my body. Rub.... *Ah,* remember, slow go. Too much change can be as bad as too little. If there is only change, how can culture survive? We want silkworms to change, but in the end we make silk by stopping their change. The purpose of change is to bring stability. That was the goal of Zhuge Liang. Your Mr. Science sounds like Zhuge Liang."

"Another Chinese substitute for my foreign ideas. But unlike Mr. Zhuge Liang, Mr. Science has no love for the emperor, and he will not fail in the end. He will not let you down. He will finish his task. Slowly."

"Good. You and your foreign ideas and foreign friends try to go too fast. I will not let you or your Mr. Science finish until I am satisfied. When I meet your friend, I will tell him he might find it easier to get rid of the emperor than to get rid of the superstitions which let the emperor rule. Maybe the new China will be like my feet. The slippers will be shiny and beautiful, but inside them bones will be broken and flesh will be rotten."

"Lao Bao, I must always try to satisfy you. Your bound feet and unbound mind opened my bound mind and body to the new. If I can not unbind your feet, you must not loosen your bound of me.

"*Ah.* But soon we will loosen together."

"*Ah.* The changes you taught me not to fear are about to happen. The empire is about to explode. The new is about to defeat the old."

"Just a little more patience. I too want the new, but no new is new enough to disappear the old. Even if China had wings, it could not fly from its history."

"The new must use the old to create a new new. In the new new people will learn to fly, but we must not fly from our destiny. There is more to China than its history."

"Much more, I feel."

"So much, I feel."

"*Ah.* As there is more to us than our bodies. Are we not flying now? When China comes together as we have, all bounds will be broken."

"*Ah,* the more bounds break, the more we come together. The Manchus are doomed...."

"Just like you dynasties rise up and fall down. But China remains the middle kingdom. We want to keep what is best of our history, but what is worst might keep us from the destiny we want. My bound feet will keep me here. Will you always stay with me as you did just now?"

They laugh together. After a while she rings a bell and Xinbao, her new treasure, young and beautiful, comes into the room. Chen's eyes follow the girl as she serves Erbao, brings her new clothes, helps her dress. When Xinbao leaves, Erbao laughs and asks, "And what will happen when you grow too old to keep up with the new?"

"I will never grow too old for the new, but when the new is too young for me, I hope I can retire with my Lao Bao and live quietly in a Shanghai without concessions and a world without servants. Except our two, Mr. Science and Mr. Democracy."

"Three men against me? I will never agree."

July 9

I tried to tell Z that when we are living together we will have many disagreements, mainly little but often appearing big because of our different backgrounds. Her response was perfect: such things can be dealt with. She is not worried about problems between us, only about me, my loyalty, what I might do with other women. I'm not worried about that at all – I know my feelings – but suspect I am more realistic about the things that get on another's nerves when two people live together; she has no experience living alone with another person, especially one whose ways will be as strange as many of mine inevitably will seem. I suppose both our worries are natural given our different backgrounds, our worlds' vastly different slants on morality and our own vastly different life experiences in those different worlds, but comparative ethnography is probably just another way of making the point I was originally trying to make. And ignoring the one she was trying to make.

This morning I was about to write her a letter, but the writing impulse got diverted into revising the novel. I lack the strength (not to mention the ability) to write a long, deep letter in Chinese. I want to tell her that of course she is right, that I am trying to go too fast, pushing too hard. I keep saying I will follow her lead, as I should in her country, but when I am alone with her I want her too much. Like a teenager unable to control his desires. I feel I have so much to say to her and it takes so long to say it. I want to be with her all the time. Even now I have much to say about this topic but no time as students are arriving.

July 10

I still wake up for hours every night full of thoughts of Z, dreams, desire, fantasies, but mainly imagined conversations we will have: books we will write together, practical conversations about what to do with her parents, how we will live, where we will live, where we will travel, etc., etc., etc. And then I imagine how she will feel in my arms when there is nothing to keep her out of my arms, the smoothness of her, our curiosity about each other's bodies. When I finally know I must go back to sleep, I apologize to her and ask her to order me back to sleep since sleep won't come when my mind is full of her. Who would have thought I would ever feel this way again? Again? Have I ever felt this way before? Probably I had similar dreams of B when I was seventeen, but there was no physical reality to those dreams. And nothing even remotely close since those teenage years.

"Shuangbao, *jie jie*, we are not young anymore. It is time you looked at your future instead of trying to relive your past. We are no longer young flowers. We grew into trees. Not so beautiful but stronger and wiser."

"You know I know that, but young flowers bloom longer in the shade of trees, and I do so like to smell them. Put my nose into the centre of their fragrance."

"And not only your nose. I know. Yet I also know how much you still like it when our old branches entangle. Our eyelashes will soon be white. We can not have every thing any more, and my little friend promises me big changes are coming, a whole new world. He is young and thinks change is a beautiful butterfly which simply pops out of its cocoon and flies free. We were young once. We were beautiful, so we thought we were butterflies too. Now we know better, and what we know is bitter. We know we are silkworms, not butterflies. The new world will be more like a tray of silkworms. They all must work very hard spinning their cocoons, yet only a few are actually allowed to change, to survive. And those who do survive end up as gray moths, not colourful butterflies. As aging courtesans we must work hard in the afternoon of life, or we will certainly be sorry in the evening of life. I bought my own house and girls so I would be free of my body, so I can enjoy its pleasures without depending on it."

"That is what we share, *mei mei*. We enjoy pleasures of the body. But you never make my mistake. You never let your body control your mind. I must stop calling you *"mei mei."* You are much wiser than I am. That is why you are a whoremaster and I am a whore.... So take me, *shifu*, master."

July 11

Returned home tired, sopping and hopping mad from too many frustrating hours of shopping and from flopping in an attempt to get travel documents from the bureaucracy. Then just as I had to leave to meet Z, Wuhan called and I ended up late, running to meet her. Of course she had arrived early. Walking back I felt really frazzled as well as the usual sopping, but the pricklings and tricklings of disaster I was feeling all over turned out to be only sweat. In the room Z's feelings soon overcame mine. She seemed particularly calm. She had thought a lot and reached her own conclusions – that if possible we should get married before I go to Wuhan so we can go together but that she won't travel with Ruby and me. Our evening was peaceful, full of our future together. That seems now to be accepted: no more pleas that I choose again. An evening of pure happiness. We sat together, she in the armchair, I in front of her in the hard chair, our legs touching – she wasn't wearing stockings and we were both wearing shorts, so I got a full feel of her wonderfully smooth legs – eventually her legs between mine, knees and calves together but gently, gently, a time of peace, not passion. Ruby lay in bed reading, but jet lag soon conked her out.

Then we got out dictionaries and Z tried to explain in detail a new idea for a novel. It takes place in old Shanghai, and I think it concerns a Chinese scholar and a naguoning (weiguoren, foreigner) whose paths cross in a brothel because they both fall in love with the same prostitute. High class Chinese prostitutes get called "sing-song girls" in English translations after their Japanese counterparts. (The Japanese actually copied the Chinese in this as in most things, Z emphasizes.) They were really courtesans, not prostitutes. They were poets, musicians and artists, not mere sex objects, and their main customers were scholars, so the plot is not as far fetched as it first seemed to me. Altho Z had just conceived the idea, she had written a lot about it and could only explain a tiny part to me (and even that took a long, lovely time). She was transparently pleased and excited by the new ideas, and the pleasure communicated itself to me even if we didn't always get the words right. I told her a bit about my ideas for a novel about a Westerner in the China of the future, which obviously has some things in common with hers, but mainly I wanted to listen to her, to suck in some of her happiness, to let it swell my own. The time did not last that long – perhaps an hour – because we had too many practical details to discuss as well, but it was a magic time, full of love and wonder. No wonder she doesn't want to tell others, to share this, to allow others to make it small. I want to shout out to others how proud and happy I am while she keeps saying no. And rightly so. We don't need or want others' congratulations or comments. That can only make our love smaller, conventional. It isn't and we must not let it become so. She knows; she is right.

I am worried about my memory. Before I started writing, I always thought my memory was great. I thought I never forgot important things. Now I keep finding many things I forgot. First I found out I wrote about Erbao before. I forgot that for many years. Even when I was writing my thesis about *Hai Shang Hua Lie Zhuan*, I did not remember that. But if I was just writing to get stuff out of me, why plan a whole novel? Yet I told Jack detailed plans. Maybe he probably did not understand them well. I do not think there was a foreigner in my plan. I did not want to write a foreigner. I wanted to marry one. But I wished my foreigner was Chinese. Of course, I could not say that to Jack, so what ever I said confused him. He heard what he wanted me to say, but I still can not remember what I did say. I am sure I did not think about Chen Du Xiu at this time. I do not remember if my hero even had a name. He was just a Chinese revolutionary hero, like the ones we were taught to admire during the Cultural Revolution. Very brave. In 1900 looking and thinking like a foreigner was very brave and revolutionary. Maybe Jack did not understand that, so he thought I was talking about two different men. Or maybe Jack wanted to be a revolutionary hero, so he turned my hero into a foreigner because his hair looked like a foreigner's. Or maybe I even said there were two different men because that was what Jack expected. He thought there should be one hero like him and the other not hero man like Huang. I do not know. I can not remember. Maybe when I was tearing the papers I was writing on, I was tearing my memory too.

Although I can not remember, but this is what I think maybe happened.

I think I wrote for myself, but I planned for Jack. Jack was always talking about his novels. He was persuading me to write at the same time I was reading *Hai Shang Hua Lie Zhuan*. That is why Erbao became my main character. That is why the story happens in a brothel. High class Shanghai brothels were fancy places. Banquet rooms were more important than bedrooms. The cooks were as famous as the courtesans. All kinds of people met there, and more business got done in them than in the stock market. I wish Jack wrote more about my then ideas that I forgot now. Such things were too complicated for our then words, but I maybe planned a whole novel to impress Jack. I did not plan to write it. Then. But I am planning to write it now. Often we trick ourselfs when we think we are tricking others. I can not remember the plan I made for Jack, but it seems like for many years it stayed locked up inside my mind trying to escape. How strange to think that there are things in our minds that we do not even know are there. One thing I do know is why my revolutionary scholar turned into Chen Du Xiu. I will tell about that later. Definitely I do not need a foreigner in my novel now. I married him. I am not like Jack. I know the difference between my life and my fiction. I keep them separate. So Chen Du Xiu is the only man I need in my novel. He was a Chinese scholar and revolutionary, and he did study abroad, and he was very interested in foreign ideas. I could not ask for more. Now. Maybe he did not really grow his hair in 1900, but he surely had ideas like that. Since what I will write about Erbao is a herstory, not a history, maybe I can make small changes like that. When I wrote those writings I tore up, I was not thinking about history or herstory. Then I was thinking about my own problems. I needed to talk to Erbao, but a lot of what I needed to say was about men and scholars. I just finished a relationship with a Chinese scientist and scholar and just started one with a Western scholar. Actually none of them were very scholarly, but they both seemed scholarly to me at that time. Now that I am a scholar too, I can be much more interested in Erbao. She is unique. The men are just men.

July 12

 For the first time this summer cicadas are in full chorus. I too feel like singing. I have just realized that since I met Z I have stopped masturbating, that thinking about her is far more pleasurable than fantasy. I made no conscious decision, but now I understand how much more in touch with my body and desires I am since I met her. And for how long I have been out of touch with them and have tried to maintain some contact thru masturbatory fantasies and realistic novels which attempted to recreate a world where my sexual desires had some basis in fact. I attributed my lack of a sex life to growing old, but in fact it was sublimation essential to continuing my relationship with P (followed by sublimation essential to continuing my relationship with life). I regret neither the fantasies nor the (probably mediocre, alas) novels, for surely they kept my hope alive while waiting for Z and perhaps enabled me to avoid settling for less.

*But how pale they seem compared to this reality. My sexual desire is more fulfilled now,
when in fact it has not been physically fulfilled and I know it cannot be for some time,
than ever it has been since Ruby's birth. The wonderful thing about it is that sexual
desire is not the foundation of the relationship. Yet it will be one of the pillars on which
that foundation is built. And it will grow and help raise everything. Perhaps the reason
for this is that Z is so natural in all her responses. Is this despite or because of her lack
of experience? Or is it simply the total of what we feel for each other (in only one of its
manifestations)?*

July 13
Dear Z,

    *It is just beginning to grow light outside. I have waked up this morning full of
things I want to tell you. I will be so happy when we are together and I can actually speak
to you, but I could not say what I am feeling in Chinese anyhow, so perhaps it is just as
well I try to write to you in a language in which I can express myself a little, even if not
enough to say half of what I feel for you.*

    *I love you. I love your spirit because it is whole. One thing that means is that your
body is part of your spirit, not separate from it. I know you think your spirit has been
broken. By poverty, by the Cultural Revolution, by your exboyfriend, by all the ideals and
all the people who have betrayed you. In fact your spirit has survived intact. No, more: it
has grown stronger and more beautiful because of your suffering. I cannot praise a fugitive
and cloistered spirit. An untested spirit's beauty is only of the surface. You told me you
were more beautiful six or seven years ago. You said you wish I could have met you then. I
would have liked that – perhaps. But perhaps I would not have recognized you then: what
I think I recognized in you is someone whose spirit has been fully tested yet survived. So
in that way you are far more beautiful now than you were then. Your beauty has depth.
Even your skin is deep. And so smooth. I love you more deeply now than perhaps I could
have then.*

    Is not that sweet? He goes on like that for pages and pages. I am really
glad I am reading his diaries. I am getting a chance to understand the love
letters he wrote to me fourteen years ago. When I first red this letter, I could not
understand it then. Almost the only thing I could understand was "I love you."
That was nice, but the whole thing is much nicer. I will have to take a shower
tonight. That is Jack's award. He gets very exciting when I take a shower because
that means he can do oral sex. Chomp, chomp. I will not let him do that unless
I am completely clean. He always wants to jump in the shower with me, but I
will not let him. He gets too exciting in the shower. And I will not tell him why
he is getting his award. Love should be a mystery. So I will not copy all the love
letter. It only means a lot to me, but it should be a mystery to any one else.

    Erbao did not have a shower, but she had a big, golden bath basin. Ahu
was good at bathing her, but when she became a madam (I used to pronounce

that word "ma damn," "mother" plus a curse word, because I thought that was its meaning) she liked her newest Xinbao to bath her. She would give the girl very good instructions how to do it. Of course, the best times were when Shaungbao could come. Shaungbao was a master bather. No instructions needed. She never got too exciting. *Ah, how nice. How relaxing and exciting at the same time. How comfortable.*

    I better write a little about Chen Du Xiu before I go back to Erbao. I am supposed to be writing about every ten years, 1890, 1900, 1910, 1920 and so on. I am doing it that way to try to give a history of Shanghai. Sort of. I mean it is not really a history, and it is only a outline of a novel. But I am a historian, and I love Shanghai, and I really feel that women like Erbao were my ancestors. We Chinese respect our ancestors and our histories and our hometowns, and I lived away from Shanghai for too long. It changed into some thing else while I was away. It became a modern city, a ordinary city, a "sprawling metropolis." I red those words some where, and I wrote them down because they describe what Shanghai is now. *Pushan Lu Yi Chen,* where I grew up, does not exist any more. My parents moved so far from the place we lived that when I visit, I feel like it would be easier to go to Suzhou than the *wei tan* (the Bund). That is almost the only part of the city I grew up in that exists any more. The city Erbao loved does not exist any more. Although governments and customs and concessions changed, but Erbao's city and my city were similar ones. Most of the buildings were the same. All those brothels still existed even if they were used for apartments. Now they are torn down. I miss them. I can not love the sprawling metropolis the way I loved the old Shanghai. Although we did not know it, but the old Shanghai was ending just when Jack and I were beginning. So I want to say goodbye to the old Shanghai through Erbao.

    And Chen Du Xiu. He is the famous one. Only I know about Erbao. That is why I love her. If I was writing a real history, the years between 1910 and 1920 would be very interesting. When I write my whole novel, those years will be the high peak for Chen. They were the years of his greatness. He was the leading new intellectual in China. Later when he became the leader of the Communist Party, Lu Xun and Hu Shih became more important intellectuals. In 1915 in Shanghai Chen started *Xin Qingnian* (*New Youth*), the magazine which led the movement to modernize China. It was revolutionary for its contents and because it used *bai hua,* spoken Chinese written down. In 1916 Chen became a professor at Beida (*Beijing Daxue,* Beijing University), the most politically advanced school in China. He led the May Fourth Movement, the most important cultural movement in modern China. It brought change by using *bai hua* in writing and literature. The classical written language could only be red by scholars. Once people began writing *bai hua,* it became possible for ordinary people to learn to read. The May Fourth Movement's main idea was to bring science and democracy to China. The movement started earlier, but it got its name from a big march in Beijing on May 4, 1919. The march protested against the Chinese government's agreement to concede Shandong Province to the Japanese. The Germans controlled it before World War One, but when the Germans were defeated in the war, the winning side decided to give Shandong to the Japanese. The emperor was overthrown out, but the Chinese government was still conceding. When the Chinese people heard about this, they were very mad. Specially the students. Specially the students at Beida. And their leader was Chen Du Xiu. May 4, 1919 is still celebrated in China as the beginning of the new China. The Communists and the Nationalists both celebrate it. But the Communists and the Nationalists both do not say that Chen Du Xiu was the May Fourth Movement's leader.

Although the famous march was held in Beijing, but Shanghai students also marched. Most of the ideas for the May Fourth Movement originally came from Shanghai. Shanghai was the centre for all new ideas. It was China's only really modern city. It is funny. I love Shanghai for being modern at that time, and I love it for being modern when I was growing up. But I do not love it for being modern now. I do not love the sprawling metropolis. My Shanghai did not sprawl. Streets were few and narrow, and lanes were more and narrower. Streets were not made for lots of traffic, and lanes were made for walkers and bike riders. People lived and worked and played close together. When people live close, they become close. When we were home, our doors were open. Even if doors were closed, it did not matter because walls were thin. We knew each other. We knew the good and the bad. When there was a argument, it was impossible to hide. When there was love, it was impossible to hide. We all knew who was doing what to who. So few people did too much. There was no room for crime. When a city begins to sprawl, there is room for crime to snake in. We were not rich like some people today, but because no one was rich, no one felt poor. We were happy. We. Up to now I always wrote I, I, I. It is a bad habit learned in North America. As soon as I talk about the old Shanghai I love, I write we, we, we. That is how it should be. As they say in Canada, we were all in it together.

July 16

Have a nasty cold and have not felt like writing, so I must compress three busy days. With Z everyday. Many raucous times with the three of us, Z and Ruby tickling me or laughing at my pronunciation of Chinese. Even in public they ridicule me. I love it. Alone with Z, mainly on long walks to her bus, things have been up and down. She is fearful about her family but mainly about our future, about my loyalty to her. She still tells me she is bad, but she also tells me of her love. Our love has become very physical without becoming sexual. We are constantly touching, little concealed touches in public or even when Ruby is by, long, close strokes when we are alone, mainly in the room but last night in People's Square, sitting on low, uncomfortable plant pots, a row of them, young lovers to the side of us engaging in very passionate necking while we were not quite necking – I didn't want to give Z my cold – yet touching with legs, shoulders, cheeks, hands, she half seriously, half jestingly concealing my big nose so passersby wouldn't see I am a foreigner. A lovely time with frequent expressions of love on both sides. Yet this after a terrible time when she was angry and wouldn't speak to me, kept trying to send me back home, said she wouldn't come to see me again. "Tomorrow?" I asked. "No." "Friday?" "No." "Saturday?" "No." Etc. Then for a long time she wouldn't talk to me at all and I mainly walked along with her, resisting all impulses to try to explain in language necessarily inadequate. But she really didn't want me to go. I felt sure she wanted (needed?) my sticking to her patiently and waiting for her. When we reached her last 46 Bus stop, it was she who suggested we go on to People's Square (after first trying to send me home one last time) where everything became beautiful again. I had been scared by her silence. So long as we are talking – even when we aren't understanding, for then we can laugh at our failure to communicate – everything is OK. I was not even sure what had caused her silence altho I was aware it had to do with some bad Western characteristic of mine, perhaps scraping the jam jar with my finger to get the last bits out for a peanut butter and jam sandwich instead of waiting patiently for Ruby, who had run out to buy more jam. Perhaps, but I knew it was more. It turned out that she was unhappy because I had said she was unhappy in front of Ruby. (But perhaps it was more than this, an expression of the fears she is feeling, the pressure she is reeling from.) Others will be the worst problem in our relationship. Alone she is wonderfully candid, willing to risk anything, but as soon as others, even Ruby, with whom she holds hands in public and seems fully at ease, enter she is fearful.

We debated – not in People's Square now, the day before – whether or not I should correct her mistakes in English (sometimes so great that only my scant knowledge of Chinese enables me to catch on: yesterday she several times said "please" when she meant "invite"; in Chinese "qing" means both). I dare not tell her how entrancing her broken English sounds. Ruby loves it too. "You and your mama two bodies live alone?" Z asked Ruby that question. (I.e., do you and your mother live alone together?) Z has guts (or love) to try to speak English when her level is so low. No other Chinese I have met would dare do so. People who have studied English a long time are often still apprehensive of speaking to me.

I think one of the things that turned around her silence last night – she insisted she wasn't angry and I'll do her the courtesy of believing Chinese has a word I do not know which expresses better than "sheng qi" what she was feeling – was my saying that once we are married she can't run away. She reacted to that when she was not reacting to other things I attempted to say, and later she brought what I said up again (at People's Square), and we improvised a long, jocular drama of her fleeing from Wuhan back to Shanghai and me telling her mother (god knows how: her mother doesn't even speak Shanghaihua, let alone putunghua) not to let her in.

Another funny scene, this one with Ruby: Z correcting my Chinese pronunciation, one of those deals where the two pronunciations sound exactly the same to me and for once they did to Ruby too, for she laughed and repeated Z's words as a joke, but Z took her literally and thought Ruby was distinguishing between the two sounds (which I still swear are one) and said "dui, dui" (right, right) and instructed me to learn from my daughter. There have been many such funny scenes, many happy moments. But also two bad moments, the second (first in matter of time since it came two nights ago) not really serious, mainly fears aroused by a letter from her sister in reply to her letter. The sister wants her to come to Qingdao and she doesn't want to go, even with me, obviously because she knows her sister will try to dissuade her. But the smaller part of her, the conventional side of her soul, echoes her sister's advice, and she fears her larger soul, which now is overcoming the lesser one, will not be able to withstand the pressure. One part of her is saying we are going too fast while the other part wants to go much faster, is probably afraid she will chicken out if she waits.

We went to the marriage bureaucracy and got a list of instructions, one of which may require letters to and from Canada (to obtain a certified copy of my divorce with the seal of both the Canadian government and the Chinese Embassy or Consulate) which will doubtless take months. When Z translated the instructions later, they sounded almost like Mulroney had to verify that I wasn't married then send the message by courier to Deng Xiao Ping. A personal phone call from Mulroney to Deng might also help. So I called the U.S. Consulate and they at least cleared up for me what is required. I have to provide documentary proof that I am not married. Hmm.... It's easy to prove you're married: you simply produce a marriage certificate. It's not so simple to produce an unmarriage certificate. A divorce decree is inadequate: you might have remarried after the divorce. The U.S. Consulate suggested I might be able to get something official looking thru a Canadian Consul in Shanghai. If there were a Canadian Consul in Shanghai. In fact one is finally being established, but it won't be up and running for several months. So I will have to call the Canadian Embassy in Beijing and see if I can get it done thru them. Once I have my unmarriage certificate, the procedure sounds straightforward. There is a new office (opened July 1) which performs marriages between Chinese and foreigners simply. Z does not want a banquet, another confirmation, if I needed another, that her motives are honorable, but she says we must distribute massive quantities of candy (100 yuan worth!). I assumed she was joking about the amount, but I am not sure she was.

Yesterday afternoon Z led Ruby and me to her house for a visit. We certainly would never have been able to find it on our own. What a labyrinth of little lanes and little houses in long rows. Yet the place was not as poor as Z had led me to expect. I've seen worse in Chicago. There are two small rooms, the upstairs one set up by and for Z, a genuine garret full of pictures, etc. She showed us her photo album, which included a picture with Qiu's former wife (or girlfriend or whatever she was) about whom, apparently, Mei knows nothing. Z is quite right about her own beauty when she was younger. She is very beautiful now, but the pictures of her six or seven years ago are spectacular, beauty queen stuff. I also met a young doctor whom she likes very much but only as a friend. He wanted to marry her, but she refused. I only saw him for a minute or two but liked him: friendly and kind, but I assume she sees him as a big brother, not a lover. Nevertheless, he is young and educated and this puts Z in a much different light than Qiu had painted

her to me (i.e., as a woman desperate to get married). I'm glad; it is another proof of what
I know, that she is marrying me, as I am her, for love. Still, I worry a bit about the stress
she places on physical beauty. Yet she has chosen me over younger, better looking men. I
assume I appeal to the romantic side of her soul just as she appeals to the romantic side of
mine. Would we have loved each other if we were from the same country, spoke the same
language etc.? That's one we'll never know.

When I seemed to develop a fever, Z and Ruby went out to get me medicine, which
Z was most earnest about my taking. The Chinese place great faith in medicine. But Z's
primary method of bringing down my fever was to prescribe the eating of huge quantities
of watermelon. She was quite disappointed in me when I ate only an average portion, and
she kept trying to stuff more down me.

I just thought a funny thought. The simple reply to Jack's novel that I
started to write turned into three stories, a history, a herstory and a ourstory.
I thought maybe I could let Jack tell the ourstory, but his story is not all of
our story. Wow. I do not know if writing in English is teaching me to love or
hate this language. Maybe English is not such a simple language as I thought.
Definitely I could not have got into such a playing of words before. I want to
write a Chinese novel about Erbao, but what would people think if I quit in the
middle of this to write that? Wow again. Maybe I am some times glad my duty
is to finish writing about Jack in English first. So I should stop playing and get
back to Jack.

Jack never worries what others think about him. He only worries because
I worry what others think. It is a characteristic of Americans, I think. They
love individualism too much. Canadians are more like us Chinese. They worry
about what others think. Before I felt very proud because I learned the word
"both." I just figured out that although Jack taught its meaning to me from
the side of Qin, but maybe I taught it to him from the side of Chu. Because
of me he began to think of both of us, not just himself. Some times. But when
he writes about my silence, he does not even consider that he might be to
blame. He does not think that what he told others about me might be to blame
because he does not care what others think. He never worries about losing his
face because he always thinks only he is right, only he is patient, I need him,
he is my saviour. Just thinking of both of us is very hard for him, and I do not
think he will ever be able to think of "all." And he calls himself a socialist.
Americans will never be socialist, and Chinese will always be. Even now, when
capitalism is fashionable in China. We always think about others. We always
worry what others will think of us. It is another thing that comes from living
close together. Even in their big cities Americans do not live close together.
They are famous for not even knowing their neighbours. Their doors are always
closed. They have many locks on them. That is because there is much crime
in America. Crime comes because people are not close. They only think of

themselfs. Jack blames me because I worry what others think, but I think he wants closeness too. That is why he loved the close old Shanghai. Americans are full of contradictions, just like me and most Chinese. Most human beings. The difference is that Americans hate to understand their contradictions. They hate to admit they have them.

I think I wrote about words before because what Jack said reminded me that recently I did not write about language and differences between Chinese and English. That is because Jack and I did not talk about that very much any more. When we were alone those days, Jack and I talked about love and getting married and what we would do after we were married, not language the way we did when we first met. But with Ruby we often talked about language again. Ruby's Chinese vocabulary was not as big as Jack's, but her ear was very good. She could hear all the sounds and tones Jack missed. So I do not believe what Jack says about her not hearing what I said. How can a man who can not hear tell what sounds sound like to others? He should be ashamed to laugh at my English. Although his vocabulary was not terrible, but his Chinese was worse than my English. Although I did not have a scant knowledge of English, but I was good at figuring out what he was trying to say in Chinese. Because I was not a individualist, I could know what he was thinking. So I could figure out what he was trying to say. Although his Chinese seemed to be better than my English at this time, but most of our misunderstandings came because he did not understand me. They were not only caused by language. They were also caused by American individualism.

Jack says I did not want a wedding banquet. This is another example of American individualism. I did not want a wedding banquet because it would delay the marriage. Before Jack met me, he agreed to teach in Wuhan. He had to be there before the end of August. Even if we got permission to marry, how could a banquet be arranged so quickly? He did not know that in China the wedding banquet is much more important than the marriage certificate. Jack mentions about Qiu and his first girl friend. That is a good example. They got a marriage certificate. They did that because they needed a official paper with a seal so they could get a apartment sooner. But they did not have a banquet or tell people about it. No one thought they were married. What people think is more important than the law. So when Qiu loved Mei, he did not have a problem marrying her. His first girlfriend protested, but there was nothing she could do. And when he got a apartment and his unit found out he was not married to the woman on the first certificate, they tried to take his apartment back, but they failed too. I did want a wedding banquet, but I could not let it be important. I knew Jack did not want one, and I knew there would be no way to have one before Jack had to go to Wuhan. Maybe we could not even get a marriage certificate before then. Candy was a middle way. It was the best I could do. When people in Shanghai get married, they always give every one they know hard candies. If we did that, we would be telling every one we were married even if we did not have a banquet. We were in my country, but I followed Jack's customs because his individualism prevented him from accepting mine. It shows how well I understood "both." I understood it from the side of Qin and the side of Chu. I sacrificed the wedding banquet for both of us. I could not have all. Jack joked about running away. Joking is another American characteristic. I never intended to run away. But I liked Jack saying that I could not run away because it meant he could not too. I told him that in Xinjiang.

July 18

Woke up this morning feeling wonderfully calm. I think the stuff being telexed from Beijing will solve the bureaucratic bullshit, and I now feel confident everything will come off and that the marriage will be one of true minds and bodies. Strange I should feel that way after seeing what I will have to contend with – Z's silence – the other night. But last night was one of calm since Z did not come yesterday, and a good night's sleep, which I needed because of my cold, did wonders. Seeing that if I was patient Z would indeed overcome her – what? fear? anger? conventional side?– really is reassuring. I was right not to try to do much but simply to wait for her. We are bound to have many disagreements, but so long as we love each other we will overcome them. And we do love each other. Every time we are together, every test we pass, proves that. Altho we have known each other such a short time and have such problems of communication, I have pretty well ceased to worry on that score. I am still curious about why Z loves me, but I cannot doubt that she does. And I also know she is doubting me less. I must tell her, however, about my anger: if her response to something she doesn't like in me is silence, mine to her will be anger, sometimes sudden, sometimes sullen and prolonged. She should be prepared and know that her method should be the same as mine, patience, waiting for the other to come around, for love to reassert itself.

What a joke for Jack to brag about being patient. People with so little history can not learn patience. I always knew Jack was not patient, but later I was surprised by Jack's anger. I did not expect a older man to have so much anger inside him. Maybe most Americans have that. Maybe that is one reason why America is such a violent place. Jack never got angry at me until after we were married, and at first it scared me. He often got angry in Xinjiang, and I did not know what to do. I was afraid he would leave me. But he did not, and later I stopped being scared. Chinese history teaches us to be patient waiting for big things like changes in government, but I am not patient about small things, and I do not like losing my face by being shouted at. So I stopped being patient at Jack. I started shouting back at him. I let myself get much angrier than he was. I taught him to be more afraid of my anger than I was of his. At first he argued back at me and we had big fights, but later he learned to stop shouting when I start. Now he shuts up fast when I shout back at him. He is the one who is silent. I act like a American. That forces him to act like a Chinese. Ha, ha.

July 19

Bureaucracy! The papers from Beijing didn't make it to Shanghai yesterday, so now we must wait until Monday. Z does not think they will be adequate, thinks they must be sealed by the Chinese Embassy in Ottawa. A Canadian seal, even a Chinese Canadian seal, even if it can balance a ball on its nose, is not good enough. It takes a Chinese seal, even a Canadian Chinese seal without a ball. The Chinese bureaucracy is downright Kafkaesque. Indeed it is no coincidence that Kafka set in China a story about the utter opacity of government to the common man: on his deathbed the emperor of China whispers a special message just for you, but never, never can the messenger reach you with the message. Deng Xiao Ping says that foreigners should be able to marry Chinese, but never, never can that message filter down thru the bureaucracy. Now I won't know for two more days and we are both on pins and needles again. Most of last night was spent trying to work out too many unworkoutable angles. When Z came Ruby and I ate while she read quietly in a chair. Even after I finished eating and wanted to talk, she obviously didn't, but not in the unhappy way of two nights ago and soon everything was fine even if we did not work out much. As usual the best part of the evening was the walk to her bus down Yanan Lu. Most of this time was spent coming to a linguistic understanding. Z asked me if I had reported our disagreement to Ruby. She was talking about a minor one tonight and meant when she was in the bathroom. I hadn't, but I thought she was talking about Wednesday again. (Glad she wasn't since that had been cleared up previously and I didn't need to be reminded of it – as is proved by the fact that I was.) I said I had told Ruby (wondering why Z was asking since that was what Wednesday's disagreement was all about) and Z became unhappy and lectured me about telling others too much. But she was neither spiteful nor refusing to talk, and when we eventually figured out we were talking about different times and I had not repeated my previous (in her eyes) sin, we had our usual big laugh and things were fine again. There must be a myriad of minor misunderstandings between us, most of which we never even realize, because of the language barrier. But I remain convinced our understanding of the big things is clear, mutual, stellar. A starfull night on a dark mountaintop. Or a moonfull night on Yanan Lu.

My physical desire for Z is very strong yet not strongly sexual, at least not in the ways to which I am accustomed. When we are together I cannot keep my eyes off her and her touch is irresistible. Her skin is the smoothest texture I have ever felt, and this is true of every part of her – presumably: I haven't touched <u>every</u> part – except palm and soles, not just one or two places (the backs of the thighs have always been my favorite) as in Western women. Opposites attract: she also likes to touch me and finds my skin hair (sweat hair the Chinese call it and it's true: my sweat also fascinates her since in this weather I am perpetually sweating. Last night I told her I loved even her sweat and she thought it terrible that I could compare love and sweat. We joked about that for some time, in the course of which she pointed out that she didn't sweat much, that "our" sweat was basically mine. I replied that my sweat was great because my love was. Altogether a lovely interlude altho I have no doubt that the comparison is quite unchinese and very strange to her) fascinating, pulling at it and stroking it (usually on my arms) frequently. Yet either because I know I must not have sex with her until after marriage (but may that come soon, soon, soon) or because (as my mother used to tell me I would, but I never have before) I respect her too much to (to use my mother's word, the proper Fifties and, I imagine, Chinese word) "violate" her, I do not find my sexual cravings for her resemble at all what they have always been towards other women. On the other hand since my teens and early twenties, (i.e., since the Sixties and its sexual revolution) I have never had a close relationship with a woman which has not become fairly quickly sexual. Perhaps I did feel this way toward the platonic lovers I had in those pre sexual revolution years. I can't remember. In any case amidst my strong physical passions there is a calm which I like very much and cannot conceive of feeling toward a Western woman. On the other hand, altho I am seldom conscious of it – I am concentrating too hard on language and on Z as a person – I know I am almost continually aroused in her presence. I am avidly looking forward to sex and can already see it will be out of sight.

Poor Jack. He was so worried about the papers with official seals. I knew they would not be good enough. Chinese officials do not take chances. If the papers were not exactly what was required, they would not accept them. They would not trust a foreign seal. Chinese do not trust foreign governments, specially Western governments. For most of its history China kept most foreigners out. That is why the Great Wall was built. In the nineteenth century Western countries went to war against China to open it up so they could make lots of money selling opium. They won the wars, but they lost the chance to be trusted. The May Fourth Movement wanted Western science and democracy, but even it did not trust Western governments. Its big protest march was against Western governments, who made a secret deal with Japan to concede a Chinese province. China does not forget its history. Why should we Chinese trust Western countries? But foreign people are different from foreign governments. Once we get to know a foreign person, we can trust him or her. Remember Marco Polo. Remember Li Matou (the first missionary to come to China in the Ming Dynasty. I do not know his Western name). Remember Jack. I now trusted Jack because I knew him, but the bureaucrats would not trust him because they did not know him. I did not think a official marriage could happen for many months. I was not sure what to do. I too sat on a rug made out of pins. That is a Chinese idiom. It is very similar to the English one about pins and needles that Jack used. The rug of pins is the reason I did not want to talk much. I did not want to tell Jack about how bad our problem really was.

But the worse our problem with the officials got, the stronger my love grew. Jack was so worried. He tried so hard to do things the way he thought I wanted them that I could not tell him I did not care, that officials some times delayed for years, that Chinese long ago learned when to ignore officials or even the emperor and to do what they needed to do, that I trusted him, that we did not have to wait. That I did not want to wait.

After 1911 China did not want to wait too. She was like me. She was like a woman who waited too long for a lover. She waited hundreds of years for the revolution that got rid of a foreign dynasty. But China was frustrated like me too. The revolution succeeded, but the country was still in seven disorders, eight messes. In my novel the years after 1911 will be full of political discussions about what to do. But that is not enough. I want to write a novel, not a documentary, a herstory, not a history. I need a personal story to make it more interesting and exciting, but Erbao and Chen Du Xiu already were in love for more than ten years. They already did all the things I wanted to do. I do not want to write just a bunch of sexy political discussions. I want to write a real novel, a deep novel, a literature novel. Writing a novel like that is more complicated than writing a history. You can not be satisfied with just facts. I will have to think how to add a fiction. But it has to be a true fiction. Herstory must not contradict history.

July 20

Last night I got to see Z among Westerners for the first time. A cousin of mine was in Shanghai on a luxury tour and we had dinner with her group on the fourteenth floor of the Park Hotel and then went to a performance by the Shanghai Acrobatic Troupe. (Will the day ever come when they dare take foreigners to a Chinese opera?) Z was worried but did fine and enjoyed herself, laughed a lot (at first nervously but progressively less so), asked the kind of embarrassing questions Chinese specialize in etc. One reason Z did well was that my cousin was surprisingly good: accepted Z and worked hard to make her comfortable. Z was full of questions about Western makeup, jewellery etc. but only after the tourists – the women did almost all the talking at dinner – asked her about her lack of such things. She told them she did not like such things, then asked me in Chinese if it was ok to say that. She thought she might be insulting them. She thought one woman, a fairly typical dark Jew with black frizzy hair, was black and marvelled at her long, polished fingernails. But it was my cousin, who wore sneakers and casual clothes with little makeup or jewellery – was this deliberate because she knew Z would not have fancy clothes? – and who is not great looking by Western standards, whom she called beautiful. Z and Ruby chattered away all night, and after the show the three of us walked openly hand in hand down Nanjing Lu to Z's bus: lovely and relaxed, the first time Z has openly held hands with me in public. Of course Ruby making us a gang of three makes it different. But no less lovely. I suspect that being accepted by a member of my family made Z feel very good. The memory of her former boyfriend's family must still rankle terribly.

Maybe I could have a foreigner in my novel after all. Erbao would not have to marry him. Specially if he was a she. In 1890, when my novel begins, foreigners were not important in the life of my city. That seems strange to say because Shanghai was mainly created by foreigners and for foreigners. It was just a fishing village before the British forced it open after the first Opium War. Although they built many fancy buildings and factories, but the foreigners were there just to make money. They only thought of us Chinese as cheap workers. They stayed in their concessions and stayed apart from us. But this changed during and after World War 1. Many more foreigners came to Shanghai, and they were not just business men. The biggest group were the White Russians, rich and noble people who were made poor by the Russian Revolution and ran away from their home country. But many other foreigners came too. For the first time many women came. Women who were not wifes. Shanghai became a really international city. Life changed a lot. So maybe my novel should show this. I think my novel will have to change around this time any how because Chen Du Xiu's life changed so much. So the changes in my novel can also show the changes in my city too. They can show the new foreign influences.

July 21

Have a nasty flu, ache all over. Also had it all day yesterday but had to keep on keeping on. Which, no doubt, is why the flu does too. The U.S. consul, who is being helpful even if he is not hopeful, piled on some more documents but told me frankly that the stuff I have is not adequate. He has been thru this before and knows. I took my documents to the foreigners' marriage bureau, which is near the U.S. Consulate, and they confirmed his fears. So now I have located a Canadian consular representative preparing for the opening of the new Canadian Consulate in Shanghai. He has the power to attest to my statements, whatever that means, another seal at the least. It feels like I am trying to snow the bureaucracy with sheer paper weight.

My perseverance may not have been rewarded but I was during an evening which included both screaming tickling matches among the three of us and serious discussion with Z. It concluded in the john (Ruby was reading in the main room) with passion too powerful to resist altho the last thing I wanted to do was give Z my flu. Earlier there had been many jokes between the three of us about the roughness of my skin, especially my beard, vs. the smoothness of Z's. In fact my stroking her silken legs led into the passion, and I continued to stroke them, up and down, the sensation rousing, the motion hypnotizing, as we stood kissing. The blank look of passion was on her face and, I'm sure, mine too. I had virtually no control of myself. How lucky Ruby was here to prevent us from going too far. "Going too far": how magnificent to use those words, my mother's cautionary words, again, to feel that way again, a way I haven't felt since boyhood, or at least since L (say seventeen years ago), and to have a woman responding so fully. The years with P obscured so much of the wonder and mystery of the human body. All our mutual sympathy, all my understanding of her, eventually my understanding of the childhood sexual abuse that made her what she was, cannot make up for what she could not give. And there is a spiritual affinity between Z and me which feels every bit as close as that between me and P. In other words I have the combination of body and spirit I have sought all my life but never before found. Oh, that it may prove to be fully true!

I got Z to agree (with numerous jokes about my letting her eat even if she brings in no money: she believes this and my mother's child in me admires the belief even as I strive to mitigate it) that unless she could find satisfying work in Wuhan, she would write, not take a crumby job. In the end she thanked me for this, confirming my suspicions that this is really what she wants to do as much as it is what I want her to do. On the other hand, she has learned what marijuana is and questioned me about that and being a hippie. She has been taught that pot is poison and hippies decadent. I became somewhat indignant over that, told her about some of the suffering I had endured trying to change a decadent society and that I didn't appreciate the people I admired and to a large extent tried to emulate labelling me decadent because I didn't choose exactly their methods, especially considering how many mistakes the moral Chinese Communist Party has made. The matter is too complicated to handle well at our present language levels, but we agreed to discuss it fully eventually. Z was not nearly as concerned as I was. She simply asked for assurances that I was not a bad person despite my hippie past, I gave them and she was content with me if not persuaded about hippies in general. Her reaction was nothing like it was to my sexual past. To what extent that is because she knows and trusts me better now and to what extent it is simply because this is not as big an issue to her as sex I don't know. She did not remember that at least once before I had told her I smoked pot, no doubt because she didn't know what it was then. She said she had just learned about it a day or two ago. I assume that means she is investigating contemporary Western life. But she trusts me more than her Chinese sources.

I do eye exercises which frequently call for covering both eyes with my palms. When I started doing them I visualized the view from my window in the Slocan Valley in my mind's eye, but since I met Z I see her image as soon as I close my eyes. That image has changed several times. In the beginning it was always the way she looked at our first meeting, when I realized we were leaning toward each other across the desk. Later there was an image of her as I sat on my floor and looked up at her sitting in the armchair, her eyes earnest (perhaps the first time she allowed herself to look directly into mine for any duration), her legs shifting about beneath her full skirt, lithe sprites revealing and covering themselves with a will and an ambiguity of their own. Today it is as she stood last night, her back to the bathroom window, her eyes, as seen thru my own unbelieving, bleary eyes, bleared with love they couldn't believe, our bodies one, those smooth, curving, restless legs alive beneath my living hands. The prose is growing purple, perhaps yellow, but who cares?

Thinking back on my walk down Nanjing Lu with my cousin's friends: two of the men (none of the women and not my cousin's husband, thank god) kept remarking about underdevelopment and overpopulation. They are money people, pure and simple. They saw, felt, smelled none of the life, the vitality, the sensuous beauty of Shanghai. Because

their senses, they themselves, are dead. Their constant question was, can China catch up?
how long will it take China to catch up? By catching up they mean become like America.
It does not occur to them that there can be any other path. What is worse is that this is
occurring less and less to the Chinese. Z, in her attack on hippies, was accepting Reagan,
bourgeois America and all it stands for, all I oppose. No wonder so many Chinese support
Reagan's warlike policies like the bombing of Libya.

Jack would not let himself think how sick he was. I kept trying to get him to stop doing so much. I wanted him to stay in bed a few days, but he would not. It was the first time I saw the man he often said he was, the American who always wanted to fight the government. I liked it because he wanted to fight for us, but it was the peaceful writer that I loved. And I knew fighting would not win. When we found out which official would decide if we could marry, I planned to find out how to bribe him. Foreign cigarettes were usually the best thing. If you can not bribe Chinese officials, the best thing is to ignore them, not fight them.

Although Jack was sick, but he was very passionate. It was very wonderful to me. I never experienced passion like this before. I thought it was because he was a foreigner. We Chinese always thought foreigners were completely different from us, more passionate. In fact I was as passionate as he was, but I thought he made me that way. I learned a lot since then. And Jack's diary gives me a hint of how to show some of what I learned.

The year is 1920. The old revolution is dead. The new one is waiting to be born. Erbao can still fit into the *qipao* of her youth. But she does in private only now, in front of her big rosewood mirror. And with Shuangbao. The two middle aged courtesans like to play as young courtesans.

Lao Ahu shows Xiao Chen into Erbao's room and pours tea. Some thing is on his mind. Erbao sees it at once, so she does not make the formal welcome his long absence entitles her to make. "Sit down, old friend," she says. She expects him to take off his clothes. She expects a political problem. Many people told her many things about Chen, and he sent her a book. *Liening.*

He sits down and stares at the rug. It is a much finer one than the one he stared at when they first met, but he never looked at it before. "Lately I am very busy," he tells the thick, patterned silk. He pauses, then goes on. "All my life I was very busy. Being a editor, writer, teacher, advisor, scholar, rebel. I have almost no time for my family."

"Ah," she replies. His family was one subject they never discussed. "You courteously do not mention another thing which some times keeps you away from your family."

Finally he looks at her. "And you courteously do not mention that it did not keep me away from my family lately."

The courtesies concluded, Erbao sits back and sips her tea. It is her sign that she is ready to listen. "It is good we keep these courtesies between us, Erbao." So it was very serious. The last time he called her Erbao was when he was studying her first rug. Then he used to call her "Erbao, *Xiansheng*." "But what is better is that we can get so far beyond them. I can not get beyond them with my wife. That is why I avoid my home."

The family again. She takes another sip of tea. It is fine tea, the best Dragon Well, buds only. He does not touch his cup. She knows he wants to say some thing very bad. So it is very hard to say because saying some bad thing can make it worse. Most Chinese try never to say bad things. But not Chen. He is not one to try to turn a comet. Erbao knows that he knows that she knows what is going through his mind. He can not let superstition control him. He lives his life to kill superstition. He lives his life to be open in a closed society. So although she is surprised by what he says, but she is not surprised that he says it directly. Even before he says it, she is thinking that he needs to say it directly so he can deal with it directly. So he does not need to pretend reality is philosophy as most intellectuals would.

"My older son ran away."

Her face looks dark. Then it lights up. "With a courtesan." She does not ask it. She declares it.

"Lao Bao, you always are full of surprises. How did you know?"

"The gossip is all around here. Jinbao ran off with a boy named Chen. I could not guess it was your son until you told me. He is like his father."

"But he does not like his father. Or know him. If he knew me, he would know he did not need to run away. I spend so little time with my family. That is why he does not know."

"Are you sure? Maybe he knows you better than you know you. You never offered to run away with me."

"I was married before I met you."

Two wifes are better than one, she wants to tell him. When did a rich Chinese man let having one wife keep him from taking another? But what she says is, "A fate he wanted to avoid. Were you or were you not looking for a wife for him?"

"I was not," Chen protests. He pauses, then admits, "But his mother was."

"*Ah.*" She does not laugh. I really am growing older and wiser, she thinks to herself. Out loud she says, "Jinbao is Erbao thirty years ago. She chose voluntarily to become a courtesan."

"Then why did she change her mind? Why does she want to marry? My son is not rich."

Erbao is silent, remembering Shi. Would she have run away with him if he was willing? Would she have cared if he was not rich? "Life is simple when you are young," she finally replies.

"I want," he begins. Then he sees the tears in her eyes and stops. After a while he asks softly, "Can you find them?"

"Why?"

It is not a silly or a easy question, he sees. "What should I do?"

"Tell them they are the new China you were seeking all these years."

Tears are flowing freely now, and not only hers. He does not have to tell her she is right. "Give me a few days," she says.

"I will talk to them. I will embrace her."

"Not too tightly," Erbao instructs, and they are able to laugh through their tears.

"You are a wonderful treasure, Lao Bao. You can solve any problem."

"Only the problems of my small world. The problems of the great world you must solve yourself."

"And I will. I found the solution, and I will use it in my own family first. I will talk to both my sons. I will tell them all the things I did not have time to tell them when they were growing up. I will make them love the new China I thought only I was building. I will tell them they are the new youth I was too busy lecturing to listen to. There is a line of English poetry. 'The child is father of the man.' I will be the first Chinese father to admit that to his sons."

Suddenly Xiao Chen is on his knees before her chair. Before she can stop him, he takes off a slipper and unwraps her bindings. He buries his face in her stinking foot, rolls his tongue over and over it. At first she is shocked. His tongue and hands kiss and massage her foot for a long time. By the time he moves higher they are laughing together.

Later they even have the political discussion she was expecting. "Now that we have solved the problems of my small world," Chen begins.

"They are far from solved," Erbao interrupts.

"They are in your hands. That is better than solved."

"I never know whether I like you for your optimism or in spite of it."

"Because you keep your bound feet on the ground, I can put my aching head back into the clouds. Up there I found a new pair of misters," Chen tells her. "Mr. *Ma Ke Se*, Marx, Marxism, and Mr. *Liening*, Lenin, *Buershiweizhuyi*, Bolshevism." He always told her foreign names as well as Chinese ones, and she always learned them so she could talk to any one without the confusion which usually accompanied foreign names. "They are a little like you and me. Marx put his head in the clouds. He taught workers about the great world we can build, a world where everyone works according to ability and receives according to need. Lenin's feet are on the ground. He teaches us the strategy to reach that world. Marx's theories did not succeed until Lenin made them work. They are working now. In *E guo*, Russia. Not such a small world, and not so far away. And you and I will help bring that new world to China."

July 22

Two hours peddling my bike in the blazing sun was not what was required to cure my flu. There's no way I can say how hot and muggy it was, how miserable I felt. Several times I had to stop because I felt faint. Z had urged me to take a taxi. Did I refuse purely out of my Jewish stinginess? Or do I feel a compulsion to do what I have to do alone, to take on the Castle myself? Call me K.

When I finally staggered back I simply collapsed. I went to bed before eight o'clock and feel a little better (if I felt worse I'd be dead) this morning but still ache all over, especially my eyes, which ache and burn simultaneously, as if yesterday's salt sweat were still coursing thru them. The worst thing is that I don't think the documents I got yesterday will do any good. The U.S. consul, who should know, didn't think they would help.

I feel so rotten that even my desire for Z seems conventional, an ordinary longing for a woman instead of a wonderful mystery which controls my being. Two nights ago, after she left, I masturbated for the first time since I met her. She had left me so excited that masturbation was automatic. Usually after we part the long walk home dispels desire at least partially, but because I was sick she persuaded me not to see her off. Did what I did turn the dark mystery into the dirty little secret? In fact I know that such thoughts are the product of my illness and will vanish when I feel better and when I am with Z, but what if bureaucratic bullshit really does prevent us from marrying before I must go to Wuhan?

Z said her mother was complaining that she was home so little. I did not pay much attention two days ago, but she must be experiencing a slew of small troubles to which I have been inattentive. I must try to understand these more and be less selfish toward her. We have committed ourselves to each other so totally that she will be in real distress if we can't marry in August.

A memory, insignificant but sweet, drifts across my mind and makes much right again. It is of Z asking me with a worried look if it was all right to express her disapproval of makeup, jewellery etc. to the American women wearing them. Her honesty was (perhaps) Western; Chinese courtesy called for a more equivocal, perhaps even an untrue, answer. But it was the honesty I originally fell in love with. Her face was much relieved when she saw I thoroughly approved of her honesty. Did she suspect when she answered that I would approve of her following her instincts rather than the ultracivilized, anti instinctual Chinese code of courtesy? I don't know, but I know a warmth spread over both of us as a result of the brief interchange. Such small warmths are important amid the threats of a cold world. (Language fails here: given the weather and yesterday's delirium induced by heat, I should say, "A chill spread over both of us.... Such small chills are important amid the threats of a hot world." I wonder if it is possible in Chinese to make that mean what I want it to mean? Probably not: Chinese fear cold even more than whatever ancients were ultimately responsible for the imagery in English. Maybe in the language of a tropical people....)

Did Jack think maybe I was pretending when I asked if it was ok to criticise the American women's makeup? He some times forgot then that he was the first

foreigner I ever met, and the only other one I met before this group was Ruby, a
child. It is even hard for me to remember that now, when the city I grew up in and
loved seems less like home to me than a cold land of mountains and trees and
wild animals. A cold land, Jack. Only a Canadian could think of making "cold"
a good word and warm a bad one. Canada might be my home, and Shanghai,
the sprawling metropolis, might seem strange to me now, but I will never like the
cold. Flowers do not grow in the cold too. Flowers have hot blood.

"Shaungbao, if I take you to the young lovers, will you promise not to try
to seduce her?"

"Why take me then?"

"For the same reason I took you in when you met the fate of all flowers
when winter freezes their petals. But you know you need more than you can get
in my house, and you will be interested in the foreign flower who made the bed
the young lovers lie in. The new world Xiao Chen searches for his son found.
But he did not go to *e guo* to find it. A *mei guo* woman, 'a mei li kan,' she says it,
hides them. She calls herself a dancer, but please do not ask her in what position
she does her dancing."

"Ah, the dance of the quaking of the quilt."

"I think so. Only the boy can understand her words, but any person will
be able to understand her movements. We could teach her some things about
subtlety."

"Ah, *naguoning* can not learn such lessons. Once I tried."

"But we can learn some things from her too. She fights with the White
Russian 'princesses' because she supports *Liening* and *Buershiweizhuyi*, and she
fights with the missionaries because she supports free love."

Because I am writing in English, I want to joke about free love and love
that does not cost money. Shuangbao might answer, "If love is free, how can
we live?" But Erbao and Shuangbao can not make that joke in any dialect of
Chinese I know. If I really knew *huahua*, I am sure I could find many jokes. I
heard that in the dialect of the Eskimos in the north of Canada are more than
twenty words for snow. The dialect of courtesans must have that many words for
different kinds of love.

Erbao would have to explain what the foreign woman means by "free
love" because maybe it is not the same as the courtesans' idea of *ziyou lianai*. "As
I understand, it means expensive love. It means she is free to love any one she
wants, and he does not have to pay her. But he always gives many gifts. Very nice
gifts. It is like what we do with our best clients, but she says she does not wait
for people to come to her. She finds them herself. And I think often she finds
women."

"Ah, then why can I not seduce <u>her</u>?"

"Because she is young, and you are not. To the lovers she is old, but to us she is young. And she makes herself feel younger by always wanting to be the seducer."

"Did she seduce Jinbao?"

"I think no. I think she did not even seduce the boy. I think what she does for them she does for her ideas. But maybe one of her ideas is to make a three cornered bed."

"Perhaps we can add more corners."

"My promise to Xiao Chen does not allow me to do such things."

"I thought you converted him."

"I converted him to taking his son and daughter into his family. But the *ameilikan* wants to destroy the family. Not just Chen's family, all families. She is bolder than we. Even a flower like me, who voluntarily left her family, still sends money back to it. And most flowers like you, who hardly remember their families, would gladly give up their rootless drifting to become a wife."

"Ah, you remind me of that young peacock Han Bangqing who wanted to make me one. I refused. I never was tempted to do that."

"Because no woman ever asked you to marry."

"Ha, you know me too well. Might the *ameilikan* ask?"

"Ah, now you discovered my hidden reason for taking you."

"You sarcastic me."

"No, you will like her, and you may be safer in her world than in ours. Maybe her world does not throw away flowers when their bloom fades. And although you are older, but she will want to seduce you just because you are Chinese. She wants to defy Chinese morality. That is why she protects the young lovers and she does not have to seduce them. But you are not like them, and she wants to learn our speech and customs. Maybe some of her customs might be good for you, *jie jie*. Because she is not loyal to the family, so maybe she is loyal to her lovers."

"Until she tires of them."

"She will not tire of you, sister. She wants to learn, and I know there is no better teacher. She will like your ideas. I do not mention your fingers and tongue."

"I think she must be tall, with long legs like yours."

"And full of fire. Come. It is worth three visits to her thatched cottage."

A few days later Erbao will ask, "How is your student learning, Shuangbao?"

"She learns quickly, but you must never let her hear you say that she is the student. She thinks she is the teacher. She thinks she is teaching a innocent old Chinese woman about the art of love between women. Ameilikan *ning* are very funny. But very exciting too. My ancient bones have found a young colour and fragrance."

I do not learn quickly. Before, in the middle of writing, I made a discovery I probably should discover years ago. For many years I lived with it, yet if I did not write this novel, I would not discover it. That is why Jack says "damn." That is why Jack writes. You do not only learn by studying or doing. You learn by writing too. Damn. Maybe it is a good word, a yell of discovery, not a curse word.

My plan for my novel took a turn I did not plan. That unplanned turn took me into a unexpected place, a place of knowledge, a place of history historians would never discover. By introducing Jinbao, I made Chen a fictional character too. I guess the Chen in my herstory always was even though Chen Du Xiu was a famous man in history. Poor Chen. He gets ignored by historians and fictionised by herstorians like me. Up to now I did not contradict history, but I need Jinbao. I need some one to keep in touch with Chen and keep connecting him to Erbao, for later he will disappear. In 1921 Chen Du Xiu was a founder and the first leader of the Chinese Communist Party. It was a mistake. He was too open a personality to play the kind of secret ghost and demon politics played in China. By 1929 his two sons were killed by the Nationalists and the *Qing Bang* (Green Gang) and he was kicked out of the Communist Party. His spirit broke.

July 23

My body remains sick in bed, but a full day resting there has let my mind rove. It is now in Kafka's (or is it Jiake's?) castle, east wing. The west wing of the castle looks like Chicago City Hall, but no marble or cut stone here: the east wing is all concrete, its functionaries all abstract. Questions elicit blank stares or incomprehensible gibberish. After much wandering thru the labyrinth of corridors, I find myself in a huge hall. Everywhere lines lead toward tiny barred windows, all of them closed. I join the shortest one. "When does it open?" I ask the man in front of me. "One o'clock," he replies. It is already two. Suddenly my luck changes; the window opens. People from other lines rush to my window, pushing aside those in the line. "Hey," I cry. "No butting in." No one pays attention; everyone is pushing forward. Two people manage to get served. Then the window closes again. People drift away. Other lines reform. A window on the other side of the room opens, and the scene is repeated. After watching several such free-for-alls, I develop a strategy. I position myself in front of a now vacant window, hoping it will be the next one to open. If it does I will grip the sides of the window and extend my elbows to keep others from pushing in front of me. Other windows open before mine, but after a long wait my window actually opens. People are pushing me from behind and both sides, but I spread my legs and stand firm. "I am in love," I tell the man behind the window. I speak softly, reverently. I am trying to gain his sympathy. "I want to get married." "Window number eight," he snaps and pulls the wooden board, closing his window. Other people have heard, so number eight now has a line. I want to claim precedence, but my vocabulary is not up to it, so I shlep to the end of the line. By the time the window opens, the line is shorter because other window openings have lured away most of those in front of me. I am now third in line and have shrewdly worked out tactics with the woman who is second. When the window opens we each grab one side of the window and lock our free arms behind the man at the head of the line, thus protecting him and holding our own places. The people in front of me are ordered to other windows, so I soon am at the window myself. I decide to be direct. "I want to get married," I tell the woman in the window. She looks me over, reaches thru the bars to feel my biceps, instructs me to turn around. "Good," she says and begins filling out a thick stack of papers. I cannot believe it. The forms are complicated, but when she finishes she says, "Congratulations. Here is a photo of your wife." I look at the photo. "Who is this?" I ask. "I don't even know her." "It is my daughter." I quickly control my anger and try to explain about Hai Bao. "Will you or won't you marry my daughter?" she asks. "I love another," I begin. She bangs shut the window. Hours later I make it to another window. "I want to marry this woman," I tell the man, showing him a photo of Hai Bao. He takes the picture. "Very nice," he says. "If you can't marry her, I will find her another man." "She doesn't want another man," I assure him. "She wants to marry me, and I want to marry her." "You can't always get what you want," he says. Does he know the Rolling Stones? "How do I know you are not already married?" I show him my twenty three documents. He leafs thru them. "No seal," he proclaims. I point out that there are many seals. "Black seals. No good. We need red seals." Makes sense, I think: Red China, red seals. I spot his chop and red inkpad. "How about that one?" He laughs. "This is light red ink. You need the darkest red. It is almost purple. Only high officials have it. They keep it in dark red boxes secured by dark red tape." I begin to cry. "Crying allowed only at window number 37," he says, and shuts his window.

The year is 1930. Erbao receives a letter from Chen, who is at his family's home in Anhui.

Dear Lao Bao,

I took off my clothes to write to you. It is my only way left to keep faith with the only person who always kept faith with me. There are tears in my eyes because I know I will never see you again. I will never return to Shanghai. The city you love, the city I once loved, is now the city of death. The city that was once full of young people and young ideas and ideals massacred all the young people and young ideas I loved. Shanghai murdered them all. Not the naguoning, the foreigners, although they helped by hiding the murderers in the international concessions, or the nadining, the outsiders, although they contracted for the massacre, but the only males who are as truly Shanghai ning as the flowers, the Qing Bang gangsters, who did the first terrible deeds that enabled the rest. The people who were outside the law enforced the new law, the law of Jiang Jie Shi, the law of death, the law which murdered my sons. But my own Party, the Party I founded and fought for, murdered my ideals. I made mistakes, terrible mistakes. We all did. We made our mistakes together. What we understood in theory became too real in practice and killed all we stood for and many who stood with us. I killed my sons by not taking seriously the things I taught them. Politics seemed like a game for intellectuals like me, but my sons are dead because of my playing. So it would not matter if my fellow players killed me. It would be better than what they did, blamed me for all the mistakes we made together. It does not matter. I will take the blame. My sons and all I loved and believed in are dead. What does it matter if they throw me down a well, then throw stones at me? Let them kick me out of the game I began, the game I am too sick to play, the game which will end in death. China will lose no matter who wins this deadly game. The new China I fought to found will become a prison whether the Guomindang or the Gongchangdang win the terrible game.

When I was a small boy, I liked to play with marbles. Each little colored glass globe was a baby world of multicoloured continents and oceans. We children all loved our marbles, so whoever won the game always returned the losers' marbles. One day a bigger boy took my marbles. I cried and went to my parents. They went to the other boy's family and forced him to return my marbles. In fact his father took his few marbles as well as my many and gave them all to my parents to give to me. When that happened I felt bad. The other boy's family was much poorer than mine. Maybe he could not get more marbles. It was the first time I understood that there were greater inequalities in the world than those of size. The next day I gave him back his marbles plus two of my prettiest ones. It was the first example of the charity which makes me unfit to play the game, unfit to live in this world. My marbles, my sons, my world. All lost. My beautiful world of "from each according to ability to each according to need." Whichever Party wins the terrible game being played now, the people will lose their marbles. The new world will be run only according to the Party's needs.

I have the same dream every night. I am riding through China in a train. I look out the windows, but the only scenery for ten thousand *li* is high prison walls. I keep thinking that if I ride far enough, I can escape the prisons, but when I look around the car I am in, I see there are bars on all the windows and doors and guards with guns to make sure no one escapes. I do not want to live to see this future. I want to die. But Jinbao will not let me. Openness is always my greatest fault. Being open and honest got me kicked out of my Party. Is it a mistake inside me, or did I spend too much time in foreign countries and foreign books? Chinese should conspire in secret. Being open always got me into trouble. Now it does not even let me suicide myself. Every time I want to do it Jinbao knows. She quickly shoves Xiaobao in with me. She knows I will not kill myself with my little granddaughter there. And the child always recalls me back to life, makes me forget my plans for death. For a little while. The first time I thought of it I was not sure and Jinbao was not prepared. She is still young and beautiful. She offered her flowery self to stop me. That is when I became sure.

Once you asked me what I would do when I grew too old for the young. Then I did not think that could ever happen, but now it has. Jinbao is very clever. She saw that. That is when she went for Xiaobao. When the old grow too old, only babies can save them.

Dear Xiao,

Keep your clothes off. I too took mine off. It is as close as I can get to you. You began what you need to do. You began to write. Write, Xiao. Do not die. You are precious to me. Our world of flowers is suffering too. The Green Gang gangsters who killed your sons now run Shanghai for Jiang Jie Shi, and they have only one idea about women. When ideas like Confucianism or Communism, Daoism or Dictatorism, Buddhism or Businessism become more precious than people, people die. Like your sons did. People suffer. Like you are, like we are, like China is. Write, Xiao. Write for me. Write for the suffering people of China. Write for you. Write to make your dead dreams come true. Write to live. Live to write until we can reach each other. Write until we can live for each other and a few precious people. Write so we can live in the middle of all this dying.

Immorality was safer than politics. Shaungbao made a lip and tooth close relationship with the Americans in Shanghai. There were several women like my *Ameilikan* in Shanghai in the 1920s. Isadora Duncan was the most famous one. Most of them did not stay too long. I imagine Shaungbao passed from one woman to another. She finds a flowerhood among foreign women who love women. When one leaves Shanghai, she arranges for Shaungbao to go to another. They all love her for her skills, which they do not know she has, and because she connects them to the Chinese life and the life of the flowers, which at least they know they do not know. I do not need the *Ameilikan* in my novel the way I need Jinbao, but I want her. I want her to show that Chen Du Xiu, who was considered China's most advanced thinker of his day and was always reading foreign books and trying to keep up with the new ideas, was out of touch with what was really happening in the West. Every one in China was. They still are. That is why I was worried because Jack was a hippie and smoked marijuana. I did not understand about North America. Although my friends in Shanghai tried to be very modern, but no one, not even returning students who studied there, understood about North America. And we should. The ancestors of the hippies were in Shanghai in the 1920s. This is my discovery. In the city that had more prostitutes than any other one in the world, all kinds of immorality were not noticed. The world of the flowers and their culture specially attracted women who loved women. The international concessions of Shanghai were a liberated area which attracted many such kinds of people. People Chinese people were afraid of. People Chinese people are still afraid of. If I knew Jack was a hippie before I met him, I would not agree to meet him. I would pretend he did not exist. Chinese work very hard not to notice what they are afraid of. So in the 1920s we did not notice the split we are now afraid of. The split between what Jack calls the old left and the new left began then. It was about personal culture, not just politics. Maybe China needs what Chinese are most afraid of, a cultural revolution. But the Communist Party will never lead it. As I told Jack when we first met, it wants to be a feudal father. It calls modern Western cultural ideas bourgeois individualism and spiritual pollution. What Mao called the *wenhua da geming*, the Great Cultural Revolution, was political, not cultural. Just as Chen Du Xiu's ideas were forty five years earlier. Chen could accept his son living with a flower only if he unflowered her. He cut her roots in the fertile world of Shanghai flowers. He insisted that she should become a traditional wife in his house that he said he wanted to be untraditional. The young couple probably wanted this too. People outside the main culture often want to get back inside. Maybe they were using the American woman to force Chen to accept them. Better a quiet wife in the house than a loud lover outside. Chen could not let his son stay with the American woman. She probably smoked marijuana.

Only a few unique flowers would understand. Flowers like Shaungbao were not afraid of marijuana. Because they had cultural ideas which most Chinese were afraid of. Which most Chinese did not notice. Which I have to discover. My sharp point is that flowers like Erbao and Shaungbao were the only ones in all of China who could understand people like the *Ameilikan*. I think they maybe did the same things quietly and sophisticatedly that Westerners made so much noise about doing. Maybe they learned more because they did them quietly. But I can only think this. I can never know because the gangsters and then the Japanese weakened the flowers by trying to make them only prostitutes, not courtesans, and then the communists called the flowers poisonous weeds and pulled up their roots when they came into power in 1949. The communists did what Chen did to Jinbao. They made wifes out of the flowers. That is why I must write a novel, a herstory, not a history. I have much more to discover. Just writing this let me make another discovery. Han Bangqing and I were both wrong. The flowers did have roots. But their roots were not in the traditional world of families. Their roots were in their own world, their own unique culture (horticulture, not whoreticulture!). They lost a lot, and Chinese culture lost more when these roots were cut.

July 24

I had a revelation yesterday, a stroke of pure genius. I realized that my divorce papers had not been finalized until after I reached China. There is a ninety day waiting period or something, and the divorce did not become final until I had been in China a month. The papers were dated late September and were mailed to me here. Since my passport proves I've been in China continuously since late August, the only place I could have got married is here, and they know I have not done that. So I took a student to translate and all my documents, especially the divorce decree and passport, to the marriage place. We talked to a new person, a man, who almost immediately agreed to accept my proof altho he could not read my documents and they did not have a Chinese seal and so, technically at least, were still inadequate. Incredible! Again I realized that the Chinese often have no actual laws or rules, that even minor bureaucrats have power to make their own decisions based on god knows what. My student was asked to translate the documents, which he spent several hours doing, and get them sealed by my unit (not Foreign Affairs or any government department!). Z must also get approval from her unit. Then we are to return tomorrow and if all our seals are in order we can marry in ten days. Amazing! Victory!!!

I rushed to Z's house to tell her the news. I should say I rushed toward her house. Finding the place (in the rain) was a major challenge. I caught Z with her hair down (and up and over, a real mess) and loved her all the more for it. I don't know why, altho I love her so much, I keep fearing disappointment, but I was in fact afraid she might disapprove of my coming. She has told me not to come without her expressed permission, and I caught her in a state of disarray, probably in the midst of her xiuxi. Instead of angry, disapproving, annoyed or even worried, she was overjoyed, even before hearing my news. As she came down the stairs, barefoot, in a ragged shirt and flimsy skirt, her hair that lovely mess, surprise and happiness smeared all over her face at first hearing my voice, the light was behind her and the outline of her legs thru the thin material utterly enchanted me, so beautiful she looked in those old clothes. We spent an evening of pure joy up in her second floor garret, passion and laughter flowing freely and together. Altho the rain had substantially cooled the temperature, Z kept insisting that her little room was too hot, that I was too hot, and kept fanning me with a feather fan even as I laughed and protested and we kissed and did everything but undress and dance the dance of the shaking of the sheets. We were both ecstatically happy, ecstatically in love, ecstatically enjoying our love. At nine o'clock her mother, watching TV below, turned off the tube and the light and went to bed. This was our signal to leave. Z insisted on a quick change out of the old clothes while I waited downstairs. She emerged in a plain white loose dress which she then encircled with an old belt and looked utterly enchanting. We walked freely and happily, mutually enchanted, oblivious to the huge metropolis around us, not resisting impulses to take each other's hands but not holding on too long, laughing, laughing, laughing, she telling me over and over "you can't" (you can't say I love you so loudly, you can't lean that way and look as if you are going to eat me when you whisper) and I overreacting and overacting. God, I love her. Everything light and lovely. She insisted on walking me to the 95 bus terminal saying she had a bus pass and would take the bus back, then running back to me to borrow five fen because she had forgotten to take her pass. As we walked I told her her health had already improved – she used to tire quickly when she walked; she also has resisted my illness – and she reminded me that I was again attempting to play the savior.

Afternoon: a sweating day of running around. Even worse for Z, who told me in a brief meeting she will have been on eight different busses. But everything go for me: the school sealed my papers in a few hours after saying not 'til tomorrow. The chairman of the department went over the translations and made corrections in one, gave me personal congratulations and a sincere invitation to return anytime. In response to a note from Z the photographer agreed to have photos by noon tomorrow. (An earlier one had told my student no one in Shanghai did it so fast.) Z is having more trouble, needed my passport and residence card to show her unit, but presumably will be successful in the end. I am waiting and hoping for her to show up altho I told her not to because she will be too tired. One of the teachers at the school was already spreading the word: turns out her husband was the man at the marriage bureau who oked things yesterday. I never cease to be astounded at what a small town Shanghai is. Yet everyone else has been caught by surprise (much to my surprise: I didn't think we had done much of a job keeping our secret). I received a veiled warning or two to be careful and oodles of good wishes. With luck all will be approved tomorrow, and we can then get officially married ten days later. And then, perhaps, go to Qingdao, a famous honeymoon spot, I am told, to see Z's family.

The ceiling in Z's room is very low. The first time she fanned me last night I leaped up in protest and banged my head hard against a beam, causing great pain and laughter.

As usual Jack wants to be the *jiushizhu*, the saviour. But Chinese culture saved us, not him. I tried to explain to him what happened at the marriage place. Maybe I explained after he wrote this day. Maybe he did not understand all my words. Definitely he does not understand how Chinese bureaucracy works. Westerners always like to talk about "the rule of law." What is so wonderful about going to court and paying lawyers and judges who know law but do not know people? We Chinese would rather pay a small bribe than a large fee. Of course there are bad bureaucrats, but there are also bad judges and lawyers. We expect to have to bribe Chinese bureaucrats. Their salaries are small. A judge's big salary and a lawyer's big fee are their bribes. The money makes sure the judge will usually judge in favour of where her money comes from, not the people he judges. Westerners say judges are paid to hold up the law. But who makes the law? Who is served by the law? The people with power and money. The rule of law is the rule of money. Although the Chinese bureaucracy runs on bribes, but it is not the rule of money. Bureaucrats are supposed to serve the people. To serve the people, you have to know the people you serve. Most Chinese bribes are usually small, a cigarette or a pack of them, a symbol to let the bureaucrat know you are human and a friend, not a enemy who might make him lose her job. The important thing is to get around all those little windows with bars that keep apart bureaucrats and the people they are supposed to serve. Then things can be decided by human contact, not law.

I thought we would have to pay a bribe to get married, but we did not.

One of the bureaucrats at the marriage place heard that the foreigner who kept coming there with useless papers worked at the school where his wife taught. He asked her about Jack and found out Jack was a good person, one who his students and his colleagues liked and respected, one who liked and respected China. Once the bureaucrat knew this, Jack became human, a friend, not a stranger who could not be trusted. The bureaucrat decided he did not need a government seal to protect himself in case Jack was trying some kind of foreigner's cheat. We did not need a law. We did not need Jack's stroke of pure genius. We did not even need my bribe.

Finding the right bureaucrat is always the key. The year is 1940, and Chen is in jail. Erbao and Shaungbao spend months looking for the right jail and the right bureaucrat. In Shanghai Erbao goes to the Uchiyama brothers, Lu Xun's and Chen's Japanese friends, and then to the Japanese Army leaders, who all know her from her brothel. She learns that Chen is not in a Japanese jail. One of Shaungbao's American friends sends to Smedley in Yanan, who goes to Mao, who laughs at the idea of helping Chen. But he supplies documents to prove that Chen was not connected to the Communist Party for many years. Out of jail Chen might cause trouble for the Japanese or the Nationalists. By finding out that Chen is not in a Japanese or a Communist jail, Erbao is able to track him to the Nationalists in Chongqing, "the capitol of free China." It is not easy to make the long trip, up the Long River, through Japanese lines to Chongqing, but four flowers, three generations of flowers, do it and find the man they think is the right bureaucrat, a warden of the jail Chen is in.

Many Shanghai flowers made the same trip earlier. They bought houses in Chongqing, so Erbao is able to get the use of one during the day. Flower power, Jack would call it. "Sisterhood Is Powerful" is the name of a book in English. *Huahua* would certainly have a good word for flowerhood, and Erbao would think about that. Flowerhood is more powerful than ever, she would think, but how different it is. Its skills keep declining. Even the best flowers now use sex more than art in their work. Being a flower is less challenging. But maybe it is more fun. Xiaobao certainly thinks so. She is only a silk flower, not a real one. But she loves her grandfather, and she loves being able to act in the little play, the real drama the real flowers created for her. I will have fun writing this scene.

The little man looked taller in their house than he did in his office. Erbao laughed to herself. She remembered how she went down on her knees to make him stand up to make her stand up. Before that he just sat in his high chair like a throne. He did not want strangers to see how short he was. Today he wore a modern type of the ancient *gao di xue* (tall sole shoes) worn on the opera stage and a purple silk gown. Good signs. Words, acting, photos and a package of American cigarettes did what her body no longer could. They lured the leader of the prison into their cave. Their cave in Chongqing was not really a cave. It was a brothel. The prostitutes were in other rooms, quietly preparing for business in the real caves, the air raid shelters. How lovely the flowers looked under the ground, where every thing else was grey and boring. Only they were not wilted in the terrible humidity that wilted every thing. Well, maybe they wilted too after a few hours under the ground, but by then their appointment books were full.

"Please sit, honoured sir," Shaungbao invited the guest. Shaungbao would present their business and Erbao would play the sad wife before Jinbao and Xiaobao came in. After many courtesies Shaungbao gets down to business. "The prisoner's name is Chen Du Xiu. I am sure you know him. He is a very famous man. He is in your jail by mistake. *Mei mei*, show him the documents.... As you can see, he was a red bandit many years ago, but the bandits kicked him out more than ten years ago." Shaungbao softens her voice to a whisper. "The bandits learned that he was a spy for the Guomindang. They wanted to murder him, but he fled to his home village. The men who arrested him there did not know of his secret mission."

"This man, this.... Chen. Is that what you said his name was?"

"Chen Du Xiu. He was a full professor at *Beida*."

"Ah. Surely such a high personage is not a resident of my humble establishment."

"*Mei mei*, please show him the admission documents."

"Ah.... Heng.... Most unregular. You have no doubt noticed that there are only two drops of water in the radical of my name."

"Very terrible. No doubt some one faked your honourable signature. That makes it even more important to get him out of your humble establishment. You will lose much face if it comes out that guests are being kept without your knowledge."

The head bowed courteously. Then he found his voice again. "We officials must serve our fellow human beings and respect the rights of others high-mindedly and honestly."

"The Generalissimo himself could not have said it better," replied Shaungbao. Indeed, thought Erbao, Jiang Jie Shi had said just those words. "And how better can you serve us poor women than by restoring the only man left in our family. As I told you, my husband and the girl's father already went before the judge of the underworld. How can we survive with no man in the family?"

Erbao did not let herself smile. These words were her cue. As the little man moved nervously in his chair, she spoke for the first time. "*Jie jie*, I just had a stroke of pure genius. Our best chance to survive is to find the right man for our Xiaobao. Why not give her as a concubine to our honoured guest. If he is a member of our family, he will surely help us."

Shaungbao pretends to be excited by the Erbao's idea. She goes out of the room and soon returns with Jinbao and Xiaobao.

When the two young women come in, the man puts on his thick eye glasses to get a better look. He did not need the glasses before. But the girl is certainly worth looking at. She knows, he decides. That is why she is looking at him. But why did not her mother teach her what his wife teaches his daughters? Not to look into a man's eyes. *Aiya.* And not to cross her legs when she is wearing a *qipao.* He quickly takes his glasses off, but as he tries to put them in his pocket, they seem to jump back onto his face. He tries to look at the older women, but quickly finds himself looking into the girl's eyes. She looks down shyly. She is innocent as well as untaught, he decides. As well as young and beautiful. He disciplines himself. Firmly he removes his glasses, puts them in their case and listens to what the old woman is saying. She is talking about music. The girl stands up, and the glasses jump back onto his face. What is she doing? She is putting a record on a gramophone. A very modern house.

What is the gramophone playing? *Ameilikan* dance music. The old woman is explaining, but he is watching the girl move shyly toward him. Of the four women only her feet are not bound. She stands by his chair. "No, no, no, I can not dance. It is strictly forbidden in the New Life Movement."

"Ah, the Master did not approve of dancing for yellow reasons, but you know that is not our reason. Even the Master approved of ritual dancing. Think of Xiaobao as part of your family, and remember that the Generalissimo is urging the Americans to help us resist the Japanese invaders. Surely they will join the war as our allies. We must be prepared to welcome them. If you come often and practice secretly, you will be prepared when they join us. You will be the most advanced official in the government."

They make a lovely couple on the dance floor. Despite the man's shoes, Xiaobao is still taller. He does not look up at her face. His eyes stare only at her modest breast, but maybe he does not see what he is looking at. His glasses are off again. His face is as red as a cooked crab.

Erbao, enjoying their entertainment, imagining herself playing Xiaobao's role, hears other music in the ear of her mind. "Jade fingers on red strings," the music of the *qin*, "the ancient grief of the Xiang River princesses, so painful to hear." The poem was written by a woman poet of the Tang Dynasty about a sadness which was already ancient more than a thousand years ago. How much finer than this noise would our music have been, thinks Erbao, remembering her youth. One of Shuangbao's treasures is a thin, hand written book of poems by flowers to flowers. A old flower gave it to Shuangbao when she was a young flower. The calligraphy is almost as beautiful as the poetry. How more sophisticated would be our seduction, thinks Erbao. "Alas, alas that the ears of common men should love the modern and not love the old." It is another Tang poem, and it brings a revelation. They have not found the right bureaucrat after all. Probably the right bureaucrat no longer exists. The ending of the Imperial Examinations, which she can remember well, means that bureaucrats no longer have to be educated. The corruption of one government after another means they reach high positions by patting the horse's ass, not by knowledge. For such a *xiao ren* (small man) as this to advance, he must have kissed the horse's ass, not just patted it. Even if such a man wanted to help, he could do nothing. Such a man can have no real power.

So the stroke of pure genius fails. The prison leader will try to free Chen Du Xiu, but such a freedom must be approved by Jiang Jie Shi personally, and Jiang Jie Shi is not a man who forgets or forgives old enemies. Chen died in jail in 1941 or 1942. We are not even sure which year.

Maybe it proves how Western I am these days, but I want a funny, sad scene like this in my novel. Why not? Even Chinese laugh at such jokes today. Jack thinks Chinese do not have a sense of humour, but as usual he is wrong. Chinese culture is full of jokes. The Master (Kongzi, Confucius) often made them. But Chinese jokes are serious jokes. They have a massage. They teach us some thing. Zhuangzi's butterfly dream is a great example. My novel will be about the death of a culture, the culture of the flowers that I am learning to love by writing about it. Maybe it will also be about the death of a city that I always loved. But it will not be a tragedy. The joke is on the murderers. My novel will show that the dead culture is not dead. Its spirit lives in me and many other unique Shanghai women. Just as the spirit of Shanghai lives some where in the sprawling metropolis. And farther away. Even in Canada. History proves that Chinese culture can not be destroyed. Qin Shi Huang failed to destroy it by burning its books. The Mongols and the Manchus were conquered by Chinese culture even though they conquered the country. Mao failed during the Cultural Revolution. My herstory will prove that Chinese women's culture also can not be destroyed. The phoenix was always the symbol of Chinese women. It does not die, but it disappears in times of war and stupidness. When people think it is dead, it reappears in a time of peace and reason. Now it was not seen in China for a long time, but it will return. So will I.

July 25

Z came late, after 7:00, and was tired, but Ruby went to sleep early – she has come down with my flu; I don't see how Z can avoid it too – and Z and I lay together on my bed. Much time was spent looking at each other and trying not to laugh since laughter causes movement and the bed creaks something awful at the slightest movement. Of course this led into a vicious circle: the more we tried not to laugh, the more we laughed, the more we laughed the more we moved, the more we moved the more the bed creaked, the more the bed creaked the more we laughed. Words are not necessary: we are both too happy. But because we are so happy, laughter is uncontainable. To keep from waking up Ruby, we adjourned to the bathroom floor. Quieter but considerably less comfortable, which is probably just as well. Physical aspects have become all important, as they should right now, and the waiting is hard on us both. Z is beginning to talk, at least indirectly, about sex, e.g., is worried about Ruby being here after our marriage. I don't doubt that she would now be willing to have sex, but I'll do things the moral Chinese way and wait. Her body is so wonderfully smooth, and, to me most wonderful of all, unimaginable in a prefreudian society, is that she has never used her body coquettishly, never used it to lure me on, never held it back to entice me. I like to think that is at least partly because I have not rushed, have tried to pace body with soul, but I also know my love is too strong and I would not want to be able to control it completely. Oh, but it is lovely to see the look of love on her face and to feel my own face responding – or initiating or mutualating (god, what a ghastly word: makes you wish love were deaf and dumb as well as blind). It seems the past does not exist, only this magnificent present and the doubly desirable future; nevertheless, as we walked to my bike (which she rode home last night and will ride back today – soon, soon, soon – when we are to go to the marriage place, Z asked about P. Because she read the Chinese translation of my divorce papers and worked out that it was I who applied for the divorce. I explained a bit about legal bullshit, but we have lots more talking to do on this subject in the future. (Not the near future, I hope: we still often misunderstand; it took me a long time to figure out what she was asking about P, and she kept starting to jump to the wrong conclusions. But, bliss, she trusts me enough now not to reach them.) She looked lovely, a white nymph, the breeze inflating her light, full dress, sailing into the night. She never looks back after she says goodbye. Soon we won't have to say goodbye.

J is back with a new baby girl. She is an American woman about the same age as Z, married to a Shanghai man of about my age who has lived in the U.S. since he was eleven. They also met and married very quickly. When I laid all this out for Z, she asked immediately if they are still happy, and when I told her yes, she was also happy. J obviously loves Shanghai, which is why she returned for a month when her husband couldn't come, but she also complained about how slowly everything moves here. E.g., they are still driving piles next to her house, as they were six months ago, when she left, and there is still no garden planted in front of her house as there is supposed to be. She said that altho there are more and more joint venture deals being made with Shanghai, all the "work" is done in Hong Kong. Businessmen won't work here because conditions are too "primitive." E.g., the phone service serves no one. So China is getting the minimum in economic benefit from all this foreign influence because it is not an "advanced capitalist country." Can it be that history is not on the side of socialism? This is perhaps an unanticipated facet of the fact that socialist revolutions have taken place first in the undeveloped world, not the developed one as Marx envisioned.

SUCCESS! All papers accepted. We will be officially married one week from today, Friday, August first. In the marriage office Z was still whispering "you can't" (meaning keep feasting my eyes on her) as we filled out the required forms. You have to give information on who introduced you and when, why you want to get married etc. Fortunately limitations of space prevented me from writing the book I have in mind.

Z has also caught my flu or maybe is just exhausted from biking around in the

*heat. I sure hope the latter. She is now taking a bath and then will sleep, as Ruby is
already doing.*

Americans should leave morality to us Chinese. We know some thing
about it. We know how to use morality and immorality, as the flowers of old
Shanghai, my ancestors, did. If Jack knew I was willing to have sex, then why did
he have to worry? Poor boy. Unable to control his love. What about me? I waited
for thirty one years. He used his unknowledge of Chinese morality to make
me keep waiting. If he was I, he would call that "moral bullshit." Why does he
have to talk that way? I hate it. "Bureaucratic bullshit." "Legal bullshit." Once
he said that word and one of his students asked what it meant. Instead of being
embarrassed, he proudly said, *"Da bian de nan niu."* That means "the manure's
man cow." That is how much he knows.

July 26
    *Alternately nurse and lover, too much in love to admit I should be a patient as well
as patient: Z and Ruby both sick (Ruby much sicker with a fever of 39°) and enjoying
ordering me about. When Ruby dropped off to sleep, Z and I lay in bed playing (well, that
is how the Chinese verb wan [wahr] is always translated), but because of her fever Ruby's
sleep was fitful. She would doze, then wake, and Z was much worried that she might see.
The next week will be most interesting as we wait for official status. I think Z is now
more impatient than I. Perhaps it is my weakened physical state, but it hardly matters to
me because I love everything about just being with Z. Merely looking at her is heaven. I
can't not look at her despite her laughing snaps of "you can't." She certainly has become
adept at those two words. Lying on the pillow, her lovely face framed by her thin arms:
irresistible. I can. But I won't. Yet.*
    *The hospital (for the physical required before marriage) was a maze, people
directing me from second to third floor and back half a dozen times before someone led
me to the right place. Why do Chinese refuse to say "I don't know?" They direct you
to a place seeming fully knowledgeable, but when you arrive an equally knowledgeable
looking person directs you back to the original place. Does saying "I don't know" entail
loss of face? Finally a kindly nurse took me in hand and led me from floor to floor so
eight different doctors could examine and squeeze my private parts. I think those parts
passed the audition. Everywhere signs proclaimed "anjing" (quiet), but nowhere was
there evidence of it. The same could be said of "ganjing" (cleanliness), but that lacked
even the signs. In one place a man lay propped on a bench in a corridor receiving oxygen
from a huge tank. He obviously belonged in intensive care. Elevators are small, crowded,
infrequent. People lean on the elevator bells as they do on horns in the streets. Out in
the street two trucks try to pass each other with an inch between them while other drivers
from both directions lean on their horns. Riding a bike you are constantly weaving in
and out of people, carts, other bikes, cars and more people. I have been doing this for two
years, so I don't know why, perhaps the heat, perhaps all the squeezing of private parts, I*

was especially impressed today by how overcrowded Shanghai is. Everywhere there is too little room: streets too narrow, sidewalks too narrow or nonexistent owing to construction, corridors too narrow, people, people everywhere but no room for them. Noise everywhere. In the hospital I was always well behind my nurse-guide. She, like every Shanghainese, was a master at weaving thru the crowds while I couldn't keep up. She just waved her hand at me to follow and kept moving, but she got me thru the maze quickly. I bet Z will have to spend three times as long. But they won't hit her for thirty kuai. At least I resisted paying in funny money.

Very tired. Just woke up from a prolonged nap. It is as if all the tiredness from being sick which I have had no time to feel this last overextended week finally hit me now that everything is accomplished except the waiting. And the end of wanting. Want to see Z. Always.

Saying "I don't know" does not entail loss of face. I will say it right now. I don't know. I do not know what to write. But I do remember. I remember every thing. I even remember more than what happened. Maybe I can not write every thing I remember, but Erbao can.

Erbao sits at her writing desk, remembering. Or does she imagine? Or dream? She is old, and the differences between remembering and imagining and dreaming are not important any more. Now often she remembers times she imagined or dreamed and imagines times she thought she remembered. Often life seems a dream.

Her red rose is wilted. Even its thorns are dropping (or drooping or dripping or flapping or flopping or flipping or some thing). Chen is tired, sick, depressed. His only children, his two sons that he tried so hard to educate, to make revolutionaries, are both dead, murdered trying to make revolution. And he is kicked out of the Communist Party he once led. She goes to him. This is not the time for words. She begins to rub his head. She pulls it into her lap. He does not resist. But he also does not respond. His head, face down in her skirt, flaps (or flops or flips or drops or droops or drips) around like a fish out of the water. Slowly she works down. His neck is loose, like it has no muscles. His shoulders are tight. They do not move when her fingers play on them like a pipa. She works harder, hammers them like a zheng until finally he groans. With a great effort she turns him over. She begins unbuttoning his Western shirt. Now that his top side is up, she can kiss him. Her mouth follows her fingers down, down his big body. Erbao likes big men. Perhaps she likes Chen too much. So much work. "I am too old," he groans. "I am older than you are, Xiao," she reminds him. But even when she has all his clothes off, even when she hikes her skirt and sits on him, he does not respond. She removes one slipper, loosens the bindings, puts the foot under his nose. "We must wipe out feudal customs," he announces, but he strokes the broken foot, then kisses it, then licks it. "I can not see your feet and think only

I suffer," he tells her. And he kisses her foot passionately. "The first time we did this, it was your idea," she tells him. While he kisses her foot, she kisses his ... stem. No thorns on this stem. "Be independent, not servile," he mutters, quoting his most famous essay. He is beginning to respond. "Be aggressive, not retiring," she answers. "Be cosmopolitan, not isolationist." "Be utilitarian, not formalistic." "Be scientific, not imaginative. Let me get on top." "No. You were wrong about that one. Mr. Science is not as important as Mr. Culture. I am where I belong. I am imagining you back to life." Yet although he is on the bottom, but her clothes and body feel wet.

July 27

    Yesterday bad, Z suddenly full of doubts. Perhaps to be expected, but I had forgotten that side amid all our happiness. I was feeling lousy too because of my flu, and no doubt Z's illness – she says she has no strength – contributed to her feelings. We were lying together on my bed, tired after she finished her hospital exam, she reading a pamphlet on birth control she had been given at the hospital. I thought she did not want me touching and bothering her as she read and so adjourned to a chair with a book. Apparently she felt abandoned, felt I had deserted her in some deeper sense. I thought I felt her feeling jealous, but I think that is what I always feel when she feels hurt. Surely she could not have felt jealous of my book. She suddenly got up and left, I in pursuit. She was hurt and scared, I angry and scared. For a long time I could not get her to talk. When she finally did she said, "I may be poor, but I am not a beggar." She insisted I knew what she was feeling and why when I didn't. Things never came quite right tho I think I cheered her up a bit as we walked, she constantly telling me to return because I had told her how lousy I felt (from the flu), I insisting on my love and mock shouting it out until she laughed and told me she also loved me. The terrible part is that for a while we were strangers to each other. No matter how much logic tells me such moments (even periods) of estrangement are inevitable between two people whose backgrounds are so different, they are still very awful, very frightening. She had left me, gone deep into that place where she is "huai," and I was feeling too weak and miserable to follow. Eventually I did follow a little way and she came out to meet me a little way and we touched before we parted. But we both had to summon up memories of previous joy for that parting touch. Much was gone from our world of love. I do not doubt that the full joy and full world will return, but I also know the time we fear will also reappear.

Dear Z,

    I love you. I love you with a love so strong, so fierce that I can say I will love you always altho my experience tells me nothing lasts forever. I love you with a love so deep that it will follow you into the abysses you call "huai." Perhaps my love will lead you into some of my own abysses, but I will also lead you out again or follow you if you know the way. If neither of us know the way, we must join hands and trust our love to lead us.

    Altho I have been sick and overburdened by bureaucracy, these past days have been

among the happiest of my life. In our happiness I had forgotten the problems. I think,
I hope, we will have many more periods of such happiness. But I am not marrying you
because I expect nothing but happiness. The problems will add depth to our relationship,
and for writers depth is life. I love you for our differences as well as our similarities. I love
you for the problems as well as the joy we will live together.

    I must talk to you about something. My exwife also used to say, "I'm bad." Early
in our relationship I did not take her words seriously, but later I watched that part of her
which she believed evil (whether I thought it was or not) take her farther and farther from
me until I could stand it no more and despaired. I have learned from that. I do not take
your assertions lightly altho I know you to be a wonderful person, not an evil one. I know
that sometimes I will have to go with you and explore those dark places inside you. I know
that such exploration will open up dark places inside me and that you may be forced to
face these as will as your own. But I also know that together we can overcome anything.
In fact we can learn more from those dark places than we can from the light ones. We
would be fools if we weren't afraid, but we would not be worthy of each other if we did not
join hands and face our fears together. Trust me. Trust our love. I love you. I will follow
you calling out my love to give us both courage. Keep calling back to me. I love you.

    How come I had so many doubts, and Jack did not have any? It is the
difference between us, between our cultures. I had doubtfulness and I had
jealousy. I was not jealous of Jack's book. I was jealous of his independence, his
American independence. I felt him leave me in his body and in his mind. He
did not need me the way I needed him. He did not understand "both" the way I
did. He did not want to be together with me all the time. I suddenly saw why he
had so many lovers. He did not need them enough. So maybe he left them, or
maybe they could not stand it and left him. I felt I knew he would want to leave
me. Maybe not soon, but definitely he would not stay always like he says in his
letter. (I was right too. Only one year later he wanted to leave me in Xinjiang.)
I would lose him or I would have to beg him not to leave. Either way would be
terrible. I would lose all my face. I was taking such a risk to marry him. If the
marriage failed, every one would laugh at me. Or they would say I told you. It
seemed to me that he would not lose any thing. He could just go on to the next
Chinese woman who wanted to marry a foreigner. Even if it did not happen that
way, that is how it seemed then.

    Jack was a typical American. He felt no past, no history. He was never able
to understand that my jealousy and doubtfulness was based on the past, his and
mine, his culture's and my culture's. His culture is immoral from the Chinese
view, and his past seemed filled with things that seemed immoral to me. My
jealousy gradually disappeared as I got used to Jack and North American culture.
All my fears and jealousies.... No, all of both of our fears and jealousies were
about our own pasts, our own cultures, much more than reality. I was jealous of
Jack because of all the fears all the stories about immoral Westerners made in me.

Jack's past seemed to be a perfect example. But Jack was not. Up to now I lived with him for fourteen years, and I never needed to be jealous of him. And his fears of my madness, which he here calls them the place I am *huai*. He feels them in his diary, and he creates them in his novel. They were not what I meant by *huai*. They come from his experience with Peg and with Western culture's madness, not me. Chinese culture's madness is different. It comes from jealousy and hate, from deliberate cruelty and torture, from fears based on these every day realities, not imaginary happenings increased by too much imagination. Westerners have a different kind of imagination from Chinese. Chinese imaginations are concrete. We worry about things that might really happen. We can imagine disaster in great detail. We do not see things from other views of points or create fantasies. And we write "eight legged essays" like intellectuals so we do not have to write about the two legged life between alive people.

So I will be unchinese when I write my Chinese novel about Erbao, who was unchinese when she imagined many of her memories of Chen. It shows that Shanghai women really are unique. We want more. We want to know more. We want to go more. We want to explore. We want to explore what is inside, not only what is outside. We want to create what we feel, not only what we live. I wonder like Erbao can you imagine a old love back to new life? Or must the rain of reality wet wishes when imagination wishes for too much? Maybe I will leave Erbao where she is while I think about that, while I remember my marriage.

July 29

Several days of misery due to my flu, which a doctor today diagnosed as "bronchitis" and gave both Ruby and me antibiotics. But the marriage is ok, and that's all that counts. Saw Z last night and, while too weak for much, we talked calmly and lovingly. Even when I feel lousy I want to touch her constantly. All will be ok. I am utterly happy whenever I am with her. I only hope ok comes by Friday.

August 1

2:00 a.m. Later today we will marry. I should be sleeping but can't. Too happy. Too full of thoughts. Yesterday Z and I kept discussing understanding, and now I have some and must write of it.

Yesterday J gave Z a birthday and prenuptial dinner, then took Ruby off to her house for a few days. Z was quite animated in the restaurant, but afterwards she became a small, scared child. I often think of her as more sophisticated than she is altho I love her just because she is not. J understood this immediately and told me (while Z was "washing her hands" – the Chinese euphemism for our euphemism, "in the bathroom") that Z is not what she expected, not a typical upwardly mobile Shanghai woman. Or, as Ruby says, she seems like a country girl altho she was born in Shanghai and has lived all her life here. Sometimes she understands so much so quickly, I give her credit for great sophistication, but really it is instinct. By some miracle I have indeed found a sea treasure, a pearl inside the oyster of her family. And what an oyster! Her brother-in-law arrived in Shanghai night before last for one day only, asked her no questions about me or her own feelings, just told her she shouldn't get married so quickly. He parroted all the cliched generalizations about foreigners, told her she was not beautiful (has he ever looked at her?) and that foreigners were interested only in beauty; therefore, I would surely desert her when I left China. And a chunk of her believed him altho she knows he knows nothing of me. That's the chunk which is the small, scared child who doesn't believe in herself. Yet also in this small, scared child is a vast faith in love and a belief in me as an embodiment of that love. (Just as I have discovered, to my astonishment, the same faith within my jaded self and the same belief in her.) She fears, she doubts, but she also loves. And her love overcomes her fears and doubts. And, inconceivably, we have somehow met thru all the tangle of Shanghai, all the walls dividing people of such opposite backgrounds as ours, the barricades erected on all sides. Oh, we will have many, many problems, but oh how I love her and how sure I am our love will overcome all the problems. Thank god we are going to Wuhan, where no one will know either of us. But wherever we go, in China or the West, there will be forces out to destroy our love, people like her brother-in-law acting from prejudice, unable to see what is in front of their noses. Needless to say, the brother-in-law acted very courteously toward me when we met. I liked him – until after he left and Z told me what he had tried to do. Yet she resisted and will come tomorrow. No: TODAY. Oh, happy, happy day.

So much to write, so many little things which happened, but perhaps I can leave them for later and now get some much needed sleep.

3:30 a.m. I still can't sleep so I'll write a bit more. Yesterday Z told me more about Qiu's first "wife." In fact there was no ceremony; they just got a license to get married (as I understand it: because law is so nebulous in China, it is unclear whether their paper was a license or a certificate; presumably ours will be a legal marriage certificate since the bureau we go to has been set up by the government to satisfy the requirements of foreigners) then had sex. She told that to Z, among many others, when they split up. So what? asks the Freudian in me. But I remember once on a bus Qiu pointing out one of his former students and roundly condemning the man for having sex with women then not marrying them. Of course Mei was there at the time. Was Qiu so passionate against the other man because he was playing a part for Mei or because he was condemning his own fault? I feel fairly certain that Qiu's immorality, not the way he pressures her, is the main reason Z often wants to avoid him of late. Z did not tell her brother-in-law when we are going to get married, did not dare after what he told her. Yet despite all her fears she is defying her family. Very quietly. I hope we will be able to remain friends with her family though I will never be able to respect some of its members. The members who act like the feudal fathers Z hates. But fathers are not the only problem. Z has no bathing suit. She likes to swim, but once she swam in the Chang Jiang. Her mother insisted it wasn't safe, became angry and cut up her bathing suit with a scissors to prevent a recurrence. Tomorrow morning we will go shopping, mainly to buy her a skirt to go with the embroidered red silk blouse I bought her (whose price she wormed out of Ruby, who told me she couldn't lie to Z), but I will also buy her a bathing suit as a symbol. Z was upset that I had spent so much money on her birthday present, but I think she accepted that I could since it also serves as a wedding present, red being the traditional color for Chinese brides. J gave us a hundred yuan FEC. She said money was the traditional Chinese wedding present. Very practical.

5:00 a.m. Still can't sleep. I am remembering Z's bare foot. After we had eaten at her house Z and Ruby adjourned to the garret to try on clothes. I sat downstairs with her mother and brother-in-law, attempting to converse in my bad putunghua and his worse English, but my mind was entirely occupied with Z and I kept looking at the open trap door where she was. There is little space up there, so periodically a foot would appear in the opening. Such a lovely foot. So different from her mother's mutilated ones. How far China has come in a generation. May Z and I help to bring it farther. But I kept looking for the body attached to the foot and, alas, it kept not appearing. Yesterday Z was already up at this hour, going to the market, buying then preparing food for her own birthday lunch. She was very tired last night. I will be today.

8:00 Finally slept, perhaps an hour. I should defend Z's mother a little. Ruby and I gave them gifts, and they put them aside as Chinese always do (not wanting to appear greedy, I assume). They wouldn't have opened them, but Ruby insisted. We gave Z's mother a dragon teapot, then discovered she is the only person in China who doesn't drink tea. I thought she didn't like it, but later she crept back to the box, took out the pot, fondled it and looked it over carefully. She obviously did like it even if she doesn't like tea and couldn't resist revealing this. Good country folks.

10:00 Z late. I was very worried, almost expected the small, scared child to try to back out, but she just had to wait for the bus. She pointed out that her brother-in-law was not saying no, just go slow, that he is not a bad person, just one with old ideas and cold feet. After all, xenophobia was taught here for centuries, long after liberation too, so his attitudes cannot be blamed entirely on "feudalicism" (as Z calls feudalism). She also pointed out that many big city Chinese, exiled to the countryside during the Cultural Revolution, did just what he was afraid I would do, married a local girl then deserted her once they were allowed to return to the city. If Chinese could act that way, what might a foreigner not do? Z has told me often that she was afraid of me, of all foreigners, before we got to know each other. And we have moved awfully fast. It isn't unreasonable to want to slow us down. But some of the things he said were unreasonable. And he never listened to her or even asked her for her feelings or opinions.

Jack always insults my family. He thinks we are all peasants. My brother-in-law came from a upper class family. That is why he had so much trouble during the Anti Rightist Movement and the Cultural Revolution. And my mother never tried to stop me from marrying Jack. She always listened to me when I told her he was good. She never listened to all the people who warned her against Jack. She is not a peasant too. She comes from the same class and herstory Erbao did. That is why she and the old courtesan I found knew each other right away. When my mother cut up my bathing suit, she worried about me. When I loved

Jack, she worried about me. She always supported me, not morality.

6:00 p.m. *"I shower finish, you...." The fade out means I then should shower begin. We both tend to do this when we are not sure how to express something in the foreign language. One day I'll have to make a record of our verbal communication. But not now. This is the moment for non verbal communication. This is the juiciest moment of my life. Z is very scared (but she will be clean). I am going very slowly, letting her lead, loving her more with every second. She just told me that when she says "wo huai," she means she is ugly (!!!), not evil, that she is not the same as P, that she won't say it anymore. I already know she is very different from P. She also questioned me about my experience, was surprised to learn I have never before made love to a virgin, thought it terrible I had tried so young (fourteen) and had sex at twenty two!*

She is like a little girl right now. And I am like a little boy. We both want to savor this moment. What a beautiful time in my life, in our life.

The wedding "ceremony" was nonexistent. They simply filled out a few papers, we signed our names (Z signing my real, i.e., Hanzi, name in parentheses after my signature), gave them 30 yuan of J's FEC, and they gave us two attractive red and gold certificates. They look quite legal: seals, Mao's picture on the outside and both of ours on the inside.

I will never forget my first sight of Jack's body. So huge, so hairy. But this is not the kind of talk a Chinese woman should talk. Jack talks very enough. There are some things I can not do. Maybe I did not say that right. A Chinese woman can do any thing. But she can not write every thing. Maybe that is why sister Erbao is in my book. A flower can talk about this kind of thing. But even Erbao should not talk here. Definitely not here.

August 3

Sometime in the middle of the night, sitting on the pot. Something is terribly wrong. I have failed miserably, disappointed Z terribly. Yet the failure has deepened our love. I hope. But I don't know how much longer I can keep failing without destroying everything. For two days I have been unable to get it up. Never have I desired to make love more, yet I have been utterly incapable of performing, of any erection, of satisfying the woman I love. I think, I hope (or do I? what if it is permanent?) the infirmity is physical, not mental. I think my half month illness has affected my glands (or perhaps the medication has). Tonight I have finally felt something, my prowess gradually beginning to return, I hope, and I think I will now be able. But Z is exhausted from trying too many times, trying too hard (too soft, it should be), and I don't want to wake her. What if it turns out to be yet another false alarm? In any case the results of all this have been, in a way, wonderful. Z, who has been waiting all her life for this moment to come and then I didn't, who has been deprived of all her hopes and certainly has fears that I am simply too old, said she would wait for me. As long as it takes. Forever. What an affirmation of her love. I know now how deep and total it is. And how deep and total mine is for her. We have cried individually and together and spoken much. It is amazing how much we can say with so few words.

She told me about her boyfriend and two previous shorter term ones. She spoke of being alone in the hospital (for an appendicitis) last fall. No visitors: her boyfriend deserted her, her parents were too old and too far away to come. Other patients had visitors but not her; she wanted to die. Yet she then said she now believes life has been just to her, gave her great and frequent sorrow but now has given her me to compensate. She said if she had married her earlier boyfriend her whole life would have been a disaster and now she is happy, will take what comes with me. She said everyone has been advising her against me and cried that not one person (J does not count since she is a Westerner and my friend, not hers) has blessed our union. Yet she has withstood these pressures. The power of those pressures caused tears to gush. Then we played, tickled, laughed, screamed. And she played with my poor, impotent penis. And I tried once more and failed. Then we slept and I woke up feeling a genuine erection for the first time since the wedding. I don't want to wake her tho. She is exhausted. Me too, I suppose, but I think, pray, that I am also ready. At last. She has had much physical and mental anguish from our efforts. She even has a big welt on her chin where my sandpaper beard rubs her silken skin when we kiss. I mustn't drag it out any more if I can help it. I mustn't.

Evening. More failures. I have just gone away from Z for the first time since Friday and experimented with myself in the bathtub. I am not right. There is nothing there. Presumably the long flu (or bronchitis or whatever) has left something wrong with my glands. Presumably they and I will recover, but what a catastrophic beginning for Z, especially since I keep asserting I'll be ok, then failing miserably again. She surely suspects I'm too old etc., yet she is sticking by me. However, she is tired and disappointed altho she has only just begun to show it a little. Her love and faith have been stupendous. I am utterly abashed and don't know what to do. More experiments in the bathtub, perhaps, but probably all I, all we, can do is wait. Both of our patience and love will be sorely tested. The terrible irony is that this whole period of my love for Z has been the most active and wondrous time sexually for me in more than fifteen years. I have had no need for masturbation, and the very thought of her gave me an erection. At least until I came down sick. Now I have such love and such overwhelming mental desire, yet physically there is nothing there. I want to cry for Z, for us. I only pray – this nonsense bids fair to make me religious; do sex (or its lack) and religion run together? – there is no permanent effect on our love.

August 4

Evening. I just managed a small ejaculation in the tub but without much of an erection. I don't know what that bodes, but at least I'm not completely impotent. I keep trying to find hope in such things; meanwhile, Z keeps suffering. And learning: she tried to "kiss" my useless appendage. I stopped her. It hurts my pride not to be able to manage myself. Fool that I am: is this a time for pride? We'll try again soon, no doubt. If nothing else, *we're persistent. I'm glad I have not counted how many times we have tried and failed.*

"I am imagining you back to life." Erbao swallows. Then she opens her eyes. She was walking in the rain. Her clothes and body feel wet, but now the sun is coming out, and a rainbow bends over the field of green vegetables she is standing in front of. It is a sign, she decides. I was right, she thinks.

The year is 1950. Erbao is just returning from her hometown. Her brother's children and grandchildren still honour her, so she went back there to escape the Communist take over of Shanghai. It was rumoured that prostitutes and former prostitutes would be executed. In fact it did not happen. They were treated well. So long as they did not try to continue in their profession. Most received training in new jobs, mainly factory jobs. Shanghai was growing like spring bamboo shoots after a rain. (You see. I told you. I always say the same thing. Maybe it is because I like to eat bamboo shoots so much.) There were many new factories. There were new jobs for all willing to work. And new men for flowers to marry.

But even if she did not have to go, Erbao is glad she went. She is much too old for factory work. The new Shanghai she and Chen dreamed of is here, but what it tells her is that she is part of old Shanghai, not new Shanghai. In the countryside she did what she long longed to do. She wrote a book. The book was a serious joke, the story of a man who did not exist written in a language which did not exist. Not Communists or Nationalists, she knew, would ever admit Chen. To the Communists the man who was their first leader did not exist because he took the wrong line in a party which did not admit wrong lines. To the Nationalists he was a communist bandit who died in their jails. Because he was betrayed there by his own comrades lowered him even more. And the language of the flowers, in which she wrote of her dead red rose, could not be admitted by the few still alive who once knew it. (But she knew it perfectly and was proud she did even if she could not admit it publicly. How much easier than writing in a language you do not know very well.) History might record its existence only in the works of people like that peacock Han Bangqing. Few enough people could read his novel, and it was not even written in real *huahua*. She would never show her book to any one because no one would be able to read it. Shaungbao would like it. She would help one of her American flowers to translate it. But Shaungbao was dead too, killed by the Japanese after they declared war on America. They took the American woman she was living with prisoner, but they murdered Shaungbao. A cultural difference.

When Erbao got off the train at North Station, she did not want to go home. She did not even know if she still had a home. She knew that some of her flowers were still living in the old brothel, so probably they would let her stay. But maybe they would get into trouble if they did. So she walked west from the train station, a old lady with bound feet and a walking stick, a granddaughter (her brother's granddaughter really, but that is what we call every one in that generation of the family) to carry her suitcase. She was so lost in her dreams that she did not even notice the light rain falling on her. Then she looked up. In front of her were fields. *Ah*, she thought. *This is Shanghai too. The city I love. The city that has every thing. Even a rainbow.* The rainbow was bent over the fields with one foot in the houses behind her. *Ah.* She told the girl to put down her suitcase, and she sat on it and looked at the rainbow. She looked and she looked. She remembered and she remembered. She imagined and she imagined. She dreamed. *A world with more culture, more colour, fewer differences. Ah.*

She did not know whether the rainbow faded or her eyes did, but when she opened them again a crescent moon was squeaking between the clouds. Her old face was no longer the crescent moon her young one was. She used the crescent moon long before Lao She. "Lao Shi, old fool, it should be, not Lao She." She spoke out loud as old people do when they think they are alone. "What does that old fool know about women and prostitutes?"

"We should go to your home, grannie," said the girl. She waited patiently by the old woman's side as she slept. Now Erbao's spoken words gave her permission to speak.

"*Ah*" is all Erbao said out loud, but she sat several minutes more. She remembered what she saw. Or was it what she dreamed? Whatever it was, it felt good. It gave her hope. She got up and went with the girl.

August 5

Last night (night number four) we finally succeeded in making love. I'm sure that's not a record, but even if it were it sure wouldn't be a record to be proud of. There was a lot of pain for Z, and she actually pushed me out the first time. Then we slept a little, woke up and completed what we began. It was still painful for her but surely the most wonderful night I have ever spent. We both spent much of the night laughing at how much she wanted sex despite the pain. Her innocent pleasure amid pain was glorious to see and experience. I have never seen anyone half so wonderful. And now it is clear that those three terrible days were not so bad, for they strengthened our love. Our overpowering love.

The year is 1960. Erbao is returning from the countryside again. For the last time, she knows. She can not take the food from the mouths of her brother's children, grandchildren and greatgrandchildren. There is not enough food in the countryside. People are hungry to starving.

At North Station she again walks west. Maybe she is searching for the rainbow she saw ten years earlier, the hope she felt, the hope a city felt, a country felt. She is now a very old woman and very alone. She must carry her own bag, but it is a small one now. One change of clothes, one manuscript. She moves very slowly. The sun is very hot. If only she had a umbrella to shade herself. She feels confused. Buildings are where fields were ten years ago. New houses, poor houses. This is Shanghai too, she tries to tell herself. It seems like forever before she finds the fields. Children are picking weeds around the planted fields. Each child has a basket to put the weeds in. One child, a little girl with a little curl and a red ribbon in her hair, is much smaller than the others. She looks very lovely. Erbao smiles at her, and she smiles back. The sun is so hot.

Then a flash, colour, the rainbow she once saw near here. Purple. The plums in the poem she is reciting to Shi. She watches his eyes fill, and Li Bai's words become her song. Later Shi brings her purple plums as a love offering. Blue. Ming porcelain. She sold her last piece, her favourite vase, to bring money to her family on her last trip to the Subei. How she loved the beauty of its painting and calligraphy. How Chen loved the politics of its ancient poetry. Green. The rice fields of home, the home of her childhood and old age. A breeze combs the light green sea of rice into curling, curving waves. Yellow. The life of a young flower, eating the wind and sleeping in the dew among other flowers, bees buzzing, silkworms spinning, spinning. One last dance with Shaungbao, their spinning a cultural revolution. Orange. Buddhism, tradition. The traditional Chinese respect for generations given the flowery twist she and Shaungbao and Jinbao and Xiaobao gave it to try to save Chen. Red. Chen. His science and democracy, which turned to bolshevism, which turned to blood. The rainbow dances before her eyes and sings in her ears, the world dances and sings and spins, a traditional opera performed in modern dress, a Shanghai opera.

August 6

Much to write about, but I only want to write about Z. Too often I have scoffed at Chinese customs for raising children and teaching young people. They may seem incredibly backward, but the results are anything but. Z is the most forward, the most wonderful, wide eyed, spontaneously joyful creature imaginable. She waited and suffered for thirty one years for this, but now her pleasure in all things, and as a result my pleasure, is beyond description. She is curious about everything, asks questions no Westerner would, does spontaneously things for which a Western woman would surely exact a price, etc. E.g., she is full of questions about sexual positions and my sexual organs and abilities (which, thank god, I seem to be recovering nicely), questions a Western woman would never ask for fear of being laughed at or thought naive. She quite voluntarily offers to "kiss my penis," as she calls it. Breaking the hymen is considerably more difficult than I imagined. I have entered her three times now, penetrating further each time. Each time there is blood and pain for her. She cries out from the pain, says she wanted to push me away every time as she did the first but didn't because she "thought I might be unhappy." I keep thinking we have finished with the pain, but who knows? Neither of us, certainly. Another lovely thing she does is after sex she sends me out to wash while she examines herself with a hand mirror. When I return, she is still sitting on the bed peering in. "Curiouser and curiouser," I comment. She does not know the reference, but she knows to laugh and is not a bit self conscious about her curiosity. Her info about sex comes from a pamphlet the hospital gave her at her marriage exam. Quite necessary since Chinese parents and schools provide no sex education. Not that the pamphlet provides much: it promulgates such gems as once a week is normal for sex. On the other hand, when we wanted condoms (her choice of birth control method), I discovered that the medicine shops had piles of them sitting in boxes on the counter free for the taking. A typical bit of Chinese enlightenment where a Westerner would never expect it, but how logical, how socialistic, in a place with such an urgent need for population control. I assume all other methods of birth control are similarly free and available. On yet another hand (you need lots of hands to talk about this contradictory country) when we traipsed to the Peace Hotel to get train tickets, the travel people were full of questions about us, questions I thought innocent Chinese curiosity until they demanded proof (a seal, of course) from Z's unit that she was indeed a Chinese married to a foreigner.

We are both full of curiosity and, as a result, usually exhausted because we stay up all night having sex and conversation. About everything: we are each fascinated by everything the other says. We are great friends as well as lovers. We have so much in common. Our communication skills are increasing by leaps and bounds. Partly this is a rapid improvement in both our language skills but also a matter of learning so much about each other that we know what is going thru the other's mind with few or no words. Outside on the street or bus I have but to glance at her for her to respond with either an I love you too glance or, more usually, a soundless laughing "you can't." Alone together anything goes; she has no inhibitions. But in public (or even with Ruby about) she shows great modesty. Except our love is slowly overcoming it: we hold hands more and more frequently. When Ruby is around she and Z hold hands in a way that tells me that Z is using Ruby as a substitute for me. The love growing between them is also lovely. Z is now teaching Ruby to write hanzi, and Ruby is working earnestly. I don't know if I'm very perceptive or very lucky to have found this prize. Is it possible that many Chinese women (whose families have not been changed by greed or learning from the West) are like her? After all, she was not considered especially desirable by Chinese men or I wouldn't have been able to find her. If this wonder woman is nothing special, Chinese methods of childrearing are infinitely superior to Western psychological ones. Or my standards are infinitely inferior. Everything the Chinese do with children is utterly different from us. I have always had full confidence in my abilities with babies and children and assumed if I had another child I would attempt to raise it almost exactly as I did Ruby, but suddenly I have doubts. Can such methods, methods which rely on freedom, work in China? Chinese babies are given huge doses of love but virtually no freedom. They never crawl because they are held constantly, most often by loving grandparents; they are toilet trained before they can walk. Z says she was twenty years old and had been working three years before she was allowed to buy her own clothes and other necessities. And her parents are liberal and easygoing. I suddenly remember the jaded ten year olds I once overheard in a Chicago ghetto. The boy wanted to play "family," but the girl was refusing. "Last time we played," she complained, "You rode me for more than half an hour." Z says even in Shanghai it is common for parents to exact a high bride price for their daughters. (I thought this was true only among the peasantry.) But Z's mother never tried to stop her (with me or previous boyfriends), and she says her father is just as good. Z has just returned home for two or three hours (thus this long journal entry), the first time she has done so since we married, bearing her marriage certificate. But the neighbors can't be told or given candy until her father returns.

Seals is one of our favorite topics. I have decided that I want my own so when the invariable Chinese question of proof arises, I can simply write what is required and seal it. Of course I'll have to learn to write in Chinese, but why fret over details? I asked to accompany Z to her factory tomorrow, and she got out the dictionary to show me "hun": everyone would faint dead away if I showed up with her. I said great: while they are all out cold, we can steal their seals and flee. Ruby, who works hard not to listen to our conversations, couldn't keep from laughing at this one and did some lovely faints, followed by a lot of tickling, screaming and suchlike antics.

On the "back door:" Z's jiefu, who has gone to a scientific conference but will soon be back to Shanghai, left her a note asking her to get him a boat ticket back to Qingdao. The back door is needed because the front door is almost always locked. Jiefu couldn't get the ticket in Qingdao because round trip tickets are unheard of, and the only time you can buy tickets in Shanghai is 6:00 a.m.! Z would have to get up at 3:00 a.m. and stand in line for four hours to hope to get a ticket. No wonder people are not willing to buy tickets in what a Westerner considers the ordinary way. When Z returned here, she immediately began calling tongzimen (classmates but in a very broad sense), three of them (on these impossible telephones that usually have to be dialed twenty times to reach one person). One of them has already called back with a no. The rules for opening a back door are exacting: the man Z was asking said he couldn't do it because the ticket was for a friend of the classmate, not the classmate herself. Why the hell can't people simply buy tickets at any time on a first come, first served basis? Everyone complains and jokes about the back door, but how can it be locked if the front door can't be used?

Maybe I should cut out every thing about seals and back doors. Maybe I should just feel all the happiness of those days of our marriage. They were wonderful, but rainbows do not last long. Except in memory they can. In my novel maybe I can make the rainbow last, but this is our story, so I better let Jack talk. Even though he talks too much.

August 7

Yesterday my back suddenly went out with great pain. I think it's because I insisted on carrying Z over the threshold and have been baoing (carrying) her and Ruby on other occasions as part of our fun and games (not, certainly, all the awkward sexual positions we have been experimenting with). What awful timing. Maybe I am getting too old for a newly married man. I feel like an old, old man lying on his deathbed, unable to move, able only to observe the life moving around him. Will I be writing in my journal then too?

A wonderfully funny, perfectly Chinese thing just happened. Z has been calling around to classmates for boat tickets. She told them she was married, and one put two and two together and figured out from her phone number at the Jin Jiang that she must have married a naguoning. *A few hours later he called back to say he had a* mei mei, *very beautiful, (aren't they all?) who wanted to marry a foreigner and could she help? Halfway thru Z's telling me this story, I figured out the punch line and we both broke out laughing. Lovely irony: one reason I fell in love with Z was that she so obviously did not want to marry a foreigner, that she loves me in spite of my being one, not because of it. Yet, perhaps not so surprisingly, there exists, often in the same people who so want contact, a hatred of foreigners. Z's jiefu, who would love to go to the West, is a case in point. He's back in town and Z's mother told him Z had married. He didn't like it one bit and managed to convince her mother, who yesterday was very happy over the marriage, that it was bad. Z said he asked her many unpleasant questions. She returned here in tears. Since I can't move, Ruby has volunteered to go back with Z to bring jiefu his boat tickets (which were just delivered courtesy of the man with the* mei mei) *and film (Kodak: available only at the foreign tourist hotels) and protect her from his wrath.*

Erbao is lying on the ground. The little girl is by her. She is not singing in the opera playing in Erbao's spinning head. She is saying, "Granny, granny, what is wrong?" The bigger children are all gone. Such a lovely child, Erbao thinks. She tries to smile, but she does not think she succeeds. "Wait here, granny," the child says. "I will get ma."

When the child is gone, Erbao really does smile. She can not get up. She could not go any where even if she wanted to. Even if she had some where to go. And the child, who was speaking *Shanghaihua* to her playmates, spoke *Subeihua* to Erbao. Erbao did not even realize this at first. She was accustomed to hearing the dialect these past years.

She thinks of her childhood friend, Sanzi, now known as Chanu, tea lady. Sanzi married into a neighbour family and never travelled far from their native village. When she became a widow she planted a few tea bushes. Every one made fun of her, for the Subei did not have a good climate for growing tea, and others tasted only tea made from the lower leaves. But Sanzi let Erbao taste the fresh bud tea. By careful cultivation and harvesting, Sanzi could make herself a better tea than could be bought in their village. There was not much of it, but she was only one woman. And now, when times were bad and others had only wind to eat, Sanzi was grinding and steaming the big, lower tea leaves and making a kind of cake which kept her alive. Erbao, dying, laughed to herself. Rainbows. Hope. One old lady writing a book in a forgotten language about a forgotten man and a forgotten culture. Another old lady growing tea in the Subei.

Luckily ma is a big, strong woman even though her feet were bound. She must be one of the last ones, Erbao thinks. The woman asks no questions. She lifts Erbao like a baby and carries her to her home. There is not much meat left on me, Erbao thinks. I am glad I lost my mirror.

At her home the woman puts Erbao on a small bed and feeds her hot water and thin porridge with the wild vegetables the child was picking. Erbao can only eat a few sips, but then she can talk. They talk a long time. They talk *Subeihua.*

August 8

"You often don't forget look woman," observed Z. When Ruby and I laughed, she changed it to, "You don't forget look woman often." We were walking (I lamely) down the street, and Z jokingly asked me what I was looking at. I said everything, and she asked, "Women?" I said yes, and she replied her usual, "You can't." We joked about that a while, during the course of which the statement I began with occurred. I'm not sure it was originally meant as a joke, but it got turned into one, my method for dealing with any hint of jealousy. After we returned to the room she said she meant that I often looked at women. So there is a bit of jealousy, but we are ecstatically happy altho my back (which is slowly improving) cuts down on a lot of activity. (The traditional Chinese doctor, whose amazingly efficacious method of back massage has been passed down through the generations in his family, told me no sex and sleep on the floor, but I expect to violate his instructions.) We talk long and late, get up early and talk more. She is constantly wanting. "I want," in her case, always refers to sex. She is out of sight, and it is out of sight that I can help her satisfy the desires of a lifetime. We discuss our love endlessly, how wonderful it is, how amazing we met and recognized each out of sight other, how we don't need money or friends so long as we have our love. We are both utterly happy, utterly exhausted. Z has just fallen asleep over her book (Faulkner's "A Rose for Emily": lots of good stuff is getting translated; one of my students is working on Lawrence's The Rainbow).*

August 9

I have always been certain that the uninhibited way I raise Ruby is the right way, but I sure am glad Z was not raised that way, and this makes me doubt all my previous ideas. Just now I was naked in front of Ruby. Z obviously disapproved, didn't want to hear my theories, escaped to the bathroom as I was explaining. This also has to do with my not satisfying her sexual needs. Her sexual desire is strongly roused, and at first I was unable, then my back went out. We still try (against doctor's orders), but I am afraid to move much and she is inexperienced. The slightest break in my concentration and/or relaxation and my erection goes: a twinge of pain, a problem putting on the rubber (last night), the fuwuyuan making noise outside the door (this morning), fear that Ruby might show up. It is terrible for her to be aroused, then not satisfied. If I fail to satisfy her desire fully, the relationship will not be the full one we both desire, but I fear that my fear of this may also affect my ability. Oh, to be young again. But who would have thought I would ever want to be a stud?*

August 11

I love watching Z hike up her skirt before sitting. She does it so unselfconsciously, so innocently. I have realized she is the woman of my dreams in more ways than one. She is, in fact, the woman I was raised to marry, has all the ideals of America in the Forties. If she were Jewish, she would be the girl of my mother's dreams for me. We have long conversations about how it doesn't matter if we are rich or poor, how we can be utterly destitute but rich so long as we have each other. Such conversations are straight out of Hollywood movies of the Forties and Fifties (and, I'm sure, out of Chinese movies as well); nevertheless, I believe every word I utter. Even now, looking the corn straight in the cob, I won't disclaim those corny ideals I was brought up on and thought I had laughed into the compost pile years ago.

Z spoke about work at her factory, says it consists mainly of sitting around, drinking tea, reading the newspaper, that most jobs are like that, that that is socialism. Of course she likes the job since it entails so little work and is worried about losing it. The whole Chinese work system, the so called "iron rice bowl," is rusty and undergoing great changes, so she fears losing her job if she asks for the three years leave we want to travel and live together in different places. She has asked for three months. At the end of that she can decide whether to throw the job over or seek a back door.

We did not have a back door in my house, but one day I opened one accidentally. The year is 1970. My mother recently retired from her factory. I return early from school, open the only door in our house, and find her reading. Ma reading? She is bent over the table with a pile of papers in front of her. "What character is this?" she asks me. I tell her. Then I ask her, "What papers are these?"

She tells me the story. I heard it many times before, how when I was small I found a old Subei woman who fainted from hunger, and ma brought her home and fed her. But today she tells parts of the story I did not hear before. Long time ago the woman was a famous courtesan, and later she wrote a book. That was what ma was trying to read. I looked at the papers. It took me a while to figure them out because they were written in *Wu* dialect, and I never saw that in writing before. But that was the only thing in them that seemed interesting to a sixteen year old girl. They were about old times and a man I never heard of before. I soon gave them back to ma. I told her she should not use them to practice reading because they were not written in *putonghua*. She told me she knew that. Then she told me they were written in *Subeihua*. I told her no, they were written in *Shanghaihua*. (They were not written in *Shanghaihua*. They were written in *huahua*, the courtesans' dialect, a kind of *Suzhouhua*, but I did not know that then.) Ma was disappointed. She put them some where, and I did not see them again for a long time.

August 12

How I love walking the streets with Z, going into shops, watching the shopkeepers react, later hearing her translations of their curious questions about us, secretly touching Z or whispering "I love you" to her, watching her face light up as she tells me "You can't," loving every minute. It struck me out walking today that I have never doubted her or my love for her. I used to worry – whether she really could love me or about some isolated characteristic I didn't like – but I never doubted. I have only to look at her, anytime, to feel an electric surge of love. Before I met her I had always doubted, even in the midst of great pleasure. I thought doubt was a part of my nature. Is it China and its relative innocence? Chinese women? only Z? I don't know, only know I have never before been so happy, so unquestioningly happy. I love the way she walks, the way she throws her legs around as if they aren't attached, like loose rice winnowed by repeatedly tossing it to the wind until the smooth, golden grain is free of chaff, the way she hikes her skirt climbing stairs, the way she squats on her heels. It's freedom, a lack of inhibition that comes thru in careless movements which reveal her attitude toward life, toward sex. Imagine waiting 'til my age to learn the real ins and outs of love, the give and take: the unadulterated pleasure she takes from life and sex gives me far more than I have ever before been able to take from love. And keeps my love growing, always growing, then its essence winnowed too, purified.

August 14

Last night Z had a nightmare that after two months of married life I fell in love with another woman and told her I was leaving her. She woke up scared and crying, a little girl whom I had to take in my arms – I should always have such chores – and comfort for a long time. She was very small, very scared and, later, very thankful for my reassurances. How beautiful to be needed in that way. I remain utterly fascinated by her, can't keep my eyes off her, especially love the silken legs she considers too skinny. I am always exhausted, want to xiuxi in the afternoons but seldom can. Today I spent the day at the American Consulate trying to help a student get a visa: failure. The waiting room was jammed with anxious people who cheered out loud when someone emerged from the inner room with the shiteating grin which announced success. Is that because the others think one success improves their chances or are the congratulations heartfelt? So many Chinese are trying to get to the U.S. And the U.S. so enjoys making them kiss its proud ass to get in, which they do so eagerly. I hate it.

There have been several recent run ins with doctors. Chinese doctors seem even more authoritarian than their Western counterparts. They love ordering patients around, often giving them superstitious rather than scientific advice. E.g., one told Z that she might get pregnant using a diaphragm and the baby might be born deformed: he apparently didn't know the difference between a diaphragm and an IUD. Since Chinese women are told nothing about sex, it is essential they be told when they are getting married, and doctors are the only ones in much of a position to tell them. But they don't. Or, worse, they lie. And apparently there are no decent books available: such books would inevitably be banned as pornographic! Z was given no choice of birth control methods. Birth control is discouraged until after a woman has had her one child. Hearing this made me realize that all the newlyweds I know have had a baby within about a year of marriage. I told Z to get measured for a diaphragm; she returned with more rubbers. Wooden rubbers, I call them, their one advantage being that they allow so little feeling that if I manage to get one on and get in, I can keep going forever. Night before last Z's delight turned to fear: I rode her too long.

August 15

Last night the mystery of the disappearing condom. When I withdrew it wasn't on me. We searched all over the bed, then I attempted to peer inside Z, then she used the mirror while I pulled up the lamp. Gone. But it must be in there, we agreed, not knowing whether to laugh or worry. Our pawing around must have made for a great comic scene. Eventually I located it with my finger and hauled it out. Then we had to examine it and try to figure out if any sperm had leaked out. How I hate using the damn things, but doctors refuse Z all other methods of birth control. If she doesn't get pregnant it will be a miracle. The Chinese have managed to get the worst of two worlds, a system of abortion but no choice.

Tonight we visited Z's teacher. I was little more than a spectator, the outsider looking in, the first time since the marriage I have found myself in that once familiar position since in our room I must be a host and the other places we have visited have been of my friends. Watching Z was lovely: her happiness is written all over her, on her face, in her voice, in her movements. She is constantly fidgeting, talking rapidly and happily, full of laughter, beautiful from the inside. How proud I, who have always been opposed to marriage, am to be married to her, and how happy we are together. But now that the word is out, we are getting less and less time alone, which is a pain. We are longing for Wuhan, where we will know no one.

This afternoon she woke me from a badly needed xiuxi, kissing me all over my body until I woke full of desire, then taking me, leading our lovemaking. It was utterly lovely, for she was so innocent in her pleasure yet so apologetic at waking me. I love her.

August 17

Z is talking on the phone. She is a different person speaking Shanghaihua, full of life and laughter, light, her voice higher, tinkling like the guniang of Chinese opera. Speaking putonghua she is

I wonder what I was going to say: at this point she hung up and came into the bathroom where I was writing and so ended the writing. The tinkling of her voice rings all kinds of bells inside me. Alas, I fear I will never be able to transcribe that voice, for it tinkles only in Shanghaihua. How many years will I have to live in this city to understand what she is saying? And will understanding the words remove the tinkle I hear? And even if it doesn't, how can I get it onto paper so it will tinkle for others? Talking to her girlfriend on the phone she seems like a young Western girl. Often she can become a little girl. Last night as I slept soundly she suddenly turned on the light. She had had a nightmare (a classmate had turned thief and her parents had cut off her hands and she died; Z was staring down at the handless corpse in its coffin) and needed reassurance. She clung to me for a long time until she felt ok. Finally she fell asleep in my arms, but by this time I was thoroughly roused and couldn't sleep. Today I am extraordinarily tired and she wonders why. I won't tell her because the last thing I want is for her to cease being that little girl. Yet she also wants very much to be a mother and often wants me, even – no, especially – in the midst of lovemaking, to call her mother and act her baby. In the midst of lovemaking she calls me her son, her father, her brother. Freud would have a ball. I'm glad he's not here. I'm glad there aren't any other men here altho maybe she isn't, for another thing she said was that she understood now why women became prostitutes and that if she were born at an earlier time maybe she would have become one. I feel nothing unnatural about any of this, at least so long as I keep my western intellectual mind from demanding to draw inferences.

Lately she has been wearing a black silk skirt and a green silk top, very loose (made as lingerie). She is constantly worried lest her bra strap is showing and so bunching up the blouse (which I think looks neat but Ruby tries to stop). At the same time when she sits down she automatically hikes up her skirt and often uses it to fan her legs, thus revealing her underpants. About this she has no compunctions. A western woman would not worry much about a bra strap but would be horrified to reveal her underpants.

Last night one of my student groups came. She said little but worried much about what I might say, so for the first time I was not always able to answer my students fully and frankly. There were a lot of jokes about bronchitis. They started when one student said I had to be careful not to catch it and I told of the bad case I had just previous to marriage. Z was very worried I might speak of the sexual consequences and kept mouthing "you can't." I didn't, but after the students left she explained that the Chinese word for a henpecked husband is homonymous with the word for bronchitis, and I suddenly understood that I had been the butt of many jokes.

Ha ha. I just learned a right word. Before I thought the word was "hen pickled." It did not make sense, but when you learn a new language, many words do not make sense. And in China, specially in Sichuan, Chinese pickle every kind of food. I knew hens must get pickled too. So I did not question that "hen pickled" did not make sense. But "henpicked" does make sense. If you watch chickens, you know that the cock almost always picks the hen. So when the hen picks the cock, it is unusual, and maybe the cock should worry. In Shanghaihua our word for henpicked is *chi guan yan*, which sounds the same as our word for bronchitis.

Z, like all Shanghai women so far as I can tell, is constantly in fear of dirt and worried about my cleanliness. She showers and bathes frequently, and today when she complained that perhaps I was dirty, I asked her what she had done before she had a bathtub and shower. It was intended as a joke, but she was insulted (with good reason) and mad and sulking for some time. Eventually I got her to talk and she said that she may have been poor but she was always clean and washed frequently without a bathtub.

I may have thought I was just joking, but I was pretty disgusting. The middle class in me does not die easily.

Neither does the smell of the sweat he is always sweating, specially in China in summer. Now I make him take a shower before he comes to bed. He used to take showers in the morning. How silly.

But I am trying not to comment about this time. What a time it was! Reading Jack's diary makes me feel like it was heaven. It was before we went to hell. Hell is what Jack called Xinjiang.

August 19

One way our personal habits differ is that Z (and the Chinese, I assume) are accustomed to washing thoroughly at night whereas we Westerners tend to shower in the morning. Every night I am ready for bed half an hour before Z. I am all set and Z is still in the tub, which she loves and plays in with great delight. For her it is a new and enchanting toy. She calls me in to view her stretched out in it, (it really is a big, nice tub) enjoys every innocent pleasure of the bath. Meanwhile, in the morning I often find no time to shower. So this morning I snuck out of bed early and showered. (Yesterday Z went to visit her mother, so I got in a nice, long xiuxi while she didn't.) Z just woke and called me in, didn't like waking alone, doesn't want me getting up before her. We hugged much but didn't make love because Ruby was due to give her dreaded morning knock on the door.

A week of constant visiting and being visited is taking its toll. We are tired, irritable and getting little accomplished. It will be good to get to Wuhan and away from friends, true or false. One of Z's friend's parents, both of whom speak good English, visited last night. They regaled me with tales of Z and their daughter, told me what good friends Z and their daughter were (true) and how much they had always liked Z (false). They told me what a frequent visitor Z had been to their home. Later Z told me that, in fact, they had always looked down on her, that she visited their home three times in fifteen years for about half an hour total. They were simply fawning on me. Z's marriage was the number one item in her factory newspaper. Also, from reports she has received, the number one item of gossip and backbiting. I suppose that stuff is much the same the world over, but I have the impression that the Chinese tend to make more judgments on less knowledge than most other people. Everyone assumes Z married me for money. What a joke. I suppose they assume I married her for her youth and beauty, but this must puzzle them since Z is not particularly young and apparently not considered a great beauty. Maybe they don't think about my motivations, just think of me as another inscrutable occidental. Anyhow, the same kind of little people are predicting the same kind of great disasters for us as they would be in the West. What a bore.

Now we have just returned from C's new house. Ruby is utterly exhausted (mainly from deciding to build her body by swimming sixty laps earlier), Z is tired and moody and I am probably worse. I should never have accepted the invitation. Altho it is late, Z is writing in her journal. So am I, so I, at least, had better stop.

August 20

Packing. What a mess. What a mass of stuff for a peripatetic to be carrying around.

Last night we had our first argument since the marriage. Fittingly, a verbal misunderstanding turned a cultural misunderstanding into something worse. We were lying in bed, tired. Z said I hadn't given her enough love. I replied that I had always given her all my love, then said, "Wo bu neng gei ni duo." My intended meaning was, "I can't give you more," but what I apparently said was "I can't give you a lot." After this a long silence ensued. A wall of ice seemed to grow between us. We pulled away from the wall, from each other, physically and mentally. Then Z got out of bed and sat shivering, covered by a towel, in the chair she had only recently vacated. It took me too long to make my move, but finally I moved about half way toward her, announcing that this was what I was doing. I don't think she understood the concept. She kept calling from the chair that I was tired – we were both exhausted – and should go to sleep. I hated her ordering me to sleep, sacrificing herself, when I knew she was even more tired than I since I had managed a nap during the day and she hadn't. After an eternity she lay down on the edge of the bed. I cried and after I finished she cried. My emotions were strong and I think surprised her. The reconciliation was good, but we have been really tired, barely moving, all today.

The bad time started riding our bikes to C's new apartment. I kept wanting to ride alongside Z, but Ruby was very tired from swimming and craved attention. Of course she went out and got mine, leaving me little time with Z, who would never be so aggressive. On the way back Z rode alone in the back most of the way. I kept slowing down and dropping back, but she slowed down too and Ruby kept urging me onward. I often looked back and waved Z forward, but she would not come. When we arrived home, she plopped in a chair with her journal and got out only when I accidentally broke a dish, at which point she came running in automatically to clean up for me. I insisted on cleaning up my own mess, a constant bone of contention: she has been raised to do all the housework for men and does not comprehend my insistence on doing half the work, is often hurt by it, insulted, as if I don't think she is capable of doing it. (In this light it seems symbolic that she would not ride forward.) She tried to take the broom from me and when I refused to give it up sulked back to her chair. I knew something was wrong but was not sure what, even wondered if I might be wrong in thinking so, but was not about to sleep until I found out what was going on. It took her an hour and a half to come to bed. She obviously wanted me to sleep before she came, but I would not, and when she finally did come I brought things to a head. I thought I could do it gently. Then she said I hadn't given her enough love.

The year is 1980. I am cleaning the house, putting things together, taking down the Mao pictures and other things left from the Cultural Revolution.

Under the bed I come upon the old courtesan's manuscript. It is very dusty. I am about to throw it away, but I start reading it first. Now I know who Chen Du Xiu was, and I am interested in courtesan life. I do not throw the manuscript away.

August 22

Last day in Shanghai. Z has been gone most of it, went to say goodbye to a friend and is now (2:00) two hours late returning. Alone at times like this I sometimes get a flash that the dream will end, that I will wake up without her. But it is not a dream and I have not a twinge of regret. We made beautiful love this morning (after a rather hurried performance last night), slow and passionate. She wants much, takes much, gives much. I am still amazed that life has such happiness, such a gift of purity, to offer. Her friends are funny. They drop by – phone from the gate and we go down to escort them up – to see if it is real too, bearing their silk covered photo album presents. No wonder the Chinese are so eager to take photos: they all receive so many albums for wedding presents that they must labor the rest of their lives to fill them.

The year is 1990. Jack and I just returned to Shanghai to be with my parents for a while. We returned to Shanghai so my parents can be with their new grandchild for a while. We returned to get my things. I want to take all my things back to Canada. June 4,1989 means Jack and I can not live in China like we planned. Looking for my things, I find the old courtesan's manuscript. I am already thinking of doing a Master's degree in the West. Maybe I can write a thesis about courtesans. Maybe I can write about *Hai Shang Hua Lie Zhuan.* Maybe I can use the manuscript. I put it in my suitcase. A few years later I have my degree. All the professors are very impressed by my thesis. They think I have a "instinctual understanding of the culture of the demimonde." They want me to write a Ph. D. thesis, but I think I will write a novel instead. Writing a thesis is like being in swaddling bands again. I cut my bands and grew up when I left China. I had to cut many of my roots. It hurt, but I gained freedom too. Now I can do what I want to do, and when I write, I want to include many new places, ideas, cultures that I found. But I have other things to do first. I have a child, a unique child, a child who never had to be in swaddling bands, to raise up. Maybe when the year is 2000 I will start my novel.

August 23

And so as Mao's red sun sinks slowly in the east, we head west into the writhing of the reform.

Another Brief Introduction

I should start writing about us again. So I have to write another brief introduction. Jack would laugh, but that is better than what he would do. He would stop here. That is what I would like to do. Then my mind could stay in Shanghai and write my novel about Erbao. How nice it would be to write in Chinese. But we Chinese do not do that way. We finish when we start. Kongzi kept looking for a good government he could serve. He kept looking a long time after he stopped believing he would find it. When he died, he was still looking. I will not do like Jack. Start a story, then stop and write some other thing else.

But I will skip some parts. If I do not, this will be too long. I will skip Wuhan. It was not a good place, but it was not a bad time. The city has terrible weather. It is one of China's oven cities, so it is terribly hot and sticky in the summer, and it rains all the time in the winter. The people who live there have bad tempers. They argue a lot. Maybe the bad weather makes them do that. But the food is not bad. There are lots of good lake fish, many vegetables and good stinky dofu. In short, Wuhan is not Shanghai. But Jack and I could not be alone together in Shanghai, and in Wuhan we were. Mostly. It was a love time. Mostly. Jack and I had some arguments in Wuhan. I remember once he shouted for me to hurry up on the street. Many people heard and looked at me. I lost my face. I shouted a lot more at him. But I waited until we got home and we were alone. Knowing the difference between public and private is another difference between Chinese and Americans. But it is not always a advantage. Until I shouted at him, Jack did not even know he did a bad thing. Jack and I were always good at having arguments, but in Wuhan they were lovers' arguments.

In Xinjiang was different. Jack stopped loving me. I do not like to remember that. I do not want to write that. But I have to. I have to finish the story even though it will be very hard to write it. Just like Erbao had to finish her story about Chen even though she did not think any one would read it. But

Chinese are not all the same, like many Westerners think. In Xinjiang Erbao would not be like me. She would know what to do. I was unexperienced. In a year of living with Jack, I only learned about our private world, but in Xinjiang we were in a world that was strange to both of us. And we were not alone together. We had no privacy. Yet I felt very alone. I did not know what to do. I could not do any thing with many people around. Yet I felt more alone than I ever felt in the wilderness in Canada. So for a long time I did no thing. It was a mistake. Erbao learned not to make it at age fifteen. I wish I will have Erbao with me, but maybe she can not be there. She was not with me in Xinjiang even though I first found her and even wrote to her a year earlier. She was just a character in a book then. She did not start to be real until I went to the Subei after we escaped from Xinjiang. But even if she can not be there, maybe to know that I know many things that Erbao knows means that now I know some things I did not know then.

Jack and I are also good at travelling. When we married, we agreed to travel all over China for a few years. Then we would live in Shanghai. After he taught one year in Wuhan, Jack was going to teach the next year in the eastnorth. So we decided to go to the westnorth on his summer vacation. Qiu and his friend Yu, a photographer, were also travelling to there that summer. Painters and photographers were allowed to travel a lot in China. That was supposed to be good for their art. We agreed to meet them in Dunhuang and travel with them in Xinjiang. That was Jack's idea, but I did not argue against it. I thought it might be good to have a small group to travel in such far away and strange places. Many people in Xinjiang did not even speak Chinese.

You would not believe how much Jack wrote when we travelled. On the train and bus he wrote almost every minute he was not talking or eating or sleeping. A lot of it is boring. I will not use most of what he wrote, but I will use some of his descriptions, even some boring ones. I think often a place partly causes how we act. I do not think what happened in Xinjiang could happen in Shanghai or even Wuhan, where people argue so much. I do not think it could happen in east China. But maybe I am wrong. Maybe it was the time, not the place. Maybe after we were married for a year, we stopped seeming like pearls and started seeming like oysters to each other. I like to eat oysters and so does Jack, but they are not pearls. Maybe we were starting to feel disappointed we opened a oyster and did not find a pearl. Maybe love could not always protect us from each other any more.

Xinjiang

July 17, 1987

On the train in Gansu province: The Chinese can still seem quaint. There are several young men in the car who are very interested in us. I talked a bit with them and Z talked much. When they aren't talking with us, they sit around speculating about us, seemingly oblivious to the fact that Z can hear it all. (Maybe they want her to?) Altho Z has given incontestable proof of her nationality – they have heard her speak fluent Shanghaihua as well as putonghua and she could identify their homes by their accents – they still wonder if she is Japanese, the notion of a Chinese being married to a Westerner is so odd to them. (On the other hand, a train fuwuyuan [attendant] asked Z many questions, obviously in an effort to learn how to go about it.) And when they heard we planned to go to Qinghai Hu and Golmud, they shivered and were horrified. Imagine strapping young males horrified because places are too cold! In the middle of the Chinese summer! Besides, they expostulated, there's nothing there but mountains. Funny, funny folks: Western city people might not want to live in such places, but they would certainly want to see them if it was possible. And they would certainly be able to figure out that they are beautiful. The photos I have seen of Qinghai Hu are breathtaking.

In Lanzhou our young males and many others disembark. Everyone else jumps off the train to buy ma pi gua, a kind of honeydew melon, very sweet and good. We have certainly come down in altitude: the weather here is hot and humid whereas it was almost cold in the mountains. Past Lanzhou, approaching the Qinghai border, everyone is harvesting wheat. Staves of it stacked everywhere and the mountains full of color, purple above, light green below with a gray stripe running horizontally across the middle.

We are in Qinghai now, the wild west, following the Yellow River. In some places the valley is narrow and there are few fields, but here it has widened again and looks little different from Gansu: plenty of crops and trees, but the wheat here is not yet ripe. The housing looks older and is mainly flat roofed, a definite difference. The roofs too are now made out of adobe, as the houses have been for hundreds of miles, altho in towns there are a few standard brick rowhouses with peaked tile roofs. One man told me the roofs are

flat in Qinghai because there are almost never heavy rains. He also says the poor part of
Qinghai, the genuine wild west, does not start until west of Xining.

Jack loved to travel by train. He could look out at the scenery like he could
not on a airplane, and it was much more comfortable than a bus. He could
move around and look out of the windows and show off his Chinese to peasants
who did not think foreigners could speak Chinese. He laughed a lot. He liked to
laugh with strangers. He thought the Chinese were very funny because they did
not want to go to the mountains, but China is a country full of mountains. They
block our views and make it hard to farm. We do not like mountains. One of
our most famous folk stories is about the foolish old man who wanted to get rid
of a mountain. Chairman Mao often told that story. Jack comes from Chicago,
where there are no mountains and it is easy to farm. He likes mountains because
he did not have to struggle against them like Chinese have to. He also does
not understand the difference between peasants and city people. The men he
was laughing at were peasants. They were very innocent. The city Chinese were
laughing at Jack because he really could not speak Chinese. His tones and his
accent were so bad that everyone laughed, but he just laughed too. He had a
good time on that train. He was very happy at the start of our trip.

July 18

*Today I saw one of those sights you see for five seconds and remember all your life. Z
and I went to the Taer Tibetan Buddhist Monastery, which was big, impressive and quite
unlike Han Buddhist temples, full of stuffed animals, su you (yak butter) sculptures and
su you itself as well as lovely, lively, deathly murals full of skulls, skeletons and ferocious
mythical beasts. On the way back we dawdled, dickering with shopkeepers and eating at
a Hui restaurant, only to arrive at the busstop and be informed the last bus to Xining had
already left. In our despair we managed to flag a truck and get a lift in the back along
with rotting eggplants and peppers. The kindly peasants in the truck even gave us extra
jackets to protect against the wind. It was still not comfortable, but looking behind us we
got a view we would never have had from the cab or in a bus. The country is beautiful,
anything but the poor, barren wasteland eastern Chinese consider it. It is especially lovely
now because the rape is in flower. Descending a steep grade in the setting sun – it sets late
out west since the whole country is on Beijing time – we round a switchback, the clouds
suddenly lift and the mountains split. In the gap sparkles a little, clear, green lake. Rising
above the lake is a fat, rounded mountain, terraced to the top, checkered in chartreuse and
yellow. Below the lake the whole valley opens, also yellow and green but several shades
of green, for it has trees as well as crops. And layered above the pied domestication glow
ranges of tall, stark, wild, distant mountains. It took my breath away. Then we rounded
another switchback and it was gone. I jumped to my feet to get a last glimpse. I was lucky
not to get thrown out of the speeding truck.*

He screamed. I thought some thing bit him, maybe a bee, maybe a snack hiding in all the vegetables in the truck. "Look, look" he shouted in the wind. "Where?" I shouted back. I was looking for the bite on his leg. He shouted again and pointed behind us. But all I saw were mountains. When he jumped up, I was scared. He might fall out of the truck. I quickly pulled him down. He held me close all the rest of the way back to Xining. That was worth more than any view.

Americans are like Tibetans. People with no history like temporary things. Five seconds to remember all your life. It is like the sculptures we saw at the temple. They were complicated and beautiful, but they were already beginning to melt because they were made of butter. Why work so long making art out of butter? We Chinese want beauty to last. We want love to last. We do not risk our life and love to make five seconds become seven. We eat butter, and we make art from stone or at least porcelain. Why can not we teach such things to Tibetans? Or Americans?

11:00: After dinner we sauntered thru Xining's night street market. I expected lots of Tibetan handiwork, but the most exotic thing we saw was peculiarly Han, a porcelain pillow. I've seen them before, and every time I do my mind pictures an upper class gentlewoman reclining on her porcelain pillow, by her side her new born babe wrapped in its silk swaddling bands: very elegant, very Chinese, not very comfortable.

July 19

8:30 a.m.: on the road to Qinghai Hu at 3,500+ meters, almost as high as the highest mountains in B.C. The road is surprisingly good, steep but paved and virtually free of traffic. What a different world China becomes without population pressure. We have just passed a shrine to Wen Chen gong zhu, a Tang princess married off to a Tibetan ruler. Apparently she passed this way. But the shrine is new, built this year, no doubt by the Hans who built this road. She is not a local heroine but a Han symbol – of China's claim of its long connection and generosity to Tibet, which traditionally began around Qinghai Hu, not the present border. The scenery is great altho visibility is severely limited by drizzle and a low cloud cover. There are more towns, good sized too, than I expected in this mountainous area. As a result many mountains are terraced and so yellow and light green (rape and wheat with some darker green vegies close to the cities). I wish they would plant trees. Where the mountains are not terraced, only grass grows. With forests this area would be as beautiful as B.C.

Suddenly the mountains are behind us. We are in a large, flat, grassy area, deserted except for a few yaks and horses. Then a town leaps out of the mist, different from the earlier ones, peaked roofs and whitewashed walls. This city, I am informed, is Han whereas the flat roofed ones were Tibetan. Then back to grasslands. The sky is clearing, the mist lifting, and the road has been transformed into an Alberta or Montana backroad, long, straight and almost free of traffic, like nothing I've previously experienced in China.

Driving is comfortable, no stop and go, proof that overpopulation is a greater problem than bad roads in eastern China. We are in the great depression in which Qinghai Hu lies, and now the lake itself slips into sight, an inland ocean but peaceful, at least today, spectacular: calm and full of colors which change with the everchanging sky.

4:30 p.m.: On the bus heading back to Xining after a day around the south side of the lake. Qinghai Hu is so beautiful because it is an alpine lake, even if there were no glaciers in sight. The same delicate alpine flowers which are found in alpine B.C. grow here in the same lovely profusion. So I was wrong about planting trees. They won't grow this high. We spent our time mainly at the "bird island," a massive flat rock a few feet from shore, completely covered with nesting birds and their guano. (Is the guano used for agriculture? I wonder.) There were no boats on the huge lake and virtually none along the shore. We were supposed to get a ride on one old scow (at 5 kuai a head), but that fell thru for reasons I did not understand. It didn't look terribly safe. The lake is a protected area. The government has wise regulations protecting the wildlife. There are barbed wire fences to prevent people from molesting the birds, and at the nesting area everyone is supposed to observe from a little house so breeding and babies are not disturbed. Not that such measures help much: a group of young males on our bus broke in and stole a whole lot of eggs. It made me angry, especially since these same guys have been cramping me the whole trip. Apparently they are back door riders, pals of the tour guide, who didn't buy tickets and so don't have seats and are sitting on the engine cover and taking up most of the little leg area I have. We have eaten almost nothing all day. We thought there would be a stop at a restaurant for lunch, but there wasn't. Being tired and hungry makes Z and me irritable. We go at each other because Z won't let me take out my irritability on the egg snatchers. I told her we should have taken the train, not this bus. We could have saved a day and the twenty three yuan bus fare by sneaking off the fast train at Goncha, on the north side of the lake, and spending the night in the hotel rumored to exist there. Then we could have rummaged around the lake for half a day and taken the slow train out in the afternoon. Of course, this is forbidden. The gong an ju (police) and everyone else claim it isn't safe, but all that means is that there is no binguan, no fancy hotel to extort money from foreigners. And that city Hans are afraid of peasants, especially nonhan peasants. Z is funny: she is starving but refuses to eat the only food we have, some pickles and a salted egg. Too salty, she says; you can only eat such things with other food; better to starve than eat without rice . We have just stopped at a village – because the egg snatchers apparently are private entrepreneurs and want to buy fish to sell along with their eggs in Xining. I guess the locals are asking a lot, for there is hard bargaining going on.

Meanwhile, the paying passengers on the bus located the local canteen. Z and I weren't the only hungry ones. At first they were buying (at double the local price, which was only two mao for a bowl of something unidentifiable), but then local males, ragged and wide eyed (not an easy feat for Chinese), began swarming in, pushing to the front and arguing with the tourists. I could make nothing of the accents and Z had remained on the bus, but looks and tones of voice told me that, for these men at least, this was the only food in town, that there was not much of it, that they were hungry and not about to sell *their food at any price. Fortunately, before the onslaught a man had been able to procure me two* mantou *(steamed buns) for two* mao *and eight* liang *of Z's back door national (as opposed to the more common provincial)* liangpiao *(grain ration tickets). The marked price was five* fen *each. Back on the bus we and the other lucky ones who managed to get food eat in total silence while we wait for the entrepreneurs, who are still bargaining. The once noisy bus is silent as an air raid shelter, the vacationers crouched in their seats looking bombed out. I do not know if this is because they had or had not previously encountered that wide, wild, hungry eyed desperation. I suspect they had. Even the entrepreneurs, when they return with their catch, are silent. Xining seems to have almost no fish and Hans love fish, so I imagine they can get a premium. Disgusting. The fish, ten to twenty pounders, are now blocking the aisle. At least they are frozen solid and won't stink. Three cheers for reform. Three cheers for socialism with Chinese characteristics. Strange how it resembles capitalism with corrupt characteristics.*

And it gets worse. As we leave the lake we come to a roadblock next to a couple of tents, a government checkpoint to make sure no one is removing contraband from the lake. The contraband is right next to the door. One glance in would reveal all. But two entrepreneurs leap off the bus and talk to the checkers, no doubt bribe them (do cigarettes suffice or do they have to dig into their wallets?), for the checkers never peek. As we drive on, the spongers are chortling among themselves, the first sounds heard on the bus since we left the village.

At first all our arguments were because we were uncomfortable. None of us Chinese tourists on the bus understood what a backward place we were going. We all thought we would stop at a restaurant, but there were no restaurants, and the bus people did not tell us that. So no one had food, and we were all hungry. If we were not hungry, maybe Jack and I would not argue. Food is very important. When you are hungry, it is easy to argue. It was just a small argument. At first I did not even think it was a argument. I thought it was one of Jack's jokes. He wanted to do some thing unlegal. He wanted to get off the train where we were not supposed to. He thought that was because he was a foreigner, but it is not only foreigners who are not allowed to get off the train any where between Xining and Golmud. I could not either. Only local people can. It really is not safe. There are many prisons and prisoners in Qinghai. Probably the men in the village where we stopped were used to be prisoners. Jack always wanted to argue with officials, and he hated to be told some place was not safe. He always said that he used to walk in the worst neighbourhoods in Chicago. He thought no place could be worse than that. But at least he could speak the language in Chicago. Even I could not always understand some of the dialects of Chinese in the west of China. And some people did not even speak Chinese. So what use would his three inches of slippery tongue be if he got in trouble? Also Jack hated *binguan*. Those were hotels for foreigners. They were much more expensive than hotels for Chinese. They were also cleaner and nicer, but Jack did not want that.

He always wanted to be with ordinary Chinese people. He did not care if they
were dirty or criminals. It was not easy to travel in China with Jack. The farther
west we went, the harder it got.

July 20

    *On the train from Xining to Golmud. At first we were going thru much the same
country as yesterday: the lush river valley, the steep ascent to the Qinghai-Tibet Plateau,
the alpine depression in which Qinghai Hu resides. Then we branched north and the
scenery changed. Here on the north side of the depression the land seems drier, the soil
sandy. There are even sand dunes. Further north the mountain tops have snow. No
glaciers that I can see but enough snow to hint that on the north side, which I cannot
see, there may be some. The depression is very large and quite flat. The lake is not yet in
sight, and the land is worked with big tractors, the first place I have seen in China which
uses Western agricultural methods. I wonder if they still have communes here since big
tractors and combines are much more conducive to communal farming than hand and
ox methods.*

    *Our train car is truly international: folks from Australia, Holland, Poland, France,
Denmark and Norway as well as the Chinese. There are also Americans and probably
other nationalities, but not in our little group. The goal of all the other foreigners is Tibet.
They will take the bus south from Golmud; we will head north. A Frenchman and a
Chinese woman, both students in Beijing, are married, on honeymoon I guess. The woman
and Z are jabbering away, comparing notes I assume. The foreigners are all young except
the Pole, who is about my age, a reporter who has worked in Beijing for over four years and
speaks excellent Chinese and English too. "Welcome to Siberia," he proclaims when we
see our first set of high stone walls and guard towers. Even before I can defend China, the
Aussie points out that the use of prisoners and prison labor to settle unsettled land is not
unique to China. I chime in, but the ring goes out of my arguments as we keep seeing more
walls and guard towers. These massive walls affect me powerfully, stir terrible memories:
of the few days I spent in jail multiplied by nightmares into the years good people I know
have had to spend behind the walls, of beautiful people murdered because they believed in
what I believe, of a time I stood outside a wall thinking of a friend inside and vowed to
make a revolution to tear down all the walls. The little, balding Pole claims that half the
population of Qinghai west of Xining is prisoners and former prisoners. Prisoners stay on
after their terms because they will be given jobs here but not in eastern China. I wonder
if the hungry eyed men we saw at Qinghai Hu yesterday were released prisoners. I have
just realized that the place where we tried to get food must have resembled the communal
dining halls of the Great Leap era. I wonder if the communes have survived out here.
But if they have, the hunger I saw means they are doing little better than they did in the
Fifties. If communes have survived, it is because communal discipline and dining halls
come in handy in a place where most residents are rough males expected to do long hours
of physical labor breaking new and marginal land, not for any of the idealistic reasons
I cherish. Can the present day rulers of China have mined Mao's ideas, discarded the*

precious metals which were to be smelted into a brave new socialism and used the dross to
forge chains of control in colonies of prisoners and semiprisoners? Or have the communes
out here and the men in them simply been forgotten? I don't know which thought is more
chilling. The Pole says communes and communism can work only as a police state and so
inevitably deteriorate into one. "Don't judge China by Poland," I tell him. "Judge it by
Marx then," he tells me. "It will look even worse." "I try not to judge," I tell him. I lie.
It's not the Pole that is getting to me. It's the walls, those enormous walls topped by guard
towers. And there are no roads on this side of Qinghai Hu. This railroad is the only way
in or out. What could be easier to guard than a railroad with relatively few stops? That's
why the authorities are so careful about who gets off or on. Even if you could get over the
walls, you would have to trek through a hundred miles of desert and mountains to reach
any place from which you might really escape. Welcome to Siberia.

    5:00: Just passed thru China's longest tunnel at an elevation of 4,080 meters,
emerging into bright sunshine, high mountain scenery, even a village at this height. I am
told there is a village on the Qinghai-Tibet border at over 5,000 meters. Just got a view of
the curved switchbacks we will now snake down: impressive. Relatives of the coolies who
built North America's railroads thru the Rockies have been at work here. The Pole says it
was prison labor. 7:30: To the north are sand dunes, but below us for the first time since
near Xining are trees, and everything is green, yellow and lovely, an oasis tho before this
it was grassland, not desert. The picture to the south is perfect, desert in the foreground,
trees, cropland and buildings in the middle, then grassland topped by layer upon layer of
mountains in the background. The Pole discourses on. He is too busy making political
points to see this beauty. I try to be too busy looking out the window to catch his political
points. I fail. Several miles west of the oasis we come to a lake but no trees or crops around
it. South and west of the lake mountains rise stark, tall, wrinkled, capped with black
clouds from which rain is falling while the valley bathes in sunlight. Horses pull rubber
wheeled carts along a dirt road. The lake is flat and looks very shallow, as if it could dry
up completely tho surely it could not since it goes on and on. It is surrounded with sand
dotted with scrub grass. The sky is full of white, grey, black clouds with the mountains
sticking thru them into blue holes and one small cloud dripping a haze of rain over one
small section of lake. There are salt flats where the water has receded and a second,
smaller lake which is probably connected to the big one at high water. On the other side
of the lake a thin arm of dark clouds stretches black fingers of drizzle over the mountains
and desert, but the sky behind it is blue, brightness transfiguring all that dread. Sand and
scrub grass – the Chinese call it camel grass, and, indeed, off in the distance grazes a herd
of camel. 10:00: still quite light. West of the lake more camel grass and desert. To keep
the sand from drifting there are miles of rectangles (about the length of graves but too
narrow to be graves) constructed of pebbles. The deadly monotony which went into their
construction is appalling to conceive. It must have been done with prison labor, the Pole
contends. "Who knows?" I reply. Shit. I know. I know that I have been judging wrongly all
these years, that I am now lying to myself. In my mind Z's words about feudal fatherhood
resound, words that once impressed me mainly because the speaker did, words I fear I am

beginning to comprehend. I look fiercely out the window. There is a line of tiny settlements along the railroad, half a dozen buildings in the middle of nowhere, and this train stops at all of them. I hold that the inhabitants were nomads before the government lured them to settle by promising life would come to them via the railroad and the power lines all the settlements have, but the Pole says they are mainly excons. In support of my theory, there are still herders living in tents, some round like yurts, dotted around, but whether they are nomads or live in the houses and only take to their tents at certain times I do not know. At least, to my vast relief, there are no prisons in sight and have not been for a while. We have come to another large lake. This one looks deeper, more permanent and less salty than the other. Many herders and animals are gathered around it.

On the train I thought Jack was mad at me. He hardly talked to me. I thought he was mad because I would not try to get off the train, but I do not think so now. He wanted to get off the train at Qinghai Hu before we took the bus there. Now he was glad to stay on the train. The reason he did not talk to me much was that he could talk to English speakers. That was very unusual for him in China. I did not know that feeling then, but I know it now. In Canada I still get excited when I can talk Chinese, specially *Shanghaihua*. Jack was very excited on the train. He was the one who was jabbering. I had to talk to the Chinese woman because the foreigners were all talking English very fast. I think some times he was mad because he was arguing with the Polish man, and he was losing. By the way, the Polish man spoke faster Chinese than Jack, and his accent was different from Jack's, but he made many mistakes and was almost as hard to understand. We say people like him have half knowledge. They know a little, but they talk like they know a lot. Jack liked to argue, but he did not like to lose. I see from his diary that they were arguing about prisons. I hardly knew what they were arguing about then. It was a silly argument. Every one in China knows there are many prisons in Qinghai. Why should Jack be unhappy about that? But he was, and I suffered because he was.

July 22
Golmud is my idea of what the Chinese should be doing: building new cities in little populated desert and mountain areas. It is not particularly being built to my specifications, but at least it is big, able to hold many immigrants from overcrowded areas. It is still mainly empty, but much construction is going on. The wide open spaces look astonishing in a Chinese city. What is built looks modern, mercury vapor street lights, for example. Yet at 6:30 a.m. it was pitch dark: the street lights were not lit to save electricity. Hardly a soul was on the streets, two bicyclists and two pedestrians in my twenty plus minute walk. I'm still fuming that I had to make that walk. The gong an ju won't let foreigners stay anywhere except the binguan. There is even a new hotel with signs in English which peasants have set up near the bus station, but the cops won't allow foreigners to stay there. It's funny: the supposedly socialist government encourages

capitalist ventures like the new hotel, but its police make sure the entrepreneurs do not reap many profits. So Z had to stay at the new hotel to get tickets and seats on the early morning bus while I had to schlep to the binguan and back. We heard many stories about the hard drinking Golmud youth, who sometimes mug and rob tourists – Z was harassed by some of them at her hotel – but surely it is more dangerous for me to walk the streets in the dark than to live in a Chinese hotel. I wanted to defy the cops, but even the hotel staff wouldn't let me stay at their hotel. The gong an ju would have closed them down, they claimed. As the Pole would have been happy to point out if he were here, the police make and enforce the rules; the people, local and foreign, suffer.

On the bus to Dunhuang, an old, overcrowded, undercomfortable bus. Around Golmud there is all sorts of construction which goes on in one form or another for fifty miles or more. That area is a huge, level depression (at 3200 meters). It is important now because most deliveries to Lhasa go by train to Golmud and then by road to Lhasa. Before this railroad was finished everything started at Liuyuan on the northern railroad, a full day's journey north of Golmud. Now that it is finished there is little traffic between Golmud and Dunhuang and Liuyuan. Everything goes south from Golmud and coming north stops at Golmud. When we missed our bus connection yesterday, we tried to find a truck to hitch on (which we were told should be easy), but none were going north.

11:15: stop at Qaidam. How strange to see a sand dune desert with glaciers above it atop utterly bare, dry mountains. And to complete the anomaly a large lake in the desert, a flat, salt lake. I assume the lake is meltwater from the glaciers altho I can see no stream. More people got on the bus than off at Qaidam, and now every inch of space is filled, my knees jammed into a woman's back, my feet on top of one bag and wedged between two more so I can't shift them. When the bus opened its doors after lunch, there was the usual wild melee to get on. I wondered why since all seats are reserved. Obviously it was to claim floor space, for one's feet if one has a seat, to bag a spot for a bag to sit on if one doesn't. The melee precipitated a big argument. There is a baby, and the father was trying to make it milk. Pouring hot water from a thermos, he spilled some on another man, who objected. Both men jumped up and yelled into each other's face for several minutes, with women trying to separate them. It is amazing that there are not more fights the way people are jammed together. This fight, like virtually every Chinese fight, did not come to blows, but why the hell didn't the parents make the baby's milk before boarding the bus? It never seems to occur to Chinese that they should avoid certain normal activities under abnormal circumstances. They do what they are accustomed to do no matter where they are. They sleep in the most godawful positions imaginable, leaning against each other or sprawled above or below, legs up, heads down or vice versa. On city busses they sleep standing, but here no one stands. I wish I could sleep. I got almost no sleep last night, kept thinking about the Pole: all he said, all the gong an ju does. But I'm in an aisle seat with no place for my head, so I'll keep scribbling tho the road be bumpy, my ass sore, my body contorted, my mind uneasy.

Sporadically out of this barren moonscape pop grassy areas, invariably strewn with the flocks and tents and/or yurts of nomadic shepherds. "See," I want to yell at the Pole, but he is long gone. Only his words remain to prod me. Beyond the good grass are large, level areas of camel grass desert with wrinkled elephant skin mountains, their ridges every shade of black and brown, down to a tan which is almost white. Light lines of tan where sand has drifted into the ruts of black mountains, jagged tops, a peak of one color rising above that of another giving the appearance of a black mountain wearing a tan hat or vice versa, stripes of grey, white, black and brown, patches of red, purple and a green which is not vegetation, a big, white salt flat with genuine green grass growing thru it. Sometimes water must flood the flat since there are horizontal lines which look like salt on the brown mountains which surround it.

        3:00 Heading thru a white pebble waste, flat and bare, toward a distant string of glaciated mountains with a low spot in the middle where the pass must be, the road utterly straight as far as the eye can see, which is a long way. Suddenly a flat lake appears, so out of place I assume it must be one of the mirages this place abounds in. Despite the large expanse of water there is no vegetation. Unlike along the railroad, where there were many small settlements and large prisons, there is virtually no settled human life here, only the one town all day and the occasional set of two or three whitewashed buildings, I assume places for road maintenance workers and equipment. And now, just because I wrote that, a small walled settlement amid the desolation. In the distance I think I can spot the reason for its existence, water and even some green, grass it must be. I suppose they can graze animals, perhaps even grow a few crops. We are lower now than we were. From the speed this decrepit bus has been making (and the attendant discomfort to my ass) I suspect we have been going down slightly tho the road looks perfectly flat. Now there is a second walled town, quite new looking and almost pretty. It uses the same long lake for water. At the third of these little settlements, which Z calls communes, – of excons? – one passenger gets off. By prearrangement twenty people are waiting and about ten of them cram into the already jammed bus. The map shows this as a swampy area, but where does the water come from? Perhaps we are close enough to the glaciers? I still see no vegetation, but the land is so flat I doubt my eyes, am not sure what is real, what mirage. I think I see a lake, green and lovely looking, in the distance. My guess from the color is that it is glacial.

        4:30 Ascending toward the pass. One glacier is bigger than any others we have seen. It must be the main source of the water. The pass is dry with a scattering of thin, light grass and a few alpine flowers, yellow and purple. The mountains catch, freeze, then slowly release what little precipitation the area gets. Just over the pass a large herd of sheep and a smaller one of horses graze. There are several herds and two yurts, one large, one smaller, where the herdsmen must live.

Jack was always uncomfortable on Chinese busses. His long legs did not fit, and he would not sleep. In his diary Jack says that the argument was because he was tired and uncomfortable. But that is not what he said on the bus.

        We are on the bus. It is a terrible bus, but I did not know how terrible then. I was never on a Western bus. I did not know you could be comfortable on a bus. Jack is sitting with his right foot up on top of one bag. His left foot is down. It is stretched the other way so it can fit on the floor between two other bags. His legs go different ways. Neither leg goes the way his body does. He has a bad back. He is sitting in this uncomfortable way. I tell him he should sleep. I tell him I will move the bags so he can lean against me and sleep. I explain how he should sit to be more comfortable. He does not move. *"Wo bu bu shufu,"* he insists. He says it the way you would in English. I am not not comfortable. I do not think that even sounds right in English, and it is impossible in Chinese. You can not use *"bu"* twice like that. He should have used *"mei you."* I do not laugh. I never laughed at his Chinese since the first time we met. I tell him his mistake. He does not listen. He saw a new mountain or some thing and is writing in his diary. He loves to describe mountains. I sleep for a while, but I can not sleep long because I am worried about him. When I wake up, I can see his face with out him knowing that I am looking. He looks very tired and unhappy. Now his left foot is on top of a bag with his knee pushed into the seat in front of us. His right foot goes over another bag into the aisle. It looks even worse than before. I tell him to sleep again. I tell him how he can put his feet so he can be more comfortable. He does not want to listen to me. *"Wo hao,"* (I am good) he says. I try to move the bags. He pushes on them so I can not move them. *"Wo bu bu shufu,"* he repeats. His voice is getting louder, and I am unhappy because this proves he did not listen to me when I told him how to say this. "Please sleep," I tell him. *"Qing rang wo* alone. *Bu nag wo,"* he says. His voice is too loud. "Shut up," I tell him softly. I just want him to speak quieter. I do not mean to be unpolite. In his typical American way, he has taught me these words without teaching me that they are unpolite. "You shut up. Stop nagging me." By the time he gets to English, he is shouting. The bus gets quiet. Every one can hear him. I begin to cry. My crying only makes him angrier, but he does not say more. He just writes in his diary.

From the north side the glaciers are even nicer, of course. I'm concentrating on them now to calm down from an argument with Z which was purely the result of this day of discomfort (perhaps coupled with memories of some of the Pole's words). It is 6:00 and all downhill to Dunhuang, two hours away. There are clouds now and looking down the colors are great, lines of dark shadows and light greens and browns, alternating bands of light and dark stretching far, far into the clear air. And behind us the glaciers. 7:00 Passing thru a land of big sand dunes, some of them sand mountains, others low, broad and full of waves like the ocean, some smooth as a calm lake, some rippled as if the breeze came up. Occasionally there are bits of green, sagebrush or camel grass. Then flat desert full of mirages.

We are in Gansu now. I assume the pass marked the border between Qinghai and Gansu. There were no prisons that I could see along the road. They must be set up to be serviced by the train. Does this mean that the batch of them along the railroad, at

least, are fairly recent? Built by the communists? And along this road they are building
communes for the released prisoners to farm? Communes in the desert, communes doomed
to bare subsistence at best. Communes to quarantine people and ideas the Party finds
inconvenient? The Pole on the train said, "From each according to the Party's need, to
each whatever the Party does not need."

Jack was always writing in his diary. I can hardly read what he wrote
because the bus made his letters shake like a snack. I put in a lot of the boring
stuff he wrote to show how useless his writing was. How silly he was.

July 23
        *The big wheat harvest in Dunhuang is pretty well all in, but the corn is still
standing high as an elephant's eye. Dunhuang – the oasis – seems even more beautiful
than the first time I was here. That was in winter, two and a half years ago. In summer
it is a sea of green surrounded by sandy beaches. From near the Magao Caves it really
looks like the sea, rippled, seemingly in motion. And the caves and their fifteen hundred
year old murals are every bit as magical as they were. What has changed is the attitude
toward them. The universal reverence I felt the first time is gone. They are now simply a
tourist attraction, a dollar maker. The hotels are all ripoffs. People are told fifteen yuan is
the cheapest room, but late comers get the same room for seven when it appears the room
may go empty. The same set of post cards with excellent pictures of the murals (which
tourists are not allowed to photograph, supposedly because flashbulbs have a deleterious
effect on the ancient paint) sells for twelve yuan at one stand and five at a second. Both
stands, presumably, are government run. But the individuals running them are allowed to
reap profits as well as salaries. At our binguan the set goes for eight yuan. To facilitate
such sharp practices the fair price is no longer marked on the folder as it used to be on all
Chinese publications. More indicative of the lack of reverence was the behavior of a bunch
of Hong Kong youth. Armed with powerful flashlights they entered every cave, literally
ran around the room making sure their lights flashed on every wall, then exited, having
spent five to ten seconds in each. Clearly their only purpose in coming was to say they had
been there. Hollow people, their headpieces stuffed with straw. Alas, I fear they are the
Chinese of the future. Their hollow music, films and books are everywhere in China. The
music (muzak really) is especially terrible because it is inescapable. One is subjected to it
constantly on omnipresent train, bus, street and school speakers.*

July 24
        *Z and I had an argument (actually two outbreaks of the same argument, one on
the bus, the other in Dunhuang) day before yesterday which the arrival of Qiu and his
friend Yu seems to have deflected. It was caused by being tired and uncomfortable for long
periods, especially on the bus. Z is too much like my mother, always full of advice; she has
a way of talking, a tone of voice, a way of saying the same thing over and over, nagging,
that is exactly like my mother's. I kept hearing my mother talking at me. In Chinese. I*

know it was just Chinese didacticism, which invariably sounds like a parent lecturing a child, but I hated it as a child, and it is even worse as an adult. Z explains and explains, nags and nags, picks and picks at me until I explode, which is very terrible to her when it happens in public. She can't see that her nagging is as awful to me as my tantrums to her. It is a matter of face. She is losing face in public and can't forget, can't see the deeper causes of the problem, constantly must assess blame. There must be a hao ren and a huai ren, a good person and a bad person, in every such situation in China, and she can't be satisfied until I admit I am the huai ren. I keep saying I will do so if she will admit to some share of the blame, but she won't and says my idea (that it takes two to make a quarrel and that they should share the blame) is wrong, that there must always be one person right and the other wrong. Her admission to any part of the blame would be another loss of face.

Qiu tells me he and his friend also had an argument on the train. The train brushed a peasant, injuring him badly. Eventually he was taken onto the train but simply laid on the filthy floor between carriages, his bloody face unwiped, no one, including a doctor, doing anything to help him, and when Qiu (who works at a medical college and whose mother is a doctor) wanted to help him, his friend and others forcibly prevented him. Qiu claims lack of what my dictionary translates as humanism but I assume is actually humanitarianism is China's greatest problem and (when I said it was the modern world's, not just China's) that this goes far back into China's history. Perhaps face and lack of humanity fit together. Perhaps when people are too concerned about their own face, they cannot consider others (faces and persons).

Jack calls it nagging, I call it doing my duty of his wife. On the bus he would not sleep. He would not even lean on me and try. I knew how tired he was. It was my duty to try to help him sleep and be comfortable. I told him many ways to put his legs and body. They would be more comfortable than the way he was sitting. His legs went one way, his body went a different way. Of course he was uncomfortable. Of course he could not sleep. If he listened to me, he would be better. He did not listen to me. He shouted at me. How can that be my fault? Why should I take any blame? Americans study psychology too much. They have too many theories about how people should act. The idea that both people are always wrong in a argument is one of them. Maybe Fraud said that. They do not think. They just use Fraud's theory. Maybe some times both people are wrong, but not this time. I was trying to do what was best for Jack and he got angry at me. He got very angry. And he would not say he was wrong. Before he always did that. In Dunhuang was the first place I thought maybe Jack was starting to stop loving me. It was some thing I always worried about. But then I thought maybe it was only because he was tired from the uncomfortable bus trip. I did not feel good either after that long trip through all that ugly country. And when Qiu and Yu came the next day, Jack was better. It was the first time in a long time I was happy to see Qiu, but now I wonder if it would not be better if Jack and I were alone. We would have to talk to each other. Jack did not talk too much to me after Qiu came. Xinjiang often seemed like a men's place, and Qiu and Yu and Jack were together in it. I was left out. The only thing we all could agree about was that the ancient caves with their paintings were very beautiful, and the Hong Kong youth with torches were very stupid.

July 25

Turpan is a big mess as was the train here, but I had fun on the train so I didn't mind that too much. After much opening of back doors and wheedling, we procured two hard sleeper tickets. However, we soon discovered that the train crew had oversold the berths and there were none available. Z showed our tickets and my nose and insisted that berths be found. For half an hour I watched her at the head of a gang of similarly frustrated ticket holders parade back and forth behind the train's leader in quest of bunks. Considering how close Z kept her nose to the leader, it's hard to believe, but she says one old guy leapt in front of her and snatched two berths which should have been hers. Another single she donated to an English friend we've made, and we ended up with one upper (there are three tiers) and a promise of another at Hami at about 1:00 a.m. At 10:45 the lights went out and we climbed up together. After a long discussion in which Z insisted on sleeping head to feet and I unmercifully chided her and Chinese prudery, we climbed in head to feet. It was lucky we did. We might have been thrown off the train for immoral conduct if our heads were together, for suddenly the lights flashed on and a shocked fuwuyuan materialized and informed us that two in a berth was bu xing. Z had no taste for argument, but I put on the best performance in Chinese of my life, a long speech in which, for the first time in my life, I felt downright articulate. I explained in detail how we bought two tickets but ended up with only one berth. The fu kept saying two people in one berth bu xing, but I countered that giving two ticket holders one berth was also bu xing, so they had one cuowu (error) and we had one cuowu: pingdung, (equal) suanle (forget it). He followed the whole spiel and burst into laughter at the end. Soon we were laughing together and I'm sure would have come to an accommodation, but several other fus turned up to help, and they were considerably more serious. I didn't want to keep the whole car up and Z was angry, so I went to visit Qiu and Yu in hard seat until Hami, when we had been promised our second berth.

On the way I got waylaid by a group of Xinjiang students in heated discussion with an American. They thought he had said that Xinjiang should separate from China. He claimed he had only made a general argument in favor of self determination and had said if Xinjiang ren wanted to separate from China they should be allowed to. A dangerous thing to say to people who speak English poorly and are extremely sensitive on the topic. I continued my streak of fluent Chinese and managed to explain his point, then had to answer many questions about myself and my views. We became friends fast, and I never did get to Qiu and Yu. These kids' education and knowledge of Chinese will make them the future leaders of a Chinese Xinjiang and they know it. What impressed me was that they did not want the right of self determination because if they had it their fellow countrymen might use it. They would not be the future leaders of an independent Xinjiang. Hmm. Now there's an unanticipated fly in the brave new ointment I would apply to our ailing world.

After a while Z came in, said she would sit with Qiu and Yu until Hami and ordered me to sleep in our berth. In fact I kept talking half an hour or more but eventually did go back and slept. Z was never given the promised berth. I'm sure they would not have treated me that way if I had stayed up, but I slept thru everything and only learned what happened the next morning.

The mess in Turpan was considerably less pleasant. It is at least 45 degrees C during the day, and a constant river of sweat flows from my head. The train station is a forty five minute drive to town and no busses were waiting. We had to walk several blocks to the bus station, then queue up in a ridiculously long and messy line for tickets. The three Shanghai ren dispatched me to a shorter line going to the wrong place, but that strategy only succeeded in pissing me off when I got to the front, couldn't get the right tickets and realized I had been used. My long nose doesn't make the impression in Xinjiang, where it is not unique, that it does in Han China, and if they want to try to use my nose they could at least give me a sniff of what they are doing. Eventually we got tickets for 10:30 (we arrived at 9:00). Altho everyone had boarded by 10:15, nothing happened until 10:45, when some officious ass started checking every ticket. There were two busses, both full, both going to the same place, and nothing to differentiate them, but the ass insisted that some tickets were for one bus, others for the other and ordered people back and forth. There would have been a fight if they had tried to put me off, hot, bothered and tired as I was, but fortunately we had made the right guess. There was one argument between two passengers, as usual much blowing of steam but no actual blows, but two girls sitting nearby fled, so the blowhard who didn't have a seat ended up in one of theirs. Everyone in the bus was steaming from being forced to sit so long in the hot sun for no reason. It was noon before we reached town.

Our approaches are very different: the three Shanghai ren are constantly asking questions of strangers, then debating their next step. I can't stand it. In this case it was noon and I had eaten only a slice of Hami melon all day and was hot and angry. I had seen a sign for the hotel, so I told them to follow me, shouldered my pack and took off. I quickly left them far in my wake, which was just as well since I wouldn't have wanted them there for the scene which ensued. Everywhere in Turpan there are grapes, ripe, luscious grapes. The sidewalks are shaded by grape arbors with big bunches dangling down. I reached up and snatched a single grape. Two thugs yelled at me from the other side of the street, ran over and blocked my way, demanding I pay protection money or whatever their racket is called. No way I was going to unless they produced some kind of official authorization. A foreigner came over and translated for me – the accent was as beastly as the thugs. He said he and his friends had just been similarly caught and made to pay seven yuan. The thugs offered to settle for five from me, which persuaded me all the more that this was a racket. These were street guys if I've ever seen them. They would have been at home hanging out on 63rd Street. I tried to walk past them. I don't

*think they actually pushed me, but the sidewalk was slanted and in poor repair and I
slipped and fell. At this point a rather more distinguished citizen came up, ordered them
to desist, and I was able to walk away, trembling with rage and shame. All this before
we even reached the* binguan.

I do not know if it was the place or the hot weather or just Jack's American
temper. It seemed like he was always mad and getting into fights on this trip.
Maybe it was my fault. Maybe I expected too much. Maybe I expected him to act
like a Chinese. Qiu, Yu and I were always trying to help him, but he was always
mad. At us. At every one. I did not know what to do. I never saw him like that
before. I was afraid that all the bad things I heard about marrying foreigners
were starting to come true.

Turpan was the hottest place I ever was in, but I still did not sweat much.
I never do. But when Jack took off the thin silk shirt I bought him for this
weather, it was covered with white stuff. At first we did not know what it was.
Then Jack tested it. It was salt. His sweat dried on his shirt. There was enough
salt to make many dishes. No Chinese could ever sweat like that. I guess he
suffered a lot in that heat. So I do not blame him for being unhappy. But he
should have controlled himself a little too. He could be hurt badly fighting with
the Xinjiang men. They are very violent people. He had hundreds of *yuan.* He
should give them five.

And he should not be angry at me. It was not my fault. In Xinjiang he
acted like I was the blame for every thing because it happened in my country.
But the people in Xinjiang are very different from us Hans. They look different.
They look like Americans. They act like Americans too. Jack recognized them.
"Thugs," he called them. Like they have in Chicago. Maybe that is why he was
angry.

July 26

Things got better yesterday. I wandered lonely as the cloudless sky while the others
xiuxied. *I bought a dress as a birthday present for Z and some grapes. The dress is pretty
and the grapes are out of this world, but buying anything requires dreadful haggling that I
hate. I do it mainly because it is language practice. Despite drinking copious quantities of
water I was in the early stages of heat exhaustion. It was forty six degrees C in the shade,
and I was in the sun much of the time. Altho I knew in theory what summer in the desert
would be like, the actuality of the heat is almost more than I can bear, and I am very
irritable. I woke up every ten minutes last night to pry the wet with sweat side of my body
from the sheet and face it toward the fan while the other side sweated. The locals all sleep
under their grape arbors. Every house has them, and they are the coolest places around.*

*Today is cloudy and the temperature a cool thirty nine. In fact it changes quickly.
We spent the day touring and constantly encountered places of cool breezes, then fresh
outbreaks of heat. Amidst change the ruins of ancient cities endure, lovely and eerie, full*

of sandblasted shapes which evoke faint memories of where I have never been: crumpled towers where a writer like me might have looked up from a manuscript to gaze out at – what? was it desert then? – holy walls devoid of worshippers, holey now, walling nothing in or out, clay brick and molded houses open to the vast desert and vaster sky, squares where no people have met for a thousand years, bygone ways and byways long gone empty. We laughed as we clambered in but soon were silenced by the weight of history, the forgotten tragedy. I'll never again be impressed by eighty year old ghost towns in the Slocan.

The Chinese are getting a kick out of being hustled by an eighteen year old hustler who arranged today's trip for us. He is of a type familiar enough to me but, judging from my friends' reactions, unknown in China, or at least to them. Like all good hustlers there is a part of him that is sincere, and the loud friendship between them is, to some extent at least, genuine on both sides. But we don't get any bargains from him: he gets us grapes and melons at the going rate, and he just added five yuan to the agreed price for driving us to the train station. The friendship mainly manifests itself in cigarettes from Qiu and Yu and the Xinjiang equivalent of kool-aid from him. Except the kool-aid was a typical hustle. He supplied us most of the trip, but on the way back we ran out; we paid enough for the resupply to cover his previous costs, I'm sure. Qiu and Yu have little conception of money and the kid does. Altho I think the kid really does like them – Yu keeps taking pictures of him and he certainly likes that – he doesn't miss a trick for making money. The Shanghai lads think it is very generous of him to let the driver take a bigger cut than he does, but it is the driver's car and the driver who does the work, after all. All the kid does is talk, and he still claims he makes two thousand kuai a month, which is many times what the others make. He knows a very few words of both English and Japanese, but Qiu and Yu are mightily impressed – they know "hello" and "bye bye." He is very solicitous of the two girls who are the other passengers on our tour (and who he says are paying more than the four of us) and calls them softly "Japanese."

You see. Jack recognized "the kid." I did not. Now I would recognize him, and not just because I went to the West. Now there are people like him in Shanghai, people who love money as much as life and do not care how they get it, people who will say any thing to get your money, people who are your friends until they have your money. But in 1987 I never met any one like him before. Shanghai people are famous for speaking fast, but he spoke faster than all of us. And thought faster too. He found people who looked very unchinese for Qiu to sketch and Yu to take pictures of. Then he told them the people were very poor. Qiu and Yu gave him money for them. But I saw him put some in his pocket before he gave it to them. I think maybe you have to think fast in a place like Xinjiang. Otherwise you will be cheated. As I said before, Xinjiang people are more like Americans, not Han Chinese. Han Chinese are proud they are not merchants. At least they used to be.

But Jack's writing is not like Xinjiang, full of delicious grapes and melons.

We say writing like where he describes the ancient cities has lots of flowers but no fruit. It seems like it is very beautiful, but it does not say much. That is because it tries to say too much. It tries to be too beautiful. It makes curved lines straight, and it bends straight lines into curves. It is unnatural. Jack usually writes that way when he is describing scenery. I noticed it before too.

July 27

I just found out that the kid tried to hustle an extra five yuan (conveniently forgetting that forty five yuan was the agreed upon price to the train station only if a fifth person, an Australian foreign expert we met, came along). We are presently (8:20 a.m.) shivering in the dining car of the train to Korla. We have been here most of an uncomfortable night, which would have been far more uncomfortable elsewhere. Last night as we ascended (in an open taxi) out of the hole which is Turofan – only the Han maps call it Turpan – it began cooling off, and by the time we reached the station I had already donned my windbreaker. There were no hard sleeper berths available on the train – we know that scene all too well – which left at 1:30 a.m. Yu worked and bullshitted hard, telling them I was an influential foreign friend who worked at the railway department in Beijing, that Z was pregnant and god knows what else. All to no avail. The conductors dispensing berths are little queens and kings in their cubicle. The people waiting dare not utter a word as the fus do their paperwork, have a snack, chat etc., all the while seemingly oblivious to the line of people waiting for them. The Chinese love to do this, and while it is a prerogative generally reserved for those in high places in the West, in China everyone who deals with the public has her or his own niche from which he or she can, and invariably does, disdain others, including influential foreign friends. On the other side (the back side) of every niche is a door. Yu loves to open these back doors. He got us thru one and onto the train platform early to give us a better shot at a seat since even the train station personnel were not sure if the train had hard sleeper cars. But the platform was packed with people, all of whom had found one back door or another. I had to laugh when I saw the result of all his apple polishing and apple buttering up. It's a funny way to run a railroad or a country, but it isn't likely to change soon: as the Pole said, "The Communist Party runs the trains and the country the same way, the way it runs the Party."

On the train stopping and starting is quite bumpy because we are going thru the mountains and need two engines to do so, but they are poorly coordinated. As we go up it grows progressively colder. Everyone is in four layers of clothing and shivering. Even I, the proud Canadian, got cold last night (in shorts and a silk teeshirt) and still am despite long pants over the shorts and a shirt, sweater and windbreaker over the teeshirt. Nevertheless, I like it a whole lot more than the heat, and at least we're out of the desert. Indeed, this place had a flood a few days ago and it's still raining. The mountains obviously catch the rain and cast a rain shadow over the desert. We have been going thru a long tunnel for several minutes. We come out of the tunnel and, unbelievably, the world is white with snow which is still falling, a white, featureless world. This place is crazy: yesterday it was forty six degrees; today it is snowing. Am I in Milton's Hell, fire and ice, the burning lake on the frozen continent?

It is 9:00, and the train staff, which has just finished eating, is lined up receiving orders from its commander in chief. Does this happen every morning or has the snow necessitated special orders? The Shanghainese, despite constant promises to speak putonghua, are grumbling away in Shanghaihua. They were sleeping away until the wonder of the snow excited a buzz which woke them. I have been writing away more from exhaustion than anything else. I can't sleep and writing is a defense against both exhaustion and Shanghaihua.

We are now at a station after having jerked our way thru a broad, yurt dotted alpine meadow right at the snowline. The meadow was green and being grazed, by horses mainly, plus a smattering of cows and other animals, but surrounding the valley the mountains resumed in a series of humps (no more than a couple hundred meters above the high valley) and these were all snow covered, some cloud covered as well. A lovely pastoral scene but cold looking and cold indeed on the train. The stop is a long one, but I can't see the town or spot the name. There does not seem to be a town here at all, just green meadow, rushing streams and placid puddles, remnants, perhaps, of melted snow or a subsided flood. No doubt the station serves many small pastoral settlements dotted about this high plain.

This train is a real change from the tourist circuit, rough looking with rough looking passengers, young males mainly. The dining car serves hot meals to the staff only. Passengers can purchase bags of fresh fruit, jars of canned fruit, etc., but it mainly and busily dispenses a variety of alcoholic beverages. Then at 11:00 (five to, in fact, no doubt another assertion by a servant of the public to her right to bossdom of her niche) the fuwuyuan closes and locks the door of her dispensary. For an hour the train has moved only in bumps, jerks and crawls. We've probably made a hundred meters in that time. For half an hour or more we've been stopped with no station in sight. The purpose, so far as I can make out, is to freeze my fingers so I can't write. The car has now filled up with people holding tickets, so apparently they are preparing to serve a passenger lunch. I guess we are now claiming our niche since the car is jammed with people eating or wanting to and we are hogging a table for no reason except our own comfort and no one dares to tell the long nose to move. My conscience tells me to do so, but my body is too tired to listen.

1:10: I would have been miles ahead and considerably warmer if I had walked to the top of the pass. Now we are crawling down beside a rushing stream, watching it grow broader and wilder as cracks open into the higher mountains and tributaries gush straight down from the snow above. Not sure why, but it feels like something out of Tolkein. Perhaps the fantastic concurrence of heat and snow have reminded me of another fantasy. At Baluntai, far enough down for some rudimentary agriculture and a scattering of deciduous trees, the river is a broad, muddy torrent. In B.C. it could look like this only in spring, never summer. On the train there are frequent, loud clashes between the crude passengers and the just as crude fuwuyuans. One female fu is particularly shrill; her voice sets my teeth on edge. Teeth on edge (of cap) is the usual method of opening the beer bottles which are dispensed here, but the male fu now selling the beer just went that one better by opening with his fingernails a bottle on which his customer's teeth had failed. As we descend the villages become less poor looking, but the basic construction remains whitewashed adobe rowhouses. An old man has set up his portable knife sharpening stand and is taking advantage of the train's lack of progress to sharpen the dining car's stock of knives. He uses two stones but mainly a T shaped blade with a short stem of very hard metal which literally shaves the steel off the knives. Then he finishes the job with a stone and a whetstone. I wouldn't want to touch the blade when he's done. Apparently the reason we are proceeding so slowly is that there is flooding ahead. I was wondering what was going on. The sky is cloudy but bright. There is no rain, but the river is a muddy torrent and all the new snow higher up is no doubt melting fast. 3:30: After a long wait we were finally allowed to proceed. The part considered dangerous was where the valley narrowed and the train crossed the river several times on a series of trestles. Altho the river had extended its banks in many places and was high and fast flowing, the bridges and tracks were high above the water level, so I can't see what the great problem was. Everything ended suddenly: flood, mountains, green, river; the narrow valley opened into a vast, vegetationless stone desert; river and tracks went their separate ways, and all that much needed water was lost somewhere in the expanse of waste. Only one narrow channel remained, leaving the railroad all the room in the huge, ugly desert world. In the end all that water had little or no effect. So now it's on to Korla, which I suppose is another oasis. I'd rather live in the small mountain villages we passed, but the Shanghainese were disgusted by their poverty as well as their temperature.

The temperature here is noticeably warmer, the sky less cloudy tho looking back one can see the solid layer over the mountains. Sticking above the arid mountains in the foreground is a single snowy peak. We are waiting again at the first station after the mountains and are told the tracks ahead are being repaired, for there is still flooding and the tracks ahead won't be so high above the water level. We're already more than an hour late and still two hours from Korla. The sun has just come out. 4:30: The staff is now assembling for a meeting. I don't imagine that's a good sign. Apparently they are assembling for an extra meal, not a meeting. That's not a good sign either. I am living on grapes: we bought five kilos in Turofan. People are just hanging out, outside as well as inside. They are all over the tracks but mainly leaning against the train for its shade. Yup: it's really hot. Nothing to do but wait. After their meal the staff had a short address from its leaders, saying it was hoped the track would be repaired soon but no one knew when. They were told to be happy, for they, at least, had eaten. Food is ever a reason for joy to Chinese. The staff then lined up briefly and returned to their posts. I wonder why they didn't look happy after being told to be. There seems to be no water left on the train – with too much outside it. 5:10: A second group of staff is preparing to eat and getting what sounds like the exact same speech the first group got. 5:30: They say we'll leave at 6:00. We'll see. We are not in any distress. Yu just got us a bowl of noodles each and we have two full canteens of tea plus bread and ham and selected munchies, so I felt ashamed eating noodles which other passengers can't get. But I ate them. We've been offered cash for our grapes several times. 6:15: Everybody is clambering back onto the train. But after *the initial rush nothing happened, and now the outside is filling up again. The latest report circulating among the staff is that we won't be able to leave for two more hours. 9:00: Still no movement but the latest rumor is 9:30. 9:29: We are moving at last. We passed the bad place very slowly, cheered on by a large crowd of laborers, male and female, with shovels. The problem was the bridge or right next to the bridge, where we crossed the river, I assume for the last time. The river had expanded from one channel to half a dozen and spilled over its banks, perhaps undermining the low bridge.*

10:00: He Jing, the first good sized city we've come to. Our arrival was loudly cheered. There is a train heading east that I assume has been awaiting our arrival. 10:30: Astonishing: we are going thru perfectly normal country, neither desert nor oasis, a land of grass, trees and farms that seems unspectacular in every way except its spectacular ordinariness in this place where nothing is ordinary.

What a place! So poor, so dirty, so crazy. One minute hot, the next minute cold, one place flooding, the next place desert. But the main thing I noticed was how poor. The villages Jack liked so much were full of broken, dirty houses and people in broken, dirty clothes. No wonder no Chinese want to go to the west of China. Shanghai people never saw any thing like this. And snow in July! Maybe the place was being punished. There is a famous play about that. It snows in the middle of summer as a punishment for the unjust execution of Dou E.

July 28

Korla is off the tourist track. What a relief: we can live in Chinese hotels and there was no line for bus tickets to Kashgar. There are no bus tickets to Turofan at all because of the flood. It's hot again but nothing compared to Turofan. Altho I like to think of myself as a hardy traveler, it seems I am now judging things from the standpoint of convenience. I suppose that is natural after all the inconveniences we have experienced, but I don't much like it. In fact the country is strange and varied enough to be interesting, and that appeals to me as much as any tourist sights and should help me put up with inconveniences, mental as well as physical. Xinjiangnese are reputed to be hard drinking. That's not surprising: one look at the scenery makes one dry. I shudder to think what the average Turofan resident consumes in drinks, soft as well as hard, in a year. The feel of the province is: go a while, drink a while, go again, drink again.

3:00: I hope we don't get into another flood situation. It was partly sunny and hot earlier, but now the sky has blackened and a few drops of rain are already falling. This kind of place gets so little rain that when it does fall the earth does not know what to do with it and disaster results. Another storm in the mountains might wipe out roads as well as train tracks and leave no way out of Korla heading west as well as east. Travelers would be trapped here. Distant rolls of thunder grow louder and longer as the storm approaches. The temperature has dropped ten degrees C – as it should for a storm, a fact I had almost forgotten because it does not in eastern China. Eastern China is tired from its long history; this place is not like that. I suppose it is I, not eastern China, which feels tired in its humid heat, but China sits on its civilization, buries it, lives off (and on) it, while Xinjiang leaves its ancient civilizations to dry and be preserved in the sun while it moves on (and off) to a new place. The strange shapes of ancient cities, melted then hardened, pointing and bowing to the sun, their destroyer and preserver, lover forever despite moods of black rage and rain. Its contrasts make looking at Xinjiang exciting, but I'm glad I don't live here. It feels like a rough, impermanent life. Somehow that sort of life, which feels normal in North America, seems out of place in China. Not that this place can really be considered China. China could never have such delightful coolness and freshness in its summer air.

More flowers without fruit writing, more straight lines curved and curved lines straight. Jack loves to tell his students and me to write simply, but he can not do it himself. I was not happy, but we did not have any more fights at this time. Because many other things were happening, so nothing was too boring or uncomfortable. But you can see that Jack is insulting China more and more. That is a bad sign. Every thing will get much worse on the long bus trip.

July 29

Bus to Kashgar, Kashi the Hans call it. "Gar" is not a possible syllable in Hanyu. All the place names seem to have two forms, native and Han. The Han name is an approximation of the native, but Hanyu is too limited in its sounds and Hans are too limited by their condescension ever to get it right. As we prepare to start, Qiu pulls out the pharmacy: he has at least twenty envelopes of pills. He and Z both have diarrhea, and he has pills for that and everything else. The boarding process has even more yelling than usual, but perhaps less fighting. People are seated in the order of their ticket numbers. This creates much noise but should avoid the usual disputes over who sits where. They are now adding or shifting baggage atop the bus and Z has gone out to supervise, as usual. She makes sure of everything. The driver and conductor's section is walled off with plastic, another good idea to protect the driver from passengers' annoyances over this long haul. 9:15: Fifteen minutes after scheduled start but still no indication of starting altho the passengers seem already to have passed that initial stage of overexcitement characteristic of Chinese starting a journey. Perhaps this is because for once they have not sold more tickets than seats. Could this be efficiency? I doubt it. Most likely there are few candidates who elect to head into this heart of desert darkness. There are still two or three empty seats in the back and I think we are being delayed because the bus people want to fill them. The mess of starting out never ceases to amaze me, but once we do start it will all be forgotten. They keep trying to shut the door, but more passengers squeeze in. They reach the seats in the back with great difficulty because by now the aisle is blocked by all the luggage the passengers refuse to trust to the rack atop the bus. More people squeeze in, and to my amazement they keep finding seats for them. A mother with a five year old has not bought a ticket for the child so must put her on her lap, which is already loaded with luggage. Instead they manage to squnch in together. It must be very tight back there, perhaps tight enough to permit departure. 9:28: We start to leave but suddenly voices ring out ordering us to stop. There is one more soldier who wants on. And so begins two and a half days of life in the sardine tin.

Except it doesn't. 9:57: back at Korla station. We drove a quarter of an hour then turned back. I assumed the motor was having trouble. It sounded like it was, but they all do. Apparently the driver simply forgot something. It just took him thirty seconds to get it but wasted thirty minutes. The army men behind us ask me if a driver in the U.S. could do that and I must reply no, only if the motor was breaking down. Otherwise, I tell them, the schedule is king. Z tells me I cannot say that, that I must not use da wang (king) in this sentence. She wants me to use "law," which is not what I want to say. Once the bus starts again, most people again instantly drop off to sleep in every conceivable and many inconceivable positions.

12:00: I have just caused an incident. They did not call this the Silk Road because of its surface. We have been going over road partially washed out by the flood. The jolting was too rough for my ass, which was in bad shape even before this, so I stood up, but while standing I leaned against my window, and between my leaning and the bumps the glass shattered. The windows are made of ordinary glass, not safety glass! Good god, what must happen when there is a crash. The glass shattered outward so no one was hurt, but now there is a big, open window, which is terrible to the Shanghainese with their paranoia of cold, but was gratefully received by the other passengers: the driver stopped to check out the window and half the bus piled out to piss. Thereafter everyone was awake, chatting and in good spirits; before everyone had been asleep. Z says the people were very nice, telling the driver the glass broke of itself, no one blaming me altho it was my fault. Apparently if I were blamed, I would be expected to pay for a new window. Korla is located on a thin sward of green hundreds of kilometers long. There must be a river in the middle, but we haven't seen it. We travel parallel to the sward, the road lying between the green and a line of dry mountains which don't look very high but contain the occasional snow covered peak. I assume this is the snow which fell a few days ago and caused the flood. The rain rolls down the mountains, making its own watercourses and depositing a layer of mud and stones on everything it crosses. Like this road. Which is what made it so rough and gave me a pain in the ass.

Maybe the rough road was not caused by the flood. Maybe this hardened over plough row is supposed to be the road. After a pit stop at a pitiful assemblage of huts on the oasis strip, the road got even worse. For an hour we chugged along at a constant but uncomfortable ten mph. Finally we reached the end of the strip, where a pathetic few workers were repairing the road. It will take them a year or more at that rate. If this represents all the good intentions that can be mustered, our road to hell will not be well paved. And so it proves: now we are indeed on a paved road, which is faster but of such poor quality that it is no easier on my ass. This is going to be a long trip.

3:00: Luntai: full of tiny plums, bowls of yogurt covered by pieces of cardboard or wood and beggars who meet the bus. It even has a book stall with everything from the big Ci Hai dictionary to glossy, if well out of date, magazines with covers showing skiers and

female body builders. No customers, however. Old Weigurs with pointed white beards and
skullcaps and very young Weigurs with pans of watermelon rinds and dirty pants' bottoms
stare at me as if I, not they, am picturesque. The bagels are delicious. 6:00: pit stop to
repair a tire. This must be a frequent occurrence on this unsilk road. We got a blessing:
the third person sitting in our seat departed and no one new boarded. What a wonderful
difference a little space makes. We are 46 kms from our night stop. The desert is in bloom,
full of purple flowers from the recent rains. We keep passing donkey and ox carts loaded
with two and even three wagonfulls of cut desert shrubs. The peasants must harvest them
as fuel. It seems a shame; surely that is no way to halt the advance of the desert, and there
is much evidence that some folks are attempting that. Near every town, even small ones,
are large plantations of saplings, very closely planted.

At 7:00 we stopped in Ku Qa and at 8:00 pulled into Xin He, our night stop. Both
are good sized cities. We are now in the Tarim Valley. We passed a beautiful lake, then the
river, which has dams everywhere. The river is used for irrigation, power and everything else
it can be. That is why so wide and fruitful a river dissipates into nothing, for in doing so it
powers a civilization. We got a lovely hotel room together at 3.50 yuan each; they couldn't
care less about foreigners. I discovered a plethora of lovely looking Xinjiangnese restaurants,
but my companions found the one Hanzu restaurant – in the bus-hotel compound – and
insisted on eating there. We have eaten nothing but Han food since we met Qiu and
Yu. Only I have snuck out and bought a few Wei items, especially the bagels. Qiu keeps
claiming he wants to eat native yang rou (mutton), but he has had a bad stomach and
was quite sick last night. On the street everyone is interested in us, laughing, wanting
their pictures taken. Indeed, out here the three Shanghai ren are as much weiguoren
(foreigners) as I am. As if to prove what I just wrote, Z returned from the john, listened to
the Xinjiang words on Qiu's portable radio and asked me, "Is that English?"

July 30
The place we ate and slept in last night is a Han stockade and must be perceived as
such by the locals. All the trucks and busses lock themselves in behind its high wood walls,
like the Europeans stockaded themselves against the Indians in the North American west.
The Hans have their own restaurant, beds and facilities plus room for many trucks and
busses on the inside. I tried to explain that this stockade mentality results from imperialism
but got nowhere with my "comrades." Americans are imperialists, never Chinese.

Back in the bus, a man is trying to rest his head on the seat in front of him and
sleep, but that seat is occupied by a young Xinjiang woman with long, flowing hair, which
the wind keeps blowing into the man's face. He shakes his head, flicks and swats at the
hair as if it were an insect, wakes up, changes position but soon slides back onto the seat
in front and repeats the movements. She sleeps on, unaware of the dance she precipitates.
Behind us an old Weigur man sings or chants, as he did much of the day yesterday, and
rolls cigarettes in carefully cut strips of newspaper. His tobacco does not look like tobacco,
has much green powdered weed in it, but does not smell like pot (some of which I saw
growing wild in Gansu) or sulphurous hades fumes or anything I can distinguish with my

nose. Only my eyes, which see and smart. Yesterday some PLA (People's Liberation Army) soldiers informed us that the old man was eighty three and had eight wives, but Qiu now corrects my misunderstanding: he has been married eight times; polygamy is not allowed; he has been divorced many times. He is obviously happy and prosperous. Life has been good to him and he seems wonderfully healthy and looks twenty years younger than his age. But what of his ex wives, their families, less prosperous members of the community? Perhaps partly because of ideas planted in my mind by the Pole such a person raises all sorts of questions in the modern world and in a country which professes to be Marxist.

11:30: piss break in the desert, the women going one way, the men the other. What a contrast between the Tarim Valley and the desert. Throughout the valley trees are planted huddled together in shallow ditches to facilitate irrigation. Everywhere the muddied waters of the Tarim flow in manmade channels, giving life at the expense of its own. Once we leave the valley, the desert colors and shapes become fantastic. For a long time we watch two purple hills glowing like distant watchtowers; slowly they grow long serrations like leg hold traps and finally turn into steep, eroded gullies from which there is no way out once you are in. I search for hobbits, Frodo and Sam in the wastes of Mordor. As we drive parallel to the endless line of mountains to the north, they resolve themselves into three layers, a low, barren string of eroded mud hills, then, at first visible only thru cracks dug by stream beds, a magnificent rainbow range of purple mountains with many streaks of red, grey, white gradually become closer and more prominent, and then, above them, tower snowy peaks, high and cloudy with rain, perhaps snow, falling on them. In the foreground the desert too keeps changing, quite bare, almost sandy, in some places, in others stony with relatively more vegetation, in yet others occasional surprisingly fruitful patches.

12:00: lunch in an oasis, Wu Tuan. As I stand outside the bus writing, a crowd gathers to discuss the phenomenon which I am. The oasis seems large and is full of melons and good looking apples, three mao per kilo of hamiguo, four mao for pinguo, but we were asked double the price other passengers paid. Now I am staying away so Z and Y can search and negotiate. They return, having paid six mao for apples, which should be four, and one fifty for watermelon, which should be one. When the PLA soldiers tell them the going prices, they are most unhappy. As I am chortling to myself about their learning how it feels to be a foreigner, they locate some Shanghai ren who have lived here since 1963, and they all explode into Shanghaihua. The animation of the rapid fire discussion which ensues fascinates me and attracts a large crowd altho neither I nor the Xinjiangnese can understand a word. To me, in putunghua, one of the Shanghainese who live here said their life was "hai keyi," not bad, but many people could understand putonghua. Back on the bus Z tells me that in Shanghaihua they expressed anger and indignation at the government and its policies toward them and cursed Deng Xiao Ping. I have read something of their history, and Z tells me more: they "volunteered" to come here as "educated youth" during the Socialist Education Movement, Mao's biggest campaign between the Great Leap and the Cultural Revolution, for which, it now seems clear, it was a sort of puppet theater dress rehearsal. The object was to bring the culture and education of the modern cities to the most backward and unsettled parts of the countryside. Shanghai's task was to *civilize and cultivate this desert. What the volunteers were not told was that it was also an attempt to redistribute population. Twenty four years into this experimental drama the actors complain that they were tricked by pious words and platitudes (Mao's) into joining a summer theater company. Now they are not allowed (by Deng) to return to real life, to Shanghai. They gave up their Shanghai hukou (residence books) when they came to Xinjiang, so they cannot move back, are forced to reenact endlessly a mock heroic fantasy. Besides this they complain that they are discriminated against here. When they came they were told they were just like the PLA, which was a great honor and a good deal then but no longer is. They live in teams, all Shanghainese together but not all in one place. Apparently there are thousands of them scattered over the desert. They say they work hard but receive only half as much money as local peasants because the government takes the rest in taxes (as, the soldiers have informed us, it does with the PLA). When they are allowed to visit their families, they are fined if they bring along the fruits they labored to grow while this is never done to the peasants. They claim they pretty much built Wu Tuan and the road to it, that there was nothing here when they first came, but that no one gives a damn now. They point out that after the Cultural Revolution people sent to the countryside were allowed to return home, but they are not. They are told that if their children pass the college entrance exams and are able to study and work in Shanghai, the children will be given residence cards, but this is true for all students, not just their children, and they know their children are at a disadvantage because of the poor quality of schools here. Even I, who moved from city to country and believe more people should, could hear the anger in their voices and feel the pathos of their predicament. I asked the mother of one teen aged boy if he could speak Shanghaihua and she said yes, but when I asked the boy he said no (tho he seemed to be able to follow others when they spoke it) and spoke in a dialect which was unrecognizable and undecipherable to me. The road has seemed better of late (or I have become better accustomed to it). Perhaps it is paved with the good intentions of the middle aged Shanghai youth trapped here. Perhaps all the good intentions of China's socialist past, the Great Leap, the Socialist Education Movement, the Cultural Revolution, have paved the road to this place of no return, this hell.*

I got to writing about hell for two reasons: Z says that is the word the Shanghainese use when they speak about this place, so their imagery corresponds exactly to mine, but also because Z inadvertently said something which made me see a parallel between my life and that of these lost Shanghai ren. What if I had been forced to stay on in Lincoln Park? I would have gone nuts if I wasn't killed first. Suddenly I saw the diabolism of being forced to abide by a choice made in the revolutionary fervor of youth. Yet if I really believed what I have always believed I believe, if I believe, with Milton, that "the mind is its own place and in itself can create a heaven of hell, a hell of heaven," why run? Am I any better than these people who believe that who they are depends on where they are? Doesn't the very fact of my running mean I agree with them? If who I was was enough to overcome where I was, I wouldn't need to run. I saw that I have spent my life choosing, then running from the consequences of my choice. When one choice didn't work, I simply chose again. But what if I couldn't cut and run, couldn't choose again? What if I were trapped in my role as these people were in their hellhole? That's another difference between China and the West: even Frodo and Sam had a way out. Once they completed their mission, they could be rescued.

Aiya. I think I swallowed another insect. This must be where it happened. I can still remember every word of talk. Jack was trying to say the Shanghai people themselfs chose to come to Xinjiang, but he did not know the Chinese word *xuanze*, so he said, "*Tamen ziji* chose *lai Xinjiang.*" We still did that some times. We still mixed Chinese and English that way. We called our language Chinglish, and usually we laughed when it happened. Usually it made us happy. It reminded us that we loved each other in despite of our differences. But not in Xinjiang. In Xinjiang our differences were things to be unhappy and fight about. "What means 'chose?'" I asked. "Like a shirt?" At first he laughed. "*Bu, bu.* That is 'clothes.' 'Chose' is the past tense of 'choose.'" I knew that word. "Ah. Choose again, Jiake." I used to say that before we were married, and I laughed when I remembered it. But Jack did not laugh. Suddenly he looked unhappy and angry. And just as suddenly I knew why. When I used to say that before, he really could choose again. Now he could not. I thought he saw that he was trapped with me the same way the Shanghai people were trapped in Xinjiang. He married a Chinese woman, and now he could not escape. For the rest of our trip I thought he was trying to escape from me. But his diary says he was not thinking of me. He was thinking of himself. He was thinking of Lincoln Park. So now I have to think what is true. I have to remember more than I wanted to.

Wu Tuan has its own river, smaller than the Tarim but exploited in the same way. I wonder if nature is objecting: one effect of all the irrigation seems to be bringing up salt. I saw one stream with wide shoulders of salt. Lack of concern for the environment, seeing it as an enemy to be subdued, not a friend to work with, seems to be a Han characteristic, but perhaps what I am noticing is simply another effect of the pressure of overpopulation. I think of overpopulation as being purely an eastern China phenomenon and of western China as being underpopulated and so a good place to shift people to, but this land simply cannot support too many people. In its way it may be as overpopulated as the east.

2:30: Akasun (clear water), a big city, the first place since Korla to look like a genuine metropolis. There is lots of construction going on, and the buildings are all brick. The city is new and clean with broad, almost trafficless streets and uncrowded sidewalks. In the background a constant flow of words streams from the speakers. Z says she hasn't heard the like since the Cultural Revolution, but the words are in Weigur and sound relatively harmonious – without shengdiao: hurray – not like exhorting. Altho our seats are reserved, my companions all reboarded the bus when they saw some locals boarding. They feel compelled to guard their places and property. This kind of travelling brings out people's real character. The caution and prejudice built into the Chinese character always amazes me and, I suspect, the Xinjiangnese as well. I would guess that deep down I have more in common with the Weigurs – we are all semites, at least – than the Hans and that if I lived here I might end up supporting them if there were an anti-Han struggle. Yet these people are still very strange to me while the Hans no longer are. I wish I could study the dynamic of the Shanghai ren in Wu Tuan. The adults are obviously quite unassimilated, but the boy, who has lived there all his life, seems very different from his parents. The situation of the Hans out here is certainly not easy. The army man behind us on the bus told us he is thirty three and has been stationed in Xinjiang for thirteen years. Once every four years he gets leave to visit his home in Hebei, not too far from Beijing. The question is, are the Hans here doing good? I loved Lincoln Park, but I couldn't save it. The Shanghai ren hate Wu Tuan, but they built it, laid roads, dug canals, planted trees, connected a lonely oasis in the middle of a desert to the outside world. I loved and left. They hated and stayed. Thank god I got out, but they have done something they can be proud of. As if they care.

I am writing this outside the bus, and one of the Weigur passengers just asked me if I was writing "English." Not Ingyu. He tried to pronounce the word properly, something that would never occur to a Han. The old Weigur man wears three layers of clothes, a pinstriped shirt much like a Western dress shirt but loose at the collar and wrinkled, then a black pinstriped jacket similar to but not quite a sportsjacket, finally an unbuttoned overcoat of sorts; he wears black pants and black boots which reach almost to the knees, a green skullcap – if he were Jewish it would be a yarmulka – with a pattern of white flowers, a wide blue cloth belt-girdle. Altogether he presents a loose, untidy appearance which is somehow attractive and certainly not dirty. His eyes are tiny and deep set but always alert. He and another old gentleman in bright blue pants and a fur lined cap sit on the ground and smoke and talk together. The women wear long, thick stockings and bloomers of sorts under their skirts. They too sit on the ground, their dresses rolled up as if they didn't notice they were wearing them. Several are breastfeeding babies.

Back on the bus there are several standees. The conductor rightly insists that people like Yu with his photographic equipment and the heavily laden PLA man behind him move their luggage and share their two person seats. The men who sit are deaf mutes and talk to each other in sign language and to others in big, good natured gestures which soon have the whole bus laughing. Pretty much the entire group which boarded at Akasun are deaf mutes, and the bus is full of their gestures. We are back in the Tarim Valley and have just crossed the river, which is very wide. Either the river gets bigger as we move toward its source or the other rivers we have crossed were channels and tributaries. After crossing the main river we also cross four deep, swift channels which are rivers in themselves. On a hill above the river is by far the largest cemetery I have seen in China. The PLA soldier behind us says one of his army friends is buried there. The cemetery is for the PLA and other Hans, like the Shanghai youth. So the Hans trapped out here get at least one advantage their eastern counterparts do not, burial in the traditional Han way. The earth out here is not crowded. Bodies can be put into it instead of being cremated. If I or my friends died here, would they put our bodies into it? So we could go from this hell on earth to a Chinese or Judeo-Christian hell under the earth? This place fills me with such gloomy bodings. The cemetery reminds me of Fred Hampton, Bruce

Johnson, Manuel Ramos, all the friends killed in a struggle I ran from. If I were buried here, my tombstone should read, "He died of shame." The PLA man also tells us that the PLA arrived in 1950 and built this entire area. I wonder if either the local people or the Shanghai youth would agree. We are now traveling in the desert, parallel to and just above the valley, dry stone above a line of lush green.

The dinner stop is in a small hole of a town, but to the delight of my companions there are wun tun. Not for the first time Z is taken for a Hong Kong ren, this time by a white faced Weigur woman baoing the dumplings. She looks terrible, her face plastered with powder moistened and runnelled with sweat. Z picks thru the filling of her wun tun, removing the meat. I put her meat into my bowl, and she looks at me with the disgust I feel toward her Shanghai daintiness so out of place here. Whiteface begins from dough and rolls it into a huge circle, folds it, cuts it into pieces, baos it quickly and efficiently. But not fast enough for one of the patrons, who complains she is too slow and starts a big argument. Other women workers rapidly come to the defense of their comrade. They take no nonsense, put down the man with the speed and dexterity he accused whiteface of lacking, leaving him stalking around in helpless frustration. I should have known from the wun tun: all the women workers except white face are Shanghai ren. When Z realizes this, she stops picking the meat out of her wun tun. You can take the girl out of Shanghai, but.... Remind me not to take the girl out of Shanghai for too long: these women show how acidic the dainty Shanghai in the girl can turn.

These women too came here twenty four years ago and hate the place. When they learn where we are heading, they make faces and tell us how dirty and foul smelling Kashi (and, by implication, this place) is. Does the native coworker they defended know what they think? I suspect she can understand some Shanghaihua; she hears it constantly, for Shanghainese will speak nothing else among themselves. She seems to be something of a convert, perhaps even a sort of groupie. The gospel of civilization, the gospel of Shanghai, must appeal to those who have never seen heaven and live out here in hell. And the animated scene of talking and complaining in Shanghaihua must be repeated every time someone from Shanghai passes thru, but probably Shanghai ren who still live in Shanghai are a rare and special treat. Later I am told that amidst all the complaining one Shanghai woman actually praised Xinjiang, said there is more room to live in and that the food is better because there are more fresh fruits and eggs. Of course her last memories of Shanghai food would have been during the three terrible famine years.

If I had stayed on in Lincoln Park and survived, I suppose I would be finding reasons to praise it as this woman does Xinjiang. Lincoln Park still haunts my memory. Even the Chinese novel I occasionally contemplate, altho it will be set in the future, is full of hidden references to Lincoln Park. I can't write anything serious without starting in Lincoln Park. Probably I'll never resolve the issues it raised for me, but I'm getting a new perspective out here in the desert. I loved it, but when the crunch came, when I knew I would either die there or go crazy, I left Lincoln Park and I left Priscilla. I chose again. I loved B.C. too. But I left B.C. and I left P to come to China. I chose again again. Yet as often as I ran from the consequences of my beliefs, I never stopped believing. Perhaps not having to pay the piper for my beliefs is what kept me believing. These poor slobs – well, there's a great instance of the word that first springs to my pen being utterly inappropriate: imagine calling Shanhai ren slobs – well, there's a great instance of my mind trying to get me off track: finding a semantic quibble to keep me from having to say what I'm going to have to say next – stopped believing yet must continue to suffer the penalty for having once believed. This really is hell for them, an eternal, inescapable punishment for their youthful faith. Meanwhile, I came to China, the happy warrior ever in quest of the faith the rest of my generation lost, and here I am, touring hell, encountering people who cannot run, watching all I believed in crumble into desert sand, hoping it can somehow hold its shape, like those ancient ghost cities.

I do not know what he said in the last half of that paragraph, but I know one thing he was thinking. He did not have to say it. He was thinking about choosing again again again. He was thinking about running away from me and China too. I felt that then, and I feel it now.

He knows no thing. He will never learn that. He is wrong about every thing. Maybe one of the women did say a few good things about Xinjiang. Those things were obvious. No place is all bad. No place in China is hell. That is just a way of talking. Only a American would take the word literally. The woman who said the good things still hated Xinjiang. All of them did. They all wanted to escape. They all wanted to go back to Shanghai. Maybe Jack did not understand this when I told him what the woman said. We have a idiom about people who hear one thing and understand ten, but Jack is a person who has to hear ten things to understand one. But maybe he wrote down these things because he did not want to understand. He wanted to think that Xinjiang was better than Shanghai. He wanted to get rid of me. All the bad things he says about Hans are really insults at me. On the bus he asked me what would happen if the people we met returned to home, to Shanghai. I told him they would not be able to get a job. They would not be able to live there for very long. In the end they would have to go back to Xinjiang. You must live where your hukou says. "No way out," he said. He looked sad, but I was not sure if he was feeling sorry for the Shanghai people or for himself because there was no way out of his marriage with me. But in his diary he keeps saying it was all about Chicago. "Zhe shi guojia huozhe jianyu?" he said then. He was trying to ask if China was a country or a jail. I pointed out that in a either/or question he had to use "haishi," not "huozhe." He looked angry again. He started speaking English, and he spoke very fast. He knew I would not be able to understand him. It seemed like he was always angry at me, and I was tired of it. I turned back to Qiu and spoke to him in Shanghaihua. I did not talk to Jack again until we got off the bus for the night.

We spend the night at Shanchakou, another Han stockade but this one's *accommodations much inferior to yesterday's. The place is in the desert with no fresh water. It seems to exist primarily because three roads meet here. The weather outdid itself this evening: a desert duststorm followed by a thunderstorm with big hail. The thunder and lightning at dusk were awe inspiring. Something was needed to settle the dust, but the storm settled it into thick mud which left us trapped in the stockade, at least if we did not want to slip and wade. I wouldn't have gone far anyhow. We didn't arrive here until 9:45, and I was both exhausted and pissed at the others because they refuse to speak putunghua no matter how much and how many times I ask them to. The bus drivers get a rakeoff, one yuan for each person they deliver to this place (and, no doubt, the other place we stopped), a Han whose family came from Guandong in 1956 informs us. Is that why we stopped here? Or is it because the Hans feel a real need for the stockade? There are Hans from many places here. I suppose they all have some complaints, but none of the others show the resentment of the ex Shanghai youth. The Pole might call all the Hans out here prison laborers because they can't leave, but only the Shanghai youth think of themselves that way. I suppose these are all exiles, but you have to think of home as paradise to think of yourself as a prisoner. If the Shanghai youth are prisoners, they are political prisoners, imprisoned because they believed in Mao's ideals. Exiled from heaven, imprisoned in hell. My exile is self imposed and I'm just passing thru.*

The place was *Sanchakou*, not *Shanchakou*. San means three. Jack knew it was a place where three roads meet, but he could not figure out that would be in the name. It seems like he was thinking mostly about politics, not language or me. Maybe I should call it Poleitics. It was ten days since he saw the Pole, but he was still worrying about the Pole's words.

July 31

I had a Freudian wish fulfilment dream last night. I dreamed my Shanghai friends were stuck in the mud, being sucked in. They cried for help, but no one came because no one could understand their dialect. They could not escape.

Wow. I can't believe I wrote that. I'm working hard to leave out much of the dream, which drenched me with dread. I woke up all in a sweat and not just because the storm caused a spike in the humidity. The lake may have been mud in the desert and mud in my dream, but it was blood in my mind. I think the little cemetery we saw yesterday must have been in the dream too because I woke with words in my head: "In the Xinjiang desert he drowned in a Chicago lake." The words on my tombstone. And my first thought when I figured out I was awake was that I was soaked in blood, not sweat. The storm may have prompted a lake of mud dream, but yesterday's thinking about Lincoln Park and my murdered friends turned the mud into my lake of blood. Like the figures in my dream, like all these lost Shanghai souls who believe that where they are is who they are, I cannot escape. What I ran from in Lincoln Park is me. It's not this place. Myself am hell.

Is Jack's dream about me or about Lincoln Park? Does he want me to sink in the mud, or is he afraid he is sinking? On the trip I was sure he wanted to get rid of me, but now some times I am sure and some times I am not. Maybe he was going through a hell in his own mind, and I suffered because of that, not because of me.

    10:30: Stop at Shuigu, which has a large blue reservoir (not Tarim water) and the most colorful mountains yet, flattopped, purple, orange, red, green, white, low and dry, streaked with an ever changing kaleidoscope of colors. Easily the nicest we have seen, yet I cannot appreciate them. I too have come down with diarrhea and am either too sick or too tired to function normally. My eyes are especially tired. Some passengers roll quite neat cigarettes out of newspaper, but others roll fat, wet, ugly stogies. Their tobacco, or whatever it is, seems especially nasty. Z's and my eyes both smart badly on the bus but are fine once we get off. Smoking should not be allowed on a closed bus, but a prohibition might be the only thing that could unite the Han and Weigur males. Of course females don't smoke or count. Did I count for anything, accomplish anything, in Lincoln Park, where I still smoked? Am I any better because I quit smoking and started running when I left?

    2:00: Coming into Kashi, the river full of people, machines and donkeys all working to build up the banks in fear of flooding. It has been an unusually wet year all over Xinjiang (and most of China too). Kashi is small and old. We passed at least two larger, much more modern cities on the way here, but they lacked the charm with which this place bubbles. It looks downright medieval. I'll try to describe it when I have more time and feel more up to it.

    First things first: I'm off the bus. Thank god. I'm off the ass busting, back breaking, body racking, lung retching, eye tearing, ideal shattering bus for good. I told the others I intend to fly to Urumqi. They can take the bus if they like, and I will meet them. Meanwhile, we start our stay in Kashi by taking a donkey cart from the bus station to the new binguan. What an improvement over the bus: I can actually move. The ride, like the city, is funny, funky, charming, quaint, but the driver spoils it by trying to hit us for five yuan when we had clearly agreed on a price of two yuan, and the place we get to is all wrong: expensive, architecturally and culturally incongruous and on the new side of town, the side with little worth looking at.

    This was my birthday, but Jack does not say that in his diary. I do not think he said it to me either. We did not talk much. Jack was still angry, and he was beginning to be sick. In China we believe that too much anger can make you sick. But so can dirty food. The food was very unclean in Xinjiang. We were all a little sick, but Jack got much sicker than the rest of us. He was usually very healthy, and he could eat any thing without getting sick. I was the one who usually got sick from unclean food, but Jack ate a lot of things I did not in Xinjiang. And he was often angry.

    Jack grew sick and I grew up in this desert, this hell. I will use Jack's curse word for it. That is what all the Shanghai people who lived there called it too.

They said the sky fell and the earth sank when they moved there. Not all of
Xinjiang was hell. Urumqi was nice, and eastnorth of Urumqi, where we did not
go, are *Tian Shan*, Heaven Mountains and *Tian Chi*, Heaven Lake. Maybe they
are called heaven because the rest of the province seems like hell. To foreigners
like Jack hell is hot, but Chinese like me do not mind heat. To us hell is dry.
Wuhan was as hot as Xinjiang, but Wuhan was not hell because it was not dry.
When we were in Xinjiang, people kept worrying about floods, but it was the
driest place I ever went to. It made me know how the wonderful, juicy grapes at
Turpan turned into raisins. I felt like I was growing old and drying up like one
of them. I was a child before I came here. That is what all the Shanghai people
in the desert said too. They said they were foolish children. They said they were
tricked into coming here. They said they learned a lot here, but they did not
want to. They wanted to stay children. They wanted to stay in Shanghai. I did
too, but I was luckier than they were. I could go back to Shanghai. But I would
not be the same. I would not be a child again.

Kashi was the capitol of hell. The Shanghai people in the desert told
me how backward Kashi was, but I did not understand until I saw it. The
Shanghai people built up the small villages in the desert. They did not have
much money, but they made them as modern as they could. They tried to
use modern machines and build modern buildings. Kashi was not like that.
Kashi was already there, and it did not change. It did not want to be modern.
Except for a few new buildings built by Hans and a big statue of Mao, it hardly
changed from how it was in the Qing Dynasty. Horses and donkeys were used
instead of cars and trucks. Later I went to Qiqihar in Heilongjiang. They used
animals there too, but that was because people were poor. They wanted cars
and trucks, but often they could not buy them. They used animals because
they had to. They used them to pull heavy loads. They rode bicycles for their
own travelling. In Kashi there were not even many bicycles. People went from
one place to another in horse and donkey carts. It seemed like the people
there wanted to stay in the past. This was interesting to me because I was a
historian. I got to see how the past looked. But I only like to study the past. I
never want to live in it. No wonder the Shanghai people could not live with
the minorities around them. Chinese people, specially Shanghai people, want
to be modern. These minorities did not want that. That is why Kashi seemed
strange at first. Later it seemed terrible.

Jack was always changing on the trip, but in Kashi was where he changed
the most. Every one changed in that dry hell. I felt like a grape that was turning
into a raisin, but Jack was much worse. He dried into a shell. When he was very
sick, it seemed like there was no thing inside him. I think I am just beginning to
understand a little. I think maybe Jack did lose some thing inside him. He lost
his American confidence. The jails and the Pole told him that he did not know
China, and the Shanghai people in the desert told him that he did not even

know himself. His pride fell until it touched the ground, but he did not do what
a Chinese would do. He did not hold his anger and swallow his voice. I think
he came to China because he was running away from what happened to him in
North America. He failed in Chicago, and he failed in his American marriage.
He came to China because he thought it was better. He thought it was socialism.
He believed in Chairman Mao. But on the trip he saw what we Chinese all saw
in the Cultural Revolution. He saw that Chairman Mao was not a god. He saw
that socialism was not perfect. He kept thinking about the jails and about what
the Pole said. He kept thinking about the Shanghai people in the desert. He
kept thinking about Lincoln Park. He thought so much it made him angry and
sick. He lost the belief inside him. At first that made him angry. That is why
we fought so much. He lost his belief in China, so he wanted to fight with his
Chinese wife. Later it made him sick, and he seemed like a empty shell.

Jack does not say this in his diary, but I can guess it. I can guess it from
what he does say and from what he said to me in Xinjiang. Jack always said
Xinjiang is not China. He thought he can understand that because he is not
Chinese too. That is just why he can not understand it. The people in Xinjiang
were Chinese, but most of them were minorities. They did not look Chinese.
Most of them did not even speak Chinese. They knew even less about Chinese
culture than Jack did. They did not follow Chinese customs. At this time Chinese
could only have one child in the family, but these minorities could have many.
We met one woman who had six young children. Does it seem like she was not
Chinese? That is what Jack would say. But the reason she could have so many
children is because she was Chinese. The Chinese government said it was ok.
We Chinese understood that Chinese minorities did not have to act Chinese.
We gave them rights we did not give ourselfs. If they were not Chinese, then we
could not give them so many rights. Jack could not understand this. He could
only see the differences.

August 1

*ONE YEAR! Mud colored boys bask naked in the sun next to the stream in
which they have been swimming. It looks as if the water has imparted its color to them.
The uniform darkness of the boys is proof that they never wear clothes when playing
in the sun. Shorts seem to be unknown in this hot land. A horse cart jingles by and
a donkey brays its strange cry. Everywhere horses and donkeys (and a few oxen) stand
about chewing or walk or trot along pulling carts. This is the first place I have ever been
where the basic means of transport is animal. The sun is hot, but the shade is mercifully
cool, especially when we sit in it sipping a drink of flavored ice. The last oasis, the oasis
at the end of the road, at the end of the world.*

At least Jack says two words about our anniversary in his diary, but was
he talking about one year of happiness or one year in jail? I can not tell. Before

we came to Xinjiang, I thought he was happy, but now I did not know. I asked him if he was happy, and he said he was, but I was not sure. He did not give me my birthday present, a dress he bought in Turpan, until today, one day late. I thought maybe that was because he was thinking that maybe he would not give it to me. Because he stopped loving me. But maybe it was because he was sick and tired. I did not know. I was worried.

August 2

    Lying in bed listening to the sounds of the outside world is pleasant, perhaps the only pleasant place in a Chinese city. Or perhaps the pleasure here is that this isn't a Chinese city. The distant and nearby braying of the donkeys, the clip clop and jingle jangle of the bells on the horse carts, the occasional shouts of the donkey drivers: how much nicer than the nasty roars of the rare motorized vehicles. How much nicer than the constant horn blaring of a Chinese city. I think – hope – I am feeling a little better today. I'm sure I will feel better if I can stop thinking about where I want the world to be and where it was and focus on where I'm at, this strange but somehow familiar world of god knows what century.

    The Kashgar Bazaar is huge, packed with fascinating people and things. We bought an oriental wool rug for three hundred yuan, leather boots for thirty yuan, two fur hats for twenty five and fifteen yuan, a dress for twelve yuan. Bargaining for rugs was an especially long, hot, arduous battle which lasted hours. We had actually bought one, larger but not as nice as the one we ended up with, for four hundred yuan, but Z carelessly flashed some FEC (which we had denied possessing) and the dealer got greedy and reneged. This surprised and angered the Jew in me. I have been taught that anything goes in the bargaining, but once a deal is struck, it is sacred. Obviously that is not the custom here, in this land which must be similar to the ones of my forefathers. Our horse cart driver on the way back also tried to get more than we had agreed to, the second time in a row that has happened. Is there no honor among these thieves? Actually the horse cart ride was worth extra – or less if you are like the Chinese, timid. It was better than a roller coaster ride and scared the shit out of Z. Me too sometimes if the truth be known, especially after we saw another horse go down on the same road. Our driver took us down a small dirt back road full of pocks and mounds, then down a steep hill and an even rougher road, all the roads thronged with other horse and donkey carts and often too narrow for two to pass. The driver had to get off and lead the horse by hand while Z and I continued to hang on for dear life. The scene from the top of the hill was straight out of an oriental Breughal, a mass of people and animals, each individual, each heading its own way. I wanted desperately to snap a photo but dared not let go of whatever I was grasping for dear life, and Z was crying out in terror much of the time, especially after she saw the other horse go down. The atmosphere of the whole day was that of a world I thought long gone, a painting by an Old Master, a page from history, not the present.

    Bargaining somehow does not seem quite so hateful to me in this place. It's part of the art, part of the atmosphere of the past. But for the same reason it's hard to conceive of this place as a part of China. And it's not just because of the strange culture or even because of all the jails we passed on the way here. These days it's hard to conceive of China as a part of China, a part of socialism. For me one essence of socialism is that it puts a fair price on everything, abolishes bargaining, eliminates the constant quest for cash and the desire to screw others to get it. The China I discovered in 1983 was full of those ideals, and altho I am willing to make an exception of Kashgar for the sake of local color, I am not willing to forgive Deng Xiao Ping and the present government for reinstating money grubbing.

No doubt the problems China is encountering are the old, musty problems of socialism in an undeveloped country. How much easier it would have been if socialism had first come to the developed world as Marx expected. Now when a revolution succeeds in an undeveloped country, the pressure for development, for the products and technology which are at present in the domain of the capitalist world, is greater than the pressure for socialism and its relative equality. Socialism gets lost in the flurry for development. If only the Chinese government would clearly state socialistic goals, admit that it is temporarily putting off achievement of them in order to develop the economy but insist that they are still the goals and must never be completely obscured by the quest for money and development. Then I might be able to accept some of the current money grubbing. But since Mao China has steadfastly refused to formulate any goals other than development – the almighty Four Modernizations – and uses socialism only as a bogeyman to prevent criticism of the Party and movement toward genuine democracy. And opponents it can't scare it puts behind those high walls, under those guard towers. Which Mao must have built. You see, you damn Pole, I can criticize China and Mao. I won't fall into your trap: you were no better than the Party; you used socialism as a bogeyman to prevent praising China. Ha, ha: I don't even know your name, but you have become my bogeyman.

I get sadistic pleasure from watching my three Han companions in this place where no one speaks their lingo. They are at a total loss, stumble from one person to another asking questions and receiving either no answers or incomprehensible ones, sinking deeper and deeper into the slough of despond, unable to believe what is happening to them in their own country, unable to grasp that this is not their country. The Hans who live here seem to stay in their own little groups and make no effort (except, probably, on direct orders from above) to learn the local language. Yu's father's friend, whom we visited, works here yet seems to know nothing of the world surrounding him, but perhaps he is a special case, a scientist working on a short term project (a study of the water situation) and not a permanent resident. The PLA men on our bus are much more permanent, and the one we talked to most knew a fair bit about Xinjiang. He knew the geography, but he did not speak the language or seem to know much about the people. And the "educated Shanghai youth" live by themselves, speak Shanghaihua and keep to themselves even after twenty four years here. In hell, they call it.

Z couldn't understand why the people here don't learn Hanyu, thought that was their only path to progress and broader horizons. Perhaps because I still feel lousy I baited her a bit, said it was as logical for the Hans to learn Uygur (I'd better start spelling it as Uygurs do, not "Weigur," as Hans do) as vice versa and that Hanyu was no better than this language (whose proper name I do not even know, but it is a melodious language, a peaceful, bubbling spring of a language full of constant rises, as if each sentence is a journey upward with a little burst of joy as it reaches the surface; it is easy to see why it is so often sung, not easy to see how it would be much good for arguing or cursing tho no doubt it, like every language, has its methods). The inborn Han sense of superiority, the four thousand years of civilization in the genes of every Han, the spirit which Great Walled out the rest of the world, which calls China tian xia, under heaven, as if the rest of the world doesn't count, is over hell, is simply too much to deal with logically. But the tiny tots of the area have a rather different perception of the world: they don't know ni hao, zai jian or any word of Hanyu, but they all can and do say "bye bye" and "hello." I pointed that out to Z, who did not find it amusing.

The people, especially the women, are lovely and friendly. One grandma walked along with us bubbling with her slight knowledge of Hanyu but speaking of the bazaar in rising bursts from her wellspring of language even when she was attempting Hanyu. A younger woman invited us into her yard to see her six children, whom Yu lined up and took many photos of but did not, even after I suggested it, take her name and address so he could send her copies. None of the Shanghainese would want many children, but there is incredible jealousy that minority people can have many and they are limited to one. The woman had a lovely courtyard garden and grape arbor – not that these grapes can compare to those of Turofan in either quantity or quality – but a glance thru a doorway revealed an almost bare, dark interior. Poverty is the concomitant of the local color. If the people could afford it, they would not be riding donkeys and horses. For back at the room it's jingle bells, jingle bells, jingle all the day.

It may be just our TV, which doesn't work well and may not draw in all the stations, but we can't get any programs not in Hanyu. If there really are no programs in Uygur, this is a gross insult to Xinjiang natives.

I could not care what was on TV, but you can see from what Jack wrote that he was already in a bad mood. We had a argument after Jack wrote this. Maybe he was just sick, but maybe he wanted to fight. Maybe that is why he said he wanted to go to a Xinjiang restaurant for dinner when he knew that I wanted to eat in the hotel. We did eat in the hotel with Qiu and Yu, but Jack was very unhappy. He did not eat much. He did not talk. During the day I thought he was feeling better, but now I could see that he was still sick. After dinner Jack and I walked together. Jack kept complaining that the food in the hotel was too bad and too expensive, but I knew he was sick, so I tried not to argue with him. Then he wanted to go in to a Weigur restaurant. I ate full, so I did not want to eat more, but he said he wanted dessert. He always wants dessert. It is a silly American idea. Why ruin the taste of a good meal with something sweet? I went in with him. The place was very dirty. How could I let him eat such dirty food? I pulled him out. He was very angry. I tried to tell him that he was already sick, and he must not eat such dirty food. He said the food was fine. He said the dirt was in my mind, or maybe he said my mind was dirty. I told him that when we went to Canada, he would have to protect me, but in China it was my duty to protect him.

That is when the argument really started, and you can see he started it. He said Xinjiang was not China. He said that to make me angry, but I tried to remember that he was sick. I tried to control myself. I explained about the history of Xinjiang in China. The more I told him about history, the more mad he got. He said many silly things. When I told him about the Sui dynasty princess who was given to marry a Xinjiang prince, he asked if Canada was a part of China too because he married me. I reminded him of the Shanghai people we met on the bus to Kashi. Why would they leave the city they loved to come to the desert? They came to Xinjiang to build China, not a foreign country. That is when he got the most angry. Now I know that is because he thought they were like him. He thought they came to Xinjiang for the same reason he came to Lincoln Park in Chicago. That is silly too. China and America are very different, so the reasons can not be the same. There was no Chairman Mao in America. There was no Socialist Education Movement. Jack came to Lincoln Park to be different from his family and his friends and his class. The Shanghai people came to Xinjiang to be the same. It was what all young people wanted to do at that time. Every one wanted to do what Chairman Mao wanted them to do. I explained this to Jack. He said that when he fought against the American government, he wanted to do what Chairman Mao wanted too. But how could a American understand Chairman Mao? Maybe I am just beginning to understand. Chairman Mao always wanted change, and Jack loved change. Deng Xiao Ping wanted stability. That is why Mao did not like Deng. That is why Jack did not like Deng. In America what Jack wanted did not matter. In America Jack was like a paper person trying to kill the paper tiger. But in China Jack was not a paper person. He was my husband. Some times his words had sharp teeth and claws.

"*Weishenma Zhongua de zhengfu bu rang renmin zhu zai ziji yao de difgang?*" Jack asked me in his bad Chinese. He was trying to ask why the Chinese government does not let people live where they want to. "Because Shanghai would sink into the ocean from all the people who came there," I told him. I was trying to be funny, and he laughed. But he did not laugh in a funny way or a nice way. "It is true," I told him. "Chinese people always want to live in Shanghai." "Fools," he said softly. Or maybe he said, "Fool." I do not know if he changed to English because he did not know the Chinese word or because he was already angry or because he did not want me to know what he said. "What means that?" I asked. "Know thyself," he said. I know that now. It is Shakespeare, I think. I did not know what he meant then, but I knew he was being unpolite even if I did not understand his words. I thought he was answering "no" to my question. *"Ni weishenma name bu keqi?"* (why are you so unpolite?) I asked. I think he got mad because he thought I understood what he said. He did not want me to understand his words. Or maybe he got mad because I talked Chinese. He knew I was getting mad because I did that. But I was not really mad yet. I was still talking *putonghua*. And I was talking softly.

"All you Shanghainese are the same," he said. "You think Shanghai is heaven." His voice kept getting louder. We were on the street. I hate being yelled at in public, and he was almost shouting now. "All you Hans are the same. You think only China is under heaven. Any one who is not a Han is a barbarian. You think I am a hairy foreign devil." That was not fair. I did not understand all he said, but I understood that. That is what Chinese called foreigners around the time of the *Yi He Tuan* Rebellion in 1900. I never said that. I never heard any Chinese say that. But I knew the words. We talked about this before. Jack knew those words were out of date. He wanted to curse me. He was cursing me by saying I was cursing him. So I really cursed him. "Tamada," I said. Softly. "Yours too," he said back. He knew that word, and he insulted my mother. So I changed to some Shanghai words he did not know, and I am afraid I did not say them so softly. And he cursed me in English. In those times all our arguments ended like that. Maybe one reason we do not argue as much now is because we usually know what the other one is saying. It is harder to forget insults you understand, so you have to be more polite. Usually he walked out after a argument. He went for a run or a walk or a bike ride. In Canada he often splits wood. I always wonder if he is hitting me in his mind with his axe. But he was too tired for any thing like that tonight, and we were already out. As soon as I shouted at him, I felt ashamed. I wanted to run back to the hotel. But I made myself walk. "*Tila, tila, tila,*" he shouted at my back. That was the way he cursed *Shanghaihua*. We often say "*tila*." It makes emphasis. It is like adding "est" to a word in English. Jack came back to the hotel later. I could smell the dirty food on his breath. It was not one of our big arguments. We had a bigger one the next night. At least that one was in private. I did not have to control myself. I do not know why I did not control myself in public. It seemed like there was some thing in the air in Xinjiang. That is why people called it hell. I would never shout on a Shanghai street.

August 3

I have just figured out the essential difference between what is happening in China and what happens in Kashgar – and, as a result, the difference in my feelings about both. Listening to the old woman describe the action at the bazaar was itself a pleasure and should have told me. These are not cold hearted business people interested only in money. They enjoy buying and selling and bargaining. So the rug salesman who reneged was not typical. That's why after a day of shopping here I didn't have the sour feelings I usually have after shopping in China. On the other hand, Han exploitation is pure money grubbing and makes me furious: we just got plane tickets to Urumqi and I must pay an extra hundred yuan for the same ticket (the Chinese pay 165 yuan, I 265). And for this room I pay double the price Z does. I hate it. There is not even a pretence of fairness. It is an arbitrary, unavoidable fraud perpetrated on me by a government I came here to help, a government which professes to believe, as I do strongly, in internationalism.

I struck out on my own today, partly because Z and I had a stupid quarrel and she won't back down even tho I did. I can't believe we had such a big fight over such a little thing. Indeed, I don't believe we had such a big fight over such a little thing. Ostensibly we were arguing about food. Actually we were arguing about this trip, about being too tired and too uncomfortable for too long and, mainly, about China, about my losing faith in China, about the underside of the mask, about Han history and characteristics. When we got to that is when things got nasty. I said some things about her people that she did not deserve. That's why I backed down and apologized for my side. But why can't she do the same? I suppose not being able to say I'm sorry is the other side of Z's lack of self confidence. In the early days of the marriage she wanted to take the blame for everything, now for nothing. It will hurt her to tears when she finally does back down. At least I hope she will. If she does not, she is asking me to treat her as I suspect she has been treated most of her life, as a pretty child who can never be wrong. But it's hard even to think of her that way here. It's as if without China Z is simply the last letter of the alphabet. She seems to be aging before my very eyes, her childlike tinkle of a voice growing harsh, her hair brittle, even her babysoft skin going ugly, drying and scaling in the desert air.

Ugly. He called me ugly. I knew it. I knew he stopped loving me.

But the main reason I left was that the Han eating habits simply became too much for me. They won't eat anywhere but in the hotel. They missed breakfast today and decided to wait four plus hours for lunch before going out. It's ludicrous. They're scared to death of anything not Han, not people so much as customs. They won't live in a local hotel: unsafe. The binguan, of course, is just another Han stockade against the natives (even tho the employees are non Hans; the bosses are Han). The one occasion when I did manage to get them into a local restaurant (because they were starving and too far from the binguan) Z supervised every aspect of the cooking, telling the cook what and what not to use (allowing no meat, e.g.) and standing over him the whole time. On my own today I got my first authentic local meal of the entire trip. I'm glad now I did not get the job I had hoped to get in Xinjiang. Living and teaching here I would be constantly siding with the Uygurs against the Hans and constantly arguing with Z about it, and that arguing would be worse than what goes on between the two of us. Personal quarrels we might be able to work out because there is a year of love on both sides, but her Han nature is thousands of years old.

He talks about love, but he still insults me and all Hans. We tried not to eat the Xinjiang food because a lot of it was dirty. It did not even test good.

In my wanderings I found the old binguan. Its sign reads "JOINT BUILDING HOTIL WITH CIVILIZATION." I was told the place was once the Russian Consulate, and it looks to have some character, which the new binguan certainly does not. Not only does it match the local color, it is cheaper than the new binguan: the Shanghainese lied to me about that. Which reminds me: last night I dreamed of Mao; he was beaming down at me. Only when I awoke did I realize it was not Mao, only a picture of him. And only when I discovered that the Shanghainese had lied to me about prices at the old binguan did I realize that the picture of Mao was the one on our marriage certificate. Would a marriage certificate with a picture of Mao have legal standing in Canada, let alone the U.S.? If I returned alone, she would never be able to follow me anyhow. What I really wish is that I could get up into those high, beautiful mountains (7600 meters!) I could see yesterday morning altho they are 190 kilometers away. During the day they are not visible altho it looks clear. It only takes a little smoke to obscure them, and this being a weekday the bureaucracy is smoking away. If I had my backpacking gear, I'd set out for them today – without asking anyone's permission.

Back at the new binguan I discover that this is a big night for Kashgar: the local news (for the week?) is shown on the local TV station – in Hanyu, read by a Han announcer, featuring news of the Hans in Xinjiang from a Han point of view. The whole thing seems to me to be a greater insult than no news at all, and since this is a locally produced program there can be no claim that doing it in Uygur is too difficult or expensive.

Jack wanted me to apologise for our argument, but I did not want to. Reading his diary tells me I was right. The argument was his fault. He stopped loving me. He stopped loving China. He wanted to escape from me. He wanted to escape from China. That is why he argued with me. The argument was not my fault. None of it was. In Kashi I tried not blame Jack too much because I knew he was tired and sick, but I was right not to take blame when I did not do any wrong thing. Chinese did that too much in the Cultural Revolution. People let themselfs lose their faces, but that did not help them. That made things bitterer, not better. Now the dry air was making my face ugly, and Jack was trying to make me lose my face by insulting my people and my country. I could not agree. I could not apologise. When he apologised, he apologised to me. He did not apologize to my country or my people. I did not really care about the government, but I thought how could he love a Chinese woman if he hated China? I remembered all the things I heard about foreigners. All the things I forgot. How quickly they fell in love, how quickly they fell out of love. Jack always had many strange, foreign habits, but this was the first time in more than a year that he seemed like a foreigner to me.

Our fighting kept on. We were fighting now, not just arguing like we did before. Before Xinjiang we might argue for one or two days, but then we would make love and forget it. Well, I think Jack forgot. I remembered, but I knew how careless Jack was. So I could forgive him for being careless because he loved me. But in Xinjiang we did not make love. At first I thought that was because we had very little private time, and when we did Jack was too hot or too sick. But now I was beginning to worry that it was because Jack stopped loving me. I did not know how to stop the fighting. I did not know what to do. I felt some terrible thing would happen, but I could not stop. That was like the Cultural Revolution too. I think when ever Chinese think of a disaster, we think of the Cultural Revolution. My teacher once said we knew we were riding toward a deep hole, but we could not pull the rope to stop the horse. It was like that in Xinjiang too. It was good when Jack and I were separate. Every time we were together it was a disaster. We argued about every little thing. We fought like children. When I remember now, I think how could grown up people say such silly things? But we were married children. I was fighting for my marriage. I did know that. I wonder if Jack did. All his words were about politics.

"Why you suddenly hate my China?" That is me talking. Jack was always criticising China these days. I have to remember. I have to write Chinglish. I am sorry, but I have to write the way we talked then. I know it was silly. But suddenly every thing was silly. Very silly and very terrible.

"*Wo bu hun Zhongguo. Wo hun jianyu. Wo hun zhengfu tou zoule renmin de freedom. Xifang de Zhongguo shi yi feichang da de jianyu.*" (I not hate China. I hate jail. I hate government steal away people's freedom. West of China one very huge jail.)

"You hate me. You say *zhengfu* (government), but you mean me. You think I take away your *ziyou* (freedom)."

That was a mistake. Arguing about freedom with Jack was always a mistake, and I should not have said he hated me. I thought he did, but maybe he did not know. Foreigners often do not know what they know. Maybe I told him. Maybe that is why he looked at me like he did. *Aiya.* What a look! I almost said he hit me. He did not hit me, but he wanted to hit me. He looked at me like he saw me for the first time and he hated what he saw. The look he looked at me felt like a hit in the face. A hard hit. But he still talked about China, not me. "*Keneng dou Zhongguo shi yi feichang da de jianyu,*" (maybe all China is one very huge jail), he said.

"I not a jail," I shouted. He just looked at me that same terrible way. "I not let you run away this jail," I shouted. He did not reply. I saw he stopped loving me. I became sad. "I try make you not sick," I said. "You want *ziyou sha ziji*" (freedom kill yourself).

He did not want to talk about us, but he was always very happy to talk about freedom. "*Suiran wo bu yao sha ziji, rugua wo yao zhe shi wo ziji de* business."

(Although I do not want kill myself, if I want, this is my own business. Jack never used "*danshi*." When you use "*suiran*" [although] in the first part of a sentence, then you have to use "*danshi*" [but] in the second part.)

"No. You married to me. You can not *sha ziji*.

"*Neng. Ruguo wo yao, mashang sha. Ni yao sha wo* to keep *wo* from *sha ziji*." (Can. If I want, immediately kill. You want to kill me to keep me from killing myself.)

"I am not American *zhengfu*. I am not Chinese *zhengfu*. Why you want fight me? I am your wife." I was starting to cry, but he was so busy shouting about his freedom to kill himself that he did not see.

"That *zhengfu* is best which governs least."

It is not easy to talk to Jack. I wanted to talk about him. I wanted to talk about us. He wanted to talk about politics. It still makes me mad. My tears turned back into shouts. "I told you I am not *zhengfu*. I am wife. You are not Mao Zhuxi. You are husband."

"*Dui. Zhe shi wo de cuo, yiji wo de cuo.*" Now I think he was only trying to say that our argument was his fault. He was just blaming me for blaming him. But it is not a good idea to sarcastic someone in a language you do not know well. What he said was, "Right. This is my mistake, always my mistake." I thought he meant it was his mistake to marry me.

I cried. I tried not to, but I could not stop myself. I was thinking that every thing I heard about foreigners was true. Foreigners loved one year, then forgot. "You mistake," I said while I was still crying. I was not trying to criticise him. I was trying not to criticise him. I was sad and confused. I wanted to tell him that what he said was wrong. I wanted to tell him that foreigners' ideas about marriage were wrong. But maybe he thought I meant that marrying him was a mistake. I was feeling that , but I did not want to say that. I wanted to explain. I tried to explain. That was my real mistake. Saying any thing was my mistake. When I cried, he started to hold me. As soon as I talked, he let me go. He let me cry. He lay down on the bed by himself and let me cry by myself. I felt alone. I was in a strange place, and my husband was a stranger. After a while I saw that Jack was asleep. How could he sleep when I was crying? I cried for a long time. I cried because I thought my marriage was over. I cried because I almost wanted it to be over because my husband was a fool. But then I thought that maybe Jack's sickness was in his brain too. Maybe if I could cure his sickness, he might become like the man I married again. I fell asleep thinking this. When I fell asleep, I did not touch Jack.

August 4

  My companions have commenced eating canned fat. I don't know how else to describe the putrid white stuff they buy in cans (for one yuan, *six* mao) *and add to the* fangbian mian *(instant noodles) they make by letting it sit in water from the thermos. I* think this is the result of my objecting to spending three yuan plus for bad food at the hotel dining room. I thought Z and I argued about food because it symbolized so much more: it symbolizes the whole Han attitude toward life, the superiority to all others Hans feel, the condescension they show. Or so I keep telling myself. The fact is that I have known of and laughed at this attitude toward life for a long time. Why then can't I laugh at their eating habits? The food is trivial, the attitude momentous. Yet I can accept and laugh at the attitude while watching them eat in Xinjiang disgusts and angers me every time. So I will eat native food on the streets. At least if I can get that far. I virtually collapsed on the street and had to stagger back to the hotel to rest. I have some sort of illness, but what isn't clear: a slightly sore throat but no other pain, just a great weakness and weariness. Perhaps what is going on between me and Z is sapping my strength. We had another emotional quarrel and reconciliation last night. This one was even dumber than the previous one, but at least it was not about food. It was about what we should be arguing about, China. Or at least so I thought. She can't understand that the very time I am beginning to see just how little freedom exists in her country is no time for her to attempt to limit my freedom. She drove me to frustration, and I drove her to tears. Only when she cried did I realize that I was talking about the political while she had been on about the personal. It was as if the realization exhausted me. I hugged her to try to say what words keep failing to say, that we must unite, not divide, the personal and the political. But this morning I felt as bad as if I didn't hug her, as if I didn't feel the grating grit of two too dry skins rubbing, as if that rub did not remind me how sick I am, how I should not be hugging and contaminating her. This morning the air between us felt as nasty as the stuff in those cans looks.

I took a long nap but woke feeling worse than ever, feeling I've got to get out of China.... Except that what's most clear, here in Kashgar, is that I am out of China. Imperialism by any other name smells just as rotten. And feels just as inescapable. Where do I run from here? East is China and West is... what I've been running from all my life.

Qiu and Yu have just returned from an expedition to the countryside on which they were insulted several times, they assume (since they can't understand the language) for wearing shorts. People rub their fingers against their cheeks at them, a sign which means shameless. Certainly the natives wear huge amounts of clothing considering the heat of the sun. Apparently this has to do with modesty, in men as well as women. Yet the children are often naked or close to it, and I always wear shorts and have never discerned a reaction. So perhaps it is one more aspect of the Uygur-Han hostility. Qiu and Yu are really down on this place. One girl even hit Qiu with a stone from a slingshot. And one horse cart driver asked them for fifty yuan for a trip which should be one yuan fifty. I asked if they could have misunderstood, but they said no, it was clear. By late afternoon, they said, the countryside was deserted, every door locked. A festival begins tonight. They start festivals in the evening like Jews. In fact there are many similarities between the two cultures despite their enmity.

Jack is not writing much from this time. Maybe I am glad about that.
Maybe he was thinking even worse things than he wrote. It is very hard for me
to read some of the things he says about me and China. I know that when he
curses China, he is cursing me too. When he wants to run away from China, he
wants to run away from me too. I have to do just what I did then. I have to keep
telling myself he was very sick. He was very sick. That is why he is not writing
much. Before I had to cut a lot out of his diary. Now I am putting in every thing
he wrote even though that is hard. It is even harder to remember our terrible
arguments, but I remember them perfectly. But I forgot our first kiss. Writing
teaches me that memory is a curse, not a.... I can not remember the word that is
the opposite of "curse." We forget the good things and only remember the bad
things. That must be one reason it is easy to fall out of love. Maybe I should stop
writing this. Maybe Jack is not writing too much because he was sick, but maybe
he was right not to write much at this time. It was too terrible. After our big fight
suddenly we were not fighting any more. Jack says we had a reconciliation, but
I did not feel reconciliated. He should have told me if he stopped hugging me
because he did not want to make me sick. He did not say that. He did not say any
thing. That is his character. He always says too much or not enough. How could
I know what he was feeling? To me it seemed like Jack did not feel any thing. I
am surprised he felt how dry our skins were. The dry air made my skin feel terrible. I rubbed many kinds of cream on it, but no thing helped. This day Jack
was very dull. He hardly said any thing. It was worse than the fights. It seemed
like every thing inside him leaked out. All his feelings for China, for life, for me,
were gone. Maybe it was better when he was cursing.

I will stop writing. But only for now. It is more than thirteen years since all
this happened. That is time for me to understand it. In Kashi I could not understand it. I did what was easy to do. I stopped talking about it. I stopped thinking
about it. I used my energy making Jack not sick. It seemed like that worked. When
he felt better, things were better between us again. So I never had to understand.
Things were better, but they were never the same. So it is time for me to think
again. But not here. Here was not the right time for thinking then, and it is not
the right time for thinking now. I will see what Jack says in his diary when he feels
better. Maybe he will say some things that will help me understand.

August 5

*Festival: the streets clogged with people and vehicles, large families packed on horse
and donkey carts, on walking tractors, on motorcycles (a man with his young son in front
and his old father behind), on foot. But not everyone is going in the same direction to the
same place as I expected. When we arrive at the mosque, the reason becomes clear. The
streets are a solid sea of people on prayer mats, shoes off, everywhere people, people, people.
But all male, male, male. Far in the rear a very few women stand minding small children,
but this is a strictly male worship. A loudspeaker atop the mosque blares out chants, and*

at times the whole sea rises or falls as men and boys stand or prostrate themselves as one. At nine o'clock the clock in the center of town (which is on Beijing time and so reads 11:00) goes off, chiming loudly, but the services go on, ignoring the infidel interruption. A little later they are over. There is no noticeable climax or ending: the speakers simply cease and the mass of people rise, but this time not as one, slowly, leisurely, standing around then gradually beginning to mill around. Atop the mosque a great, long hornpipe sounds, then drums. The worshippers who were inside the mosque flow out to mingle with those on the outside, again like water, for surely there was no space for all those additional solid bodies. The music lasts only a minute or two but continues to echo in the ear, strange, exotic, enchanting. A few men wear robes and turbans, priests no doubt. There are many beggars in the crowd, probably doing well. After an interval the drums and horn sound again, now much more lively, and a young man and a boy begin dancing. The music is fine, but then the loudspeakers come on with competing noise and music until someone manages to turn them off. The sound and tempo of the hornpipe and drums increase, but others do not join the dance, and after a while the young man gives it up. Men simply mill about amidst the music. I am too weak for the tiger sun and sit in the shade of a building and listen. The crowd is thinning, constantly thinning. After half an hour or more at the same tempo the music slows, swells, then quickens just as I thought it was concluding. At 10:00 (noon Beijing time) the drums cease and the horn finishes off. Then the loudspeakers boom an announcement and it is over.

I thought there would be no money dealings today, but here the custom differs from Judaism. After the service at the mosque the bazaar bustles altho the big item shops, like the ones which sell carpets, seem to be closed. There is no problem getting a horse cart, thank god, Allah if necessary. Life proceeds, festival or no festival, illness or no illness. And I am ill and glad to be back at the room where I can sleep.

And sleep: I think I have slept twenty of the last twenty four hours. A strange sickness, no pain but a vast weariness and inability to move, to act, to think. To write.

Jack was very sick all this day. He was not strong enough to fight, but looking at the empty shell of him, I could not think that was good. I told him he should stay in bed, but he wanted to see the festival. He sat behind in the shade watching and writing. I went into the crowd with Qiu and Yu. I often looked back at Jack. He looked tired, small, empty, a dried up shell of himself. Some times I thought he went to sleep. When we went back to the hotel, he did go to sleep. He slept all afternoon. When I saw how sick he was, I felt sorry for fighting with him. But how could I know? He did not say how sick he was. He never does. Americans always pretend to be brave. I knew he was sick, but I could not guess how sick until this day. Now I told him he had to stay in bed. He listened this time because he was too sick to go out. Qiu and Yu left early, so I went to the festival alone this night. I heard there would be dancing, and I wanted to see. I could not bear to look at the shell of Jack, and he could sleep better if I was not there.

That night I found out there were worse foreigners than Jack. Chinese foreigners. There was dancing on the street that night, but the dancers were all men. Only men on the street again. Terrible men. They called me. I do not know what names, but I am sure they were bad ones. They made signs for me to come. They pushed against me in the crowd. They squeezed me. They tried to touch my every place. One man slapped me. Compared to them the worst of Jack's hate was love. They were animals. I felt like I was in a tiger cage with no way out. Maybe they would kill me. A PLA woman saved me. She was in uniform with a gun. She walked me all the way to the hotel. She was in Xinjiang twenty years. She told me never to go on the street alone. A woman needed a man or a gun to protect her in Xinjiang. How terrible. How different from China.

When I got in the room, Jack was asleep. I was crying. I wanted to wake Jack up, but when I touched him he was burning, and he did not wake up. So I knew he was really sick. Usually he wakes up very easy. I let him sleep, but I could not. I could not stop thinking about what happened to me. I could not stop thinking about the Xinjiang men. They were animals, not men. Then maybe I did fall asleep. I am not sure. I kept seeing the men. I could see their faces, but I could see more too. I could see the animals behind their faces, fierce tigers, wolfs, bears and other terrible animals. Maybe I cried out or jumped because Jack woke up. Usually if I wake Jack up in the midnight he is angry, but this night he was too sick to be angry. I told him what happened. I cried. He held me. I felt very cold, and his body was very hot. We needed each other. I fell asleep thinking that. When I woke up, it was light, and Jack was still asleep. I wondered if I was dreaming when I thought he woke up. He did not say any thing. He just held me. I did not know what was dream and what was real. But the Xinjiang men were real. Too real. Too fierce. They looked like Westerners, but Jack was not like them. Thank heaven and earth.

And he did wake up at midnight. He did hear what I said. His diary says so. I did not tell him the next day. I did not want to talk about it any more. I did not want to think about it. I still do not.

August 6

Thank god we're getting out of Kashgar. Z had a horrendous experience at the festival last night. If I stayed much longer I fear I'd conclude that these two utterly dissimilar races deserve each other, deserve to oppress each other. As they do. Even the hospital is closed for the holiday. On the way back from the hospital we walked away from a horse cart without paying. Part way to the hotel the driver tried to up the ante. I couldn't take anymore. These bastards keep agreeing to a price, then raising it. Z told him that if he insisted we would leave. I doubt that she intended to, but I did. He actually drove us more than half way and got nothing. I expected him to follow us and relent, but he didn't. Perhaps it was a matter of pride for him: one doesn't beg the animals, which I am more and more coming to think they consider us. This is why all the rules of business

don't apply to us. Among themselves I think business is conducted simply and fairly. I'm
utterly depressed and don't know which is depressing me more, the fact that I am coming
to share the Chinese hatred of and prejudice against these people and the fear of what
they might do (to themselves as well as China) if they were independent, or seeing the
face behind the Chinese mask of ancient wisdom and gentle courtesy, the sophisticated,
pedantic, condescending bullying which is so much worse (if only because it is done by
those I have come to love) than the juvenile bullying of the Xinjiangnese. The first might
be like unlocking the cage of a tiger in the middle of a city. But the Chinese would do
that with some kind of electronic control on the beast. They would do it to watch the fun
which ensues. Later they would electronically subdue the creature with great fanfare and
say its escape proves that tigers – like ordinary folks – must be kept in cages. They would
enjoy the bloody lesson they could preach.

    Jack was too sick to write. I think he wrote this later. I think he wrote it
on the plane. The last day in Kashi was very terrible. It was almost as bad as the
night before. Jack was very sick, but he did not want to do any thing about it.
There was no thing inside him to struggle against his sickness. He did not want
to go to the hospital. Did he know it was going to be closed? How can a hospital
close? If people get sick during a festival, are they supposed to die? Maybe I was
even worse than Jack. I kept trying not to think about the night before, and I
kept thinking about it. I was sure that Jack did not love me any more. I kept
trying not to think about that, and I kept thinking about that too. I was sure he
was going to leave me. He seemed like he already left me in his mind. He did
not look at me. He did not look at any thing. He seemed like he was some where
else. But he was very sick. I could see that. His body was burning. Getting him
to a doctor was a thing I thought I could do. I kept trying to blame all the bad
things on Jack's sickness. I thought if I could make him well, he would thank
me. Maybe he would not leave me.

    I almost had to dress Jack and carry him outside myself. He just wanted
to lie in bed until we had to go to the plane. I wish I let him. But I could not.
He was very sick, and by making him do things I made myself think he was here,
not another place like it seemed to me. The first horse cart driver was very bad.
I was still seeing the animals behind all the Xinjiang men. This one seemed like
a rat, small and fast moving but very bad, very tricky. He charged too much, but
I was afraid of him, and Jack was too sick to argue. At least I thought he was. I
am sure the driver knew the hospital was closed, but he did not tell us. He saw
how sick Jack was. I am sure he knew where a doctor was, but he did not tell us.
He took us to the hospital and left. We tried to get in. We tried every door. We
banged on every door. No one was there. Or maybe there were people there, but
they would not open the door. It was very terrible. The second horse cart driver
was different from the first one, but he looked even worse. He was very big, like
a bear, a big, fierce, stupid bear. I thought he would hurt us. Jack hardly said any

thing all day. He was too sick. But when the driver tried to raise the price and I told him we already agreed about the price, Jack suddenly shouted, *"Ting"* (stop). The driver was so surprised that he stopped. Jack got out. I wanted to tell him not to because he was too sick, but I could not argue in front of the driver, and I wanted to get away from that bear too. I did not think Jack could walk back to the hotel, but he did. He was angry, and that made him strong enough. At the hotel Jack got in bed and went back to sleep. He did not get up until we had to leave for the plane.

August 7
*   Haven't felt like writing and still don't, but I must force myself to write about Urumqi, (or Urumuqi, as the Chinese pronounce it, adding the obligatory Han syllable) where we are now. We are staying at Qiu's sister's husband's brother in law's house. Of course the Chinese have one word for this relationship, which I have simplified because I should state younger or older for each relationship. Urumqi apartments obviously have more room than those in eastern China, the city is spread out comfortably and the traffic is the most rational I have seen in China. Qiu's relatives have lived here for over twenty years (but were not volunteers from the Socialist Education Movement), but everyone including their twelve year old son speaks Shanghaihua. This is because the city is full of Shanghainese. There are also many other Hans; this is a Han, not a Uygur, city and so, for the first time since coming to Xinjiang, I feel like I am in China. I have to admit it feels good. I'd like to say it feels like coming home, but I can't say that altho I would have a month ago. It feels good only compared to how I felt in the rest of Xinjiang. Visible in the three and a half by five meter living room are a refrigerator, freezer, washing machine, TV, fan, stereo tape recorder and tropical fish aquarium. The floor is neat linoleum. All in all the most middle class living quarters I think I have seen in China. After traveling around Urumqi by bus my comment was, "Why can't this be the capitol of China?" It seems to be the first logical city to get around and live in I have encountered in China.*
*   I don't know which method of seeing a doctor, the front door or the back door, is faster. We waited for an hour for Qiu and Yu to see their acquaintance, who is head of the Urumqi Railroad Hospital, and during that time all I wanted to do was enter the hospital thru the front door and get in line. However, once the preliminaries were accomplished, I have been moved right along and given excellent care. The result apparently is going to be penicillin, which is what I have been trying to prescribe for myself from the gitgo. They will also do blood tests and x-rays, much needed I think. The interesting thing is that this is all routine. The back door saves no money and avoids no paperwork; it simply greases the wheels and insures that I get all I am entitled to with some dispatch. What I'm getting is a complete check up. At each stage one pays separately; for each test one gets a bill, takes it to a cashier, pays it, gets a receipt and presents it to the tester. It seems a bureaucratic waste, but it has moved right along. Like the city the hospital is not overcrowded. One problem it shares with eastern China is that antibiotics are given only by injection. There*

are no penicillin pills, so I will have to come in every day for a shot. I wonder why that is. It just makes that much more work for both doctor and patient as well as more paperwork. There is the usual assembly line of patients pulling their pants down for a shot in the ass. Chinese modesty stops at the hospital entrance. They administer the injections amazingly slowly. I clocked the second (and longer) shot: it took over nine minutes! Supposedly this is less painful, but it is a strange sensation, lying with my ass sticking up and a needle sticking out of it while several nurses and friends look over it and discuss me and Xinjiang. Kashi is still backward but much better than it used to be, the Han nurses assured Qiu and Yu. To me such knowledge is a pain in the ass. All these Hans prefer the roar of truck motors to the jingle of harness bells, the characterless new binguan to the old joint building hotil with civilization.

But they helped me. I found refuge in this little, misplaced but efficient corner of Shanghai just in time. My temperature had shot up and I was in pretty bad shape. The Shanghai ren acted quickly, and five different injections have helped as has a big, delicious meal, which I surprised myself by eating a whole lot of. Qiu's relatives like Urumqi, prefer it to Shanghai, for all the obvious reasons: room to live in, a convenient, uncrowded life etc. I was impressed by the ease with which they put together the feast and by the way the man automatically did the dishes and cleaned up after the meal. I feel the possibility of living like a human being again for the first time in many days.

Jack and I agree about one thing. It was good to get out of Kashi. It was great. Kashi was the worst place I ever was in. It was dirty, dusty, grubby, backward, uncivilised, unfriendly, unethical, shifty, cruel, sadistic, merciless, mercenary, immoral. And many other words I could say if I was not tired of looking through my dictionary. Jack is right. It was hell. It was specially hell for him because he was sick. It was hell for me because it was hell. The Shanghai people in the desert were right to call it that.

Urumuqi seemed like heaven to him compared to Kashi. To me too, but it was still Urumuqi, not Shanghai. The Shanghai people in Urumuqi liked it because it was convenient. Life there was more comfortable, but it was not Shanghai. They still missed Shanghai. They missed the old Shanghai, the one I miss too. They did not have to say that. That is why they kept on speaking *Shanghaihua.* When we first went to Wuhan, Jack once asked me for a special word that told why Shanghai was better than other places. I told him the word was "Shanghai." "Shanghai" means better than any other place. Every one in China knows that. Jack did not know it because he is Jack, a American. He can have many ideas about Shanghai. He can even love it, but he can not understand why. So Urumuqi seemed better than Shanghai to him. One reason it seemed better is that it cured him when he was sick. But it also seemed better because Urumuqi is logical and Shanghai is not. The sharp point is that is exactly why it is not better. Shanghai is not as convenient and comfortable and logical as Urumuqi. But it is Shanghai. There is no other place like it. It is unique. What makes it

Shanghai is that it is not logical. It is a mixture of all things which it is not logical to mix. That is why I want to write a novel about Erbao. Erbao understood that. Her life was like that too. She mixed immorality with morality, art with politics, culture with money. She was like Shanghai, and Shanghai made her beautiful. In the countryside before she came to Shanghai she was just a ordinary girl. In the countryside after she left Shanghai she seemed like such a ordinary woman that every one thought she was a widow. No one guessed she was a courtesan. But in Shanghai she was so special that the leading intellectual of the May Fourth Movement fell in love with her. Maybe her love and her ideas, Shanghai love and the crazy mixture of ideas possible only in Shanghai, helped make him the leading intellectual of the May Fourth Movement. Many more people fell in love with her. Men and women too. Me too. I love her because I found her where I needed to go to save my marriage. Then she showed me how to make myself a unique Shanghai woman who does not need to be married to have a full life. Maybe I even loved her when I was a child. Maybe she loved me. Maybe her love was as important to me as Jack's love. Maybe she showed me how to love Jack when I thought I lost him. Maybe her love showed me how to love Jack when he thought he lost me. I can not understand it all. That is why I will have to write my novel about her and Shanghai and love. My unique novel, my herstory.

August 9

The penicillin is working. I feel better today, so Z and I went to visit a Kazakh friend, a student we met in Wuhan when I mistook him for a Westerner (which he is, a western Chinese who looks and is ethnically European). Our friend wasn't there (he is in the north, Ili, near the Soviet border), but his mother insisted on inviting us in and feeding us traditional Kazakh delicacies including very sour yogurt and dried yogurt, something completely new to me, light brown chunks, very solid and tough to chew but unmistakably yogurt. Their language sounds like Uygur and is related – the two groups can generally understand each other – but not the same. Everyone in the family, parents and five kids ranging in age from a college graduate to a middle school student, speaks good putonghua. This is because the father, who has a Communist Party tattoo on his hand, studied four years in Shenyang (at university but as a member of the PLA) and is now a road bridge engineer. The woman is a teacher, and both parents say that all their coworkers are Han. Their apartment is big by Shanghai standards but smaller than Qiu's relatives' place and brightly painted, much brighter than any Han residence I have seen. One wall was covered by a huge oriental rug, three times the size of ours for two thirds the price. So our bargaining in Kashgar did not get us nearly as good a deal as we thought.

Early in our talking there came a knock on the door. A little girl brought a letter from a friend, a woman whose mother-in-law often beats and curses her. The woman had actually thrown the note out of a window because the mother-in-law had locked her in her apartment and wouldn't let her out. The note asked her friend to contact the husband's gege (older brother) because the husband is out of town on business. Our friend's mother tried but couldn't get in touch. But some time later the note thrower escaped and rushed in with two children. She and her friend conferred in private, so my main contact was with the smaller of the children, a big eyed, scared to death girl of about seven. She never said a word. There were huge quantities of food on the table and everyone tried to give her tasty morsels and encouraged her to help herself, but she just stood there, trembling and wide eyed. Altho she knew everyone in the room except Z and me, she never touched the food or spoke a word. Her mother's purpose was to leave the children here in safety while she returned to her horrible home. A classmate from out of town was coming there to meet her, and the mother-in-law's disapproval of this had started the fight. But when the mother tried to sneak out alone, the child screamed a frightful scream, ran to her and refused to let her go. So she had to take the children back with her. The family tragedy was written all over the little girl's face. After they left we were told that the husband usually supported his mother and beat his wife, saying he could get another wife but had only one mother. I had been thinking of the problem as a manifestation of Xinjiang's Muslim culture until I heard these words. On more than one occasion I have heard Hans say much the same thing. It was easy for everyone left in the room to agree the whole thing was feudal, but no one thought anything could be done about it unless the woman wanted to attempt to get a divorce.

Jack was feeling better, and we were not fighting. But we were not the same. There was a space inside him and a space between us, a silence. We did not talk about us. We did not talk about China. For the first time since we got married there were many things we did not talk about, many things we were afraid to talk about. That is why it was good to have this terrible thing to talk about. Jack did not say to me what he said in his diary. He did not say Hans were like the Xinjiang people. If he said that, we might argue again. I thought we agreed that people who did like the woman's mother-in-law and husband were very different from Chinese. I expected my husband to love me. It was his duty to love me. It was my duty to love him. And I did love him. Even though I thought he did not love me any more. There was a space between our bodies too. Jack almost did not touch me any more. Before he always wanted to touch me.

August 10

The penicillin has done its work: yesterday I felt better, and today I think I'm back to normal. Physically at least. Trying to purchase train tickets is not conducive to mental health and has left me feeling even more depressed about China. I wanted to escape Xinjiang fast, so when we got to Urumqi, Z came to the train station to buy tickets. She was told they have to be bought the day before we want to leave. Today we were informed she should have bought them then. Turns out yingzuo (hard seat) and yingwo (hard sleeper) require different methods of purchase, but of course there are no signs or any other indication of that. So we are now in a Kafkaesque process of being shuffled from one line to another.

In our previous line another American foreign expert got even more pissed off than I do at the way people crash the line and was shouting and physically preventing them. Then the ticket seller in charge of that niche opened her window and let people look at her while she spent twenty minutes talking on a personal phone call before she dealt with the first person in her line. Maybe she was showing off to outsiders that Urumqi has a phone system that actually seems to work. Everyone was fuming, but no one dared speak out since what they all wanted depended on her. My next place was simply a closed door with some people milling around waiting while others entered and shut the door behind them. Finally someone opened from the inside and instructed people to line up, and people barged toward the front no matter how long they had been waiting. The other American expert has worked in Nanjing for two years and says he is really fed up with China. I understand his feeling. Well. All these special lines in which we have been standing are for people who can't get tickets in straightforward ways. Now my big nose has gotten me somewhere: a slip of paper entitling me to stand in the line I originally attempted to get into when we arrived two hours ago. Unfortunately it shows little tendency to move. The other American managed to circumvent one of my lines and is up ahead trying to keep crashers out. Uh oh. His circumvention was in vain: he was refused a ticket and Z is now leading him to the line he circumvented.

The eventual result was that they agreed to let him buy tickets for the day after tomorrow (which is what he wanted) but said he could not pick them up until earlier that day. This did not satisfy him and he blew up, cursing China at the top of his lungs and complaining that he had spent hours in line only to be told he couldn't do what he had been asking all along to do. Surely this is one of the more disgusting aspects of the transportation mess – and other messes – in China: no one ever tells you right off what you can and can't do. You end up wasting hours of your time before you are given the no you could have been given at the start.

I have now learned that had we been apprised of the proper way to buy yingwo tickets, the procedure would have been as follows: four days ahead of time Z would have had to tell the ticket authorities we wanted tickets. Then every morning she would have had to report to the railway station (at the other end of town, a forty five minute trip each way even with convenient and efficient busses), wait for her number to be called out and shouted "dao" (present). After three days of such waste, on the fourth she would have been entitled to purchase the tickets. So we actually saved time by wasting half a day in the station since otherwise we would have had to waste several hours on each of four days. What a country. While I was not impressed by the other expert's ugly American conduct, I was in full sympathy with his desire to clear out.

August 11

In the ticket line yesterday Z detected a Subei accent, talked to the speaker and, incredibly, discovered she was a relative originally from Binhai. As a result we were invited to the woman's family's home, spent a pleasant evening, got a huge meal and learned *some fascinating family history. The woman is actually from Z's mother's older sister's husband's family, a family hated and reviled by Z's mother's family, she claims unjustly. I think her father was Z's aunt's husband's older brother. Z's aunt's husband was supposedly a bandit who was killed attempting to rob a landlord, but his relative says that in 1985 it was announced that in fact he was a Communist Party member who was robbing landlords of their weapons to turn them over to the PLA. More of this anon.*

The other part of the story has to do with Z's aunt, her mother's second sister. The woman who fed us so well claims that Z's mother's older sister poisoned her own son. She says the Party investigated by placing silver (or was it quicksilver?) in the dead boy's mouth: when it turned black, this indicated poison. In any case the Party executed the woman (when? I thought she said the late forties, but if the Communist Party was in power it must have been at least 1949 and probably 1950 or 51) by stabbing (not shooting in the back of the head, the usual method and the way Z originally heard the story). Later this woman's father and other relatives mutilated the corpse, cutting it into pieces. Z's mother's family repieced and buried her. Enmity persists between the two families among the older generation, but Z and the woman could agree it was all a tragedy of the old society and that that society, not individuals from either family, was to blame.

Another Chinese mess, but what a fascinating one. What wild ways the Party works. The old bandit, who is universally reviled by Z's family and most others in Binhai, was a Communist Party member, yet it took almost forty years for this to be revealed, and it was revealed so poorly that until now Z and her family did not know it. Apparently an investigation is being conducted (very slowly) to determine all the circumstances. According to our informant the question is not whether or not he was a Party member but whether or not he was a member who went astray. When that is determined, the facts will be published. Or some facts will be published. Maybe. Does one ever find out the truth in this place? How I would love to know it. How I would love to tell the story.

Jack says many things in my second aunt's story wrong, but it is not always his fault. The woman told many things wrong. Maybe she did not know all the facts, or maybe she lied some times to make her own family look better. I do not know. I still do not know what is true and what is false about this history. The only things I for sure know is that after my second aunt's first husband was killed, she remarried again. Then her son died and the first husband's family said she killed the boy and she was killed. It happened in 1947 or 1948. The Communist Party did have power in the Subei then. I think the woman's family killed my aunt. I think the woman's father did it. But the Communist Party told them they could do it. It was done in the market where many people could watch. That is supposed to teach a lesson. "Kill one, frighten a hundred." It frightened my mother and taught her a lesson, but not the one it was supposed to teach. Other people learned other wrong lessons because every one knew my aunt did not poison her son. That part is silly. There are many silly stories and rumours about my aunt. But maybe some of them are true. I still do not know if her first husband was really a Communist Party member. It does not matter. It was wrong to kill my aunt. She was very famous for her beauty. I do not know if she was very brave to remarry again or just very poor. Those were very hard times to live in. Maybe some day I will find out the truth and write a history. Maybe some day I will not find out the truth and write a novel. Maybe the novel will be more true than the history. What is truth? Maybe the novel will be the same one that I write about Erbao. In my mind second sister and sister Erbao are connected. That is because when I went to the Subei to look for second sister, I found Erbao. But maybe they were connected in my mind even before I went to the Subei.

It has already worked its way into my dreams. Last night I dreamed of the lake of blood. My worst nightmare, my own personal hell. Just as I'm about to escape one hell, am I going to be trapped in another? I hadn't seen or even thought about that bloody lake in years, not since before I came to China, but this is the second time it has seeped into my dreams lately. But last night Z saved me. Her aunt's body parts were strewn over the lake, floating alongside the bodies of my Chicago friends. I must have cried out in my sleep or something because when I awoke Z was holding me. I'm not sure she was even awake. Indeed, given what our relationship has been lately, I'm pretty sure she was not awake. I am sure her holding me enabled me to go back to sleep. When I did, the lake was gone. Z and I were together, searching for something, some missing piece of her aunt, I think, her heart, I think.

I dreamed about Erbao that night. It must be that night. Maybe second sister's story made me think about her. It reminded me what life was like for a beautiful woman who stayed in the countryside. Erbao could never be unique in the countryside. She had to escape to Shanghai. Like my mother did. If my mother stayed in the Subei, maybe she might be killed like her sister was. If she remarried again there, she would get in big trouble. I wonder if I was holding Jack because I was dreaming about Erbao. I dreamed about her when I first met Jack, but I did not dream about her for a long time. Not since I married Jack. I started dreaming about her again at this time. When I was in the Subei, I dreamed about her almost every night. The dreams did not tell me what to do to save my marriage. I figured that out. I did that. But the dreams gave me strength. The dreams helped make me I.

August 12
On the train from Urumqi to Beijing, somewhere in eastern Xinjiang. The province is huge. It seems appropriate that we have been travelling all night but are still in Xinjiang, still in the desert, for this morning I think I felt the healing fountain start. Z woke up full of excitement and a novel she wants us to write based on the story of her family she heard from the in-law in Urumqi. She wants to go to the Subei, to the hometown she has never seen, to research it. It is exciting to see her excited like this, makes

me feel better. I'm still not great, but I sure am glad to be heading out of Xinjiang. I've felt too lousy for too long here. It's a shame to leave without seeing Ili or Heaven Lake, where Qiu and Yu have gone, but my body itches and my soul feels dry in this desert. I need to be washed in the blood of Z's aunt and her bandit/communist husband. What a novel they will make. Will the woman face death defiantly? Or will she be innocent to the end, her eyes huge, like a baby's, then, as the knife is raised, bulge with horror before glazing over? Just when I am most down on China, something like this happens to remind me that, for all their all too obvious faults, the Chinese, who on the surface are the most cautious, the most pedestrian of people, in reality, beneath the surface, beneath the mask, are never dull. Just when I think I have stopped loving this place, something reseduces me, reminds me I can't.

I may have come to China seeking socialism but what I found – and fell in love with – was a culture. I found it my first full day in the country when, exhausted and sopping with sweat, I stumbled into People's Park and stumbled upon the strangest music I ever heard. I was caught, as foreigners from Kubla Khan and Marco Polo to Matthew Ricci to Bertrand Russell, have been caught by this strange, contradictory land. When I try to think about it logically, when I consider its politics or economics, when I meditate about what Mao really accomplished, I lose it. Then I hear a story like that of Second Sister, and I find it all over again. And I just found more. Second Sister is so far out that I neglected something closer to home. There is another character, Z's mother: she suffered the murder of a sister she loved, respected, looked up to; yet she struggled on to assert her rights, women's rights, lived among threats, some subtle, many not so subtle, until she knew she would be killed or driven crazy. Then she ran, ran until she reached Shanghai. Now who does that remind me of?

Me. When he talks about Ma, I see he is talking about me, not just China. It is happening now like it happened then. In Urumuchi I still did not know what to do then, and I did not know what to think now. I still thought Jack stopped loving me then, and even after all these years it still seems funny that the terrible story about my second aunt made Jack love me again. It is so strange that I want to laugh. Strange but maybe true. Jack is very unchinese. He is very romantic. Like Chairman Mao. That is why he liked Chairman Mao. That is why he loved China. That is why he loved me. Except Chairman Mao, Chinese are not romantic. Our words for "romantic" mean wasteful or idle dreamer. But it is a characteristic of our "strange, contradictory land" that we admire romantic people. So we admire Chairman Mao even though we hate many of the things he did. Maybe that is why I admired Jack. Maybe that is why maybe I still some times love him even though I hate many of the things he did.

Here is what I think. In Xinjiang every thing changed when we heard about my second aunt. When I said I would write a novel with Jack, I started to become me. I, not just China. I grew up. I became a woman, a Chinese woman, a Chinese woman who was starting to become unique. At that time I was not even sure Jack knew that he talked all the day we got on the train about my second aunt and her bandit husband and what a wonderful novel their story would make. So I felt excited the next morning on the train because I figured out how much he would like it if I said I would write the novel too. I really did want to write a novel, but even more I wanted to fight for my marriage, and the novel was the way I did it. I turned defeat into victory. I turned danger into safety. I see now that getting married was not the turning time in my life. This was. Just like choosing to become a courtesan was not the turning time in Erbao's life. After Shi left her and Lai wrecked her house was. Han Bangqing's novel ends there. Mine will begin there. That was when Erbao had to grow up and understand what her choice to become a courtesan meant. That was when she really chose. She chose the same thing again. So did I. Our first year of marriage was too new. It was too exciting to me. I kept thinking about sex. I became a sex object. Jack married me for my mind too, not just my body. I forgot that. Erbao could keep the love of a intellectual like Chen Du Xiu because of her mind, not just her body. She understood about that before she met Chen. After Shi and Lai, she worked much harder to educate herself. She wrote poetry and prose. After Xinjiang I worked harder to educate myself too. I started to think. I did not write much, but I thought much about writing. Jack liked that. He started to like me again. He started to love me again. He says China reseduced him, but I did too. So even when he lost his love for China in 1989, he could still love me. I grew up. I got smarter and stronger. Me became I. The object became the subject.

August 13

Woke up this morning quite cool and still in the Gansu Corridor. It always surprises me how long it is, how big the west of China is, how vast the desert. It changes constantly from sand to pebble to rock, from bare to camel scrub to oasis, from flat to mountainous, from drab to technicolored, but it goes on and on. Here the Corridor has widened a bit and the northern mountains have receded into a morning mist – is there such a thing as a dry mist? – but two layers of mountains are discernable to the south, the second layer snowcapped. There is much more snow around than there was three years ago. And that was winter while this is summer. As usual everything is cockeyed in China. Where but in China could I find a woman with a family history like Z's? The mist must come when opposites attract, when mountain snow couples with dessert warmth. We have been traveling at a good clip for a day and a half, so we must be nearing the end of the Corridor, but the land still reverts to desert anywhere it is not irrigated. "Here is no water but only rock,... mountains of rock without water." Last month's floods are shadowy memories like the play of sun and shade on the wide, dried stonecourses that are watercourses a couple of weeks a year.

3:30: The speakers blast on, an abrupt awakening from a much needed xiuxi to a dramatic orchestral fanfare and a more dramatic scene outside the window. Stunning, striped mountains, purple striped gray and gray striped purple. The weather is suddenly

hot and sultry after the refreshing cool of the pass. We are approaching Lanzhou, getting
back into the east China climate. The land is not dry, the fields no longer dependent on
irrigation, everywhere productive, not just a few irrigated spots. There are rivers, muddy
and sluggish. The dramatic transformation from west to east of China is made even more
dramatic by my xiuxi and sudden awakening to loud, stirring music. There are still a few
tall dryland trees, but shorter, stockier ones are taking their place, including many fruit
trees. The land is lush, a natural lushness, not a lushness imposed by the exertions of man
or a freak desert oasis, not an isolated lushness to astonish but a pervasive lushness to
accept. China.

East of Lanzhou the ti tian (terraced fields) are beautiful even when, as now, they
are mainly bare. The magnificent colors of last month's wheat and rape are gone and most
of the fields are being prepared for the fall crop. Still the bare terraces stretch towards infin-
ity, winding up and around in dizzying, labyrinthine patterns to the tops of uncountable
loess hills. Water has hollowed out holes in the loess and everywhere are hills of various
sizes and shapes, all terraced, some in big steps, some in small, some large lumps of fields,
some neat little ones. But everywhere every inch is utilized.

Every train in China is geared to Beijing. No train goes thru Beijing: you must
get off, buy new tickets and change trains, no simple procedure. We will almost surely
be forced to spend two nights at Beijing's inflated prices. But the funniest thing is the
numbers. Train numbers change depending on whether the train is heading towards or
away from Beijing (even towards, odd away). E.g., the little train from Changsha to
Chaling must have two numbers each way, 513/516 and 514/515, because Changsha
to Liling is toward Beijing while Liling to Chaling is away, so the number of the train
must change at Liling, where the train turns south or west. Talk about deliberate and
senseless confusion. We won't be out of Gansu until after midnight. In other words, well
over two thirds of the trip is in Xinjiang and Gansu – and of course we did not begin
in Western Xinjiang.

I am presently listening to four Hans make fun of Uygurhua – in Shanghaihua:
we are all provincials locked inside the little world of our language. But Z is less provincial
than I thought, less provincial than I am in at least one way. She has more languages, so
more worlds are open to her. She can use her Subeihua to research the novel I would love
to write but know I can't alone. Most of my pleasure will have to be vicarious, but the
pleasure of letting her think the idea was hers is already worth much.

So Jack did know he was trying to get me to write the novel. That is ok.
That is even good. It means that he wanted to save the marriage too. Although
I do not think he knew that he was doing that. He would never think he was using something as high as literature to save something as low as marriage. Maybe
he thought he was using his marriage to create literature. Like he did with his
novel. Except did not he say some where in the novel that he was writing to try
to save our marriage? Maybe I will have to read his silly novel again. Maybe what
happened in Xinjiang made Jack grow up too. I do know that he started writing

his novel in Qiqihar, right after he got there from Xinjiang. While I was in the Subei looking for mine. Maybe I will have to think more about that, but not now. I want to think about Erbao now.

Writing about Xinjiang prepared me to write about Erbao just like writing about Erbao prepared me to write about Xinjiang. Erbao helped me understand myself, and understanding myself helps me understand Erbao. I am almost finished with this history I have been writing for so long. I think I am ready to write my novel now. Not the novel I went to the Subei to find. The novel I found in the Subei. The herstory that found me thanks to my mother. Not the herstory my mother had to live thanks to her older sister. But maybe I will write that one too. Writing this history makes me feel like a writer. *Ah, you snacky Jacky.*

August 14

I don't know where we are, but it is east China with a vengeance: dull, overcast, dripping, clammy, misty. Also green and lush. And my throat, for the first time in weeks I realize, is not parched, painful and foul tasting upon awakening. Goodbye desert, hello China. On the train the speakers belt out moral homilies: how to take care of children, cleanliness for passengers etc. Several people are wearing teeshirts which read, "Happy Our Country Being Famous For Its Rich And Strong." But not for its English. Outside I see traditional Chinese roofs, the first time in a month I have seen that trim little curve. And altho there is no sun, my body is sticky with sweat, that pervasive feeling in the east China summer which I have not felt for a month. Z is overjoyed to feel it again; I am less enthusiastic but must confess that I didn't relish the dryness either. China is a land of extremes. Despite being named the middle kingdom, it seems to have no middle ground. The only good places (climate wise) are high but south, like Kunming.

Z just threw away a packet of pickles after I told her not to. She waited until she thought I wasn't looking. I managed not to say anything. I suspect I wouldn't have been able to restrain myself in the desert. Her abilities to convince herself food is bad are prodigious. When we had pickles she liked, she thought nothing of keeping and eating them for a week in greater heat than this, but this brand she doesn't like so she says they are spoiled after one day. What makes her action different from the way a Westerner would react is that I didn't ask her to eat them, just to let me eat them, but for me to feel different from her is intolerable to her and she wants to enforce a senseless conformity. She is like the fus who periodically march thru the cars correcting every towel which is not hung in precisely the prescribed manner.

He wrote much more than this. I have to cut his diary again. On the train he wrote lots, but most of it is boring. It is about scenery. I will only put in the interesting parts and the parts about us. The last part shows that he does not understand about his own body. He was so sick for so long, but as soon as he felt a little better, he wanted to eat bad food again. He did not care if he made himself sick again. He is like a child. He needs me to look over him all the time. On the train we talked a lot about the second sister novel. We decided that when we got to Beijing, I would go to the Subei to research the novel and he would go to Qiqihar alone. I did not like to let him. I knew he would not be able to set up our apartment alone, but I also knew the school officials would help him more if I was not there. I wrote a letter for him to give to them. It told them to help him a lot until I came. I knew they would do it. Chinese know how much help foreigners need to live in China. In Beijing I would be close to the Subei, but in Qiqihar it would be a long way. And I decided a short time away from each other might be good for us both. I was right too. On the train my breasts were telling me my period was coming. That meant we did not make love for a month. Maybe I could make Jack stay with me, but all his talk about jails showed me I did not want a prisoner. I wanted a lover even more than I wanted a husband.

Jack thought he only needed a lover, but he really needed me to be a wife and a mother too. Here is another thing he wrote in his diary. He wrote this in Beijing.

On the train we had an astonishing half joking, half serious discussion in which Z's basic position was that I wanted her to stop nagging me because I wanted her to stop loving me, that she could not stop nagging me as long as she loved me. What the hell am I supposed to do with that?

You are supposed to be glad that you have a Chinese woman who is willing to worry about you and take care of you, Jack. So quit writing and try to get some sleep. He stayed up writing the whole night we spent in the Beijing Railway Station. More than ten pages in his diary. Most of it is boring. He is lucky he did not make himself sick again.

August 15

A night in the Beijing train station. We arrived late at night and it seemed preferable to walking the streets in the rain or paying 350 yuan to sleep at the Changwen, the only hotel near the station in which foreigners are allowed. The station is the choice of thousands of other travellers trapped in this idiotic city by a system of transportation which takes all trains to Beijing and none thru it. These are not bums. Most in the area we are in are well dressed, have wristwatches and expensive luggage. They spread out bits of plastic, cardboard, bags or newspapers, then sprawl on the marble floor using their suitcases as pillows. It is a peaceful scene, everywhere bodies, almost all of them asleep. Only a few aristocrats like me sit awake, unable to sack out, reading, chatting quietly, staring into space from sitting positions. I was surprised that we were able to find chairs but no longer am: the floor is preferable for sleeping.

I saw two different arrests. There are obviously many plainclothes cops circulating, maybe more than there are pickpockets. The first bust occurred right next to me as I was walking around. I heard a click, turned and saw that one man had just slapped hand-

cuffs on another. He then led his prisoner off by the scruff of the neck, but after a few paces he suddenly started slapping the helpless man around. I don't know why anymore than I know what caused the arrest. I could see everything and the man made no effort to resist or escape. If he said anything, he said it very quietly, under his breath, for I was close enough to hear even a normal tone of voice. The slaps were delivered open handed and were so loud that they quickly drew a crowd. After five or six hard slaps the man was again led off but this time in the opposite direction. The brutality seemed entirely gratuitous. There seemed no reason for it. For that matter there seemed no reason for the bust. The other arrest was farther away. Mainly I saw a crowd and a man being hustled away, again with physical stuff. This is a hard, cold city, the capitol of everything I dislike about China.

The man who was arrested was trying to pick your pocket, Jack. I thought he knew that. Foreigners always have lots of money and do not know how to protect themselfs. Pickpockets go to them. But so do policemen.

5:25 a.m.: The Chinese are truly amazing. As Z and I bit into our apples, the man sleeping in the chair next to mine half woke up, asked in a drowsy voice how much we had paid for our apples and volunteered how much he had recently bought some for. Then returned to sleep. I would have laughed if I weren't so tired I feared falling off my chair.

2:30 p.m.: We have managed to get a room at the out of the way "cheap" hotel for foreigners. In the early morning Z managed to get us both tickets for tomorrow. This miracle was aided by her spotting a man selling his ticket to Harbin, which she bought for me after much hesitation and fear that it might be counterfeit. I slept two hours here then awoke realizing how badly I need to shower. Alas, one of the reasons this hotel is cheaper is that there is no hot water from 2:00 to 6:00. So here I lie looking at Z on the other bed. Sprawled beneath an oversized blue towel of the sort the Chinese use for blankets in the summer, she sleeps, a perfect picture of innocence and beauty, one lovely leg peeping out. How I want to ravish her. I must not, for she is menstruating and was feeling feverish from our exhausting night in the station. Nevertheless, I creep from beneath my yellow towel blanket and touch the lovely limb. She sighs contentedly in her sleep, so I run my fingers lightly along the exposed flesh. Her skin is silk again. Which is more amazing, that I have known such beauty so intimately or that there was a time in the desert when I did not desire it in every nerve ending of my body, every fiber of my being? Where was Z's aunt's second husband when they killed her? Surely he should try to save her.

Chinese do not make futile heroic gestures. Even the emperor could not save Yang Gui Fei.

Qiqihar

August 17

The train from Beijing arrived in Harbin exactly on time and there was a train to
Qiqihar waiting, so passengers simply had to cross the platform and get on. We can buy
tickets on the train. How convenient. How astonishingly convenient. It feels good to be in
the north again. Light is coming into the sky before 5:00 a.m., and the weather is blessedly
cool. I am wearing long pants for the first time in months. Outside the window conifers.
It might be B.C., except there are no mountains and the trees are planted only along the
railroad tracks. Beyond them are fields, Western type fields planted and cultivated by
tractor in long strips. Mainly corn. There are even headlands near the tracks for the tractors to turn in. Imagine: uncultivated land in China. And pastures. Pastures! With dairy
cows, Guernseys from the black and white look of them, and occasional bunches of sheep
and horses. All in all the place feels familiar, perhaps the first place in China I have been
tempted to say that of. Even the transportation system in the Dongbei (Northeast, tho it is
written eastnorth) feels familiar, efficient: lots of tracks, no pulling onto sidings to let other
trains by, trains on time and connections convenient. It was developed by the Russians and
the Japanese. The question is, why don't the Chinese choose to develop transportation in
the rest of the country along these lines? I will no longer accept the cop out notion I used to
use to excuse so much: that most of the country is too crowded. The government simply does
not want the convenient mobility such a transportation system provides. It does not want
people to be able to move about freely and easily.

August 18

On to Qiqihar – Or Is It Back?

My train of sleep runs straight to dream:
Look out the window at the moving world
Moved through always strangely unmoved;
Listen to the strangers on board

Murmur together in a foreign tongue,
The words familiar as the whistle
Heard as a child, heard as a symbol,
Heard as eternal as loneliness
In the strange land recognized as home.

August 25

Every morning I wake as I did in Kashgar, to the pleasant sound of distant donkey braying. Like Kashgar Qiqihar is isolated enough to rely heavily on animals for transportation, but there the similarity ends. Kashgar is an ancient city; it feels middle eastern, like something out of the Bible – whoops, the Koran. Qiqihar is a frontier town, something out of the American wild west. Being China, of course, the west is in the east and the east is in the west. In Qiqihar there are more cars and, because it is flat, many bicycles, so the animals are used mainly for heavy work, hauling produce, metal pipes, concrete blocks etc. Only their cries seem exotic: no jingle bells or surreys with the fringe on top here. Carts are humble affairs, big and inelegant, reminiscent of ones I can just remember clopping thru the alleys of my boyhood in Chicago. The frequent train whistles sound even more eerily familiar. Yet despite these and other similarities this place is utterly Chinese altho I can't put my finger on exactly what makes it so. Perhaps the language: how wonderful to live in a place where people speak putonghua, speak a dialect I can occasionally understand. But it's more than that: altho the place feels different from any place I have been in China, it feels a hundred percent Chinese. When Z arrives she will be able to tell me why because she will feel at home.

Except for the weather. She won't like that. They tell me I live farther north than any other foreigner in China (one room farther north than the other foreign teacher at our school). The weather is cool, windy – Qiqihar is called "the windy city!" – and rainy. It has rained almost every day since I arrived. The rain is not the torrential downpour of the south but the steady drip of the north, often merely a drizzle, sometimes harder but always wet and unpleasant with the cutting wind blowing it in your face. July and August are the rainy months here, I am told. Good for the crops, I am assured. The crops: Z won't find those familiar: big fields of corn planted and cultivated in black soil by big tractors. It looks like the Midwest. Imagine: a place in which Z and I can both feel at home.

September 6

Z returns today. Hooray!!! I wouldn't have encouraged her to go to the Subei if I had any conception how hard, how damned hard, it would be without her. And speaking of "damned," that's the first word in the novel I have begun: "Damned if I know how a sidestreet in Chicago can lead into the marketplace in the Subei where Second Sister's heart was cut from her body." I like that sentence, but little more has been forthcoming. To write a character well a writer must become the character, but the character I want to become is Z, not her aunt. I thought it would be enough to conceive of second sister as an earlier version of Z, but it is not enough. I want Z herself, not a stand in. Maybe having

*Z back will enable me to write about second sister instead of her. I keep trying to write
about second sister and her husband and end up thinking about us. Z's history and mine
as a politico in Chicago must parallel, not replace, her ancestors' story. None of us were
notably successful, but Z and I survived. To tell their story. I hope Z returns with enough
details to let us tell it. But in fact the same thing is happening now that keeps happening:
I can think only of Z's return, not the research she has been doing. And I don't care if we
write together so long as we are together.*

I cried the first time I red that last sentence. Jack did love me. My history
is ended, I thought. Then I thought, that is what Jack would do. He would
stop writing here. But I am Chinese. It is my duty to finish what I started. So
I kept writing, and I kept reading the diary, and I kept thinking. Why did not
I know? Did Jack say? It would be just like Jack not to say. He always says the
things he should not say, but he often does not say the things he should say. But
he did say this. He did start saying he loved me again. But how could I be sure
after Xinjiang? There was a question mark behind our marriage since Xinjiang.
Maybe I should know Jack loved me again? Maybe if he was Chinese, I would be
sure. Maybe if I was innocent, like Americans, I could be satisfied. Some times
we Shanghai Chinese are too clever. Some times innocence can be wiser than
civilisation. But Jack changed so much in Xinjiang. Could that happen if he
really loved me? Could it happen again? He changed so fast, just like we always
heard foreigners did. But he changed back just as fast after he got out of that
place he called hell. The funny thing is that in Shanghai we called Heilongjiang
hell. At least Xinjiang was not cold.

September 7

*She is sleeping now and I am reliving our remeeting. I see her wobbling along
lugging a heavy suitcase and rush to relieve her of her burden, but as I take the bag I get
a close look at her face. I had forgotten how beautiful she is. My knees turn to mush, the
suitcase slips from my grasp. As I am about to fall over, she catches me, embraces me. In
public. She embraces me in public. We kiss. In front of hundreds of people in the Qiqihar
Train Station we kiss. A long, hard kiss which turns into a longer, fluid French kiss. She
is back. Love has returned.*

I cried again. I forgot about this kiss too. Reading Jack's diary was getting
to be like the movies we used to go to in China. At the high peak you could
hear all the people in the theatre crying. That is our Chinese character. We cry
when things come out the way they should. Jack's words show his character too.
He does not think. He does not analyse. He just feels. "Love has returned."
Through my tears I kept thinking why did it go away?

It is hard to get to and from Binhai. There are no trains there. You have to
change many busses and trains. And in Beijing you have to get off and buy a new

ticket. I was very tired on the trains in the Eastnorth, but I could not sleep. I was worried about Jack. I was worried that he stopped loving me. I thought I could keep holding him by using writing, but I did not find out much about second sister, and I was afraid his passion dried up in the desert. If his passion dried up, mine would too. I knew that. The more I thought, the more I could feel it drying up. Why did he stop loving me in Xinjiang? I did not do any bad thing. I did not stop loving him. If he could stop loving me so easy, maybe I should not love him so much? That bitter question bothered me on the whole train trip. My better love had a question mark. Then I saw him in Qiqihar. As soon as he looked at me, I saw he loved me again. It was great. He fell into my arms. I caught him. I was the strong one. He was the child. I knew that for many seconds when I held him and kissed him. I do not know if I could do that in Shanghai, but Qiqihar was a wild place, full of wild people. I saw the wild country and the wild people in the train. *Aiya*, this was the *da bei huang*, the great northern waste, hell. When I thought that, I laughed out loud. How embarrassing, but no one on the train in that wild place even noticed. I laughed because I knew Jack would say that Shanghai people call every place that is far from Shanghai hell. Maybe he is right, but this was a different hell from Xinjiang. We use different words for it. This was the place where many young Chinese were sent in the Cultural Revolution. Every one in my generation red many terrible stories about it. Xinjiang was hell because it was so strange that it seemed like it was not earth, but this was hell on the earth. This was hell in China. But it was wild China, the China we Chinese worked hard to civilise. I think it must be what Jack calls the China under the mask. I do not think I wear a mask. I am proud to be unique. I am proud to be strong. I am proud to be civilised. I think I began to learn that in Qiqihar. Maybe in the *da bei huang* I became a little wild myself. Maybe Qiqihar made me strong enough to live in another wild place far from Shanghai. A wild place that is not hell even though it is cold. Maybe Qiqihar made me strong enough to live in Canada.

Thinking all this made me stop crying. When I looked at Jack's diary again, I saw stains on the writing. From my tears, I thought. I tried to wipe them, but the page was dry. *Ah.* So Jack cried too when he wrote this. We were crying together. That made me think more. Maybe I am not so unique, I thought. Maybe I am not so Chinese even. Maybe I am like Jack. Maybe I am Jack and Jack is I. We are human beings. We are both all. Maybe we human beings are alike like beans after all. The first time I heard Jack say "human beings," I asked him why he was calling people "beans." It was in Shanghai, the first time we were in his room at the Jin Jiang Hotel. He laughed. He wrote the two words and explained the difference between "beings" and "beans." Then he said that when he was a child, he made the same mistake. He could not understand why people were called beans until he learned to read and saw the word written. We laughed and laughed together. We were one. We were all. We are all barbarians.

We are all civilised. We are all human. We are all together. Now I remembered.
I knew this too at the Qiqihar train station.

I know now that I knew many of the things I learned writing this history
in the few seconds I held and kissed Jack in the Qiqihar train station. But then
I forgot. I was so tired. And Jack made me forget. He took me home and treated
me like a princess again, like a child, like a delicate butterfly. It was wonderful,
but it made me forget. How can a butterfly remember that it was once a worm?
Writing this history makes me see that I forgot so much. And when I forgot, I
remembered the question mark from the train. I think maybe that is another
Chinese characteristic. No, a human characteristic. We never forget a bad thing,
but we are not so great at remembering the good things. I learned a lot of things
I forgot writing this history. I learned that silkworm love lasts much longer than
butterfly love. So maybe it is not important if I can not remember our first
butterfly kiss? I do not know. I only know I have a lot more to learn, and not
only things I forgot. I know there are many things I do not know, many things I
want to know. So I must write my novel about sister Erbao. You learn old things
writing a history. I wish I will learn new things writing a novel that is herstory.

Jack's school sent a man and a woman in a van to pick me up at the train
station. They wanted to take us to a restaurant, but Jack kept saying, "*Hai Bao
tai lei*" (Hai Bao is too tired), and he was right. He made them take us home. He
already cooked the spaghetti source. While the noodles were cooking, he put
me in the bathtub. It was not as big as the one at the Jin Jiang Hotel, but it felt
so nice. I did not have a bath since we left Shanghai. He washed me all over. He
often had to run out to check his noodles. When my bath was over, he wiped
me with a big, soft towel, the kind we use as blankets in the summer. He locked
the door and took off his clothes. We both ate naked. He saw how tired I was
from the long trip, so he did not ask many questions. He did not say any thing
about the novel. We did not talk much. We did not have to. But I did tell him
how good his spaghetti was. It really was great.

After we ate, he took me to the bed. He told me to lay down. "*Bu neng
dong,*" he said. I knew he wanted to say *bu yao dong,* do not move, but his wrong
Chinese was right this time. He said I was not able to move, and it was true. I was
too tired to move or to correct his Chinese. I would like to describe the making
love just for practice because maybe I will have to use that kind of description in
my novel about Erbao. But I can not. Although I lived a long time in Canada,
but I am still Chinese. And I was so sleepy after the long trip and the hot bath
and the big meal that I do not know what was love and what was dream. Jack
said he wanted to kiss my body's every piece. He started with my feet because
usually I like him to kiss my feet. My feet are thin and long. Not Golden Lilies,
which is what bound feet were called, but very lovely, I think. But before Jack got
up to my knees, I was falling to sleep. I pulled him up, and we made love very
softly. We did not make love all the time we were in Xinjiang. We did not make

love in almost two months. No wonder we fought. Jack was excited, but he saw how tired I was, and he fell into my feelings. We made long, slow, quiet love. We made love like we were in a very gentle dream. We made love like two butterflies making love for the first time. No. It was not like the first time. It was like the first time should be. It was like both of our dreams of love came true. We made love with 俨然, *yan ran*, "solemn awe," as it is translated in Jack's translation of *Mudan Ting* (Peony Pavilion). But it does not mean exactly that. The whole line means the lovers knew each other in some past life, so now they recognized each other. How wonderful. But awful too because this wonderful love happened in a dream. Making love to Jack, I felt like I was in Du Li Niang's dream of her willow lover, the beautiful dream that cast a awful spell over all her life. She wanted her dream love so much that it killed her. She had to go to hell to get permission for her ghost to look for the man she dreamed of. The ghost found him and made him dream of her. Then the ghost taught the man how to bring her back to life. So both of their dreams of love came true. Now I wanted my dream of Du Li Niang's dream to be true. It was not the first time I dreamed that dream. I dreamed it before I met Jack. It scared me then. Now it seemed to come true in a beautiful way, perfect, not scary at all. But later I wondered if it did come true. Maybe it really was only a dream. Maybe I fell asleep and dreamed that wonderful, peaceful love.

Softly come, softly go,
River run, gently flow.

The dream ran on and on. I kept waking up, seeing Jack floating on top of me, knowing I was dreaming, drifting back into my perfect dream. But some times I thought maybe making love was the dream. If this is a dream, I remember thinking, I wish I will never wake up. And some times I thought the dream was even bigger. I thought the trip, the Da Bei Huang, the Subei, the Xinjiang, was all part of the dream. What if the whole trip was a bad dream that was ending in a good dream?

When I waked up the next day, the sun was shining and Jack's body was not on top of mine. I was afraid. Maybe Jack's body was part of the dream too. Maybe no thing was real. Maybe love was a dream. Then Jack saw I was awake. He put down his diary and we made love again. I knew that was real. But the love we made in the morning was ordinary love. I needed to pee so much that I hardly enjoyed it. Later we made love again and again, but it was never again like the dream time, so I always wondered if the dream was real. I looked in Jack's diary to see what he said, but he does not say about that first night. I guess I waked up too soon. He must have stopped writing when he started crying. Then we got too busy for him to write again. But maybe that kind of love does only happen in dreams? Another question mark. That was the problem. There were too many question marks. I was too not certain. Love was very good in Qiqihar, that wild place, but maybe because I wanted to be back in Shanghai I kept remembering all the question marks civilisation wrote.

So I still do not know if the "solemn awe" love I felt in the night came from the dream or if the dream came from the love. That must be why Jack used Zhuangzi in his novel. Maybe that night he dreamed of butterfly love too. He did not know what was dream and what was real too. We both were not satisfied with simple silkworm love. Silkworms never are. Every worm dreams of flying. Jack and I both wanted to be butterflies even though we knew we could not know if we were. He tried to find out by writing like he was me. He wrote his novel to try to make silk out of the cocoon he was trapped inside. He was not sure I loved him like I did at first. So he had to write his silly novel, and I had to read it and write my funny history to learn he really loved me. But writing it taught me that Zhuangzi was wrong. It does not matter if the dream love was a dream. Du Li Niang was right. Love can make a dream true. And art can make a dream real. Like the silkworm makes its dream of flying real by spinning its silk cocoon. Jack's love is truly real. And so is mine. We both had to write to find out. Writing is like cooking. You love the banquet you make more than the one some one else makes. That is the good moral at the end of my story.

The moral at the end of a story is very important. I wanted to say it better, but I could not in English. So I wrote it in Chinese and asked Jack to help me translate. This is what we wrote together: The sympathy I could not feel when Jack was writing about me I have come to feel by writing about him. About us. Writing is to loving as cooking is to eating. You have to create to appreciate. Now it is dinnertime. Maybe it will be a feast. We both hope our fictitious feast will last a long time.

The end of my story is the beginning of my novel. In Binhai my relatives were very nice to me. They were very poor, but they always made feasts for me. They always cooked chicken and fish and other expensive dishes. One time I returned early from one relative's house to the other's. I saw the simple, one dish, no meat meal that they usually ate. I felt ashamed that they wasted so much money buying food for me. I gave them all presents, but I could not pay them back. I learned a lot about my family in the *Subei*. But I did not learn much about my second aunt. My relatives did not want to talk about that, and they would not let me look for anyone in her first husband's family. I knew the woman I met in Xinjiang was in Binhai. She was buying tickets to go there when I met her. But my family would not let me try to contact with her. The two families are still enemies. The newspapers did not have any papers that old either. I did get some books of local history, but none of them talked about what happened to my second aunt. In one of them I found a short article about a virtuous widow named Zhang Erbao. Maybe Han Bangqing changed the surname? Zhang is a common name, but maybe she was related to me a little. The article said that Zhang Erbao was writing a biography of her husband, the late Mr. Chen, who was killed in the Japanese war. You can see why the local Binhai scholars would be impressed by a 75 year old woman who spent her whole adult life in Shanghai returning home to write a biography. Maybe she told the story that she was a widow and it was her late husband's biography, but maybe the local male scholars just jumped a great leap to that conclusion. They could not think what she really was. They did not realize she was writing about Chen Du Xiu, or they did not remember his name that was once so famous.

My novel will be tragic, but maybe it will have a happy ending. I have a idea for the last scene. Erbao and Chen are reunited again. They sit together in Erbao's house, too happy to be together to make love. I will leave them there while I think about how to get them there. They are naked because they are talking politics. They hold hands, munch sour fruits, look out the window. The window has very thin curtains, so the world outside it looks misty. It should look like that because what they are talking is about the future of their city. In the mist they can see other houses in their lane, foreign houses with different coloured doors, and behind them tall foreign buildings, the Cercle Sportif Francais and Grosvenor House. In the future Grosvenor House will be called the Jin Jiang Hotel. It will be my first home of married life. On the first night of our marriage Jack and I also sat naked, unable to make love, holding hands and looking out the window at houses like the one Erbao and Chen sat in. I told him about growing up on Pushan Lu, and he told me about Bissel Street.

Chinese/English Glossary

B

bai hua – the modern way of writing Chinese, brought in by May Fourth Movement reforms

Beiquan – Chinese pronunciation of Norman Bethune (1890-1939), a Canadian doctor who organized medical services for the Communist Eighth Route Army and died at this work

binguan – fancy hotel in which foreigners are allowed to live

Binhai – small city in the Subei, home of Hai Bao's parents

Bund – the main part of downtown Shanghai, along the Huangpu River, full of tall Western buildings, the heritage of Shanghai's colonial past, when this was the heart of the International Concession

C

Cao Xueqin – 1715?-1764, novelist, author of Hong Lou Meng

Cao Cao – Character in San Guo (Three Kingdoms), a Ming Dynasty novel often performed on the opera stage

Chang Yang Hao – Yuan Dynasty poet (13th and 14th century)

cun – a Chinese inch (actually a bit longer than an inch: 3.3 centimeters)

D

danwei – work unit

Dies Irai, Lachrymosa, Tuba Mirum, Confutatis, Libera Me – sections of the Requiem

dizi – a high pitched bamboo flute

Dou E – heroine of Yuan Dynasty playwright Guan Hanqing's Snow in Midsummer

Du Li Niang – heroine of Mudan Ting (Peony Pavilion)

E

erhu – a two stringed, bowed Chinese musical instrument

F

FEC – Foreign Exchange Certificate, also referred to as funny money. During this time the Chinese government exchanged foreign currency for FECs, which could then be used to purchase certain luxury items not available to people with ordinary Chinese money

fen – cent, the smallest denomination of Chinese money

fu wu yuan (sometimes shortened to fu) – attendant

G
gong an ju – police

Gongchangdang – Communist Party

Great Leap Forward – political movement of the late 1950s

Guan Yu – one of the heros of *San Guo* (*Three Kingdoms*), famous for his bravery

guniang – girl

Guomingdang – Nationalist Party

H
Hai Shang Hua Lie Zhuan – late Qing Dynasty novel by Han Bangqing, usually translated *Lives of Shanghai Singsong Girls*, more literally *Lives of the Flowers of Shanghai*, published 1894

Han Shan – Tang Dynasty poet (8th and 9th century)

Han Bangqing – novelist, author of *Hai Shang Lie Zhuan*

hao – good, bravo

Hengshan Lu – a Shanghai street famous for its large, Western style houses, homes of wealthy foreigners before the revolution

Hong Lou Meng – *A Dream of Red Mansions*, early Qing Dynasty novel by Cao Xueqin

Huai Hai – a river, site of a battle in northern Jiangsu Province

Huangshan – Yellow Mountain, the most famous and beautiful tourist mountain in China

hukou – residence book

hun dun – usually known in English by its Cantonese pronunciation, won ton

J
Jade Emperor's Peach Garden – The Jade Emperor rules heaven. His peaches

confer immortality and were plundered by Sun Wu Kong, who thus became immortal.

Jiang Jie Shi – Chiang Kai Shek (the Cantonese pronunciation)

jiao (or mao) – ten Chinese cents (fen)

jiaozi – dumplings, sometimes called potstickers in English

jie jie – older sister

Jinggangshan – mountains along the border between the provinces of Hunan and Jiangxi, where Mao organized the first Red Army and Liberated Area

June 4, 1989 – date of the Tiananmen Massacre

K
Kongzi – Confucius, 551-478 B.C. China's most famous philosopher and teacher

kuai – slang for yuan, the Chinese dollar

L
Lao – old, a polite address before the name of an older person

Lao She (1899-1966), Chinese novelist and playwright. He committed suicide during the Cultural Revolution.

Lei Feng – a People's Liberation Army soldier canonized by the Chinese Communist Party in the 1950s. He was selfless, a boyscout constantly performing good deeds and supporting the Communist Party and government

li – Chinese measure of distance, half a kilometer or a third of a mile

Li Matou – Mathew Ricci, a Jesuit priest who arrived in Beijing in 1601

Li Bai – 701-762, Tang Dynasty poet

Lin Biao – Communist Party leader, second in command to Mao during the first part of the Cultural Revolution. He died in a plane crash in September, 1971, attempting to flee China, allegedly after attempting a coup

Liu Shao Qi – Communist Party leader, accused of taking the capitalist road during the Cultural Revolution longxiapian – a Chinese snack, pink puffs which expand when fried in oil

lu – street

Lu Xun – 1881-1936, Twentieth century China's most famous writer and critic

M
Master – Kongzi (Confucius)

May Fourth Movement – Movement to modernize China, named after its most famous demonstration, May 4, 1919

May Seventh Camp – (Wu Qi Gan Xiao), places in the countryside where party members and intellectuals were sent to reform their thinking during the Cultural Revolution

ma la dofu – hot, spicy tofu

mei mei – younger sister

Mei Guo – the United States

Mengzi – Mencius, 372-289 B.C., Chinese philosopher

Monkey King – see Sun Wu Kong

Mr. Science, Mr. Democracy – the two most important symbols of the May Fourth Movement

mu – Chinese measurement of area, approximately 1/15th hectare or 1/6 acre

Mudan Ting – *Peony Pavilion*, a play by Tang Xianzhu (1550-1616) often performed as an opera

N
naguoning – Shanghai dialect for weiguoren, foreigner

Nanjing Lu – the main east west street in Shanghai, famous for its shops

ning – Shanghai dialect for ren, person

Ningbo – a seaport in Zhejiang, south of Shanghai

O
old emperor – Pu Yi, China's last emperor, who became a gardener under the Communists

P

palanquin – sedan chair, traditionally a red one carried a bride to her new husband's family

Peng De Huai – Chinese Communist military leader. In 1959 he criticized Mao's Great Leap Forward and was removed from the Party leadership. Subsequently he was tortured and died during the Cultural Revolution.

pigu – ass

pippa – traditional Chinese stringed instrument

Pu Shan Lu – a street (*Lu*) in Shanghai; it means something like be charitable to everyone in need

putunghua – Common speech, Mandarin, the official dialect of Chinese

Q

Qin, Chu – two states during the Warring States period (481-221 B.C.)

Qin Shi Huang – (d. 210 B.C.), King of the State of Qin, then founder of the Qin Dynasty (221-206 B.C.)

Qing Bang – (Green Gang), gangsters who controlled Shanghai much as Al Capone and his gang did in Chicago

Qingdao – port city in Shandong Province

Qinghai – a northwestern province famous for its prisons

Qingming – a Chinese festival which honors the dead; it is celebrated on April 5

Qufu – city in Shandong Province, birthplace of Kongzi (Confucius)

R

ren – person

rightists – people imprisoned or sent to the countryside for "reform by labor;" many were intellectuals who criticized the government after being urged to do so during the "hundred flowers movement" of 1957

S

Shandong – Province directly north of Jiangsu

Shanghaihua – Shanghai dialect

Shaoxing – a city in Zhejiang Province, home of Shaoxing Opera, a style performed exclusively by women

shengdiao – tones; because there are a limited number of syllables in Chinese, the way a syllable is pronounced changes its meaning; there are four tones in Mandarin

shengjian mantou – literally raw fried steamed bread, little fried meat filled dumplings

Sima Qian – 145-86 B.C. Chinese historian of the Han Dynasty

Spring Festival – The Chinese Lunar New Year, the biggest festival in China, it lasts 15 days from the new moon to the full moon

Su Fan Movement – a Communist Party rectification campaign of 1955. It means clean out the counter revolutionaries.

Subei – Northern Jiangsu Province, north of the Yangtze River

Sunan – Southern Jiangsu Province, south of the Yangtze River

Sun Wu Kong – The Monkey King, hero of the Ming Dynasty novel *Xi You Ji* (*Journey to the West*)

Sun Zhongshan – Sun Yat Sen (the English pronunciation is based on Cantonese)

T
tai ji, tai chi quan – a popular Chinese type of exercise

tamada – your mother's, a Chinese curse word

Tang Xianzu – 1550-1616, novelist, author of *Mudan Ting* (*Peony Pavilion*)

thatched cottage, thatched hut – in *San Guo* (Three Kingdoms) Liu Bei makes three visits to Zhuge Liang's thatched cottage to persuade Zhuge Liang to join his forces

Tianshan – Mountain in Shandong Province

tongzhi – comrade

W

wenhua da geming – the Cultural Revolution, literally cultural great revolution

White Snake – *Bai She*, a famous Beijing Opera

Wu – the area which includes Shanghai, Suzhou, Hangzhou: they all speak forms of Wu dialect

Wuchang – a city in Hubei Province, part of Wuhan

X

xiao – a bamboo flute, lower in pitch than the dizi

Xiao – little, a polite address before the name of a younger person

xioajie – maiden, literally little older sister

xiuxi – rest, nap

Xuzhou – City in northwestern Jiangsu Province

Y

Yang Gui Fei – lover of Emperor Ming Huang of the Tang Dynasty. His troops blamed her for the rebellion of An Lu Shan (755 A.D.) and demanded her execution. Ming Huang reluctantly complied. The incident is the subject of many poems, plays, operas and paintings.

Year of the Dragon – in Chinese astrology every year is named after one of 12 animal symbols

yuan – the Chinese unit of currency, it has fluctuated in value, presently worth about 12 cents US (2006)

Z

Zhang – the most common surname in China (China has only a few hundred surnames)

zheng – traditional Chinese stringed musical instrument

zhongshan – Sun Zhongshan

Zhu De – 1886-1976, one of the leaders of the Communist Revolution

Zhuangzi – ancient Chinese daoist philosopher, 4th and 3rd century, B.C.

Zhuge Liang – Character from *San Guo* (*Three Kingdoms*), a Ming Dynasty novel often performed on the opera stage